# Reviews for
# The Triempery Revelations

"Two elements elevate this work above standard fare. First, it's a character study at its heart, driven by the growth and evolving relationships of complex people, vibrant and varied, without any reduced to stereotypes of good or bad. Second, the mysteries of the Rill and the Wall are compelling and drive readers to explore this world more  deeply. Stephens serves up a terrific first entry to a fascinating new series."
—*Booklist*

"An incredible introduction to a new fantasy series… layered, flawed characters within a fascinating world with a rich history and intriguing magic system that you can't wait to learn more about."
—*Smyco*

"*The Kheld King* takes all the elements that made *Sordaneon* great and expands them. A character-driven story with high stakes, with politics as the main focus of this fantasy."
—*Jamreads*

"If *Dune, Lord of the Rings* & *Game of Thrones* all got together and made a book baby, it would be rather like *Sordaneon*, which is to say that it's brilliantly done… It was easy to sink into the world along with Dorilian and the others. I'm absolutely in awe of how many layers Stephens brought to the strange world of the Rill and all those fighting for power."
—*Rebecca Crunden*

ESSERA
THE RIFT
GWEROVEN
Ennsa
Askyllon
HESPIRIAN MTS.
Stauberg
ELEUTHERON
Bynum
SERRAIN
Aral
DANNUTH PLAINS
Kyrbasillon
DANNUTH
The Maw
TAHLWENT
Elithegh
Trulo
Gustan
Tramyff
Tuala
Omadawn
AMALLAR
Eastmeary Brenna
Rhodhur
Hwothylwel
Garfallow

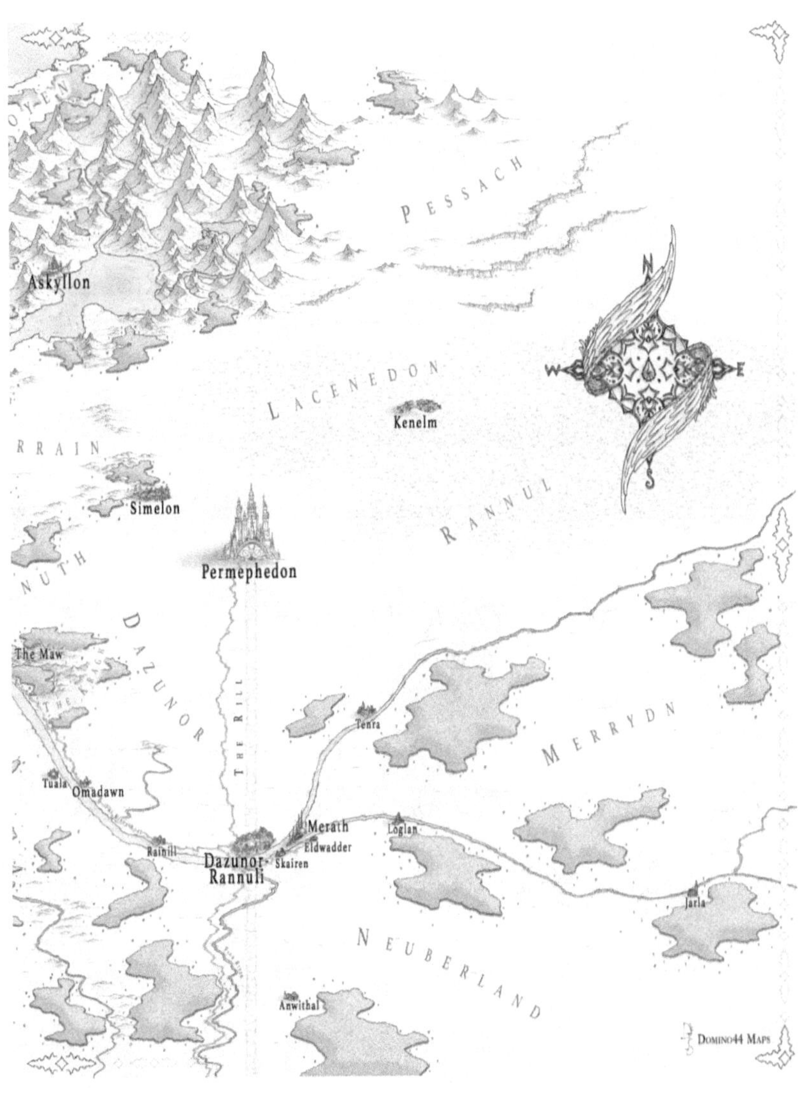
OYEN
PESSACH
Askyllon
LACENEDON
Kenelm
N
W E
S
RRAIN
Simelon
RANNUL
NUTH
Permephedon
DAZUNOR
The Maw
THE RILL
Tenra
MERRYDN
Tuala
Omadawn
Merath
Loglan
Rainill
Eldwadder
Dazunor-
Rannuli
Skairen
Jarla
NEUBERLAND
Anwithal
DOMINO44 MAPS

# BIBLIOGRAPHY

The Triempery Revelations

*Sordaneon*
*The Kheld King*
*The Second Stone*
*The God Spear*
*The Walled City*

*The Rill Lord*
(forthcoming)

*Moon Blood and Salt Flowers*

# THE WALLED CITY

### THE TRIEMPERY REVELATIONS
- BOOK V -

## L. L. STEPHENS

# Copyright Information

## *THE WALLED CITY*
### Published by

Forest
Path
Books

*The Walled City* Copyright © 2024 by L. L. Stephens. All rights reserved.

This is a work of fiction. All characters in the publication are fictitious, or are historical figures whose words and actions are fictitious. Any other resemblance to names, incidents, or real persons, living or dead, is purely coincidental.

Forest Path Books supports writers and copyright. This book is licensed for your personal enjoyment only. Thank you for helping us to defend our authors' rights and livelihood by acquiring an authorized edition of this book, and by complying with copyright laws by not using, reproducing, transmitting, or distributing any part of this book without permission.

Forest Path Books publications may be purchased for educational, business, or sales/promotional use. For information, please address the publishers at: *info@forestpathbooks.com*
or
Forest Path Books, LLC
P. O. Box 847, Stanwood, WA 98292 USA

Stay informed on our releases and news!
Join the reading group/newsletter at:
*https://forestpathbooks.com/into-the-forest*

Front cover art © 2025 by Larry Rostant *https://rostant.com*
Map © 2024 Domino44
PR Compass Rose font © Peter Rempel (licensed for use)
Cover and interior design by Mahli *https://bookdesignbymahli.com*
Cover content is for illustrative purposes only, and any person depicted on the cover is a model.

Library of Congress Control Number: 2024920666
ISBNs:
978-1-951293-82-6 (hardcover)
978-1-951293-81-9 (trade paper)
978-1-951293-83-3 (e-book)

To my wonderful sons, Michael, Anthony, and Kenneth, whose childhoods served as a great counterbalance to my writing ambitions. I wrote the first version of *The Walled City* when they were in grade school... and the final version this year, when their own children are now in grade school. I've watched my boys squabble, bargain, aspire, throw tantrums, battle, and prevail. Every character in the Triempery series owes them much.

# THE WALLED CITY

# 1

It occurred to me the other day that we ourselves are
expressions of Leur. We're born, we grow, we learn, we
try to nail things down, make them forever—but we never
succeed at permanence. We are the stuff of Leur's
Creation and we change constantly.
HANDURIN STAUBERG-RANDOLPH, *REFLECTIONS*

The day following the Rill Coming brought solemn crowds to the High Place of Bellan Toregh. As dawn gilded the sky and hills to the east with bands of rose, a thousand men and women hiked to the hilltop to watch their own people, their leaders and loved ones, go to an enemy country. The prevailing mood was that if the Rill didn't kill them first, maybe Sordan would later.

As the delegates chosen by the Witan stood arrayed upon the Rill platform, dwarfed by the *charys* that had rested all night in the slip at their backs, they were wrapped in the best of winter furs and dressed in summer finery. As cold as it was in Amallar, they would soon be in Sordan's sun and warm weather, where true winter never settled.

Hans had spent another nearly sleepless night, tutoring Arne and Aubrey for the trip to Sordan in the morning. Arne at least knew some of the people they would be meeting. And Aubrey would be by far the better ambassador, Hans knew, though he refrained from telling Arne this. Aubrey's Stauba contained the refined inflections of Essera and she detected nuances of position and power. Hans suspected she could hold her own at any Staubaun court.

"A few years in Neuberland can teach a woman a lot about Staubauns," she said as they waited for Nalf and the rest of the Cruihcila leadership to arrive. "Staubauns create their own manner of blindness. If you play into their expectations, they leave the gates unguarded and are easily fooled."

"There will be people in Sordan you won't be able to fool." Hans turned to Arne, with whom he'd also mulled over the letters to be sent on the mission. "You already know some of the dignitaries we will have to deal with. I would have enlisted Robdan, because of his experience, but I sent him away with, well—you know." Naming Dorilian would be a mistake with so many Kheld ears nearby. "At least I still have you."

"I reckon you do have me, for what it's worth. But Hans, I don't know anybody."

"You know Levyathan. You know Tiflan, don't you?"

Aubrey gave them both a sharp look. "Well, I don't. Who are they?"

Hans wanted to roll his eyes but managed not to. "Remember that book in which you found Dorilian's name? They're in there too, probably right beside him. Levyathan is Dorilian's son, his Heir. And Tiflan is his cousin, the Bas of Teremar. A very important man. In fact, Arne has probably met most of the important men in the land. He just didn't bother to take notice."

Hans turned back to Arne. "This time you'll have to make sure to take notice, and remember people's names, if you want to be my lieutenant."

"Lieutenant? Me?" Though he had always held that position in an unofficial capacity, Arne couldn't help but be pleased to have his role made official. He'd had few occasions in his life where he felt important. "Well," he conceded, "I will be the only one of this lot who's ever been there before. And if there's to be an alliance, I suppose I'll be seeing more of them. Heck, I've seen more of their cursed Hierarch than they have, the last couple months."

"And that's something else you can do—you can tell them he's safe. Only you and Aubrey know that."

Nalf Rhys, dressed in his best furs and accompanied by Old Mothers and Cruihcil high elders, arrived on the platform and joined the line of delegates as dawn pushed the sun above the feathery eastern horizon. As if with the dawn, the boarding bars inlaid alongside the slip lighted, glowing blue, and the *charys* opened, its interior gently lit, a ramp extending from the platform to seal the minimal space between the vessel and the landing. The *charys* was ready, but there was yet time.

"Friends will meet you in Sordan." As he spoke to the delegation, which in addition to Aubrey and Arne included Bellan

Toregh's headman along with two chieftains and one adventurous blacksmith, Hans repeated what Dorilian had told him. "The Highborn Sordaneons and others who are trusted. Your coming has not been made public and may not be. That is at the discretion of your hosts. But you will return in the morning, bringing with you a delegation from Sordan who will be empowered to negotiate a treaty between our two nations and maintain Rill operation until then. This I have on the word of the Sordaneons."

Nalf Rhys then stepped forward and made a brief speech, praising the emissaries for their courage and honor, exhorting them to remember that they were Khelds and, by damn, they'd better carry themselves with pride! Hans didn't doubt they would. The Thegnard had chosen his six emissaries for no other reason than that they were too proud of being Kheld to succumb to the lures and luxuries of the rich Staubaun Hierarchate. Hans rested his own hopes elsewhere. Now, more than ever, he wished Dorilian was going with them. And he wished just as much that his uncle Robdan was going too. This was precisely the right situation for Robdan's diplomatic skills and knowledge. Robdan would have loved to see Sordan, would have embraced that opportunity, not be shaken with fear as were some of these other men. But maybe, just maybe, it was better this way. In his own city, Dorilian might well have proven difficult and changeable even for Robdan, whereas now only the Hierarch's last and favorable instructions would be followed by his subjects.

A series of high-pitched tones emitted from the *charys*, alerting passengers to an imminent departure.

"See you in the morning." Hans gave Aubrey his most encouraging smile. She looked apprehensive but determined as she stepped into the *charys*. The chains binding her to this trip were ones she herself had forged, but Hans knew she would think to the end that she went to Sordan of her own free will. Arne, when it came his turn, swallowed bravely then entered the *charys*.

The dawn was bright, the sun fully risen, when a second series of high-pitched tones sounded and the boarding bar on the landing flashed vibrant red, the portals closing and boarding ramp retracting. Hans felt a subtle surge of energy. Slowly, barely perceptible at first, the *charys* rose from its holding berth and slid into the first acceleration arm. Cupped suddenly in the flaring energy fields of the propulsion mechanism, the *charys* leaped forward, a low drone sounding as each successive field shifted, departing with wildly increasing speed until it too vanished.

The last whine drifted across Bellan Toregh.

"It's gone." Nalf Rhys stared after the flash of light that had carried his countrymen south to lands none of them had ever thought to see.

"It sure is," said Hans. He felt more alone than he had in ages. For the first time since meeting Arne on the docks at Ben Aranath on a hot spring night so many months ago, he was completely on his own. "But it will return. And when it does, we're going to make Amallar a Rill nation."

# 2



The Rill was a tunnel. It did not *look* like a tunnel from without.
Yet, from within a *charys*, the way ahead was a wall of streaming
colors and not-colors rushing toward Aubrey from a point far ahead
where blue sky could still be seen. It took only a heartbeat for Bellan
Toregh's snow-covered hills and woodlands to vanish. The tunnel
turned white. A mountain loomed and then was gone. *I'm breathing.
I feel no movement at all… but those were the Great Telarkans!*

To either side of her, men clutched white-knuckled at the curves
of softly molded cocoons. The one in which she sat cupped her
firmly, its contours fitting her body so well she could almost forget
it was there. But ahead, ahead… the tunnel shot into a country that
was gold and blue, flat and vast, flowing like a two-colored river.

Bare moments later and too soon, she felt a pull, featherlight.
That pull was followed by another, then another, another…. Far
ahead, the tunnel was collapsing into discernible scenery. Aubrey
saw a great crescent of blue water awash with sun and, rising from
it, an island of white that swelled in her sight until its immensity
and grandeur caught at her heart and tore it in two.

"Sordan," Aubrey heard Arne say and the men seated nearby repeat in hushed choruses.

*Great Mother of us all*, she thought. *It's beautiful!*

Wrenching her gaze from the vision of Sordan, she looked out the side, at the lake below. Many boats, their striped sails swelling with breeze, skimmed the blue waters beneath her, and she could make out the faces and figures of people smiling and waving, the warm, casual welcome of folk who were accustomed to watching a *charys* come home. For them, the Rill had never stopped running. Ahead, across that water, building like a dream, Sordan crowded forward to meet them as the *charys* passed above courtyards and houses, wide streets and narrow. People went about their morning business as the vessel glided overhead toward unfurling arches that gathered it in. Within moments the *charys* and its passengers plunged into shadow, engulfed by staggered terraces of which Bellan Toregh was but a suggestion.

"Oh, Mother," Aubrey muttered to Arne, who sat beside her. "It's too much. It's too *big*!"

"Stop thinking of *him*, will you, or the whole thing will be too much for you!" Arne hissed beside her ear. Aubrey knew Hans hadn't told Arne more than he needed to know, but that proved he suspected a lot. "Those will be his kin outside. So keep it! Yeah, I see them," he pitched his voice louder, for the benefit of the others, and pointed out the welcoming delegation waiting on the platform. Aubrey noted they were all men, along with one child.

"The big one?" Arne continued. "That's Tiflan—he kept Hans and me safe the first day we got here. He ain't shrunk at all, either. Just be prepared to look up a lot!"

"Who's the boy?" one of the delegates from the Witan wanted to know.

The *charys* opened before Arne could answer. The platform resembled Bellan Toregh, but vaster and more enclosed, with a pleasant coolness and the humming echoes of background noise, music to the ears of eight people who had endured a journey of perfect, if self-imposed, silence.

Arne led them across the platform to the grouping of several men who awaited and spoke to the boy. "Hello, uh… Sir?"

The title was warranted. The child had dressed for ceremony and a crown of emerald stones encircled his blond head.

A lean Staubaun with a protective mien and wearing the uniform of a commander of the guards interceded. "Your Thrice Royal Highness," he said, crisply providing Arne with the proper form.

The Thrice Royal Highness flashed a smile. He possessed the confident warmth of one for whom titles mattered less than his guardians would have liked. "Welcome, Arne Anseldson," he said. "We are happy that you have returned to our City. Some of us have missed your company. Your abrupt departure did not allow us to wish you a safe journey to your homeland."

"Well, Your Thrice Royal Highness," Arne stressed with a sideways glance at the Staubaun commander, who nodded, "we weren't all that sure you would."

"I hope you are now reassured." Only then did the boy look beyond Arne to the remaining delegation.

Aubrey stared, knowing who she saw, seeking signs of another. The boy's looks were more Staubaun than his famous father's, with eyes so golden they might have been fashioned of that precious metal. He met Aubrey's gaze with an instant of perplexity, as if he, too, were seeing for the first time something that did not quite match its description. He *knew* her, and she could not even guess how.

"My kinswoman, Aubrey Thegn Amundda," Arne said, leaning into the notice. While the other Khelds glared at having her introduced out of order, ahead of her elders, Arne seemed to scarcely notice. "And Aubrey, this here is His Thrice Royal Highness, Levyathan Sordaneon, His Grace the Hierarch of Sordan's son and Heir, which is also his title... one of them anyway."

"Thrice Royal." In speaking those words, Aubrey felt the full weight and meaning of that title. Dorilian's son. A Highborn Heir. Her runes, then, had been wrong. Where there was a son, there was or had been a woman—almost certainly a wife.

Did Sordan's Hierarch have a wife? Aubrey tried to remember but could not. People never talked about one.

Nor was there opportunity to learn more, as the line of Kheldish delegates was presented, not only to the young Heir, His Thrice Royal Highness Levyathan Sordaneon, but to those others in attendance. Tiflan Morevyen, Bas of Teremar, with a warmth of smile that indicated he might be, as Arne had suggested, as good-natured as he was imposing, greeted them next, as did Legon Rebiran, the commander who had prompted Arne about titles and whose name was closely associated with the Hierarch's most elite circle. Several other high Lords passed before Aubrey's eyes and ears. The Speaker of Sordan's Halia. An admiral. A leader of their High Council. When at last introductions were done and letters of identity presented to their hosts, Levyathan offered official greetings and the pledge of his Sordaneon name for their safety.

One of the bearded Kheld delegates, hard of hearing and looking dissatisfied, bowed forward politely, although impatiently. "Your pardon," he said, forgetting the royal title altogether. "But aren't you a bit young, lad, to be making such promises?"

The surrounding guards froze, the onlooking Sordani nobles now taut in the lip. Tiflan of Teremar's eyebrows lowered, and his golden gaze glinted with displeasure. That a mistake had been made was clear.

Arne jabbed the offender in the ribs. "Not that way, Renwitt!" he hissed. "He's the Hierarch's own son, and Highborn himself and all. Nobody talks to him that way—not these Lords, not you, not Hans, not nobody!"

Levyathan flashed Renwitt a smile. "He's right. Until recently, I thought 'Thrice Royal Highness' was my name. Even my nurse called me that when I was a babe in the cradle. It was a tremendous awakening to me when I heard my given name. It still is." He smoothed over the offense with a grace that belied childishness. The Khelds nodded amongst themselves and relaxed as the young Heir continued, indicating the awesome emptiness to all sides. "Your party is here in secret. We have commandeered this terminal for the hour. Usually it is crowded with travelers and cargo. The City will for the most part be unaware you are here. That is why it was decided you should be greeted not by a lesser but by a less obvious member of the royal family. Sordan requires certain attentions and my cousin, Bas Deleus, is seeing to matters of State while my royal father is elsewhere occupied. That left only me. Naturally, we did not wish to insult Handurin by not greeting his emissaries personally. I assure you, I have every authority." Levyathan eyed the delegation levelly. "Do not mistake what I am. While I may be young, I am no less Sordaneon."

He spoke the name as if it were an honor guard, a bastion in itself. Even the most cynical of the Khelds seemed impressed. If this was a child, what were the men like?

As they left behind the airy honeycomb of Rill structures for the cool interior and the passageway that would take them to their destination, a cohort of the Sordaneon bodyguard took positions well to the rear, the possible threat against which they had been guarding no longer to be feared. A respectful search had revealed the Khelds to be unarmed.

Aubrey, from her place at Arne's side, found herself privy to snatches of conversation. Much to her surprise, Arne fell into an effortless banter with the young Highborn Heir and his companions, a pattern of easy questions and easy answers.

"How is Handurin?"

"Fine, real good in fact. Happy the Rill didn't run him down. And how's yourself? And where's Fahme?"

"What could trouble me in Sordan? And Fahme is well. She is at Rhondda pursuing voice studies."

So, for all his blather, Arne had better connections than he had cared to boast about. That towering giant, Tiflan of Teremar, a man renowned and respected in every land of the Triempery, had not held himself above measuring Arne to see if he had grown. Aubrey couldn't help but notice the pleasantness of their association, the laughing ease of their exchange. It was more proof that Hans might have been well treated in Sordan, even as he had claimed. Whatever relationship he had developed with Dorilian, the foundation Hans had laid here was serving him well.

A question, itself inevitable, came from one of the other men in the delegation, spoken half in trepidation. "Where is your father, the Hierarch Dorilian?"

"I'm afraid he is out of the City. His affairs are such that he is unable to be here."

"We will want to see him."

"That may not be possible."

So Dorilian was not here. The ruling authority very likely did rest in Dorilian's son, this gold-haired, clear-eyed boy whose laughter even now commanded his courtiers to smile in unison with the young Heir's perceived mood. Yes, Aubrey could see that Hans had courted the Sordaneons.

Or was it Hans they courted? Perhaps he was not cautious enough.

Later, much later, when night had fallen upon the City, when the beauty and power of Sordan that had overawed the delegation all that day took on a sharper and more brilliant edge in darkness, Aubrey's feelings at last caught up with her.

They were being treated to a private showing of a circus, the most extraordinary performances any of them had ever seen. They watched dancers toss flaming swords, boys tumble on horseback, a girl who flew through the air on wings of gossamer, and a woman who commanded strange beasts. During the show, while flames spun circles on the floor, a man joined the Sordani nobles at their seats. Tiflan moved to allow him a place. Glancing over to see what was happening, Aubrey felt her heart nearly stop, though just for a moment. Just until she saw it was not Dorilian who had joined them. She looked upon a man of similar build, Dorilian's same height and way of moving, and a resemblance that on the surface could be easily mistaken.

Because Arne was seated near, Aubrey figured she might as well ask. "Who is he?"

"Deleus, Bas of Suddekar. He's some kind of cousin to the Hierarch. I think their mothers were sisters."

As Arne had warned, they were among Dorilian's kin. Family relationships, clearly, bore as much import to royalty as they did to Khelds. That book of Staubaun lineages Aubrey had borrowed from Robdan had told her Tiflan's mother was similarly related.

One or two of her fellow Khelds seemed to detect a resemblance, but they had not yet made the connection. To link a man they'd seen but once or twice in their own country to the Sordaneons was obviously a leap too far. Besides, a trio of young women had just taken to performing acrobatics on wire strung over their heads.

Arne, at least, seemed to know Deleus. "How's Pallas these days, Most Noble? Didn't expect to see him greeting us, but there he was," Aubrey heard Arne ask in a quiet aside. He was at least attempting to employ the Stauba tongue of the upper classes, not the Sordanish the natives were speaking.

"As expected, old Pallas issued a diatribe against the proposal made this morning." Deleus sounded less like Dorilian than he looked. "Still, we predict he will ultimately be agreeable." He added, with a wry smile at young Levyathan, "We may have underestimated our Speaker's affection for his Hierarch."

"Pallas wants to limit Dorilian, cousin, not be rid of him."

"And so the fox is a dog after all. Indeed, his loyalty is so firmly placed, he insists on being party to the delegation tomorrow."

"Pallas?" Both Levyathan and Arne's expressions turned incredulous. The applause of the crowd for the acrobats briefly caught their attention. Then Levyathan laughed softly in an undertone. "He probably wants to ensure that any terms are set as near as possible to the Halia's."

"We got a few like that ourselves," Arne confided. "We call 'em Stefanites." One of their own delegates, a Stefanite, glared at him, though his Stauba was not quite excellent enough to confirm any slight.

For Aubrey, however, the circus had become mere background, the performances no longer enough to engage her. Her gaze kept straying to the royal Bas Deleus, cousin to the Hierarch. Had she doubted for a moment after meeting Levyathan this morning, she did not doubt now. The man she had met in Amallar, the man who had called himself Thron Estol Bevvan, could be—surely must be—Dorilian Sordaneon. The family resemblance was too striking. Deleus had the same way of shaping a smile, of turning his head, of acknowledging a greeting. Now Aubrey understood how Sordan had not noticed, until recently, the absence of its Hierarch.

As night deepened and the other Khelds had sought their beds, Aubrey remained restless. The terrace beckoned, so she sought the coolness and quiet of Rillglow-brightened stone. The Kheld delegation was being housed in the Sordaneons' own wing, and she, being the only woman, had been given an apartment of her own. Even the garden outside her door was isolated and private, meandering between terraces and walks from which the City could be viewed.

*Is this where you stood, so many weeks ago, when you contemplated going to Amallar?* She could imagine Dorilian here. This magnificence suited his arrogance. *Why did you come to Amallar when you had all this? Is it any wonder that to you we seem so small? Hans is right: we could not have taken this from you. But that man in Essera, the Mormantaloran—can he?*

How powerful, then, Nammuor must be, to pose a threat to this City and the people in it. That had an Entity standing guard. And what of Amallar, which had not Sordan's defenses? How had its leaders allowed themselves to fall into the trap of believing that all Staubaun countries were like Essera, divided and corrupt, without growth and without honor? Was it because they were blind? Or were they merely envious?

"Envy seeks to destroy what might outshine it. Better a world in darkness than one that might seek another star."

Startled, Aubrey spun and pressed her hands against the wall at her back as a shadow emerged from the trees. She had not seen anyone there nor heard any approach. Her visitor's clothing of muted silver and gray blended with the night. Levyathan studied her as he came into the soft light of the Rill and the moon. Even as it did in Amallar, a full moon rode the skies above Sordan.

"I know you," he told Aubrey, "because *he* did." Something about the young Sordaneon Heir was changed from the boy she had seen earlier. Levyathan cocked his head to one side. "He was supposed to come back; he was supposed to be here tonight. Few knew where he had gone, and few knew to expect his return, so no one has questioned. I have explained it to them, and they know better than to dispute what I say. But I knew two nights ago Dorilian would not be returning, that he had to flee Amallar prematurely. I knew he had been driven from danger into danger. Do you wonder that I was prepared to hate you?" He sighed and turned, placing his elbows upon the rampart at her side. "I thought you would be awful. But you're not."

Stunned, Aubrey could not help but stare. Two nights ago would be the night she had discovered who Dorilian was. How could that news have reached Sordan so swiftly? Thron—Dorilian—had not had access to the Rill that night, not with the Faeduadan swarming all over the Rill mount, making sacrifices. He would not have taken the chance of getting caught.

"What do you know about that? Did Hans write that in his letter?" It chilled Aubrey to think Hans would have betrayed her.

Levyathan shook his head. "No. Handurin keeps women's secrets as closely as those of men. In time he will become a trove of them. Yours is but one of the first."

"Then how?" she demanded, uncaring entirely that this was a Highborn Prince for all his youth, forgetting he was a boy.

Levyathan looked straight at her and spoke in perfect Khelda. "Do you really want to know—lady?"

*Mother save me, he even says it with the same tone of voice, the same inflection!* Aubrey, though she felt a sudden chill in the cool night air, could not look away from that penetrating gaze. Levyathan was not asking what had happened—because he already *knew*.

"You don't know what we are," he told her. "You have no idea."

"I understand that now." She looked away from him, out from the rampart and across a City that outshone the moon. This boy knew what she had done. That she had lured Dorilian, that she had kissed him, that... *Dear Mother.*

Something bright broke from the structures behind the Serat and shot southward, toward distant Teremar, its passage punctuated by a resonant pulse that followed in its wake, a deep note as if from a massive drum. *Rill Lord.*

"Is it always like that?" she asked. "Between you and him?"

Levyathan frowned. "Not usually. His mind is too strong. Something happened to let his control slip."

Yes, she had witnessed that too. She ducked her head. "For what it's worth, I don't hate him. I... I no longer know what I feel."

Unnerved, feeling faintly silly for being on the defensive before a child, Aubrey turned and walked away from the view over the City, following the terrace to where it skirted one of the garden's curves and fronted abruptly upon a wide flight of broad steps. Halting before them, uncertain, she tried to discern what it was that lay in the shadows of that upper landing. Aubrey sensed Levyathan still beside her, a definable presence, a breath of something still curious.

"It's only another part of the Serat. Do you want to see?" He ascended the first few steps and extended his hand. "Come, lady."

It was an invitation... and also a command. Drawn by his quiet insistence, she accepted Levyathan's slight, boyish hand and let him lead her up those stairs of smooth marble to the secluded heights of a terrace garden. Here, upon a point about which the island itself seemed to have been shaped, the great glowing bowl of the City and harbor could be seen giving way to moonlit expanses of water and forest, and between them wide strands of silvered shore like a highway between kingdoms.

"See." Levyathan offered a smile. "We have the best view."

It *was* the best view. "I thank your Thrice Royal Highness," Aubrey said sincerely, seeing now the charm that had won over Arne. "Your City is lovely."

"And terrible too. Sordan has two faces." He leaned upon the wall, his chin resting upon his arms as together they admired the glowing beauty of the display before them. "One face is hard and cold, because it must be, to rule. Few know about the other, which is generous and loyal, but wary of strangers and locked behind secrets. It is so hidden, that face, most never look upon it. Neither do they know to look for it. People are quick to see a thing as they wish to see it."

"Are you warning me?"

"I'm trying to help you understand."

"Dorilian?"

"Dorilian is something astounding. I am hoping you can see past the layers of lies, and the wall of secrets, to know him for what he is. He is not the image others have created of him, or even the one he has been forced to create so he might live among them. Misperceptions protect him, but they harm him too." Levyathan's face, painted by moonlight, faintly luminous in its serene, childlike features, contained emotions she could not unravel. "Even now, Khelds are saying he is not here to greet them because of the enmity he bears toward your people."

It was true. Aubrey lowered her head, knowing she had played a part in the surface misperceptions about which Levyathan warned her. What sort of strange child was she speaking with? "Why are you telling me this?"

"You would not believe me if I revealed it. But you will see him again, and if you do so through a membrane of lies, you will never know him."

Aubrey shot him a cross frown. "As if I ever knew him. And don't talk to me about lies. He was a lie all along. I knew a man named Thron Estol Bevvan. I have never met Dorilian Sordaneon."

"Don't be so sure. His reality is deep. Whatever you knew in Thron Estol Bevvan must belong also to Dorilian, else he could not have been that man." Levyathan looked very young and serious in the dark that obscured them both with a veil of shadows. "You have known the man, but you have yet to meet the Highborn Hierarch about whom so many tales are told. You have yet to see the man in your mind and the Hierarch as one and the same."

And did she even want to? Was there no other way to reconcile the demon that came to her in the night, other than to let Dorilian's reality destroy what she knew? Aubrey sighed and turned her back on the City. "It may not matter. He's gone, and I have even forgotten what he looks like."

"Have you? Come, lady, and I will show you."

Levyathan led her to a place where the terrace broadened to a great verandah, its classical grandeur rising from the foliage in white columns and arches, silent and beckoning across silver tiles that gleamed like water beneath their feet. As though she walked into a mist, that evocative outer beauty gave way to inner splendor as terrace melted into gallery, gallery into hall, entering rooms richer and more elegantly appointed than any Aubrey had ever seen.

"No." She pulled back, afraid again. "This is where you live."

Only the Highborn, with their vast wealth and privilege, could possibly afford to surround themselves with such sumptuous seclusion, furnishings the least of which would cost a Kheld merchant his entire fortune to have in his home. And Aubrey found she did not want to see the way Dorilian lived, the truth of an existence so alien to one in which she'd played a part. That existence had been false, doomed to fail when confronted with this.

"It's the shortest way. Come. There is no one about, and there is something I would show you. It is but around the corner."

Along one of its faces, the walkway opened onto a long, airy gallery with white floors and walls and high domed ceiling. It looked like a place where visitors might wait for audiences. Elegant couches, with lines simple and functional for all their understated luxury, stood at various points around the room as the lighting flared at Levyathan's touch upon the wall, revealing its appointments.

"All the Hierarchs of Sordan reside here."

Levyathan drew her into a gallery lined with portraits. The echoing silence of the place, empty at this time of night, lent his words a hushed gravity. Pausing before one of the pictures, he bade Aubrey look. The man portrayed stared back at her with eyes the color of spring leaves, a narrow, handsome face marked by sensitivity and pride beneath a coronet of silver and emeralds intricately wrought about a glittering green stone.

"The Sordan Coronal is one of the fabled enhancers used by the Aryati," Levyathan said. "Not all of them were destroyed. This one is only worn on ceremonial occasions. The man wearing it is Deben I, the eldest son of the Rill god, Derlon. He was also Sordan's first Hierarch."

"He doesn't have gold hair." Aubrey spoke aloud what most surprised her.

"No. His mother was Neryllia of the Lilies. You'll see portraits of her too." Levyathan pointed to the next portrait. "And that man is his son, Deben II, who was just as great, and next to him is Deben III, who was magnificent. History knows them as the Three Debens. Under them, Sordan was glorious, a center of culture and prosperity in the Triempery for over five hundred years."

As Aubrey and Levyathan continued on into the gallery, a score or more portraits gazed from the walls, each as beautifully executed as its neighbors, details so finely brought to light that the subjects seemed to live still beneath the flatness of their likenesses. Only when Aubrey drew near to one likeness that especially intrigued her did she notice that these portraits showed no mark of paint or tint, but were instead smooth and flawlessly sketched, even as the likeness of Hans had been from Mena'tantaureus. It was not painting, but something else, a kind of magic that had captured them in life and transferred that moment onto this strange surface. Each man looked much like his predecessor, formidable rulers with intelligent faces and auras of authority, who retained generation after generation the golden-brown eyes, bright hair, and pale complexions of the Staubaun Lords. In their eyes, Aubrey saw the look of eagles.

"That is Davan II." Levyathan indicated a portrait of one long-dead ancestor. "He was Hierarch of Sordan for less than a year before he was killed at the mouth of Trongor Pass during the Last War with Ardaen, just minutes before the Kheld forces from Amallar would have reached him. And that," he pointed to another of the portraits, "is Tarlon Sordaneon, his son. The last true Rill Lord. Tarlon held afterward that the Khelds did not seriously attempt to aid his father, that they allowed Ardaen to kill Davan because Davan had argued against Kheld settlements in Neuberland. Tarlon never allowed another Kheld into his presence, even in Essera. He won many battles in the Great War with Ardaen and as part of the treaty ending that war, he gave one of his sons into a marriage with an Ardaenan princess. The Malyrdeons never did like sullying their linens." His words were so gently spoken that Aubrey couldn't tell if his observation was bitter or merely pertinent. Noting her attention, he smiled and added, "It is said Tarlon had his eye on Essera's throne. He probably did. Endurin was his friend as well as Highborn kin, and the mother of Endurin's Heir was Sordaneon, the daughter of Tarlon's younger brother. That half-Sordaneon Heir died, but not before he had fathered the mother of Marc Frederick Stauberg-Randolph. We Sordaneons, however, have never counted Marc Frederick among our relations."

Marc Frederick had been part Sordaneon. She had not known that. That meant Hans, too, carried some small part of that blood within him. Among Khelds such a relation was near enough to be counted. But she had heard that, among the Highborn, only the male members carried on the lineage.

It was then they came to a portrait whose subject cast a shadow on those men who preceded him both in looks and history. Aubrey looked in wonder on the likeness of a man whose appearance was dark and predatory, throwing off the golden heritage of the Staubaun race for the black hair, bronzed skin, and sea-gray eyes of the Ardaenan kings. *Labran*, Aubrey knew, even before Levyathan said the name. *He challenged Marc Frederick and lost—and was held hostage in Essera for thirty-five years.*

"Yes," Levyathan answered quietly. "It was a lesson we never forgot. His son, Deben IV, Dorilian's father"—he indicated the portrait at the end of the gallery—"ruled over a captive nation. He became a bitter man after his father was imprisoned, and never left this island but once, the day he died. Essera had ceased to be our brother and became our enemy. You see, lady, how the lesson lingers. We will never be brothers to Essera again, not even should Handurin move toward that goal."

"You mean, not if Dorilian should have his way."

"He *is* Sordan. And he has always had his way." Levyathan led Aubrey out of the gallery through a door opposite the one they had entered, then drew her into a wide, high-ceilinged chamber at the end of which stood a raised dais and a simple throne used for private audiences. Hung in honor behind it was a work of art magnificent to behold. "Dorilian had his coronation—and Essera had not even one representative in attendance."

The portrait showed the newly crowned Hierarch of Sordan seated on his eagle-winged throne, flanked by his court in full royal attire and pageantry. Behind him stood the imposing giant, Tiflan of Teremar, golden and powerful. Legon was there too, helm on arm, and a younger Deleus standing beside a tall older woman. A host of others, Staubaun and Estol and dignitaries of far-flung lands, stood in grim support of the youthful Hierarch. Like Stefan that same year, Dorilian had been twenty-one. The Rill Stone gleamed like an emerald star upon his hand where it rested on the gilded arm of the Eagle Throne. And the man seated there....

Aubrey dared to mount the dais and stare him in the eye. *Yes,* she thought, meeting the smooth gaze of the triumphant and arrogant youth who had been crowned Hierarch the same year Stefan had been crowned Essera's King. *I remember you. I met you in Amallar on a day when rain clouds thundered across the hills and the leaves were damp beneath our feet. Did I really put my dagger to your throat? Would that I had it there again.* Her Sordani spy, this man who years before she had ever met him had posed in his royal garments and device-crown, its jewels a blaze of green fire upon his brow. She shuddered that a likeness so perfect should have caught the soul-shattering coldness in Dorilian's silver eyes in his moment of attainment, the icy aura of defiance in the way he sat his throne, held sway over that bejeweled gathering. *You were born to rule them.* Aubrey had never been so certain of anything in her life as that which she knew upon seeing him clearly. *You were born to bring kings and empires to their knees. What's more, you know it.*

*And I was born to help a man named Hans Thegn turn your heart.*

She stood before the mural a long time, unable to tear herself away from that portrait, to stop looking at the handsome men, the beautiful women. Especially the women.

"Which one is your mother?" she asked softly. Levyathan stood silently beside her, watching her study the splendid picture on the wall.

He answered with the biting tones of frost as it snaps underfoot. "She is not there. She died the same day Deben did. Do not mention her to him, lady—not ever—for he will not forgive you for it. He hates even her memory."

"Will you tell me why?"

"How many reasons do you need?" The strange smile that tugged at Levyathan's lips was not that of a child. "She was Nammuor's sister."

Though morning dawned soft and silent, Aubrey's recent pain, far from being laid to rest, found fresh ways to remain bright. No matter where she turned in this Serat, what corridor she walked or person she met, Dorilian's name hovered at the edge of each conversation and the possibility of him lurked around every corner. Aubrey even felt him acutely when she met with Asphalladra early that day. Aubrey had requested to meet with Cullen's widow, who she had learned dwelt in the Serat in a small apartment adjacent to a pretty garden.

"Thank you for asking to see us." Asphalladra looked just as Aubrey had imagined she would: Staubaun tall, flaxen-haired, and perfect. "I wouldn't have known about you being here."

"They didn't tell you?"

Asphalladra shook her head, though she looked amused. "I'm a refugee in residence, not a member of the family."

They sat in the garden. Above the hedges, fountains, and main buildings of the sprawling palace, Rill rings and arches rose like surreal sculpture, rotating into new positions as *charysi* entered or departed. The thrums and whines of Rill movement were an ever-present song in this place.

Aubrey welcomed Asphalladra's offer to have the children brought to join them, a boy and a girl so like Cullen that Aubrey felt her heart swell. Eight-year-old Ranwulf had his father's wide mouth and smile, even had the same freckles dusted across his nose and cheeks. Allysa was brown-eyed and lively and fascinated by Aubrey's sash of Thegn plaid. "Like Da's!" the girl lisped. That Allysa spoke those words in Khelda brightened even sad thoughts. Heartstruck to see Cullen's children happy and safe, and regretting her previous hard thoughts about their mother, Aubrey spoke with her little cousins for several minutes until their governess took them to their morning lessons.

"In Amallar, everyone's sure they're dead." Aubrey watched the ample, laughing governess usher them away. As painful as the admission was, it was more painful knowing whom she had accused of those deaths.

"Erenor pronounced them so after we left," Asphalladra acknowledged. "He needed Cullen's heirs to be deceased. Out of the way. I believe I was pronounced a whore."

"Yes. The Hierarch's."

Aubrey craved Asphalladra's answer. Everything about it mattered. For a full year, Khelds had endured the shame of hearing that Cullen Brodheson's wife had run off to Sordan to become Dorilian Sordaneon's mistress.

Asphalladra's head tilted back, and it took her another moment to speak. "And that is how they kill off the last vestige of the man I love. They seek to remove him even from memory by placing me in the bed of a man so hated that every mention eclipses Cullen completely." The woman's pinned hair and soft gown of gauzy blue cotton were suited to Sordan's mild climate. Her Stauba, however, bore warm inflections true to Essera. Cultured. Privileged. *Foreign.* She and her children were indeed exiles.

"I never slept with the Hierarch." Tears lining her lashes, Asphalladra lowered her gaze. "Why would I? Why would *he*?

Dorilian helped me because he and Cullen knew each other. At Gustan, at the King's table those years ago—they conversed, they shared meals. That's how Cullen knew so much about the Rill and why he so hoped the Rill might come to Amallar. Because he listened, because Dorilian *said* things. Except it all changed. Marc Frederick died, and Stefan made the Rill impossible. If only Cullen could have lived to see this! A year has gone, just one year… and the world has changed and… dear Leur." She broke into a sob. "Cullen missed it by only that much."

Aubrey hadn't known. She had thought Dorilian Sordaneon knew no Khelds at all. Only now did she see that he must have known at least some. And Asphalladra had never been Dorilian's lover, could never have been, not when she still mourned her dead husband so deeply.

The Khelds left Sordan the next day at midmorning, accompanied by a delegation of Sordani representatives and a penned agreement of safe passage that would enable them to negotiate in Amallar. The Rill platform shimmered with a dreamy, sleeping haze of silent wonder as the Khelds said quiet goodbyes to their hosts. There would be no war with Sordan, of that Aubrey was now sure. No person who had seen Sordan would ever contemplate waging war upon it, except—and here she shuddered—a man with so much power that he could foresee the smashing of this City with its tall towers and watery approaches. Nammuor the Mormantaloran loomed much larger than he ever had before.

Just before leaving, Aubrey found herself drawn away from the others, around a corner, where Levyathan self-consciously placed a package in her hands.

"For you, lady, to take north."

Neatly tied in a plain wrapper he had surely put on with his own hands, the parcel was surprisingly light and not so large that it would not fit among the things Aubrey carried. Despite herself, Aubrey smiled. "What is it?"

"A gift, upon one condition: that you take it with you always and do not open it until you have nothing else fit to wear." Unfazed by her questioning look, Levyathan smiled and pressed another object into Aubrey's hand. "And this, from me, in remembrance of Sordan." It filled her hand with shimmering color, a hair ornament wrought in the shape of dragonflies, cast from a lustrous silver-blue metal. "It once belonged to another beautiful lady, one who also had dark hair. Here, let me show you." With fumbling hands, he placed it in her hair. "There," he said, then admitted, "I wish Fahme were here. She would do it better."

"Fahme?"

"My sister. She has clever fingers. You should hear her play the lute."

Dorilian had a daughter. And a son. A very strange son. Aubrey tried to make sense of both children but couldn't. Not here.

Though the ornament dragged heavily, not quite properly seated, Aubrey stammered her thanks, thinking it was almost certainly proper to decline such a personal gift but not knowing how to refuse it. Levyathan led her back to where the men gathered. Kheld and Sordani alike scrutinized her with a strangely respectful curiosity.

To the surprise of them all, Tiflan of Teremar strode onto the platform, a brace of youths loading his bags onto the baggage rack in a clear indication that he was joining them. Even before he came to stand with their group, awaiting the signal to enter the *charys*, Tiflan looked grim.

"Bad news," he said as he walked up. His golden eyes showed shadows of concern. "We're getting reports out of Trongor, just arrived. More details about something that happened ten days past at Ogarth."

"What would that be?" Arne asked, curious. Aubrey surmised that Arne hoped nothing had happened to Herberth, who he—and many at Rhodhur—had rather got to liking.

Tiflan frowned. "We don't know anything for certain yet. Information is scant and nothing firsthand. But it doesn't sound good." A high tone chimed, and he ushered the now silent and worried delegation onto the *charys*. Taking his seat, he said to the Kheldish elder beside him, "I think you will be wanting to send troops to the Pass."

# 3

Amynas awoke in a strange land where people worshipped
him in the manner of men who had come before him.
*Wind walkers*, the people called his kind, *light bringers*. His
mind, however, was uneasy when he saw that the Aryati
had made for themselves a perfect world where rain fell
and seas were smoothed because the diadem-wearers
wished it, and the people offered up their children and
their toil to appease a race of gods.
CIBULITUS, *ANNALS OF THE RETURN*

Hans spent the day following the Rill Coming listening to an endless gamut of Kheldish demands. Most had to do with politics and barely addressed economics. Should Staubauns be allowed to disembark at their station? How many at a time would be allowed to reside in Bellan Toregh? What about Estols, Ardaenans, Gae, and the damn Sordanish? Which domains were to be favored as trading partners, which relegated to gold-haired stepchildren?

Orem Darm, whose life spent on the Dazun River in sight of Dazunor-Rannuli had given him the opportunity to see Rill operations firsthand and who better understood the complexities that would emerge, soon proclaimed such discussions pointless.

"If we are not open to all, we are still closed—and might as well not have it, for all the good it will do. Without investment in warehouses and partnerships, goods or markets, the Rill is just a very fast horse."

Hans silently blessed Orem and marked him as an adviser.

As the discussion wound into late afternoon, even Nalf Rhys threw up his hands.

"We'll have decided all the rules and we don't even got us a game!" He'd sought out Hans during a necessary break between rounds of talk. "That cursed Rill had better make its return appearance in the morning, or I won't be the only one ready to string up the next Sordani messenger he sees!" It still rankled Nalf that Sordan's spy had made off just before the Rill had come. He would have been happier with a hostage.

"Just don't string up the Sordani delegation," Hans reminded him.

They walked from the Bridge and Chimney Inn, having taken a meal there, and made their way down the packed street toward the meeting hall. The crowds of the day before had not dwindled. Instead, word of the Rill coming had raced across the region and, in its wake, even more people had made their way to Bellan Toregh. The curious swelled a population already at the limit of the town's ability to handle them. Had Hans not been who he was, and Nalf Rhys Thegnard of Amallar, the inn would have turned them away. As it was, the innkeeper had leaped at the chance to not only feed men of renown but have some of his questions answered.

"They ask so many questions!" the innkeeper complained, without irony. "They want to know if there is only one silver sled that travels on it, or many? How does it move, and so swiftly?" Hans was unable to answer, though he promised the innkeeper that people were coming who could.

Just as he and Nalf were nearing the town's hall, a pair of riders made their way through the crowd, shouting.

"Hans Thegn!" It was Brec Anseldson, and by the look of him, he had ridden hard. He and the rider with him dismounted, the latter to hold their horses at ready. "Foreigners have come! You must return to the compound, and Nalf Rhys too, to decide what to do!"

Nalf glared at the young man, then at Hans. Clearly he was as unhappy with having his role usurped as by the news. "What kind of foreigners?" he demanded. Like Hans, he quickly swung up onto one of the horses.

Brec shook his head, his face taut and grim. The man who'd ridden with him had quickly recruited some of the elders and leaders who'd begun to pour out of the Witan meeting hall to help hold back the crowd, now alerted to something happening. "You ain't gonna believe it" was all he would say.

The compound swarmed with soldiers. The yard alone, before they even reached the buildings, overflowed with Kheld rangers and horsemen, at least a hundred by the look of them. Hans surmised they had come from the surrounding forests and hills and might be part of that force Nalf and Fran had assembled in anticipation of Sordani treachery. His heart dropped.

*Dorilian! They must have caught him!*

Hans urged his horse forward as the Khelds moved aside to make way. That there were no shouts, no condemnations, just scattered looks of expectancy, seemed all wrong. When he made his way to the center, he saw why. Within that circle of armed men, dismounted and sitting in relative comfort despite their situation, were two dozen other men wearing unfamiliar colors and garb. These, too, had the look of fighting men and women, though not precisely the air of soldiers. Even an initial glance showed them to be worn and grim, displaying the black hair and gray eyes of folk from Ardaen. They in turn guarded another man.

"Handurin! You look splendid, lad. Rusticity suits you!" One of the men bounced up from the bench on which he had been sitting, holding a fur hood in his hands.

"Endelarin?"

For once, Brec had understated the truth. Hans really couldn't believe it. Although apparently in good health and spirits, the Ardaenan king had not made the journey without hardship. His clothing, though elegant, was neither the cut nor fashion for hard travel and the purple velvets and tan leather showed rips and stains from rough terrain and foul weather. Only the many rings on his fingers and the modest jewels in Endelarin's crown had given the Khelds reason to credit his claim.

Hans dismounted and ran over to the gathered Ardaenans, all of whom stood to bow to him. "What are you doing here?"

Fran Gorseddson, who had arrived before Hans, grabbed his arm. "You mean he's who he says he is?"

"If he says he's Endelarin, King of Ardaen—yes!" Hans turned to Nalf and the others who gathered near. "Call off the soldiers and make the king and his guard welcome." When his simple pronouncement left Nalf looking unconvinced, Hans provided a stronger introduction. "This man is Endelarin Nemenor. I told you about him. I met him in Sordan, and he helped Arne and me get to Ogarth when our boat was damaged by a storm. We would have drowned at sea but for him. I don't know what the hells he's doing in Amallar, or how he got here, but he's a friend."

"A very *good* friend." Endelarin gave Nalf a toothy affirmation. "I gave your countrymen not only a free ride but reams of good advice. Some of which, I hear, he's taken."

Nalf grumbled in his throat. Seafaring Ardaenans had frequented neither Amallar nor Essera in recent years. The last time the two peoples had interacted to any degree had been during the Triempery's Second War with Ardaen, during which Kheld ancestors had found glory in battle against formidable foes. Endelarin's crew looked far from terrifying. No wonder the Khelds cast a skeptical eye.

"If you're such a fine friend," Nalf asked, "why is it our border patrol found you sneaking into Amallar?"

"I take exception to that accusation!" Endelarin straightened with apparently every bit of royal dignity he could muster. "One look at me will tell you that I am not the sort of man who sneaks! I do not have to. I have spies for that. On the contrary, my men and I were fleeing for our lives! And we're but the first. We were determined to reach you quickly." His expression turned grim. "I speak the truth: there are more on the way! Within a week, you will have more Trongorians than Trongor will—what's left of it."

"What do you mean?" Hans remembered his dream and his heart sank. Ogarth, its merchant-palaces and warehouses of stone, vanishing into the mist....

"Nammuor, that's what! He attacked without warning! Ogarth is gone and the Sorcerer has unleashed monsters on the land!"

The story came out over the course of the next few hours. Although pressed for details, Endelarin insisted that he and his people be fed before he could possibly undertake such an ordeal. "Harrowing," he said, "and we've eaten only the occasional rabbit or field mouse since. And drunk only water! Surely you have some wine?"

To Hans's surprise, Endelarin spoke passable Khelda, though none of his crew did. "One of the benefits of matrimony," the king explained with a wink. He had settled into the more comfortable surroundings of Hans's residence outside of town, to which all interested parties had retreated. Tables and chairs for Endelarin's escort, and a warm fire in the hearth, had done much to cheer the

King. "Two of my loveliest wives are Kheld women, blue-eyed flowers I plucked from Stauberg's garden years ago, before Khelds murdered the Wall and left the place. Women are wonderful for languages! They teach a man all the words needed to please them, which I am more than happy to learn… and do."

Out of curiosity and the goodness of their hearts, the Khelds fed the Ardaenans who had descended so unexpectedly upon them. Most townsfolk were too astonished to know what to make of the Ardaenan king and his bedraggled band. They were relieved to learn this was not the vanguard of a larger invasion, though why Ardaen should want to invade Amallar was not something anyone who floated that theory ever bothered to explain. When it became clear that Endelarin would reveal nothing until he had eaten, the Khelds provided the best they had to offer and raced to the nearest inn to fetch the cook there. The innkeeper himself served the meal and waited until Endelarin had pronounced it fitting fare.

"A fine feast! You are a master among cooks!" Endelarin declared after the first few bites. The innkeeper retreated to the admiration of onlookers, impressed that one of their own had earned royal praise. To Hans and the Kheld leadership seated at the table with him, Endelarin spoke between mouthfuls. "Our deprivation was extreme. We fled Ogarth with no supplies at all."

"You said you would explain that," Hans reminded him.

Heaving a sigh, Endelarin nodded. "You must be told, of course. It will be easier telling you, I hope, than it was telling Herberth. We encountered him trying to reach Ogarth at the same time we were riding as fast as we could to get away from it. He'd made a tour of the northern part of the country to do a bit of politicking. That diversion may well have saved his life, for surely Trongor will need him now. Indeed, it was he who told us we could find you here. Something about a plan."

The sea king's gaze clouded mournfully as he continued. "And to think that just two days before, I had awoken to a very fine morning! Two young Trongorian maids, absolute beauties—sisters too—after spending the night composing music with me had agreed to become wives. Honeymoons being what they are, I looked forward to a melodious voyage home and sent my pretty girls off to spend a last night with their mother. The weather was foul and so I passed the night on land. I keep a discreet little palace there. Or rather, I did, for I fear it is gone now. That very morning, a mist rolled into the harbor. My palace was on high ground and I could see"—Endelarin gazed unflinchingly at his listeners, his commonly merry face grim—"the ships were distorting, changing shape. Dissolving into the sea. One by one, I watched the masts and prows sink away. We Ardaenans are seafolk, and what happened to Zepheron and his ship is burned into our brains. We avoid Mormantalorus on the high seas. Nammuor does not sail into the Kolpos because, until now, he has chosen not to challenge Sordan or Ardaen. But I sensed at once what foul thing was happening."

He looked to Hans. "I knew the extent to which Herberth had helped you, which is to say not a whole lot—but to those not involved it probably looked like more. And I knew that the word must be out. No amount of talk about the Rill stopping and speculation about you still being held in Sordan was going to spare Herberth now. Nammuor is not where he is today because he thinks other people's business is their own. In less time than it just took me to describe our ordeal, I dismissed my household, rallied my people about me—as many as I could mount—and we took off for the hills. Even as we left the gate, we heard the howls and screams of the dying. Not only the ships and the buildings were disintegrating in that mist."

By now scores of men and women had gathered in the house. All were silent, listening to the tale. Though the place had grown warm from the press of many bodies, something in the air itself seemed to strike the listeners cold.

"I had clearly lost my ship, which is to say my way home. At first I tried to make my way by land to Ardaen using the road to Caerdon. But as we attempted to leave the city we spied ships at anchor, merchantmen all. They flew many flags but none were what they seemed. While we watched, those ships disgorged a fearsome cargo. Monstrous beasts! Ravening clawed things that turned on anything human, even their handlers, and with bloodied teeth tore them limb from limb and feasted on the carcasses. These, the Southlanders set loose in a horde to plague the countryside. Hundreds of them, thousands for all I know. Unfortunately, it was the countryside I had hoped to travel. I weighed my odds and, finding them not good, fled away from the coast, toward the mountains.

"It was then we met with Herberth's party on the road and apprised him of the situation. He agreed with my assessment. By then, refugees had begun to make their way along the road, and their tales were uniformly horrible. Ogarth was destroyed, every building turned soft and collapsing in upon itself, and every human being touched by the mist was doing the same. Those who fled were being devoured by monsters. I wished Herberth well, as he was determined to lead Trongor through this trouble and in the battle to come. It is clear that Nammuor has begun the war in the south. As Trongor's Elector, Herberth prevailed upon me that I would find the most safety to leave Trongor altogether, make my way through the Pass into Amallar. He then put upon me the grave task of warning you, which I said I would do. And, oh"—Endelarin pulled an envelope from his pocket and extended it to Hans—"this is for you. In his own words."

"How many people?" Hans took the note, still warm from Endelarin's body. He wished he could drive from his mind the images that had taken root there. "How many people have died?"

Whatever weariness Endelarin had pushed aside in the telling of his escape now came back upon him. His ordeal showed in his face. "I could not tell you. Ogarth was home to tens of thousands of souls. Many tens of thousands."

"All dead?"

"Most of them. Some escaped, as we did, but they were not many, nor do we know what has befallen them. Certainly, those in the countryside had better chances." Endelarin looked at the men and women seated and standing so grimly around the crowded room. "Is it wrong to hope that they might find refuge among your folk?"

"Aye, they might," Nalf Rhys granted, reluctantly it seemed. He glanced at Hans's guard of Trongorian rangers, all ten of which were seated nearby, looking grim. "Trongor's folk are a doughty lot—so long as they don't settle in, get too comfortable."

"I'm sure you can see to that," Endelarin said.

Hans knew argument would ensue and hoped the Khelds would continue their ancient hospitality. Amallar could absorb Trongor's refugees. He knew the Khelds well enough now to know they would be kindhearted to men and women fleeing from a terrible enemy. Kheld leaders might fret about the numbers or allowing a foreign presence on their soil, but they would not turn away people in their time of need.

"What of yourself?" Hans asked the Ardaenan king, turning the conversation in a different direction. "I don't suppose you're planning a lengthy stay?"

"Hardly. I can find much warmer company. No, my original plan was to take the road to Leseos and then to Randpory, where I might travel by Rill to Sordan. Once there, I am sure cousin Dorilian would provide me with a way off his island." Endelarin perked at the thought, adding hopefully, "If it's true the Rill has started up again and stops here now, perhaps I could catch it tomorrow? I believe I have warned you sufficiently."

"And about what?" Fran Gorseddson challenged, looking unsatisfied. "We've had no reports of any of this. Not of monsters and not of Trongorians crossing the mountains, either. How do we know it's not Sordan has set you up to this, seeing as you and the Sordaneon are cousins and all?"

Endelarin snorted. "The only thing my royal cousin and I have ever done together is argue! And I can assure you he could do better than to send an underarmed force of Ardaenans led by an inept soldier such as myself into Amallar!"

One look at the bedraggled Endelarin and his tattered companions bore out that they little resembled a fearsome force. The Sordaneon, they knew, was capable of much more. Blowing out a sigh, Nalf Rhys silenced Fran's protest with a look and spoke more reasonably to the Ardaenan king. "We got us a lot of Sordan stuff going on just now. You already heard how the damn Rill showed up. And one of their spies fled out just the night before that. Now you come to us with this Trongor story."

Endelarin was not mollified. "My only charge was to deliver the message. Whether you believe it or not isn't something I promised to ensure. I am now most concerned with getting back to Ardaen, provided the Sorcerer hasn't unleashed something even worse on my poor kingdom. It's entirely possible he now knows that *I* gave Handurin passage! Who knows what horrors he might visit on Ardaen? At the very least, my subjects do not know now if I am alive or dead. My sister the Queen, formidable as she is, may be overmatched. My wives will be inconsolable, and my heirs may be overly ambitious. Things are not going well, and if you choose not to believe it, that is the least of my problems."

The Khelds looked dismayed and unsure. Ardaen had always been a distant foe of theirs, one with which none of them in living memory had ever battled. Yet every Kheld child was raised under the auspices of the ancient trust put upon them by Erydon the Gift-Giver when he had first ceded them their land: that they should stand ever vigilant against Ardaen. Twice, they knew, the Highborn Triempery had warred with that nation. Though there had been no war in more than one hundred fifty years, and Marc Frederick had often received the Ardaenan king and ambassadors at his court, Stefan had been less friendly and Amallar was not convinced that Ardaen no longer presented a threat. More than a few of the Khelds in the room wondered if perhaps the Ardaenans were not simply being crafty.

Hans, however, thought Endelarin looked too grim, his sunniness too shadowed, for there not to be truth to the horror he had witnessed. Not only that but Hans, too, felt something had gone very wrong. *Nammuor wants to frighten away any who would support me. By doing this, he robs me of Trongor and sends a message to other nations. And he strikes a blow at Sordan as well.* Now Sordan would need to worry about similar battles near its own territory. An insight came to him—blinding, sharp, and true.

*Nammuor wants to keep Dorilian in Sordan. Or give him reason to return. Trongor is just a gruesome diversion.*

Let this Sorcerer try to frighten away potential allies. Hans was not about to let those efforts frighten him or keep him from his purpose. But maybe he could offer help to Trongor.

"We'll find out soon enough if what King Endelarin says is true," Hans told the Khelds gathered in the room. "Until then we should see to his comfort and good treatment. At the very least, he'll spend the night as my guest. Brec and his lads can see to the Pass. He can take the force the *keld* chiefs have gathered here."

"Not a chance." Nalf crossed his arms over his chest. "Sordan could still send a bellyful of soldiers at us. This could be a trick."

"Don't tell me we're going to do nothing about the Pass."

Brec stepped forward. "I'll take any fighting men that want to go with me. We got towns on the way, and I left a company of good men at the Pass. I can send word by wing within the hour. We know how to block the mountain. If there's a problem, we can put up a fight."

That resolved the issue for the time being. There were still Rill issues and more to talk about, as the elders reminded them, and the Khelds willingly went back to the town's hall for discussions, knowing Endelarin and his folk would still be there in the morning. Hans stayed with Endelarin, sitting by the table, watching the townspeople leave.

"Suspicious lot you've taken up with." Endelarin sank back into his chair. "Are you sure they're your best option for a people to lead?"

Hans sighed. "They're not always that way. Like Nalf, the Thegnard, said, it's been an unusual couple of days."

"For all concerned. At least I will thank them for the hospitality and a good night's sleep. Khelds certainly are a prickly crowd! My wives had led me to think they would be more... fun!" Though haggard, Endelarin looked at Hans shrewdly. "So the Rill does run here now, which must mean you've patched up things with Dorilian. Good! He makes a bad enemy, as Stefan found out. I can think of few situations worse than having Nammuor wanting to kill you on one hand and Dorilian behaving like a stone wall on the other." He leaned nearer, his voice dropping to a tone more confidential. "But whatever did you do, that he would send the Rill here, to this untidy little backwater of less-than-friendly natives?"

"I asked him for it."

"Asked him?" Endelarin chortled softly to himself. His travel-stained leathers rumpled as he leaned back in his creaking chair. "Well, there would be a new approach. And just when did you ask him?"

The next day saw the return of cloudy skies, the smell of hams being smoked, boat traffic on the river, and the Rill. Hans waited on the broad white platform with an apprehension barely less acute than when he had waited for it two days before. What if something had gone wrong in Sordan? Endelarin stood with him while the Trongorian and Ardaenan men at arms waited below to ease lingering Kheld suspicion that they might be party to some diabolical Sordani plot.

"I'm sure your people are safe enough. Sordan is not an uncivilized City. People there know how to treat emissaries. They don't generally resort to murder most foul or taking hostages or... anything as barbaric as that." Endelarin appeared not to notice the scowl Nalf Rhys directed his way.

Rill whine split the morning with its distinctive signature. Just as it had more than a day ago, only now from the south, there came a pinpoint, a blaze, a great disk of light that assumed the shape of a *charys* before their eyes. Their ears warmed to the reverberations of deceleration. Those Khelds watching cheered roundly as the *charys* eased once more to a stop where they stood. When the vessel's portals opened and the Kheld delegation emerged, obviously unharmed and smiling, there was another round of cheers. Hans embraced Aubrey and Arne and greeted the rest of the Khelds, including an elder named Renwitt, who leaned near to him and whispered, "They have fooled us all. They are ruled by a boy!"

Hans greeted the Sordani delegation, noting a few members with surprise. Tiflan grinned at seeing him again, but Pallas Trophoneos accorded only a stiffly proper bow upon acknowledging him. As Nalf launched into a welcoming speech, Endelarin looked around from behind Hans and waved. Tiflan and Pallas frowned with disapproval while Nalf explained that it was high time for negotiations, given the trouble in Trongor and the general state of Essera.

"And now it seems we got us wickedness in every corner and it's time to get out the broom," Nalf Rhys said, indulging in Kheld fondness for metaphor. "Let's see if we can sweep away enough dust to find the floor and get down to what we have to do."

As the welcome ceremony wound down and the rest of the Sordani delegation went with Nalf to their accommodations, Hans stayed behind with Tiflan and Endelarin to watch the unloading of the Rill car. In the spirit of important negotiations, the Sordani had come bearing gifts. Among the first to be unloaded were many fine horses, one of them an ivory, blue-hoofed beauty, a gift to Hans from Levyathan Sordaneon. "He thought you should have him to ride north," Tiflan said.

Hans ran his hand appreciatively over the gelding's sleek shoulder. "A mount fit for a king."

"Which you are."

Endelarin, for his part, skirted the beast and peered inside the *charys*. "I should say there's room enough in here now for my crew and myself, and our horses too."

Taking renewed notice of the Ardaenan king, Tiflan fixed him with a puzzled frown. "You are the last person I would have thought to find here. The nearest seaworthy port to this station is in Trongor!"

"And so, last I heard, is Nammuor!" Endelarin would hear no more criticism. "After what happened to me in Ogarth, I suggest you stay well clear of him yourself. It was Amallar or death, I tell you, and Amallar suddenly seemed very suitable. Until I got here, that is. Kings can't just sally forth into other nations, you know. They thought I was invading them!"

His frown deepening, Tiflan turned to where Hans stood with Arne and Aubrey. "Your countrymen were wrong only in that the real foe was on Endelarin's heels. Now you must be wary that Nammuor will seek to invade Amallar by the same passes that Ardaen has often used."

"Our rangers can call on the forest *kelds* and hold back Mormantalorans just as fiercely as we last fought with Ardaen," Aubrey asserted. "Unless," she worried at a new thought, "the Sorcerer can conjure up an army."

"No, he can't do that," Tiflan assured them. "Unless he has mastered a higher sorcery than any Diadem wearer before him, the only man he can conjure from one place to another is himself."

"Well, he got those ships in. Dorilian should replace his admiral." Endelarin peeked again at the *charys*. "How long will this thing sit here? My men are still at the bottom of the hill. I need to get back to Ardaen and the business of keeping Nammuor out of the Kolpos. Dorilian certainly won't have a problem with my help in doing *that*! All I will ask of him is a good meal and perhaps, for once, some pleasant conversation. He is capable of it, you know."

"Not currently." Tiflan looked out across the snowy countryside. "He's out of the City. But Levyathan can see to whatever you need."

"Dorilian not in his City at a time like this! With Nammuor running amok?" Endelarin looked from one person to another, quickly grasping that he would get no answers. Following a sigh, he fixed his attention on Aubrey. "You're the only one here worth looking at," he said warmly. His grin became positively brilliant. "Would you consider being a royal bride? I have a lot to offer: jewels, clothes, palaces, riches beyond your wildest dr—"

"—Headaches as endless as his penchant for babbling," Tiflan interceded. As Aubrey gaped in astonishment, the tall Bas grasped Endelarin by the elbow and propelled him along the platform. "I suggest you do get on this *charys*. We brought an Epopte to run things, so I'll write you a pass. Now go fetch your men."

"—And I'm a lot of fun, in bed and out!" Endelarin finished before Tiflan had him out of sight.

Watching them, Hans both grinned and sighed.

Aubrey shook her head. "I don't know about trusting Ardaen to keep Nammuor from bringing troops into Trongor," she said.

"Endelarin has more wits than people give him credit for. And I've heard only good things about his sister the Queen. He'll do what he says. The minute he gets to Sordan, he'll have access to ships and ambassadors and the rest of the machinery of diplomacy and war. He's related to the Sordaneons, remember. He'll tell them what he saw."

Arne looked at Hans. "*He* won't know." Arne would not say that name, out of habit, and also because Aubrey stood near, even though she surely had to know who was meant. "Levyathan is the only Sordaneon in Sordan now."

But Hans felt something bigger taking place, even on the glistening white platform where they stood. "He'll know," he asserted, sure of it. "He probably already does."

Beside him, Aubrey blanched but nodded. "Yes," she said, "and if he doesn't, he'll know as soon as Levyathan knows."

# 4

Our race perceives manifold chronological vectors, but
our ability to time-bind is one-directional—we cannot
transfer information to previous generations, only those
contemporary with us or which come after us. But
consider the Entities, that they exist throughout the
whole of Time. Through them, might we not exchange
information with both future and past?
EMRYSEN MALYRDEON, *ERGEIRON AND DALN: A STUDY IN LEUR*

"Nammuor's *sister*?"

Hans and Aubrey stood inside an audience chamber of Bellan Toregh's Rill sanctuary, which Tharos had just opened, along with other public spaces half of the Kheld elders in attendance had just inspected. Before leaving, the elders had pronounced the room strangely given to windows. In the rare moments of solitude, Aubrey laid out everything she'd learned during her time in Sordan: how Deleus's resemblance had maintained the illusion of Dorilian still being in the City, Levyathan's strange knowledge of distant events, the horrible news out of Trongor.

And the truth of Dorilian's marriage.

Endelarin's hushed hint at the Feast of Coming hadn't even touched the surface. *A scandal from the very first vow.*

Tiflan returned upon the end of that last revelation. Hans found himself looking to the solid, frowning presence, hoping he would fill in the rest. But Tiflan was evasive. Having seen Endelarin off on the return Rill to Sordan, he'd joined Hans and Aubrey in the sanctuary, not guessing he would be waylaid with difficult questions.

"It's enough you know that much. Dorilian has nearly succeeded in erasing her from the Mind. As for the rest, I'm not going to lay out the personal details of my cousin's life for you."

"But it's true?"

"Levyathan would not lie." The big man sighed. The north-facing portals of the room looked out across Amallar's wintery hills; those to the east overlooked the platform, where observers could watch the loading or unloading of the Rill. People going about their business outside would not know they were being observed.

If Tiflan had hoped Hans would send Aubrey away, he was soon disappointed. Hans wanted Aubrey to hear this—and to hear it himself. At last Tiflan relented enough to tell them a little. "Her name was Daimonaeris, daughter of Camas of Voret. Her father was Highborn, a Malyrdeon by lineage, and Nuarch of Mormantalorus. The line went *gynekos* and he was the last of them."

"Nammuor is Highborn?"

"No. Same mother but different father. Camas raised him and sired Nammuor's sister. There were twenty years between them." Tiflan studied the design set into the tabletop—smooth, polished, flowing like molten metal. He looked thoughtful. And troubled. "Royal marriages, you must understand, belong to politics, not love. Dynasties, not individuals, matter. Bloodlines and inheritances. Alliances and heirs. Dorilian was sixteen and Heir to Sordan. He didn't want a wife. He didn't know what he wanted. Deben wanted her."

"For his son," Hans clarified.

Tiflan gazed at him evenly. "For Sordan. Dorilian is who she *wed*."

Hans realized it then. "But not who she slept with."

Nearby, in front of a view of snow and sky, Aubrey stood stiff and alert, clearly unwilling to say anything that might stop the flow of revelations.

Tiflan's mouth firmed bitterly. "People believe those things they find obvious. Truth can be concealed by assumptions. The Highborn live long, in part because they come slowly to physical maturity. They cannot reproduce in their teens. Dorilian was typical in that. He didn't reach full height until he was twenty-five. He very likely couldn't have sired a child until then."

"Levyathan's not his son."

Tiflan nodded, acknowledging that truth. "Only in name. But he is Sordaneon. The boy was born of Deben's seed."

Not Dorilian's son, his brother. The child of betrayal. Yet

Levyathan was just as Highborn, just as Sordaneon, and just as powerfully, stubbornly loved. Hans knew he had not mistaken that affection. "And Dorilian isn't angry about it?"

"There's more to it. Some things are beyond anger, beyond vengeance. This thing has a scope you cannot imagine. Do not discredit Dorilian's ability to perceive the plots others direct against him or discern between perpetrator and victim. Nor should you underestimate what he will do to salvage those he loves."

"Maybe someday he'll tell me. I'm willing to wait for that." Hans respected what Tiflan was trying to do. "It's just that...." He couldn't see a sensitive way to put it. "If Levyathan is Nammuor's nephew—he's also his Heir! I studied law about that stuff. Grandson of the body and legal successor of Mormantalorus's last Nuarch. Not to mention Levyathan may be Nammuor's only blood relation. I haven't heard of any others, have you?"

"No."

"That's significant, Tiflan."

"Yes, it is." Tiflan never lost his pleasant expression, though he remained thoughtful. "Obviously, Levyathan thought it something you should know, you and this young woman. Nammuor's ambition did not start with Essera. His first attempt was at Sordan. The City along with the Sordaneon Rill birthright and the family's claim to Essera's throne were to be his through Daimonaeris's son. You see, he knew that Deben sired sons, not daughters. The marriage to Dorilian was never intended to be anything but a sham. Once Nammuor had his heir, all the Sordaneons save the infant would be murdered. But Dorilian turned out to be a surprise. Maybe he had the Rill gift—maybe not. Maybe he and Levyathan his brother possessed a degree of Highborn sorcery—maybe not. Nammuor couldn't tell. No one could tell, not even Marenthro with all his ways. The Sordaneons were too secretive, and Dorilian's shields against the outside world were too strong. Our grandfather, Sebbord, had made sure of that."

"What you said... about Dorilian salvaging those he loves." Hans had been working the timeline in his head. The events surrounding the brothers. In his mind, he was once more in Sordan, standing on the terrace high above the flagstone court... the screaming, the falling... the mad dancing of costumed sorcerers before the towers bloodied by sunset as Second Day hurtled toward darkness. Had Nammuor been there? "The day his brother died..."

Perhaps sensing those thoughts, Tiflan shook his head. "Do not go there. It's not a good place. His brother's death was a terrible day—and not one I can explain. Dorilian lost his mind with grief. Levyathan—*this* Levyathan—was born a year later."

"But to give the child the same name?" Aubrey whispered. Both men heard her and turned to look. "They're uncanny, both of them are... because of that? Was he trying to wish his brother back to life?"

Tiflan rose and picked up his things. "No one knows. He's never said." He made for the doorway, paused, then looked back. To Hans he said, "They're Highborn and they're brothers. They share thoughts and memories—and life itself. They share everything, even death. A few drops of Nammuor's blood won't come between them. Even Nammuor knows better than that."

"And what happened to Daimonaeris?" Hans asked.

Tiflan nodded to Aubrey. "Just as Levyathan told her. She died the same day Deben did. Dorilian cut off her head."

# 5



As Dorilian left the hills behind and descended the road toward the Dazun and Merath, even the air changed. Heavy now—redolent with scents of wet vegetation, brackish freshwater wetlands, and muck stirred up by frogs and eels—it smelled like Gustan. Every breath reminded him of a fateful season and the man with whom he had spent and squandered a year. He would give back every day of the last twelve years of his life to have that year with Marc Frederick returned to him, to spend it again and remake the World. Had Dorilian awakened the Trestethion node then, with Marc Frederick at his side, would the Khelds still have hated him? Probably... though maybe less than they did now.

And yet here he was, in thrice-cursed Amallar, on *this* road. The road from Trestethion, from Bellan Toregh. And ahead of him lay a river. Always before, Dorilian had seen the mighty Dazun as a highway. Today the river was an obstacle. It and the Kheld town of Eldwadder stood between him and the safety of Merath.

"Six riders, a day behind. Pressing hard." The man speaking was one of Farrl's rangers, a man named Amel, whose nondescript looks allowed him to better blend in among the Khelds. He had just ridden in from watching to see if anyone followed. "They're stopping at inns, taverns, farmholds along the way. Asking about Trongorians. Spies. The townsfolk who've met us are giving us up."

"A day behind?" Farrl confirmed.

Amel nodded. "No more than that. I outrode them to get here. Once past where the road forks to Dazunor-Rannuli, no more need for asking or stopping. They'll finger us for the bridge at Eldwadder."

A complication. Dorilian had hoped to reach Merath without incident. He might still do so, though it was midday already. When Farrl offered a plan, he listened.

"The bridge is a half day ahead, sir." By not employing proper address in front of his men, Farrl maintained the pretense that Dorilian, while a man of import, was not royal. "We might make Merath tonight if we press the horses."

"No," Dorilian said. The threat of pursuit did not override caution. They would reach Eldwadder and the High River Bridge ahead of their pursuers, but if they were to reach safety they must also *cross* it. Though Khelds kept an eye on travelers who entered their country, they little cared about any leaving. Merath, on the other hand, would be sure to question the passage of armed men from Amallar. Best not to court being turned back. "Sordan has an embassy in Merath—and my ambassador there will honor this order." Dorilian handed Farrl a locked cylinder with his personal seal. "Choose two men and ride ahead. Take the fittest horses and press to cross the bridge tonight. You have the diplomatic passes Herberth left you. The ambassador, Vaneus Pindar, is reliable. He will deploy the embassy's guard to await my arrival."

"If I may ask, sir? Should we not approach Merrydn's Princess?" As Amel and the other rangers dispersed to prepare for that day's ride, Farrl spoke more freely, but softly. "I know I presume, but... are you not kin to her?"

"Kinship counts for little these days. I will give her no notice by which to close her gates against me."

Farrl gave a subtle bow and went to select the men who would ride with him into the city.

Dorilian, who would journey at a less pressed pace with the rest of the men, knew he was being unfair. It was proper form to notify his royal kinswoman that he was entering her city. To not inform her until after he arrived was a slap in the face, but he had never liked Ionais Malyrdeonis. Though they were related doubly through the Highborn blood of their fathers and his mother, in his mind she would always be the woman Jonthan Stauberg-Randolph had married and then tragically widowed, leaving the Malyrdeon plan for the Triempery ruined. From their very first meeting, Ionais's attitude toward Dorilian had smacked of contempt, marked by deletions of etiquette no woman born into a Highborn house would ever commit in ignorance.

Neither had it helped that Dorilian's youthful pride had magnified every slight, turning oversights into insults, every dismissal to personal attack. Though their ranks were carved in eternal stone, their personal positions had changed in ways Ionais and her fellow aristocrats had yet to realize.

*I have slipped their chains. I could be their king if I wanted that. And they do not yet know I have wrenched the Rill out from under their feet.*

His success at the latter accorded an unimaginable freedom, striking away shackles Dorilian had not even known he was wearing. Covert strictures, invisible and ulterior, passed on through generations. Marc Frederick had hinted at them but only now, in hindsight, did Dorilian perceive them. At last, he commanded true power—beyond that of the name he carried, more than bestowed by a crown on his head or a sword in his hand. The power of his Entity filled his body like blood.

*Rill Lord.* For years, he had declined to test the greatest part of his birthright. Others had suspected his affinity and crafted designs. Ambitions to be attained. Fears and paralysis to hold him. A memory bubbled to the surface and he felt Nammuor's horrible finger on his cheek, the hated voice inserting a needle of fear.

*The Seven Houses would pay a lot to get their hands on you.*

Dorilian shuddered and his horse, sensing a change in its rider, slowed its pace.

"Is something wrong?" The Kheld elder, Robdan, eased his mount alongside him. Dorilian had almost forgotten him.

"No," he answered.

True, of course... though not entirely. Nammuor's existence haunted this Second Creation. That malignant presence was with Dorilian always, creeping tendrils of hate that vibrated the strands of his psyche the same way touch vibrated a web. Nammuor's Diadem was a palpable thing even here on the farthest edges of its influence, its alien energies pushing against the fragile stasis shields within which Leur had encased the recreated World. Those shields rendered most weapons ineffective but for blades—Leur magic or

Leur physics, the energy threshold rules were unbreakable—but their protections governed only the forces of physics, not those generated by arcane devices. Or Entities.

Nammuor's crazed Entity stood poised to unmake the Creation—and perhaps even sought that.

The damned Diadem needed to be broken once and for all.

A cold wind pierced Dorilian's coat, and he shivered. Allowing Rill plasm to reside, even temporarily, in his skin augmented his senses but also opened channels he preferred be left closed. When in contact with it he felt everything—everyone—as alien. Sharp-boned. Acute.

As he had felt Aubrey that night. Intensely, intimately, so vividly alive. Had his awareness been due to the Rill or something more?

It was just as well he had placed some distance between himself and the Rill's active field. From *her*. From complicated entanglements. With senses freed from the conundrums that plagued him, Dorilian could imagine himself ordinary again, merely human, as he rode to Merath along muddy roads through fields and snowbound woods.

With Farrl gone, Dorilian assumed command of the remaining men. Because being found at an inn or holding would be too risky, they stopped for the night in some woods beside the river road of Eldwadder, a Kheld town on the bank of the Dazun and within a stone's throw of the bridge. Out of an excess of precaution, neither Khelds nor the Merrydni allowed traffic to cross at night. It was just as well; the men needed food and the horses could use the rest. Always with a man on watch, the escort huddled together to eat boiled eggs and dried beef. The horses were picketed out for some forage, though they remained saddled and ready to be mounted on short notice.

The meal was a poor one, barely enough, and Dorilian thought about sending a man to one of the town's many inns to procure tastier fare. Not just for himself, but his escort as well. Tonight, at least, he would not eat better than his men. Even without the swordmaster's scowling presence, Tutto's lessons endured. While with his soldiers—even these soldiers whom he had taken on for having no other choice—Dorilian was one of their number. Responsible for them. He had the place of command and while they guarded his life, he must also guard theirs.

The best guarantee of his life was to not endanger theirs. Not even make a simple purchase that might draw attention. And so he ate cold eggs and stale bread and dreamed of Gerd's cooking, of the sweet buns and egg puddings and tender lamb stews he regretted leaving behind.

When dawn came, and with it knowledge that the bridge was open again to travel, they set out. Even across the broad sweep of the Dazun, Merath was beautiful, a great city guarded by stone towers and strong walls that had served for centuries as defense against foreign invaders and Kheld barbarians. Khelds hadn't attacked that bastion in three hundred years, so the bridge to Amallar was less heavily guarded these days than the even grander bridges that crossed the Rannul River into Dazunor. Merath presided at the confluence of both the Rannul and Dazun—and it flaunted Esseran prosperity from the high walls of its many palaces.

The sun had barely nudged above the trees, but on the river it poured broad ribbons of pink light between banks lined by the city and town. Eldwadder itself had awakened and the bridgefront street stirred with early traffic. Farmers headed to market with their goods while merchants set up stalls in front of their shops. Already there were customers and people readying to cross. As were all bridges throughout the land, the span over the Dazun river was subject to Triemperal law and kept open to travelers; but Dorilian had overheard enough talk along the way to know that guards on the Kheld side made the crossing unpleasant for those they did not favor. A party of sturdy Khelds, some mounted and all armed, met them on the approach to the bridge. More Khelds lounged near the guardhouse. Men and horses alike breathed frost into the chilled morning mist as Robdan rode forward to meet them.

"Sir." The ranger Amel rode up beside Dorilian, directing his attention to their rear.

Eldwadder's shops and sundry businesses still appeared calm enough. However, an unusual flurry of movement for so early an hour stirred at a curve where one of the town's main roads turned toward the river. Riders. Several of them. Possibly their pursuers.

*Damn.* Dorilian must get himself and his men past the guards on the bridge... and then he must hope upon Leur that Farrl had succeeded in alerting the embassy.

"Speak your business," one of the Khelds demanded of Robdan, loudly enough for all to hear.

Robdan cleared his throat. "Well, you see, we're on our way to Merath."

"You don't say."

"Wait, Cadfarch." One of the other guards nudged his mount forward. "I know this man. This here is Robdan Aelfricson, my own uncle from Rhodhur!"

"The Archcouncilman?" Cadfarch scrutinized Robdan with new respect.

The other guard, stout and bearded, nodded. "Don't you remember me, Uncle?"

"Why, it's Holweck, isn't it?" Robdan gave a harder look. "I haven't seen Euneth in more than an age—but I can see you've turned into your father instead of her."

Dorilian recognized what was happening. It was pure Kheld custom that Robdan would do a bit of kin sharing. He prayed the exchange would not waste too much time. Dorilian leaned to Amel and, keeping his voice low, spoke in Esta. "Signal the men. If those Khelds ride toward us, we charge past these guards. Our safety lies on the other side."

Though Amel nodded, there was no mistaking his concern regarding that plan. He too had clearly spied archers among the bridge's Kheld guards.

Holweck chuckled and kept speaking to Robdan. "Got business, do you, Uncle? Over river?"

"Hans Thegn has sent us to see about working something out with Merrydn."

"Ain't he something?" Holweck took in hand the passes Robdan extended. "Heard talk he's set on getting back the King's throne in Essera. Said something at Witan about getting the Rill to come. Think that's true, is it? Got message by bird that it might have happened."

"Oh, yes, I think it maybe has. That's what he said would happen, anyway. But it's been days since we left, you know."

"I envy you meeting him at all, but it makes sense given your place. Ain't it something, though. Here. Go on." Holweck handed the passes to Cadfarch, who did not even glance at the papers before passing them back to Robdan.

Dorilian edged his horse forward to join Robdan and signaled the other men to do so also. The riders at the far end of town had noticed them and regrouped. Only moments more remained.

"Heard about Hans Thegn's Trongorians." Cadfarch assessed them solemnly above a full, seldom-trimmed beard he probably found useful for irritating Staubauns who attempted the crossing. "If it's for him, you're good with us."

Cadfarch waved them through.

They were clear of the guard. Ahead of them, passage across the bridge lay open, though they were not alone in crossing the long span. Carts and wagons, as well as other travelers, also occupied the way but at this hour there were not many. Most were headed into Amallar, not leaving. Between these groups were stretches of open bridge.

The Kheld guards would slow their pursuers... but possibly not for long. Already those riders were at the guard post. Upon turning to look back, Dorilian saw them gesticulating and trying to break through.

"Ride," Dorilian urged. There was too much bridge yet to cross. A hard clamp of his knees caused his mount to quicken pace and he leaned into it, low to his horse's neck. Near his side, Robdan lurched and grasped at the horn of his saddle to keep his seat when his horse leaped to follow. The Trongorians, alerted, quickly assumed formation behind and to the fore. Together, they fled at high speed across the remaining bridge.

Deep and gray, the Dazun flowed in leaden currents under the tall bridge's graceful arches. The hoofs of their horses sounded a dull passage as they left Amallar behind. Shouts followed, but no arrows. No doubt the Kheld guards were loath to let arrows fly upon unsuspecting travelers, merchants and their beasts. Racing now, Dorilian and his escort wove around a tarp-covered wagon, spooking the wagoners and their oxen. Merath loomed before them, a vista of blue stone towers and moss-stained walls as dark as the water beneath the bridge.

Ahead, not quite half the way across, stood a wall of uniformed Merrydni guards, their blue leathers barred and trimmed with black. What had caused their advance could be seen behind them: a mounted force wearing Sordani green and silver. Dorilian and his escort reached the guards, who parted to let them through, then closed ranks to every side of them.

A tall man, helmet festooned with an officer's crest, ran forward to confront Dorilian.

"Are you the emissary?" the officer asked urgently.

"I am more than that." Dorilian gestured toward the Sordani guards. Vaneus Pindar was with them, attired in diplomatic blue. Farrl rode with him.

The approaching pursuers, undissuaded by the guards on foot, slowed only for a moment. Encouraged as the Merrydni soldiers hesitated, the pursuers pressed forward, shouting and waving their weapons. At once the embassy's troops, already on high alert, charged through the stunned Merrydni line to bar the way. Faced with a wall of horses and men armed with steel, the six Kheld pursuers reined to a halt. That didn't keep them from shouting invectives.

The angry Merrydni captain confronted Dorilian, who had positioned his horse at the side of Vaneus's. "Halt! Ambassador, I must protest! I must speak with my commander. We have an agreement with these people!"

"Not about me," Dorilian said. He signaled for the mounted guards to attend him. The captain of the Sordani embassy guard bowed and obeyed, ordering his troops, despite not knowing he was in the presence of his Hierarch. Projective empathy had its uses. Farrl gathered his men also, including the nearly forgotten and frightened-looking Robdan. To the Merrydni captain, Dorilian said, "I will be certain to tell your Princess that you performed your duty this day."

"S—sir," the man stammered, taking in all signs that he was in the presence of a man of rank, but uncertain of how and why.

"Send the Khelds back unharmed. Don't let them through." As he turned his horse to leave the bridge, Dorilian said to Vaneus. "I suppose I need to tell my cousin this is not an invasion."

"Of course, Thrice Royal," Vaneus kept his voice low. "I will personally deliver reassurances to the palace and the Princess."

Dorilian nodded. Heads of state were not without their obligations. "Bear my personal greetings to my royal cousin. Announce my presence and request, respectfully, an audience. I have no doubt it shall be soon. You will bear her answer to me at your residence, where I shall be staying."

Vaneus bowed and left for the palace with his own bodyguard and two of the Merrydni guards. A detachment of Merath's city guard, called from their posts, also mounted to form an escort appropriate to the entrance of a foreign force. Thus protected, Dorilian and his entourage progressed unhindered across the park and into the city, proceeding along streets lined with city dwellers amazed by the sight.

# 6

That boy doesn't need another enemy—those, he has in abundance. Enemies have defined his entire existence. Don't let his define yours. Should the time come when Dorilian Sordaneon extends his hand to you, don't be the one to put a sword in it.
MARC FREDERICK STAUBERG-RANDOLPH,
LETTER TO HIS GRANDSON STEFAN

It took only six days for the Sordani and Amallaran delegations to hammer out the terms of their alliance. Even Hans was surprised by how quickly the pieces he had envisioned had fallen into place. Now that the Rill gleamed in silver promise above the station at Bellan Toregh, the Khelds wanted it badly. Centuries of dreams and denial distilled into a few golden hours of opportunity many feared might never come their way again. They worried that Dorilian would change his mind and withdraw the offer as precipitously as, it seemed to them, he had offered it. They wasted no time in making certain they had the Sordan alliance signed and sealed with every promise they could place upon it. Their agreement to terms about which they'd sworn never to compromise, they explained away by pointing to the Rill.

Hans saw that Sordan's ambassadors also grappled with changes and upheaval. Dorilian had not been wrong about what the cost to him might be. His delegates saw Dorilian as taking on dimensions they both marveled at and feared, seeking alliances they in the same breath understood and distrusted. That he might abandon Sordan haunted them. That he should gift Amallar with the Rill struck Dorilian's own subjects as a godlike gesture, comprehensible only in that context. Day by day Hans watched their struggles to understand their Hierarch's reasoning. Whenever they asked Hans's opinion, he pointed to the one conclusion that he had himself reached: Dorilian meant to seize the last vestiges of Rill control from Essera by opening another station that, like Hestya, would be completely outside the sphere of their adversaries. That Bellan Toregh did not in any way fall under Sordani control simply indicated what they must negotiate.

Dorilian had made one thing clear: the Khelds would have Rill access only by way of an agreement with Sordan.

Agreement didn't come easily to any of the others, either. Some Neuberlanders were less than satisfied—not with the Rill, which they acknowledged would greatly benefit their settlements—but with terms that stipulated Gignastha would not be deemed a Kheld Lordship. It was a point Hans himself had insisted on, saying he did not want the scandal associated with it. "That domain has brought my family nothing but grief," he told anyone who asked. "I want to grow a future that's new and strong, not old and twisted." Emissaries on both sides agreed that Gignastha's ultimate dispensation could be decided at a future date, that it remained on the table, with the concession that Khelds would be represented in the decision making.

More reluctantly, Khelds accepted as valid, strictly as a point of Highborn law, Dorilian's claim to Essera—but they did not want him to ever sit on its throne. Instead they agreed to accept rule by joint committee, with Essera, Amallar, and Sordan represented equally if something should happen to Hans and Emyli or any Heirs—so long as Rill service and all other provisions of the treaty continued to be honored. Amallar would become autonomous and henceforth have equal standing with Essera and Sordan.

Nalf Rhys had argued loudly for Hans to marry before leaving Amallar, but there had been such disagreement over the matter— not just resistance from the Old Mothers but also because so many prospective brides were being suggested by arguing factions—that Nalf had given up on it. The Khelds were happier with the Sordaneon concession acknowledging Kheld settlement rights in Neuberland and establishment of the sovereignty of the Gignastha Principate within the borders Marc Frederick had drawn. Dorilian Sordaneon, they knew, had already withdrawn one of Sordan's armies from that region; now they demanded and received assurances that the second army would leave also and Gignastha would field its own troops. Negotiating the presence of Sordani military ships and troops in Trongor, a potentially sticky situation, proved to be minor. Endelarin's account had been widely disbursed and the Trongorians and Hans spoke up fervently on behalf of that domain's distress. Sordan's agreement to restrict its activities to Trongor and not cross into Amallar—while the Khelds were not comfortable believing it—was deemed acceptable due to war.

*Nammuor misjudged.* Hans barely restrained his satisfaction. *He didn't know about the Rill or that I would be able to bring the Khelds to this alliance. I'm doing things he never dreamed I would do. And so is Dorilian.* It thrilled him to think of the advantage he had gained. In addition to establishing the first formal relationship between the Khelds and Sordan, complete with provisions for an exchange of ambassadors, the alliance also included provisions for Neuberland to have joint Staubaun and Kheld representation to the Archhalia, something Dorilian as Highborn had the power to dictate—and had written in a communication for all to see. Hans would later have the opportunity to formalize the arrangement through the Archhalia.

For the first time, Khelds would have an official voice in administering a land other than Amallar.

It was a fragile truce but a promising alliance. Many Khelds who had known nothing of Sordan, beyond a litany of well-used reasons to hate the distant Hierarchate, found themselves grudgingly admiring the Sordani delegation. Dorilian had chosen his ambassadors brilliantly. His most significant move had been to place Tiflan at their head. The presence of the tall, easy-going Bas, ruler of a major domain in his own right and a close blood relation to both the Sordaneons and the ruling family of Merrydn, made a suitably important statement, but Tiflan's jovial manner graced a mind at once sharp and fair, a combination Khelds adored. He humanized the Sordani company more effectively than Hans or Arne ever could have, telling stories of his youth in the lands to the south and even, once, reducing his Kheld audience to tears of laughter while relating how Dorilian at age fourteen had first bested him in a sword fight.

"Little did I know he had been so infuriated over losing to me that he would spend every moment of the next two months practicing the sword using his left hand! So there I am, minding my own business in Askorras, and he calls me out and wagers his best horse that he can beat me. Now mind you, he still owns fine horses, but that beast was as glorious as any that ever graced a

Highborn Prince's stable. Of course I accepted and started counting my winnings. Next thing I know, I am beset by the young whelp's blade and it is coming at me in directions I never expected. In all the years I had known him, he had fought right-handed. Now he fought as expertly with his left as his right! And he would switch hands between blows! When Legon tossed him a second blade, I knew I was done. I was fortunate to escape with just a sword jab to my ass. I have challenged him since, but he always says he's already made his point."

The other Sordani delegates were less entertaining but had been selected with just as much care. Although Hans at first doubted the wisdom of including Pallas Trophoneos, the Speaker's presence ensured that any alliance would meet approval by Sordan's noble and public legislatures. The rigid Haliast gradually warmed somewhat to the Amallaran delegates, in particular Orem Darm, with whom Pallas shared a fondness for a certain northern card game. Although never entirely comfortable with Kheldish demands, Pallas nonetheless recognized that the time had come for pragmatism: Hans knew Trongor's fate sat heavily upon Pallas's thoughts, as did the unspoken peril his people faced should evil befall the Sordaneons. Similarly, the aged former ambassador, Auleos Periskleron, brought with him to the table his family's vast experience in Neuberland and years of Sordaneon appointments to Marc Frederick's court, and the elder statesman eventually smoothed several key points with his grasp of Esseran alliances and diplomacy. One delegate had pleased Hans especially, the Epopte Tharos Odakkon, whose advocacy on behalf of the Rill as Entity tempered expectations while at the same time laying the groundwork for a fair-minded working relationship between the Khelds and the Rill community they so desperately wanted to join. Using the Rill to communicate with Permephedon, Tharos had immediately spoken with the Brotherhood and presented Dorilian's stipulation that reactivation of Dazunor-Rannuli was to be dependent on immediate recognition and inclusion of the new Bellan Toregh node. At the end of negotiations, Nalf Rhys was overheard to say that if Essera didn't have men like these, they should get some.

"The damned Sordani know what they want, I'll grant them that,"

Nalf told Aubrey one night as she helped him with his notes. "Guarding Leseos like wolves, showing their teeth over a few border towns."

"They're allies of Leseos. The Rill runs there."

"And now it runs here too." The Thegnard's eyes gleamed with what Aubrey knew were thoughts of what that might mean. Bellan Toregh would become a more prosperous town, a center for trade and commerce. He had spoken about how in a few years they might need to move the seat of government. He'd even said how it satisfied him to no end that now Amallar was tied physically to Sordan and Essera, that his people had gained a foothold on that silver strand of commerce and communication between cities. To his mind, the only really daunting task was that few persons outside of Amallar and Neuberland spoke Khelda.

It was that, in fact, that had kept Aubrey at Hans's side. She at first had balked at interacting with the Sordani. Although she found Tiflan easy to be with, the others reminded Aubrey only too clearly of a hard truth she both needed to accept and wanted to deny. She had fixed her interest on the wrong man. It was easier not to face her humiliation at all, and she had contemplated returning to Saemoregh. But Hans had insisted he needed her.

"Aubrey," he pleaded, "no one else speaks decent Stauba!"

It was true that few Khelds ever bothered to learn tongues other than their own. With Robdan gone north, Hans had soon discovered that only Nalf Rhys and Orem Darm—and to some degree Arne—among the Kheld delegates spoke reasonably good Stauba. A few others spoke enough to carry on a conversation—of sorts. Most Khelds who spoke any Stauba at all were traveling traders who spoke as Arne had when they'd first met, using a polyglot of different dialects. They would have to learn.

"I need someone I can trust, Aubrey," Hans had said over her objections. "It's not just getting the words right. It's getting the *spirit*."

And so she found herself sitting in on the talks along with Hans and Orem Darm, painstakingly translating the language of each document or interpreting for the Kheld delegates in sensitive discussions.

"The first time I met him," Hans confided to Aubrey about Pallas when they found themselves catching a few minutes between rounds of talks, "he and the Sordan Halia sentenced me to death by beheading."

"And dismemberment," Arne reminded Hans. Arne had

brought his friends something to eat from the kitchens. "Both of us." The day was a cold one and they shared a blanket as they gathered before a brazier heaped with coals.

Aubrey gaped at the two in astonishment—and outrage. "He did that? How can you sit at the same table with him?"

Hans laughed. "It wasn't personal. He didn't know who I was."

"I'm not sure it would have mattered," said Arne with a grin.

"Besides, every time he looks at me now, and Arne too, he has to be thinking about it—that he actually gave that order."

"Beheading." Arne nodded.

"And dismemberment."

The two young men laughed, but Aubrey found much to be thoughtful about in what they'd said. She, too, had said things to a man without knowing the truth about who he was, said things—and done things—that now made her want to crawl into the earth. Would she ever be able to look that man in the face again? She regarded Pallas far kindlier thereafter.

That night, as she walked back from the inn after an evening spent arguing with Fran Gorseddson over whether Hans had been right to yield Gignastha, Aubrey looked up at the shining strangeness of the Rill mount, burning white against the night above the snowy town. Amallar was forever changed.

And so was she.

The Rill was forever. Dorilian Sordaneon had given it to them—to Hans—and then he had moved on. From such a gesture, he had moved on. Only for a moment had Amallar occupied his mind. Whatever he had gone to meet was greater than the Khelds or their squabbles over land. Greater even than the Rill. The chill that seized Aubrey then went deeper than bone. Even gone, Dorilian made her feel small.

She would never make him fit into her world again. But neither would she ever fit so well within it as she had before she'd known him. The Rill structures arching in pale arms over the town didn't guard any past Amallar had ever known. Aubrey could almost feel the world growing vast, something ancient falling away.

# 7

Merath is a city of pinnacles and spires crowning the hills
between two wide rivers. Three splendid stone bridges
span the Rannul, including the twelve-arched
Haralambdos Bridge that is the easternmost point of the
King's Road. Only one bridge, however, crosses the
Dazun from Amallar into Merath. As travelers enter the
city, they pass beneath an arch with a sign that reads, "No
whores, no thieves, no beards."
ROBDAN AELFRICSON, *JOURNAL OF THE RILL WAR*

"We did our duty, which was to escort you to safety. We wish no reward but that you find a way to help our poor country." Still clad in garments he'd worn on the road, Farrl stood in the center of the ambassador's private study and looked ill at ease. Robdan felt for the man.

Dorilian had released the ten Trongorian rangers from his service, saying that the two hundred men of his ambassador's guard would be sufficient unless Merrydn's Princess proved false—and if that were the case, ten Trongorians would not make a difference. News of Trongor's destruction had reached their party upon their arrival in Merath. The Trongorians were anxious to return to their people.

"Sordan has sent aid already, and it should reach there soon. I have received word that Ardaen shall help also—and I will personally prevail upon Lahgael to send assistance."

The mask had returned and Dorilian sounded royal again. Like he had always spoken at the Archhalia.

Farrl noted this too, for he bent his neck. "Thank you, Thrice Royal."

"You are continuing to keep secret from your men just who they escorted north?"

"Yes, Thrice Royal. I believe even the ambassador's troops and staff are yet unaware."

Upon receiving a glance, Vaneus Pindar nodded. He was seated at his desk, a grand affair that took up half the room, and continued placing documents into an envelope.

"Keep that secret," Dorilian instructed. "I would rather my enemies not know where to find me."

"Yes, Thrice Royal. You have my word."

"And you have mine that I will help Trongor. First, you and your company will rest here in Merath. A day or two to recover your strength. I have already made things right with the Princess for Trongor having invaded Merrydn."

Robdan fought a laugh. The purported offense barely qualified, but he had enjoyed finding out that the Trongorians, not Dorilian, had actually done the invading. Trongor was a foreign power; Dorilian was Highborn. Being Highborn meant he could not be denied entry into any Triemperal land or city—at least not legally. Because the Trongorians had been his guard, not representing Trongor, the matter had resolved upon that point.

"I will see to it you and your men leave here with more horses and weapons. And nice fat purses, of course. You will personally bear letters from me to Prince Handurin—and to your people, many of whom, I have learned, are now in Amallar. Give the letters to whomever leads them."

"I will do so, Thrice Royal. Thank you." Farrl bowed, first to Dorilian and then to Vaneus and Robdan, before he left, closing the door behind him.

"An excellent man," said Vaneus. He finished with the leather envelope and tied off its silver and green ribbons. "Will Trongor continue to be allies with us in this war?"

"I think at this point they have no choice but to be. Sordan is now a lifeline." Dorilian wandered toward the nearest of the room's three windows, where he joined Robdan in looking out over the city.

"I've not been to Merath before today," Robdan said, "though I have seen Merrydn's Princess at meetings of the Archhalia." He gazed with wonder at the fine view. The Crescent Palace's blue-glazed towers pierced the day's heavy gray clouds. He paused, then ventured, cautious, "The Princess is not always your friend when it comes to the vote."

Dorilian drew a deep breath. "Ionais is almost *never* my friend. She doesn't like me." His tone suggested the feeling was mutual.

"Yet you believe you are safe here?" Robdan watched Dorilian turn away, to all appearances unconcerned that his protections were few and their loyal guard of the last several days was leaving.

"I'm safe enough. Ionais dislikes me, but she loathes Erenor Tholeros—and she understands better than most the danger Nammuor presents. She lost as many people at Permephedon as I did—people she loved. Her father taught her well and she doesn't believe lies. She will not betray me to harm."

He didn't sound convinced. Robdan frowned.

Vaneus stood from his desk, envelope tucked against his side. "Nor is the Princess the only dignitary of Highborn birth in residence. The Gracious Princesses Sapphia and Margarid Dannutheonea live here in exile and will almost certainly wish to speak with Your Thrice Royal Grace."

Robdan saw no way for Dorilian to avoid such a meeting. The Sordaneon Hierarch would naturally interest the widowed Esseran Princesses whose husbands Stefan had slaughtered. He watched as Dorilian, his expression newly thoughtful, retreated toward the hearth and its bright fire. His pacing betrayed a barely chained energy Robdan didn't know how to read.

Dorilian glanced back over his shoulder toward the window and its view of the castle before shaking his head at some decision he had made.

Vaneus opened a hand. "If you do not wish to go, Thrice Royal—"

"No. Send your messages. It's time I get this over with."

Ionais Malyrdeonis e Theslaeon, Princess of Merrydn and daughter of the last Highborn Prince of that land, awaited her visitors in state, wearing the robes of a ruler over a gown of hazy cornflower-blue silk. She was flanked by three women no less elegant. Her regal calm and their equanimity were but natural extensions of the birthrights they enjoyed. Robdan had seen that look of entitlement before in the man they confronted. Ionais's smile almost belied the dislike that lurked beneath her welcome.

"Cousin." She greeted Dorilian with well-feigned warmth.

"Forgive us for the informality of your welcome. It is not like you to arrive unannounced. Or at all."

Ionais's head, her golden hair topped with a circlet of blue gems, barely tilted to her kinsman. A subtle discourtesy, given Dorilian's higher rank. Ionais of Merrydn was as beautiful near as she had seemed from afar. Robdan knew the Princess only from his tenure in the Archhalia, wherein she'd sat near the head of that long chamber, and he at the very rear. Now Robdan inhaled Ionais's perfume, light with the scent of lilies, and gazed upon the porcelain perfection of skin as flawless as a young maid's, despite being a woman of forty years.

Dorilian managed a nod. "My apologies. But I did send a man ahead."

"A man who but came in the morning? And yourself by afternoon?"

"Short warnings make for short visits. I don't intend to overstay my welcome."

With a lift of her chin, Ionais turned to present the other women, each of whom executed a curtsey upon introduction to Dorilian. For his own part, Robdan bowed as deeply to each of them as he had to Merrydn's Princess. By names alone, these women merited veneration: during Stefan's reign, Princess Sapphia had been wife of Rheger Dannutheon, Prince of Dannuth and later Prince of Stauberg; Princess Margarid had been wife of Elhanan, Rheger and Sapphia's son and Heir. The third woman, Euella Rannuleonis Metagoras, was the ruling Basarchessa of Rannul. Robdan had seen Euella only once, at the Archhalia meeting that had confirmed Hans as Stefan's successor. As Robdan recalled, Euella had voted for doing so.

In the presence of such royalty, Robdan was glad of Dorilian's attention to detail. At the ambassador's residence they had bathed away the dirt of the road and exchanged their travel garments for finer attire. Robdan's clothing remained quite plain. His borrowed garments, hastily fitted, had come from the ambassador's staff. Dorilian, however, had found that the husband of Vaneus's daughter possessed both suitable proportions and a reasonably good wardrobe, from which he'd purchased several items. What the man who had contributed those articles of clothing thought about having given over his wardrobe to a hastily arrived emissary, Robdan didn't know. For his own part, he was glad he'd been able to shave.

Dorilian nodded to the women. Vaneus executed a perfect

diplomatic tilt of the head. After making his bows, Robdan did his best to emulate that posture. By the simple fact of being present, Robdan had just assumed the position of Handurin Stauberg-Randolph's emissary. The tension beneath the domed and vaulted splendor of the Crescent Palace's vast and storied hall was visceral.

"Dorilian." Ionais employed the familiar name crisply, with the directness of a peer. "We must talk."

Robdan watched the way cold purpose settled across his companion's features.

"Yes, Ionais," Dorilian said. "This time I think we will."

# 8

The daughters of Essera's Princes are regarded as only slightly less high than their fathers. While few inherited thrones, history has recorded these women as lionesses who founded, protected and ensured the survival of great families.
ASPHODE MADIOS,
LETTER TO NABOE THOMES, DENIZEN OF PHAER

Dorilian had few kin left in Essera. The Malyrdeon Princes were gone, all murdered. Only a handful of their daughters remained. Of these, Ionais, as the sitting Princess of a domain, ranked the highest. Her grandmother had been first cousin to one of Dorilian's grandfathers, and her father, Regelon, had been a staunch ally of Marc Frederick. In a dynastic move celebrated by all of Essera, she had been wed to Jonthan Stauberg-Randolph, though no issue had come of that short union. Dorilian had liked Jonthan far more than he liked Ionais. She had been cold to him for years, even preceding Jonthan's death, in which Dorilian had played an unfortunate part. Jon's death still haunted him, but he cared little one way or another for Ionais and her opinion.

As Hierarch of Sordan, however, Dorilian could not dismiss outright the Princess of Merrydn, especially not when he had entered her country with few guards and no promises of protection.

Which was why Dorilian sat at a table with Ionais and her guests, honoring kin bonds and enduring questions. Those guests had informed him of the terrible hardships his stoppage of the Rill had caused in Merrydn and Rannul, as well as the priceless knowledge that the two-year-old girl Erenor had banned from being Princess of Stauberg could now quote passages of her grandfather's poetry.

As a poet, Rheger had been well regarded—but Dorilian declined Ionais's offer to have the child brought in to perform. He thought Sapphia and Margarid looked grateful.

"And where have you been these last two months?" As Ionais signaled the placing of a post-meats course, her voice remained light, though unconvincingly disinterested. "Rumor alone placed you in Sordan."

She looked lovely. All the women were especially elegant tonight and the men presented themselves impressively with the exception of Robdan, who even in better clothing appeared out of place. Even the room was dazzling, but then everything about the Crescent Palace was beautiful, from its gates of blue agate to the marvel that loomed behind the seated royals, a musical curtain of falling water. Waterglobes cast pure soft light upon the spent elegance of scented tapers held in arms of silver. The table at which they were seated remained laden with the remnants of a meal Dorilian had not eaten. A minor tragedy, considering the fine reputation of Ionais's cook. He had considered using Robdan as a taster but decided not to do so when he determined that the Kheld did not fully understand the role. Instead Dorilian had watched Robdan enjoy the meal, and nibbled not even a morsel of his own, a slight that turned whatever goodwill Ionais had borne him to frost.

"And where do rumors place me now?" Conversation at least would keep his thoughts from food.

"Name a place and I have heard a rumor that put you there. Some few claimed you were in Merced securing a bride, but a little mouse in your palace told me you sent her home unsatisfied. Your court asserted that you were hiding out with antediluvian mystics in Jharbala—but I know you favor the orthodoxy of Cibulitans. For myself," Ionais's clever gaze swept Dorilian's face, "seeing as you have turned up on my doorstep with Trongorian mercenaries, I have a notion you were in Ogarth, which is why Nammuor attacked it—though you had already made your way to Randpory. Rumor places you there also, and in Gignastha or even Annech."

"Not far wrong, fair cousin. Did you not hear? I crossed your bridge this morning— from Amallar."

Dorilian catalogued their responses. Euella, seated at Ionais's right hand, openly gaped, pink lips parted. Sapphia's slender eyebrows lifted. The man sitting to Ionais's left, Euden Staubaun

Mezeon, frowned. Euden was Merrydn's foremost general and one of only three men other than Dorilian at the table.

"Yes," said Ionais, gaze narrowing. "About those Trongorians—"

"I required an escort."

"You created an incident. My men at the bridge barely held back a horde of rampaging Khelds!"

"The Khelds were pursuing *me*. They weren't trying to invade your city—or even cross the bridge."

"They're baying for us to turn over a spy!"

Her pique amused him. "But I'm not a spy. You can honestly say that none entered your city."

"Though given this morning's events we must believe you indeed arrived by that bridge, that you were ever in Amallar beggars belief." Ionais paused to bestow a long and questioning look at Robdan, then lifted her golden chalice before speaking to Dorilian again. "What else could it be but one of your sick misdirections. You, of all of us, would not dare to go to that forsaken country."

"I don't see why not."

Ionais's lips tightened smugly. She exchanged glances with Sapphia, whose steady gaze also weighed Dorilian. "Erydon's Promise. You are obligated to uphold it."

"Which I did. I kept Erydon's Promise. I neither attacked Amallar nor invaded it. I but paid a visit. My intentions were pure."

At that, Ionais laughed. "Your intentions are never pure, least of all toward Khelds or any of Stefan's breed. Indeed, it's debatable who hates the other more: you them, or them you."

"Hate? Not me, certainly, and not all of them." Dorilian relaxed into his chair. As long as he wasn't eating, he might as well be comfortable. "The fact remains, I went to Amallar and the Khelds were none the wiser." Every guest at the table, save Robdan, wore the same incredulous look. "You don't believe me?"

"I suppose I must, though I wonder how you pulled it off."

"Oh, come, Ionais, you have said often enough that my looks belong in a wharfside stall. I have myself heard people mutter behind my back that my eyes remind them of dead fish tossed up on the beach."

"'Twas never so." Ionais knew when to abandon an argument. Seeking less prickly ground, she directed a question to Robdan instead. "Tell me, Master Kheld, how did our cousin come to you? Was it unexpected, or planned?"

"Not planned, Your Royal Highness." Robdan possessed the training to speak to so high a personage. Dorilian noted the Kheld's innate diplomacy under pressure, just enough deference in his gaze and self-effacement in his words. That Robdan employed excellent Stauba helped keep the conversation civil. Ionais would not attempt to converse around him. "Indeed, his Thrice Royal Grace's arrival was most unexpected. A complete surprise! Only Handurin Stauberg-Randolph, I and Herberth of Trongor—and also Prince Handurin's companion who had been with him in Sordan—knew who he was. And all that time he remained undiscovered."

"That must be true. Else certainly we would have heard of it the length and breadth of the Triempery. But then, my cousin is an actor." Ionais cast another gaze around her table, commanding all to attend her words. "Surely, you've noticed—Dorilian changes to suit the play nearly as expertly as he changes the play to suit him." With soft snicker she turned her attention back. "And how, do tell, did you manage to keep the secret in Sordan?"

Dorilian shrugged. "My City. My kin. My habit of privacy. And you can ask, dear cousin? As if I would choose to satisfy your curiosity. You and your friends—indeed, your guests here tonight—would as soon I stayed there to rot. But why not ask why I left? Or what have I done? Or are you so certain that I have done nothing, and will do nothing, without your approval?"

"You? Do nothing? Ha!" Even Ionais found the notion laughable. "Oh, no, Dorilian, not you. What you have done? Much of that we already know. Our shipments and our profits languish in Dazunor-Rannuli and you stopped answering anyone's letters. But what you did in Amallar? That all the World would dearly love to know. And will, I'm sure, or you would not be sitting at this table with this Kheld at hand, baiting me to ask that question. But why did you leave Sordan? That I can guess." Ionais leaned forward imperiously, not even attempting to mask the consuming nature of her concern. "People will say you come to Essera to seek its throne. I need to know if this is true."

"If I wanted that throne, I could have had it long before Nammuor arrived at Aral to complicate matters." Dorilian picked up the wine cup in front of him. He swirled the contents and studied the sediment. Poison? Unlikely. A sedative, more like. His body resisted those, but Ionais would know which to use. He put the cup down again with a hollow ring of glass on metal. "Handurin can have you, cousin, the lot of you. Essera is his if he wants it, and it seems he does. I wage my grievances against Nammuor only. I shall drive him from Stauberg and I shall drive him from Essera—yes, that I will do, because in Essera he is a threat to me. And in time I shall rid him from his southern strongholds as well, smash the Diadem into his skull and from there to the core of the World or the ball of the sun if that is what's needed. But once Nammuor is gone from Essera, I pray never to set foot here again! I want it not, and never have."

"You did when Stefan had it."

"Did I? I don't recall trying to take it from him."

"You waste your breath if you think you can be coy with me," Ionais sniped. "No one in all Essera believes you mean to give us to yet another Stauberg-Randolph. Not after Stefan's wretched reign. Why not proclaim yourself and be done with it?"

"There's nothing to proclaim."

"As if we would have you."

Dorilian had reached the limit of his desire to be civil. He leaned forward again, little caring what Robdan or the others might make of his words. "Ionais, you would not have me even if I would consent to sire the next Highborn dynasty upon you. Nor would I consider having you. I offer you only armies, no options and no kingship—why else do you think I have supported Handurin but to put him in that place? And he is agreeable, else how would I have left Amallar? Because I followed him there! Followed him there to propose an alliance which I have secured!"

"With Khelds?"

"Who else? Will the Royal North follow Handurin? Will you?"

"Why would we?"

The table's silence put a sharp edge on that question, but Dorilian held its answer. "Me," he said. "Or have you forgotten the nature of your wager?"

Ionais's hand fled to her throat, where a necklace of Merrydn's fabled sapphires swathed her neck with blue fire. Her fingers trembled as she picked up her spoon to sample the dessert.

In the ensuing silence Princess Sapphia spoke for the first time. "Oh, but we do remember, Thrice Royal. We remember only too well the wager our husbands and fathers made upon an Entity's cryptic guidance. Now we but wait to see if their hope was in vain. Because when it comes to hope, you offer none."

That cold pronouncement shattered argument. The Wall stood sheathed within it. Faced with the sacrifices these women had made, Dorilian reined back his judgment of them. Now that he was in Essera, building bridges would serve better than burning them. Nor did he wish to offend Sapphia, whose late husband had risked so much on Dorilian's behalf.

"I admit my actions have been difficult to understand."

"Try impossible," Ionais muttered.

Dorilian ground his teeth. He looked to Sapphia, whose cool amber gaze at last yielded a ghost of appreciation. A hint, though barely, that while *he* might be regarded as hopeless, his prospects were not. "Then let me make myself clear. None of us know the full scope of that wager. Perhaps Marenthro does, but he has not passed knowledge of the Wall's intention to *me*. When I speak of wagers, I do not speak of the Wall or its paradigms. Another Entity works through me. I speak of the wager made by fools in Essera to subvert the Rill to their ends only."

Ionais laid down her spoon and signaled for the dish before her to be removed. "Is that what this show of Rill threats and poverty is all about? To bring Epoptes and fools into line?"

"No. Rather to create opportunity."

"For whom? Yourself? Because Stefan's half-breed brother will not be accepted with much good grace."

Now, at last, they'd reached bedrock. Dorilian noted that Robdan, though he looked dismayed, kept silent.

"Oh, if I can take your petty slurs, I'm sure Handurin can. Our situations are not much different, I've found."

"And his Khelds?" Margarid asked. Soft and pretty, she sat stiff-backed at Sapphia's side. Anger lurked within her direct gaze. "Will he bring them with him?"

Revulsion roiled from Margarid's every gesture, even the tiniest. Dorilian tasted her hatred upon the very air. The bitterness shocked him. Had he felt like this to others of his kind those years ago? If so, it had been for less reason.

"Handurin is not Stefan," he countered as gently as he was able.

Ionais persisted in the younger princess's place. "No. But what do we know of him other than that he is of the same stock?" She pointedly ignored Robdan, dismissing him as easily as she did her small dogs, which lounged under the table about their feet. "Will this Handurin subject us to yet another plague of foreign ministers and taxes? Another barbarian horde to ravage Essera? You show an unsubtle cruelty in this game."

Dorilian faced the thoughtful general seated at her side. "What think you, General Mezeon? Is this a game? A diversion such as the Princes of Tahlwent and Lacenedon once played about their evening tables, plotting how to keep my grandfather from what was rightfully his—and how to strip Sordan of her riches? Did they roll dice for which plum Sordan appointment to give to which of their cronies? Which inheritance to confiscate or Rill slots to expropriate? Which widows or daughters to forcibly wed? Why do they now act as though by winning they lost?" Dorilian was satisfied to see Euden's mouth tighten as the General's gaze dropped from his. To Ionais, Dorilian resumed. "Stefan was Marc Frederick's Heir, so be it. You granted me no help in my battle with him. You pawed the line the more to obscure it, but not once did you cross it to my side. I stood alone when he tried to annex Gignastha, alone when Nammuor sallied into Suddekar, alone when Stefan tried to force Trongor to cease its trade with me and then, when Trongor would not, took to using Mormantaloran ships. When Palaistea's palace burned and the Royal North rebelled, what did you do? Did you call on me to help? No! You stood by until Stefan ordered the deaths of the last two Highborn Princes in Essera. Stefan hated me so much, and listened to Nammuor so well, that he would kill all of my race—and yours—and *you stood silent!* I warned you Stefan was cutting his throat, that he was cutting all our throats, and that this was not the end of it, but the beginning."

His anger silenced Ionais, and all of them, as Dorilian had intended. "When Stefan died, yes, I wanted Essera—I wanted Essera to survive! Who played games then? It was my right to claim that throne. It still is—and ever will be. You could have had me then, but suddenly Sordan seemed the better cage. So you tolerated Nammuor in Stauberg and his damned lackey Erenor to be Handurin's Regent—and then placed Erenor's paid men on the Regency Council, so many that Emyli would not put herself in the same room with them, and who could blame her? Did you think I would stand by and idly allow it, and forgive the slap when all was done? But you had no fear of me then, so long as I could be held to Sordan. Yet I stood with you when you made your feeble move, nearly too late—I voted Sordan's block with your minority to bring Handurin back from hiding when you needed him to keep Erenor from becoming King! I brought him back for you! How dare you now say that you do not want him!"

Ionais struggled to maintain her well-practiced composure. "Nammuor restrains himself lately. He holds to what he has and does not press for more."

"Every person here, even you, is too intelligent to believe such tripe." Dorilian was getting heated. He must cool this conversation to land his points. "Winter approaches, cousin. Nammour's supply lines by sea are drawn out and the Rill no longer supplies him from Dazunor-Rannuli. Nor does he want to drive Essera's remaining free nobles to Handurin. Amallar threatens no less than Sordan to unseat Erenor, whom Nammuor still needs."

General Mezeon surprised Dorilian by interjecting. "This is so, Most Royal. The Mormantaloran does this neither out of goodwill nor gratitude. He overran Dazunor this spring, after waiting the winter."

"And will not overrun Lacenedon following *this* one, have I anything to say about it," said Dorilian firmly. "Hebron did in secret ask my help and I've pledged it to him. Already I have sent one of my armies north to his aid."

"And none to mine? That army crossed my land before your embassy made known that it wasn't the aid you promised *me*." Ionais glowered with suppressed anger but there was nothing she could do about that transgression. Dorilian's army had passed into Lacenedon weeks ago. "What of Handurin and his Khelds?" Ionais asked. That point clearly pressed her more. "What say the bearded rabble about your troop movements? They cannot like seeing you move armies into Essera." Her gaze slid momentarily to Robdan, who wisely held his tongue and instead filled his fork with a mouthful of savory pudding.

Though Margarid's face hardened, Sapphia's attention turned inquisitive.

"I left soon after the Khelds learned about it. They were not happy," Dorilian conceded.

"Hah! And neither are we!"

"Yet you haven't asked me to withdraw that army. And neither will the Khelds. Handurin and I are agreed on one thing: Nammuor must be defeated and the Diadem destroyed. Handurin is as convinced as I am of the evil of the thing. Don't ask me how Handurin came to know of it, locked away in some sister World. He glimpsed his brother's death somehow and perhaps he saw it then. It would not be unlike Marenthro to have granted some kind of vision. Be sure Handurin handles his Khelds well." Which was more than Dorilian could say for himself at the moment. He eyed the bread of which Robdan had eaten enough to satisfy half a troop. If there were poisons in it, the Kheld would be dead by now instead of digging into a custard. Dorilian reached over and tore off a hunk.

Sapphia laughed aloud, and Dorilian knew why. She had spent many years with Rheger's Highborn appetites. Even Ionais snickered.

"Where does Marenthro stand in this?" Sapphia asked, notes of merriment still in her voice.

"As always, we do not know," Dorilian answered. The bread was good. Dense, with a fruity crust bearing a hint of fig. "And even if we did, we would know nothing."

Ionais signaled to a servant bearing a tray of sweet cordials. The bitch. "Still showing your teeth at his reflection? But you show Handurin naught but smiles, it seems. What then of these rumors that you were holding him your prisoner in Sordan? All that was on good authority."

"By design, to see him safely north. The boy inherited his brother's enemies along with his titles."

"And you not the least of those."

"The way I despised Stefan? And with the Khelds trumpeting far and wide that he was to be their King? Come, who would not credit it?" The servant presented the tray of cordials. Dorilian gestured for Robdan to take one for him also.

"Indeed." Ionais took a glass in hand. "Yet it seems no one has credited the truth, whatever that may be. You may be Highborn, and able to ferret the truth from between men's teeth and ears, but the rest of us are not so gifted with an ability to see yours. You have told us nothing of the Rill and when Dazunor-Rannuli can expect to see more of it. Nothing at all. You have yet to explain your actions and your plans remain unclear."

"Then let me clarify them. I came here to Merath for but two things: my ambassador's bodyguard, which I intend to take with me, and to deliver an ultimatum." He watched how Ionais's gaze narrowed at the word. She had never liked being ordered, not even by her father. Certainly not by Dorilian himself. "If you are with me, Ionais, daughter of Regelon, if you stand by my Highborn blood, then you will make your peace with Handurin by whatever means it takes you to do it. All of you will. And you will join with him. Because if you do not, we will mark you with the enemy and you shall find yourselves between the jaws of a different beast than has ever ruled this land."

Dorilian laid his fingertips against the glass of cordial—and tipped it. The glass rang onto the table, the creamy white liqueur spilling over the tabletop of silvered glass, signaling an end to their conversation.

As Dorilian stood with Vaneus in the Crescent Palace's reception hall, waiting for the signal that his escort was ready to depart, he noted the approach of a lone woman. Older, poised and with hair of bright silver gold. A cloak of white fox pelts draped her shoulders and provided some protection from the cold that permeated the open space. Dorilian was himself cloaked again in winter gear. He signaled to the armed guard that stood between him and Sapphia that she should be allowed to approach.

"Princess," he acknowledged.

"Hierarch." Sapphia's low voice bestowed respect, though little warmth. Her gaze briefly followed Vaneus when, with a deep bow, he moved to join Robdan at a spot nearer the door.

Dorilian wondered what Sapphia had come to say to him. The possibilities were endless and ranged from accusations of murder to vows of vengeance. His only communications with her had been short and infrequent, death-centered.

Her words bore no hostility. "Rheger trusted you," she said.

"And I him. He was a great loss—to Essera and all of us. Elhanan too. I... wish I had known them better."

Sapphia's gaze met his. "I know why you could not save them. Their deaths happened too quickly. And even had you known, you could not have traveled to Stauberg quickly enough." She smiled as Dorilian realized her corroboration of his ability to translocate. She knew, too, that he would have needed access to a device as well as intimate knowledge of the location to be visited. Neither had been at hand at that moment. Sapphia did not mention Dorilian's promise to not go to Essera while Stefan lived. "But I wonder—we all do—did you know ahead? The Wall—" She broke off speaking and looked toward the tall doors beyond which the view rolled past Merath's city walls to the night-misted west. Toward the Entity that had ruled her and her husband's lives. And which might possibly still be operating within the shadows of events. "They talked about you, the men of my family. Rheger and Ostemun whispered about how Austell slipped his mind because of you. Because of the Wall and the Rill and... they implied you might yourself have seen Wall visions that day."

"Nothing that made sense to me—or them."

"Then. What about now?"

What was she asking? Sapphia was a Malyrdeon. Daughter, wife, and mother to Princes for whom the Wall was an intimate presence and about which she knew more than even Dorilian did—and he had studied that Entity for years from afar.

His answer delivered on her question. "Are you asking whether Handurin will succeed? I do not know that. I saw nothing of him at all. Whether I will succeed? I don't know that either. I foresaw the Demise—but so did *they*. None of us prevented it. As for after—" He broke gaze and turned to look elsewhere. For a moment, at least, the door would suffice. "I saw a palace in flames, myself on a throne. Do those make sense now? To me they do. Stefan, I saw also... but now Stefan is gone. No visions of him remain. That makes sense too.

"I'm not a Wall Lord," he reminded Sapphia. "I cannot foresee which visions will happen and which will not. I only know for certain after they have happened."

"As did Elhanan." She granted a bitter smile. "The Wall showed him what Stefan was. But of you he saw too little. If the Wall knows what you are, Dorilian Sordaneon, Elhanan did not discern your final shape. The Wall, I believe with all my heart, has kept you well hidden—and maybe this Handurin too." Sapphia looked back over her shoulder to where Ionais and the two other women, Margarid and Euella, stood at the foot of the grand staircase leading into the palace. "Essera will not be reclaimed without battle. Had I an army I would hand it to your command."

"You have access to people with armies," he pointed out.

Amusement crinkled fine creases around Sapphia's eyes. "I will send messages. You will find Margarid's brother a friend and Gweroyen a staunch ally. And my nephew Hebron is firmly your compatriot. As for Rannul and Euella... with her you have made a conquest already."

*Spare me.* Dorilian declined to look at the woman in question. "Do not suggest—"

"I would not presume."

Yet she had. Sapphia's reputation as an aggressive matchmaker was well earned. He would set her on Handurin instead. A letter in the morning would suffice.

Military barks of command sounded in the courtyard. The ambassador's full guard had arrived. Robdan and Vaneus had already mounted and waited in the rain for Dorilian to join them on the ride back to Sordan's heavily fortified embassy, where he was to spend the night. He gave Sapphia, then Ionais and the other women, polite nods before he turned to walk away.

"Your will may be made of adamant, Dorilian Sordaneon, but your body is not," Sapphia said in parting. "Let what happened to the line of Ergeiron be a warning. Do not forget you are mortal. It rests on you to see to the next generation."

He stopped to again face proud Sapphia, behind whom Ionais had stepped forward to level a glare of agreement. Margarid and Euella, too, both watched wide-eyed and tense. All four reminded him of why he steered clear of women.

"A next generation? Why would any of us want that?" Dorilian was certain his lowered voice would reach the ears of all four women. "Did the Wall tell your husbands and fathers nothing? Because it showed one thing of which I am certain: that as much as the blood of Leur might yet prove the salvation of this Creation, we also stand as its greatest threat. Stefan knew this," he snarled to Sapphia. "Your son Elhanan showed him." He did not flinch from her stunned expression. "I was in the Mind with them that day. I know why Stefan killed them and became more determined than ever to kill me, and Levyathan too. Nammuor's cursed Diadem wants us—to breed, to inhabit, to corrupt utterly. Ask yourselves why."

Dorilian left without looking back again, his bootfalls sharp upon the marble floor and leaving only silence behind him.

# 9

The Malyrdeons were paralyzed by their own visions;
blinded by their own Entity. Which path did it wish them
to take, which path to avoid? They could not discern
between them and so they died in the dark. I will not. If
the Wall has some great plan, I know nothing of it.
DORILIAN SORDANEON, LETTER TO HANDURIN

Robdan had hardly been in his bed an hour when the door to his small room—located on a higher floor than the suites of more important Embassy guests—opened and Dorilian stepped in. Without a word, though it was dark and Robdan had not had time to set a light, the Hierarch stretched beside him on the bed.

"I will sleep here tonight, Master Aelfricson." A silvering of moonlight through the window traced the sharp outline of Dorilian's profile. "I do not trust Ionais so fully that I would sleep where she knows to find me. And who would think to find me with you? They don't know that I've grown used to Kheld beds. Farrl knows I am here, and my ambassador sleeps in my bed tonight."

"But… I don't understand." Robdan found it disconcerting that Dorilian was fully clothed—and armed. The bright gleam of an unsheathed blade vanished under covers.

"She would not kill me, Master Aelfricson, I don't fear that. It would be sacrilege, render her anathema to her Entity. Also, she needs me to be sure of the Rill. Reason enough to keep me alive, and a better one to imprison me here. It would not take so very much, a few guards for my 'protection.' I know the game for having played it." The rich tone of his voice drifted into lighter notes of mingled sleep and laughter. "It would be well for Vaneus to catch her in the act. Her embarrassment would be extreme, and she would then cease to trouble me for fear that I would hold her plot against her."

"What could she do to you?" Robdan found it fascinating, this look into the inner lives of royalty.

"Not very much, given her loyalties. She would not turn me over to Nammuor. More likely she would seek to force me to wed. Her or one of her nieces, perhaps that girl Euella—or the baby, Elhana. A Princess of Stauberg is a suitable match for a man of my rank. Suffice I do not care to tempt the possibilities. Sleep, Master Aelfricson, and let me sleep. We rise before dawn to continue on our way."

"The Rill." Robdan wanted to know one thing more. "You did not mention it to her, or them, what you did at Bellan Toregh."

"No, though they surely know already that a *charys* left Permephedon. They would know also that it did not stop in Dazunor-Rannuli. Soon they will learn that none since have stopped there— or will until I am satisfied. We will answer those questions in the morning. Then we can ride away with Ionais's wrath on our heels and not on our heads."

Of course. Dorilian's reasons ultimately made great sense. But for Robdan, the bed, though large enough to sleep a Kheld family, had become crowded. He lay stiff, unwilling to move, afraid of disturbing or touching the Hierarch. For a long time, he courted sleep but did not find it, until at last, somewhere in the gloom and without even knowing it, he nodded off.

In the morning, he awoke to find Dorilian gone without a trace. One of the ambassador's soldiers stood at the end of the bed, telling him they were preparing to leave.

Dorilian's departure from Merath was greatly different from his arrival. The two-hundred-man combined guard of the Sordan embassy had replaced the Trongorians. Sordan's ambassadorial garrison was a formidable fighting force, the first Robdan had ridden with, stern proud men who unflinchingly served a ruler most of them had never seen in person until that morning. Robdan huddled in the penetrating cold outside the city, upon a fresh horse, this one a large gray beast of the breed Staubauns preferred for their own use.

The man beside him, with whom Robdan had struck up a diffident acquaintance, was one of Vaneus Pindar's deputies—in charge, he said, of the embassy's purse. He revealed that the ambassador's sleep had gone undisturbed. "The Princess has played it fairly." The man made no pretense about finding his role as an onlooker exciting. "It was her best move. I do not doubt our Hierarch would have proved to be a troublesome guest. The last man who tried to make a prisoner of him lived to regret it."

"I remember," Robdan said, thoughts drifting to Stefan.

"Yes, we all do."

Merath's blue towers looked ghostly, barely visible through mist thrown up by the city's two rivers. Princess Ionais and her retinue arrived on horses of pale frosty colors that blended with the very air. She was accompanied also by the three royal ladies from the night before. The pearly beauty of so many velvets and furs recalled old tales of Highborn glory as they paraded beneath the naked arching limbs of waterside willows.

"Where is your Hierarch?" Ionais demanded when she had reached the meeting place.

The ambassador's deputy bowed his white-haired head. "The Thrice Royal had business to attend at the embassy, Most Royal."

"And none to attend here?"

"A man of his position," he demurred.

"Yes, yes," she snapped impatiently.

Waterfowl hooted upon the gray slate water of the river Rannul, a lovely, faraway sound across a cold, flat land. *Where is he?* Robdan wondered. It occurred to him that Dorilian might have elected to depart in secret, though it didn't seem likely he would leave without a fighting force. That thought vanished when Dorilian, mounted on an ivory warhorse and bringing with him the ambassador and an entourage of yet more armed men, came into sight along the river road.

Dorilian had prepared for this parting. Gone were the plain riding leathers of the other morning and the Trongorian garments that had served him so well. Gone too the silken court fashions purchased from the man who had wed the ambassador's daughter. In their place Dorilian had donned travel attire befitting a Highborn Prince: sleek dark leather beneath rich furs that clothed him like a pelt, velvet sleeves laced with pearls, and upon his head a helm of gold-chased leather lined with fur. His appearance was far changed from that of the pursued man who had entered

Merrydn the day before. Dorilian reined his horse in front of the Princess's party, nodded to his ambassador, and then to the royal ladies.

"Cousin," he addressed Ionais. "It is time we leave you. But we thank you for your hospitality, the nature of which has not gone unnoticed."

Ionais graciously bowed her head in acceptance of the verdict. "Your Thrice Royal Grace is welcome in Merath, as ever he has been. Will you be going to Permephedon, cousin? The High Citadel is not besieged and is yet free."

"No. I do not intend to court that leopard. He can always find me when he is inclined to show his spots."

"And Dazunor-Rannuli?" Ionais lifted her chin. "You will require the Rill node there. When will service resume to that port?"

"You know, then, that the Rill has resumed operations?"

Secure in her information, she smiled acknowledgement. "The system reactivated four days ago. We know a *charys* that originated at Permephedon bypassed Dazunor-Rannuli's Mount. Since then at least two more *charysi* have passed through going north."

"Then you don't know?"

"Know what?"

"That they stopped in between. I no longer have need of Dazunor-Rannuli. I opened the node at Trestethion. In Amallar."

Ionais's fur cloak flew high and wide as she flung it from her arms, freeing them. She kicked her horse forward from the other women and the line of silent courtiers, all of whom wore shocked expressions. "You would not! You *cannot*!"

"Cannot? You might want to think again about what I can and cannot do."

"But why? That rabble does not need the Rill—*we* do! We have a Covenant!"

"Then consider this: I am Sordaneon and my actions *are* Covenant! Mind your own house, Ionais, because I mind *mine*. The Rill will serve me or it will serve no one." Dorilian had never feared this woman's rage. Instead the time had come for her to fear his. "Essera failed in its obligations and handed the Rill to its enemies. *My* enemies. The Rill is forfeit, cousin, because you failed in your duty, not I in mine!"

"Failed!"

"When Nammuor wished access to Dazunor-Rannuli, you gave it to him, not openly, but by consent, for Merrydn but protested lightly. Faint scolding for the start of an invasion! I would have done more, but no! Essera's fat lords forbade me, crying Covenant but not holding to their part. The Seven Houses plotted for power and you let them seize it! Mormantalorus swaggered on the platforms and its armies slaughtered cities in Dannuth and Dazunor, while Merath and Dazunor-Rannuli profited from the Rill. Since my options then were fewer, I was forced to submit while Nammuor and his thugs gorged on Teremar grain, grown in *my* fields, and sponsored men who warred on me in Neuberland with weapons forged from my own steel. Finished by my own weaponers! One year I have watched, and warred and waited, but no more. I stopped the thing, and him, and you, and now I have found better hands to hold its gift.

"You were blind, Ionais. You and all Essera. All you saw was the Rill and that if Nammuor needed it too, your interests were secure. You never considered that I might turn to other options."

"*Khelds?*" Ionais's shrill voice sliced the cold air like an icy sword.

Dorilian shook his head. "Not Khelds. Handurin."

"You are mad!" she hissed. "Marenthro was wrong to call you sane!"

"Remember that. Handurin is far saner than I am. Deal well with him—he may surprise you." With a deft pull on the reins, Dorilian turned his horse. He had barely ridden two paces when a female voice called after him.

"Thrice Royal!" she called. "Please hold. I have something for you!"

Dorilian stopped and looked. One of the mounted women who had accompanied Ionais had ridden forward. A vision in mauve and pink silk with a cap of pure white feathers atop her bright hair and a flat box braced before her on the saddle, Euella of Rannul rode her ivory horse across the mist-frosted lawn. Bedewed seedheads scattered sunlit droplets at her approach. When Vaneus protectively manuevered his mount near, Dorilian raised his hand, signaling the ambassador should wait.

Upon reaching Dorilian, Euella bent her neck before speaking. "You will have safe passage through Rannul, Thrice Royal. I have sent word."

Though already rumor was certain to precede him, Dorilian had hoped for more secrecy. "I have no wish to confront troops of yours on my way."

"They will not confront you; neither will they seek you. These are loyal men. Their commander fought for my brother Burelan against Stefan and Erenor and has been in hiding. Indeed, I have helped to hide him." At seeing Dorilian's interest sharpen, Euella's lips curved with a slight, self-conscious smile. "Stefan killed my brother and forced me to wed one of his loyal lords. I know better than most that rebellions are costly and paid for with blood. The man to whom Stefan wed me was decent and noble, which may be why Erenor killed *him*. I will not wait on the sidelines for any man to decide to whom they will wed me next. I throw my lot with you, Thrice Royal—my domain and my people—and I will do so today, because I believe I have something you might put to good use."

Euella lifted the box and opened it to show the contents.

Against a bed of blue velvet blazed a diadem of brilliant stones set in a band of starlight. Sapphires and flame garnets, alternating—*lr* stones, to judge by their inner fire. Not just a royal crown, but a device.

"The Circle Kissed by the Sun," Dorilian said, naming one of the lesser enhancers.

"Rannul's crown."

"I thought they had all been taken." By Stefan, after the murders of Dannuth's princes. And then by Nammuor. It served Nammuor's interest to account for all the Highborn devices.

"A few have not been, this one and Merath's among them. Burelan hid it before he went to engage Stefan. He sent it to Merath." She ducked her head before raising her eyes again to meet his. "I cannot use it, Thrice Royal. I think that perhaps you can."

In Euella's unswerving gaze Dorilian saw lingering belief in rumors he had striven for years to extinguish. Euella clearly hoped that he might bear the gifts needed to wield this device; that he might through this crown somehow summon the power to defeat the forces aligned against her domain—against all their domains and people. In her faith Dorilian glimpsed an echo of Handurin's half-formed hope. *Would this power you are tempted to seek make you strong enough to defeat Nammuor?*

*Maybe*, Dorilian had wanted to say on that day. *Maybe, if all the stars align and Leur smiles and the dead rise from their graves.*

And look... the stars were aligning.

"Lady," he demurred.

"I want you to have it." Euella lifted her delicate chin. "Princess Sapphia told me... when I asked her. She told me what her husband said, that maybe you could use it. To escape them. To be safe—and free."

He had trained his gifts through a greater enhancer than this one. Yet with this lesser device he could do much. Certainly he would be able to translocate. Flee if necessary to avoid capture. First he would need to ascertain if it had been tampered with or altered. Dorilian reached to take the box from Euella's gloved hands. As he did so he closed the lid.

"My thanks. I hope not to need it for long."

Her shy smile deepened. "Rannul would someday like it back. Perhaps in time for when my son becomes Rannul's Bas?"

He nearly laughed at that. Rannul's young Heir was but an infant. "In time for that, indeed, Most Noble Lady. If this war we face is to end in our favor, it must end quickly."

After giving Euella a deep nod, Dorilian motioned to Robdan and Vaneus that the time had come to depart. The bodyguard fell into formation behind as the party left Merath by way of the north road. He had received a cylinder that morning from Levyathan, bearing news that the Khelds had signed a treaty. Legon had departed for Permephedon with a full battalion of the Eagle Guard and with any luck would join Dorilian within a few days.

All Dorilian had to do now was stay ahead of the news of his arrival in Essera.

# 10

Kheld men I can put into positions of authority. They
understand that power works through hierarchy. Kheld
women, though, consult runes and lay Wheels. They
wrestle with riddles and ponder enigmas. They never get
anything done.
STEFAN STAUBERG-RANDOLPH, LETTER TO CULLEN BRODHESON

The Sordani delegation's return to Sordan with a treaty to be ratified temporarily secured the Rill as a fixture in Amallar with Tharos and a brace of cantors from Sordan to run things until the final terms of its operation could be negotiated. That process might take weeks, but it was a start. A grace period of Rill service, with the promise of an eternity more in exchange for their alliance, far surpassed anything Khelds had hoped to gain. Hans wasn't content to dwell on that success though. He needed to mobilize and make his way north.

And he needed to do so against an enemy who was expecting him.

"I don't want Nammuor focusing all his forces on Sordan—or on us either. Not after what he showed us in Trongor."

Hans studied the faces of his most trusted advisors, whom he'd gathered in his room at the house outside Bellan Toregh. In addition to Nalf Rhys, whose trust Hans had at long last earned, that core group included: Arne and Aubrey; Tye, senior officer of the remaining Trongorians; Ednowa Faldenda, a local Old Mother with knowledge of existing supply stores and distribution; Fran Gorseddson for his experience in leading troops; and Orem Darm, whose familiarity with the lands they would be discussing was invaluable. Hans needed Khelds he could count on to keep a clear head when it came to matters involving the world outside of

Amallar and Neuberland. "I want Nammuor to divide his energy. We're inland, so he can't use ships against us. That means armies. If we can gather enough troops, I think we should engage the enemy in Dazunor."

"In Trongor Nammuor delivered poison and monsters by sea. Can he do that by land?" Fran asked.

"I don't know," Hans confessed.

"If he does bring monsters, we can set up bear bolts," Arne proposed. He and a group of Khelds interested in weapons making had been working on the problem. "We can kill some of them."

Nalf scratched at his beard. "And death clouds that eat stone and flesh?"

A fair question, one about which Hans had been thinking. "It's not just Nammuor we'll be fighting. It's Erenor and other lords with interests at stake. None of them want to see what happened to Trongor happen to Dazunor. Neither monsters nor poison, but especially poison clouds dissolving things they need, like roads and warehouses—and food. Nammuor will hold off on that kind of thing unless we start winning too much."

"You're not suggesting we lose?" Nalf sought to clarify that point.

"No. I'm saying we need to win quickly—and big. An overwhelming assault."

"And you have a plan for that?"

"Not yet. That's why we're here. To come up with one."

"So it's Dazunor for our big surprise, but by what road?" Orem leaned over the map, a detailed rendering obtained from the Sordani and finer than any in Amallar. He indicated the line of the Dazun River between Dazunor-Rannuli and a town called Omadawn. "West of this town, the hills get tall and crowd the river. There are no sure crossings save by ferry. Rivermen tell us the Sorcerer has an army at Trulo and occupies everything to the west. To attack him there would be perilous. You would do better to divide the Regent Erenor's armies to the east." Orem pointed to a brace of well-marked bridges. "But Dazunor-Rannuli is even more dangerous; there are bridges we might use but the city is surely well defended. You would be attacking a Rill port."

They had talked of other plans, but any attack that did not liberate Dazunor-Rannuli risked a two-front war. As things now stood, Erenor could not use the Rill to supply his troops, but neither would Hans be able to use it to further his own military operation unless he took the city—and Dorilian resumed Rill service there. Tharos had confirmed that Rill operation had resumed to Permephedon, but *not* to Leseos or Dazunor-Rannuli.

"I would rather see Merrydn at our backs," said Aubrey. "Erenor, your Regent, has concentrated his troops in Dazunor where he's besieging Dannuth."

"Where is that?" asked Arne. He leaned over the map, his brow furrowing as he studied lands that a year ago he'd probably figured he never would see.

"There." Nalf pointed to the spot.

"I expect Princess Ionais is eager to see the Rill station at Dazunor-Rannuli liberated and restored." That morning Hans had received a communication from Levyathan containing a packet of letters. Dorilian had safely reached Merath and would soon be joined in Lacenedon by Legon and the Hierarch's Eagle Guard. Farrl was being sent back with supplies and promises. Merrydn was trustworthy and Rannul too was an ally. It felt good to be getting intelligence from reliable sources. "Merrydn's army is strong and well commanded. Princess Ionais has given that command to Euden Mezeon, Archon of Mezeras. He captained Marc Frederick's Suddekar garrison for many years and is highly respected. And Rannul will send an army under a man named Albin Metagoras."

Another thought occurred to Hans. "Does anyone here know what Erenor's former commands might have been?" He wished he'd done more study about his usurping regent while in Sordan.

"He was commander of Stefan's King's Guard until being made Bas of Tahlwent," Nalf said. "Before that, under Marc Frederick, he was Captain of the Dragoon Cadets."

"Sounds like he started out honorably," said Orem Darm.

"Honor's easy when it amounts to the same thing as self-interest." Hans frowned. "Erenor turned on Stefan quickly enough once the Malyrdeons were out of the picture. I still suspect he had a direct hand in my brother's death—and my mother confirmed that suspicion. She told me in a letter."

Aubrey looked thoughtful. Perhaps she remembered her own proclamations on that subject. "So Erenor will be a desperate man. If his gains are ill-gotten, he won't want to answer for them."

"I may find a lot of that in Essera." Hans sighed and rolled up the map. "We'll head for the bridge at Merath."

Aubrey had just turned the corner to the canal bridge of the Bridge and Chimney when a distant thrum reverberated above the town. Half the people in the street stopped what they were doing to look overhead, toward the town's great hill. Aubrey stopped too, but not for the same reasons. She'd seen a cloaked figure, slight and nearly obscured by shadows, perched on the footing of the stone bridge over the Floh. Rill light spilled upon Lark's upturned face and parted lips.

Another thrum sounded and then another, followed by a succession of softer, lower notes. Overhead, the Rill's giant limbs reached toward the south and elongated to the north. Aubrey watched Lark inhale with amazement, a childlike wonder pouring across her face as a silver *charys* appeared as if out of nowhere and glided into place atop the mount. Aubrey didn't even have to see it to understand. She'd watched earlier arrivals with the same awe.

She strode across the road to stand beside her friend. "Supplies," Aubrey said when Lark looked to acknowledge her. "Tents. Wagons. Food. Horses. Food for horses. Weapons too. However many men we can muster, Sordan will arm for war."

"Change."

"More than we ever dreamed."

A group of fur-cloaked men crossed the canal-spanning bridge and hurried on to the inn there. The street resumed its normal activity now that the Rill's massive structures had ceased to move. Glow from the mount permeated the night, painting buildings silver and blotting out the stars. Only the quarter moon shone through, a pale ghost of what would elsewhere be a queenly presence.

"What brings you here?" Aubrey had never expected to find Lark so far from home. To her knowledge, Lark had never set foot east of the Gates of the Frendel.

"Grandmother. She sends a message. Her Wheel has revealed mighty portents."

"Let me guess." Aubrey waved toward the hill.

"The Rill brings a great coming together. People speak Hans Thegn's name in the same breath as hope. They cheer wealth for themselves and our people. They gather an army to make him King. They do not see the other thing."

"What other thing?" Aubrey wished she didn't always need to pry Lark's words into focus.

"The change."

*Change.* The Old Mothers' readings of Hans consistently raised that portent. The question always circled around whether the change would be good—or dire. Even now. Hans's path was not finished; it was ongoing.

Again Aubrey pointed to the Rill. "If you want to see change, there it is."

"The Toregh has changed. The Rill has changed. Perhaps even Hans Thegn has changed." Lark removed her gaze from the hilltop and her eyes, eerily blue by Rill light, slid to Aubrey. "Has Amallar?"

"Are you going to try to tell me we haven't?"

"No. Just look at what has changed... and what has not yet."

Sometimes Aubrey forgot how uncanny Rappeleye Mothers could be at divining portents. What if there were something deeper at work? Rhodhur's Old Mothers and their Wheel had foreseen the Faedic Prophecy and that Hans would be subject to it. The very existence of that prophecy had constrained the Old Mothers who had convened for the Witan. No Old Mother had stood to defend Hans when he had been pushed into the Spear's Path.

And none of them—neither the Old Mothers nor the Faeduadan—had foreseen that Hans was not working alone, that another man worked alongside him. Or that Dorilian had brought his god.

Amallar had changed, yes—but much as it pained Aubrey to admit, maybe not that much.

"What did Grandmother Rappeleye see?" Aubrey asked. "That Hans would overcome the Faedic Prophecy created to chain him? Because everyone else missed that."

Lark's hood slipped from her head and silver light teased the strands as she shook out her mane of dark hair. "Lud's Oracle is unchanged, its prophecy in motion. Hans Thegn has been set upon its path."

A path shrouded in a design none could unravel.

"Aren't you getting cold sitting on that stone? Let's walk across the canal. There's a woman on the other side who sells mulled mead. It's early still. Maybe she hasn't closed her stall."

The weather had lifted and, because the day had been a sunny one, the bridge was clear of snow, as was the arched passage beneath the inn. Nearer the river on the other side, drifts piled beside walls or in places where shadows lingered longest. The mead mistress's stall still showed a lamp and the hearty woman at the counter was happy to take Aubrey's coin for two mugs drawn from that night's last kettle. Aubrey and Lark sat on a lonely wooden bench facing the river. Boats bumped a nearby wharf.

Aubrey sought to relate that astonishing hour when Hans had faced down the Faeduadan. "They tricked him. Hans told me how they maneuvered him into consecrating the Horse."

"Their deceit does not invalidate the oracle or its prophecy."

"Maybe not," Aubrey conceded, "but it has made Hans pull back from us. He used to be more innocent."

Lark's wide, searching gaze weighed her. Aubrey felt a need to explain. "Because of the priesthood's methods, he distrusts the oracle and will not heed it. He looks at our people and sees what we were willing to do—what we *are* willing to do—to him and now his plans. He dislikes falsehoods of all kinds. The Faeduadan's prophecy was dark. Amallar's heart divided. Men fleeing the field of battle. Witchcraft and treachery." Aubrey took a long drink from the deep bowl of her mead cup. A cloying scent of honey teased her nose.

"What kind of witchcraft?"

A fair question. So many malignant forces inhabited the world. "The oracle wasn't clear. Highborn magic, maybe. Legend has it they can fly and we've seen for ourselves how they explode things."

"They build things too." Lark pointed to the Rill.

"No one built that. It was there already. Hans told me. Waiting. Sleeping."

"Awakening."

It had done that too. Aubrey sighed. "The thing is, the prophecy never said anything about the Rill at all. Not one thing other than that Lud would not show his Spear. Except Lud *did* show it. Only it wasn't Lud." Very few Khelds understood just who *had* shown his spear.

Lark's night-shadowed smile teased that truth. "The Rill belongs to another god. Lud cannot prophesy it."

"Can runes? Can Wheels?"

"If the Rill belongs to the Mother's sphere."

Which it didn't.

The mead in the cup called to Aubrey. Sweet. Warm. She drew another swallow. Nights were good for drink, drink was good for dulling the mind, and a dull mind—was good for forgetting.

"Hans is gathering an army and supplies. Swords, armor, horses... Sordan sends so much, I know it was set up ahead of this. Maybe not for Bellan Toregh, but—" The coming war was painfully real, and for Dorilian it had been real all along. He had come to Amallar to advance a needed alliance, had awakened the Rill to secure a path to Essera. He had needed *this*... for *that*. Aubrey was still trying to understand what had brought so singular a man to Amallar and into her life. "I think Hans means to leave before the next waning. He said his mother is arranging help for him in the north. Money. Supplies. A few allies. I hope he survives the winter."

"Then strengthen him. Go with him." Steam from Lark's cup mingled with a puff of breath when she licked her lips.

"Me? Hans has better help than anything I can give. He has advisors now, real ones. Men of importance and experience. He has an alliance with Sordan. He only needed me to translate portions of the treaty so Old Mothers and men on the Cruihcil would understand what we were negotiating and agreeing to. And then I helped translate the negotiated parts back into Stauba."

"At Aurdollen you tried to teach Stauba to Nilla and me. It didn't seem important then."

"It wasn't important when we were *twelve*. It's important now."

On the other side of the canal, wagon wheels rumbled along the rutted road. Cargo from the Rill, brought down the mount by technology Khelds had never guessed lived within their hill and carted away, almost certainly toward the King's Bridge and the bustling military camp outside of town.

Lark's assessment sharpened. "What are you going to do?"

Yes, what? Aubrey's life had taken on a course nearly as frightening as that of the River Floh, and that was certain to become a far more important highway of trade now that Bellan Toregh was a Rill port. Part of her wished to be small again. She swirled the contents of her nearly empty mug.

"Perhaps I'll return to Amundhal. I have responsibilities there." She cherished the big stone house with its pond and mill and golden crown oaks lining the road over a stone bridge. Her father had planted those oaks. Toward the back of the house, in a manicured garden overlooking the stream, stood her Mother Oak, still young, grown from a seedling of the Thegn Oak that towered over the Barrowwood.

Her mother had planted that seedling. She, however, had planted nothing at all. "Amundhal has missed my attention for too long."

A sideways glance showed Lark watching with a half frown. Lark wasn't buying Aubrey's reasons.

Aubrey wasn't sure she did, herself. She spent more time away from Amundhal than she did managing it. The business of procuring supplies for Neuberland's rebels or of overseeing the release of captured enemies interested her more. The only future she had ever glimpsed at Amundhal lurked in the acquisitive gazes of men who aspired to gain her bed, and with that her land.

She tried again. "Neuberland needs leadership now, and more than ever because of the war effort. Saemoregh and the Cruihcil could both use my influence. All the men of importance or good use are riding to join Hans."

"They can turn to old men to lead them. And women of any age. So can Amundhal."

Because change would not wait. Neither would war. At least not for Amallar, or Neuberland, or them. Aubrey sensed what Lark wanted of her. "Amundhal has fighting men for protection. They provide me—and Amundhal too—with defense because I have wealth, not because I aspire to the kind of power men wield. Wodd and my men... their families live on my land. My welfare ensures theirs. They trust me to lead them."

"But Amundhal's future and yours—all of our futures—are bound with that of Hans Thegn."

"Is that why you're here? To tell me that?"

"Ha! As if you need me to tell you anything."

*No.* From the moment she had noticed that Thron had an unusual bond with Hans, Aubrey had sensed that her path was linked somehow to their pairing. Every time she was with one or the other of them, the Mother approved. Though events atop Bellan Toregh had laid bare its existence, the precise shape of Her path remained hidden enough that few others had discerned it. War-minded men like Nalf and hotheads like Fran saw only what they wanted to see—and the Old Mothers and Rappeleye Mothers alike had missed the crucial alignment.

*Lahd.* Aubrey alone had divined the key stone. Dorilian. Even in thought the name made her flinch. For her, Dorilian too had changed, everything about him. No longer did she believe theirs had been a chance encounter. Somehow, for some reason, the

Mother had moved Aubrey to engage with the man, meant for her to know him, maybe even bind him. For she and Dorilian were bound together now in ways Aubrey found terrifying. At least her course had flowed this moon as normal and they were not bound in *that* way. She had never felt such relief.

Cheeks burning, Aubrey remembered how she had told Hans she wanted to see Dorilian again. And how she still wanted that.

Lark's clever gaze weighed her reaction. Aubrey owed her friend more explanation. She gestured over her shoulder, at the source of the town's silver glow. "I rode it. To Sordan. Hans and the Witan chose me because I know Staubaun ways and speak Stauba."

"Is it as beautiful as the stories say?"

"Yes. All towers and sunlight. I... understand a great many more things now than I did before."

"Good reasons, then, why you should go with Hans Thegn. You've seen their City and do not fear them. You don't bow down before their wealth, their gods. Their Wall. Their Rill."

That was true enough.

Lark gave a little half smile and leaned nearer. "I became the Mother's servant. I spent a night under the Hill, with a man, as was foreseen by the Crone."

"That's not what the old witch meant—and you know it!"

"I don't know that it didn't. And I know one thing more—only one path remains." She pointed to the light-crowned hill. "The cold trees."

And here they sat, two survivors of that day, striving against the tatters of a childhood curse. Nilla had died. But Aubrey and Lark still breathed and trod the Crone's fateful words. Aubrey's stomach turned. Lark didn't know, could not possibly know about what she had done—or with whom. Besides, she'd only bedded the damned Rill Lord, not wed him. Lark's mittened fingers settled over hers and Aubrey looked again into her friend's cat-sharp gaze.

"You are part of this," Lark said.

"I don't see how." Another lie. Another thing Aubrey resented was how Lark had always been able to see through her.

"Ha. You see more than that. You see *why*."

They finished their drinks in silence, then rose and set their empty mugs on the mead stall's wooden counter, thanking the woman for her brew. The silence between Aubrey and Lark thickened as they walked across the canal bridge to the inn.

"We don't see the Mother's Path from where we stand." Lark was still trying to convince her. "We see only the choices."

"Our choices *are* her Path."

"Yes."

Aubrey detected an icy change of seasons in the air that touched her tongue and teeth, as sharp and cold as the Rill glow spilling down from the mount. She lifted her face to it. She could almost taste the silver of that kiss. "Then I've already laid my path," she said. "I think I've set something free that should have stayed caged."

Lark followed Aubrey's gaze. "That?"

"No. I could never have stopped that."

"Remember Gifu's teaching. If a woman sets a path, she must follow it."

"Find out where it goes."

Lark nodded. "Finish your part. If you don't, the path goes wild. Or dies."

This one wouldn't. The path Aubrey had set would only die if Dorilian died. Or Hans. Or the Rill itself. Of that, she was certain. If unfollowed, though, it might twist into another shape, spawn outcomes over which she would have no power at all. That part of the Mother's wisdom still had teeth.

She and Hans and Dorilian too... they followed the same path—and the only way to kill or tame the thing they'd set in motion was to follow it into Essera.

# 11

It is for each generation to guard its endowment. Look
upon our advantages: a stable society, bountiful wealth
and privilege, and the stature of a people great and
admired. That we have achieved this stature is no accident
of biology. That we are stronger than other races, more
beautiful, more intelligent, and possess healthy longevity
are the gifts of our fathers and mothers before us who
mated wisely. Like the very horses we breed with such
pride, we do not mingle our seed with lesser blood.
CLAUDAS STAUBAUN BERSULES, *A PURIST DIALOGUE*

Dorilian had never seen a land as lonely as Lacenedon. Snow
carpeted a nearly featureless plain broken only by occasional
ridges and shadowed hollows. The basins, unlike those to the
south, were barren of ore. Wastelands. Rannul and Dazunor were
richer. Lacenedon was simply vast.

A few days earlier, while passing near Permephedon, Dorilian's
party had picked up an additional four thousand mounted men from
his elite Eagle Guard, turning his well-armed escort into a small but
formidable army. With them was Legon Rebiran, Commander of
the Eagle Guard, who made no secret of his belief that Dorilian was
vulnerable in the field. That they rode swiftly and over long distances
toward an army belonging to an ally reassured Legon not one bit.

"You trust him," Legon said of the Bas of Lacenedon. "I don't.
His men aren't going to catch mine without swords in hand."

Legon trusted no one when it came to his liege. He barely
tolerated that Dorilian insisted on keeping Robdan at his side. The
Kheld alliance, while Legon knew it to be a fact, brought with it
memories of Stefan. But more and more Dorilian saw the advantage
of having Robdan near at hand. Not only did the man have a head

on his shoulders that was good enough to be worth protecting, but Robdan, like Marc Frederick, made a point of keeping a journal detailing his travels and thoughts. At the very least, any information sent to Handurin would be well documented.

Outriders from Lacenedon's camped army spied Dorilian's approach first and soon a greeting party of thirty riders crested the rise ahead of them. All wore thick woven coverings of pale gray wool upon their heads, crowned by helms of dull metal-banded leather. The leader, his lean body encased in ash-hued garb, rode a white horse draped with a blanket of summer-sky-blue embroidered in black thread: backdrop for Lacenedon's heraldic Bear.

Soon the two groups of horsemen neared each other, and both leaders met in the center of the resulting knot of riders. Dorilian had directed Robdan to wear a fine cloak of marten fur that had been purchased for him in Merath. For himself, in addition to a cloak of Sordaneon green and silver, Dorilian wore a circlet of bright stones upon his brow.

"Your Thrice Royal Grace." The gray-clad Lacendoni horseman bowed deep in the saddle and displayed open palms. As he did so, every man with him did the same. "For once, I am glad to see you."

Dorilian recognized Hebron of Lacenedon more by voice than other means. He had met Hebron at only one Archhalia and then mostly had listened to arguments against Emyli and Handurin. Now the man before Dorilian pulled aside the gray scarf to reveal an austere countenance, narrow and creased with dignified lines of middle age.

"And I am glad to meet again, cousin." The kinship Dorilian acknowledged was marginal, at best. The honor was that he used it. "We would ask your hospitality, Bas Ursenos."

Hebron bent his neck, accepting the courtesy. "It has always been yours to enjoy, Thrice Royal, although you have not seen fit to favor us."

"Your domain's climate chills my enthusiasm."

"Not every land is blessed with Sordan's benign seasons. I can assure you, though, our summers are mild and worthy of even a Highborn Prince's days."

Dorilian nodded agreeably. "If we are still around this summer, I will ask you to show me this land of yours. Have you any idea where my army is in this featureless plain?"

"Fifteen thousand at my stronghold of Askyllon." Hebron gazed grimly to the northwest. "It is by virtue of that army I still hold the north end of the lake above Tranchosa."

"How far?" Dorilian asked.

"Three days. For tonight, please accept the hospitality of my camp. Tomorrow, we shall ride with my five thousand added to yours."

"The way is dangerous then?"

Hebron's somber features darkened. He turned his horse, and his men rode ahead as they made toward the ridge and his camp. Legon kept at Dorilian's side, with Robdan beside him, and the Eagle Guard fanned in positions to the rear. "The land between here and Bynum is menaced by Erenor's soldiers and Nammuor's plunderous minions. I hold Lacenedon but by vigilance and the cold arm of winter." Hebron sighed and shook his head, speaking through clenched teeth. "Erenor rallies his forces forth from Stauberg and his troops hold the Eleutheron. My capital of Kenelm is secure, but I fear it will be besieged come summer. Never did I think to see the day we of Essera would war upon our own."

"Essera has done so for generations."

"You speak of Sordan's occupation, and rightly. Rill greed and ruin. And now foul reversal has fallen on us. The traitor Erenor grows daily stronger under the Sorcerer's wing. To think I voted that monster to sit atop this heap of a Kingdom."

"Which monster? Erenor or Nammuor?"

"Get one and get the other. I recall you voted differently. Ah, well, 'tis done. What we got from it was war." Hebron turned his gaze upon Dorilian appreciatively. "I see you wear a device."

"Rannul's crown. On loan from a lovely lady."

"Let us pray you have no need to use it."

Dorilian hadn't so far. His journey north had been without incident. Though Dorilian had thought often about what he might do if he'd been attacked, he still did not know what course he would have chosen. Flight, while less obvious than the unleashing of power, sat poorly with his principles.

From the top of the next ridge, they spied Hebron's force camped upon the plain, hundreds of ground-hugging mounds glistening like gooseflesh on the land's white skin. From a distance, such an encampment could hardly be seen. Hebron pulled to a halt before one low mound.

Dorilian dismounted, Legon alongside him. When Dorilian turned, however, he witnessed the Kheld, Robdan, nearly tumble from his horse onto stiff legs only to fall ass backward in the snow. When Robdan finally lurched to his feet, Dorilian signaled for the Kheld to join him. Together they followed Hebron through a snow-coated flap held aloft by one of the guards. Legon would stand as protection outside.

Within, they found a hollow formed beneath the snow cover by an arrangement of lightweight frames and skins of *vrkarsa*, a heavily furred animal found only in the icy reaches of the Cjta. Bright woven hangings lined this framework with warm patterns of blue and crimson. A massive brass brazier squatted in the center of the chamber, throwing off so much heat it was necessary to remove their heavy outer garments. A brace of small waterglobes ensconced in lanterns cast a golden light. Robdan looked amazed to find such sumptuous surroundings in the midst of an icy wilderness. Dorilian was no less surprised: he had never imagined Hebron Ursenos to be anything but spartan.

"Hebron," he said, allowing an element of familiarity. "I had not thought you favored decadence."

Their host motioned for his guests to be seated upon scattered cushions after his aide departed into a side chamber with everyone's shed outer garments. A faint smile tugged at Hebron's mouth. "The least of vices, I assure you."

"War disagrees with your sensibilities?"

"Immensely. Tell me not that you prefer it otherwise." Hebron let his gaze drift to his other guest. "Good welcome, Robdan Aelfricson. I had hardly expected to find you or any of your kind in company with His Thrice Royal Grace—no matter how strongly recent events point to the reason."

Robdan bowed his head, accepting the welcome while overlooking the implication that only the company he kept made him worth speaking to. Lacenedon was distant from Amallar, and Khelds seldom ventured into that purely Staubaun domain.

An aide knelt to present pots of bitterswell heated to steaming richness, served in gilded cups. These Hebron passed to his guests. "Tell me, Thrice Royal," he said plainly. "What of young Handurin? It seems odd that you would promote him. No matter which rumor one credits, he is as Kheld by birth as Stefan was."

Robdan simply sat back and sipped his cup of bitter brew.

Dorilian answered evenly, "Handurin's other qualities recommend him. To be frank, he reminds me of Marc Frederick." He had not said so before. Now it felt... what? Provocative? Real?

"Truly?" Hebron's proud mouth firmed. "A First Creation castaway, then, for that has been the rumor of his location—and that is worse. Especially now that news places Handurin as chief among the Khelds, as was his late brother whose reign is best forgotten." He continued with barely concealed discontent, "The Rill runs to Trestethion, I hear."

"What difference to Lacenedon? It runs no less to Permephedon for that."

"And is that how you purchased the Khelds?"

Robdan stifled a cough. Hebron had used the Staubaun term most offensive in its suggestion.

Dorilian held the other man's gaze. "I pander my birthright to no one. Not Nammuor, not the Seven Houses—not even the Epoptes who believe they order the Entity's every move. Or do you miss the old days, when Essera commanded the Rill's choices? Those days are gone. They died with Stefan's last breath and deed against me." He swirled the dark liquor in his cup before taking a drink. "If the Rill serves my ends, so be it. Such is the Mind of Leur."

"The Mind of Leur, I would ask—or the mind of Dorilian?"

"Is there a difference? Now that most of my kind have been murdered, where else would the Mind reside?" Challenge laced those words. "You forget who I am. *What* I am. Even the Epoptes do not deny that I am Derlon's Heir. Leur blood flows in my veins. Shall I allow my patrimony to be used by those who would destroy me? I warned a thousand times that I would not allow it, and Essera took no measures to safeguard the Covenant, one of the first articles of which states that the Rill shall not be used against Sordaneon interests."

"I could not protect it," Hebron protested. "The Rill runs not through my lands!"

"You could not. Ionais could not. The Seven Houses could not. And since Essera is so unable, what choice have I but to seek more able guardians? And the Rill *does* run through Amallar."

"But the Khelds are savages! Barbarians! Their commerce is the raising of goats and mayhem. What can the Rill do for them but spread their filth farther into our domains?"

"Oh, they are not so primitive as all that." Dorilian noted the way Robdan clutched his cup of bitters more tightly. "I found Khelds difficult, to be sure, but not uncivilized. They're capable and industrious. Best of all, they have excellent cooks. Indeed, I believe they have untapped potential."

"*You* found them so?" Only then did Hebron realize what was meant. "Where? Not in Amallar, surely?"

Dorilian glanced in Robdan's direction, reinforcing the Kheld's presence. "Yes, I was in Amallar. How else did I empower the Trestethion node?"

"You were *there*." A swallow and a head shake of disbelief. "I had not thought—I did not believe it possible. Least of all that you would step foot in Amallar! The Promise—"

"I entered as an act of peace."

"But the Khelds—"

"Never guessed who I was, save Robdan here. And Handurin, of course. I masqueraded as an Estol from Trongor."

"They thought the Rill dropped from the heavens, then, when it arrived at their door?"

Dorilian reached for the bitters pot, refilling his own cup. "As far as Khelds know, it can be done by relay from Sordan, as you believed. Indeed, as most people will. I expect Handurin has taken full honors for the thing. He will give me my due—of that I am sure—or I would not have done it. If the Rill lifts Amallar from my back and discomfits my enemies, the opening of Trestethion serves me well."

Hebron's gaze flicked briefly to Robdan and then back to Dorilian. "Think you the Khelds will deal honorably? Stefan poisoned them to death against you."

"Me? They hate me too well. But they will deal honorably with Sordan. Two nations can oft agree when rulers are not at issue. And they must ally with Sordan if they hope to gain the Rill as a permanent fixture. I'm fully capable of repossessing what is at this point merely a token of goodwill. My goodwill flags when not returned and is not offered again soon, as Stefan found out. No, my attentions are spent on Handurin, and more profitably."

"I should say so, with your treasury to fund his endeavors," Hebron observed sourly. "Between that and the Rill, the boy outdoes even his grandsire for alliances."

"I'm quite the prize—as you well know."

Silence, then a dark side gaze to Robdan. "And the Khelds now know this also?"

"We do," Robdan conceded. "Though it took much persuading."

"Of that, I am certain." Hebron sighed. After taking a long drink from his cup, he put it aside and addressed Dorilian again. "You have ever been the seed of change, and I fear you now bring great ones. Is this some manner of punishment? That we must now suffer barbarians because we chose not to suffer your will? The Epoptes meet to frame an opposition to you, and the Rill stops the next day—"

"My plans do not revolve around punishing Essera."

"What then? Am I to truly believe they revolve around Handurin?"

The silent aide returned with platters of meat rolls stuffed with wild grains and dried fruits, and golden-fried cakes sprinkled with nut meats and honey. The kneeling youth offered first to the Hierarch, then to Bas Hebron, and lastly to Robdan before departing once more.

"You say you left the boy in Amallar?" Hebron appeared resigned to having his questions unanswered.

Dorilian nodded. "Prince Handurin? Yes. He is well placed to guard my royal back, don't you think?"

"Or to put a knife in it." Hebron's Staubaun-dark eyes glimmered with solemn reflection. "What is to stop him from doing so? You have few forces here and fewer friends. Nammuor, your enemy, will soon enough know that you are here, and then move against you as swiftly as he dares. Handurin has you in a place like no other. You are in more peril now than you have ever been."

"Not so. Handurin could have taken me in Amallar far more easily. I was alone, very much at the mercy of his goodwill, surrounded by an enemy that, once aware of who I was, would kill me quicker than even Nammuor would. Why think you Handurin did not?"

"I dare not guess. I would rather know."

Dorilian put down his barely touched platter. His gaze challenged Hebron's understanding across the low table between them. "For the same reasons I did not hold Handurin in Sordan. Because I could not. Not without cutting my own throat. That would have been a pretty sight—Nammuor and half of Essera waited on it. You, I count among the few who sent fair warning, though I needed it not. No great insight was necessary to know that to continue holding Handurin in Sordan would mean all-out war with Amallar come winter. As I have Nammuor hammering at the gates of Suddekar even now and overrunning Trongor to provoke me, why would I court such a liability?" Again, Dorilian frowned, irritated by those who overlooked his ability to recognize obvious maneuverings. "As for Handurin, had he done other than as he did—what stood he to gain but Sordan tearing at his knees and Nammuor chopping at his head. His choices were even fewer than mine. Imprison me and he would have had war. Kill me, and it would then be holy war. At best, the difference lies in definition."

"True." Hebron nodded. "You placed him where he could not do otherwise. And at the same time you proved him not your enemy. But what of us? It's hardly enough that we battle Nammuor for our very lives, but you would face us now with Amallar!"

"Then face it. You've always known it was there. You were content to create the beast, now sleep with it."

"I would slay it before it stirs had I but the sword that would do it!" Hebron's grim face flushed with blood, his fierce gaze darting to Robdan with pure contempt. "Were it not for Stefan and his filthy barbarian horde, would we be where we are? You of all men know better! That you would go among them is your own special brand of recklessness, for the foul Khelds would as soon eradicate the Highborn from the face of this Creation as remember who it was that gave them their place among us. Did they not slay the Princes of Leseos and Gignastha and dance in their blood? Did they not remove the heads of Rheger Dannutheon and his son? They crowd our borders, fingering our lands, plundering all that falls within their grasp—demanding, always demanding. Let them run loose in Essera and they will not be content until they have not only Stauberg but Permephedon as well. How long then until they crowd at Sordan, claiming that they have not enough and you have so much? Erydon intended not that his gift should be turned against us."

"It will not be so!" Robdan cried out in protest, but Dorilian forestalled his argument.

"These foul Khelds, as you call them, may well prove to be the gift that saves us all. Essera is no fine prize. This land is weak, easily won, its splendid roots forgotten as soon as adversity knocks at the door. I could cut a swath through it so wide, the rest would fall into the damned chasm and be swallowed along with it. And who knows but that I will yet do it, if only to take Nammuor with you! Aral opened her arms to Nammuor before Stefan ever died, Tahlwent followed shortly after, thrice-holy Stauberg has become Nammuor's whore, and this spring Dazunor fell into his lap. Erydon was a Wall Lord—remember that. Who is to say that he did not see the danger and moved to provide us ahead of the need? It is an old rumor of my race that we see things to which mortal eyes are blind."

"And what do your Highborn eyes see? Something we do not?"

Dorilian's silver gaze touched Hebron's with chilling certainty. "Perhaps I do. I see Handurin on the Star Throne of the Malyrdeons."

# 12



The Khelds had never mounted such an army as rode from Bellan Toregh toward Merrydn. Every day saw more people pour in from the western forests and hills. Smiths and farriers, wagoners and wranglers, Khelds of every ilk joined the ranks of those willing to bear arms. More than anything, what Hans commanded resembled a nation on the move.

Also, though to no one's joy, not surprisingly, Endelarin's predictions of an influx of refugees from Trongor proved accurate. They came in a steady stream of the war weary and hungry, seeking sanctuary and food. Tye, until Farrl could return, took command of a growing contingent of his tough-minded countrymen who wished to fight. Those folk of Trongor not eager to fight in Essera agreed instead to help defend the Pass or returned to their country as armed companies. Having found Amallar a safe haven for themselves and their families, the Trongorians pledged to help safeguard the country—and Prince—that had offered them refuge. They pledged themselves for Handurin.

The bulk of the Kheld forces, however, came from the populous towns of Amallar and nearby Neuberland. Fran Gorseddson returned from the Gero valley with a small army of his own. "Good men that've been fighting for years," he told Hans with a grin. "And they're spoiling to fight some more."

The army started out along the road to Merath and gathered

volunteers as it went, growing daily until it straggled out for leagues. Some parts were well organized. In addition to the Trongorians and Fran's disciplined forces, Arne had spent part of his time at Rhodhur putting together a crack team of Amallaran archers, all of whom were also good with *skifr* and sword. His brother Brec and several other experienced rangers had undertaken to command recruits from the Frendel valley. Even Aubrey's loose cohort of Saemoregh rangers gathered enough recruits from that region to become a respectable troop led by Wodd. The Lords of Annech and Gobba, though they did not send troops, had honored admonitions about the prospective treaty being ratified in Sordan and withdrawn their forces back over the Gero. The new treaty stipulated the Sordani garrison still at Gignastha would respect existing Kheld settlements in Neuberland and send aid to their defense.

Hans spent his first days on the road observing who made the most effective leaders. As they drew near the Dazun and the land began to break into lower, rolling hills, he rode through the Amallaran ranks, meeting with each *keld* and its chieftains, confirming its organization. Volunteers without *keld* affiliations he assigned to either Brec or Fran.

Nalf Rhys, as head of the Thegn *keld*, was pleased to find that his clan's volunteers numbered more than five thousand and rode proudly in advance of that column. From somewhere, probably the women of his household, he'd obtained a length of cloth upon which they'd appliquéd the emblem of a spear in honor of Treowdan Almarreson. Nalf's display prompted the other *kelds* to follow suit and soon the impromptu army was aflutter with ensigns, all borne high and proud. Even the Trongorians carried a flag of red and blue silk bearing the Golden Ship emblem of that domain.

"I'm the only one who doesn't have one!" Hans laughed. He was glad of the spirit being displayed, even if it was impressive only in its sheer enthusiasm.

From where she rode beside him, Aubrey looked around and joined in his delight. Saemoregh had contributed a fine banner with seven stones, in honor of Aubrey's runes. "You will have a much finer one," she assured Hans. "Once we get north." Aubrey had seen the banners displayed by the Staubaun Lords of Leseos whenever they sallied forth from their city and knew that a proper ensign for the arriving Prince of Dazunor would have to be more splendid than anything a Kheld woman in her tent might fashion.

Maybe in Merath they would be able to find a skilled seamstress with the proper materials to make one.

That night, however, Hans experienced the first dread he had felt in months. His dreams filled with visions of fire, the sky tearing open… and water.

A touch on his arm made him bolt upright in bed, his sword nearly drawn but for Tye's hand on his wrist. "You must see this, Prince Handurin!" The urgency in the man's whisper was reason enough for Hans to rise and follow him.

The sky to the east was purple and red, malignant—but not with dawn. It was hours until sunrise. Rubrous strands unfurled across the heavens, rapidly shifting through orange, then yellow and, finally, bright white as the dome they created encased the horizon.

"What is it?" Hans asked.

"We don't know." Tye's voice mirrored his expression, tight and anxious. "It has not the look of the Rift."

*I've seen the Rift.* Mulsor and madness. Seeing Arne run up to join him wearing but a tunic and leggings only reinforced the memory. The end-of-the-World violence they'd seen that storm-tossed night hadn't looked like this though.

Arne asked the same question Hans had just asked. "What is that?"

"Don't know."

*Volcano?* he wondered. But no. There was too much light, and even that was dying. As Hans watched, joined by men in the night guard and those they had awakened, the fiery illumination to the east dissipated, contracted, and then—almost too suddenly—was gone. Had some catastrophe struck? Something from the heavens fallen to their World to wreak destruction? Whatever it was, Hans saw no reason to spread panic.

Nalf Rhys lumbered to the ridge upon which the watchers stood, looking around and muttering. "What's going on? I don't see a thing."

"It's gone," Hans answered, "whatever it was."

"A blood-red sky, they said. Could be an omen."

"It wasn't blood-red." Because no one was going to leave the ridge unless he did, Hans led the others back to their tents and their beds. The cold ground penetrated through his slippers. With a few more words, he reassured them and was content that most of the army, at least, would sleep out the night undisturbed. His own eyes would not close, however; neither could he sleep. *The sky was not blood-red*, he kept thinking as he lay in his cot and stared at the dark striations of his tent overhead. Over and over, his mind repeated what he had not said to the others. *It was hotter than that.*

For two days he watched the sky, wondering if he would see currents of ash or dust darkening the horizons. He saw only clouds, swift-flying overhead, white and unthreatening, while sunrises were pink and bright. By the fourth day, he resolved that he might never know what had happened.

A week after leaving Bellan Toregh, and foregoing the road to Dazunor-Rannuli, the Khelds were within a day's march of Merath and the bridge at Eldwadder. Clouds from the west moved heavily across the sky and by late afternoon the army marched in rain. The white snow that had made the countryside look so clean had long since melted away. There was a cry on the road ahead, and a flurry of hoofs as two men on horseback rode up. "Hans Thegn!" They shouted and pointed ahead, toward the river. "It's over the banks! For miles and miles! The Dazun has flooded!"

Wheeling his horse around, Hans looked toward the Dazun's distant headwaters. The rain pelting them was ordinary, moderate. Not a towering storm. Not the kind that caused floods—and it had come from the west. Not the east, from which the Dazun flowed. A searing prickle of realization crawled across the skin of Hans's brain. *Nammuor. What did you do? What did you do that night the sky burned with fire?*

"It's not just flooded." Orem Darm gestured toward the valley. "Look at the Mother-crazed thing—water all the way over the bridges! I can't even see the rooftops of Dullegh or Onoddel. I tell you, the towns are gone!"

Hans and the Kheld chieftains stood on a hillside overlooking the Dazun. Brown waters churned against the wooded banks for as far as they could see. The towns Orem had named should have been directly below, Kheld river communities just downriver of Eldwadder and the great bridge at Merath. The gathered Khelds grew quiet and worried.

Hans resolved to tell them his fears about Nammuor and sorcery, only to find that other rumors, easily believed, had already taken root.

"And doesn't that just point to the cursed Sordaneon having popped up in the Royal North, his own self." Nalf Rhys scowled and nodded to acknowledge the looks his announcement awakened. "That's right! He's up there! Birds carried the news. Man out of Merrydn said Dorilian Sordaneon was welcomed at the Crescent Palace! While we were talking peace and thinking ourselves clever, he got himself north, took the Rill behind our backs!" The Thegnard frowned at the river. "As fine a piece of backstabbing as I've ever seen."

"Reckon he did it, then, that evil bastard," Fran judged. "Got his army north and himself too... and then this to make sure we couldn't come after him!"

"That's ridiculous." Hans stared them both down. "Think about it. If Dorilian Sordaneon could do stuff like this, Stefan would have had his hands full with bad weather every week." He gave up for the moment on trying to persuade them that Nammuor was an evil sorcerer. All he could do was keep reminding Khelds of it until they saw for themselves. For now, because the flooded river was a problem needing to be addressed, he directed riders to head east and west along the river to assess the damage and look for possible places to cross.

Later, Hans delivered his news to Arne and Aubrey as they walked back toward his tent. "It has to be Nammuor's doing. I studied the Dazun while I was in Sordan. The river originates east of here in mountains girdled by World-binding palisades of ice. The Pillars of the Sky. I think Nammuor melted that ice, at least some of it."

Camp was on high ground well away from the still-rising waters. A few of the other captains were waiting for them there. A strategy was needed, and Hans counted on seasoned veterans to make up, at least somewhat, for his lack of military experience.

However, his commanders were at as much of a loss as he was. Like him, they had never seen anything like it.

Orem Darm, especially, wouldn't accept that the river had flooded so suddenly. He sank down on the floor of the tent and stared out at the slashing rain. "Born I was on that river and learned from the tales of graybeards all my life, and though the Dazun floods often in spring, when the snows melt and the rains descend, never has it risen so high as if overnight. You heard the townsfolk who made it to high ground—there was no high water even hours before, no sign of the river rising until it descended upon them."

"This flood isn't natural… and it isn't just about us." The more Hans thought about it, the more certain he was that Nammuor had caused some kind of glacial melt. One glacier or several hardly mattered. "Nammuor is capable of something like this; the device he uses commands great forces. Marenthro warned me how terrible it—and Nammuor—could become. I think he raised the river so we can't cross—and also so Dorilian and his armies can't. Nammuor would like nothing better than to keep our forces from joining." Nammuor probably also hoped to trap Dorilian in Essera. But only the Trongorians looked to be impressed by that argument.

"Floods don't last forever. Only a few days." Aubrey sounded more hopeful than certain. She took a seat near the brazier and wrapped her arms around her raised knees.

"It's already done the damage Nammuor wants." Hans had thought about that too. Nammuor's goals weren't only military; Essera's economy and communications were also compromised. *Hans's* economy and communications. "The bridges are washed away, here for sure and maybe all of them, all the way to Gustan. Every bridge from Amallar into Essera. That was Nammuor's real goal. It'll take weeks, maybe months, to build a new bridge, even after the floodwaters have receded. We have to find some other way to get across—and supply our troops until the Rill Mount reopens in Dazunor-Rannuli."

Although Dorilian had seen the ratified treaty that secured the Kheld Rill port at Bellan Toregh, he would not facilitate release of Dazunor-Rannuli's Mount until he'd viewed a document signed by the Seven Houses and Brotherhood of Epoptes, saying they agreed to his terms.

"We got us the Rill," Arne said. "We got supplies moving down the Floh. Maybe the enemy can keep us from crossing the Dazun, but they don't control the Rill one bit. Maybe we should head back to Bellan Toregh and hop to Permephedon, then sneak back on them."

Though most of the others nodded, Aubrey looked unconvinced. "I don't like that we wouldn't have an overland supply or escape route," she said. "We could just as easily get bottled in at Permephedon."

"And I think that's what the enemy wants us to do, use the Rill to Permephedon. Get us deep in Essera, like Aubrey said, then we'll be more vulnerable. That's not where we need to be." Hans pondered the news from Nalf Rhys's informant, sent by bird, that the Mormantalorans had moved troops east from the Kyrbasillon siege and toward the High Citadel. Erenor, too, had moved troops north out of Dazunor-Rannuli.

"Should be safe enough at the Great Citadel. Place is big as a mountain and can well hold an army." Nalf Rhys walked into the tent. He'd stayed behind a few minutes to direct men toward the hewing of rafts and makeshift boats. He slapped his gloves down on the crate that served as a table and gestured behind him, toward the now-closed tent flap. "We have no options here. We can make a slew of gods-cursed rafts, and fast work of it, but rafts are slow crossing and no good in fast water. You have to build them where you use them, for one thing. The enemy would peg us and have troops in place before we got 'em all in the water, much less across."

"What about pontoons?"

"Too far across," said Orem Darm. Life on the river had taught him much, not least of which was a deep respect for its power. The Dazun's strength as a border lay in the formidable obstacle it presented. "Even without the flood, the currents would snap rope, the river's that strong."

"It wouldn't snap cable." Hans looked around the table and saw only blank faces. That and the fact he needed to use a Staubaun word told him there would be no cable in Amallar. He thought, then asked, "How long would it take to get a messenger to Bellan Toregh?"

"Two days by fast relay," Fran spoke first. Others nodded.

Hans got out a sheet of paper. "Fetch a rider. And send this message to Sordan."

Hans pulled his army back from the river and had them disperse to surrounding villages. The next morning he held another meeting in a small but dry woodcutter's cottage he'd taken over to be his headquarters. From there he ordered men under Fran Gorseddson, with two companies of Thegn horse soldiers to accompany them, to Bellan Toregh. "Take the Rill to Permephedon," he said. "Make a production of it. Unload supplies, even if the barrels are empty. Take a few days about it."

"What are you up to?" Nalf Rhys wanted to know. He wasn't the only one sitting at the room's single plank of a table to scowl. "I won't send good men on a sham!"

"You aren't sending them and it's not a sham. They're going to

Permephedon so they can strike from there at Dazunor-Rannuli. They're just going to take a few days getting there. And they're going to take a letter from me to Marenthro Dru'vida." Hans turned to Aubrey, standing nearby, and she handed over two sealed documents. Aubrey's experience with official correspondence ensured the letter to Marenthro, as well as another written to Hans's mother, would be properly addressed.

It occurred to Hans that he could go himself, deliver the letters personally. It would be good to see Marenthro again. And his mother. He had more questions now than ever.

So many questions. And so far, the only answers he had found rested with a man now fighting in the frozen northlands, whose well-being had come to mean as much to Hans as his own. Though Nammuor was after them both, recent actions confirmed that Dorilian was the greater prey. For that reason alone, Hans was determined to stay with his army, force it across the Dazun and harry both Nammuor's and Erenor's flanks until he'd achieved the second front Dorilian needed.

The woodcutter's cottage boasted little in the way of appointments. Other than the table on which the captains had spread their maps, the cottage's best feature was a tiny alcove to the back with a bed Hans could sleep in. Given that the main room's hearth was also tiny and provided little heat, Hans was glad of the number of warm bodies he'd assembled. He lifted his head when he heard horses outside and the challenge of his Trongorian guard turned suddenly joyful.

"Captain!" Their cries penetrated the frame and wattle walls.

The door creaked open and Farrl entered, accompanied by two strangers. The man with dark hair and blue eyes was undeniably Kheld, while the other man was tall and broad, with the gold-bright hair and brown eyes of a Staubaun. Farrl bowed and the new arrivals did also, doffed headgear in their hands.

"Prince Handurin," Farrl said. He looked weary but otherwise hale and happy to have returned. "I met these men on the road from Jarla. They claim an urgent need to speak with you."

"And so do folk from every drowned town on the Dazun," grumbled Nalf, who'd spent the morning directing flood victims to shelters.

The Kheld—a striking, handsome man wearing a jacket of fine blue leather beneath his weather-battered cloak—cocked his head and frowned. Everyone in the room, however, noted the Staubaun's sharp glare and tense stance. Time to step forward.

"Farrl! You made it. Before the flood." Hans could not hold back a grin. "I feared you might have been caught on the other side."

"Indeed not, sir, though I and my men might have been arrested had we sought to cross at the Merath bridge. Heard tell they're still chasing a spy. We left the city and crossed at Loglan." Farrl extended an envelope. "I bear letters from Merath."

"Thank you—for these and for returning with your men. A lot has happened." Hans took the packet in hand. He would talk with Farrl later about whether he could continue to rely on the Trongorian rangers for his guard. When he looked to the two newcomers, Hans caught the Kheld man studying him with a slight, apologetic smile.

Hans guessed the reason. "I know. I don't look like my brother."

The man ducked his head. "I never met him. I'm Cam Gereggson, from Tualla. This is my partner, Ralen Ornichos." He indicated the Staubaun, whose rough face, with an oft-broken nose and scars, scowled at the snorts of disbelief prompted by that claim.

There was good reason for the stares of those in the room. Khelds and Staubauns never... partnered. They fought, or eyed each other hostilely across crowded rooms, or maybe occasionally played a spirited game of dice—then fought about that. The most common relationship between a Kheld and a Staubaun was for one to accuse the other of cheating. Already murmurs flew, mostly expressing misgivings over having an unknown Staubaun in their midst. That lasted only until Fran stepped to the Staubaun man's side.

"Hey! Ralen's chips are good!" Half the room showed surprise over hearing Fran speak up in a Staubaun's defense. "I know him from Neuberland. He runs boats on the river and has smuggled swords and other arms to us for years. Damn Gobbans even threw him in prison for it."

"Is that true?" Hans asked. Usually he or Fran was the tallest person in the room, but Ralen, he noticed, topped them both by half a head.

Ralen nodded and spoke in a voice as rough as his face. "Prison brand on my hand to show for it, if you need proof. Highness." He added the last reluctantly—in perfect Khelda.

Orem Darm also stepped forward. "And if Fran's word is not enough, take mine. I and my *kilth* will vouch for both these men," he said. "Those of us on the river have long known that Cam Gereggson has a partner among the Staubauns and that between them their barges move more hard trade among Kheld ports than any other."

Nalf fluffed his bushy beard over the chain of office about his throat and leveled a skeptical gaze at the pair. "Well, I've heard of Cam Gereggson. Built that canal, he did, on the Frendel, and a fine town, too, at Tramyff. Comes from good kin on the Essera side. But if he has a Staubaun partner, then how come I never heard of him?"

"Ignorance," Ralen muttered underbreath. Fortunately, only those nearest heard. Hans suppressed a chuckle. He liked these two.

Cam settled the matter. "My traffic is on the Dazun, nowhere else, and people who don't live or do business along the river know little about my affairs—or Ralen's." The way his gaze settled on Ralen conveyed the solidity of their bond, which Hans sensed was deeply personal. "You see, Ralen and I operate without support from merchant cartels—or princes. We just conduct our business. Although"—he gestured in the general direction of the river—"I may not have any business left."

"You?" Hans grasped the point of emphasis. Cam and Ralen owned distinct operations. "That's why you have to get across the river, to find out what—if anything—either of you still has."

"My barges are certain to have been scattered, if not destroyed by the flood, sir," Cam reported, not without regret. "I don't foresee many of my vessels having escaped, if indeed any could have. My warehouses, too, might be gone; that remains to be seen. However, we think some of Ralen's barges may have escaped damage. They were berthed up the Rannul."

"How far up the Rannul?" Aubrey asked. She moved to the table where the maps lay spread.

"The flood will have caused backflow," Ralen warned. "But not nearly the same volume or force as along the Dazun." From his jacket he withdrew a crude drawing with lines and symbols, which he proffered. Aubrey took the paper and smoothed it atop the map. "My berths are located on the Rannul side, at Lekos. Twelve barges. Four deep draft, three wide hull flat, and five short haul. With Rill traffic at a standstill, so were they. If Dazunor-Rannuli's floodwalls held, we may have other boats there."

"Barges." Hans's mind raced toward the possibilities. He perused the map with interest. Rannul, according to Dorilian's just received letter, was an ally.

Aubrey bent forward at Hans's side. Late sunlight streaming through the cottage window touched the details of the map with golden highlights as she shot him a grin. "Flood or no flood, you will have to establish a presence on the river. We could use those barges."

Hans nodded understanding. "We still have to cross the river first, as planned. But afterward—"

"Yes," Aubrey agreed eagerly. "And we can also use what these men know about the Dazun: its ports, its capacities. And not just the river—the city. Dazunor-Rannuli. We need to know more about it."

Hans turned toward Ralen and Cam. "Aubrey's right. I think I've figured out a way to get my army across the river. Even with the flood. It's going to take a few days, but... I will let you cross with us, if you will negotiate use of your barges after. To move and supply my troops. And I'll want you to meet with my map makers. Let's talk."

The answer to Hans's call for help from Sordan came that next day in the form of a royal engineer. Davon Artos arrived at Bellan Toregh with two assistants, two score able-bodied workers, and enough of the requested cable and equipment to require two dozen heavy wagons and several dozen draft animals—also sent by Rill— to haul it. He and his first assistant arrived ahead of his materials, riding a brace of the swift Suddekan horses for which the Sordani were renowned. Alerted to Davon's arrival by courier and in possession of letters from both Levyathan and Tiflan, Hans found the Sordani engineer standing atop a ridge upstream from a Kheld hill fort, peering out at the troubled waters.

The flood had crested the day before, but the Dazun was still an awe-inspiring sight. The giant river's turgid waters had gouged the banks to either side, leaving behind eddies of mud and broken trees.

A solidly built Estol of middle years, with dark hair, hazel eyes, and a ready smile, Davon projected the kind of unassuming competence Hans had come to expect from those men Dorilian favored in his service. As outlined in Tiflan's letter of introduction, Davon's reputation rested on having overseen the design and construction of a string of dams, floodwalls, and bridges, including replacing the royal bridge at Randpory and restoration of the aqueduct at Gignastha. Not only that, but he also spoke passable Khelda.

"I understand you have a rogue sorcerer to thank for this."

Davon stopped often as they walked along the ridge, surveying the destruction wrought by the river. "I've seen worse along the Randpory, believe it or not. Telarkan runoffs regularly wash out bridges there. But the Dazun is usually better behaved."

Hans nodded grimly. "Two weeks ago there was some kind of event to the east—we don't know how far—that lit up the night sky. Purples, whites... something violent. The timing is consistent with when word of the Rill operating in Amallar and of the Hierarch arriving in Essera would have reached ears there. Whether natural catastrophe or sorcery, I'm left with the same result. The river has become impassable. It's taken out all the bridges between Merath and Dazunor-Rannuli, and possibly all the way to Gustan."

Davon shook his head, clearly remembering the ancient structures fondly. "Now there's a shame! Ergeiron would unmake the Wall and the Debens turn in their graves if they knew all their hard work on the Dazun bridges had come to this. I spent a summer on a barge in my youth, studying them. The like of those spans cannot be made again. Now such drawings as I sketched in my books are all we will ever have of them." Shoving his hands into his pockets, he looked over at Hans and rocked back on his heels. "Good bridges take a while to build. We can dive into that job later. I surmise you want the cable to string something temporary."

"Pontoons, maybe. I don't know. I'm not looking to control the river in any way. I just want to cross it. I'm not a military strategist, really, and I'm sure as Sordan not an engineer."

"You don't need to be an engineer." Davon's intelligent eyes twinkled. "That's why you have me. And I think we shall use Bondar as your strategist."

"Bondar?"

"An Ardaenan. He died five hundred years ago, but he made a hell of a brilliant crossing of the Dazun before one of the Malyrdeons sliced him in two. Better yet, he kept excellent notes on how he did it. Last year, I conducted an exercise based on his Dazun stratagem for the Hierarch's generals." Davon removed his gloves and together with Hans started back down the hill. "I heard your men have been building rafts and boats?"

Hans nodded, already looking at Davon in amazement. The man was wasting no time!

"Excellent! We can move quickly, then. My assistant will talk with your woodsmen about constructing movable plank sections for a roadbed. The more of those we can make ahead, the better. More slack means less likelihood of failure. Also, you will want to send some groups out as a diversion to a decoy point to make it look as if you're making rafts for a crossing. I want to talk with men who know the river and, in particular, I would like to see some maps showing the natural channel."

"Would you look at that!" Nalf stood at the edge of the hastily cleared road to the river. A scrub-covered point bar just downriver screened the site. Their river experts were certain the natural feature would conceal their efforts from being observed on the other side. The river bank swarmed with workers and equipment.

At his side, Aubrey could but stare in wonder. She had seen quite a lot in her life, at Leseos and along the Floh, but never anything like this.

Young Kheld lasses and lads gathered along the roadside and gaped in amazement at the great machine, its recumbent metal form gleaming like something out of legend.

"What do you figure that is?" one boy asked.

"Dunno," said another.

"It's a pulley." A young Sordani lad leaned against his wagon, in patient wait for the signal to drive down to the waterfront. This machine's twin already had been hauled into place and anchored by cable strapping attached to enormous spikes driven deep into rock. Davon had told Hans and the Kheld captains that morning that the real challenge lay in making a reliable temporary pulley on the other side so the raft bearing this one could be hauled over. Once the pulley was mounted on the other side, setting up a horse-pulled ferry would be easy. "You tree squirrels can touch it if you want," the lad continued, "but don't stick your arms or legs in anywhere. There's moving parts."

"That so? Then why don't you have it blocked?" The youth challenging the other boy was Snearly Darm, who'd grown up along the banks of the Dazun and had picked up a river rat version of Stauba.

"It *is* blocked," the Sordani youth asserted. "You don't think we transport them spinning like damn toys, do you? But no one with half a brain sticks body parts anywhere they don't need to, even if it's blocked. All it would take is the load to shift to get chewed up something nasty."

"Don't," growled Nalf when Snearly sought to put his hand on the alloy pulley that had been brought up from Sordan's shipworks. The boy obeyed and to Aubrey, Nalf added, "Already touched it myself, and that thing's not natural. No metal's that cold or smooth. Hurt my hand to feel it!"

"And I've never seen a pulley that big, or one shaped that way." Aubrey glanced toward the bank, where Hans stood with Davon Artos and Orem Darm. The real wonder was what was happening on the river, attached to ropes and Gulvang Darm's sturdy boat. The slow uncoiling of metal rope from the first pulley now stretched halfway across the Dazun. As thick as a strong man's arm, it glinted dully in the sun, gray as the water. One of the engineer's assistants regulated the thing so it didn't spin out too fast or become unwieldy for the boat. On the other side of the river waited a corps of Kheld and Sordani workers ferried over ahead of time. This one, they said, would make short work of moving an army.

"Metal rope," Nalf marveled. "Who even knew they made the stuff?"

"Hans knew," said Aubrey. She was seeing more every day just how much Hans knew, and not just about metal rope. Dorilian. Hans understood a man for whom metal rope and giant pulleys and god-machines were ordinary.

Nalf nodded and puffed out his chest. "It'll be as smooth a passage as Lud himself could make once they have that. Look at all that stuff! I asked one of the bosses about it. He laughed when I asked how long it would take one ferry to carry over all Hans Thegn's men. 'Wait and see,' he said. I think there's going to be more than one. I think there's going to be a dozen of them!"

With a smile, Aubrey concurred. She needed to rejoin her Saemoregh contingent. Her unit would be among the first, not last, to cross. Neuberlanders knew more Stauba, more Staubauns, and Essera was full of those. "We're doing this," she told Nalf. "They'll know we're coming, but we'll be too many."

By nightfall, there were five ferries operating. By the time daylight brushed the river with rose, a bridge of rafts and planks hewn by Kheld woodsmen and secured by dual cable runs bellied in a shining curve across the Dazun. Empty. Handurin's army of Khelds had long since crossed over.

# 13



After a hard night of marching and riding, Hans's army gathered in the mists at the edge of the recently flooded plain that cradled the Staubaun city of Dazunor-Rannuli. They would reach the city itself by nightfall. Hans dared to hope it could be taken without fighting, but he doubted it. The lords of that city, the secretive and powerful Seven Houses, despised Khelds—and Hans—too fiercely to surrender to an army of infidels. Hans saw that he must give them no option to do otherwise.

He had organized his troops and taken on an advisor from Sordan, Soter Kometes, whose expertise lay in logistics. The Khelds weren't happy about Soter, except with the part about him being Hans's to command.

"My Hierarch has given me to Your Royal Highness's service," Soter stated upon introduction. "I was trained in the Military College of Simelon and served under General Vidyamemnon in Suddekar. I am a constructor of camps."

And an expert in keeping armies on the move. At the moment, the camp in which they'd spent the night, as well defended as any town, was being torn down and packed up to every side. Attended by his captains, Hans spread a map with fresh notation on a makeshift table where his command tent had stood.

"The tactic of sending supplies and troops to Permephedon worked." He pointed to broad purple arrows north of their location. "Fran and his men are within a day of us. Nalf's spies tell us that our ploy—and the flood—convinced the Regent's forces to move north of the city, here. Even if they don't end up fighting Fran, they won't be able to move back fast enough to engage us before we reach Dazunor-Rannuli."

"I don't like it that Sordan sent even more troops to Lacenedon." Nalf Rhys glowered above crossed arms. His birds had also brought that bit of news. He wasn't the only Kheld to scowl at Soter Kometes. Any reminder that Sordan, too, had troops in Essera awakened harsh sentiment.

"Those troops are needed there. It'll be a two-pronged war," Hans reminded them. For his own part, he was glad of the reinforcements Sordan had sent to Permephedon. For several days, the influx of arms and soldiers had bolstered the appearance of portending invasion, with the immediate bonus of expanding Fran's arsenal. "Dorilian's presence in the Royal North ties up half of Erenor's military—and most of Nammuor's attention. If we can get Erenor out of Stauberg, all the better!"

"We'd best start here then, seems to me," said Arne.

"Yes." Hans seized that opening. "Because I have a plan. You, and Nalf too, are going to attack where they won't expect it." He drew his finger along the blue line of the river, toward the wharfs. Then he pointed to the main road. "And I will attack where they are expecting."

"But down by the river is all marshes and fens!" Nalf's scowl and wide eyes questioned whether Hans had lost his mind.

Hans let Orem Darm handle that one.

"Cam Gereggson knows people," Orem said. "And I know people. We found some to guide you into the city through the Beardfen."

"Is that even there still, after the flood?" Aubrey asked. She'd told Hans about the Beardfen when he'd first asked questions about the city they were attacking. Khelds lived in Dazunor-Rannuli, as they did in many parts of Essera along the Dazun

River... but they weren't welcome in the city itself. Khelds primarily lived beyond the city limits in low areas where there weren't even streets, only footpaths and hovels built on stilts.

Orem nodded to Aubrey and Nalf, and to Arne too when he looked interested. "There are ridges built by floods over the years. Paths. When the water retreats, these emerge again. Dazunor-Rannuli's Khelds know the fen. They know where to walk... they know how to get through."

"And they'll get us through," concluded Nalf.

"All the way to the Kheld Port," said Orem Darm.

"A whole army," said Arne.

Soter Kometes took an appreciative breath, then smiled.

"Yeah," said Hans. "A whole army."

"They won't be expecting me and my troops, I hope." Hans took Arne aside to say a few parting words. They'd helped each other strap on armor and swords. It was the first time either of them would see battle. "You and your men should be drawing most of the attention."

"I figure we will. Folk in the city won't like one bit waking up to see an army of Khelds running at them through the swamp." Arne grinned. On the other side of the mists, guides from the Beardfen were already leading Kheld warriors through the watery morass that was the shortest path to the city. Their guides had said Khelds fleeing the rising waters had been denied entry into the protected city, with many perishing because of that. Now that the waters had receded and left behind paths through the fen, Dazunor-Rannuli's Khelds were more than willing to help the invaders.

Hans nodded and looked out over the army that was already parting ways in the mists. Soon the sun would rise high enough to burn away most of the haze. All traces of snow were now long vanished, but mornings still bore winter's chill frost. "I hope they aren't expecting us at all."

With a cock of his head, Arne expressed his lone worry. "And we don't know what to expect when we get there. Don't suppose many here has ever set foot in Dazunor-Rannuli. Or any Staubaun city. Me, at least, I've been to Sordan, and I caught an eyeful of Ogarth when we were there, before the Sorcerer got it. Them cities are damn big! I don't expect this one will be any smaller."

"No, I reckon not." Arne had a point—most Khelds had never

seen a Staubaun city, much less a city that was one of the jewels of the Triempery. Hans adjusted his gloves. "I'm not sure how much resistance we'll encounter. Dazunor-Rannuli lives for trade. It hates to have the rhythm of that trade disrupted. That's exactly what Dorilian did when he stopped the Rill. But that's not going to be what they fear, not this time. They're going to fear that we will be looters and vandals, that we'll plunder their treasures and rape and kill their families. So that's precisely what we won't do. I've given the order to every captain that any person caught doing anything not related to fighting in battle—be it rape or thieving or purposeful destruction of property—is to be arrested. I will not stand for it. Ours is a just battle, not one for pillage and plunder."

Dazunor-Rannuli had reason to fear being plundered. No city in Essera was richer. Stauberg, with its Highborn history and impregnable Wall, was more fabled—high seat of the Malyrdeon Kings and beloved of Staubauns whatever their nation. Aral was more beautiful, with its soaring cliffs and palaces and plunging gorges filled with rainbows and mists. Permephedon was more majestic, one of the Five Cities, a center of learning and Rill terminus where dwelt the immortal and mysterious Marenthro. Yet all of those cities together did not have the wealth that filled Dazunor-Rannuli. Its mighty Houses, fortressed palaces, and vast warehouses burst with the gold and treasure of centuries of Rill and river traffic. The golden domes of those palaces gleamed above the city like rising suns, all given birth by the silver passage of the Rill. When Khelds over the centuries had looked across the river at the Rill city of the Staubauns, all they had ever seen was everything they could not have.

"They fear for their gold." Nalf Rhys had found Hans. It was time for Nalf and Arne both to enter the Beardfen. "Not letting men plunder, that's going to fail, you know." He raised a hand when Hans moved to protest. "But you're our prince. If that's what you want, that's what we'll do!"

"That's what I want. I'm their Prince too. Prince of Dazunor, remember?"

"King of Essera, that's what I want to make of you." Nalf's armor was polished so it glinted in the faint light. "Are you ready, lad?"

"I'm—" There was nothing to say. Not really. "I just want this day to be done."

Arne clapped Hans on the shoulder. "And we'll do it, just like we planned. Nalf and his boys, and mine too! We'll get through in secret, take the Kheld Port and then the big bridge—"

"And the Old Fort after that," Nalf affirmed. "Move fast. Set posts."

"They're going to fight you," Hans warned. "The people of this city, they're either going to hide in their homes or they're going to be trying to kill you."

"Aye, they should," said Nalf. "But we'll take a stab at your plan. Leave them alone to prove themselves cowards." A great sound of derision came from deep in Nalf's throat as he clapped Arne's shoulder and drew him into a trot after the gesturing guides. "Let them hide behind closed windows! We've beat them already and they know it. We have their Rill! Let 'em stew!"

"Even if your men get through and secure the Lower Canal, more enemy troops wait to the west of the city."

Hans grimaced because Soter's warning was apt. There were Mormantaloran troops but a day or two away, commanded by Nammuor's dangerous minion Salkren Zel. Hans's success ultimately hinged on whether he could succeed quickly. Deliver the killing blow. To do that he needed to seize Dazunor-Rannuli's core. The Rill Mount.

He had crafted his plan using history. He'd studied the city... its maps... its letters and lore. Dazunor-Rannuli and its Rill Mount had not been attacked since the Malyrdeons had bought peace with the Khelds by giving them Amallar. Defenders and attackers alike respected the Rill's potential for ceaselessly deploying fresh troops and supplies.

And therein lay Dazunor-Rannuli's weakness. It had never been attacked. No one knew how to defend it.

Nor was the Rill going to help them.

Though the bulk of the Kheld troops had gone with Nalf and Arne and the other Amallar captains, Hans still commanded a sizeable force. From astride his ivory horse he led four units of Kheld infantry, a cavalry consisting of various ranger units and Aubrey's Neuberlanders, and a mix of Trongorian foot and horse soldiers. He also had his Trongorian guards, forty strong under Farrl. What Hans had to do now was use his army to achieve two ends: he must divert attention from the surprise attack being launched nearer the river and he must capture the heart of the city. Doing so meant advancing on Dazunor-Rannuli from the east, along wide avenues and great bridges over the city's storied canals.

"You have the maps?" Hans asked Soter, who nodded. The deeper into the city they went, and the more canals they encountered, the more they would need the maps Sordan had provided.

"I have some too," said Aubrey. She was already mounted. A saddle envelope beside her leg held a set of simplified sketches she'd assured everyone would be helpful.

"If this plan works, they'll be expecting us." Hans mounted his horse.

The sun had risen just enough to have vanquished the earlier haze. He and his troops would be visible to the city. It would be foolish to think they hadn't been noticed already.

Hans kept his captains with him as he took his place at the head of the army. Doing so felt right. He would be visible and visibility projected confidence, even if he was feeling anything but. Dorilian had given him the best advice: *Pick good generals. Tell them what you want to do... then let them do it.*

Unfortunately, some of his generals were as unseasoned by actual war as Hans was.

As Hans's force crested the lone ridge between them and the city, Soter pointed to the west. "You're not alone in this confrontation, Prince Handurin," said the Sordani advisor. "In the Rill, they see my Hierarch standing with you. It holds them as nothing else could."

Indeed now they could see that the Rill stood frozen and unmoving above the great city. No silver *charysi* slid with graceful entry into its rings beneath white arms that arched like dead things above those golden towers. That affirmation as much as any other emboldened the Khelds and urged them on to seize intact the first jewel in Handurin's crown.

"The Khelds hold the eastern perimeter and command the roads to Jermyn and Merath, General." The scout pointed out the roads from the ridge overlooking the lowlands where Dazunor-Rannuli lay besieged. "Prince Handurin's cavalry has captured the outlying towns of Sanant and Pryddor. He already controls the bridges of the Upper Canal." The scout was crudely dressed and could have passed for a fleeing peasant. He made his report to three men riding ivory horses, their armor inlaid with royal colors and ensigns identifying them as High Lords of the Merrydni. Behind the hill were arrayed a thousand men on horseback, an emissary fighting force in the service of their Princess.

General Euden Mezeon pondered the news. "And the citizens of the Outer City?"

"Surrendered. Prince Handurin has promised clemency and full protection to all who do not fight him."

*And so they buy their property with his peace.* Euden's noble mouth contracted, neither grimace nor smile. He already knew that Prince Regent Erenor's army had engaged north of the city with a Kheld force that had swept down from Permephedon. Not only had young Prince Handurin stunned Essera by a brilliant crossing of the Dazun, he was also parlaying his unilateral Rill access into a victory. "What of the Mormantalorans?" Euden named the sole remaining force of any consequence. "Are they not within leagues of the city?"

The scout nodded. "They advance, Noble Lord. Along the Dazun Road toward the Kheld positions at the west bunkers of the Old Fort. And the Seven Houses have directed the City Guard to stand back. They are leaving it to the Prince Regent's troops to defend the city proper."

*And the Khelds to defend them from Mormantalorus.*

Euden Mezeon calmly turned his gaze toward the golden domes that even now glinted through the haze of battle. Erenor's forces would defend the Inner City fiercely. He would not engage that battle—but there remained a way to secure it. Deciding, he picked up his horse's reins again and gestured to his aides and captains. "Our lot is with Handurin. We will fight the Mormantalorans. Sweep three prongs below Handurin's lines and use the Sidon Bridge. Join the Khelds at the west encounter." He donned his helm of command. "We will seek out whoever is commanding them after securing the flank."

"I'd feel better if they'd just come at us." Arne shouldered against Orem Darm as they peered over the earthwork wall. Arne's archers and Orem's rivermen had led the attack against the first of the Old Fort's massive earthen walls, the one nearest the river, and had captured it easily. It had been only sparsely defended. The city hadn't thought that Hans would find a way to cross the flooded river, or that its citizens would face an attack from the riverfront. Dazunor-Rannuli hadn't given enough weight to the notion that Khelds living in the Beardfen would provide passage and aid. Downhill from the Old Fort, among great docks crowded with barges, were the warehouses of Dazunor-Rannuli's Lower Canal. So far, there was no sign of anyone down that way looking to cause trouble.

"It's like they don't care if we're here so long as we leave them alone." Orem Darm eased back from the crest of the outlook and to a sitting position, pulling out the crude map he'd scratched on a piece of precious paper.

"That damn Sordani advisor was right about this fort," Arne noted. "Easy to take and it sits high over the city. Though nothing sits as high as that." He squinted along the watery line of the Canal to where the Rill Mount's soaring crown lifted above the jumble of buildings that was the Merchant Quarter. The gold domes nearby would be the Palaces of the Denizens, the Seven Houses. If there was fighting anywhere near there, it would be Hans doing it.

Arne returned his attention to the villages in the distance, west along the road that followed the Dazun River. Hans had said there was an army out there, though so far Arne hadn't seen any sign of one. The road blurred and he rubbed his eyes. Then he rubbed them again.

The Dazun Road hadn't blurred. Neither had the hill across the way. Both were swarming with men.

"They're here! The damn Southlanders are on us!" he yelled, jabbing Orem Darm with his elbow before grabbing his sword and running to order his archers.

The Outer City, those palaces and noble edifices lining the serene waters of the Upper Canal and its branches, surrendered without a single blade being drawn. Emissaries from the inhabitants of those suburbs met with Handurin and his foremost captains at the bridges, accepting terms sent beforehand by way of Beardfen Khelds. Hans made clear that he wanted little from Dazunor-Rannuli's residents except assurances that they accepted him as Stefan's Heir, Prince of Dazunor and their King, and that they would honor their current laws and his authority in their city. In return, he would ensure that no harm would come to peaceful citizens, as well as no looting or confiscation of their property. Those who did not swear fealty could look forward to having their property seized and turned over to Hans's agents to distribute. For most, that suggested distribution to Khelds, and the vanquished quickly began to police their neighbors to be sure none opposed the young victor. Hans left behind enough men to secure the area, choosing a phalanx of Staubaun-speaking Trongorians and a contingent of East Amallaran Khelds accustomed to Staubauns. He then proceeded with the remainder of his army to enter Dazunor-Rannuli proper.

It was there that the fighting began. Not all of Prince Regent Erenor's forces were north of the city, fighting Fran Gorseddson. Hundreds of the Regent Erenor's soldiers ringed the merchant palaces, and the Rill Mount with steel.

The Old Fort's earthworks swarmed. It was not men on foot the Khelds faced, but mounted swordsmen. Arne was glad of his archers. They were able to cut down many of the horsemen before they reached the wall, but many outer bunkers were overrun. Those men would soon lose a clear line of retreat if they stayed. Arne ordered his archers to abandon the earthwork. "Fall back!"

Using riderless horses captured in the fighting to carry their wounded, the Khelds methodically retreated to the Old Fort, from which they would defend the river's warehouses and the bridge into the Inner City.

Two hours of fighting had captured part of Dazunor-Rannuli. Hans remained behind the front line of the fighting, guarded by Farrl's Trongorians and the leaders of two units of Kheld horsemen, including Aubrey's rangers. They had taken and now occupied a sprawling palace situated on a low hill that overlooked neighborhoods and bridges, the port and Inner City. Just beyond them rose the richest prize of all: the marble palaces of the Seven Houses Customhouse and the towering majesty of the city's Rill Mount, a complex of structures and multiple platforms that dwarfed Bellan Toregh's several times over.

"We must show the enemy no quarter." Farrl referred to the troops still defending the district. "Once we force their hand, only then will the Seven Houses reconsider their position. You must appear willing to engage them."

"That's not difficult." Hans saw for himself that the resistance was becoming fiercer. "I *am* willing to engage them. I can't just leave them here festering like an abscess."

At his side, Aubrey scanned the golden domes and splendid buildings that opposed them. She sat astride her horse in full fighting gear. The leather armor, helm and shoulder guards, the stout sword at her side and rack of *skifren* mounted on her saddle, depleted to but three, gave evidence of having seen battle. Aubrey wasn't the only Kheld woman bearing arms in the fighting. Two of Arne's sisters were among his archers.

"I'll tell you all you need to know about the Seven Houses," Aubrey offered. She too had been talking with Sordani advisors. "They're not your allies. Neither are they famed for fighting. They pay others to do it for them. Once Erenor's men are defeated, they may not have sufficient soldiers of their own."

Hans grinned at her. "That's what we're going to find out."

Farrl exchanged a sharp look with Aubrey and frowned at Hans. "That's what others will find out for you, Prince Handurin. You will stay here. This lady and her men will protect you. Until the city is taken, the danger to you would be too great."

"We don't have so many troops that we can afford to hold any back," Hans argued. Though he understood Farrl's reasoning, he hoped to avoid any accusations that he had sent men to their deaths but hadn't led the battle.

"And we don't have so many princes that we can afford to risk our only one in combat!" Aubrey snapped. The warning in her blue gaze was clear: the Khelds were not about to lose their Prince while she had anything to say about it.

So it was from the safety of the palace terrace that Hans watched, now guarded by Aubrey and Wodd, as Farrl's men joined with the other company of Kheld riders to engage the Regent's soldiers holding one of the great canal bridges. It took several minutes to cut a swath through the line of well-armed men. Hans felt his gut seize when he saw men fall and heard their screams.

*How many poor souls are dying today? And for what? If this is what it will take for me to be their King, do I even want it?*

He caught Aubrey looking at him. "I'm not used to butchery," Hans admitted. He had not been close to the fighting before.

"You have a sword," she pointed out. "Haven't you ever used it outside of practice?"

*No*, he wanted to tell her, but didn't. He didn't want Aubrey to think less of him or feel he needed her protection. *Dorilian taught me how to use a blade*, Hans reminded himself, recalling the many hours they had sparred. *He taught me again… and again, to be sure the lessons stuck*. Only now did he see why. "I've used it," he told her.

"Aubrey!" Wodd interrupted. His wolfskin-sheathed right arm raised to point to the next bridge. The small Kheld force there, men on foot, had nearly fought its way through, but was now being beset by a second party of soldiers coming at them from behind. The Khelds were trapped on the bridge between the two forces.

"Hells!" Aubrey cursed. "Stinking Staubauns! They kept some men back!"

"There are thirty of us," Hans said. "We can help them!"

Aubrey was clearly torn. If she sent off Wodd and her riders, she and Hans would be left as good as defenseless themselves. But she never got the chance to make that decision. Wodd and the Saemoregh men were only too ready to ride to the aid of their fellow Khelds, so Hans spurred his horse to the fore and gave them the reason they needed. Seeing how the direction of the battle had turned, Aubrey urged her horse after her rangers, joining Hans at their head. If they were to fight, it was as good a place to start as any.

Nalf Rhys pulled his sword out of a Staubaun corpse and deflected another blow with a swing of his mace. It entangled the blade and pulled aside. With a brutal yank Nalf unhorsed that man and ran him through. He wasn't proud of killing men, but he was good at it. The northmost bunker he and his *keldanes* defended was fast becoming a slaughterhouse, but at least it was not a slaughterhouse for Khelds alone.

Cries rang in Nalf's ears but he didn't stop to attend them, only to turn to the next attack, to fight the next man. It was out of the corner of his eye that he saw the flash of banners, a burst of horses and men moving at angles through the Mormantaloran troops. Blue-clothed men astride blue-draped horses, cutting the attack. He found himself without a foe, all around him slain, other Kheldmen coming to join him.

"They're not ours," someone said, eyes wide.

"Merrydn." Nalf noted the banner. He lifted his sword and mace again, ready to hold ground against any cursed Southlander that made it through that line of horses and steel. "Stand! They're with Hans Thegn!"

The arrival of the Merrydni horsemen altered the thrust of the Mormantaloran attack and threw the forward troops into confusion. The Merrydni entered the battle at three key points, weakening the enemy offensive by dislocating its core units. Soon the center of the battle was in disarray, the edges fraying. Though at two points the Kheld line had been breached, the Mormantalorans had failed to take the Old Fort or advance into the city. Red-cloaked corpses littered the field, men and horses dead or dying. The riders of Merrydn pulled back as well, though they did not leave the field but simply allowed the Khelds to reestablish their perimeter and assume command of the defenses. Nalf Rhys, joined by Arne and Orem Darm who'd come down from the Old Fort, walked out to greet the Staubaun leaders.

"By the grace of my Princess, Ionais of Merrydn, we have bought your Prince time and opportunity." The Merrydni general was clearly a noble. "We, however, will not enter the city. We honor standing agreements with the Denizens of the Seven Houses."

"But you'll help keep the Southlanders off our backs?" Nalf demanded.

The man nodded. "Yes, that we will do. We have no ties to Mormantalorus and would see them gone from these lands."

"Good!" Nalf nodded. He turned to his Khelds. "Half of you stay here! Orem! Get your rivermen on the canals. Arne, you and your archers stay here. Help these horsemen hold the fort." Nalf then pointed to a knot of warriors with blood-dripping weapons. "You lot follow me into the city. That's where the fighting is now and that's where we're needed!" He had only to gesture to the city for them to know what he meant. Fires already burned deep within those canyons of storehouses and dwellings, and it was not fire alone that turned the canal waters red.

Hans had nearly reached the Rill Mount before he lost his horse.

A wooden beam launched from a warehouse platform crashed into his mount's shoulder, sending it down. He scrambled free and immediately brandished his sword, well aware that the fighting in this quarter was chaotic. The bridge had been but the beginning. There'd been alleys and narrow streets that dead-ended at canals. And now this. The men he and his Khelds pursued had led them into a square thick with traps. Hans got to his feet only to find himself fighting at every turn. One man, seeing the colors Hans wore, yelled and lunged at him, sword high.

Hans leaped to the side, bringing his own sword up, steel ringing against steel. The man attacked again before Hans could think. His body responded as though he were in training again, reflex-sure and quick, so that this time he was able to knock the man's sword aside and bring his own blade back fast enough to get in a blow. His foe staggered, then crumpled, arm nearly severed. Hans stumbled back, and turned, only to face more armed men. Hours of sword work became his lifeline as he fought and hacked, relying on muscles and reflexes shaped months before.

Now he was glad for the unending practice—and for his opponent then. He might never have bested Dorilian with a sword, but he had learned to hold his own against a man famed both for strength and agility. Compared to the man who'd taught him, Hans's foes, while still dangerous, were readily mastered. He killed five men, and possibly more, before Aubrey and three of her rangers joined him and they were able to fight their way to the others. Then Farrl and his Trongorians were there too. Slashing. Stabbing. Spilling guts and blood.

The sunlight changed. Stronger, casting walls into shadow. The ringing of steel no longer filled every moment. Hans retreated a few steps, happy to have Farrl at his back, and looked around. More Khelds had come. Many more Khelds. He recognized Orem Darm and his rivermen and that they had somehow come out of the warehouse district to take control of the big bridge leading to the Rill Mount. And there was Nalf Rhys with his Kheld infantry, cutting the body of the defending forces in half and hacking them away from Hans and his beleaguered Trongorians and Khelds. Of the men immediately surrounding Hans, several of the Kheld fighters were dead and many more wounded, though only one of the men of Trongor had taken serious hurt.

"Your Khelds fought bravely, but they are unseasoned in battle. Experience makes men harder to kill," Farrl told Hans when the fighting moved away. Together they surveyed their group. The survivors tended the wounded. "With each battle, your Khelds will become stronger. Win enough, and they will become formidable fighters."

"They won't have a choice." Hans recalled the disorder first at the bridge and then later, men leaping into the fight. Khelds fought as they argued: exuberantly chasing the obvious. He'd hardly done any better, riding into battle the way he had. He sure hoped Arne's part had been less bloody, that he'd come through all right. Aubrey at least was unhurt; Hans had seen her ministering to the wounded men. As he walked with Farrl toward the bridge to the Rill Mount, Hans averted his eyes from the bodies of his slain Kheldmen—and the Esserans too. A man wearing Stauberg blue sat propped against marble stairs, futilely trying to hold in spilled intestines. Certain to die. He met the man's gaze and found it hate-filled.

*He wants me to die. To go away, to never have come back at all. Because if I had stayed put, none of this would have happened.*

Some wounded man's unearthly howl rose above the general clatter and Hans turned in its direction. A Kheld man, bloodied and broken, was being lifted and carried from the street to make room for horsemen charging over the Rill bridge. A sword blow had taken half the man's face. Brain matter leaked through a missing cheek and eye to slide as pink clots into the dying man's beard.

*Oh gods.*

Hans darted to the nearest structure of any size, the high grand steps of a nearby building. A bronze bull, life-size and imposing, stood guard upon an impressive stone plinth. Good. It was big and might hide him. Dropping to his knees behind the plinth, he heaved over and vomited onto the flagstones. Wet and hot, bile splashed onto his trousers.

The stain mingled with the blood of men he had killed.

A shadow fell upon him. "Well aren't you a pretty sight! A damn king who can't stand battle gore."

From his knees, Hans glanced up at Nalf. Battered and blood-streaked, the Thegnard wore a frown like a condemning judge. Hans's stomach rebelled again and he bent over, heaving, then catching back his breath. To his surprise, he felt a hand on his shoulder. Firm. Reassuring.

"First battle?"

Hans nodded. His sickness seemed to have passed. He hoped it had passed. Maybe it would if he could just close his mind to the gore. Tentatively, he wiped his sleeve across his mouth. Blood... and now vomit. The blood was someone else's; he had taken no wounds.

"So you're alive and they're not. You could look happier about it." Nalf gave Hans's shoulder a final squeeze. "Pull yourself together, lad. Say you've seen all seven hells and be done with that.

But find your balls and get on your feet. People don't want to see their damn king on his knees! They deserve better than that!"

It took an effort for Hans to push his shaking body to standing, to face this man squarely. Nalf looked war tested enough for them both, with a slash on his chin staining his beard and one sleeve ragged and soaked with blood. It took almost as much effort for Hans to speak.

"I never wanted this." He swallowed the sour taste of bile and wished the air he breathed didn't smell of death and shit. That the cries for help of the wounded and dying didn't fill his ears. "I never imagined... I didn't know what my coming back to this World would mean, that people would follow me... or that they would die because of that! I never thought I would be doing the killing! I wanted to make things better!"

"Better? You know what makes war better? Not dying!" Nalf crowded forward. Hans took a step back only to bump hard against a wall. "Not one person today wanted to get cut to ribbons or meet his end on the point of a spear. But every damned one of us wanted to fight! For you! And what we need right now is for our king to show he has the stomach to be one! There's more fighting to come, lots more! And it's going to be ugly, because fighting always is. More people are going to die. It's your job to make sure you're not one of them. So for the love of the Mother, show our lads you have a good head, not a spanked ass!"

For Hans to show that he was in for the long haul, standing beside them, a man they could follow. A man... not a boy. *I am waiting for you to grow up*, Dorilian had said.

*Arne will be all right*, Hans told himself. That too was a fear. *Orem Darm and Nalf made it, and he will too. There's nothing I can do now but wait for him to show up.*

Hans straightened and gave Nalf a brief nod.

Past Nalf's shoulder the street had been cleared. Bodies, Kheld and Estol, and not a few bright-haired Staubauns, lay sprawled next to building walls and on steps of time-polished stone. The sounds of fighting still to be heard were distant and few, barely rising above the cries of the wounded. Today's battle was dying away. Hans dared to hope his forces had taken the city. That *he* had taken it—and that the cost would not be too high.

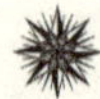

Although the highest ground to be found in Dazunor-Rannuli, the Rill Mount had not been prepared for military use and offered little resistance. Most of its defenders had fled upon seeing how the fighting in the city below had turned against them. The Regent's forces had been run out of the city. The arrival of Merrydn's force broke what little will remained, confirming that their neighboring Princess had taken the side of Prince Handurin.

Hans gathered the troops nearest him—Aubrey's rangers, Nalf's men, and the Trongorians—to climb the Mount. Only the Epoptes waited for them—surprisingly many, a sea of yellow robed figures kneeling at the distant end of the platform in row upon sun-colored row.

At the near end of the platform stood a solitary man wearing a ceremonial hood and stole. Above him soared the Mount's white crown of silent Rill structures. Behind him loomed the serene and storied buildings of the Brotherhood's renowned College.

"Prince Handurin." The man bowed deeply. Elegantly so, Hans noted. "I am Pitar Kisthoda, this Mount's Archmage and Prime. My Order and the staff and students here gathered have not participated in this conflict, nor in any deed that might offend you. We submit to your authority over the city."

Hans glanced up in open appreciation at the structures surrounding them. "And the Rill?" Compared to this Mount, Bellan Toregh was *tiny*.

Pitar's head cocked to one side. His look was genuinely quizzical. "Your victory gives you control of this Mount and this city—and of we who stand here. But not of the Rill."

Hans shot him a reassuring smile. "No. Dorilian has that."

Something, perhaps confirmation, found birth in Pitar's still cautious gaze. Or maybe he was just surprised by how easily Hans used Dorilian's name.

Even more politely than before, Pitar asked the critical question. "Does Your Royal Highness have the ability, or authority, to revive this node?"

Hans shook his head. "No. We're working on that." He drew a breath and was glad that up here the air was fresh and sharp, clear of the taint of blood and death. "Tell them that, the Seven Houses, when they come to you."

The cost in lives would have been higher had resistance in the city not been limited to Erenor's troops. Few of the citizens of Dazunor-Rannuli had lost their lives. But the Khelds counted their dead and calculated the price. They honored the restrictions Hans placed upon them, however, and few instances saw them taking anything that belonged to another. Those that did were quickly punished. "Hans Thegn got the better part of this city not to fight with that promise," Nalf Rhys was heard to say, "so hold to it, and maybe we won't have to fight so bloody hard the next damn city we take."

Dazunor-Rannuli counted among its residents some of the richest families in the Triempery. Only the Sordaneons, it was said, possessing both an unending stream of Rill revenue and the domains and riches of a Highborn dynasty, controlled more wealth than the secretive Seven Houses, the merchant families of this proud city. Their strongholds in the center of town, ringing the mount like gold-crowned teeth, would require months of siege to take by force. Fortunately, Hans would not need to.

*They are a cesspool of murky alliances,* Dorilian had once confided. *They'd sooner betray you than see you in their chambers. But you have what they need to survive—remember that always.*

The Seven Houses had intermarried with lesser members of the Highborn Malyrdeons and had until recently controlled the ruling houses of Leseos and Rannul. The Epoptes accorded them special status and favors; cartel lords funded the regimes and pulled the strings of rulers from the Bas of Leseos to the false Prince Erenor. And now the Seven Houses would be watching the Stauberg-Randolph Prince Handurin, striving to ascertain whether to invest their influence with him or hold to their shadow alliance with Nammuor.

Notably, the Seven Houses had let Mormantalorus and Erenor's troops fight to defend the city. Not a single soldier of theirs had issued forth from behind those closed and guarded walls.

Hans looked upon those massive keeps and smiled.

# 14

When it comes to human societies, change is not a passive
event. It doesn't just occur one day for no reason; it
requires an agent or catalyst. Nothing in society changes
until something in the Creation changes it.
AUBREY AMUNDDA, SPEECH TO THE FAETHAN ARGOELLIN

Arne rejoined Hans and the main force long after dark on the
Rill platform overlooking the wide plain toward the west. Hans
and his generals had met there to confer with the Brotherhood of
Epoptes, primarily on behalf of the College located on the Mount,
and remained after to decide the next day's strategy. After the
others left, Hans stayed behind with Arne and embraced him as he
deserved.

"We did it," Hans said. "We made it."

"You had a good plan, taking the Fort the way we did, sneaking
in through the Beardfen. We held it, too, that Fort. Fought the
Southlanders back, so now they're setting fires to make sure we
don't follow. But we're staying put." Arne pointed west to the
orange glow in the outlying villages from which he'd just arrived.

The retreating Mormantaloran forces had set whole towns to
the torch to create a smoke line, preventing Kheldish and
Merrydni pursuit. Though bloodied himself, with a few gashes to
the face and arm, Arne was jubilant about having beaten back the
enemy and secured the Canal Bridge. He also had words of warning
for Hans.

"I had no idea it'd be this big! Dazunor-Rannuli is as big as
Sordan! It has more people than we have army!"

"It does. Which is why we need to remember they're not the
enemy." Hans had been making the point all day that Dazunor-

Rannuli's people were not disposed to fight. "They're more scared than anything else," he pointed out. "They don't want war. They don't want their city destroyed and they don't want their families terrorized the way Mormantalorus has been doing to the towns along the Dazun, saying it's Sordan's soldiers. I've talked with many of this city's leaders. If I leave the citizens of Dazunor-Rannuli intact and to their own order, they'll offer no resistance. That's why we must be disciplined, Arne—no looting, no chasing down women—"

"We know," Arne assured Hans as they left the quiet environ of the Rill Mount and began walking down the broad road to the ramparts of the commercial buildings below. "You gave us the talk and we're holding to it, not asking for food or water or nothing— nor taking it when they offer, seeing as it could be poisoned and all with the enemy still not long gone. We're keeping to our own."

"Good." Hans clasped one of Arne's shoulders. They both were wearing Staubaun-styled leather battle armor now. It was a far cry from what they'd worn the day they'd met in Ben Aranath. "I'm glad to see you back in one piece."

"You and me both." They walked past the looming black shadows of towering lifts and cranes, ghosts of the mercantile might that clung to the district surrounding the Rill mount. Arne hefted his sword. "And I'm damn glad I learned how to use this!"

The next morning, Dazunor-Rannuli unfurled its finery along the short distance from the Rill Mount to the expansive open plaza of the Denizens' Quarter. Banners fluttered down from balconies, lining the street with ribbons of color. Relieved that Handurin wished to keep most of their city's institutions and leadership intact, the populace embraced him enthusiastically. He had already, since the night before and for much of that morning, met with representatives of the city's noble Staubaun families and its citizen councils—including the powerful merchant guilds—all of whom had accepted his lenient terms in exchange for their pledges of fealty. Only the golden palaces of the Seven Houses had remained closed to him, staring down in disdain. They had not stayed closed for long, however. A messenger arrived midmorning from Pitar Kisthoda, bearing a joint request from the Brotherhood of Epoptes and the Seven Houses, to ask for an audience and to propose the initiation of discussions about resuming Rill service to the city.

Hans had what the Seven Houses wanted, just as Dorilian had said. The Rill gleamed before their eyes no less brightly than it had before the eyes of the gathered Cruihcila of Amallar and Neuberland—if not brighter. The Seven Houses had come to being because of the Rill. They served it, depended on it, used it to transport their goods. The Rill had shaped their history, their mindset, their lives. For a time, during Marc Frederick's reign, when the Sordaneons had been powerless and Essera's ascendance over Sordan at its zenith, much of the World had treated the Rill as the franchise of the Seven Houses. Goods and gold had flowed into their coffers. Entire domains were held captive to the policies and whims that issued from behind the closed doors of the high secret chambers of the Customhouse in Dazunor-Rannuli.

That situation had changed. Any pretense that the Seven Houses controlled the Rill had ceased when the god-machine stopped running to Essera, and not all the gold and might of the Seven Houses had given them a means by which to move it.

And now the Rill ran again—to Permephedon and even to Amallar—but it sailed above the strongholds of the Seven Houses and did not stop at the mighty Mount at Dazunor-Rannuli. Nor would it, until Dorilian was satisfied that the Rill would not be used to aid and supply Nammuor.

Hans alone knew what it would take to satisfy the Sordaneon Hierarch. Not only metal and pulleys had come from Sordan. Even before crossing the Dazun Hans had received a missive written in that strange ink Dorilian alone seemed to use. The letter outlined the Hierarch's requirements for restoring Dazunor-Rannuli's station, and his trust in Hans to act as Dorilian's surrogate in negotiations. Much as that trust pleased him, Hans had already decided he would agree to nothing about the Rill, nothing at all, until he had satisfied his own misgivings about the Lords of the Seven Houses.

On the handful of occasions when the Seven Houses had cropped up in their conversation, Dorilian had been unusually cryptic. Though Hans sensed clearly that there was no love lost between the Hierarch and the merchant lords, no details of their conflict had emerged. Conversations with Robdan and, more recently, Endelarin and the Epopte Tharos, had been more revealing. The Seven Houses had masterminded numerous plots against the Sordaneons, not the least of which included Labran Sordaneon's imprisonment. Their offenses against the Sordaneons were many. Indeed, just before his death, Stefan had crafted a strategy with the Seven Houses that had effectively seized control of shipments through Dazunor-Rannuli. In return for the Seven Houses diverting some shipments of weapons and food destined for Lacenedon to Dazunor-Rannuli and then overland to Neuberland, Stefan had assigned control of a significant portion of the crown's Rill slots to the cartel. Those slots, for Rill service from both Dazunor-Rannuli and Permephedon, had given the Seven Houses, and their allies among the Epoptes, control of shipment movement in Essera. Stefan had secured more and better weapons for the Khelds—but to do so he had given the Seven Houses control of nearly all of Dazunor-Rannuli's Rill traffic.

"Fran told me about the weapons," Hans said to Aubrey and Arne just before they left the big house on the Lower Canal where they'd spent the night. Located in an older part of the city near the wharfs, the manse was a grand, tall building with access to both the canal and the street. It was also owned by Cam Gereggson and Ralen Ornichos and had been deemed by Khelds to be a suitable place for their leaders to regroup. "Fran boasted about it, how all the blades and armor he and his fighters got were from Sordan's forges. How they'd gotten rich selling them, too! He made it pretty clear I haven't done anything yet to match Stefan."

"You told me the Hierarch wasn't too happy about that," Arne said. He stood beside the big table in the manse's entry. A shiny brass scale, a big one, occupied the center of the table and he'd spent much of the morning placing different objects in its pans.

"He was furious. I heard him threaten Quirin, the leader of the Epoptes about it," Hans confirmed. "I think it contributed a lot to why he stopped the Rill."

"But our lads needed the weapons, Hans." Aubrey folded her arms over the heavy wool of her knitted overblouse. Though the sun was up and the streets bright, the room's impressive brazier did not completely remove the chill.

"And Fran needs to understand that Stefan gave them a few swords—but I want to take back the Rill. I'm trying to gain standing and financial independence. We all have weapons now, new ones, and we need to learn how to use them."

"Like now?" Aubrey asked. "Against the Seven Houses?" She frowned as Arne, bored with placing weights on the scale, settled a book onto one of the pans. The shelves upstairs had yielded two volumes of poetry Aubrey had begun reading that morning.

"Especially against the Seven Houses. Until I can get the better of them, I don't control this city. This meeting with them is going to be as big a battle as the one we just fought." Hans lifted his head at the sound of horses outside the street entrance and saw the main door open to admit Nalf and Orem Darm.

They were preparing to depart the gated house when a small commotion just outside took their attention. A silver-haired man, tall and lean, waved a packet of ribboned and bound letters at the soldiers who'd stopped him. The soldiers, seeing the emerald and silver of Sordaneon flourishes on the letters, were glad to turn the matter over to Hans.

The letter introduced the newcomer as Sinon Kouranos, Sordan's representative to the Archhalia. "Ambassador," Hans greeted.

"Your Royal Highness," Sinon acknowledged along with a deep bow. "My Hierarch has directed me to assist you in whatever way I can. I traveled all night and have just arrived from Permephedon. My entourage is exhausted, and I have sent them on to the house I keep in this city. I, however, am at your immediate disposal."

"I'm just about to pay a visit to the Customhouse of the Seven Houses." Hans wondered if this obviously travel-worn man, covered with dust from the road, should join them.

Brown eyes turned skyward, new purpose enlivening the grave, intelligent features of Sinon's face. "Thank Leur for the day. Then I have arrived none too soon, for most certainly you will be needing me."

# 15

Dorilian Sordaneon came to power at a critical juncture in which his Highborn lineage faced extinction. Upon the deaths of the Malyrdeons, the Wall had lost its mortal aspect and its gifts were no longer experienced directly among men. The Rill had become a tool of imperial rapists, its benefits increasingly restricted to the Seven Houses, its being victimized by politics. The demise of the Sordaneons would deliver the Rill to such interests completely.
PITAR KISTHODA, *ASSUMPTIONS: GODHEAD REVEALED*

Hans perceived the underlying structures of cartel politics even before he passed beneath the golden wheat sheaves adorning the grand arches of the Customhouse Gate. Though he'd brought enough soldiers with him to make any double-cross by the Seven Houses costly, his most powerful weapon was the blade Dorilian had already laid across their throats: the knife edge of Rill dominion. It promised surer death to these proud merchant princes than any Stauberg-Randolph army. Hans had glimpsed the laden barges waiting to be relieved of cargo, and the omnipresent sour smells of grains going to must and the burning of fouled meat. He had also noted the filled warehouses and idle workmen, confirmation of what Hans already suspected. Small wonder that for centuries the Sordaneons had been the natural enemy of the Seven Houses. One controlled what the other must have.

Few people, however high, could say they'd set foot inside the secretive fastness of the Customhouse. No Kheld ever had stepped inside, or at least none had been acknowledged. Persistent rumors of Kheld girls and boys bought and sold for pleasure had never been substantiated. Neither had cartel involvement in the lucrative business of providing Kheld slaves, prisoners in the Neuberland war, to labor in the poisoned mines and quarries of Leseos and Randpory. All Seven Houses transactions took place within codified confidentialities so secret and obscured, no merchant not of their guild could name for certain the merchant lord through whom they'd done their business.

The Seven Houses had used Marc Frederick to achieve their ends and had despised Stefan even more. The Stauberg-Randolphs would find no alliance here.

The only thing Hans would come away with would be knowing the face this enemy would present to him.

*They cannot be bought*, Hans reminded himself. *They are here only to assess how they might buy* me.

The Customhouse looked deceptively plain for what was essentially a seat of government. The main highway into Dazunor-Rannuli traveled high ground untraversed by canals, bisecting the west end of the city. That road ended at a plaza ringed by tall buildings, most of which housed important merchants or vendors of commodities. One side of the plaza bore only a high wall of stone carved with emblems of commerce. A single gate, immense and imposing, dominated the wall, the plaza and indeed everything around it—except for that which could be seen overhead. The Rill crowned it no less than it did the rest of the city. Sheaves of flaxen wheat, perfect even in the individual kernels on the heads and the spikes of beard, clothed the gate's pillars, which were crowned by gilded scales holding in balance stalks of ripened grain. Seven banners of gold cloth, each emblazoned with the emblem of one of the cartel's constituent Houses, drifted from the arch to flutter above the heads of all who passed beneath. The place Hans entered constituted a foreign power in his own land—and when he left, it would still be one.

Sinon introduced the men who greeted Hans and his retinue as Rhynos Staubaun Kheprion, Eptor of House Koillos, and Thirzan Staubaun Esdras, Denizen of House Haralambdos. Mentally, Hans placed them in the roster of names he had learned from Dorilian. Koillos was one of the most shadowy and treacherous of the Seven Houses. Haralambdos, on the other hand, bore the dubious distinction of being the only House with which Dorilian did any business. Notable by their absences were representatives of the other Houses, in particular the Denizen of Phaer, the formidable Chyralane, about whom Dorilian had warned him.

*Evil, with a side serving of vile.*

Sinon had cautioned Hans against trying to unravel the cartel's history with either the Sordaneons or his own family. "It's far too complicated. Just listen carefully to what they say they want—and realize that they mean not a word of it. What they really want they will never say to the likes of you."

Sinon had changed from his travel attire and had even chosen Hans's attire for the occasion, sending an assistant to commandeer deep-hued velvets, blue leathers, and pale silk brocades from the closets of nearby nobleborn. "You must dress as a Highborn Prince," the ambassador explained, adjusting a sash by affixing a jeweled brooch. "Your grandfather did so for every meeting. Now let us find you a more fitting circlet—something... flashy."

Sinon had similarly adjusted the garb of those who accompanied Hans. Euden Mezeon, who appeared every inch the Archon, met Sinon's approval. However, Arne, Aubrey, Nalf and Orem now looked more like well-off Kheld merchants than victorious soldiers. "Threats don't impress them unless they know you can deliver," Sinon pronounced. "Therefore, look like the kind of people who can deliver the threat."

Here the Khelds met at last the Staubaun power they had enshrined in tales. Now more than ever before, they encountered the wide gulf between their world and the one they wished to join. Despite their new accessories, their best furs looked out of place. Their boots, hard heeled and rough, scratched floors of pure blue onyx. Though Hans strove to look unimpressed, his Kheld companions gaped and stared at rooms paved with agate and marble, above which soared vaulted ceilings, faced by walls of mosaics depicting a glorious, Rill-based history. Furnishings in the public rooms were few, but not the signs of wealth.

Bows and introductions gave way to formalities, the three representatives showing their guests into a room with high, sky-revealing windows, dominated by a table arranged for diplomacy. All took their seats.

"Denizens of the Seven Houses," Hans acknowledged, keeping his nod polite. He remained standing, an act of authority his hosts did not challenge. "It seems we have a common goal."

The walls were filled with eyes. Hans sensed them the moment he spoke. Watchers lurked behind tapestries and screens, at peepholes secreted within ornate mosaics, pillars veined with gold and worked with scenes drawn from the river and the Rill. Everything Hans and his party did was worthy of notice: every movement, gesture, and word. He was certain ears sprouted here, too, assigning meaning even to their silences and intent on picking up whispers. Those at the table strove to elicit more than policy.

Hans noted, with an inner smile, that Aubrey wasn't too cowed to look. She catalogued each nuance, each mannerism, alert for signs of trickery. The clothing Sinon had dictated for her included a gown of deep, subtle indigo with voluminous sleeves and a headpiece of velvet set with dark, mysterious pearls. Hans liked the effect. He liked even more that Aubrey had concealed slips of paper along with a bit of writing chalk within her gown's wide sleeves.

*She suspects we're being watched. She senses the larger picture.*

"If it please Your Royal Highness," Rhynos managed to sound insincere even with those opening words, "we intend to cooperate fully in the restoration of service to Dazunor-Rannuli. To show our tacit public and private support, we shall make available to your use our full complement of Rill slots. Please, we beg you, be seated."

Hans sat. "I have no doubt the Seven Houses will cooperate." Long talks with Dorilian and Endelarin, sessions with the Epopte Tharos, and even conversation with Sinon on the way over just this morning, now served Hans well in framing his response. "However, it is not me you need to satisfy. The Rill is not mine to bestow. I honor the birthright of the Sordaneons. The Hierarch has seen fit to restore Rill service throughout these lands, as I am sure you have learned by now. However, he requires that I send him personal assurances regarding integrity of service to Dazunor-Rannuli. Only then will he release the Rill service here. You understand his concerns."

"We understand he is overvigilant."

"He explained his reasons. Now I ask you to understand mine. I'm not my brother. I'm not interested in wresting Rill control from the Sordaneons. I *am* interested in seeing to it that the Rill is used in ways that assist my military campaign and benefit the kingdom to which I am the rightful Heir." Hans regarded his opponents, one by one. By their expressions, he knew he had surprised them. Good! "To that end, I will send the assurances that will convince the Hierarch to return service to Dazunor-Rannuli's Mount—on two conditions. First, that transit and cargo origins and destination will be held open to all citizens, with the only exception being for my second condition: that Rill service not benefit either the person or purposes of Nammuor the Mormantaloran or his minions."

Rhynos leaned forward in his seat. He moved his hand, closing it over the handle of a carafe holding a vivid green liquid. "Your Royal Highness need have no concerns in that regard. Please, refresh yourselves." He filled his glass and invited his guests to do the same from similar vessels set about the table. "The Seven Houses have the needed experience in these matters. We will see to it that Rill operations run smoothly and equitably."

As extended, the reply was suitably vague. Hans detected Aubrey's hand on his, passing a slip of paper under the table. He glanced at it.

"You misunderstand," Hans said. He took his glass and inverted it on the table, signaling he would not drink. "I intend to keep full authority over Dazunor-Rannuli and its Rill operations in my own hands—at least until such time as I have established and assured peace in this land. The Seven Houses will have to be patient."

The word chosen was a laden one. Every nuance had been marked and they had detected the redirection.

"Be patient? By that you mean we will not have a voice." Denizen Thirzan leaned forward to crowd the table with his richly robed frame. The Seven Houses were not accustomed to having terms dictated to them. Especially not by a Stauberg-Randolph. "Rethink yourself, Prince who would be King. We control sixty percent of Essera's Rill slots!"

There it was, the first of many threats Hans would face from men who, unlike Khelds, would not admire him for besting them.

"Sixty-two percent," said Sinon in a practiced monotone. He had filled his glass and now lifted it to the light to examine the color and clarity of the contents. "With contractual options for two percent more."

Hans settled back in his chair, keeping his expression neutral. He wanted his hosts to chew on the extent of his influence, what inroads he might already have made in Sordan and Essera. "Configuration and allocation of Dazunor-Rannuli's Rill slots are being re-examined."

"Re-examined?" Rhynos sounded alarmed. He looked sharply from one man to the other. "By whom?"

"Dorilian Sordaneon."

In the silence that followed, even the walls seemed to hum. If one looked closely, tapestries stirred and eyeholes opened. Sinon, with a sigh, gave Hans a look that said the session would prove long. He brought out a linen bag which he set on the table. From it, he began to remove some small green nuts, which he broke open to get at the sweet purple meat, discarding the dainty hard shells in a pile on the table.

Denizen Thirzan's neck swelled as though he were strangling in his ruff of office. "Use of the Rill is ordained according to the Covenant. Even this Sordaneon cannot overturn the Covenant! It is a holy obligation—it is a *vow*!"

Sinon nodded at that answer. "A vow that my Hierarch maintains was broken a half century ago at your instigation. Proof that the vow was broken lies, perhaps, in the fact that he was *able* to stop the Rill." Sinon cracked another nut between his fingers, fishing out the morsel inside. "It presents an interesting question," he conceded, "as the Covenant binds men as regards the Rill, but not the Rill as regards to Itself." His eyebrows drew together thoughtfully as his gaze wandered into open thought. "This is always a conundrum when dealing with the Highborn and their Entities, this matter of boundaries."

Rhynos bestowed a withering glare upon the ambassador. "Dorilian Sordaneon is *not* the Rill!"

Sinon raised a gray eyebrow and popped the purple nutmeat into his mouth. He chewed for a few moments. "Whether he is or isn't... is a moot point, don't you think? Considering what's happened? He might as well be. The Rill follows his mind. It goes where he wishes it to go and does not go where he wishes it to pass by. At the moment, because he wishes it thus, the Rill is passing by Dazunor-Rannuli. You, on the other hand, wish to change that. I would think it a sane policy—one that young Handurin and these intelligent Khelds of his seem to follow—to treat my Hierarch as if he *is* the Rill. That way, you are much more likely to get what you want."

"Then your Hierarch is mad!"

Sinon shrugged and dropped another shell onto the pile. "Unprovable. And immaterial."

Hans leaned forward to interrupt them. "Covenant or no Covenant, lords of the Seven Houses, your Rill slots here amount to nothing if Dazunor-Rannuli is bypassed."

Clearly unhappy, Rhynos and Thirzan eyed each other, weighing their options. That the Covenant might be overthrown and, with it, centuries of Rill agreements, worried them. Dorilian's reasons for wishing to do so were too well known to them not to be persuasive.

"And the Permephedon slots?" Thirzan asked, bringing up a key, and now also delicate, point. The Seven Houses controlled those as well.

"A portion of those belong to the Crown too. That is to say—me."

"We have arrangements with your Regent!"

"Agreements that concern Rill slots turned over to your use by my brother and administered by Erenor after Stefan's death. Those proxies are now invalid. When I was pronounced Stefan's Heir, Crown Rill rights reverted to me."

Thirzan conferred with an unobtrusively dressed man who had appeared at his elbow, leaning to whisper to him. Orders? Or more information? Hans exchanged glances with Aubrey and Arne, both of whom returned looks saying that they didn't know what it was about. The expression on Sinon's face said more, as did his gesture indicating Hans to remain calm.

"You have yet to be confirmed in your status by the Archhalia, Prince Handurin," Thirzan said after the man had retreated from the room. As he regarded Hans from across the table, the man's patrician face displayed only calm assurance. "You cannot legally claim the Dazunor titles until then—and therefore have no Crown interest."

With a sigh that announced he had expected this argument, Sinon reached into the leather portfolio he had kept with him at all times. "I have it somewhere. Yes, here." He retrieved a document from within. He perused, then summarized its contents. "Two months after the death of King Stefan, his brother Handurin Marc Frederick Stauberg-Randolph was invested by the Archhalia as Heir to the late King's titles and domains. I recall distinctly my Hierarch Dorilian Sordaneon in person voting against this investiture." The ambassador gave Hans a knowing arch of his eyebrow. "My Hierarch was at that time indisposed to the arrangement. It passed nonetheless."

"Naming Handurin as Heir," Rhynos emphasized. "Not titular Prince."

"True, as my Hierarch did not veto it." Sinon pulled another document. "That brings us to a second Archhalial action, at that same session. This action made Erenor Tholeros regent for Handurin until, and I quote, 'such time as Handurin is invested in his domain and titles by a majority of the Archhalia.'"

"Your Hierarch also voted against that."

"True. But again, he did not exercise his veto, which many thought he would. In any event, the action was adopted by Essera, which was all that was needed."

"And Erenor remains Regent. Handurin has not been invested in his domain and titles by the Archhalia."

"I offer that he has. This past summer, the Dodecai of Sordan met and invested Handurin fully in his domains and titles. This document was entered into the record." With a flourish, Sinon laid the document out before them, its ribbons of state gleaming against the rich wood. "I have proxies here from Gweroyen, Dannuth, Lacenedon, Amallar, and Princess Emyli on behalf of their seats investing Handurin Marc Frederick Stauberg-Randolph as Prince of Dazunor." He laid those documents out as well. "By my count, that makes sixteen votes to fourteen, a simple majority. As my Thrice Royal Hierarch Dorilian Sordaneon has furthermore added his most significant Highborn vote for the action, I believe we can consider it... done."

Hans flashed back to the white heat of a Sordan summer and the day Dorilian had hauled him before the Dodecai, subjecting him to them, asking their indulgence. So this was what Dorilian had been leading to! The Hierarch had anticipated the legal challenge and had arranged behind the scenes and in back rooms to obtain the needed proxies, assuring that Hans would be granted his full investiture and titles by Archhalial rules but under the Archhalia's tables. Hans tried to keep his expression clear of what he was feeling, to give the impression that he had known all along. His companions were less successful. Arne looked puzzled; Aubrey amazed. Nalf, seated alongside Orem, stared at Sinon as if he were some kind of strange magician. Euden Mezeon merely lifted his eyebrows. Sinon, as usual, betrayed only that he was doing his job.

Rhynos and Thirzan thumbed through the papers, examining each proxy. "These are not equivalent to an Archhalia vote!"

"Investiture of title does not require a vote in chambers," Sinon reminded them. "If a rightful heir to a title meets the legal requirements, he becomes the ruler of his domain. The regency is indeed, at that point, *ex-officium*. Handurin was proclaimed by the Dodecai to have met the legal requirements for inheritance. Indeed, I recall that at the time the Archhalia undertook at great length discussions on the appropriateness—or lack thereof—of my Thrice Royal Hierarch's declaration of house arrest for a titular Prince. In fact, I have documents—"

"I am certain you do." Thirzan scowled.

Sinon continued, "The Archhalia itself has acknowledged Handurin as titular Prince."

"Yes, yes. But Erenor does not consider the regency to have ended," Rhynos pointed out. "I believe in Rill matters he still votes the Permephedon slots according to the Epoptean Brotherhood rules of conduct."

"Another moot point," Hans interrupted the back-and-forth with a grim smile, feeling the power of his new status settle about his shoulders, in his hands. "You see, one of Dorilian's terms for restoring *this* Rill node is that the Epoptean Brotherhood's charter be suspended."

# 16

If great fortune is great slavery, what might we make of
those who believe truly that their god gems their robes
and be-dews their crowns?
ZAMENES, *On the Nature of Gods and Men*

By the end of the second day after the battle, Hans had taken up
residence in Dazunor-Rannuli's Emrysen Palace. It took a day
longer for him to fully absorb the fact that the place was truly his.
He walked long corridors through archways and vaults formed of
fantastic materials, and into rooms that, like Rhondda's, displayed
the careless wonder and wealth of nearly fifteen hundred years of
royal habitation. No one barred his passage or placed limits on
where he might go. Even the household staff, which had seen three
rulers come and go in but a year, melted away whenever he
approached, acknowledging the Prince's right to enjoy his
inheritance. Marc Frederick had inherited more from Endurin
Malyrdeon than the mandate to rule; there were also vast estates
and grand palaces, wealth beyond any Hans had ever known.

Hans felt a profound ache. *This is all they ever wanted*, he realized.
*Erenor for certain. Even Stefan, who wanted it for the Khelds. They
wanted this—this wealth, this show, this power. They want it still.*

*But Nammuor wants something more. For him all this splendor is
but glitter and dust.*

Hans looked out through windows of unblemished glass across
a terrace paved with a living carpet of blue moss tipped by frost.
Beyond the terrace stretched a green-purple lawn dusted with snow
and a cypress-lined road along which a party bearing Merrydni
standards was riding toward the city.

Sinon Kouranos, who'd attended that morning's negotiations,

joined Hans at the window. The midmorning sunlight lifted the golden threads that banded the emerald stripes of Sinon's diplomat's robe. "The Princes of Merrydn have long been solid allies of your family. It's heartening to see your grandfather's legacy hold fast in such times as these. Only the Brotherhood of Epoptes has yet to make its stance final, but I don't think you need be concerned."

The Brotherhood's envoy had departed that morning to Permephedon. "So you think they'll do what Dorilian wants?"

"I think he's made clear that they have no other choice." Sinon turned his head slightly, acknowledging Arne, who stood nearby. "By the time your representatives, and mine, reach Permephedon, you may be sure the Brotherhood will have acted."

Hans figured that was probably true: Pitar Kisthoda had left Dazunor-Rannuli immediately after learning Dorilian's terms for releasing the Rill. All manner of things were moving more quickly than Hans had ever imagined they could. In the courtyard outside, grooms loped into view, bringing more horses. Sinon's work at the palace was finished for the day.

"Thank you for your help these past few days," Hans said. Not only had Sinon masterfully handled the Seven Houses, but he had given Hans a deep and needed introduction to Essera politics.

"My Hierarch conveyed to me that I am to serve you in this as I would serve him." Sinon's cryptic smile displayed surprisingly little weariness for someone who had spent two days negotiating with representatives of various Esseran factions. "To better serve the both of you, I will remain in this city that I might function as a diplomatic liaison—a resource, if you will. There is little about Essera and its powerful that I do not know."

"Are you yourself a northerner?" Many of the past day's interactions with different emissaries, details noted but unspoken, had led Hans to wonder. As he walked with Sinon toward the open door, where Arne stood with a brace of Trongorians who were standing guard, he noted two men wearing diplomatic livery waiting at the foot of the landing. One held the ambassador's horse. Notably, the animal was not ivory white but a well-bred gray. Sinon, then, was not himself of royal birth. It fit a pattern Hans had already pegged: Dorilian bestowed few civil posts of importance on his fellow aristocrats.

"No, Your Royal Highness. I was born in Sordan." Sinon looked contemplative as he paused in the doorway. "In those days the Triempery was united. I was fourteen when I went north to attend the Paranus Academy in Stauberg and was recruited into the diplomatic corps under King Endurin. My father remained in service to the Sordaneon Royal Household. He commanded and died with the guards trying to defend Labran Sordaneon from being taken prisoner. I was at the time an ambassadorial aide stationed in Leseos. I offered my resignation, but Marc Frederick, your grandfather, persuaded me to remain. For many years I served him in numerous capacities, including as Triemperal Administrator in Sordan during the last year of Deben's protracted regency. After that, I was Governor of Neuberland. During your brother's reign, I was for a time his Ambassador to the Archhalia." He cocked an eyebrow at Hans's look of surprise. "Now what is that about, young Prince? Does my experience perplex you?"

"No. Your affiliations. You served my grandfather all those years, and Stefan too, not the Sordaneons. Yet Dorilian chose you to be his representative."

"Perhaps it was I who chose him." Sinon picked up his diplomatic pouch from the table he had set it on while donning his cloak and tucked the envelope under his arm in a solemn grip. He bowed, acknowledging Hans and those with him as he prepared to go. "I am at your service, so long as it goes in hand with my allegiance to the Hierarch."

After the Sordaneon diplomatic cadre had disappeared down the road, Hans led Arne back to the library. Aubrey was already there, seated at the opposite end of the table, to all appearances engaged in writing. Surrounded again by quiet and books, Hans walked to the large table where he and the emissaries had been talking not long before and picked up a stack of papers. Arne broke the silence.

"I was starting to like old Sinon, until he got smart there at the end."

"He just pointed out that good ambassadors don't simply pop up along the road. Dorilian's ability to collect exceptional people is about as uncanny a talent as his gift for making enemies." Hans settled in a chair before the document-laden table. He wished Arne would just drop this topic and signaled that wish by starting to read the papers in his hand.

"It's that Highborn thing he's got going for him," Arne reckoned, oblivious, "though damned if I've figured out yet what it means. They're just a fancy kind of Staubaun if you ask me. But lots of folk follow it blind. Highborn this and Thrice Royal that, as if it matters." He straddled a chair and laid his hands across the back, his chin upon them, watching Hans glumly.

Hans decided he might as well answer. Tiptoeing around the topic of Dorilian had never been easy and was now nearly impossible. "It matters, Arne, if your ancestor is a god, and it matters double if that god is the Rill. At least in *this* city, it matters. When we met the Seven Houses, you saw just how much. They didn't open their doors because I've suddenly become powerful. Or even useful for that matter. And my name sure doesn't grease any wheels. It's Dorilian they fear—and they fear my alliance with him. They won't cross him now that he's shown he can command the Rill. The Rill is their god—but they're not sure what he is."

"Well, I'm not sure, either, but I'd put my last copper down that he ain't no god. Reckon that's because there's no Staubaun in me." Arne pondered what Hans was doing, then asked, "Why do you keep going over those papers? That writing ain't going to change. It still says the same thing each time."

"I want to be sure of that. The Seven Houses are intent on getting the Rill to run again in Dazunor-Rannuli and they're not above doing something underhanded to make it happen. And I still don't understand the Epoptes." Hans reviewed the papers before him. It had taken two days to negotiate an agreement with the Seven Houses and the Brotherhood of Epoptes that both he and Sinon had found satisfactory. *Relinquishment of all confiscated Sordaneon property in Seven Houses hands or the hands of persons associated with same, to be returned at once to Dorilian. Relinquishment of crown Rill slots, to be restored to me… relinquishment of Principate of Dazunor Rill slots, to me… relinquishment of Halasseon Rill slots, also to me… all other former Malyrdeon slots confiscated during Stefan's or Erenor's reigns to be conveyed into the trusted custody of the College of Sages pending settlement of claims… agreement to realign the Brotherhood of Epoptes pursuant to the Order retaining its charter… replace the Order's Psilant with a candidate acceptable to the Hierarchate and the Crown… all of the Order's Trestethion slots to be negotiated by a committee including representatives from Amallar…. The Seven Houses to be limited to minority partner participation also determined by a committee including representatives from Amallar. The Seven Houses to turn their barges to supplying the armies of Dazunor under my direction…*

"They've made powerful concessions." Aubrey was going over the documents as well, noting key points into Hans's log and the duplicate log she sent daily by messenger to Rhodhur for safekeeping. She sat back in the chair opposite him and rubbed at an ink stain on her fingers.

Hans nodded in agreement. "They're afraid Dorilian will get stubborn on them and decide not to resume Rill service to Dazunor-Rannuli at all."

"Would he do that?"

"Get stubborn? Yes. You haven't seen him in his best form yet. Not run the Rill to Dazunor-Rannuli? Maybe. If he thought it would punish his enemies more to *not* have it than it benefits his interests for them *to* have it, then certainly. The Seven Houses know they're being watched. They want to convince Dorilian that they're agreeing to terms that will cripple them." Which they were. While not ruinous, the agreement significantly reduced cartel dominance of Dazunor-Rannuli Rill operations. Hans signed the personal note he'd written to go along with the signed treaty in the packet he'd put together. He was using the 'invisible' ink Sinon had given him. It was difficult to read in the firelight, but he knew Dorilian would appreciate his efforts to keep their correspondence private.

"You're the only person I know who will use that stuff. How can you write when you can't see what you're writing?" Aubrey wondered.

"Says he *can* see it," Arne told her.

"I can speak for myself," Hans informed them. He calmly dropped wax on the folded paper and sealed it. "It's magic ink or something. Dorilian said it's only visible to the writer and the intended reader."

"Strange magic," was Aubrey's assessment.

"No stranger than runes."

She shrugged, then smiled. "Shall I tell you what my runes said this morning?"

*Oh, no!* Hans shot a look at Arne. Both of them knew that tone of voice. "What?" he asked.

"That I'm going to Lacenedon along with this signed agreement, and your letter, and the signed treaty with Sordan." She returned the fierce scowl Arne directed her way.

The silence that followed Aubrey's announcement said more than it concealed.

"That is where you're sending these, isn't it?" she persisted. "To the Hierarch, in Lacenedon?"

Hans didn't deny it. "Aubrey, I'm not sending you riding into Lacenedon in winter."

"Ha! You don't know that land any more than I do, but we can be sure Staubaun lands are not without roads."

Hans had hoped she'd buy that excuse. "You're right. I've never been there, but I have been in very harsh winters. The snow, the cold, the wind. I wouldn't send Arne if I didn't need to send my own right hand. And the weather's not even the worst part. Lacenedon is the heart of the Royal North. Bas Hebron is a Purist. He hates Khelds. He opposed Stefan and voted against my return because I have Kheldish blood. The only reason he broke with Erenor is that he couldn't stomach Nammuor bringing in troops— and he thinks other people have a better claim. People who had Highborn fathers, like Ionais of Merrydn or the baby Princess of Stauberg. That vote for me to be invested with my titles? That was Dorilian's doing. He promised Hebron troops to help liberate Stauberg. Hebron is Dorilian's ally far more than he is mine."

"If that's what awaits, even more reason to send me! I speak better Stauba than anyone else you have, except for the Staubauns, and you can't trust them the way you can trust me. Ask the Seven Houses about my qualifications. Ask the Denizen of Hedys."

"I haven't forgotten how you nailed down that agreement to secure his barges."

"Then you know why you need me now, and there. There's that agreement with the Epoptes to look at. There are first impressions to make." Aubrey presented a determination Hans could tell already would be difficult to break down. "Arne will follow your instructions, you know that. But I'm the better spokesperson."

Arne frowned and folded his arms.

Hans spoke before Arne could say something heated. "Maybe you are, if what I needed was a spokesperson. But I'm not sending Arne to recruit the Lacenedoni. He's going to deliver the agreement with the Seven Houses to Dorilian. That and the signed treaty with Sordan. That's it. Dorilian knows Arne and trusts him. The agreement with the Epoptes is separate, between Dorilian and them. I don't have to approve it. If Dorilian is satisfied, then Arne will return to Bellan Toregh with whatever we need to restore service to Dazunor-Rannuli."

"But you're not sending him alone," Aubrey pointed out.

"I thought I might send Orem Darm." Hans watched Aubrey warily, even more because he could read what she was trying to do.

"Orem won't make nearly the impression I will."

"Orem knows Staubauns and speaks Stauba as well as you do—and he doesn't have any fights to pick with Dorilian," Hans told her bluntly. "He's not going to say or do anything to cause the kind of serious trouble you could find yourself in."

Firelight reflected red along the writing stick Aubrey tapped against her cheek as she studied him. "Why? Because of what happened?" She let Hans know she had weighed that possibility. "Dorilian's political. We've both seen just how much. This alliance is important to him. He's perfectly aware of my status among Khelds and that I'm related to you. He knows he misled me in Amallar and he's not going to say or do anything to let others know about that. I'm not worried about him."

"Neither am I. I'm worried about you. I can't afford to be represented by someone who might forget who Dorilian is."

"Shadrach! The whole world knows who he is! Except Orem Darm." Aubrey's smile coolly acknowledged Hans's dawning realization. "What will Orem think when he knows who your 'spy' was? How many people will he tell?"

When Hans looked to Arne, he got a quietly mouthed expletive in answer. It was too soon, the truth too incendiary, for any of this.

"He'll tell more than I've told." Aubrey persisted. She threw up her hands. "I know who Dorilian is. He's the Thrice Royal Hierarch of Sordan, Rill Lord and Highborn and the Staubauns think he's a god, that he's the embodiment of every holy thing their cursed race holds sacred. People are supposed to bow and scrape—and hold their tongues. Do you think I don't know how to do that? You've seen me with the Seven Houses, as well as Euden Mezeon and other Esseran nobles who've come to you offering their allegiance. You even sent me to Sordan. I comport myself fine. I understand forms of address, how low to bow, to whom, and when. I know what to do."

"But will you do it?" Hans closed the pouch in front of him, locking the keyed latches. "I trust you to be silent, but you're proud when you address the Lords of the Seven Houses, Aubrey—and with Esseran lords too. When they stare, you stare right back. You don't defer to men; you let them know what you think. And that has been the way to handle them so far. The Seven Houses. The Denizen of Hedys. This city's merchants and lords. They accepted it because they had to, because things have changed for them with me as their Prince and Khelds as my allies. Dorilian is... not me. He makes everything different. You can't be proud with him—not in front of the high lords and ladies of the Royal North— because they won't let you. And neither will he. He might even be unhappy to see you. Or have you forgotten what happened at your last meeting?"

Hans watched the high color that burned across Aubrey's cheeks and knew she was remembering not only being intimate with Dorilian but that she had also felled him with a blow to the head and bound him. Interrogated him. She could be certain Dorilian had not forgotten any part of that encounter. Even Arne looked uncomfortable that they'd brought it up.

"I told you I would want to see him again," Aubrey reminded Hans tightly. "That was the price of my silence. You agreed that I would."

"Sure, someday. Maybe a little closer to home. And I had in mind a meeting at which I would be present."

That earned Hans a smile. "Which of us would you be protecting?"

"Both of you." He shook his head, frustrated at getting nowhere. "I'm in the midst of a war, Aubrey, and so is Dorilian. Neither of us needs this kind of palace politics. Why now?"

"Because it's time to put a stop to all the questions. I don't want them hanging over our heads—over my head and yours... and his!"

"Aubrey—"

"Orem Darm should stay as your representative *here*. This is where he can do the most good. I'm the one who should handle the Rill restoration."

With a sigh, Hans weighed what to do. Lacenedon was an important domain, and its Bas, Hebron Ursenos, was someone to be handled carefully, if not yet an ally then at least a man Hans did not wish to offend. Aubrey was not wrong to suggest Hans needed to send capable—and articulate—representatives. In any other circumstance, he would send her. Aubrey and Arne together made a good team. What gave Hans pause was that Aubrey was still deeply conflicted about the man she would be going north to see.

Reaching over, he laid his hand on hers, warm atop the ink-marked papers. "What if you see Dorilian and it just adds to the hurt? What if what you make real is the monster you've always feared?"

Eyes large and shining with feelings she would never let become tears, Aubrey averted her gaze. She looked toward the windows that framed a view of the Upper Canal. "Then at least I would know that," she said softly. "But you and I both know that I won't find the monster our people have made of him—that what I will find is a man. Maybe a terrible man, maybe a proud one. But only a man."

*But what if you're mistaken? What if you find out he is something else? Would you even be able to see it?*

He could not deny Aubrey the chance to confront the demon that howled in her mind. Only if she faced it would it cease to torment her. She had upheld her part of their bargain. Hadn't Hans asked Marenthro to be sent back in time so that he might know his enemy's face?

Hans squeezed Aubrey's hand. "Find out what you need to know," he said, to her surprise. He rose as Arne gaped at him.

"You're letting her go?"

"Yes. She's right about needing to maintain secrecy, and I really could use Orem here to help with the barges and the port." Hans nodded before turning his attention back to Aubrey. "You and Arne should be safe under diplomatic banner and you'll pick up a Sordani escort at Jorma. That army Nalf and Fran are still spluttering about left a garrison of troops there before moving north."

Later, after they had gone over the papers and plans and received final instructions, Aubrey left for bed. Like all Hans's companions, she had been given a chamber in the royal wing and would sleep on down quilts if she liked, beneath silken covers. Already, because of Hans, Aubrey's place in the world was changing. All of their places were changing.

"It's gotten real, Hans." Arne spoke with a kind of wonder as they spent a few minutes before the fire. "Sometimes I can't believe it, you and me talking like this, in this room and all. Hell, just that we're in Dazunor-Rannuli! It's a long stretch from Sordan, ain't it?"

Hans looked around the magnificent library, the marble walls lined with scrolls and priceless books, the maps and columns scribed in gold with passages from *The Cibulitan.* If he wanted anything, he had but to gesture toward the room's discreetly screened alcove and a member of the palace staff would appear. He wondered how many people would give in and stop fighting and be happy with this. "It's a long stretch from Sordan," Hans agreed. "But something tells me we aren't even close to where we're going."

He wished he had Dorilian to talk with, right now, here and in this room. That morning Hans had gone to the Rill Mount, just to stand upon its monumental structures and feel the pulse of the city. Of the World. For a fleeting moment, he'd discerned something cognizant, impressions of battle and horses and snow. Of blood and distant cities rising in strange shapes above white hills and men who watched him without seeing him at all.

He did not doubt for a moment that Dorilian knew already Hans had taken Dazunor-Rannuli.

# 17

---



---

"I don't care if you do dress like a man, or even if you act or think like one!" Nalf Rhys was having none of Aubrey's explanations. "The fact is you're a woman. And no Staubaun man ever born can be trusted around one of our women."

"Uncle, don't be absurd." Aubrey lowered her voice as others passed them in the corridor leading to the State Entrance. The palace had assumed the trappings of a prince's headquarters and it swarmed with delegates, officers, and petitioners. "Look outside. I'll be riding with soldiers! I've Arne with me as well as six well-armed Sordani fighting men from the Ambassador's bodyguard! And I'll be meeting with people who will know I'm Prince Handurin's cousin."

"And they won't like it! They won't like it one bit." Nalf's stern expression dissolved into a scowl. "Not a one of them has ever recognized a Kheldish nobility. And worse if they do, seeing as they're always sniffing for ways to worm into a prince's affairs. An alliance is all the better if it gets them a beauty in their bed." He took hold of Aubrey's arm as she tried to walk away. "Don't brush me off, lass. Or have you forgotten how your mother got her Staubaun blood?"

She turned on him fiercely. "She got it because my grandmother was some lord's doxy!"

"That she was, but not by choice. No! She was abducted!" At

the surprised look Aubrey shot him, Nalf nodded. "It's time you knew. She was hauled into some lord's coach in Stauberg and carried off. She never said by whom. And do you know why?" Nalf pulled Aubrey around so that his gaze stabbed full into hers. "Because he was high. Whoever that bastard was that took her, that raped her, that filled her with his seed—he was so high that even the King, even Marc Frederick himself, couldn't do nothing to him. So they counseled silence. They got her out of Stauberg and they never told anyone she bore a child. And why was that? Because that man would have seen it killed."

Though she no longer fought her uncle's grip, Aubrey could not continue to look at him, at the hate that turned Nalf's face harder than she'd ever seen it. "She went away with him, they told me," she said. "Left her child and never came back."

Nalf sighed, swearing under his breath, perhaps regretting now what he had told her. "There was nothing to come back to. Elsleth Brodhesda was looked upon as a Staubaun Lord's whore, even when the King got her back, because of the time she was with the man who took her. Gave the babe to her brother's wife to raise and left for where none knew her."

"Because her own people chased her away. If she found more welcome among strangers, whose fault is that?"

Arne, stockier and more broad-shouldered in outdoor gear, came around the corner. "Aubrey, get on, will you? I've been out there waiting. And you should have talked her out of this last night, Nalf, if you wanted to keep her from going. You might have stood a chance, then."

"Well, she oughtn't go, and you know why!" Nalf now had another target for his ire. "I'm minding you to keep an eye to her. I don't know what Hans Thegn's about, sending her off to the icy north. No good ever came from there and I don't hold with sending our women into Staubaun lands."

"Aw, Aubrey'll be all right. She's good with a blade, and she speaks Stauba so damn well she'll just talk circles around any trouble. But we got to get going or we'll never get there."

Nalf stepped back to let Aubrey move past him. She gave Nalf a wan smile and embraced him quickly. "Thank you, Uncle, for telling me." Though she had more questions than ever, Aubrey couldn't voice them with Arne standing at hand, impatiently letting her know she was making them late. It was probably best she give her thoughts time to fully sort out. "I'll be careful." She made her promise as she closed her heavy winter riding coat. "I've never had a good word for any Staubaun lord and I'm not starting now. Any man who tries to abduct me I'll open from pie hole to rooster." Patting her sword, she flashed a grin as she went to Arne.

"Damn you, girl!" Nalf Rhys laughed bitterly and followed them out to the yard.

They found Hans outside waiting to see them off. Nalf went to stand with him. "Can't say I like her going," Aubrey overheard Nalf say as she walked away after they'd exchanged goodbyes. "But I see what you're about, letting the Sordaneon and those high-nosed Lords know you're keeping with your Kheld ties by sending our kind along with the papers. And he'll need to use them to send 'em back. That's crafty, and I like it! Forcing him to deal with Kheld folk."

Hans watched Arne and Aubrey ride off and was about to go back inside with Nalf and Fran Gorseddson and a handful of curious visitors when distant shouts made him turn around again. Alerted to arrivals on the road, he took position at Nalf's side on the broad moss steps to the colonnade.

The soldiers entrusted with guarding the royal compound had halted a group of riders on the lawn. At least one rider rode a horse of purest, blue-hoofed ivory, and there were others riding richly caparisoned grays. Standards proclaimed a royal party, as did the newcomers' apparel. They were clearly attempting to approach, thinking they had business there. One of the visiting Staubaun nobles who had come to the palace that morning to arrange terms for use of his property asked permission to approach Hans, who granted it.

"That is the standard of Royal Dannuth, My Prince." The man pointed to the banners flying on the party's upraised spears. "The domain's Bas rides with them."

"Is that so?" Nalf said. "And how can you tell that?"

"By the crown regnant upon the standard."

Nalf grunted at that. "That may be," he said aside to Hans, "but Dannuth was a thorn in Stefan's side. They conspired with the Sordaneon to swing Essera over to the side of their Highborn Prince, but Stefan cut that short. Stefan killed their Prince later—for sedition! I say they're likely to be trouble."

Hans studied the newly arrived horsemen. He could see for himself that the banner was a royal one. Although Dannuth had been among the last domains to have Highborn rule and had therefore resisted many of Stefan's reforms, the current ruler opposed Erenor strenuously and had voted for Hans to return. Dannuth continued to resist Erenor from the besieged city of Kyrbasillon. Hans didn't see anything to be gained by turning this party away, not with a westward push across Dazunor looming in the next few weeks. But neither would it do for him to be careless.

"Give me a sword." He turned to the men around him. Fran Gorseddson, who had not taken his eyes off the strangers even for a moment, unbuckled his and handed it over. Hans belted the weapon about his waist, then signaled the guard to let the newcomers approach. He walked back down the steps to greet them.

The riders, observing the cautions of war, dismounted to walk the rest of the way. Hans saw now that there were six of them— and the foremost one an adolescent youth, who wore a royal circlet of silvery metal crowned by golden spear-tip points.

"Your Royal Highness." The youth spoke first. Only briefly did his clear golden gaze sweep Hans with barely concealed curiosity before he dropped to one knee and, unbuckling his sword, took it by the scabbard to hold it out. "I am Kerr Aigelleros é Dannutheon, Bas of Dannuth and Archon of Aillirod. I am here to offer you my sword."

His sword? He looked barely old enough to be wearing one. Hans took the sword, noting as he did so that the weapon was a royal one, the rich leather scabbard embossed with regal insignia and chased with gold. The hilt itself, crusted with gold and garnets, was worth a prince's ransom. "Thank you, Bas Aigelleros," Hans said simply. He declined for the moment to draw the blade in completion of the proffered act. "Before I go any further, I want you to stand, that we can discuss what service you believe I might wish from you."

Kerr rose. Already tall, he was still slender, in the first stages of a lankiness that would plague his next few years. There was no denying the determination in his expression, however. "I offer myself and my men. I would offer the resources of my domain as well—were it not engaged already in war with your enemy."

"First, I need to be sure you know who I am." Hans smiled at the youth's eagerness.

Kerr looked surprised. "Why, you are Prince Handurin, of the Stauberg-Randolphs. Unless—" Looking flustered, his gaze strayed to the other men arrayed before the palace.

"You can relax. I just wanted to be sure. You didn't say at first, and I will not accept service until I'm certain the person offering it knows what he's doing. You know, then, that I'm in Dazunor to reclaim my rightful lands?"

The bright face flashed that knowledge back at him. "More than that, I should hope! Do you not mean to restore the Stauberg-Randolphs to the Esseran Kingship?"

"As a matter of fact, I do. Here." Hans drew Kerr's blade so that it glittered briefly before the gathered company, then returned it to its regal housing. "I accept your service, Bas Kerr, and promise to do it honor." Hans handed the weapon back to Kerr with the proper ceremony, marking the young man's smile as he buckled it back into its usual place.

"You are a noble Prince, whatever some say about your army and that you would see Dazunor overrun with Khelds."

Taking offense, Fran reached for his sword, only to find that Hans was still wearing it. But Fran's glare and that of Nalf and others warned Kerr that he had strayed into troubled territory.

"It is not I that believe it," Kerr hastened to add, "only that the rumor precedes you. I think you might find it to your benefit to now have some Staubaun troops!"

"Troops?" Nalf visibly perked at the mention.

"How many fighting men do you bring?" Hans asked. There would likely be a day of sorting through such alliances.

"Five hundred," Kerr declared. "Most of Dannuth's army is defending my capital at Kyrbasillon. My father is holding the city for me. I was in studies at Permephedon when Erenor laid siege, which is why I am able to come to you here."

"Permephedon?" Hans smiled. "Does Marenthro know you've abandoned your studies? Let's go inside."

The palace opened before them, great doors leading to even greater rooms, the corridors and halls already filled with hopeful petitioners, most of whom would leave disappointed. Kerr's brows pulled down thoughtfully as they entered. "Marenthro is seldom seen anymore, and he is certainly not teaching pupils! I haven't seen him in months. But I have seen your Lady Mother, the Princess Emyli, Sire, and can tell you she is well."

Hans winced. His mother. He'd been back for months, several of those but minutes away by Rill, in Sordan and at Bellan Toregh—and he had yet to visit her. Of course, entering Essera at all had been out of the question for him until recently, and Emyli had explained in letters why staying at Permephedon was best for her. Hans had sent only two letters since leaving Sordan, both carried by Sordani couriers from Bellan Toregh.

"I owe my mother a visit," he explained to Nalf and Fran, not just to Kerr. "Traveling overland to Permephedon just sounds, well, risky. I could get cut off from my army here if some of the powers in this city were to rebel in my absence. It would be better for me to hole up here for a couple of weeks until we get the Rill in order. Solidify what we've gained. Then when the Rill resumes service, I can take a day to go to the High Citadel."

Kerr stopped cold, his expression one of alarm. "Prince Handurin, you cannot wait here, not even a day. You cannot give Salkren Zel that kind of time! Do you not know what he is doing?"

Fran Gorseddson laughed. "He's running for the hills with a spanked bottom!"

From the midst of Kheld laughter, Kerr looked to the older men who had ridden with him. The ones nearest him looked grim. He spoke again, this time slowly, as did justice to the news. "He runs nowhere, but to his master's purpose! As we were riding into the outer villages this morning, we heard that he has put three Kheld settlements to the sword, then burned them to the ground. Those who attempt to escape are run through with spears, then tossed back into the flames. Already the Dazun Road is lined with corpses and the river swarms with those who flee him. Mormantalorus is purging Dazunor of every drop of Kheldish blood!"

# 18

The Leur was the sole remnant of the Creator godhead,
all others having dispersed in the Sacrifice of Daln. He
greatly regretted that he alone should remain and the
burden of immortality weighed heavily upon him.
Turning to his friend Amynas, he said, "Forever is a long
time to spend alone. It does not have to be that way." At
that, Amynas laughed, for though it had been a goal of the
Aryati to attain the immortality of Leur, his kind, as
creations, remained a mortal race. From that moment,
however, the possibility of life eternal shimmered before
him like a sword he had but to grasp.
CIBULITUS, *ANNALS OF THE RETURN*

Quirin stared in fury at the gathered Arch-Epoptes who sat, arrayed in ceremonial stoles, along the length of the table that filled the Grand Chamber of the Covenant. Permephedon's towers rose in graceful terraces outside the Rill complex windows, otherworldly shimmers outlined by the ruddy glow of a winter sunset.

"You cannot do this," Quirin told the gathered men stiffly. That they were seated while he stood at the head of the table lent his words the proper weight. "My primacy is ordained, not situational. The Seventh Article of the Great Consignation states clearly that my position ends only at death."

Pitar Kisthoda, who had arrived that morning after journeying by road from Dazunor-Rannuli, now stood also. He tipped his velvet-crowned head. "Yes, but with exceptions for incapacity, apostasy, or other crimes against the Consignation, as laid out by the Eleventh Conclave according to articles of the Covenant."

One by one, the seated Arch-Epoptes and Mages placed their obsidian staffs of office upon the table's gleaming surface. Quirin stiffened. The meeting was being given over to Pitar's move to dismiss him. They wanted Quirin out as Psilant. All of them did.

"I am not incapacitated—and I have committed no crimes!"

"But you have committed apostasy."

The accusation did not surprise Quirin; he knew from whom it had come. "Dorilian Sordaneon's accusations—"

"Were investigated," Pitar reminded Quirin. "I presented the findings to the Conclave and you should recall that your actions toward the Hierarch caused our Brotherhood no end of discussion and concern. Disruption of the Conclave suspended the hearing, which led to no conclusion and therefore no action at that time. Due to the great importance of recent matters, the Conclave is yet seated—and we just now voted to revisit the evidence."

This should not be happening. Dorilian's list of grievances had been addressed and debunked. Quirin's allies in the Brotherhood had stood solidly behind his determination to keep the Sordaneon Hierarch in his proper place—in Sordan—to be held powerless, watched over by the Brotherhood. Until the Rill had stopped running to Essera. Until Dorilian had challenged and become necessary to everything the Brotherhood defined itself to be.

And now the Conclave was "revisiting" evidence.

Quirin attempted to calm those waters. "What I said to the Hierarch—"

"Yes, that." Pitar's soft words amounted to a sigh. "Your barbs to the Hierarch constituted direct denial of the Rill's divine continuity through Derlon's descendants. Others were present, Quirin, including Prince Handurin of Dazunor, from whom I obtained a statement while in Dazunor-Rannuli. His testimony confirmed the statements of the three Brothers our investigators spoke with in Sordan, who verified that your words against the Hierarch were in fact hostile and questioned the Hierarch's bond to the Rill."

Pitar straightened and addressed Quirin directly. It was an insult. Gone was the subservience that had formerly marked their interactions. "The First Article of the Covenant made with the god Derlon states that the Sordaneons hold an enduring primacy that supersedes yours or any man's. They are never to be denied transport—yet you threatened to place an injunction on Dorilian's travel and communications. And the Rill is never to be used against them—yet you directly stated to the Hierarch that the Brotherhood could and would turn a deaf ear to his complaints that the Rill was being used to benefit his enemies."

"His complaints were unfounded."

"Then why not investigate his complaints? Perhaps they were true and his welfare needed protecting. The affidavit before us is Dorilian's own statement that he felt stopping the Rill was a necessary move for Sordan's protection, and by extension his own."

*Damn him!* The moves being laid out at this table were clear. Dorilian had established a rationale for Rill stoppage that left Quirin holding the blame. Along with every other member of the Brotherhood's ruling council, Quirin had read the papers Pitar had brought from Daziunor-Rannuli: Sordan's signed treaty with Amallar, the Sordaneon Rill agreement for Trestethion, and the Hierarch's terms for resuming Rill operation in Dazunor-Rannuli. This meeting addressed only that last matter.

Dorilian wanted Quirin removed as Psilant. He would accept whatever other Epopte the Brotherhood voted into that office, whether qualified or not, but he wanted Quirin gone. Nammuor had predicted correctly.

"This travesty of an indictment has no basis or merit." Quirin locked gazes again with Pitar Kisthoda, hating that their long years of service to the Rill had come to this. It took no prescience to know he looked upon his replacement. "I never sought to harm Dorilian Sordaneon, nor have I ever denied his stature as a son of Derlon. But look—look well—at what he is doing! At the harm he has done already and continues to do! The Rill is godbound—by Covenant, by Promises—to serve this Triempery and its people! Who is Dorilian serving now, at this moment? Some barbarians who invaded us and were given land to keep them away from our cities? Ruinous Stefan's bastard brother whose purposes we do not yet know nor understand? Think of the harm being done here! Dorilian is dismantling the Triempery!"

"Peace, Quirin," Pitar admonished. Though Quirin sought support from the other men around the table, too few looked disturbed; most merely looked resigned. "I met with Handurin in Dazunor-Rannuli. I and the Seven Houses. The Brotherhood was included in the discussions that led to these documents. Handurin wages war against Erenor and pursues a rightful inheritance. He is no threat to us or the Triempery—or the Rill."

"Handurin? Dorilian is the threat here, not that insipid boy."

"The Hierarch is willing to negotiate."

"But not about me."

"No. About wanting you removed, he has been unyielding."

Because Dorilian saw Quirin in the same light as he saw Nammuor. As an enemy. Quirin bit into that fruit and found it bitter. The Rill was his life, his everything.

Pitar continued. "You understand, I hope, that the matter before us is the obstacle that you present if you do not step down as Psilant. All other matters pertaining to resuming operation are resolved. Removing you from office is the one term standing in the way of restoring the Rill to Dazunor-Rannuli."

A city and Rill port too important to Essera's economy, indeed the economy of the very World, to leave languishing when one simple act—one stupid, futile act—would set prosperity's gears once more in motion. Would see food flow to feed a hungering population and serve once more as its lifeblood, move goods to again swell the purses of warehouse owners and merchants and gild the lofty profits of aristocracy.

One simple act that would happen whether Quirin wished it or not.

"I will not resign my office," he stated. Though hot fury burned within Quirin's brain, cold reason controlled his tongue. "If this Conclave wants me gone, you must formally condemn me for this apostasy you would foist upon my name. And then you must remove me from this post by your wills, not mine." *Their wills and Dorilian's.*

Rings glinting on unflinching hands, each Arch-Epopte picked up his staff. Each spoke his vote for removal on the basis that Quirin had broken the Covenant, that he had denied the Sordaneon god-right and thereby committed apostasy. While he stood unflinching before his Brothers at the table, suffering their witness and pity, Quirin knew more humiliation was yet to be visited upon him. The wearer of the Third Ring of Order approached and with reverent hands lifted from Quirin's shoulders the white and gold ceremonial stole denoting the primacy of Psilant. Next, at Pitar's bidding, Quirin drew over his head the heavy chain woven of mage metals. This he handed over. Only then from his finger did he twist the First Ring of Order until it came free. He had worn the holy device for more than fifty years.

"Quirin Chrysolemnos, of this ring and these enhancements you are divested. You are no longer Psilant of this Order; you stand no longer at the head of this Brotherhood." Despite his light voice, Pitar's solemn pronouncement felt heavy. Quirin experienced not liberation, but chains. Not relinquishment, but exile. Though he remained an Epopte, eagle-marked and bound by his vows, he was cast out of power.

Without the First Ring of Order, Quirin would never again walk alone into the Rill's secret places. Nevermore would he seek in private its hidden wonders or stand in solitary awe in witness of the Entity's energy flows, hoping to find answers.

Dorilian Sordaneon was not just removing Quirin from influence, he was taking Quirin's god from him.

Coram Barzanes had just reached the moment of climax when he felt Nammuor enter the room. Detecting that sinister presence banished any thought of pleasure from Coram's mind and withered his lust at the root. Rolling from atop the girl he had been enjoying so thoroughly, he blanched at his red-cloaked Master's look of amused dismissal.

"Begone," Nammour said to the girl. The order sent her running from the room without even a thought of modesty, and Nammuor's darkly glowing gaze followed her until the heavy door of carved wood slammed shut, leaving only the two men in a room with a great altar of a bed from which hung curtains the color of blood. "A toothsome bit. At least she's Staubaun. I appreciate your enthusiasm for repopulating Tahlwent with common bastards."

Coram had reached for his pants and was already putting them on. Of late only his bed had offered refuge from the cold. "Well-born ladies have fathers who wish them duly wed."

"As you will be. I have gathered twenty and five heiresses of pure blood to be wed to my loyal captains this day."

"This day? But I'm already wed to the mother of my sons in Teleg."

Nammuor's countenance froze Coram's protests. "What does that matter? You will have another wife this afternoon, and sire other heirs to inherit their grandfather's lands. It will be a marriage of state with no other pretense. Your wife in Teleg will bow to the necessity. And you will be no less free to pursue your usual appetites."

Coram held his tongue. Nammuor had been in an ill temper for weeks. Pacing the azure halls of the Halasseon Serat like a caged wolf, plotting sorceries he could not put into action because too many recent uses of the Diadem had weakened him. Coram felt only relief at seeing that Nammuor was not wearing the device. The Diadem's central jewel, compound and disturbing, possessed a blood-tinged malevolence none could long look upon. How Nammuor bore it was something Coram preferred not to think about.

But a month ago, mere weeks after raining destruction on Ogarth and without nearly enough days spent in regeneration, Nammuor had traveled to the Pillars of the Sky. He had been accompanied by three mages, those armed with powerful devices upon their brows. Only Nammuor had returned, pale and wasted. Like Ogarth before, that sorcery had succeeded. The Dazun had flooded such as it had not done in even the memories of Essera's gods. But Nammuor could not use the Diadem again, not so soon, and his inability was fueling a great impatience.

Nammuor studied the items on the bedside table. Finding a small dagger, he picked it up and turned it over. Locating a tiny switch on the embossed leather handle, he triggered it, releasing two spring-loaded swiping claws gleaming silver with poisoned tips. "This is a clever blade. Superb craftsmanship."

"Aral is filled with such treasures as this one. It was made by the Aryati in Gweroyen a thousand years ago." More than a thousand, though surely Nammuor already knew that. Mormantalorus too housed a treasury of Aryati devices, many of which Nammuor had catalogued and adapted to his own purposes.

The blade tapped against stone, claws clicked back into hiding and set down with a calculated care. "We are in those lands where legends come to life again," Nammuor noted, all too casually. "Gods settled here first and Immortals dwell here still. Who knows what forces we might awaken?"

"The Wall is fixed. So is the Rill. And Marenthro does nothing." Having accounted for the Immortals, Coram took a seat on his bed again and searched the floor for his boots.

A smile colder than Nammour's eyes touched his pale lips. "Not because he cannot. Because we never see his true shape, it's easy to underestimate him as an obstacle. Do not make that mistake. Marenthro's designs are masterful. Look what he has accomplished with Handurin. And Dorilian Sordaneon is no longer trapped in Sordan. The Highborn eagle now flies in Essera."

Coram laughed. "He hates Essera."

"Does he? Dorilian is in Lacenedon."

"What? That cannot be—"

"My information is good."

Then it must be true. "He has ever been a creature of action. Many have predicted he would not like being held without recourse in Sordan. So he found a way to unlock the bars."

"The Khelds were ever a weak link."

"They seemed strongly against him."

Nammuor eyed Coram balefully. "You take your eye off the design. Marenthro tossed my Sordaneon a fine piece to play, a Kheldish Prince—and Dorilian knew how to use him. Surely you can see by now that Handurin is but an elegant distraction?" Again, Nammuor glanced at the dagger, its deadliness well hidden. "I know Dorilian's mind. I know he plays games within games, and not least of them the game of his Highborn birthright."

Coram lifted a questioning eyebrow. He stood and began to belt his sword. "Derlon's heir to Derlon's powers born? Old tales. He shows no sign of that power."

"The Rill now goes to Amallar. That god awakened quietly— after it lurked for years beneath a veneer of dormancy."

"The Rill gift, great as it is, will not help him in battle. If Dorilian goes to war, his skill with a sword will do him more good than his Rill god."

Nammuor's gaze upon Coram darkened, that feral mind following every move, every gesture, assigning value. "You are a fool."

Not even a shadow of doubt touched Coram's certainty. He had slain many men in Nammuor's service, some of them Highborn. That Dorilian might be dangerous, he knew. The man was unpredictable and persistent, a superior opponent and swordsman—and that Dorilian healed from wounds that might kill common mortals was something even a man in the service of sorcery might respect.

"I know your plans for him," Coram assured Nammuor. "I but present his situation. His sorcery is unproved, as is this Handurin's leadership of the Khelds, all rumor and no substance. I do not spend all my time abed, Master. Perhaps your commanding of the Dazun to flood did not prevent the Sordaneon from joining his strategically repositioned army in Essera, perhaps that too was part of your design—but the Dazun surely thwarted Handurin and the Khelds. You have shown them the power they would face. They will think twice now before they try to cross."

"Did it thwart them?" Nammuor waved the door open, and together they stepped into the cold, smoothly lit corridor filled with light reflected from the sea. Even here the smell of salt hung in the air, recalling the warm sun and ocean breezes of distant Mormantalorus. Nammuor's red garment caught a gust that tugged it about his frame, a casual reminder that he still wore human flesh.

"Yes," Coram replied. "And the Khelds would have heard of what happened to their Trongorian friends by now. As other events in Essera filter to their ears, Handurin will soon strike the barbarians as more liability than bargain." Coram had barely spoken the words when an invisible hand of sorcerous power swirled its grasp around him and slammed him to his knees. Nammuor thrust a fistful of paper in Coram's face. Maps and missives. On them could be seen the bold strokes of Salkren Zel's writing and that of his archivist.

Coram went cold. *Missives.* Nammuor must have received them by way of array. Aside from Stauberg, the nearest one was at Trulo. In Dazunor.

"That flood stopped neither of them!" Nammuor tightened the sorcerous grip, gradually strangling Coram. "Handurin and his horde of filthy Khelds have taken Dazunor-Rannuli! Erenor respected that city's autonomy too well. He caved to the Seven Houses and the Rill-addled Epoptes and failed to fortify the city. He left it to them and, craven cowards that they are, they surrendered! They schemed to keep their Rill from me and now they do not have it at all. They'll dance to any tune Dorilian plays."

Coram gasped gratefully for air when the tight hold on his throat abruptly released. "Master, I—"

"You," Nammuor commanded, turning away from Coram, his mage-cloaked minions falling into line as he prepared to leave this corridor to which he seldom ventured, "will wed the three daughters of the Enlad of Bethan, thereby securing the old man's allegiance and his lands. You will then have a period to impregnate them." Like a malevolent wind, his crimson cloak twisting about him, Nammuor swept from Coram's gasping presence. The sea itself seemed to crash at the walls, the wind howling down the corridors, Nammour's voice trailing after. "Enjoy your nuptial moon. We leave after for Stauberg to battle with a man whom you and others have clearly underestimated."

# 19

My father's friendships with the Highborn were extensive
and profound. He counted among his close friends
Enreddon Malyrdeon and Sebbord Teremareon. Loss of
the latter friendship saddened him, and he regretted the
politics that kept them at cross-purposes. "Sebbord chose
Labran—as I would have done in his place," he said. "He
could not turn his back on his Hierarch and remain true to
his god or himself."
EMYLI STAUBERG-RANDOLPH, *REFLECTIONS OF THE KING*

The time had come to engage the Mormantalorans.

Hans assigned defense of Dazunor-Rannuli, still under threat from Erenor's troops in the Royal North, to Ionais of Merrydn, Euella of Rannul, and Emyli. Dorilian had told Hans Ionais could be trusted. And Emyli had funded an army of professional soldiers from Merrydn and Rannul to Hans's cause. The citizens of the city, including the Epoptes and the Denizens of three of the Seven Houses openly supported this move. Hans also left Orem Darm's river-wise Khelds, along with Davon Artos and a Sordani advisor, to arrange for provisioning Hans's troops during the next leg of his Esseran campaign: namely, to chase down a butcher.

Nammuor's general, Salkren Zel, outraged over having lost Dazunor-Rannuli, sought to squelch any support for Hans in the countryside. Keeping always a day ahead, Zel laid waste each village and farming compound, slaughtering all inhabitants but for those unfortunates he left behind to convey the message he wished to send.

At what had been a prosperous farm outside of Dyfern, a patrol from Hans's army found an old Kheld couple left alive. Zel's soldiers had blinded one and cut out the tongue of the other.

"I'll never hear my sweet wife's voice again," the old man

lamented. They clung to each other like infants who feared to let go. What they had witnessed let neither sleep. Hans's troops could do nothing for them but give them blankets and a promise of safety for the night, then a ride to a camp for refugees in the morning. There were too many such victims to care for them all.

"Damn them!" Nalf Rhys had developed a new hatred for their enemy. "They leave behind nothing but charred meat and fear!"

"It's not Khelds they're angry against!" the old man cried out piteously. "They told us. It's the Prince—he's in bed with the serpent. Khelds now breed with snakes, said they. Stefan rid the land of them, but Handurin has returned the Highborn evil to this land. He ought not do this wicked thing! Consorting with Sordan is the source of all our woes."

Though Nalf Rhys had craft enough of his own to see clearly what the enemy was doing, the lament remained the same at every turn, every burned town and pitiful refugee. Before the week was out, a trail of horror led from Dazunor-Rannuli to Orfudd, and the land was filled with pleas for Hans to break with his ally. Even many in his army came to believe he should do it. Only Euden Mezeon with his Merrydn cavalry, now over two thousand in number, the Trongorians under Farrl, and Kerr's Dannuthi force of five hundred stood against the Kheld disapproval.

"Where are *his* soldiers? Safely away from battle, tucked in Lacenedon, growing strong while waiting us out!" Fran protested heatedly. "We don't need the Sordaneon. *You* don't! Haven't we proven that? Keep your peace with him, if you must, but bid him go! Then the Southlanders will leave these people alone."

"No." Hans answered with the resolve he had begun to employ every time the matter arose. "Don't you see? The reason Nammuor's doing this isn't to drive Sordan from Essera, but to weaken *me*. Us! He prefers Sordan over Khelds a thousand times over. He's sowing division in *this* army!"

Nalf Rhys, too, added words of reason. "I've my own spears to take up with Sordan, but now's not the time. This alliance is what has got us this far and we'd be fools to turn our backs on it now! We'd do better to spend our wind catching those damn Southlanders! This madness is nothing that can't be stopped by putting our swords in their gullets!"

Most of the Khelds bore swords now and many had horses as well. Far from being ragtag, the army Hans commanded had coalesced into a respectable and well-provisioned fighting force. The Khelds knew the Rill had contributed to their stature, but few stopped to consider that the swords, armor, and horses had not simply appeared because they needed them. Those that did think about it assumed their Prince had paid for their good fortune. Particularly after seeing Dazunor-Rannuli and the newly retaken royal palaces there, they were convinced that Hans Thegn, like Stefan before him, now controlled the boundless riches of a royal treasury. Hans didn't tell them that, in one form or another, all of it came from Dorilian. There were many Khelds who might have thrown their swords to the ground had they known that, and Hans wanted every man well armed.

*All that I have, all that I am, I will now give over to battle*, Dorilian had told him. At the time, Hans had not stopped to think what that meant. Even now, he wondered.

There were times he simply watched in amazement as the vast production and wealth of the Sordaneons poured into arming the Khelds.

"It's getting colder," Nalf Rhys said to Hans as they camped beside the broken walls of a ruined stronghold. It had fallen centuries before to Ardaen, one of the Dannuthi soldiers had said. "Some of the lads are asking what's in it for them if they go on."

Hans turned in surprise. "In it for them?"

Nalf lifted an eloquent eyebrow, the hairs there stiff as spikes. "Lands, titles, commissions. What do they get?"

Hans shook his head. He'd begun hearing complaints from some Khelds that they were fighting too hard, and for what? He hadn't let them loot Dazunor-Rannuli and the Southlanders hadn't been leaving behind anything much worth looting in the towns they'd seen since. More and more, it seemed to Hans that his army of Khelds might not last through the winter.

He answered Nalf Rhys, quietly: "They'll get a Kheld as their King, not a Staubaun ruler who'd oppress them. They'll get peace in their lands, not war that will take their lands from them. They'll get a sword and a horse, and good pay while they're soldiers, with the opportunity to make whatever they want of their lives after." He stirred the fire with a stick, his gaze following the shower of sparks that flew up, dancing, in the air. "As for rewards, I plan to appoint Khelds to high office, but only those who are qualified to hold them. I plan to reward loyal people who distinguish themselves in my service with lands, but only lands that are vacant or forfeit to the crown. I plan to repeal any laws that prevent Khelds from owning property or engaging in commerce in any land in which I have authority. Once I am King, any person who has served honorably with me, or their widow or children, will be entitled to other things—but I will have to find out how much money I have left first." He met Nalf's answering guffaw with a grin.

Nalf regarded Hans slyly. "You know how the game is played, but you keep aiming to make your own rules."

"I'm not sure of much about being a king, but I don't want to be king of a nation of brigands. That would make me the greatest brigand of all."

"Now that is something your grandfather might have said." Nalf fixed his cup in a forked stick and held it for a minute in the fire to warm his grog. When he pulled it out, he caught the cup in his gloved hand and held it before his face for warmth before taking a sip. "I know what you're thinking: that Stefan gave in, let us fall into greed and indolence and that's what ruined him. But he talked like you did when he started. He meant it, then."

Hans believed it. Everything he'd learned about his brother pointed to a fervent and well-intentioned desire to lift the Khelds into Essera's mainstream. The patterns that had destroyed Stefan had come later. "He was misled, somewhere along the way."

"Maybe so. But he also had great enemies, powerful forces against him. You haven't fought against what he had to. He had the Highborn insurrection to deal with. He had them to fight. The Sordaneon may be the last one now, but he wasn't the last one then."

"Rheger Dannutheon." Hans pulled the name from memory. He had learned it from his tutors in Sordan and through conversations with Dorilian and others. Kerr ruled Dannuth because his mother had been Rheger's niece, daughter of the Prince who had died at Permephedon. Who Hans had seen die.

Nalf sighed. "The same. There were Malyrdeons still when Stefan became king. Marc Frederick had tamed them, married one's daughter, kept them in close counsel. But Stefan—they scorned him for being a Kheldman's son. Even our best blood wasn't good enough to groom their gardens."

"That attitude isn't dead."

"No, and that's another plank to hammer. But the Highborn and their sorcery, that's something you need to know about."

"I think I know enough."

"If nothing is enough. Because that's what you know if you think there's nothing to it." Nalf scowled darkly, warning him to listen. "They steal men's thoughts, the Highborn do, they suck men's souls. They live and breathe a different air than we do. They wear a different skin."

Hans stared at Nalf in disbelief. A different skin?

Nalf returned the stare, nodding. "You think I'm mad. That because you've met this Sordaneon and he wears the face of a man, that means he is one. Maybe he's just close to one, close enough to fool the world. Think of that."

"I'm not going to listen to this."

"You'd listen to Stefan if he told you. And he would. Because Rheger Dannutheon and that son of his taught him what the Highborn are."

Across the camp burned the bright fires of forges where smithies worked throughout the night to repair the machines and hardware of war. Hans listened to the clang of iron, the shouts, and the clatter. "Was that before—or after—Stefan killed them?"

Hans saw right away that his flippancy had angered Nalf. They often exchanged heated words leading to an inevitable impasse. This time, however, Nalf frowned and took a deep breath before pressing the point. "Before… and after. I was there with Stefan that day at Stauberg." Seeing that he had Hans's attention, Nalf continued, his words heavier than they had been. "He'd arrested them there for plotting insurrection. They'd gone to their Wall and were using it against him. They deserved to die for treason— but he'd sentenced them to house arrest."

Surprised, Hans looked up.

"Oh, yes." Nalf set down his cup. He removed his glove and blew into his hand. "Stefan wasn't eager to spill that blood. We all knew the tales, about their gods. About them. And the people were afraid. Staubauns. The Estol common folk. All of them. Afraid of what might happen because of it, to the Wall… to the World. The Staubauns, you know, had this Highborn holy idea that the Wall would end without their godborn royals. The Rill too. Maybe the World. And so Stefan promised. Promised he wouldn't hurt a hair on their heads.

"Instead he meant to send them away. Erenor and some troops of his waited to take the Highborn Princes to a ship in the harbor that would carry them to Aral. A palace for a prison. As soft an exile as any could ask for. Only thing is, the damned Princes didn't want to go. So Stefan said to those Highborn traitors, 'It's that or death. Give me a good enough reason to kill you, and I will.' I was there, so I heard it, and I saw. Rheger and Stefan faced each other, man to man. Something terrible happened between them then. Something terrible was said. The man's son attacked. Elhanan was his name. That was when the killing happened. Stefan had no choice but to order our lads to cut off their heads. But I saw Rheger smile first. Before they did it, I saw him smile."

Hans forced his tongue across dry lips. "But why?" he whispered, not sure how he should believe what he'd just heard. He sensed that Nalf was telling the truth. "They were unarmed. Why did Stefan kill them? He didn't have to."

Thin acknowledgment of something bitter curled Nalf's lip. "Why? Because the damned Highborn monster made him do it, that's why! Possessed him, and laughed, and would have turned him against his own men if Stefan hadn't killed him! Because if they'd lived, if they'd got away, they'd have only bred more monsters! That's when Stefan said they all must die, the Highborn. All of 'em. Before they breed more of their monstrous kind. He let Elhanan's baby live only because it was a girl child."

Stefan had been willing to kill *babies*?

Nalf cocked a look at the horror he saw on Hans's face. "See there? Stefan ruled an uneasy land and a treacherous people. And you know what the worst of it was? There in Stauberg? The Wall. It shook to its foundations, the city's foundations. The cursed thing knew they'd died. It howled like a beast wounded. The population saw that and went mad, the whole damn city, and ran screaming through the streets killing any Kheld they could get their hands on. We had to fight our way out for our very lives! But that Wall didn't die itself like all the naysayers who'd told Stefan not to execute those Highborn Princes said it would. It remained standing. It's standing there still, proud as ever. Even after its own blood was spilled, even after Stefan killed the last Highborn Princes in Essera, it's standing. But that day it shook and moaned to the winds—and there weren't a Kheldman who would stay in Stauberg after. Not one day. And there ain't none that will set foot in it since."

The next day the army moved toward Rainill on the river road to Trulo, the city that had for a time during Stefan's reign housed his court and capital. As the road began to wind into hills and forest, Hans made his way on horseback to the side of young Kerr, who smiled at Hans with the pleasant reserve that so marked the royal Staubaun caste. Hans eased his horse alongside that of the adolescent Bas.

"My brother ordered your uncle's death and your cousin's. So why have you joined me? Why don't you hate me?"

Kerr ducked his head, looking to each side to see if he could speak freely. "There are people who will think I should."

"You don't?"

"No. I don't hate Stefan either. It's difficult to explain."

"I'd like to hear it."

"Perhaps you can understand. You've met Dorilian. I haven't, but... you may have some idea. The way the Highborn view the World can be quite perplexing." Kerr looked behind him, toward the ensigns of his bodyguard. The older men were conversing with Hans's Trongorian guards. "The Highborn keep their secrets perhaps too well. My uncle Rheger was a noble man, distant at times, but meditative and devoted to the Cibulitan philosophy that existence defines truth. That the Mind cannot hold falsehoods— and that if the Mind does hold a lie, it also holds the truth that cancels it. It's Highborn thinking. I only know how the Mind worked in this case because Rheger did not die without having spoken about the matters that led to his demise. He was falsely accused of his treason. But not by Stefan."

"By whom, then?"

"Erenor."

Of course. Erenor had been setting into place his own eventual grab for power. Removing the last pillars of Highborn rule—the rightful successors to Stefan's throne—had surely been part of that plan. Hans regarded the youth beside him, wondering to what extent Kerr resembled the ruler he'd succeeded. He was still young but would soon make a handsome man with a will as durable as any Kheld's. Erenor had gambled on an ineffective guardianship, not foreseeing that the next in Dannuth's royal line would be a strong-minded boy sprung from even stronger-minded parents. Through Sinon Kouranos, Hans had heard the tale of how Grenant Staubaun Aigelleros, though but a minor lord who'd wooed and wed a

Highborn Prince's daughter for love, had after Stefan's death refused to swear allegiance to Erenor, punctuating the refusal by denying Erenor a garrison in Dannuth. The domain's capital of Kyrbasillon had been under siege ever since. Kerr himself had been left unmolested at Permephedon with the hope that when he took power he would be more malleable than his father.

"But why did Stefan kill Rheger and Elhanan?" Hans couldn't put the question out of his mind. "Do you know that?"

Kerr lifted his young face, and the wind blew his pale-gold hair back against the fur of his cap. "No. No one knows why he did that. Except—" His gaze found refuge in the sight of the supply wagons being drawn along the road.

"Except what?" Hans prodded. Nalf Rhys and Rannuf approached across a trodden field. People had noticed the two royal persons were sharing company.

"Rheger didn't condemn him for it. Neither did Elhanan." Something light filled the words. Wonder, perhaps. "This is going to sound strange because you haven't grown up with them, but the Highborn don't read men's thoughts. Not really. They feel them. But they can *be in* men's thoughts. Especially the Malyrdeons when they are in Stauberg. Their affinity with the Wall Entity is strongest there. I think that's how Rheger and Elhanan were in my thoughts that last day. And not mine only. My father, my mother, even some of the retainers of our household. The doomed men's thoughts"— Kerr sighed—"were not against Stefan. Not completely. They felt themselves unjustly condemned, yes, and they believed Stefan tragically misguided. Rheger's mind, especially, was thick with apprehension of something—or someone—else."

"Erenor?" Hans asked. "Or Nammuor?"

"I don't know. Feelings are ephemeral and can be difficult to assign. But I think the Sordaneon might know, being Highborn himself. He would have been in the Mind with them."

Nalf was in earshot now, and others would soon join them. Hans smiled at Kerr and clapped his arm. What he had learned was enough. Great as Stefan's crime in executing the last Highborn Princes of Dannuth had been, whatever his part in making that awful event come to pass, Rheger Dannutheon himself had not died cursing Stefan's name, but another's. And Dorilian had known whose. However much Dorilian might damn what Stefan had done, he could not deny a truth.

Hans remembered something else, something Dorilian had said about Stefan having given Nammuor control of Stauberg's seas. How Stefan had allowed Nammuor to establish a bridgehead in Essera—at Aral.

*Nammuor.* Stefan had been about to send the Dannutheons away, but not to an honorable exile. A vicious predator had been lying in wait. A sorcerer who enslaved Highborn lives in malignant crystals.

Something cold seized Hans's gut and clawed toward his heart. His dream came back to him, the one visioned within a shaman's spell in Chuquiago. Stefan's haunted eyes and boast. *I killed the rest of his demon-breed.*

At last Hans knew why Stefan had done that—and why Nammuor had killed him for it.

# 20

The Trans-Hesperian northlands of the Eleutheron,
Gweroyen and the Lakes region of Lacenedon are wildly
beautiful. The mountains there stand tall even where they
crowd the sea. The lakes of the Ulnossi, however, water
the most serene and lovely land in the Royal North, home
to vineyards and orchards, pastures and estates. Staubauns
have long guarded it well—from invasions and each other.
PATROLOCUS, *JOURNEYS TO MANY LANDS*

A line of men and horses crossed the featureless white plain
that, in summer, would be a lake. It was winter, and the long
body of fresh water that defended the east face of Askyllon had
frozen. Aubrey had glimpsed Askyllon's clifftop battlements on the
last occasion she'd raised her head to take a look, but she hadn't
looked for quite a long while. It unsettled her to know she walked
atop water that was fathoms deep.

The Lacenedoni soldier leading the way glanced back over his
shoulder and shook his head. *Khelds!* Aubrey heard him mutter.
*Useless!*

The party had come upon Askyllon's guard outpost that
morning. They'd presented documents attesting their purpose, and
it had fallen to one of the post's soldiers to guide them across the
trackless lake, by far the shortest route to the fortress. Judging by
the soldier's stares, Aubrey and Arne were either the first Khelds
he'd ever seen or unlike any other Khelds he'd seen. The soldier
rolled his eyes every time any member of the party, including two
men sent by Sinon Kouranos and a score of well-armed Sordani
guards, were clumsy on the ice. Sadly, they were clumsy every
other step. Even their horses were inexperienced and were being
led behind them, making their progress even slower.

"Step it up, will you?" Their guide pointed to the west. "You want to be on solid ground before it gets dark, don't you?"

Aubrey looked. Clouds trooped along the Ulnossi mountain chain in threatening overtures to a storm.

"Speaking of solid ground, you promised there'd be some." Arne distrusted the ice so much he hadn't lifted his head even once.

"Of course there is! This isn't the Lost Sea, you know. But it won't dash out to meet you. You want solid land, you got to *get* to it. If you would take your eyes off the lake, you'd see that the fortress is big as any man could hope for. It's right there in front of you. It would cheer you up if you'd just take a peek."

"No thanks." Arne was having problems enough dealing with walking across the slick, glassy surface.

Aubrey thought the surface felt solid enough, even though the water beneath it was said to be as deep as the mountains were tall. So far the Royal North was proving to be a land of frozen beauty and heart-stopping wonder. On their journey to the Bas of Lacenedon's fortress, Aubrey and her party had seen primarily vistas of frost-flowered hills and prosperous farms. Since skirting Permephedon, where Sordan's emissaries had picked up documents from the Brotherhood of Epoptes, the delegation had avoided the region's many flourishing towns. The towering High Citadel had been daunting enough. For two nights Permephedon's arcane nature had burned white in the distance, visible across the Lacenedon plain, its towers taller and grander even than Sordan.

Inspired by the guide, Aubrey ventured to raise her head for a better look at Askyllon, built atop a high cliff at the edge of the lake. Although massive, the fortress did not meet her expectations. She had thought to see shining towers and smooth surfaces gleaming even in the gloom of this overcast sky. Instead, what she saw reminded her more of Rhodhur: strong walls of dark stone and stalwart architecture, framed by supporting buttresses and arched gates. There was even wood to be glimpsed in the roofs and portals, and the road scaling the bluffs to the fortress was of coarse gravel and chopped ice.

"That's it?" she asked, disappointed.

"Expecting Permephedon, were you?" the soldier snapped.

By the time they reached shore and set foot upon the road that would take them to the fortress, cobwebs of rivulets had begun to freeze upon the road. The stones themselves seemed to grow diamonds. The party mounted their horses again and made better progress. Where they topped the bluffs, the path led onto a broad plateau crowned by the fortress. Though Aubrey noticed they had but a short distance to ride, she saw that every field to the east and north of the road bristled, dotted with the tents and constructions of a huge encampment. By its green-bordered silver wolf banners, they knew they had found the Sordani army that had left Neuberland and made its way north, bypassing Rannul and Merrydn. Here, on this desolate highland, that force had joined with Lacenedon's army. Banners of emerald bordered with silver, black, or gold waved in a wide current along the southern edge of a solid field of cerulean, light and dark, broken by yellow and red. Against the gray afternoon sky, the banners and the men with them filled the plain. No greater army had been assembled in Essera in living memory.

Arne gave Aubrey a look that asked why, if there had been this great a Sordani force in Neuberland, the Khelds hadn't been annihilated. She answered with a glare.

Walls that had seemed rough and formidable from a distance loomed even more fearsome, lichen-covered and enduring. The fortress had taken forty years to build, their guide told them, and in a thousand years had never fallen to an enemy nor known a Kheldish foot until a week ago. They passed beneath three ranks of iron gates into Askyllon's cavernous maw.

Under the scrutiny of watchtowers, an immense courtyard capable of harboring a thousand mounted men opened before them. Mountain gravel gave way to flagstones set on beds of sand, uncluttered and clean. A line of mounted guards conducted formations near the far wall but the small party of Sordani and Khelds passed no other troops as they entered. By dint of a length greater than its width, the yard directed all eyes to the largest and grandest of the resident structures, the Keep, which dominated the yard. Approached by wide stairs and terraced landings, it was also the only building boasting arched, paned windows in its daunting facade. Colossal stone bears stood guard at the foot of the landing, menacing all arrivals. Golden claws and teeth glinted in the thin light.

Upon entering the courtyard, Aubrey followed the others of the party by dismounting where directed. A bevy of boys in blue and black livery ran from positions beside the stairs to grasp bridles and hold the animals while the riders secured their gear. Not sure what to do next, Aubrey shouldered her pack and looked to Arne.

"I say we do what they do." Arne indicated the two Sordani emissaries, who had just walked confidently to the foot of the stair leading to the Keep. Aubrey nodded. Lacenedon was unknown territory. It was best in this case to let the Sordani lead the way.

Several men emerged from the Keep and descended to meet the newly arrived delegation on the broad middle landing. Aubrey counted three nobles attended by two youths and four guards. Two of the nobles merely nodded but deferred to a tall man richly garbed in a long cloak of gray-brown bearskin over a tunic of embroidered velvet, gold adornments showing at his throat and wrist. Despite the man's finery, he was bareheaded. Gold-bright hair almost completely gone to silver accentuated the chiseled perfection of his features and the cool manner with which he greeted his guests. Both Sordani emissaries bowed deeply, which earned polite accord, but only that. For the bows of Aubrey and Arne, the man gave no response at all.

*Bas Hebron Staubaun Ursenos.* Aubrey noted the bear crest on the gilded jacket and was glad to have spent so many extra hours studying Robdan's books. Through his mother, Hebron was grandson of a Highborn Prince and grandnephew of Lacenedon's last Highborn ruler. His father's mother had been similarly royal. Twice royal, then. Hebron would have needed to be Highborn himself to be any higher.

The emissary to whom Sinon Kouranos had entrusted Sordan's official messages bowed and gave his name and that of his aide before stating his mission. "Most Noble, we have business for the Thrice Royal's personal attention from the hand of his Archhalial ambassador. Where might we find him?"

"It would please me to oblige you immediately." Hebron spoke using the tight, slightly archaic consonants of the north. "However, His Thrice Royal Grace rode out this morning to review his troops and has yet to return. We expect him soon. Until then, accept our hospitality." Hebron's gaze slipped to Arne and Aubrey, standing nearby in their woolen wrappings and hoods, and his mouth curved sourly. "Your companions should seek shelter outside the gate."

"You must speak about that with them, Most Noble."

"We're also part of the business," said Arne.

Hebron frowned. Arne had not addressed him in proper form.

A shout from the watchtower lifted heads throughout the fortress and cut short any impending answer. Armed men wearing

Sordan's colors emerged from the guard towers to line the courtyard approach. Bas Hebron turned to the alerted couriers.

"You're in luck. The Hierarch returns." Aubrey noted how Hebron's gaze slid again to her and Arne and lingered for their reaction.

An echoing clatter broke the quiet within the courtyard, preceding a sweep of color and men into the open space. Three horses of shining ivory cantered through the arches of the gate, followed by an escort of twenty men mounted on steeds caparisoned in emerald silk emblazoned with the Sordaneon eagle. Aubrey studied each ivory horse and its rider when they pulled to a halt before the stairs.

There was no mistaking Dorilian. It wasn't just that his horse was magnificent, its trappings resplendent with gems and its hoofs encased in the rare bright-hard silver of royalty. Neither was it because Dorilian was clothed in outstanding richness or that every soldier in the courtyard dropped to one knee. All these things appeared *natural*. Aubrey wasn't surprised. In every way, Dorilian stood out from other men. He always had, even in Amallar. One of the noble Lacenedoni youths, not a stable boy, ran down the steps to grasp the white stallion by its heavy bridle while Sordan's ruler dismounted without any of the awkwardness one might have expected from a man wearing light armor and bearing a battle sword.

Although he must have noticed Arne and Aubrey before he ascended the steps, Dorilian gave no sign of recognition. He greeted Bas Hebron, who bowed deeply, and then turned to acknowledge the Sordani emissaries. Both weathered men dropped to their knees and touched Dorilian's extended hand in gestures that conveyed genuine joy at being honored. The Sordani nobles who had just ridden in also dismounted and ascended to stand with their Hierarch.

"We bring messages for Your Thrice Royal Grace from Sordan. A letter also from your ambassador." The first Sordani courier extended the packet he bore. "And we bring greetings from Prince Handurin Stauberg-Randolph of Dazunor."

No introduction for her or Arne, Aubrey noticed. She couldn't tell if the lapse was deliberate. Dorilian simply nodded his satisfaction. "We will have to see about getting him properly installed there." Just hearing his voice again made Aubrey's heart pound. "Will he advance to Permephedon?"

"I do not know, Thrice Royal. When we left him, he was in Dazunor-Rannuli."

Dorilian took the bundled letters in hand and passed the packet to the man standing beside him. Aubrey recognized Legon Rebiran, now very changed from the man she had met in Sordan. Legon still projected an unsettling aura of warning, but that alertness now had focus. While the Witan had been hammering out its agreement with Sordan, Legon had traveled by Rill to Permephedon and then made his way north along with added troops to his Hierarch's side.

Aubrey focused on breathing as if the world had not shattered into pieces.

She had known seeing Dorilian again would be difficult, but she'd not expected the experience to be so forceful. She knew this man by the way he moved, the tug of his smile, the caress of his voice, and bite of his words. His reality was so sharp that it hurt. She could not see him as a stranger. That he might dismiss her and Arne, assigning them no significance, wounded her and let her know he held a weapon she herself had put into his hand.

His next words felt distant, unanchored. "The Khelds are to be accorded the status of ambassadors and housed in the Keep. They're also to attend the banquet tonight. I will take my two men with me and see to their quarters myself. The soldiers of their escort will join the Seventh outside the walls."

"Of course, Thrice Royal." Everything about Hebron was cool, even his response.

Legon walked ahead and was first through the door, which the third Sordani noble held open. Dorilian, however, paused on the doorstep, trailed by the two emissaries, and pondered something, then turned back. "And Hebron, please inform Master Aelfricson of the Khelds' arrival. He'll be pleased to know his kinsfolk are here—especially his niece."

Hebron's dark eyes became visibly rounder. "Niece?"

Hebron was not alone in following the Hierarch's gaze to see which of the new guests was not masculine. Aubrey felt her cheeks burn and she glared back into Dorilian's gray eyes. They regarded her with cynical amusement. He had recognized her from the first.

*There you are*, Aubrey thought, feeling the ice from his hard, cold smile slide between her ribs. *I have finally met you, Dorilian Sordaneon. And I don't think I like you.*

A result he appeared determined to be set in stone. "Yes, we have ourselves a lady in our midst, although one would never guess it by her appearance. It might be to her benefit to find herself in the company of your Gwenna."

The bewildered Hebron responded with a nod of agreement. He continued to stare unabashed at Aubrey, frankly examining her as though trying to decide what kind of woman would travel a great and dangerous distance in the company of soldiers and with but one male companion. Hebron waited until Dorilian and his men had disappeared into the Keep before he spoke to his Kheldish guests.

"We have only recently had your people as guests. You are welcome on the word of my godborn cousin and on behalf of your Prince. We do have rules. You are not to leave these walls and would be wise to stay within the confines of the Keep. I expect you to follow the conventions of proper address and form while you are in my court. We have a great many persons of high rank in residence and I will not have my guests insulted by improper manners or inattention to their privileges."

Without waiting for their response, Hebron directed his white-haired chamberlain to hold the heavy door and led the way into the Keep. Aubrey and Arne followed into a vast entry hall. Perhaps in light other than the dim, powdery sunbeams drifting through high, narrow windows, the room would have acquired a less oppressive grandeur. The floors were beautifully inlaid of many kinds of wood and carpeted with thick rugs, examples of which also hung on the walls alongside other works of art. Huge braziers shaped like flowers or trees warmed the lofty chamber. Two staircases, one on each side of the hall, led to the upper levels. It was there, at a landing between the staircases, that Hebron left them in the care of the chamberlain.

"See to them, Isvan."

Arne watched Hebron walk away before leaning over to Aubrey and speaking in Khelda. "We sure have a Staubaun in that one, don't we?"

Aubrey nodded and rolled her eyes. A Staubaun Lord, to be sure. And a Highborn Hierarch, too, under the same roof. If ever arrogance could be compounded, they'd found the height of it.

Aubrey looked about the room she had been given and knew she should be more impressed. Located on an upper floor of the central tower, the chamber was beautifully appointed and, though she was sure it was not the best to be had, it was nonetheless a nest of luxury in these barren reaches of Essera. It certainly surpassed the tent in which she'd slept the last several days. She wondered how much to make of her accommodations. Among Staubauns, the quality of a room revealed a thousand nuances about a person's status. She had no illusion about how she had come to this largesse.

Pushing the hood from her head, Aubrey slumped onto the bench at the foot of the pretty bed. She studied the contrast her rough boots made on the elegant carpet, how shapeless her winter gear looked in the full-length mirror that ludicrously caught her eye. She saw herself: dark-haired, wary-eyed, wild. Did she really look like that? Her expression would terrify a highwayman. Moved to test that image, she smiled, then stopped, stunned by the change.

*It's not as though you've never looked in a mirror before!* she chided herself.

Restless, she stood again and stripped off her cloak and outer leathers. She almost missed hearing the soft knock on the door.

"Lady?" a light, female voice called.

"Who's there?"

"Laavi, a maid. Come to see you settled. May I come in?" The door cracked open just enough for a pale face and two bright eyes to peer around it.

Aubrey waved her visitor in. For a moment, she and Laavi stared at each other. The girl had looked shorter at first only because she had bent over to peer around the door. In truth, Laavi was Staubaun tall, with great braids of golden hair neatly falling below her shoulders. She was the first to smile, with self-conscious welcome.

"Pardon me for staring, lady, but I have never seen a woman of the Kheld people before. Or any Kheld at all! I'm so glad you speak Stauba!" She spoke in the melodiously inflected Stauba of the Royal North.

"So am I, though I was not expecting a Staubaun lady," Aubrey admitted. She wondered if this meek creature was Gwenna.

"A lady? Or Staubaun? Oh, no, lady, I am an Estol girl of no rank at all! I'm a servant-in-training to the Lady Gwenna, Bas Hebron's favorite."

"Oh." The lapse flustered Aubrey. She should have known that in Essera she would meet fair-haired folk who were not Staubaun. Nor was she accustomed to servants. Khelds had few servants, and Hebron's fortress seemed to have little else. They even had servants-in-training.

"I've been instructed to see to your bath, lady, and your preparations for the banquet tonight. You have been summoned to attend."

Aubrey froze. "Summoned?"

"By the Thrice Royal Hierarch Sordaneon. Bas Hebron said."

"Oh, that," Aubrey recalled, adding a shrug. She had told Arne to inform Robdan she would not attend. "It was just a request."

Laavi's brown eyes widened. "The Thrice Royal doesn't make requests. It is as he wishes."

Of course. Among Staubauns anything Dorilian Sordaneon said would be carried out without question—and he had said Aubrey and Arne were to be at the banquet.

"Great! As he wishes." Aubrey sighed and dropped her pack, which she had been holding all the while. It landed on the floor with such a thud that Laavi could only stare at it. The girl quickly regained her composure.

"Oh, lady, surely it will be fine. I'll draw a hot bath and wash your hair and dress it for you. I'm training to be a lady's maid and, though I'm not yet accomplished in all things, I'm very good at hair! And let's take a look at your gowns." Laavi glanced around. "Have you your baggage?"

"This is it." Aubrey nudged her pack.

The girl could not believe it. "That? No trunk of gowns? Have you no jewel case or box of toiletries?"

"No. Just some plain clothes such as I have on now, a nice silk blouse and my very best overdress. It was good enough in Dazunor-Rannuli. Water, some food, medicines. But nothing fine. I don't usually need it."

Perplexity reigned on Laavi's young face. "But surely, lady, you have occasion. Bas Hebron said you are cousin to Prince Handurin of Dazunor, and I cannot believe a Prince of Dazunor would not give parties! Have you no dress to wear at all?"

"I have nothing to wear to some lord's fancy banquet." Aubrey stopped abruptly, remembering. "Oh, wait! I have this." She knelt and retrieved from her pack, where she had carried it with her, just as Levyathan had told her to and only because it was so lightweight and thin, the small cask of silvery wood. She rose and laid it on the bed, where both young women stood, silently looking at it.

"What is it?" Laavi asked at last.

"I don't know. The one who gave it to me said that I should only open it when I had nothing to wear. And I just said that I didn't."

"If there's something to wear in that little box, it's probably not much more than a slip! Just the sort of thing a man would do!"

"No. He's not a man—well, not exactly." Aubrey still wasn't completely at ease with the boy she'd met in Sordan, whose words had carried so many meanings. "But he wasn't the kind to give bad gifts." It took her two attempts to get the latch, but then the cask opened, the top sliding neatly to one side. Inside gleamed the sheen of fine fabric.

"Why, look at that!" Laavi gasped in delight. She helped Aubrey pull the dress out and together they held it up in amazement. Both of them looked back at the casket, knowing that what they held could never be put back within. More amazing still was that the garment looked ready to be worn, without a hint of crease or disorder. A bodice of silvery green adorned with seed pearls and beads of finest jade flowed into a satin skirt of smoothly mellow gold striped with that same misty forest color.

"It's gorgeous, lady!" Laavi ran the fabric through her hands, again and again. "I have not seen finer in all of Lacenedon! And look!" she exclaimed, her amazement redoubled. "There are slippers too!" She reached into the box again and held up a pair of velvet slippers, embroidered as the dress was with jade beads and pearls.

Aubrey swallowed. Her throat was dry. "I don't suppose there are any jewels in there?" She figured she might as well ask.

Her faith now fixed on wonders, Laavi looked. "No, lady. Nothing of that. But can you believe all this in that little box? I would like to meet this man of yours!"

Easing herself to sit on the bed, Aubrey continued to stare at the box, the dress laid out beside it. How had Levyathan known? How *could* he have known? Her mind swarmed with half-forgotten tales of the Sordaneons and their strangeness, that they were the descendants of demons and that the Highborn either saw or created the future.

And then she laughed, not caring how or why.

*He knew I'd need something to wear!*

Her heart lightened, Aubrey turned to Laavi, who was posing in the mirror, holding the gown before her and admiring it from every angle. Part of the plan for the evening, Aubrey was certain, would be for the Staubaun gathering to show off their finery. Well, she, at least, was going to look as fine as any lady in the room!

"I think I'll be wanting that bath, Laavi. And your services as a hairdresser too. Now that I have something to wear," Aubrey declared with a fierce grin, "I'll have a thing or two to show any man who would set me in my place."

# 21

Staubaun table manners are more than they seem. As among our folk, people get to eat in peace without fighting for their every morsel or getting stabbed for a joint of beef. But Staubaun manners also create opportunities to converse with people similarly constrained to converse with you. In the grandest sense, their etiquette allows for displays of culture, hierarchy, and prowess. When you get down to it, Staubaun table manners are a mating game.
Tobold Forbasson, *A North Country Primer*

The lights were bright, and the music wafted soft and low. There was something of an air of Sordan about Askyllon that night, a suggestion of warmer places and merrier circumstances, prompted perhaps by the influx of Sordani nobles into the staid Lacenedoni ranks. Or, Robdan thought, maybe it was the Hierarch himself who called to mind the distant land that was his home. As he sat at the head of the table, flanked by Hebron Ursenos and the fortress's commander, Dorilian Sordaneon fascinated the crowded hall with the same regal presence that kept Sordan's royal court in thrall. His attire was rich—splendid, even—but he did not need gems for brilliance or the gleam of gold to look invaluable. Dorilian was invaluable. He was Rillborn and, more than that, he was rare: a living reminder and promise of a race nearly extinct. The noble persons seated at the royal table seemed to draw radiance from the Highborn presence among them, to be enlarged, and they spoke with the animation and flavor of a chosen people. Privilege draped them like the gift of beneficent gods.

In such society, Robdan Aelfricson felt like a blot. He knew that he also looked like one. He'd elected to dress in dark colors, the reason being that he had packed nothing else. He'd also brought no coin with which to attempt to purchase something more festive, and even to borrow something better would have required too much of a tailor. He was shorter than any of them, half-grown youths aside. Robdan consoled himself by observing that Dorilian also wore dark colors and an uncluttered style. He was equally quick to admit that the effect was vastly different. Dorilian wore rich deep colors to accentuate the bright tones in his hair and the fairness to be found in his features, with the purpose of heightening his apparent Staubaunness. Robdan simply didn't wear his vestments with the same authority. He lacked something. Presence, perhaps.

Robdan glanced to the other table where Aubrey sat and approved of what he saw. He was happy she had chosen to attend the banquet. It did Khelds no good to hide out of view, letting Staubauns think them too uncivilized for proper company. But that gown she was wearing—where had she gotten it? It clothed her in refined beauty, as flattering as it was appropriate, even if it was cut in Staubaun fashion and revealed her body in ways that alarmed him. Gifts only hinted at when wrapped in homespun woolens showed through enticingly once clothed in silk and Aubrey's own shimmering loveliness. Robdan noticed that some of the Staubaun men could barely take their eyes off her. And yet that didn't worry him nearly as much as what he noticed when he followed Aubrey's frequent glances to the head of the table. *Mother be merciful! Did she have her heart set on* that *one?* Aubrey could have any man at the table tonight if she wanted, from the Staubaun nobleman seeking to converse with her on her left to Bas Hebron himself, whose gaze was overtly bold. Even Arne, as alarmed as Robdan at the attention she was garnering, glowered at Aubrey to stop.

This night, Robdan thought, was not going to end well.

Aubrey ignored her kinsmen's attempts to restrain her. Until recently she'd seldom been in purely Staubaun—or noble—company and was not about to give up this opportunity to exercise valuable social skills. Might she be out of her element? Perhaps, but she wasn't too far out... and she was not to be slighted. She dared anyone to tell her she didn't belong here. Her missions to Sordan and the Seven Houses had taught her much. Prior to sitting for dinner she had conversed with the Bas of Gweroyen and his father, answering questions about Hans's success in Dazunor-Rannuli. If this was the world into which Hans Thegn and the Rill would propel her people, then Aubrey would learn the way of it. She watched a bright stream of after-dinner cordial ripple to fill a glass as fragile as melting ice. Her fingers traced the dainty stem, wondering if it would snap between them. But the liqueur within, when Aubrey sipped it, reminded her of Sordan too, with a taste of oranges just short of sweet and a heat like that of the southern sun. She set the glass aside and smiled.

"*Marmairein*." Her Staubaun neighbor gave Aubrey a warm, masculine look that invited conversation. "The elixir of golden Teremar."

"Teremar, yes. I remember." Aubrey thought back to her night in Sordan and the food and entertainment at the Teremari Bas's table. "Tiflan's country."

"*Tiflan*, is it?" His laughter was as free of guile as his gaze. "Leave it to a Kheld to get on name terms with the highest folk in the land and then flaunt it in your face!"

Aubrey joined him in laughter. She knew Staubaun rules of formal address. *Bas* Tiflan, she should have called him. In Sordan, however, he had told Aubrey to call him by name and she had gotten used to thinking of Tiflan that way during the negotiations in Amallar. Most Staubauns would have frowned at Aubrey's lapse, yet her dinner companion found her amusing. Curiosity moved her to consider him more carefully. He was Sordani, to judge by his light accent. And he was noble, or he wouldn't be seated at the left hand of one of Hebron's nobles. Aubrey recalled the third rider who had arrived with Dorilian and Legon earlier that afternoon, the officer she hadn't taken the time then to notice. She saw him now as a handsome man of perhaps forty years, with chiseled aristocratic features in a lean face. Although the pale track of a scar cut from his left cheek into the golden hair at his temple, she thought it did not detract from his good looks.

"And you are?" Aubrey perused him above the rim of her glass as she took another sip of *marmairein*.

"Bersyas Staubaun Garheleon, at your service."

Aubrey's jaw dropped. She'd heard of Bersyas—many times. "I believe The Neuberland Warmonger is your current sobriquet." She bit back several more cutting remarks for the sake of the company she kept.

Bersyas gave her a mocking smile. "I believe it is, among Khelds. I'm also called the Hound of Bane and the Bastard of Sar'Pryannis. My Hierarch warned me to expect your hostility. Do I have it?"

"You certainly do!"

"That's unfortunate. Yet strange alliances often breed interesting bedfellows." Bersyas drew a finger along his scar. "A *skifr* gave me this. Two years ago. Kettlebreck Hill. And don't tell me you launched it."

Aubrey examined the scar, which had knitted cleanly and well, then smiled at him sweetly. "I'm afraid not. I have better aim than that."

He burst out with a purely masculine laugh of appreciation. "Kheld to the bone, you are. A lovely lady, and one who can wield a weapon as sharp as her tongue."

"Where I come from, women know that a tongue is a poor weapon if not backed up with a blade."

Newly appraising, Bersyas settled back in his chair. "So it's true you're from Neuberland? I could have guessed it, so much fire and such finely honed words."

Aubrey turned the pretty glass in her fingers, studying Bersyas across its glittering shape. "I'm surprised your Hierarch didn't tell you that."

"He only said the topic would be delicate. Apparently, it was for me to learn why."

"It might have something to do with your army burning the village of Tredargh last winter." She met his glower with one of her own. "The displacement of all the people and slaughtering of livestock, destroying the Afmarren bridge."

"I remember the village," he said, evenly. "It was not supposed to be there."

"Neither were you."

Bersyas laughed. "But there I was. And there they were. Surely one had to give way to the other. They were wise to flee my cavalry." He leaned toward Aubrey, his tone dropping to something warmer. "Don't tell me you were there and that I overlooked you."

"No. I was in the hills of Saemoregh, tending to the people you drove from their homes."

"Saemoregh. The town is well defended. Stefan kept a garrison there."

"And now Prince Handurin does." Aubrey had seen to that before agreeing to join him.

"What a pity you are determined to hate me." Bersyas smiled with the first hints of persistence and leaned nearer still. "You don't look as though you'd be averse to a hot-blooded man or a good tumble in bed."

Aubrey looked at him in astonishment: Bersyas had spoken in a Khelda that was only slightly imperfect, bearing traces of both Sordan and Neuberland Stauba accents. More revealing was that he'd used an idiom of Neuberland origin. He must have had close association with Khelds to have developed such fluency. Only then did Aubrey notice the intense and curious glances directed at them from around the room at hearing a barbarous tongue being spoken.

Hebron was the first to raise the matter. "General Bersyas. What words are so secret they cannot be spoken in a civilized language?"

Bersyas recovered his formal demeanor and bowed his head as he addressed the Bas. "Most Noble, I ask pardon if my words have offended. I was but complimenting the lady in her own language, hoping to please her."

"And is she pleased?" Dorilian inquired. Aubrey wondered if he had been listening—or if Bersyas, any of them, knew that Dorilian too spoke Aubrey's language.

She gave Dorilian and the rest of the royal gathering a shattering smile. "Indeed I am, Thrice Royal. Though the compliment did not strike the mark."

Aubrey knew as well as the other diners about General Bersyas's fondness for Kheldish women and that he was known to have kept a succession of Kheldish mistresses.

Dorilian frowned. "We understand your ambitions for the lady, Bersyas," he said to his chastened general. "However, we feel you should find some other activity to which you could devote your energy this evening."

"Yes, Sire."

As though the table had rotated to exclude them, conversation returned to its ebbing tide of politics. Aubrey could not escape a baleful glance from Robdan expressing his displeasure with her deportment.

For his part, Arne simply drew his finger across his throat, indicating to her his feelings about what he wanted Aubrey to do... or perhaps what Aubrey could expect from Arne later.

On the eve of war, even doomed men might dance. Dorilian watched the sea of glittering couples moving upon the dance floor, and wondered which ones would not return from Stauberg's cold white fields. He could have told it, were he a Malyrdeon. A Wall Lord could have looked into each man's life and seen where it would take him. But that was a power he had never sought, afraid that if he should ever start looking into the fates of others, he would see his own.

He had been in this forsaken land long enough to have acquired a deeper hatred for it. Six weeks of armies and camp tents and Hebron's cold company—of trying to forge a smattering of northern lords into a coalition that might succeed in wresting the Royal North out of Erenor's grasp. They might do it yet if his conversation this evening with emissaries from Gweroyen and the Eleutheron bore the desired fruit.

"Surely you will join the dance, Thrice Royal?" Gwenna, the soft-spoken female who had taken the seat to his right at the advent of post-meal dances, was lovely and accommodating; precisely what Dorilian expected of Hebron's taste in women.

He shook his head. "Surely not. I have no desire to turn this pretty party into a spectacle."

"We would be honored if you would do so."

He studied the dancers and their movements. "Have you ever wondered why we dance?"

Gwenna's amber eyes twinkled when she smiled. "Because Leur once danced on the skin of forever and the firmament gave birth to the Child of Dawn?"

Dorilian looked at her, surprised. He had not thought her profound—or did she merely repeat ancient stories? Dance ran parallel with Creation. The Leur of *that* story had danced alone within the Void and given birth to Itself. Yet most people danced, as did these high folks tonight, where others might see them. Why was that? Because it was important that others should see? Because, for some, it was their only opportunity to be with someone they otherwise must pretend did not interest them?

Dorilian let his gaze wander the room until he found Aubrey, standing with her kinsman Arne near the windows. No one stood with the Khelds or talked with them. That might be in part due to

Dorilian's earlier quashing of Bersyas for attempting it. Yet, Aubrey was easily the most beautiful woman in the room and the most desirable. Though she may not have known it, he'd watched her all evening. Only Bersyas, until Dorilian had put him in his place, had paid her more notice. He watched Arne walk away to join Robdan again at the tables.

In this gathering of hundreds, none attended the Khelds, yet every Staubaun at Askyllon was aware of them. Disdain barely covered their fear of what the presence of Khelds among them might mean. They read portents in every gesture, every article of clothing, in the beauty of the woman and the somber inadequacy of the men.

He noticed Aubrey leave abruptly, exiting through the tall doors leading to the terrace. Bersyas followed.

Damn him.

"Excuse me, Lady." Dorilian made his apology to Gwenna. He gestured to Legon to follow him.

He caught Bersyas standing on the other side of the door, hanging back from going out on the terrace, but watching. The general startled when Dorilian tapped him.

"Leave."

Bersyas looked from the Hierarch to the young woman, then back again, confusion in his gaze.

But he left.

# 22

Years of experience have made clear to me that, of Leur's creations, human emotion is the most wondrous. Passion reduces distance to nothing and renders Time toothless.
MYRON, LETTER TO HIS MUSE

The terrace extending from Askyllon's ballroom was barren of all but a promise of icy solitude. Carved out of the mountain to clear a view over the lake, it did not fully front the hall but occupied a jutting spur of basalt overlooking sheer cliffs. Aubrey wrapped her arms over her breasts and stayed close to the walls of the Keep, which afforded protection from the wind. Moonlight silvered the frozen lake and turned the thin high clouds to wraiths.

The cold soothed her turmoil.

*How I hate these Staubauns and their high places!* She blinked back tears as she glared out over the harsh landscape. *They're so lofty, they think they need no one, nothing. Peacocks breeding in a wasteland.*

*This is what destroyed Stefan. This Staubaun scorn of everything but their own vastly imagined perfection. Hans should have nothing to do with them!*

When Aubrey heard a footstep and knew that she was not alone, she sighed and stomped her foot, thinking it would be her uncle or Arne. Instead, she heard only silence… and waiting. She turned.

"Thinking is cold work if you insist on doing it out here." Dorilian's voice wore the same dark tones as the night.

"I was thinking so loudly I was afraid they might hear me. They're rumored to read minds, you know." But the truth, Aubrey knew, was different. *I just wanted to get away from their eyes!*

Dorilian nodded. In the pale light he looked thoughtful himself, and Aubrey sensed that he measured every word, every gesture. "They can't read minds, but they can read situations. Give them but the breath of a reason and they will resort to their favorite pastime."

He wanted her to ask, so she did. "What would that be?"

"Plotting. They're very good at it."

"Is that where you learned to scheme?" Aubrey asked archly.

"No. I learned from better than these. Marc Frederick kept second-rate nobles as lap dogs. Nammuor castrates them for sport. And Marenthro still has them all fooled."

*And what about you?* Aubrey wondered. Except she already knew the answer. None of them, not even the wizard of Permephedon, had ever mastered Dorilian Sordaneon. The chill she felt was not only in the air. All about her, mountains gleamed in the moonlight like teeth. And Dorilian, too, wore a remote look, high and proud, like the Staubauns he ruled.

"What brought you here?" he asked.

Aubrey knew he did not ask what had brought her out on the terrace. It was simplest to tell him the truth. "I wanted to see you again."

Dorilian accepted that answer before demanding another. "Why?"

"I don't know."

"What if I said that I do?"

Aubrey had no answer and averted her gaze. It was unreal somehow to think that Dorilian could understand the tumult in Aubrey's soul. If that were true, if Dorilian *could* understand, it would put him ahead of Aubrey herself. She could not possibly sort out the mad rush of feelings that accompanied finding herself once more in Dorilian's presence. She'd underestimated how many things encountering him again would force her to rethink and redefine; it was important now, more than ever, to do so. To believe in Thron Estol was to believe in a phantom. Here, in the icy reaches of the Royal North, Aubrey's Sordani spy had come into his own—into infamy and power—and Aubrey could barely fathom the magnitude of the distance between them. Had she really ever pried those proud Highborn lips apart with a kiss? And had the return kiss been only a dream?

Embarrassed—and hoping Dorilian, even more than the Staubauns Aubrey sought to avoid, could not read her thoughts— she turned away, too confused to speak.

"I thought you would hate me," Dorilian said.

*Does he care about that?* Aubrey remembered his parting words. Was it possible he had spoken not with conviction, but regret?

"I did hate you… at first," Aubrey conceded. "I spared Hans nothing in the way of threats against your person. Your men in there would flay me if they knew the things I said that night, or thought, or did." She smiled into the frosty distance where mountain shadows vied with those cast by the thousand torches of the Keep. "Yes, I hated you, just as you knew I would. I hated you because you weren't Thron and then later I hated you because you were. I could not reconcile the terrible things I believed with the man I thought I knew." Aubrey cut a sidelong glance at Dorilian. "Hans worked very hard at repairing your reputation."

He almost laughed. "Be wary, lady," he murmured with a smile of his own. "Handurin may be even better than I am at casting glamour."

Aubrey felt a lurch in her stomach and recognized it—the same heightened awareness she had always felt around him. Dressed as he was now, in all the power of his station, Dorilian retained every bit of his former appeal and more.

He leaned on the rampart beside Aubrey.

"Where did you get that dress?" he wanted to know.

She shrugged. "A boy I met in Sordan. He said… he said I should carry the package with me and not open it until I had nothing else to wear."

He frowned then, abruptly, puzzled. "Did he? He didn't tell me."

"Maybe it was supposed to be a surprise."

Aubrey noticed the way Dorilian's gaze sharpened upon her. "Yes, I'm sure it was. He's full of surprises these days. It must be impending adolescence." Dorilian turned and stood Aubrey so he could look at her. She obeyed his handling, finding no malice in it. With one fingertip, Dorilian brushed the jade beads and bright pearls of her bodice, then trailed lightly over the bared tops of her breasts just above the beautiful fabric. Aubrey's skin flushed as a shiver danced through her.

"Do you know what you do to men, dressed like this?" Ever so lightly, Dorilian's finger rested on Aubrey's skin, a lingering command.

"It's just a fantasy."

"Some fantasies have more power than truth."

Aubrey's heart pounded. Her chest rose and fell. Dorilian's touch burned like passion itself—and her body craved that heat. "Maybe it's just the dress," she whispered. Suddenly, without reason, she was afraid.

Dorilian lifted his finger from Aubrey's breast to her cheek, then played his thumb across the soft yielding of her parted lips. Aubrey inhaled sharply, recognizing what he was doing. It was the forge all over again. Only now it was he who exposed Aubrey, layer by layer… desire by desire.

"Don't you see, lady?" Dorilian murmured. "It doesn't matter if it's just the dress. They won't make that distinction. All that would matter to them would be that I take notice. Do you realize what that would do to them?"

"No."

"I suggest you learn before it kills you. You must always remember." Dorilian dropped his hand, turning back to the rampart and the broad, shining-white mantle of Ulan-Sana so far below, and sighed. "There is much you do not know about me and my place in this World. Most especially how to behave toward me in public."

No windows overlooked this small corner, and none could see them so long as Legon Rebiran stood watch, a shadowy figure just beyond the closed doors. Aubrey noticed only now the suggestion of a human shape framed by frosted glass. Legon's presence reminded her that this was time Dorilian had stolen from others to be with her. If so, she would use it.

She lifted her chin. "Maybe I know all I need to know about the great and terrible Dorilian Sordaneon."

His light eyes gleamed with more than moonlight. "I very much doubt that."

Behind his words, Aubrey sensed an entire hidden world, glittering and remote, its battlements unassailable. The Staubaun world Hans had said was dying had never looked so formidable. The Highborn world remained unknown.

Dorilian's gaze narrowed. "Or maybe you don't remember that you called me inhuman."

"Not you. *Him.*" Aubrey shook her head. "The man the world talks about and fears. The one they mistake for a god." She refused to succumb to Staubaun mystery just because it surrounded her with moldering walls of belief. "That these Staubauns give you a place in their world, and it flatters you to accept it, does not mean they know you. They don't even see you—they see only their myths. So do Khelds. So does the World. Sordan's Highborn Prince. Rill Lord. Amallar's implacable enemy. You know what that version of you means to people."

"Far more than you ever will."

"I'm sure that is true. But I've seen what they have never seen. I've been with you in ways they never will be. I know you better than they ever could."

"Do you?"

The question teased Aubrey's skin. Dorilian pressed his fingers under her chin, turning Aubrey's face up so he might see her answer.

"I do. Because they are trying to enlarge an enemy or know a god. But in Amallar I knew the man," she whispered. "A very human man." Not knowing what it was that made her bold—the dress, the night, the myriad things unspoken between them, or maybe just that she had drunk too much sweet *marmairein*—Aubrey placed her hands on Dorilian's shoulders and leaned close, her bodice of pearls softly crushing the emerald velvet covering his chest. Cold as the night was, he had the heat to banish it. Like a moth drawn to flame, Aubrey touched her lips to his.

All at once she felt the blaze of every thought she'd ever had of him and the pull of other thoughts—wonder and pleasure; amusement and hunger and fear.

When they parted, the moisture of that contact still hung between them, turning to frost in the night. Though he said nothing, Dorilian's gaze never left hers. He regarded Aubrey for what seemed an eternity, his expression unreadable. She feared she'd said too much, taken liberties now beyond her station. The music from the hall intruded. Aubrey turned to listen.

"You haven't danced." Dorilian said it matter-of-factly.

Aubrey looked away, afraid of what Dorilian might read into her thoughts. "I haven't been asked," she said. "I think Bersyas meant to, had he not thought better of it—but northern lords don't dance with Kheld girls, do they?"

He answered slowly. "No, they don't." Then, "Would you like to dance with me?" He held out his hand, his gaze asking a different question.

Her answer was the same to both. "Yes."

Dorilian's fingers closed over hers. On one, she saw the gleaming emerald signet she had marked in Amallar and had taken from him. The Rill Stone encircled his finger with shining green fire, silver eagle ascendent. And then he was leading Aubrey into the room again, Legon Rebiran retreating from the door as though he had never been there. The music filled her ears until there were no voices in the room at all. Just Dorilian. And light. And the people in the room melting away like ice in the sun.

"I don't know this dance!" She abruptly realized where they were.

"That doesn't matter." Dorilian pulled Aubrey close with an expertise born of a life she could not even imagine. He lowered his head for a moment and she felt the warm breath of his whisper. "Let me do it. Allow your body to follow mine; it will know what to do. Trust me." And then they moved into the center of the floor.

*What is he doing?* Robdan's heart nearly stopped as he watched the glittering entrance of the Hierarch of Sordan onto the dance floor, Dorilian's arm around Aubrey as he led her in a dance. All about them, the room had gone icy silent and still. Only the musicians played on in the gallery above, unaware of events below. *Is he mad? Is she?*

The dance was the *araesan*, the sweeping, beautiful dance of the south, less mannered and more sensual than northern patterns, played in honor of the Sordani. But the Sordani couples that had been dancing, the noble captains and their ladies for the evening, gradually left the dance floor as they became aware of the only couple in the room that mattered. Or maybe it was just that they so seldom saw the dance as it played out before them now: Dorilian moving with the sensual grace he displayed in all things, his Highbornness suddenly, blatantly, there for all to see as he dictated the steps of the dance, his dark-haired partner in her Sordani gown following like a shadow in misty green and gold.

Robdan looked around, seeing women standing resplendent, hard-eyed in their astonishment and disapproval, and the men... the men were alert, their expressions assessing. Before them all, the couple seemed to become familiar, their movements more fluid— the dance spinning out like a dream. Intricacy upon intricacy, mirroring each other, they circled before the gathered nobility of the Royal North as though oblivious to the world.

And maybe they were. Robdan could see that Aubrey had eyes only for her partner, who occasionally met her smile with his own. But what Dorilian thought, none could tell.

And then the dance was done. They had entered it halfway. To the total silence in the room, before all the frozen onlookers, the couple stopped. And broke, Dorilian releasing his partner's hand. Now the focus of all eyes, Aubrey appeared to awaken to where she was and with whom.

She stood proudly, triumphant, her beauty marked and soon to be discussed to the ends of the Triempery, her blue eyes locked on something no one else in the room could see. And then, as though some cord were cut, Aubrey lifted her hand to her mouth and dropped to her knees, her gown spilling around her on the pale blond floor.

It was but three heartbeats that Dorilian stood over Aubrey, looking down at her with an expression none could decipher. Robdan didn't think it was anger. Whatever it was, Dorilian tore himself from it and, with a signal that summoned his courtiers to him, silently turned and walked away. He left the room then, every vestige of warmth seeming to go with him. The ballroom plunged into realms of frost.

Aubrey, visibly shaken, got to her feet and looked around at the Staubaun nobility still watching her in silence, their gazes hard and condemning. With a gasp, white-faced, she too then fled. Her footfalls shattered the silence of that high place. Robdan and Arne ran after her.

Only once he and Arne had gone, their unwelcome presence banished from that Staubaun gathering, did Robdan hear the music begin again and the room burst into sound.

The grand entry of the Keep loomed high and cold. Dark stone arches disappeared into soaring vaults overhead to keep company with echoes. Shadows gathered between pillars which themselves spilled darkness across the gray stone floor. Aubrey had run there without knowing where she ran, or even why. Only that she had to escape their eyes. Some instinct had brought her here, to the lonely entrance to this place.

"I didn't know you could dance like that!" Arne caught up with Aubrey first, grabbing her arm and halting her flight until their uncle could join them. "What did that bastard do? Did he force you into it?"

"No!" Aubrey shook her head, her voice still trembling with the fear that had gripped her in the ballroom. "And I can't dance, Arne, not like that. Not like a Staubaun lady. I don't know how he did it, but… I think because I wanted to, he showed me how."

"Aubrey, lass. Are… are you all right?" Robdan caught up at last. He was breathing hard and fast.

"I'm fine. Really, it's nothing. I don't know what came over me." Only now was Aubrey realizing what she had done and why.

"What do you mean you don't know? Either he forced you or he didn't! The whole room saw!" Arne persisted.

"Yes! But… he didn't force me. I can't explain it." She walked away. The stone floors chilled her feet through her slippers. The cavernous hall swallowed everything, even voices.

"But why, Aubrey?" Robdan followed after. "Why throw it in their faces?"

"I don't know. I don't know why. He… he asked me to dance." Bizarrely, the reason sounded flimsy and incomplete. Why had Dorilian done it? It wasn't for love of dancing—or was it? Had he simply liked the way their bodies moved together? Or was it just a Highborn Hierarch's caprice, a joke on them all?

Aubrey's legs went weak again. She sank onto a bench.

Robdan sat beside her. "Do you realize he danced with no one else all night? Not one noble lady graced his arm. He might as well have snubbed them. As a Highborn Prince, he is expected to observe every decorum, and especially the unwritten ones. But they'll blame you more. Even if it was his idea to dance with you, they can't let themselves think that. It's too threatening to them."

*All that would matter would be that I take notice. Do you realize what that would do to them?* Now, at last, Dorilian's words acquired their full meaning. Aubrey rubbed her arms miserably.

"I can't understand it." Robdan's frown grew more puzzled and a bit angry. "He's their ruler, after all, born to his position. He knew what they would think. He knows the dangers! He should never have put you in such a position."

"No, Uncle. He was showing me something. Something I needed to know." Something new and fearful thickened in Aubrey's throat.

"Or something he wanted the world to know, us and them." Arne's anger continued to bleed through. "They've been treating us like dirt all evening, even when we're at their tables."

Was that true? Aubrey ducked her head. She'd been testing her new skills, having her fun, not watching Arne and Robdan—or realizing until this very moment that Bas Hebron had seated her with Bersyas on purpose. "Dorilian put an end to that."

"He tried, I guess," was Arne's opinion.

Robdan looked dismal. "Don't you see? It's so much more complicated than that. Our standing in the Triempery has always been that of outsiders, to be *kept* outside—of their society, their economy, their politics. What little progress we make or wealth we accumulate, they tolerate because we continue to remain outside, without influence. Kheld animosity toward Sordan is accepted and even embraced by Essera's lords. In all truth, they have encouraged that estrangement for centuries. I don't think they appreciate being reminded of Sordan's alliance with us—or that Dorilian is bound to Hans by that alliance. I even think they're alarmed by the extent to which Dorilian honors it. For all that they have opposed him themselves over the years, they fear nothing more than a fall from Highborn favor."

Such cold logic suited the darkness—and helped Aubrey focus. This night was full of nuances that cut at her soul like knives. "They don't need that alliance at all, do they, these northern lords?" Truth held a bitter sting. "Hans wants it. Maybe Dorilian wants it. Even we want it now. But these Staubauns don't want it at all." *No more than do the Seven Houses.*

Robdan granted Aubrey a weary sigh. "They want it only because it gets them *him*. He reminds them of past glory, when Highborn Princes ruled in Essera. They crave that power. And Rill power too. They dare to hope Dorilian will have no need for this alliance once Nammuor is defeated. Lass, they sense their world slipping away. The lords in this fortress don't want Hans as their King—no more than they ever wanted Stefan. They want Highborn blood to resume its place amongst them."

Arne's jaw dropped open. "Him? Well, if that doesn't beat it!" He looked around as if he would charge off to confront Dorilian about that very thing.

Robdan stayed any further argument with a warning hand. "I've seen no indication that Dorilian is so inclined. He despises them more than we do. From what I have seen these weeks with him, his only goal is to break the Prince Regent's hold and put Hans on Essera's throne. That and defeat Mormantalorus. But this isn't the stuff of Witans and old men talking, nor even two princes agreeing what they will do. In these lands, we navigate colder wills and greater power than ever has been seen in Amallar. Stefan swam in these waters—and look how that turned out. I remind you now that we are in the halls of empire, among lords and houses that have ruled by iron and will for a thousand years. These northerners court Dorilian and will walk carefully where Hans is concerned, but they have no use for us. As Khelds, we just detract from their plans and must tread carefully."

"So we're treading careful. But the damn Hierarch sure isn't. Why the hells did he dance with our Aubrey?" Arne sounded more suspicious now than ever.

To that, Robdan could only spread his hands. "I will have to ask him. Maybe he did it to forcefully remind them of Sordan's alliance with Hans and Amallar. He's accustomed to making policy statements through his actions. I wouldn't put it past him. Here, lass," Robdan wrapped his cloak about Aubrey's shoulders, "let's get you to your room now. And we must get to ours. In the morning, we all need to be going our separate ways."

# 23

Who summoned the tempest? Not Ariande's joyless bed,
the cold marriage from which she fled, her dark beauty
clothed in precious sapphires.
Perhaps the Wall encouraged her to seek her father's
grave,
to brave the god-brightened sea.
Heavy of heart she sailed from Stauberg—escape
accomplished; destiny thwarted.
But think of this: who summoned the tempest?
MYRON, "TEMPEST," *TWELVE POEMS*

"Perhaps the Hierarch was just putting her in her place?" The oldest of the gathered lords liked that suggestion. "From what I saw, he looked most unhappy."

"And what place would that be?" Hebron intoned darkly. His bootsteps echoed no less resonantly off the stone walls. "On his arm? In his bed? Open your eyes! The man spent six weeks unaccounted for in Amallar."

"And the Khelds now have the Rill," someone else noted.

That observation was enough to silence them all.

The meditation chamber in Askyllon Keep hosted few meetings. More fortress than palace, Askyllon seldom housed even its own Bas, let alone noble lords in sufficient numbers to make secret meetings necessary. This inner chamber with its whitewashed walls and vaulted ceiling made a fine place for such discussions, however, and the men who had gathered there felt reassured by its aura of seclusion. Gilded triptychs depicting the Return of Amynas and the Fall of Gweroyen adorned the room, and alcoves provided places for thoughtful reflection on the Cibulitan passages deeply inscribed with golden letters upon plain walls.

The Lord of Pessach leaned against the wall and smirked at Hebron's concern. "It's more likely Dorilian ensorcelled her. She looked horrified. Come, we know the Khelds have hated him for years. And, I might add, his disdain for them is beyond famous. We all know how perverse he can be. I knew this Sordaneon at Marc Frederick's court and he was a nasty handful then. The King bent over backwards constantly to keep him from lashing out. Now Marc Frederick is dead, and Stefan after him—and Dorilian lords over their Prince and their dominions. Who is there to put the brake on his impulses? I venture any man here would like to find himself clasped between that pretty Kheld's legs tonight. What if he tried to have his way and she said no?"

The gathered men nodded. What better way to humiliate a woman for being proud than to compel her to dance, publicly and against her will, with her people's mortal enemy and then at the end force her to bow abjectly before him? It fit what they knew of him.

Hebron scoffed at the idea. "Dorilian? I've never known a more disciplined man. Nor one as unlikely to bed a woman for sport. He calculated every move of that dance. There was something going on there, and I would like to know what. But it was not that the Kheld wench said no to him. She was saying anything but no."

"Might she be another Brenna?" The most aged lord raised another possibility.

They fell silent, then, recalling the Kheldish beauty who had been mistress to the Highborn Prince Estevan, Endurin's Heir. Brenna's daughter by that Prince had later given birth to Marc Frederick. From that single coupling, in their eyes, had sprung a plague of woes. Dorilian's child on a Kheld would be a catastrophe.

To all in the room, Aubrey had suddenly become as dangerous to Essera as Nammuor.

After saying good night to Robdan, Aubrey closed the door behind her and glanced about her pretty room, resenting its soft colors and flounces. Everything about it looked false. Not only had she not found what she'd sought in the Royal North, she had uncovered a handful of perils and armfuls more questions. She threw herself backward upon the mattress, to lay atop a sea of misty silk and stare up at bedcurtains embroidered with lilies. The lilies came together in the shapes of crowns.

Dorilian had shown Aubrey what would happen if she loved him.

Glory. Desire. Passion. She'd seen it all, what it would mean to be Dorilian's lover. His kisses, his body. Dances on floors of gold and Sordan gleaming by moonlight. But there had been more: poison in the wine or food; knives in the dark; cold eyes forever on her and colder hearts, knowing that none wished her well. Deception and lies from the lips of corrupt men and women even more corrupted. A life of trusting no one.

That gloss Hans had talked about, that Highborn gloss polished to such a sheen that no one ever really saw Dorilian, ever knew him—now Aubrey knew why Dorilian had embraced it. She had seen this all as their fingers had parted to the dying strains of music from a land she saw nightly in her dreams—and seen too how another land, this one, haunted Dorilian's.

*A city of towers and a blue table shattering, a floor covered with the dead. A Staubaun woman beautiful beyond description, screaming as she saw the sword in his hand. Stefan shouting beneath archways of azure, "It's because of you that he is dead!"*

Had he shown these things to Hans too? It would explain so much.

*…Dorilian's body and hers entwined on a floor of clay at Bellan Toregh…*

And overarching all this was the Rill. The visions had shown it to Aubrey in a hundred facets, that powerful, brilliant Entity. And Dorilian had shown himself: bound to the Rill, mortal, crowned, and terrible; standing between all of humanity and their god.

Aubrey had fallen to her knees before him, knowing what she did.

*Highborn.* The sorcerer race, godborn, shielded from the world. Dorilian was one of them.

*It's not just the Rill. He is what Stefan said he was, what all the world says he is. Not human. He's something more. And he let me know that, tonight. Because I said I knew him… because I said I knew all I needed to know about Dorilian Sordaneon.*

Once more Aubrey felt herself surrounded by hard, hate-filled Staubaun eyes, as Dorilian had left her standing alone in their midst.

Alone.

As he was. Always.

Aubrey rose and walked to the window. She wondered if, in the ballroom where she had danced with him, Dorilian had returned and the festivities had resumed. Probably not. *He despises them more than we do.* Yes, what Robdan said was true. But there was power in Essera, might and allies even a Sordaneon might find in his interests to court. Here in these towering icy halls, Hans's war assumed a Staubaun face.

For these golden lords and ladies, the war was not about restoring Hans to Essera's throne. Neither was it about Nammuor. It was about securing a Staubaun kingdom and a Staubaun future. Aubrey's every hope grew cold as she realized these nobles would reject Hans too if the opportunity arose. Hans had known from the outset that his alliance with Sordan would be fragile and aligned with forces poised to tear it from him. Or him from it.

A knock on the door preceded it opening. Bas Hebron entered the room along with two of his men. Seeing Aubrey, Hebron nodded to the men, who then exited to wait outside.

"You will be leaving shortly," the Bas informed her curtly. "If you need assistance with packing, I will summon Laavi to attend you."

Mindful of the men outside the door, Aubrey swallowed the sour taste of alarm. "I have no intention of going anywhere tonight. I am here with my kinsman on the business of—"

"I know whose business you attend here. I believe you are done with it. Your kinsman is also leaving."

With that, Aubrey understood. She pulled herself straighter. "Does His Grace the Hierarch know of this decision?"

Hebron's fine features hardened. It had been the wrong question to ask. "No. This isn't his fortress. It's mine. He's as much my guest here as you are. The difference is that he's welcome." He surveyed Aubrey standing before the window in her fine gown. "You are a beautiful woman. However, this is a garrison full of men on the eve of war. I would not wish to have to explain to Prince Handurin or His Thrice Royal Grace that you chose to wander the Keep carelessly and met with some… unfortunate circumstance."

Mouth dry, Aubrey lowered her eyes and then her head, accepting the veiled threat. They did, indeed, do it well—so well she had no difficulty envisioning an accident on the narrow mountain road leading from the Keep, or a Kheld man and woman vanishing into the tents of the armies camped outside its walls. To trust Hebron to keep herself and Arne safe was no longer prudent.

"I cannot travel in this gown." Aubrey spread her skirt with her hands. The light fabric filled her fingers with promises soon to be discarded. "May I have the privacy in which to change? And may I have Laavi to assist me?"

Hebron pondered, his gaze lingering. Aubrey sensed the thoughts behind his dark eyes, thoughts she as a Kheld woman recognized only too well. Did all Staubaun men lust for women they considered beneath them? To her relief, Hebron bowed to her wish. "The servant girl will be sent in to you. I will be outside the door."

Hebron waited patiently and then impatiently. He knew women could be long about their business. His Gwenna often took an hour to dress. He had thought Khelds would be less leisurely, this one in particular. He did not recall her having brought much with her, but perhaps she had brought more upon the pack animals. That dress she had worn....

It was common knowledge Kheld women enjoyed carnal relations with men. Their goddess encouraged it. The way they displayed their bodies, looked men in the eye... awakened lustful thoughts. Consequently, they often stirred even dedicated Staubaun men to foolishness. Though he was aware of this weakness, Hebron was surprised to find himself beset. It had always been his stance that Khelds were a lesser race unsuitable for men of Staubaun breeding and that the men who sought them out were barely better than Khelds themselves: impulsive and infirm of conviction, indulging crude animal sensation without regard to higher ideals. It distressed him that his mind wandered more often than was seemly to images of this Kheld female as she looked in her gown. Confident, proud, her bold gaze inviting men to think of the pleasure that glorious body might give them. That Dorilian, too, had clearly noticed only served to confirm the woman's allure.

The thought of putting this Kheldish beauty in her place by using her for his release was not an option Hebron entertained for more than a moment. That he was even thinking of it appalled him. This female *must* be removed from Askyllon.

"What's taking so long?" he muttered. He rapped on the door.

No answer.

With a sharp look to his men, Hebron sent them in first. What they saw told the tale: the window flung open, draperies flying in a brutal wind that had pulled them through. On the floor, propped against the bed and tied hand and foot, eyes wide above the gag that had silenced her, Laavi wriggled for attention. Hebron knelt down and released the gag. "Where did she go?" he demanded.

"Oh, Most Noble Lord, I don't know," Laavi sobbed. "I helped her out of the dress there"—she indicated the gown thrown carelessly across the bedcover—"but then, when my back was turned, she tied this scarf around my neck and pulled until I fainted! And I woke up like this!"

At the window, the soldiers leaned out and peered around, though there was little chance they would see anything in the dark. Hebron glared at the servant girl as he unloosed her bonds. The Kheld had tied them expertly. "Where did the bitch get the rope? Can you tell me that?"

Laavi sniffled. "She carried it with her. Had just a pack, she did, when she came here. She's a barbarian, sir! This morning she had a sword!"

Hebron's captain came over. "The Khelds arm even their women and children," the man said. "Many a man has followed a Kheld woman into a room only to get steel in his gut. We must assume she is carrying the weapon with her."

Nodding, Hebron rose. "I don't want a general alarm. Search for her in secret but find her!" The man summoned his soldiers and hurriedly left. Hebron quickly assessed the room. Of the Kheld and her belongings, only the dress remained, flung upon the bed. And Laavi, now on her feet, holding a pair of dress slippers to her chest as she shivered in the icy wind that roared into the room.

"Close the damn window!" Hebron barked. The miserable girl scurried to obey before Hebron had even walked out the door.

# 24

If we accept as true that all things of the World, except
Leur, are subject to forces of entropy and atrophy, then it
also follows that just because Staubaun society has no
wish to change does not mean that change will not take
place—only that it will take place despite them.
MARC FREDERICK STAUBERG-RANDOLPH, *WORLDS APART*

"He's gone."

Laavi pulled the wardrobe door open and helped Aubrey emerge from behind racks of heavy velvet gowns and ancient silk dresses once favored by Bas Hebron's grandmother. Aubrey herself wore only the chemise from beneath her gown—that, and the sword in her hand.

"Thank you," she said.

Laavi stared round-eyed at the blade. "Well, I know how they are. Bas Hebron claims his rights with all the girls." When Aubrey looked at her in surprise, Laavi ducked her head and lifted her shoulders. "He isn't so bad. He's clean and quick, and gentle enough while he's about it. It's just not fun is all."

"I'd kill him first."

"Is that what Kheld women do? Slay a man for being a man and not thinking between the ears?"

"No. We slay men who behave as beasts and think it sport to mount helpless women." Aubrey looked around for something to wear. "I can't believe you took all my clothes!"

"I had to wash them! All dirty with travel. No lady—"

Aubrey turned in exasperation. "Will you get it in your head? I don't have the luxury of being a lady, especially now! These fine lords of yours are going to take me out somewhere and do gods know what to me if I don't get away. I need some clothes!" She plucked at the flimsy chemise. "Some real ones!"

"Take mine." Laavi began at once to untie her servant's garb. She had barely unlaced the overfrock, however, when they heard soldiers approaching. Laavi gaped at Aubrey, then at the window. "Oh, Lords! They're coming back, probably to go out the window the way they think you did! Follow me!" Leaping into action, the girl turned and dashed from the room, her arms waving, and ran to the approaching men, her skirts flying about her ankles. "Help!" she screamed. "Help! Help!"

Grasping what Laavi was doing, Aubrey tightened her grip on her sword and darted out the door. With any luck, the soldiers would focus for a few precious moments on distraction. It was all the break she needed. Stopping for nothing, not even to see if Laavi's frantic run carried her into a startled soldier's brawny arms, Aubrey turned the corner and ran the other way.

The soldiers cried out an alarm. Aubrey ran as fast as she could. The interior of Askyllon Keep opened before her as corridors drawn from a nightmare.

Midnight flooded the lower levels of the castle with darkness. Though the passage was lined with torches, most had burnt out hours ago and the remaining, sputtering few afforded little light. Aubrey pressed into the shadow formed by the stone rib of an immense pillar. Overhead, the ceiling's unseen arches created an echoing vault. Worse than the darkness and the silence was the cold. Her bare feet ached from it.

She had avoided Hebron's men thus far, but the search showed no signs of letting up. The doors lining the corridor bore chalk marks denoting occupancy of the rooms beyond, but the symbols meant nothing to Aubrey and one part of this Staubaun building looked like another.

More footsteps echoed and clattered into the passage. Aubrey retreated deeper into her stony crevice. Her ears strained for clues as to who approached. A pale glow, the light of a torch, preceded the approaching soldiers. When they were near, she peeked around the column and was relieved to see two men in Sordani military dress. Her relief leaped even more so when one of the men turned to the other man in a way that showed a sharp-featured face she recognized.

"Legon!" With a cry of thanks to the Mother, Aubrey darted from hiding. Her bare feet slapped hard stone tiles.

Legon put out his hands to catch her.

"What the—?" It took Legon a moment to rearrange his surprised expression into something more commanding. "Lady, what are you doing in these parts? And where are your clothes? You stand a good chance of getting hauled off and raped running around dressed in next to nothing!"

The other man, handsome and wearing officer's bars on his collar, snickered. "Raped? Not by us!"

Legon snarled at the other man to be silent. To judge by their glassy eyes and winey breath, both men had been drinking.

"Legon, please," Aubrey entreated, "you've got to take me to the Hierarch." Dorilian would not dismiss her, not about this.

"Dressed like that?" Legon shouldered aside his companion and shushed the comment on the man's lips. "I had best see you to Bas Hebron's Lord Chamberlain. He would know where your proper room is."

"No! That would be the worst thing! Please. I'm freezing cold. You have to take me to your Hierarch, and quickly, before some of Bas Hebron's men make you turn me over to them!" Aubrey tugged on the embroidered sleeve of the same formal jacket she'd seen earlier.

Annoyed, Legon slapped at her hand until she released him. "Control yourself! And address me as Commander." Every trace of surprise had fled. "What is this about Bas Hebron's men?"

"I don't have time to explain. Just take me to Dorilian."

Aubrey noticed that the companion's jaw fell open and his eyes grew round. She'd done it again.

"His Thrice Royal Grace," Legon corrected pointedly and sharply, "likes his sleep. And he likes it uninterrupted. I'll be a short man in Amallar before I dare disturb him in his bed." In the space of the last few statements, Legon appeared to have shaken off the effects of drink. "Now tell me what's your trouble with Bas Hebron's men or, by the Leur, I will root some of them out and have them tell me."

She would get no further. Only Legon's Highborn liege could issue commands he would follow. Aubrey wasn't giving him the respect he deserved. Crossing her arms over her barely covered breasts, trying hard not to shiver, she looked down at the floor and spoke in a more respectful tone. "It's not Hebron's men. It's

Hebron himself. He... refused to be discouraged." It was the most believable explanation.

Aubrey's glance showed Legon's dark eyes widening with understanding. The companion was finally silent. Now both men looked thoughtful. Legon maneuvered Aubrey aside until the pillar stood between them and the other man. "Bas Hebron accosted you?" His voice dropped to a growl. "What do you want me to do? I'm not going to confront him to defend your honor."

"No," Aubrey agreed. "That's not your place. But I think your Hierarch will want to prevent the Bas from doing something foolish."

Legon stared and Aubrey stared back. She took satisfaction in that he hesitated at all. An alliance alone would not have prompted a pause. With a great sigh and a snap order to his companion to go to his room and stay there and speak to no one, Legon removed his fur-lined cloak and flung it over Aubrey's bare shoulders.

"I'll be damned if I'm forced to bare my steel over a half-dressed Kheld wench." Taking her by the arm, he steered an unceremonious course down the long hallway. "Here, give me that sword." He snatched it. "Even I couldn't get you in to see him if you're armed like an assassin!"

Steps loomed ahead. Soon dank lower levels gave way to loftier corridors lined with polished stone and warm light from wall-braced lanterns. One corridor opened to high ceilings and a stairway she had not seen before. Telltale signs announced they had entered the part of the Keep controlled by Sordan. The presence here was martial, and the soldiers wore Sordaneon green and silver. A dozen armed men guarded a massive door, but they gave no challenge to Legon when he simply led Aubrey past them. Within was a chamber of elegant, paneled walls, stark furnishings, and a scattering of tables and chairs. Intricate lamps hung on the walls. Several more men, armed and alert, rose to attention upon their entrance.

"Commander." The officer presented his sword fist to chest in a salute, and his soldiers did likewise. Aubrey could well imagine other men waiting in the rooms beyond. She pulled Legon's cloak about her body more tightly.

"No one passes." Legon gave the order even as he manuevered past the soldiers.

She drew herself straighter and wished she need not endure the soldiers' cold, deliberate scrutiny. Her state of undress almost certainly suggested conclusions she'd rather not encourage. Mercifully, Legon's almost singular position as the Hierarch's trusted friend meant obtaining access without having to explain himself. Moments later, they entered another room—larger, grander, and empty but for an enormous table and a handful of chairs.

"Sit here."

Aubrey plunked down where indicated and watched as Legon adjusted his clothing and raked fingers through his hair before his reflection in an expanse of mullioned windows. Then he rapped on the door. A low suggestion of a reply prompted Legon's sour look in her direction before he went into the next room.

His conversation filtered back. "Your pardon, but I... that lady of the Kheld folk, the one from Amallar that you danced with, has requested to see you."

A long pause. "Did she give a reason?"

"I would rather she explained. I can't talk with these Khelds. They're never quite direct. But it has something to do with Bas Hebron."

A moment later, Legon appeared at the door to gesture that Aubrey should enter.

The chamber beyond resembled a treasure room. A wooden floor flowed like amber glass except where covered by rugs in deep hues of red and blue. The fire from the hearth reflected glowing tones to the room's lavish paneling and tapestries. Books lined gilded shelves, except for one that held a collection of porcelain horses caparisoned in gold and jewels. A heavy carved desk and some chairs occupied a corner near the windows, suggesting that area of the room, not the bed glimpsed through a half-closed door, was the seat of activity and function. Dorilian sat at the desk, surrounded by papers, pens, and cylinders of brass. For the first time, it struck Aubrey that Dorilian's lofty title was not just ceremonial. It came with responsibilities as well.

At least he was not in bed as Legon had feared. Dorilian still wore his formal clothing from earlier in the evening, although he'd undone the buttons of the shirt and the jeweled clasps of his jacket, both of which hung open. The crown that had graced his head now glinted on the table atop some papers.

"Where is your dress?" Dorilian indicated that Legon should reclaim his heavy leather cloak. It embarrassed Aubrey to realize how she must look, with her hair loose and disordered, her limbs wrapped in a soldier's cloak, and wearing nothing on her feet.

Aubrey yielded the fur-lined garment. Though her borrowed chemise was skimpy at best, it was pretty and covered the most essential parts. At least this carpeted, royal chamber was not icy cold like the rest of the Keep. Resigned, she shrugged and let both men stare at her. "I left my dress, and everything else I own, save my sword, in the room with Bas Hebron. He graciously allowed me the option of removing my gown."

"The Bas attempted to molest her!" Legon explained grimly.

"No, he didn't," Aubrey corrected, quickly, to head off misunderstanding.

Legon's head shot up and he glared, near enough to bite and baring his teeth as though he meant to. "You said—"

"I lied. I needed help and didn't want you to dismiss me." She gave Legon a look of sincere apology. "Bas Hebron came to my room to inform me that I am to be escorted out of Askyllon, tonight, I know not where or why." By Legon's narrow look, he knew why—and, at the moment, concurred. Nor did Dorilian need guess at Hebron's motives, to judge by his expression. Aubrey tried not to look desperate as she explained further. "They have Arne too. At least, I was told he would be leaving with me. I don't know more than that. I didn't trust what the Bas said he was doing, and I made my exit by way of a trick. He and his men are searching for me as we speak. I fear for my safety and that of my kinsman."

The silence in the room told her she was being taken seriously.

"Have you heard anything of this?" Dorilian asked of Legon.

"No." Legon frowned. His alert look suggested he had a few thoughts on the matter. "Bas Hebron can be canny with his politics and usually treads carefully, but his fear of miscegenation with Khelds or other peoples is notorious. Clearly, he seeks to remove the lady and her kinsman quickly. By not informing you, he would make it possible for you to truthfully say you knew nothing. Thus, he protects his alliance, but he also hopes to conceal his participation."

"That he does not want me to know will be what keeps this matter secret. Did any of Hebron's people see you bring Lady Aubrey here?"

"I think not. When I found her, she was in quarters assigned our senior officers. Don't ask me how she found her way there. She was armed for protection. Here is her sword, of which I relieved her." Legon laid the sword on the desk, near to Dorilian's hand and far from Aubrey's. "Only Paunas and I saw her until we reached this floor. I can make certain he doesn't talk, and you know your Eagle Guards won't."

Dorilian gave a satisfied nod. "Do that. Then find Arne Anseldson, wherever Hebron has stashed him, and deliver him to Master Robdan's chamber. Do it stealthily. Make it look as though he made his own escape, or Hebron's soldiers did him in—I do not care. Hebron is to guess at what I know, not be certain of it. And tell no one where the lady is. Only my guard, Master Robdan, and Master Anseldson, once you have him, are to know. I want Hebron to sweat."

Legon nodded. His reputation as a dangerous foe resided in such attention to detail. He left more quickly than he had arrived, Sordan's dog set loose.

Dorilian leaned back in his chair with a sigh. He tapped his pen against a stack of leather envelopes for a few moments before throwing it down. When he rose, he went to a tall closet, from which he pulled a heavy robe. "You," he said to Aubrey as he draped the robe about her, "are more trouble to me than Handurin ever was."

Aubrey snatched the robe about her shoulders, pulling it to cover her breasts and conceal her thighs. It was dark blue, its hems embroidered with golden spear points. "I didn't ask for trouble. It simply showed up."

"No, Lady. *You* simply showed up. Lacenedon is no land for a Kheld woman, even one who is sharp and good with a blade. You had no way of knowing what your welcome would be."

Aubrey wasn't about to let Dorilian shift the night's events onto her shoulders. "My welcome was merely cool until *you* danced with me! In front of all of them. Only then did they turn on me like some loathsome disease." She eyed him unhappily. "You knew what would happen."

"As you should have—before you ever set foot upon the path that led you here. You knew me for who and what I am. This time you knew! Yet your flirtation could not have been more obvious all evening."

"Flirtation?"

"Tell me I'm wrong."

Aubrey frowned. "I don't think anyone ever tells you you're wrong."

"Not often. And only when they're sure of it. You're not."

"All right. Fine. Hans warned me."

"You should have listened." Dorilian led Aubrey to the hearth, where he sat her on a divan facing the fire. He pulled over a low chair for himself and sat facing her. He looked like Thron again, though wearing richer clothes and in surroundings Aubrey would never have imagined. Some of Thron's ease, and mannerisms, had returned as well, and Aubrey had to force herself to recall that the man she looked upon was not the man she had known in Amallar. This man was harder and colder. This was the Hierarch of Sordan.

"Lady"—the tone of Dorilian's voice indicated he was accustomed to the full attention of any to whom he spoke—"all my life I have faced enemies determined to control or kill me. Essera opposed my very birth. Its lords coveted my inheritance, my birthright, and my lands. My mother was murdered when I was seven, my cousins when I was twelve, my grandfather when I was seventeen. My enemies subjected me to guardians I did not want, tutors whose purposes I distrusted, and plots designed to imprison me because of my name, my nation, and my god. I survived them all. On the night I first met Handurin in Sordan, he had unwittingly stepped into a plot of monstrous intent. The only thing about it that surprised me was to find him in its midst."

He shook his head, somehow managing to look amused. "Your people are arrogant enough to think Khelds are first and foremost of those who seek my demise. That conceit is laughable. It was not Khelds who killed my mother, nor my brother, nor my father—and those they did kill, they killed in ignorance or by the designs of others. The enemies I fear most are hidden, inhuman, and have plans beyond the grave. They have ways of getting close to me. Khelds do not. At worst, your people have been an irritant to me, at best an amusement... but never, until now, a danger."

Aubrey lowered her gaze. "You mean me."

"At the moment, I see no one closer. Not to mention it is thanks to you that I came north without Handurin and tore asunder my own designs. *You* forced me here. You forced me to flee Bellan Toregh, to flee for my life. Only one other person has ever put me to that." Dorilian's gaze hardened. "Do you have any idea how much I dislike Esseran winters?"

"No." Aubrey knew next to nothing about Dorilian, really. And yet, she knew so much. The scent of his skin and the texture of his hair. His quick temper born of intelligence and action. The humor that so often lurked beneath his acidic observations. It was hard to reconcile such very human things with this Rill Lord and ruler of nations. How many truly knew this man? Few men had the opportunity and fewer women, if what Aubrey knew of Staubaun society held true. Even Dorilian's own lords did not often speak with him as she did now. To them he gave orders, edicts, opinions... but never explanations. The intimacy of his conversation this night was as singular as her knowledge of him, brilliant and priceless, but still undefined, perhaps even by him.

"You say you hate Essera, yet you are here by choice." Aubrey wrapped her fingers in the wool and pulled the robe more snugly around her. It felt warm and substantial, like him. Even tenuous conversation bridged the awkwardness. "Not even winter could keep you from Permephedon and the Rill, or Sordan itself, if that were where you wished to go." It was truth. Dorilian commanded entire nations.

"While I can place myself within this World, there's a part of it I cannot master. Time, lady. Of all Leur creations the most unstoppable. Handurin and I fight as we must, where we must. Our enemy's power grows by the day. We must attack while there's still a chance of defeating him."

Somehow, Dorilian saying it made the danger feel more imminent. Except for the Dazun's fearsome flood, Aubrey and her countrymen had seen little evidence of the enemy's sorcery. Or Dorilian's for that matter. Since girlhood, she had heard talk crediting the Sordaneons with arcane powers. Highborn powers, it was said, Rill-given, such as the lightning that had shattered the aqueduct at Gignastha.

Which called another question to mind, something she had heard lords raise in Dazunor-Rannuli and again just that evening. "I heard these lords and generals say the end goal of your campaign is to take Stauberg. But how? Do you have a plan to surmount Stauberg's Wall?"

"If you truly want to know... yes."

"How?"

"If I told you that... let's just say secrecy prevails where plans too well known go astray." The confidence of his thin smile reassured her. "Stauberg's Wall is not the mystery to me it is to others. Even Nammuor does not truly understand its being."

"It's like the Rill?"

"No. It's not like the Rill."

Aubrey sensed a hint of irritation at the question, the lifelong impatience of a man who understood things he could not explain, confronted by someone who barely grasped the rudiments of his Entities.

"Is the treaty what you wanted? Will you release Dazunor-Rannuli's Rill node?" These were answers Aubrey wanted to bring back with her. Dorilian had said nothing of it, though Arne had given him Hans's letter. And Sordan's emissaries had stated that the Brotherhood of Epoptes had signed Dorilian's terms.

"I have the order on my desk. I've prepared a cylinder that bears my code seal and will carry what's needed. The signed treaty and orders will be sent to Permephedon in the morning—along with you."

Aubrey felt a warm flush of chagrin. Even though she far preferred Dorilian's intervention to finding whatever fate Hebron had prepared for her, it stung to know she needed the help. "Why did you ask me to dance?" she asked again. The question was too important to leave unanswered.

A look she had not seen since Amallar settled across Dorilian's features. His regard warmed, familiar again, the man she remembered. "The most beautiful woman in Askyllon wanted to dance with me."

"Every woman in Askyllon wanted to dance with you," Aubrey retorted. But the pronouncement pleased her. A blush rose in her cheeks.

"No. Every woman in Askyllon wanted *me* to dance with *her*. They wanted to be seen dancing with me, or to have danced with me. To tell those who might care that they had danced with me. In reality, they would have been dancing with themselves, for themselves, for the room to see and the World to know—for everyone but me. I know the difference, lady, and I have enough ways of being alone without subjecting myself to that."

Aubrey bowed her head, only to feel a touch under her chin, lifting her face again to his. Images and feelings swirled like driven leaves, that evening's dance coming back to her, all moonlight and frost.

"To what end did you pursue me to Lacenedon, Aubrey Amundda?" Genuine curiosity threaded the words. "To what end did we dance?"

"I was not pursuing you."

"Call it what you will."

Again, Dorilian pinned her with truth. It clung to her in telltale threads, refusing to let her lie... to either of them. What had it been on her part if not pursuit? She'd badgered Hans to let her come north. "I needed to find out... about you."

He didn't ask what about him Aubrey had come to Lacenedon to discover. The expression on his face said that Dorilian, too, craved resolution.

"That night"—he removed his hand and only his gaze continued to touch her—"I was angry. At you. At myself, at my lack of control. At having too many feelings and not enough reason. At having put myself in that position at all. What happened between us—"

"Was not what I'd planned."

"That hardly matters. We both encountered other than we expected."

To that Aubrey could only nod, though she winced. "I wanted to get you alone." She was doing it still.

"You wanted more than that."

Aubrey ducked her head. She'd long since given up on counting the number of mistakes she'd made that night—or this one. Telling the truth was less humiliating. "I hoped to gain an advantage. I thought I could maybe get you to... I did it because I... I wanted you, in other ways."

That Dorilian didn't look away felt promising. "But the man you wanted—"

"Was you. I've thought about this a lot and I know that now. *You* were in my arms that night, not some other man." Emboldened, Aubrey dared to touch Dorilian's cheek, then jaw, finding his features warm and human, and noble too. He didn't pull away from her assessment. "I came to Lacenedon wondering who I would find. A lie or the truth. I needed to know if what I felt was real." It was all she could say and was not even close to what she meant. What did she want to prove was real? Dorilian? Her feelings? His history with her people? Questions shattered upon his sharp contradictions.

Dorilian continued to study Aubrey intently, as one would an unwary child.

"You should be more afraid of me," he said. "You should be terrified. Do you know *anything* about me?"

"I know that you're the man I met in Amallar. That I chose you over all other men when I joined with you that night. That I was right about you all along and still managed to be completely wrong. I cannot dismiss what I feel." Aubrey hated that she would have preferred Dorilian to be cruel, to be horrible, if that would kill the confusion in her heart and, with it, her pain.

"But what of those things others say about me? Surely you've heard."

Yes. Of course, as had the whole world. "That you hate Khelds and wish to destroy us? I know that's not true, or you wouldn't have given us the Rill. And Hans told me you didn't kill Stefan, or the Old King, or the martyred Princes people say you murdered at Permephedon. I believe him."

"He speaks the truth. I murdered none of them. But there are other truths that, when held to light, remain. People are dead because of me, many by my own hand."

"Were any of them Kheld? Kin to me?"

"None that I know of."

Aubrey drew a breath before admitting, "I've killed people too."

"Kin to me?"

Aubrey shook her head. "None that I know of."

Dorilian nodded. There was more to say, so he said it. "And what of the tale that I killed my wife? That I cut off her head?"

Had Tiflan told him what Aubrey had learned? Levyathan, quite the contrary, had cautioned not to make that inquiry. Now, to Aubrey's dismay, Dorilian had raised the atrocity himself. Dry-mouthed, she did her best to answer. "It was a violent time. In fact, it sounds unreal." She could not finish.

"You don't know me very well at all if you don't believe me capable of that."

Had Aubrey really hoped for a denial? Or known that she wouldn't get one? That terrible moment had been among the visions Dorilian had shown following their dance. "She must have done something terrible for you to do that to her."

"She did." But he wasn't going to say what.

"Why are you trying to frighten me?"

"Because nothing else is working."

Aubrey turned her hand and ran the backs of her fingers down Dorilian's cheek, along the Staubaun-smooth curve of beardless jaw. No tension lingered there, no anger, only acceptance of where they were. Of how they were, tonight and in this place. Dorilian leaned his face into the touch and Aubrey closed her eyes. So near. Even the air—rich with notes of applewood, spiceroot, and *him*—tasted of promises. When Dorilian slid his fingers into Aubrey's hair and then combed it back, cupped her head to pull her closer, she opened her lips to the kiss. Here. Here was the answer Aubrey had sought. The kiss filled every empty space between them with something hot and familiar, uniquely theirs.

Dorilian withdrew, resolve regained; Aubrey saw that when she opened her eyes. Felt the pulse of it beneath her fingers, now on his collarbone. Her last question left her lips as a whisper. "Do you want me to go?"

"No," Dorilian said.

Aubrey wanted him. *Him*.

Not the Hierarchate of Sordan. Not his name or his titles or the divine dynasty he embodied. Not his claim to the Star Throne of the Malyrdeons or the riches of eighteen hundred years of Rill hegemony. Not the god-spawned powers he was rumored to possess or the temporal power he wielded. Not that through him she might gain a child to secure for her and her tribe a legacy above all others.

This woman of the Khelds, this Aubrey, with her dark-haired beauty and rebellious female pride, wanted *him*.

When Dorilian looked at her, touched her, no hidden purposes looked back, no veiled agendas stirred within her bones. Aubrey's desires were as naked as the promises of her body, born of skin and blood and mortal things. Her immediacy lured Dorilian, summoned something wild. He looked at her and true passion looked back, a hot yearning of the flesh, wanting only to join, to know, to possess and become. He recognized the raw impetus of propagation and the forces that dictated desire for him. The same forces also moved him.

She thought that she loved him. Because he was a stranger and looked Staubaun enough to awaken forbidden attractions she as a Kheld would never acknowledge or name. Because he intrigued her, had bested her, and she knew he could do so again. Because she wanted to hate him and could not do it, she thought it was love.

And maybe it was.

Had he not relived daily, even hourly, the feel of her body straining against his in the forge, her desire hot upon his mouth, her hands pulling him down? His body had answered hers no less ardently, an animal hunger that had left him breathless. And Aubrey's voice, afterward, the irony of her words. *I hate him, your Hierarch...*

She hadn't known. And in not knowing, she had given him both the gift and the curse of experiencing what it was to be wanted apart from being a Rill-born Prince. Of being, simply and seductively, a man.

He had feared he would never know it again, never again feel the pleasure of being with a woman who wanted him simply because she found his body appealing, his person worthwhile, who embraced so fully the parts of him that she knew. The pain of that knowledge had cut him as deeply as a death. To be wanted for himself and then not wanted because of who he was! The irony replayed itself again and again in Dorilian's mind, until at last he had managed to find it ludicrous in the way profound truths often are, that he should be so singularly cursed that love for him should be impossible.

And now, here she was, in Askyllon, wanting to know if what she felt was real.

To his amazement, learning his identity had not destroyed him in her eyes. On the terrace, shared with the icy breath of winter on both their lips, Aubrey had betrayed just how deeply he still moved her. He had danced with her because it was the one pleasure he would have that night. Because he was selfish. Because he could. Because if they danced, he could draw her, however briefly, into the brilliant blaze of his life, let her glimpse the beauty and terrible power of his station... because then Aubrey might, even a little, understand why he could not be with her. That she should show up in his chamber later, shivering, Legon's cloak about her shoulders because these Esseran Lords had done as Dorilian had known they might and tried to keep her from him, was beyond fate.

If only for the gift of knowing, however briefly, the full force of trust and desire, he could very well love her.

Aubrey had known from the first she wouldn't leave this room tonight. How could she? Any woman would have understood the male tension that emanated from Dorilian, the heat in his gaze that announced his reasons. Somewhere within a mind stunned both by him and her body's unhidden answer, Aubrey grasped the import of the decision. Something hinged upon it, but she knew not what.

When he pulled her to him, she gave herself to that embrace, encountering the crush of velvet and leather, jewels and heat. "Please," she gasped, not knowing what it was she was pleading for. She rejoiced when he angled his face to meet hers, his lips insistently moving over hers until she responded with a kiss just as hungry.

"Stay." Rough with feeling, Dorilian's command warmed Aubrey's cheek just before he buried his face in her hair, his mouth brushing her neck. His hair, reddened by firelight, caressed her face and smelled of bergamot, of summer.

Aubrey inhaled that scent, wonder flaring alongside desire. "I will," she whispered. Loosened by the contact of their bodies, the robe she wore slid from her shoulders.

"Be very sure, lady," Dorilian murmured. "What we do tonight, we cannot pretend away. If any learn that you have been with me, your own people will denounce you, and you will find no refuge with mine."

"None of them frighten me."

His fingers tightened in the tangle of Aubrey's hair and pulled her head back, forcing her to look at him. "Then say my name."

She had never spoken it to him.

"Dorilian," she said, and there was no more pretending.

He spoke hers, too, minutes later, after they'd entered the next chamber, after his clothing also found the floor and the bed yielded to their weight. His mouth traced the hidden valleys of Aubrey's body with a ferocity that claimed her completely. Hands eager and grasping, Aubrey caressed and claimed Dorilian's skin, the hard muscles of his shoulders, his thighs. The powerful curve of his back. In creating him, the Mother had not merely smiled but done her finest work.

Surely no other man in all Her creation ever pleased a woman so well.

# 25



"I didn't protect you. I could have—"

"Don't," Aubrey interrupted Dorilian's sleepy vibrato. She buried her cheek against his arm, curling deeper into his sleek, solid warmth. Bare months ago she would have called this man a monster. Now, skin on skin with him, Dorilian felt inevitable.

"I thought I could protect myself," Aubrey confided. "From them. From you, from my feelings for you. Follow the rules, be ever so proper—circumspect and clever—but I suppose I broke a rule along the way, and I wasn't clever at all, because look, I had to turn to you for help. I didn't want to do that. That was never my intent. But here I am."

Strong arms drew Aubrey closer and she felt his warm breath brush her nape. "Yes," Dorilian said a moment later, surprisingly pensive. "Here we are."

The hesitation and the resoluteness within which he'd wrapped the word "we" invited exploration, but the bed was warm and Aubrey was too close to slumber for passing impressions to find purchase. Tugged by sleep, she slipped beneath such things, surrendering instead to the sweetness of being held and cherished and utterly safe.

Aubrey woke to pearl-gray dawn spilling through high windows she had not even noticed the night before. Deep pillows and soft blankets cradled her body in a warm, soft nest, and a lingering scent—fennel and summer and musk—awakened memory of having been with a man. She felt proof of that encounter in her hips, her thighs, when she stretched and smiled. The man she'd chosen might not be to anyone's liking but hers, but she had never favored the kind of men others would choose for her.

Finding herself alone in the bed, Aubrey pushed onto one elbow. A pinkish light filtered through the open bed curtains on her right, softly setting aglow the rose silk fringe. It was morning. She had spent the entire night. Wanting to see what lay beyond the curtain, she scooted to the opening and looked at the room beyond the bed.

It was the same bedchamber into which Dorilian had carried her during their embrace. The same high ceiling beamed with heartwood. The same rich appointments. The same bed. The simple fact she was still in this room, this bed, told her much.

Dorilian had not sent her away and would now need to explain her presence.

Aubrey swung her legs over the floor and sat up. The robe from the night before lay there, abandoned along with the pretty chemise. Seeing nothing else by way of clothing, she slipped back into both. Barefoot, she trod dense silk carpets to the door and peeked into the next room. Dorilian stood at the desk. Unlike her, he had dressed for the day and, though his silk and velvet garments were those of a prince, Aubrey found his appearance familiar—controlled, cool, deeply focused on what he was doing.

He looked up to see Aubrey in the doorway, then indicated she should approach.

"I'm almost finished."

As Aubrey watched, Dorilian lifted the sword resting on the desktop, turned his left hand, the one wearing the Rill Stone, and nicked his fingertip upon the sharp, unsheathed tip. Ruby drops of blood welled but for a moment. He put down the sword and pressed his blooded finger to the dull leaden surface of a ringed disk that lay on the desk. Aubrey did not recognize the metal.

Immediately upon being touched, blue-green tracery, like writing, scrolled to fill the disk until a silver eagle spread wings at the center. Dorilian tapped it again with the finger with the Rill Stone and the disk's metal fanned into segments that collapsed upward and inward to form a much smaller shape: a cone ringed with symbols. He lifted the cone between his fingers and displayed it.

"Behold the message."

"That will unlock the Rill?"

"In conjunction with the key. That, too, will require the message."

Not just the message. *This* message, crafted of Highborn magic. Metal and blood. Aubrey decided to be pleased Dorilian trusted her enough to let her witness it. Deftly, he placed his creation into a message cylinder and locked it, then handed it to her. Aubrey took it. The ornate tube felt light, almost insubstantial.

"I bear no love for Dazunor-Rannuli," Dorilian said. "This I do for Handurin's gain and Nammuor's defeat." He placed his other hand atop Aubrey's before she could take it away. "Now I will ask something of *you*."

Of course. Aubrey nodded and quipped, "Leave quickly? Because I will. Arne and I both. We—"

"Have no choice in that matter. You will both leave Askyllon immediately. That is... as soon you dress. What I want is for you to go to Bellan Toregh, give this message to Tharos Odakkon, and then *stay* in Amallar. By coming here, you have put your life in danger. Don't do it again. Let your people protect you while I cannot. Promise me that."

Protection. That again. Last night's events had given him reason to think Aubrey would need it. Though even a Mother could not dictate a woman's choices, that Dorilian desired to protect her melted Aubrey's resistance. The warning clearly expressed a degree of care for her. Events still shaping both their lives had convinced her Essera was even more dangerous than she could have imagined when first she'd made her decision to ride north with Hans. Much less her choice to come here to Lacenedon.

"I can't make such a promise," she answered. "My people— Hans—depend on me for too many things."

"I'll write to Handurin and he will understand. I'm not exaggerating the danger to you."

*Shadrach!* If Dorilian wrote to Hans, Hans would do whatever the letter asked. Theirs would always be the primary alliance. Dismayed, Aubrey shook her head, wishing she faced some other coalition.

If only she had her runes, some way to read this situation. This was probably not the time to ask if she might retrieve them from her room.

Dorilian took Aubrey's distraction as signaling a need for further explanation. "Lady, I have just signed a treaty fiercely opposed by every man in this fortress. It will be just as fiercely opposed by every powerful Lord and Lady in Essera, and by important allies and subjects of mine in Sordan as well. I would be a fool to think there will not be consequences. Some of those consequences may well fall upon you, as happened last night. For both our sakes, I am going to ask Handurin to give you duties elsewhere. I would rather you agree to my request and spare him the trouble."

Could he sound more serious? Aubrey sought a middle ground. "If Hans is still in Dazunor-Rannuli—"

"Stay away. From there especially."

"Why?"

"You've been there, and you can ask that question?"

Aubrey had seen for herself that the city could be hostile toward Khelds. But she'd cajoled barges from the Denizen of Hedys, hadn't she? She'd enlisted Dazunor-Rannuli's nobles and merchants to Hans's cause. "Hans controls the city, he and his allies." When Dorilian's expression didn't change, Aubrey acknowledged the concern. "Does this really mean so much to you?"

"Yes. I need your word."

Would Aubrey be allowed to leave if she did not give it? Or would she be forced to stay by Dorilian—and increase the danger for them both? Dorilian or no Dorilian, Aubrey didn't wish to remain anywhere near Bas Hebron. For good or ill, every choice, even the least one, took her further along the Mother's Path.

Hadn't the Bog Crone herself placed Aubrey on this one? *To one girl a king, to one a man, to the other the cold trees...* "I promise, then. I will take your key to Bellan Toregh and stay in Amallar, away from the war in Essera."

Maybe Dorilian could read the truth as he gazed deep into Aubrey's eyes, because just before he nodded, she felt the weight of his trust. It felt like sunlight and steel. Aubrey hoped Dorilian would kiss her, but he did not, and she felt too uncertain to attempt to kiss him.

Legon Rebiran escorted Aubrey to Robdan's room through passageways Legon himself had cleared of prying eyes. No one witnessed the move, which occurred in the wing of the Keep controlled by Sordan. He had succeeded in finding Arne and had placed him, too, in Robdan's custody, but had nothing more to say about it after telling Aubrey that. Not even when she expressed her thanks and relief. She sensed disapproval behind Legon's silence. She also knew that he would never ask for or reveal the particulars of her overlong stay in Dorilian's chamber. Legon dropped Aubrey off along with her possessions from her own room, to which she was forbidden to return. Even when a quick inventory provided reason.

While Arne and Robdan conferred in the next room, Aubrey searched her packed gear. She'd found the rich leather bag with her runestones, and also the beautiful dress and slippers, but her small case of medicinals was missing.

"My healer's bag," she noted. "It's not here."

"What's not here?"

"My herbs. Potions. Powders—"

"Poisons? Bas Hebron's soldiers would have taken anything they considered dangerous." Legon raised eyebrows at Aubrey's look of offense, then crisply informed her, "You and your kinsman will leave the Keep within the hour. The diplomatic emissaries you arrived with will remain for another few days for talks. An escort from the Thrice Royal's Eagle Guard will accompany you to Permephedon and see that you board a *charys* to Bellan Toregh."

"Thank you, Commander Rebiran." Aubrey wore her sword again and was glad to be back in trousers and boots. What Dorilian had told his own men about having had her in his chamber, she did not know, or if he had told them anything at all. That he might, indeed, be able to weave spells over men's minds, Aubrey no longer doubted. In her pack, now light one healing case, she carried letters meant for Hans and Sinon Kouranos, as well as missives regarding the campaigns in Dazunor and Lacenedon and the sealed cylinder with what was needed to resume Rill service to Dazunor-Rannuli.

Legon continued to frown. "No good will come from this strain with Bas Hebron," he said. "That we should imperil an important alliance over Khelds cannot be in anyone's interest, not even my Hierarch's."

"If there is strain because you saved our lives, Commander, the fault is with the Bas. Sordan proved more honorable."

"My Hierarch keeps his word. Always."

"I think you do too."

Something in Legon's countenance relented. "Always."

Accompanied by Legon and forty elite Eagle guards, Aubrey and Arne set out into fog thrown off by the hot springs in the valley, taking a different road to the lake than the one by which they'd arrived. Soon Askyllon was behind them, shrouded in mist, its dark walls but a memory. Before they began their descent to the lake, Legon halted the party. He indicated to Arne that a rider wearing Sordaneon colors waited on the way they had just come.

"Go with him." Legon placed his horse to prevent Aubrey from joining them. "On the Hierarch's orders, Lady, you are to stay with me."

"What for?" Arne asked. He'd sworn to Robdan he would not leave Aubrey alone with any Staubaun types again until they were back in friendlier lands. He eyed the other rider suspiciously. "You said earlier you were to take us to Permephedon. *Both* of us."

Legon answered with a soldier's deliberation. "That man is one of my captains. The lady is safe with me and my men," he assured Arne. "She will be here still when you return."

Not quite mollified but given no other choice, Arne rode his horse back up the path and dismounted where told. There was a bridge and a ghostly waterfall carved like some sculpture of pillars and columns of ice. He felt no surprise, not even a little, at finding Dorilian there, though it still caused every bit of unease. Arne had wondered when they would speak, and it made a kind of sense that it would be here, away from Hebron's place and Hebron's spies, with Sordan's army between them and discovery.

"This army goes to Stauberg." Dorilian spoke directly, though fog hid the force to which he referred. "I have my own spears to sharpen there, but I will sharpen Handurin's as well. The city will be his if he wants it. I have no ambition to win it for myself. Sordan is my domain and always will be."

"Not to give offense or anything, but Khelds will believe that when we see it, and not a moment before then. The winning and the leaving. No one's ever taken Stauberg because no one's ever gotten past the Malyrdeon Wall. Don't matter how big your army is if you can't do that."

"I'm aware of the difficulty. I have reason to think I will prevail. Nammuor's weakness will lie in that he thinks I'm being rash. I have that reputation." Dorilian reached into his jacket and extracted a leather envelope sealed with official ribbons. "I want you to deliver this, by hand, to Handurin. It's a personal note from me."

Arne took it hesitantly. He'd never taken anything from the Hierarch's hand before. "I'll make sure he gets it."

"You suffered no mistreatment from Hebron's men?"

Arne stammered in surprise that Dorilian would ask. "Just the usual roughing up. Nothing serious."

Dorilian nodded. He turned to go.

It might be their last chance to speak. Arne decided he wasn't about to let it slip by. "About Aubrey. I wouldn't speak up, but—" Arne gulped, seeing that Dorilian had stopped to listen. Arne decided to plunge on, rushing to get it out. "She's good family, and kin of mine, and I sure hope you aren't playing the same games Staubaun men have played with our women since Alm walked out of the Bogs."

A flicker of amusement answered him. "Is that what you think?"

"I don't know what to think. I never do, about you." It was true. Arne didn't quite know what to make of Aubrey spending all night in the Hierarch's chambers, 'under his protection' as Legon had put it. He remembered that he and Hans had been similarly protected at one point and hadn't had to share a chamber with Dorilian. Still, it didn't make sense that this man would take a Kheld woman even for sport. Nor had Aubrey given any indication this morning that she'd done anything but get a good night's sleep. Even so, there had been that dance last night, and the way Aubrey looked at Dorilian, and Arne knew as well as any how other men would talk. "It's just that we don't like seeing our women toyed with. Like that Bersyas last night, there's a fine example. I'm glad you stopped him. Not that she'd have gone for him or anything, knowing his ways as she does."

"She has better taste than that," Dorilian concurred.

"Yeah, she ought to." Arne realized how that sounded and dropped the topic awkwardly. Then he added, because it needed saying, "Her own people would stone her if they thought she was with you in any way. I just want you to know that. There's those already that want to see Robdan brought to answer for being up here, even if Hans sent him. And another bunch on top of them that thinks you need killing badly. So, I don't want even a whisper to get back to Amallar that Aubrey spent the night with you—not even if the two of you were as chaste as the stone virgins of Ghastra!"

Dorilian granted another look of amusement. "Rest assured, Master Anseldson, it's even more in my interest than hers that there be no whispers about the lady. Only a handful know where she was last night. I can guarantee my men will hold their tongues because I will have their heads if they do not. And Lady Aubrey and I will say nothing. Nor, do I think, will Robdan. That leaves only you."

"Well, I won't say nothing!"

"You are false before you start. I know you will tell Handurin."

Arne glowered. "I reckon I will. He should know."

"And indeed, he shall. Now, are you through interrogating me about my intentions?"

It was the best Arne could do. He'd never know for sure what had happened between the Hierarch and Aubrey, both so set on holding their tongues. That neither outright denied anything dismayed Arne. Little as he liked the thought, he could imagine them together.

"Tell Handurin one more thing." Dorilian put on his gloves. "I have summoned my second Neuberland army from beyond the Gero. Now that we have a signed treaty, I feel safe in relocating that force. My enemy is in Essera. If your crazy Khelds want to take Neuberland so badly, now is your chance."

"Can't say as some won't think about it. But we're all fighting in Essera now, looks like."

"At long last, yes, we are."

The first true sun of morning touched the Kerastes glacier so that it shone blue, mists rising from its fractured surface.

"Hans believes in you." Arne felt something serene at saying what he knew, as if putting it into words made that knowledge true. "He said at first it was Marenthro's word he took. Now it's yours. I can't say I'm all behind that, but I think I know why he feels it. These Staubauns scare the Mother's love out of me." The larger Staubaun world the Khelds had encountered in Lacenedon and Dazunor-Rannuli terrified Arne in the way it overarched everything, even Sordan and the Rill and Permephedon itself. It was a country he did not want to know. Dorilian's ability to navigate it awed him.

"You glimpse but the surface and let the currents sweep you away. But look deeper and you would see that their world is dying."

"Dying?"

Dorilian glanced at the cold, beautiful land. "Handurin knows. It was he who first showed it to me. And now I must ride the beast in its death throes. Either I will kill it, or it will kill me." He gave Arne a bitter smile. "You might wish for both."

# 26



"They always manage to keep ahead." Fran pointed to the enemy encampments across the thread of water that was the Dazun tributary of Nema. "See how clever they are, the way they do it? It just looks like they're camping there, but there are more tents than men. I asked Farrl, had him send some of his Trongorians out to look. They climbed that ridge." Fran and Hans looked to the hulking shoulder of the rise heralding the much larger hills to come in Dannuth and Tahlwent. "The main body of Southlanders is way behind, other side of that woods."

"A trap?"

Fran looked uncertain. "Could be. Or it could be just their way of concealing their main force."

"What does Euden Mezeon say? Or Soter Kometes?"

"We don't need the damned Staubauns to tell us what to do." Fran slammed his spyglass back into the carrying case slung on his horse's saddle.

It took an exercise of royal will for Hans not to show a flash of anger. Kheld antipathy toward Staubauns, for all that it had fired the different Kheld clans into becoming a cohesive army, was wildly indiscriminate in its choice of targets. Neuberland Khelds, in particular, tended to hate Sordan Staubauns and Esseran Staubauns just as intensely as, and perhaps even more than, they hated Nammuor's troops. Fran barely tolerated Kerr's Dannuthi troops and made no secret of his dislike of Euden Mezeon. Soter, the Sordani advisor, Fran despised and avoided.

"I want their advice as well as yours and Farrl's." Hans affirmed his position for what felt like the tenth time that day. "We'll meet in my tent later, after duties assignment." He turned his horse and headed back down the slope toward his own army's encampment.

*How am I ever going to forge them into a nation?* Staubauns were afraid the Khelds would take whatever wealth and power they still had, and the Khelds couldn't get around their burden of old hurts. And Hans was just about the only person who could talk to both sides.

By the time Hans reached his campaign quarters it was dark, and he wanted to be alone. He dismissed his guard and informed his newly acquired page, Snearly Darm, that he would eat in his tent that night. Having staff at his beck and call was something Hans had yet to get used to, but his Staubaun subjects approved that he should have people to attend him—and Khelds were adamant those people be Khelds. Snearly was a good lad. Washing up, however, didn't ease Hans's mood, nor did listening to the Kheldish music that swelled from troops sitting about their fires, laughing boisterously as they shared bread and company. On other nights, he would have sought them out or made his way over to the Staubaun ranks where Kerr and Euden supped with their ranking officers. The Staubaun nobles, although quieter, nonetheless took part in a far-ranging discourse Hans found engaging and informative. Tonight, though, for some reason, music seemed jarring and the mere thought of conversation repellent.

*I wish they'd all go away, the whole world just go away, and stop looking to me for answers. Everywhere I turn, they saddle me with expectations.*

Hans shook his head, clearing away emotions that were at once jarringly out of place and too diffuse to pull into focus. He was irritable with no clue as to why.

His cot was serviceable, and he welcomed the comfort of its thick mattress, even for sitting. Though the tent also boasted a chair, it was less padded, and Hans preferred the cot's space for laying out maps and papers. Over the last weeks he'd become more familiar with his Esseran birthright than he'd ever thought possible. Somewhat to his surprise, he'd learned that Dazunor's flat plain lay only in the east, near Permephedon and Dazunor-Rannuli. To the west, Dazunor was all rolling hills and winding rivers, rich with farms and famous for forges—the latter logical in that those hills sat astride the great ore fields of what had been the region's largest city.

*Gyges.*

Dorilian's descriptions of Gyges had enthralled Hans. Beneath these hills that lay ahead of them, an Aryati treasure city built of metals gathered from the stars had melted. Then the land had gone dark, and silent... and it had cooled.

*Ore flow.* Hans tried to envision it the way he had once envisioned the forgotten cities of one of this Creation's many lost pasts. Had the city's streets become veins of gold? Of rarer metals? If he unearthed its buildings, what secrets might he find?

The images in his head blurred and shifted, dreamlike but clear.

...ice-crowned mountains, so near... soaring above him, high and cold, while below him a lake shattered silver moonlight... Aubrey, dark-haired and beautiful in moonlight, wearing a dress of frost and pearl, gazing through eyes filled with wonder. Fear... desire. Aubrey leaned near, her soft lips touching, warm...

*Aubrey.* Hans gasped, startled that he could feel anything like... that. About her. Aubrey was a friend. Someone Hans liked and trusted, practically a sister. It had to be something else, maybe the music, because a strange melody too filled his mind, softer, sensual... but music shouldn't be causing him to feel like Aubrey was actually with him, her body molding to his.

Hans sat up, fingers raking through his hair, looking around his tent for distraction.

"Sir?" Snearly's clear young voice cut through into Hans's thoughts, rendering them to mere ribbons of feeling. "Got you something to eat. One of the mule drivers caught himself a fat young snouter and has it roasting. I carved you the best bit off the leg." Snearly set a wooden trencher piled with crudely sliced slabs of meat onto the small folding table beside the cot.

"Thank you, Snearly." Hans smiled at Snearly, who by dint of trying succeeded in making himself more useful every day.

"It's better than what most have to eat. Men are saying it's coming down to them or the horses."

Hans knew his army wasn't starving. "Why do they say that?" He gestured that Snearly should sit down to share the meat. Having someone else there would keep Hans's mind where it belonged, and not on far-fetched imaginings. "Here, have a slice. No, that one's all fat and skin. That one—"

Beaming with pleasure at being asked to share a plate with his prince, Snearly sat down and picked up the sliver of meat. He bit into it, juices running down his fingers. "Well, you see," he explained between chewing and swallowing, "seems most of the wagons coming in from Dazunor-Rannuli, they have nothing in them but grain and hay for the horses!"

"That's what I ordered."

"No food for men, just for horses?"

Hans nodded. "And cattle. We herd cattle with us, because the enemy is driving off or slaughtering all the cattle in the towns and farms. Men can hunt food, like this driver just did," he hoisted a piece of meat on his fork, "but I would rather have my men's meals on the hoof in the surrounding villages, even if that means feeding those cattle with purchased grain stores. And horses must eat too so they can carry men into battle." He had to grin at Snearly's look of agreement. "Not to mention grain makes for bread and gruel. You haven't seen any of the men going hungry, have you?"

"Don't see as I have," Snearly conceded. "But they maybe get tired marching all the time and fighting and then getting only dry bread to eat when they get bread at all. But we're staying put here now for a while, you think?"

Hans shrugged and poured more wine from the ewer on the table. "I'm not sure. The weather is turning. I'm meeting with the captains tonight and we'll decide something then." But he already knew what he would do. If Fran and the Neuberlanders wanted to harass Zel's positions, Hans would let them. But he would hold back his main force and stay east of the flat, wide, and not yet frozen Nema River to consolidate his gains. One of his first moves would be to fortify his storehouses. *Zel wants me to be impetuous, to attack the way a Kheld would and leap upon what looks like an easy victory. I need to be the one doing the surprising.*

Later that evening, Hans met with his captains in the main part of his tent, where three large braziers cast off enough heat for the men to remove their cloaks. A single suspended waterglobe burned brightly with sufficient light by which to read correspondence and maps. Nalf had brought along a new map, freshly sketched by one of several spies in Essera, that detailed the positions of the enemy forces near Kyrbasillon. The enemy troops there showed no signs of moving.

"They don't think we're much of a threat, looks like," said Fran.

"They know Zel is carving up the Dazun Road." Nalf had dressed to impress, in a wolfskin cape as splendid and striking in its way as the shining mail of the Staubaun Lords. Golden trophies taken from slain enemies dangled from the rings on his wide boarskin belt. "And they know we're not heading their way. It's clear as day itself that we're cutting here, across the underbelly." He stabbed with his finger at Trulo. Despite having lost its bridge across the Dazun, the city served as gateway to the richly forested lands of western Essera—and the sea. "They may have a mind to come at us should we push Zel out of Trulo and into the stinking Glainoi." The hill country Nalf named had been the heartland of Essera for many centuries, a land famous for great estates and magnificent farms from which sprang horses with bloodlines rivaling those of their owners in antiquity. Khelds had long been unwelcome there, even as grooms or house servants.

"That's why I intend to set camp here for a while." Hans traced the line of the river to show that they already controlled the approaches to Dazunor-Rannuli and the ore fields. Their current position was a good and defensible one. "I want to build granaries. Construct depots. Give the men some rest."

From outside the tent came sounds of horses arriving, of harnesses and the muffled commands and curses of agitated men. The Trongorian guard let in a pair of Khelds dragging another man. That man was clearly Staubaun, and his travel gear boasted the rich detailing of the upper caste. Both his headgear and the jacket under his elegant cloak of fox fur displayed ornate stitching and jeweled embroidery. He glared pure disdain at the men who'd ushered him in, then singled out Hans among the men he faced.

"If you would prove yourself a Prince," he challenged, "tell your unwashed creatures to unhand me."

Though he disliked the man's demeanor, Hans identified no hook upon which to hang a suspicion. Disrespect from high-handed locals was an everyday insult. He looked to the Khelds. "Where did you find him?"

"Practically rode up to camp. Said he wanted to talk to you, but then got all snotty about it."

To Khelds, there were many reasons a Staubaun might want to see their leader, but none that allowed bad manners.

"Asked him to wait, did you?"

One of the Khelds snorted. "Did that. Then he got smart, bragged he was some high fancy lord. As we reckoned he might be, by the clothes. And we figured you or these lords here," he acknowledged the other Staubaun men in the tent, "would want to know more about that."

The man lifted his head and offered his own defense. "I am Aedes Kopelates, Enlad of Saldis. I represent a consortium of local men of rank weary of the foreign presence in our land. We might be persuaded to formally recognize your royal standing in return for suitable promises."

Ignoring the affronted expressions of his captains, Hans eyed Aedes with interest. It was unusual to hear such a proposal presented openly. "What kind of promises?"

Lifting his chin, Aedes turned slowly and scanned the room, marking with whom he stood. A golden topaz the size of a horse's eye glinted against the dark leather covering his chest. "That you leave our lands and other holdings intact. Furthermore, we demand you seize none of our crops, buildings, accounts, or other goods in support of your army, nor will you molest our families and fortunes."

"Is that the same deal you made with Erenor Tholeros?"

The dry chuckle that broke the ensuing silence came from Nalf Rhys. Euden Mezeon and Kerr exchanged glances. Hans knew he was right in his suspicions. Aedes turned back with dark eyes suddenly and newly wary. "Prince Handurin, you cannot afford to dismiss the interests—and support—of the lords of these lands you would rule."

"What I cannot afford is worthless promises. You've already promised to Erenor, and for all I know to Nammuor also, the same support you now offer to me, in return for the same interests. Your empty words would hold good while I prevail, but any promises would disappear the moment I'd actually need them. For all your demands, you offer me nothing tangible, not a single soldier or sack of grain. As for the safety of your families and crops, the rules of conduct for my soldiers are well known. I see no reason to promise you anything." Hans watched as Aedes's expression lost some of its composure, gained a sneering edge of calculation.

"And so we get no surety?"

"Go back to your frightened lords and your family, Aedes Kopelates," Hans said. "Tell them that their rightful ruler has no intention of dishonoring them. However, this land is at war, and I will make no guarantees as to their futures. I will pay a fair price for your crops or other goods should I have need of them. Whether you keep your lands or your fortunes will depend on other things." It was common knowledge that Hans didn't intend to extend Erenor's grants of property or titles without adjudication.

With a thin grimace of acknowledgment, Aedes nodded. "And these men with you, this smug lot of thieves, what are you granting them in return for their service?"

Hans discreetly gestured to Farrl as Kheld and Staubaun captains alike took offense. *There's more to this!* Ever alert to even Hans's slightest movements, Farrl stepped between the angered captains and the increasingly divisive Aedes. *Not the situation, the man.* Hans focused. *There is something about the man.*

Why had Aedes chosen to confront Hans here? Why now? Because Aedes had watched from outside the camp... had seen the captains file into the command tent? Perhaps had even known that it was Hans's custom to hold these meetings almost nightly, after evening duties?

Not only that, but Aedes moved in an odd way, turning his body and not just his head, his eyes. *He has another eye...*

As Hans's gaze touched the golden topaz, something within looked back. Hans recognized the presence there. *Nammuor.* Nammuor was watching. Possibly listening as well. The Sorcerer and his mages had access to Aryati devices and ways, employing technologies most of the people of these lands no longer recognized. Hans had spent a whole week in Sordan with Tutto Rhunnard, who had discussed in some detail the many kinds of Aryati devices Hans might encounter.

*Careful.* It would be a mistake to let Nammuor know Hans had become suspicious. Neither could Hans move freely. Any attempt to signal Farrl now would only further reveal Hans's recently devised code system of hand gestures to the enemy's watching eye.

"These men have my loyalty and gratitude, Aedes Kopelates." It was essential that Hans force his own men to refocus, listen to him. He stepped around from behind the table, making himself more of a target. Assassination wasn't beyond Nammuor's possible intent. "I welcome all men and women who come to me honestly with a desire to respect their rightful King." Hans meant the words for Nammuor, now that he knew what the jewel was.

"Sordan's claim is higher."

The pattern was there, discernable, Aedes moving so that the jewel's sorcerous gaze might assess the reactions of other men to those words. A carefully calculated movement of Euden Mezeon's head alerted Hans that he too had detected that they were being watched. And provoked.

*I can play this game. Neither this man nor Nammuor knows what my understanding with Dorilian really is.* Hans shrugged with a lightness he did not feel. "Dorilian wants to see Essera free of Marc Frederick's and Stefan's murderers. As do I." Hans walked to a stand where he'd placed on a small easel a portrait of his grandfather that he had found in Dazunor-Rannuli. Looking at it reminded him of a death yet to be avenged. He touched the frame and felt strengthened even more than usual by Marc Frederick's memory.

Aedes smirked and looked about confidently. "Then this Sordaneon should himself leave Essera. All in this land know he did the murders. Or is it your plan to have Dorilian secure your throne so you may then seize him for yourself?"

The men around Hans reacted each in his own way, from glares of affront to snickers betraying underlying approval of such a plan.

"How dare you suggest that Handurin would do such a monstrous thing!" Young Kerr would have stepped forward had not Euden Mezeon gripped him by the arm.

*Now*, Hans thought. Draped on the chair beside the table was his heavy cloak, thrown aside earlier. Snearly had not thought to hang it on a peg. Hans grabbed the cloak by its embroidered edge and tossed it, flaring, over Aedes' head. The substantial, fur-lined leather fell heavily, covering the topaz just below the man's throat. Seeing what Hans had done, Euden Mezeon leaped upon Aedes, wrapping his strong warrior's arms about the man.

"Open!" Euden shouted to the guard. The guard tore aside the tent flap. Euden flung Aedes from the tent so that he rolled onto the hard-packed earth outside. Wrapped in his rich cloak, Aedes fell onto his back and those watching saw his body convulse in a great, arching spasm.

"Master! No!" Aedes's muffled voice entreated, before a raw scream was ripped from his throat. Now that the device was discovered, it was useless to Nammuor—as was its wearer. Light flared beneath the cloak, then pierced it.

"Down!" someone shouted.

Farrl, nearest to Hans, pulled him to the floor of the tent as a crackling sheet of energy burst outward from the screaming man, searing the air with the stink of ignited gases and burning silk, hair, and flesh. The body jerked and twisted in flames. The screaming died only when Aedes did.

"Madrock's hells!" Fran climbed to his feet and went to stand over the charred, still burning remains of the man. Light from campfires showed but shadows of smoke and glints of gold. A few tents nearby had caught fire and shouting had ensued as men scrambled to fight the flames. From within the curtain of smoke, wounded men screamed. "What demon's work was *that*?"

"Nammuor's." Hans got to his feet and gave nods of thanks to Euden Mezeon, who looked as shaken as any of the Khelds, and to Farrl for his tackle. Even Nalf Rhys looked ghostly pale as he scanned the growing circle of men drawn by the event. At least two of the outside soldiers had been cleaved through by the lightning, not having known to avoid it. By the look of the bodies, one of them was dead and the other likely to die.

"It was an altered *lr* crystal." Euden looked grim as he said it. "A mage device that can be in two places at once. I haven't seen one since the Demise. Such crystals are difficult to use. Only the Highborn and Epoptes yet know the making of them, although rumors have for years credited Mormantalorus with their manufacture. That Leur-built City is Sordan's twin and sister to Permephedon."

"If the Highborn make them, what makes you so sure it wasn't the Sordaneon who sent it?" Fran challenged. "Find out our plans regarding him?"

"Dorilian already knows my plans regarding him. And he wouldn't need to do this." Covering his mouth and nose against the stench, Hans walked over to the body and used his dagger to lift what remained of the chain about Aede's neck. The blackened setting gaped like an empty socket.

"Nor do the Highborn have others call them 'Master,'" Euden Mezeon noted. His noble countenance gave him a grim assurance. "It is an ancient prohibition."

"It's true I never heard them called so," Nalf Rhys agreed reluctantly. His frown deepened as he looked upon the scene, evaluating the hundred things it told him. "Well, we always heard the stinking Southlander was a sorcerer. Stefan himself said it enough. And now, by the looks of it, he's decided you're worth his attention." Nalf weighed Hans with a newly respectful stare.

Hans nodded, himself shaken. "Unfortunately, he also now knows who is with me and what we look like. And that there's dissension among us. Don't think for a moment he wasn't analyzing our responses for signs of weakness—or that he didn't find any. Or that he wasn't prepared to kill us all." Several soldiers gathered, intent upon removing the body. "Keep what's left of the device. I'll want to look at it in the morning in daylight." Wanting to restore normalcy, Hans added, "We start on the granaries tomorrow." Dismissing the captains, he went back into the tent and closed the flap behind him.

He'd known it would come to this. Not just physical battle, not just the cold and bad weather and armies. *Can I fight a sorcerer? I was lucky this time. What if I don't recognize his next attack in time? How many will die then?*

Feeling drained, Hans sank onto the welcome softness of his cot and lay back, glad for the soft glow of the tiny waterglobe nestled on his table. Darkness would have sparked too much imagination. What he had witnessed of the Demise at Permephedon burned through his fevered thoughts: Marc Frederick's last, doomed stand against the death Nammuor had decreed for him. Nammuor couldn't break the Leur's Ring, but he could destroy the mortal flesh of the man who wore it. *You are all that is left here worth saving! Run!*

Until now, Hans had been hidden. Nammuor had not even known who Hans was. Until now, Nammour had not assigned Hans any value beyond that of a lineage and name, a nuisance simply for existing, a minor prince to be mopped up later. *Marenthro knew what he was doing, keeping me hidden, inactive. All these months, all these years, Nammuor noticed only Dorilian, saw only Dorilian.*

Dorilian Sordaneon, brilliant as a sun, had blinded entire nations.

Nalf was right. Hans was no longer hidden. The Sorcerer had taken notice.

# 27

There is a small fruit of Sansordan's desert, a tiny growth,
easy to overlook because it lives in the shadows of rocks
that shield it from the sun and view. It doesn't look like
much at all: lumpy, green, and common. That is, until it
is opened and prepared with care, upon which it becomes
a delicacy, rare and wonderful.
UBBEN CHUPARA,
LETTER TO HIS FATHER, UMMKAR PREQUOYAH IV

"This better get done," Arne complained quietly, though
Aubrey was sure Tharos and probably half the delegation of
Kheld elders waiting on the platform would hear him. "Because
I'm not going all the way back *there* to tell the Hierarch to get it
right. Damn Hebron and his lot might just take the opportunity to
finish me off."

"We won't have to go back," Aubrey replied. "Dorilian wants
this to work, right? So it'll work—we just need to be patient."

Upon arriving in Bellan Toregh the night before, Arne had
waved the cylinder in the air above his and Aubrey's heads and
proclaimed they'd secured the key. His pronouncement had
brought on rounds of cheers and golden brew. They'd been the
toast of the town while the ale lasted.

Now Aubrey and Arne were the only ones who knew that while
Tharos had received the key, he'd not been able to use it. Which
was why they were all waiting on the empty platform for a *charys*
to arrive.

Wind pushed at the beards and garments of the small crowd
atop the Toregh. After weeks of waiting, leaders and common folk
alike were eager for Rill service to Dazunor-Rannuli to begin.
Bellan Toregh had not yet built such structures as graced other Rill
mounts, like permanent shelters where passengers could wait in

comfort, so people huddled in what protection the square columns of the station colonnade offered. Aubrey overheard quite a few people grouse about Dorilian's intentions, whether he would truly revive Dazunor-Rannuli's Rill. About Hans' and their boys' parts in the war, she and Arne heard in plenty. Word on what the Hierarch was doing was scant.

*Holed up in Askyllon, waiting it out,* was the usual sneer.

A few stone troughs and fine wooden carvings had been put around the place and piled with winter greenery in an attempt to convey cheer. Aubrey was glad to see her countryfolk had made an effort. Far from resting dormant all these weeks, Bellan Toregh's Rill mount had become a place of business. Though dawn barely lifted the clouds to the east, passengers gathered on benches arranged near the carts and stalls of that day's vendors. Many held wrappers filled with griddle cake or egg hash pies, and steam wafted from the stall of a branroot vendor. On the other side of the platform, the station's elevators had been working all night and laborers swarmed, moving and stacking cargo for lading. Trade was on all minds, but the first order of business was to begin sending provisions and supplies to their fighting force by way of Dazunor-Rannuli.

Tharos, attired in full Epoptean robe and sashes, stood beside Aubrey and looked as tense as a man anticipating a backstabbing. Instead of providing a usable means by which he might bespeak the Rill, the message cylinder had instructed Tharos first send a second, encased and coded message to Sordan. What had followed was a brisk, anonymous response to that message: *Message received. Await charys.*

Though he feared a more skilled Epopte was being sent or some Sordaneon device fetched, Tharos chose to be sanguine about it. "The Hierarch trusts no one. He made certain that if the message was intercepted by his enemies, nothing could be done with it but compliance. The key was in Sordan all along."

"I figured he had it with him. I mean, he's the one that stopped the damn thing." Arne hardly looked convinced.

Tharos sighed. "He *is* Rill flesh. Making it so someone else can bespeak the Rill specifically to override his bidding would be nearly impossible to implement. The Brotherhood has been attempting from the first hour to configure a Rill command to release Dazunor-Rannuli."

Of that, Aubrey was certain. She'd seen and heard enough on

her own to know the Seven Houses and the Brotherhood of
Epoptes were Essera's true unholy alliance. Hans said he and
Dorilian had spoken for hours about how to manage the politics
certain to accompany Rill restoration. Releasing a sigh of her own,
Aubrey leaned against the nearest column and looked out into the
dawn now crowning Neuberland. From this height, she could just
see the outskirts of the town at the foot of the mount, beyond
which lay the rolling, mist-drenched hills where Saemoregh would
be found.

Aubrey's holding lay within that distance. Fallow now, with
harvested fields. Dorilian had all but ordered Aubrey to stay in
Amallar and, now that she was far away from him again, the request
rankled. It should not have. Though she felt no pull to be there,
Amundhal was her home. Her holders would be weaving and crafting
at this season and she could spend her time on studies. What sat
awry was that her holding had little need of her. All important
activity was taking place north of the Dazun. Did Dorilian really
think Aubrey should spend this war carding wool or milking cows
with her crofters? Or communing with the Old Mothers at
Rhodhur? The only place farther from anything at all was the
Rappeleye Motherhome at the edge of the Bogs and the World.

*I agreed too quickly. I was too flattered with thoughts that Dorilian
cared about me.*

Maybe, if she went to Amundhal and Saemoregh, Aubrey could
do something useful like plan a new springhouse or set up a school.
The latter would be a good use of her time. Both in Amallar and
Neuberland, Kheld children—and men and women too—would
be needing more and different schools than those they now had.

"Might as well tell me what you're thinking," said Arne. "I can
see from here you're not headed back to Rhodhur."

Aubrey had told Arne that plan. Apparently, she'd done as little
to convince Arne as herself.

"Saemoregh is closer."

"At least it makes sense."

Conversation ceased as Tharos straightened. "Rill sign."

The Rill's rings rearranged and a distant thrum reached their
ears. Mere heartbeats passed before the silver shape of a *charys*
appeared, coming from Sordan. Upon arrival, it settled in the
center of the run and all could see it differed from the usual
conveyance. Green and silver, horned and elegant. The combined

Kheld and Epoptean guard stepped forward to bar the way. Gasps erupted when the *charys* opened and a score of soldiers in the green and silver uniforms of the Sordaneon Eagle Guard emerged, surrounding a lone small figure.

The child who exited the Rill onto Bellan Toregh's platform commanded all eyes. Round-faced with wide dark eyes, she glowed with the bloom of a girl just entering maidenhood. A dress of yellow silk fell in pleats from a yoke of ornately figured gold. Beaded shoes bright as sunbeams dazzled on her feet. A circlet of gold filigree, arrayed with tiny enamel flowers of yellow, white, and orange, crowned her fall of glossy, shoulder-length brown hair. Excitement heightened the pink in her sun-brown cheeks. Against the gray and stark winter landscape surrounding the mount, she looked like a breath of another season.

Arne ran forward. "Fahme! What are you doing here?"

The Eagle Guards closed rank, which stopped Arne in his tracks, but Fahme ordered them aside. "Please stay behind me like I told you." She stepped to the front and beamed at Arne, then at the yellow-robed Tharos, who looked completely stunned. "I'm here to help. I am the key."

Following Tharos's lead, Aubrey and Arne whisked Fahme into the station. Not only was it warmer within but removing the Sordaneon Princess from the jostling and shouting crowd made her guards less nervous. They had only allowed Arne inside because Fahme knew him. When the gathered Khelds insisted an elder, one of Bellan Toregh's Old Mothers, be allowed to observe whatever was going on, Aubrey too was allowed inside to interpret.

"She's the Hierarch's daughter. Adopted," Tharos said.

Fahme, heeding Tharos's warning to touch nothing, stood with Arne near the consoles and the station's panoramic windows. Fahme practically bounced with delight over what she was seeing.

Tharos added, "This is the first time I have met her. I know, however, that she petitioned to study at the Order's college."

"Denied, I'm sure." Aubrey had learned in Dazunor-Rannuli that only youths born to the purest of Staubaun bloodlines qualified for training. She relayed the details to the Old Mother. Ednowa Vesl Faldenda smiled with approval of the child as Tharos continued.

"She doesn't meet *any* of the criteria."

"I have absolute pitch!" Fahme and Arne had decided to rejoin them.

Tharos smiled. "So do donkeys."

"She tells everyone who'll listen she wants to work with the Rill." Arne spoke to Ednowa in Khelda, which Aubrey dutifully interpreted to the captain of Fahme's guard. "But they only train boys and pure-bloods, and don't like Sordaneons much either." To Aubrey Arne said, in Stauba, "It's a damn shame she wasn't in Sordan when we went."

From his side, Fahme answered with great solemnity: "I was in seclusion. Perfecting my instrument."

Aubrey pondered the girl. It was difficult to place Dorilian alongside her. The great expectation was that he might someday sire sons. Daughters but placed the Sordaneon line at the edge of extinction. Though she had heard Fahme mentioned by Hans and Arne, and even Levyathan, Aubrey hadn't expected a girl like this one, clothed in yellow and utterly sure of her place in the world. Just as surprising was to see Tharos bend in a deep bow.

"You say you have the key, Princess?"

"No. I told you, I *am* the key. Father designed it. I've been training my whole life for this!" Fahme spread her hands and twirled, yellow gown flaring about her ankles, to include the room. "He told me one day I would be inside a node. And look where I am! I'm here to bespeak the Rill."

Aubrey had never heard song so pure as that which rose from Fahme's throat. The girl stood before the black orb Tharos called the Overlay link, which appeared after insertion of a small cone-shaped device into the center console. Young hands held before her as if in supplication, her body straight and her throat slightly extended, Fahme drew a breath and her lips parted to release a string of perfect, golden notes. Maybe they were words, maybe just exultations of joy and hope, but the result was sheer beauty. Motes of light born in the heart of the Overlay swarmed within its orb like a flock of birds, gathered and parted and rearranged. A clear strong tone sounded from the console overlooking the platform.

Tharos placed something into the hair beside his ear and began talking to unseen persons. "Dazunor-Rannuli is responding again! So is Leseos!"

Fahme stood, hand on throat, smiling and laughing. "I was sure I could do it! Father listened and told me I could. I studied and studied. I studied so hard!"

"Beautiful," Ednowa said, speaking the Stauba word. "Mother's gift."

"I never heard anyone sing like that." Arne's wide-eyed admiration remained high.

"Dazunor-Rannuli is reporting full restoration of operations. *All* operations." Tharos sank back into the floating chair and beamed. "They are receiving a *charys* from Permephedon as we speak. And they eagerly wait to welcome ours as soon as we can send it."

"Can I borrow him?" Arne spoke to Fahme as he pointed to the head Eagle Guard.

The officer and Fahme exchanged a look. "You need a guard?" she asked.

"I need to make an announcement, and… well, he looks really important, with all that green and silver armor and all, so I thought maybe—"

Fahme nodded. "Presentation. Go with him, Ordan, and strive to look your most important."

Arne left, accompanied by Ednowa and Ordan, to bursts of cheering as soon as they appeared on the platform. The door closed behind, restoring silence, but those inside could watch the effect of the announcement on the crowd. People jumped with excitement, some ran to give Arne and Ednowa—and Ordan too—horns of beer.

"What you sang. Were those words?" Aubrey wasn't sure which astounded her more: that the Rill had listened to a child, or that Dorilian had entrusted a child with so powerful a secret.

Cheeks bunching with pride, Fahme grinned and nodded. While Tharos worked the console and looked as happy as he had in weeks, Aubrey walked with Fahme to the other side of the operations room and a viewing area that overlooked the Floh and the town of Bellan Toregh. Fahme had already stated she would be leaving as soon as the crowd could be controlled and access to her *charys* regained.

"*Leur'alta*. Leursong! Not words exactly and not Aryati, which the Epoptes use in setting schedules. Father taught me a Rill speech they don't use. Leur is the language of Creation, of which the Rill is part. The language Derlon knew first."

Song, it was said, had lifted the Five Cities. Aubrey was learning a great deal about a man who embodied more mysteries than known truths. "Your father," she told Fahme, "has a knack for delivering surprises." Dorilian had hidden a key where no one, especially the Epoptes or Seven Houses, would ever look.

"People are easy to fool. They thought because he hadn't done anything about the Rill, that meant he couldn't." Fahme's small hands clenched in fists. "Same as me. People don't want me to be his daughter, just because his body didn't make mine. They call me a pretend Princess and my father frivolous."

"I can't believe anyone would call Dorilian frivolous."

"People do, behind his back. Behind mine. Ha! I showed them."

Aubrey battled her laugh. "I think you both did!"

Fahme grinned fierce satisfaction. "Just like he said. The night before Father left Sordan, he came to my room and told me not to sing Rillsong for anyone unless I got a message from him saying to wear my yellow dress. And that when I did, I would show the world whose daughter I am."

Fahme had gone back to Sordan as brightly as she'd arrived, clearing the run for the massive cargo transport that now occupied the space. "Her real father tried to kill him. Did kill all those Princes and the Old King too, at Permephedon. He was the man who poisoned the wine." Arne was telling Aubrey what he knew about Fahme and Dorilian too.

"And Dorilian still took her in." There was another wonder.

"Because of her mother. Her mother was his brother's wet nurse, part of the family. I'll grant him one thing: he's fierce loyal to any that are loyal to him. Levyathan told me Fahme's mother was that way. Met him when he was seven years old, the day his mother died, and stayed with him 'til she got murdered by that wife of his."

The more Aubrey heard about Daimonaeris, the more she understood why Dorilian had cut off her head. Loyalty spoke to him, deeply. As did promises. Just thinking it brought on a wince.

"Now what?" Arne shot Aubrey a look.

"This shipment. Are you seeing it?" Even with equipment brought in from Sordan during the last weeks, and workers trained to use it, loading the *charys* was taking longer than scheduled.

"They're new at it. They'll get faster."

"They'd better get faster soon. I think Tharos is tearing his hair out."

Arne grinned. "The only Epopte I ever saw before him was bald. I guess that would explain it."

A loud rumbling came from the road, along with shouts and other sounds of confusion. Aubrey and Arne followed it to the plaza where the access road joined the platform. A convoy of wagons, cloth covers billowing above wide beds, groaned on their wheels as teams of dusty horses attempted to pull them onto the platform. The wagons' drivers ignored the gesticulations and warnings from guards. A tall, yellow-banded officer and his similarly attired men from the station's contingent of Epoptean guards placed themselves in front of the wagons and tried to turn them back.

"Halt! This is the passenger side. No cargo."

"But I have to get my hams on!" A portly figure climbed down from the lead wagon. Even dressed in dusty travel clothes, including a jaunty cap with a feather in it, there was no mistaking Gerd Ralfson.

The officer looked on in disbelief. "You're trying to board hams?"

"Khelds eat hams. Tell him, Arne Anseldson." Gerd singled Arne out as someone who might have importance enough to assist. Aubrey still found Arne being in charge of anything quite amusing.

Arne turned to the officer. "If he says he needs hams, he needs hams."

"Hams aren't people. They go on the lading side!"

To that, Arne could but shrug. Gerd looked lost. It was as good a moment as any for Aubrey to step in with an important question. "Gerd? Why are you here? Hams or no hams, you should be keeping the inn at Rhodhur Hall."

Gerd drew a breath and provided the answer. "I got a letter. Hans Thegn's kitchens and provisions are, well, a mess. Not being run properly at all. I've been asked to come put things right. I don't know anything about feeding armies, but I know how to cook for a crowd. Figured I would start with hams. Proper warrior's fare, those hams."

Tharos rushed up. "What is this? There's no lading on this side."

Aubrey put a hand on his arm. "This is Gerd Ralfson, an important man here in Amallar. He has the ear of Prince Handurin, who has sent for him. There aren't many passengers. Surely these few wagons can fit."

Tharos's mouth pressed tight before he spoke in measured tones. "The *charys* can be configured to accommodate them, yes, but I also have to change the lading weight and assign a new fee. Does he have the fee? Because he's not on the list, and neither are his hams—or the wagons or horses!"

Rill fees. The scourge of this new way of transport. Gerd must have heard of such fees because he blanched.

"How much?" Aubrey snapped. After hemming and hawing, Tharos managed an estimate. "I'll pay. For him and the hams. Everything. I'll write a draft the Order can present to my bank in Leseos."

"And for unlading in Dazunor-Rannuli?" Tharos prompted. "Are arrangements made?"

"Made for what?" Arne wanted to know.

"To get these wagons and their cargo off the Mount. It's an island, there are tolls. You can handle that, I suppose," Tharos said dryly. "If you know your way around."

Arne threw his hands in the air and waved them. "Hans has a man for that."

Aubrey shot Arne a look. "Prince Handurin," she said to Tharos, "has retained a broker, a man named Egidius Mogens to handle unlading of supplies and... other things. But Mogens doesn't know about Gerd. Arne will have to tell him."

"Me?" Arne challenged. Aside from having sat in with the Seven Houses, he hadn't taken part in mercantile negotiations. "That was all you and Orem Darm."

"Oh, for the Mother's Tears."

"There's also the Seven Houses," inserted Tharos. "House Koillos specifically. They're claiming priority on the schedule."

Arne turned to Aubrey in alarm. "I can't argue with them about that! They use words I never heard in my life!"

"We have priority," Aubrey stated. She'd interpreted those very parts of the Rill treaty—and memorized them so well she could reproduce them if necessary. "Prince Handurin and his army and his allies have priority." So did Sordan. If necessary Aubrey would drag Sinon Kouranos into this matter. To Arne she said, "Looks like I'm going with you."

"To Dazunor-Rannuli?" Arne looked conflicted.

"I need to make sure everything's smooth on that end. I'll come right back after."

This transport was needed. It also would be making a statement. Hans needed the supplies for his army, but Aubrey's people needed it to go off without a hitch—if only to prove Khelds could be reliable partners in their new Rill enterprise. Arne would work his ass off to get the job done, but Aubrey was the one who'd negotiated the arrangement with Mogens and she was better positioned than either Arne or Orem Darm to deal with the agents of House Koillos.

*I'll come right back*, Aubrey vowed. *I'll go to Saemoregh.*

What she would not do was leave the first transport to Dazunor-Rannuli in a lurch.

# 28



It was one thing to send a Rill load of goods. Warehousing and moving those goods was a different problem altogether. To this end, and because no one else was doing so, Aubrey had encouraged Hans to form relationships with Esseran merchants and brokers. Noble lords and ladies provided horses and troops; merchants provided warehouses and barges and wagons. Egidius Mogens was a purveyor of the latter three. Aubrey was surprised—and delighted—to learn that the warehouses leased by Mogens for Amallar's shipments included one owned by Cam Gereggson and Ralen Ornichos.

Aubrey had liked the pair on first meeting them in Darluum, where Hans had gained an agreement that gave him use of their barges. Other Khelds remained suspicious of the partnership, but Aubrey had seen early on that Ralen's devotion to Cam was absolute—as was Cam's to Ralen. Kheld and Staubaun, not fully accepted by either side, the two men navigated the turbulent and often hostile world of Dazun river commerce too successfully to be ignored.

"Ralen is more than the muscle," Egidus said when Aubrey asked which man was the one in charge, "and Cam is more than the brains. I suggest seeing them as one person."

As Egidius led both Aubrey and Arne to a large warehouse, he explained that Ralen had just purchased the warehouse from the estate of a man who had supported Erenor and, upon having had to flee the city, had forfeited the property. Aubrey admired the move—and something else Egidius had just told her. It shone through in the subtle bow of the merchant's head, and his tone of regard when Ralen welcomed them to his place of business.

Seeing Cam walk toward the group from the far end of the warehouse dock where he'd moored a small boat brought on a smile. Though plainly dressed, he looked prosperous—and rather too handsome for such rough surroundings. He greeted Ralen first, then Aubrey and Arne.

"Where have you both been?" Cam's wide smile was inclusive of them all. "In Lacenedon, as rumor has it?"

He had almost certainly heard the rest of the rumor, that Aubrey and Arne had brought back the signed treaty. "In Lacenedon, yes," Aubrey answered. "As deep into Staubaun lands as any Kheld should ever have to go. I won't be going again." She was uncomfortable enough being *this* north of the Dazun—the cold waters of which she would be able to see if she stood atop some nearby boxes.

"That unpleasant?" Cam looked surprised. He, clearly, had never been to Lacenedon.

Arne snorted. "You think the Seven Houses are bad? You haven't met Bas Hebron's lot."

*Thrum.* A series of deep reverberations sounded across the city, at a distance but imminent. All on the warehouse dock watched a vast shape appear overhead where before there had been only air, its immense mass effortlessly entering shape-shifting arches and slowing until it came to a stop, suspended above the nearby Rill Mount like a sword in midthrust.

"Marvelous," said Egidius.

"And just in time to make good on our investment," Ralen snickered to Cam.

"Maybe we can get our other warehouse out of hock."

Ralen laughed aloud and grinned at the Mount, upon which elevators had begun to climb. He slapped Egidius on the shoulder and the two men walked along the quay to talk business. Aubrey seized the opportunity to pin Cam with a question.

"Is it true? Do you and Ralen own a Rill slot?"

Acknowledgment warmed Cam's blue eyes. "Yes. Rill slot owners often buy their portions on credit and then leverage those portions through brokers, especially commodities slot futures.

So"—he explained with a short head nod toward the Mount—"when the Rill stopped, not all the slot owners could meet the payments demanded by their creditors. Neither could they get their credit extended because, well, the Rill was stopped. And no one knew when, if ever, it would start up again. Panic everywhere. You have no idea. But Ralen and I had never owned Rill portions or futures. We didn't operate in that stratum."

"Meaning what?" Arne asked.

"We're common traders," Cam explained. "Boats and barges. Short term carrier agreements. But—"

Aubrey grinned and said to Arne, "They had money."

Cam chuckled quietly. "We had *lots* of money—and even with the Rill stopped our routes remained profitable. So we helped one of those men out by buying his useless Rill slot."

"His *no longer* useless Rill slot."

"True. So now Ralen and I own an entire slot: Dazunor-Rannuli to Sordan. It cost a fortune—but we're about to make a bigger one."

"I had a cousin who owned a Rill slot," Arne confided. "Well, his wife did, but he managed it. Cullen Brodheson."

It was strange, Aubrey thought, the way a Rill triumph could make her feel sad. She stopped reminiscing when she saw Cam's expression shift from joy to condolences. "You knew Cullen?"

"King Stefan's Trade Minister. Of course we did. I did mostly. I... handled that end of things during Stefan's reign. Cullen Thegn was good and decent. It was a crime what happened to him."

"He would have been happy to see... this." Aubrey waved her hand at the Rill.

Cam nodded, also frowning up at the Mount. "I don't care how much coin I make, I will never think that thing is natural."

That a man so clearly sophisticated should hold such very Kheld views made Aubrey laugh. She looked over as Ralen rejoined them with Gerd in tow. Having traveled by Rill and now being again in the city where he had served as Cullen's cook years before had Gerd aglow with excitement.

"This fine man has said he will transport my hams! Bring them down from the Mount and put them on barges. All my hams and potatoes and crates of crockery—and the wagons to carry them."

"See, I told you, Gerd," Arne said. He went to stand at the beaming innkeeper's side. "Aubrey got it all arranged with that man Mogens." Egidius was nowhere to be seen and had probably gone back to his counting house.

"So she did! And best of all, I can leave this very afternoon! Hans Thegn will not have to wait a day longer than it takes to get there."

"Where would that be?" Cam asked.

"Rainill, I figure, is the nearest port," said Ralen.

"It is. But I was just there. The wharf at Rainill has heavy lumber for building cranes, but only one pulley could be salvaged from the wreck the Mormantalorans made of the piers. When I left there was no working block and tackle for unloading."

Some of the elevators on the Mount were descending, headed toward the warehouse loading docks. At least one load of Gerd's hams, however, was already at hand, piled high on a horse-drawn wagon. Aubrey watched the course of Ralen's thoughts, from frown to determination.

"I think I can get one." Ralen rubbed a hand over his face, then through his rough-cut hair "I've made friends with Sordan's quartermaster. River ports are essential to the war effort. He'll get me a block and tackle, likely within the hour." He gave Gerd a rakish smirk. "Come, friend, let's go bribe the man with a ham."

"Will that work?"

"It should."

"Oh good! Wait." Gerd trotted to the wagon and wrestled two hefty bundles from under the tarp. He carried these back and pushed one into Cam's arms. "This one's for you and your partner here. Your partner, truly? How times have changed!" Armed with a ham, Gerd joined Ralen again and they hurried off.

While Arne went with Ralen and Gerd to see about securing a block and tackle, Cam stayed behind with Aubrey to talk.

"Come to dinner tonight," Cam invited. "Rill revival is a good occasion to celebrate, and"—he shifted the ham in his arms—"there will be more than enough ham."

A fair offer and one Aubrey probably should accept. She might even enjoy the company. Aubrey looked around at the bustling sights of the city center. The palaces of the Seven Houses crowded the Lower Canal with their ornately tiled walls and landings. Larger and even more splendid were the gold-faced walls of the Rillhome Palace with its glittering domes and towers, standing imposingly at the head of the Lagos, the central lagoon across which could be seen the spires of other, more distant Highborn palaces. Cullen had lived at the Rillhome Palace and worked from there following Stefan's confiscation of it. The just-signed treaty had restored it to the Sordaneons, so that now all it did was remind Aubrey, again, that she wasn't keeping her promise to Dorilian to stay in Amallar.

Instead she was here, being given one invitation after another.

"I would enjoy a Kheldish ham," she said, hoping it conveyed real disappointment. "It would remind me that even in this city it's possible to find good company and a bit of home. But Arne and I have promised Egidius that we'll go with him to a reception at the house of the Dannuthi ambassador. It will send the right message."

"What message is that?"

"That Khelds have come up in the world and we can no longer be excluded."

"I don't think that many people outside of Prince Handurin's circle are ready for that message just yet," Cam said. He set the ham down on a nearby crate and sat beside it.

"You may be right. But I think it falls on those of us in position to do so to try. He—Egidius—is lending me a dress, something borrowed from one of his daughters. I didn't bring one with me and, well, the fancy dress I do have is too alluring. I drew far too much attention in Lacenedon the night I wore it."

Why did Cam slide her such a sharp look? "There's talk in this city that Prince Handurin may be eyeing you for a bride."

Aubrey restrained a sigh. Kheld men plotting the Esseran succession was bad enough. Staubaun fears, on the other hand... "Me? Never. And Hans won't wed anyone until he's defeated Nammuor. He says that if he should sire an Heir in a land without peace, it would be too tempting for Essera's nobles to kill him in hope of establishing themselves in a regency."

"Smart young man. But then he's still chasing his own regent through the kingdom."

"Which is one more reason it's important to send the right message. Hans needs every ally he can get."

Another thrum announced a new Rill arrival, this one from the north. Dazunor-Rannuli's three active runs ensured almost constant arrivals and departures. Cam looked down the Lower Canal's gond-filled expanse, toward the river and the location of the house he and Ralen shared. Aubrey had visited the waterfront manse once before, during her previous stay right after Hans had secured the city.

"If you get the chance tonight, stop by. Our parties often run late." Cam had a smile that could win over any argument. "I guarantee our guests will be more fun. Ralen and I don't follow society and we like interesting people. Like Mennud, whose songs offend everyone"—Aubrey laughed at that and so did Cam—"and Haliast Tauros, who never votes for anything, or the famous courtesan Nuessil, who knows everyone's secrets. And there'll be a reading by the poet Myron."

Aubrey grasped the dense wool sleeve of Cam's upper arm. His look of shock embarrassed her enough to release the fabric. "*Myron*? The one who wrote 'The Hills We Die On?'"

"The poet. Yes."

"He's *here*?"

"Where did you think he lived?"

"Stauberg?"

Except Aubrey hadn't thought about it, not at all. She had read Myron's poetry for pleasure and not scholarship and so had missed the obvious. She should have picked up from his verses that Myron was not a northern Esseran... that he lived in Dazunor-Rannuli. What luck that he should be at Cam and Ralen's party tonight affording a chance to meet him. Aubrey had never met a famous poet before, only a handful of itinerant bards.

Cam chuckled. "It's surprising that you know of Myron."

"I'm just as surprised *you* do."

"Well, I do I live here."

Here, in the heart of Essera, alongside Staubauns and bankers and the Rill. Aubrey, however, had never considered that a more worldly Kheld like Cam might also know songwriters and poets and famous courtesans. It could be amusing to meet one of those also. His party did sound more fun. Arne had returned to the dockside along with Gerd and Ralen; all three now walked Aubrey's way. Aubrey stood and turned to Cam. She needed to speak quickly.

"I want to meet Myron," she said, prompting an inquisitive head tilt from Cam. "I'll find some way to stop by your party, but don't let him leave before I get there."

# 29

What do the Highborn give us? Access to the Wall and Rill, of course, but they also represent key elements of a legacy written in blood. The gifts of Leur lie not in the Entities only; those gifts are also found in Highborn ability to use the many artifacts their ancestors left behind.

MILATES AMBROS, *PAPER TO THE FIFTY-FIFTH CONCLAVE*

*Grandmother sends her regards. I have begun corresponding with her.* Dorilian felt his jaw tense. Damn the boy! Levyathan was developing far too much of his own mind. *Don't visit Ermenthalia,* he warned. *Her loyalties stand too close to Nammuor. I placed restrictions on her for good reason.*

*I understand. She may possess a means to translocate me. I have Tiflan here to advise me. He's very good at these things.*

Yes. Between Tutto and Tiflan, Levyathan's protection against magic-adjacent attacks was exceptional. Being in Sordan also afforded a high level of security.

*Where are you now?* Levyathan wanted to know.

*Danae. Near Bynum.* Dorilian sat upon a stony outcrop at the top of a hill overlooking the Eleutheron capital. His army and Hebron's darkened the fields to each side of the main road. From here he could also look upon another hill, one that told a separate tale. Dorilian had made a small detour to see for himself the ruins of the Danae Palace, to feel for himself its horrifying residue. A winter-kissed hilltop. Columns of char and ash. Death and anguish. Loss—but somehow incomplete. He could not fully define his dissatisfaction. Palaistea had died here along with her children. Dorilian should have felt those lost lives more acutely and thought maybe too much time had passed.

*Closer to Stauberg.*

*Yes*, Dorilian confirmed. *Erenor's army has chosen this place to make a stand. I am not marching to Stauberg; I must fight my way there.*

*And Nammuor?*

*Will be waiting.*

Dorilian had tried, once or twice, to detect his enemy in the firmament and found only the slightest trace. Nammuor's Diadem was alien to the Creation and in no way a part of it. Only Nammuor himself inhabited Leur's work, and Nammuor's presence was dark, infected, increasingly more shadow than substance. But Dorilian had heard enough rumor of Nammuor's recent activities to know that he had to have used the Diadem's powers to cause the Dazun to flood. If Nammuor had channeled that much power, he had to be weakened for now. The only question was for how long.

*You cannot face him.* Levyathan's worry was finite, familiar.

*I can. I will. I have the Rill.*

*And the Wall?*

*That depends on what happens at Stauberg.*

Dorilian withdrew from the contact and settled his mind. This day would see battle and he must be ready. There had been only sporadic fighting so far. That a Highborn Prince—a Sordaneon—rode with the invading armies greatly dissuaded local militias. Only Erenor's regulars, mustered from lords beholden to the Prince Regent and intent on protecting ill-gained grants of lands and titles, had offered up much resistance. Dorilian held Sordan's troops in reserve as much as possible, letting the armies of the Royal North—Lacenedon, Gweroyen, Pessach, and rebels from the Eleutheron—carry the battle standards and the burden of fighting.

He received frequent reports from Sinon Kouranos, his advisors in Handurin's camp, and the Hierarchate's sources in Merath and Dazunor-Rannuli about progress of the campaign in Dazunor. After overcoming the flood, Handurin had proven capable in the field. Bed talk from Aubrey had revealed Handurin's almost-disaster in Dazunor-Rannuli, but Dorilian had heard better news since. A young man more interested in being a just and mindful leader than a warrior in search of renown was not the worst thing for beleaguered Essera. Among the reports Dorilian saw were many that assessed Handurin favorably.

The main fear remained the Khelds. Much of Essera believed that Handurin's army amounted to a horde of barbarians. And that Dorilian's army was little more than that.

Great swaths of meadowgrass lay brown and broken, trampled into the cold soil between the two armies, and even the hedgerows looked like they had given up hope. Erenor's troops occupied the south shore of the lake called the Little Sister, the lesser body of water attached to the western end of Ulan-Sana. Fires still burned fitfully in Bynum, where armed rebels had mounted resistance and caused Erenor's commander, an Archon named Bragord, to abandon the city in favor of confronting the allied host of Sordan and Lacenedon in the open. Another allied force, from Gweroyen, was gathered beyond the hills to the west. Dorilian did not foresee Gweroyen taking part in this battle.

Gweroyen lay in wait for another day, however, and Erenor's commanders had to feel a bit... boxed.

So why was the enemy not making a move either to cede the battlefield or secure it?

"They're waiting for us to attack," Hebron concluded.

Attack. Which inevitably Hebron would. Or Pessach would. Or the rebels would. But Dorilian would not. He acknowledged Hebron, mounted at his side. "Your battle. My troops in reserve."

Horsetail crest of command whipped by the wind, Hebron nodded. He urged his mount down the hill. Dorilian tightened his knees to keep his charger from following. Though trained for battle, and eager for it, the great horse would see none today. Just as Dorilian, armed for war, would not test his devices—neither the Gweroyen Sword nor Derlon's Armor. Legon had brought the famed artifacts north, packed in ways none would suspect. Since Askyllon, Dorilian wore these things openly for all to see and either take heart or despair.

He had worn Derlon's Armor before, most often for show. The breastplate had even saved him from injury a time a two during the early years of his Hierarchate. Few knew that Dorilian had also practiced using the Armor's other pieces and attributes. Derlon himself had crafted the Armor—some said in Sordan, some said in Olympos—during the last years of Exile and had worn it in the Wars of Return. His son Deben had used it also in the Gweroyen Wars during the first decades of the Return, when the young Highborn race had fought the Aryati here in these very lands. The pieces were made of a metal so light, so unknown, its like had never been replicated; legend said Derlon had created the metal solely for the purpose of making the Armor. In addition to providing nearly impervious defense against attack, the breastplate, gauntlets, and greaves enhanced strength and motion, allowing the wearer to run, leap, and move faster than any merely human body was able. During his test wearing of the Armor at Rhondda, employing calculations and cautions gleaned from one of Sebbord's books, Dorilian had leaped from the beach to the top of the cliffs overlooking the lake. A single leap. He had done thus again at the Serat in Sordan later, running along the rooftops and jumping between buildings.

Wearing Derlon's Armor, any man verged on being a god.

Dorilian became aware of Robdan, a quiet presence astride a gray horse not far from Dorilian's ivory one atop this strategic ridgeline. He had ordered Legon to keep the Kheld near. It was not only for the sake of Sordan's alliance; Robdan had a scholarly bent of mind and genuine curiosity about his hosts and surroundings, a rare combination that fostered the sort of late-night conversations Dorilian relished.

"What are you staring at, Master Aelfricson?"

Robdan flushed at having been caught in an impropriety. Now Legon was frowning at him also. "You're dressed for ceremony."

Onlookers might think so. They only ever saw Derlon's Armor on such occasions. "Presentation. I am on display."

"Yes. Armor you never need and a sword you never draw." Robdan had noted the artifact-sword Dorilian wore strapped to his back: its intricate scabbard and hilt made of shining metal the color of mist—a thing of a time come and gone. Having studied ancient weapons, Robdan might even know what sword it was.

"People like having them around." *And me, they like having me around*, Dorilian might have added. He felt like a museum piece sometimes, revered for reasons embedded in the past. The last compendium of the godborn.

Below on the field, Hebron was riding his army out, four thousand horsemen flanked by ranks of infantry in formation. Pessach's smaller army established position to the south, closer to Dorilian's Sordan troops, which remained behind the hill. The enemy would know they were there, of course—and were perhaps hoping to draw them out. Doing so would fuel too well the rampant fears of Essera's still-hesitant domains should they see Sordaneon troops take their lands or cities by force.

"Look." Bersyas indicated the field below. He and the Seventh's standard-bearer were positioned to Dorilian's left, Red Hound on white flying beneath the Hierarch's banner of silver Eagle on emerald.

*How peculiar.* Bragord's forces marched in tight formation, not toward Hebron's advancing troops but toward the city. Toward Bynum, from the unfortified fringe of which bands of rebels had emerged to join the battle.

"What are they doing?" Dorilian asked of Bersyas, a seasoned general who had seen more battle.

"Hiding something." Frowning, Bersyas passed the spyglass he had been using. The brass tube glinted with knobs and rotating lens housings. Dorilian put it to his eye and focused the device as he listened to his general. "See? There's another formation just like it not far behind. Notice how many soldiers are holding spears up, presented as if formally guarding something, close together, not as men on the march. The spears so close together obscure what is at the center of the formation. But you can make it out. There's something big, being pulled by large beasts."

Large beasts... and also unusual. Immense, gray-skinned, and clumsy, spiked along the spine. Dorilian had seen mention of the like in recent reports. "*Ulygma.*"

He had used the Aryati word, to which the ever-curious Robdan asked, "What does that mean?"

Bersyas answered tensely. "Mormantaloran abominations. Foul, unnatural creatures. They do not breed and must be made."

Made, yes, but not so unnatural they could not be killed. Especially these slow, plodding creatures. These were not the fearsome monsters that had terrorized Trongor. Why use them at all? Dorilian trained the spyglass on what the beasts pulled behind them. Palisaded. Covered. Not tall enough to be a war machine, but a conveyance massive enough to need powerful creatures to pull it.

"What's inside?" he asked, though he did not expect Bersyas to know the answer. Lowering the glass, Dorilian acted on intuition. "Whatever that thing is will be to our detriment. Bring up the long bolts. Quickly. Set along that ridge." Gauntlets glinting, he pointed to a spine of high ground where Hebron's horse units had passed. "Take out the beasts. Stop that conveyance and any others that come our way."

"Yes, Thrice Royal!"

Upon Bersyas's signal, the Seventh's standard-bearer raised a third banner, the Phoenix, to join those of the Hound and Eagle. Bersyas wheeled his horse and charged down the rear slope of the hill toward the units of his army.

"Something dangerous?" Robdan asked. He had picked up on the urgency, so different from previous encounters.

"I don't know yet." But Dorilian sensed something amiss. Creatures such as these, created and not bred, were surely Mormantaloran in origin. If Erenor had gotten assistance from Nammuor, it would be more than just a few draft beasts to pull his wagons. The threat here was neither the beasts nor the wagon, but what was inside. A Mormantaloran war machine might deploy poisons or magic. But the latter was only possible if Nammuor had also sent along the mages needed to work the magic. Setting crystals and wielding devices required men or women trained in *Ir* technology. *Skilled* at doing so. Maybe there was a mage in that box. Maybe several. But it made no sense for Nammuor to risk high level mages in a battle with such low stakes. Bynum was nothing to him.

Neither was Erenor.

As for poison... to release poison here would deliver death to Erenor's troops as well as his foe's—not to mention that to eradicate Bynum the way Nammuor had eradicated Ogarth would brand Erenor a monster in every land north of Suddekar.

So what was in the box?

Dorilian signaled and Legon edged closer. "What war machine would be needed to mount a successful siege of Bynum?"

"None." Legon looked mystified. "There has been no war in this land since your forefathers defeated the Aryati. The city has no gates, no walls, and few defenses—certainly none that would require a machine to overwhelm. It sits beside a lake and could be invaded also by water. By water or land, the barricades erected over the last few weeks by the rebels can be easily breached by projectiles and accelerants."

Possibly that. An overpowering assault. A brace of war machines might reduce the city to rubble, which would dishearten the rebels.

"Message Bersyas. As soon as he has set up the long bolts, have him target that box. Use fire."

The conveyance was approaching too near the city for Dorilian's liking. Hebron's cavalry engaged Bragord's horsemen on the right flank, and the swords and pikes of Lacenedoni infantry flashed as those units surged against those of other commanders to the left. Screams and the clashing of metal and wood carried up from the field. But no opposing forces assailed Bynum's barricades. Erenor's commanders had arranged their forces in such a way as to facilitate moving the damn box.

The why of that became clear moments later when the powerful draft beasts, though pricked with many arrows from the rebels behind the barricades, separated from the conveyance after the coupling was released and moved away, herded by handlers. The spear-bearing soldiers scattered as the front of the box dropped free to land hard on the ground, where it bounced and settled to become a ramp. The sides of the conveyance parted also and fell away, and something dark and immense erupted from within.

A black monstrous shape, toothed and bristling, burst out among the handlers and the beasts. With a huge limb that ended in claws longer than swords, the creature swiped at all things in its path. Bodies scattered, as did legs and torsos in a display of gore. Guts flew like party streamers. Those beasts and men not fallen ran from the destruction, screaming and squealing. The creature rose on its rear legs and roared.

Though Dorilian and Legon kept control of their horses, Robdan's mount wheeled and bolted down the backside of the ridge, its rider clinging to the saddle. At least it fled toward Sordan's camp and safety, Dorilian noted. Good. One less noncombatant on the field. The standard-bearers looked to him, tight-faced.

*Stand*, Dorilian silently ordered. None of the men with him could leave until he did, and for him to leave the field now might cause disaster.

By the monster's appearance, the beasts from which it had been fashioned might have been bears. Massive and furred, but so enlarged, so twisted that the resemblance was only that of having four limbs with huge, clawed paws and an ursine, wedge-shaped head. Knobbed, stretched, with three pairs of blood-colored eyes above a broad muzzle and a maw of yellow fangs, it roared again as it turned toward the barricades from which Bynum's rebel archers had unleashed a storm of arrows. From the bones of the monster's visibly scarred cheek and brow blazed the bright gold of embedded *lr* jewels large as eggs. A metal spiked collar high on its thick neck glittered with the same.

Disorder ran through the surge of Hebron's attack as horses reared and the formation broke. The charge disintegrated into chaos. Erenor's infantry fell back to give the beast no impediment to where it might ravage.

"Dor! Back! Follow the damn Kheld! That thing's the size of a house!" Legon overstepped his rank—but not his role of securing his Hierarch's safety.

"Yes! And it is being controlled. Find the mage—"

"I am not leaving you!".

"And I'm telling you to kill the mage!" Dorilian snapped. Leaning outward from the saddle, he wrapped his fist around the Eagle standard and yanked it from the startled standard-bearer's hands, then wheeled his mount and rode with all speed down the hill. This day's disaster attended the *beast*.

With Legon close on his heels, Dorilian reached the ridge occupied by the long-bolt line. The unit's commander dropped to his knee when Dorilian dismounted and released his horse. He would not need a mount for this. He kept the standard in his hand. To Legon, still mounted and looking distressed, Dorilian repeated his command. "The mage. There may be two monsters, so two mages. Use any weapon at hand, including the long bolts." To the unit commander, Dorilian gave a different order.

"The creature is bent only on destruction. It will kill Bynum's defenders—and too many of us. I don't want that thing to get into the city. We must show that we can defend it."

"But Thrice Royal, the long bolts—"

"Aim for the body and only the body. The creature has *lr* crystals welded to its skull and neck. If those crystals are disrupted, the energy released could kill everyone on the battlefield. Possibly me as well."

"Sire?"

There was no time to explain. The reason was about to become evident. "Hold your bolts until I am clear of the creature, then let loose."

*Now.*

Dorilian tightened his grip on the Eagle standard in his hand— and moved. Just one step activated the Armor—foot firmly to the ground, calf muscle tensed to create the magical bond to his body— and sent the beat of his blood and the wind of his breath to his ears, immersing him in the pulse of god-bestowed power. Dorilian's next step covered the stride of a horse at full gallop. Three even longer strides to cover half the distance to the beast... two more for him to leap upon the monster's back. His right foot slipped on the oily fur, but his left foot held. He regained balance, wrapping both hands around the Eagle standard he still carried and raising it high. With all his strength, and the force of a god's armor behind it, Dorilian planted the pole of the standard deep between the creature's shoulders, through the pelt into muscle, fat, and bone. So deep that only death would dislodge it.

He leaped off as the creature roared and twisted, clawing at him in agony and protest. Landing squarely, legs bent and fist to the ground, beyond range of the beast's teeth and claws, Dorilian watched as his order was obeyed, the long bolts launched. Metal shafts the length of wagon beds slammed into the monster's ribcage, throwing it onto its side. Maddened, the wounded creature screamed and thrashed. With a jump to his feet, Dorilian reached for the sword on his back. Raising aloft the shining blue-green blade of the Gweroyen Sword, its glow reflected on the eagle wings of Derlon's Armor spread across his chest, he knew himself armed as a god.

What did they see, those men watching on the ridge... the ones behind the barricades... the soldiers of the enemy? What did the monster see as it turned upon its tormentor?

Carefully balancing his movement as the creature lurched to its feet, Dorilian darted sideways. He had worn the Armor in battle once before, but defensively; he had not used it as an enhancer. He found it exhilarating. Acceleration and angles. To his surprise, the beast lunged faster than he'd thought it would. One massive paw swiped him and he curled to let the Armor take the force of that blow, felt himself lifted and thrown. A claw, or something, caught him under the ribs, scraped over the Armor, but the force dissipated, absorbed. He barely felt anything at all from that or the fall. No damage—but he had dropped the sword. Probably a good thing, given its properties. The weapon shone in the trampled grass several body lengths away. But when Dorilian sprang again to his feet, propelling himself to where the sword lay, a shearing pain ripped through the back of his right leg. With a cry, he crumpled to the ground.

*Not now!*

He had been warned—had read about—the risk of subjecting

mortal flesh to the arcane dynamics of the Armor. He had practiced, of course, had attempted again and again to perfect his kinetics, but in the heat of combat he'd acted purely on instinct, had failed to exercise caution. With this result.

Teeth clenched against the pain, Dorilian reached forward from where his ill-advised movement had landed him and grasped the sword, then forced his legs to work. The left leg functioned as normal and he could still move the right by using the Armor, though it cost him greatly in pain and he risked making the damage worse. Ungracefully, he pushed to his feet and again lifted the sword. This time when the wounded monster, bolts embedded in its shoulder and torso, swung its bloodied claws his way, Dorilian swung first. The Gweroyen Sword's *tullun* blade cut cleanly through the creature's forepaw, smoothly separating three toes, each tipped with rapier-long claws. Blood spurted, three streams of gore danced through the air, some of it hitting the Armor and running down in beads as Dorilian used his left leg to launch away from the beast. The beast lunged at him again and this time he hurled beneath its limb and struck at the creature's bolt-bloodied chest, the green-bright blade of the sword slicing deep into the great hairy side, cutting a path through bone, through meat, carving a piece nearly off. Furious, the massive body reared, foul flesh hanging from its ribs, as Dorilian executed a one-legged leap and roll that took him out of range of slashing claws.

*Shoot it again!*

What were they waiting for? He was clear of the beast.

"Loose!" Dorilian heard Legon's command from afar. Had he dealt with the mages? Or was he doing so now? That command was followed by another, then the whistle of long-bolts flying through the air. With another roar, the creature fell back again, a bolt lodged in its throat.

Somewhere behind the beast and its hulking mass, black smoke billowed against the cold blue sky. The other conveyance? Perhaps, because a second creature's unworldly shrieks joined the sounds of battle and death. The beast Dorilian faced, however, was not yet dead. And the placement of the last bolt, buried in the thick muscles of the creature's neck, warned him that he could not risk a misfire. The *Ir* crystals of the collar were almost certainly low-grade and therefore might not release sufficient energy to level him and Hebron's somewhat reorganized men, or those from the barricades who were now rushing forward—but Dorilian didn't want to risk the possibility. These common soldiers would not know how to approach and disarm *Ir* weaponry.

He had to finish this.

Nor was Dorilian's leg his only issue. As did all enhancers, Derlon's Armor commanded that the wearer's metabolism provide the base energy for its amplifications. That Dorilian was Highborn—and Sordaneon, bound to the Rill—meant he could summon more energy than most, but the results were familiar: throbbing headache, dizziness, nausea, and the impending certainty that soon his limbs would start shaking. He could not keep up this fight indefinitely.

Though his injured leg throbbed violently and threatened to buckle, Dorilian relied on the Armor itself to keep him upright. The greave and thigh piece supported his right leg while he used his left to propel himself behind the hunkering beast's rear limbs. Swinging again, gauging his shoulder's strength and angle of delivery so as not to tear that joint too asunder, he swung the Gweroyen Sword into the creature's tendons, severing them along with much of the leg bone. The beast dropped to the ground. What Dorilian's use of the Armor had nearly done to his own right leg, he now did to this monster, immobilizing his foe for what he must do next.

Hobbling along the creature's heaving side to the forelimbs, he hewed the tendons of the second leg, rendering both helpless. Though the monster tossed its ursine head and gnashed yellowed teeth, blood loss had weakened it. The commander on the ridge had wisely ceased to fling long bolts at the fallen thing. The second conveyance, its walls blackened and whatever had been within its box spilled in smoking ruin on the ground, was reduced to wreckage. A fresh barrage of bolts flew toward a ridge well to the rear of the fallen creatures and their wagons. The mages were under assault and, if any fortune was to be had, were dead already. As for the monster Dorilian confronted… though its red eyes blinked and its jaws moved, it made no move toward him when he came up along its throat and slashed deep into the soft meat under its jaw, cutting arteries and releasing what was left of its misbegotten lifeblood to flow. Red bubbled thick about Dorilian's feet.

He lowered the Gweroyen Sword and looked around. The battle had turned. All fighting was now taking place behind what had been the enemy's lines. Enemy and friendly forces alike had seen a godborn Prince engage Erenor's battle beast, had watched legends reborn.

And Dorilian would be damned if he would let any of them see him limp off the field—or vomit all over the god's thrice-cursed Armor.

After bringing Dorilian's horse, Legon climbed fur and blood to retrieve the Eagle standard from the monster's corpse, drawing eyes away from his lord. Using the dead beast and the horse's great body as a shield made it easy for Dorilian to mount while hiding how debilitated he had become. Only when he had returned to the Seventh's secure camp—with Legon again assisting him in dismounting—and was again in his tent safe from prying eyes, did Dorilian surrender to the price his use of the Armor commanded. Part of that price was having to listen to Legon berate him.

"You were reckless. Tutto would chew on your ass."

Dorilian hunched on the edge of the bed, his right leg propped on a footstool piled with cushions, his arms on a low table as he glared up from the wide, deep bowl into which he had just vomited. The bowl was gold, magnificent, molded in shapes of ancient heroes wrestling bulls, the perfect vessel for a Hierarch's spew. Though Dorilian had drunk two full flasks of restorative, his body had yet to completely cease its torments. His pain had dulled and the vomiting had stopped, but the dizziness was unrelenting. He had never felt so sick.

"Those abominations would have killed a hundred men at the barricades, and many more in the city had they and the enemy gotten inside. As things stand now they did not even kill *me*."

"They could have."

"Not while I was wearing the Armor." Dorilian had removed it—or rather Legon had removed it from him.

Sounds from the front of the partitioned tent alerted them that they were being joined by a new arrival, though not an unexpected one. The Eagle Guard would allow no one through unless either the Hierarch or their Commander had given that person clearance. A noticeably tentative hand parted the heavy brocade curtain enough for a just as hesitant voice to make an inquiry.

"Your Thrice Royal Grace? You asked for me?" Robdan's

head, graying hair not yet dry from having been washed, peeked around the curtain fringe.

The Kheld's politeness never failed.

"You may enter, Master Aelfricson."

After performing a deep bow to Dorilian, Robdan gave a smaller bow to Legon, who did not acknowledge it. "My appreciation that Your Grace still can look upon me after the way I fled the field earlier."

"Do you call yourself a coward? I thought to credit your horse. You have yet to master one that I have noticed."

"Well, yes, there's that I suppose."

"I forgive all horses who flee monstrous beasts and all riders who cannot control panicking creatures many times their size."

Robdan ducked his head. "My gratitude, Thrice Royal, for your understanding of my predicament." Perhaps hoping to recoup from his embarrassment, he hastened to add, "I did watch your battle. From a distance, of course. General Bersyas saw my horse bolt and, well, he sent a man to get me. I was with him on the ridge. What you did, the weapons you bore and the way you slew the beast, was amazing." He looked to Legon, whose now deeper frown persuaded Robdan to cease issuing praise.

Dorilian indicated for Legon to leave. They had talked earlier about getting some food. Despite still feeling queasy, Dorilian was hungry. Famished, even. Legon, however, hesitated, hand on the curtain.

"Are you certain?" Legon wasn't asking about the food.

"Master Aelfricson can be trusted. While in Amallar he was my sole companion on many occasions, including while I slept. Also, to my knowledge, Robdan has never betrayed a confidence. At this moment, aside from you, he is the only man in this camp I would agree to be alone with—and you are the only one I trust to get my food. And ice. I could use more ice."

Issuing a crisp nod, Legon departed. The curtain fell heavily in his wake, a sweep of gold and emerald. Dorilian turned away and saw Robdan quickly avert his gaze from the golden bowl.

"I've been vomiting." Dorilian saw no harm in letting Robdan learn about some of the joys of having Highborn gifts. "My reward for using *that*." He indicated a nearby frame upon which Derlon's Armor hung in shining glory. "Powerful—and dangerous. Most artifacts are, and enhancers especially so."

"An enhancer? Truly?" Robdan peered again at the Armor, his face bright with wonder.

"More than just an enhancer, but... yes. Not dangerous at all to wear, if all one wants of it is decoration or protection, but perilous to use."

A mote of understanding brightened Robdan's amazed expression. "I have read about these devices of great power, though I never imagined I would see one. It explains, I suppose, how you were able to run so fast and jump on the beast's back with your standard in hand... and other things. The way you moved—"

"The Armor made that possible. And also the way I tore the muscles at the back of my leg. I cannot even bend the knee." Dorilian indicated the affected joint and limb, snugly wrapped and elevated. "You see, Derlon, who first created and wore the Armor, was a god and I... am not. Legon is bringing back ice for the pain and swelling. My mortal flesh will heal, of course, but that will take a few days and"—Dorilian sighed and pointed to a nearby table with a big silver ewer and some goblets—"for now I have a bit of difficulty getting around. If you would pour me some water? I dismissed my valet and have been relying on Legon for assistance. I don't want anyone to know I am hurt. My soldiers—and allies— think I'm nigh invulnerable, and I prefer they continue to think that."

Though he looked surprised by the request, Robdan complied ably. He poured water into a gold-chased glass goblet and brought it over. Dorilian took it with a nod of thanks.

"Are you asking me to help you conceal your impairment?" Robdan completed the unspoken part of the request, just to be sure.

"Yes." Dorilian drank the water, then set the empty glass alongside the golden bowl. Among other things for which he was grateful was feeling his stomach accept the liquid. "Legon will tell no one, and if you promise me—"

"You have my word: I will tell no one." Robdan's grave delivery recalled another occasion on which he had given his word, and kept it, atop Trestethion. "Although I would be greatly honored if during this convalescence you would indulge me with conversation... or perhaps allow me to read a book or two."

Robdan must have noticed that a few of the latter rested on a table nearby. Dorilian had ordered a selection of tomes brought from his personal library.

"You may," Dorilian agreed, "though be warned that one is written in Aryata. A treatise on how to use this Armor. But I think you might find the others interesting."

"If I am to be so much in your company, how will you explain it to your generals and others?"

"However I choose. You and Legon can tell them you are teaching me Khelda."

Robdan laughed and Dorilian wished he could laugh with him. He was feeling sick again, his stomach rising and the room spinning. He desperately needed either to drink more restorative... or eat. He also needed to build up greater tolerance to arcane demands upon his body if he was to use his gifts again—which might be soon.

*Nammuor is human. I am not. I recover far more quickly.*

But was he godborn enough to engage a god's weapons against the Undying Crown? Or the Wall?

In the meantime, he should not subject to discomfort the man helping his recovery. "Sit," Dorilian directed. He indicated a nearby cross frame chair inlaid with ivory and gold and bearing a brocade cushion. "At least we can be thankful that whatever argument I give for wanting your company will not excite speculation that I have taken you for a lover."

To judge by his startlement, it was a good thing Robdan was already seated. The very notion made him blink. Then, with a cock of his head and a lift of his eyebrows, Robdan grimly acknowledged the root of that remark.

Closing his eyes, Dorilian leaned back, willing his dizziness to cease and for Legon to return with a plate of food. Another complication. Dorilian's name was becoming too bound up with Khelds. Marc Frederick's trap—and Stefan's legacy. And the Wall, of course. One must never overlook the Wall.

That damn Entity wove its very plots into lives and generations.

# 30


Do not ask me what I feel. You could not begin to
comprehend the answer.
DORILIAN SORDANEON, PER ZAMENES,
*ON THE NATURE OF ENTITIES*

Chyralane Rannuleonis, Denizen of Phaer, bowed her head over a brazier of coals and sprinkled a fine dust over the glow. At once the room blossomed with scents of orange petals and Lahgaelan spice.

"He is not the fool Stefan was." Iphithus, one of three great-nephews who had gained Chyralane's confidence, sounded surprised. "Where Stefan was all bluster and pride, Handurin is quiet and confidence."

"As well he might be, with Dorilian Sordaneon as his bulwark." Chyralane set aside the wide-bodied jar in her hand with a precision that attested to its costliness. She rearranged the silken folds of her gown. "How did that alliance happen, I wonder?"

And how had it happened without the Seven Houses knowing? The Epoptes at Sordan, whose reports she paid exorbitantly to procure, had failed to detect the true chemistry of that pairing. Overlooking the nuances, they had but clamored with the multitude and brayed at the obvious. Even the normally astute Psilant Quirin had counseled that the Seven Houses had no cause for concern. Small wonder he had wailed loudest when Dorilian, taking the Brotherhood completely by surprise, paralyzed the Rill. Quirin was howling again now that the bold Hierarch had opened the station at Trestethion. Chyralane was not surprised that the Brotherhood had removed Quirin from his Psilancy.

The only thing left to wonder was whose plan it had been to

subvert the Rill so completely to Handurin's gain. The realignment of the Brotherhood aside, it did not bear the stamp of a deed Dorilian would have originated.

"You think it a true alliance, then? I find that difficult to believe." Iphithus was not alone in that. History spoke for itself. The Sordaneons had opposed the imperial pretensions of the Stauberg-Randolphs since their arrival on the scene. Dorilian and Handurin were far from equals.

Chyralane pondered. Her long fingers gripped more tightly the staff she used to assist her movements. "If they are allied, it is because the Sordaneon wants it that way. Even if it's true Emyli conspires in the shadows, this fledgling Prince cannot possibly be Dorilian's only reason. No, there is something here that begs examination."

"Perhaps a love match?" Iphithus raised an old innuendo. "The boy is well favored. Fair of appearance and blonder than I thought he would be with those parents. He has good height, but Emyli's blue eyes. Or Marc Frederick's." His voice dripped with meaning.

*Yes, Marc Frederick indeed.* Chyralane remembered the man for having known him well. Dorilian's attachment to the late King must be considered, as it undoubtedly played a part—though not the one Iphithus proposed. Marc Frederick had not been at all interested in men as lovers. That old speculation was now causing men who should know better to overlook the obvious. Another rumor had come to hand this morning out of Lacenedon.

"What do you know of these Khelds Handurin has brought north with him?" Chyralane asked, offhandedly. "Their families and allegiances?"

Iphithus made an effort to look surprised, then shrugged. Most members of the Seven Houses knew very little about the barbarians occupying the commercial wasteland between Dazunor-Rannuli and Leseos, which made his network of contacts an exception. Although he surely understood Chyralane to know more than most, Iphithus proceeded to provide the clarifications she sought.

"There is no recognized Kheldish nobility, despite Stefan's attempts to create one, and their allegiances are strictly internal. They are loosely organized in several clans and there are a handful of leading families in them. The Thegn, Vesl, and Darm clans are the most numerous, with the Thegn holding sway in western Amallar, the Vesl in the midlands, and the Darm along the Dazun and Floh rivers. The Thegn command the most recognizable Kheld leadership positions, including a cabal of women called the Old Mothers, and have long been the most visible faction in Essera." Iphithus drew on his carefully gleaned knowledge of the Khelds, presenting concise analyses as he had for a generation of cartel lords. His maternal House, Koillos, with its extensive trade ties in Leseos and marriages to powerful families there, had long provided useful information to those Houses participating in the forbidden trade of Kheldish slaves, as well as the provision of contraband arms to Neuberland's rebels.

He continued, "Amallar's Archhalia representative, Robdan Aelfricson, who took the seat last year after Erenor's purge, is Thegn. His family is an old one and highly respected. Marc Frederick was of Thegn heritage, as was the rebel Erwan, who was Stefan's father. Those Thegn ties produced much of Stefan's core of Kheld supporters, many of whom were carried over from Marc Frederick's administrative appointments. Currently, Handurin draws much of his base support from that clan. The man they call their Thegnard, a clan chief named Nalf Rhys, is a cousin of the late Triemperal chamberlain, Tobold Forbasson, and was uncle to Cullen Brodheson, Stefan's trade minister. He exerts strong influence among the Khelds and is said to be both tough and clever. His influence over Handurin, however, is uncertain." Iphithus's high brow gathered into thoughtful furrows. "Handurin's most visible association is with a Kheld youth from the Thegn named Arne Anseldson, a distant cousin of his and related, as Khelds tend to be, to just about everyone. Robdan Aelfricson remains influential—including, we now think, with Dorilian himself."

Chyralane slowly nodded. About the latter, she had heard as much from the Princess of Merrydn, whose short letter following the Hierarch's stop in Merath had stirred only misgivings. *I fear his interaction with the Khelds may have consequences you will not like.* It was not just that Sordan's Hierarch was for reasons of his own promoting this half-Kheld Prince. Dorilian's allegiance to Marc Frederick's legitimate Heir, despite what had been a harrowing history with Stefan, was predictable.

Chyralane thought little of those in her cartel who had gone to great efforts to oust Emyli as Regent, thinking it would pave the way to putting aside the Stauberg-Randolphs permanently in favor of true Staubaun rule. Erenor Tholeros had ambition, but his alliances were shaky. An even worse mistake would be to think Dorilian might be that Staubaun ruler.

That man was Highborn, yes, but he was *not* Staubaun.

Not since Tarentar Sordaneon had sired Labran on an Ardaenan princess had the Sordaneons been truly Staubaun. That same treaty had instilled the crude blood of Nemenor into the noble Sordani families of Alphareon and Kellados, from which it had trickled by marriage into the Highborn lines of Teremar and Suddekar. The resulting breed was feral, violent, and willful. Dorilian was proof of that.

And where had Essera been during that transformation? Where the Seven Houses? Rejoicing that the Malyrdeons had been kept pure of taint. Celebrating the weakening of Sordan's Highborn strain for purposes of Rill hegemony and never guessing that a hundred and fifty years would strip Essera of its own Highborn Princes and powers.

What cared Dorilian Sordaneon—whose grandfather Essera had betrayed and imprisoned, mother murdered, and father kept in humiliating regency all his reign—about true Staubaun rule? He intended to thrust Handurin upon them without a second thought. It took no prescience to know Dorilian's ends did not include preserving the Seven Houses.

But neither did Chyralane favor, as others did, handing Dorilian to Nammuor. Such short-sightedness alarmed Chyralane no less than had Stefan's genocidal paranoia. No, the splendid legacy of Leur, the blood of Amynas Malyrdys that flowed all too potently in Dorilian's veins, was too singular to pander to Nammuor's obvious designs. If, for the sake of that blood's continuance, Dorilian was to be brought down, chained and bred like a beast, at least let it be for ends the Seven Houses envisioned. The Rill Lord's fate must be bound to the salvation—and perpetuation—of the Rill.

How best to get their hands on him was a plot yet to be woven. The Hierarch's caution was legendary. He was never without bodyguards, never in unsecured surroundings. Except, it now seemed, he had been so in Amallar. That Dorilian had been so accessible might yet prove an even greater misstep to Staubaun designs than failing to anticipate his readiness to abandon ancient allegiances. As for Handurin—that Prince, too, raised questions of bloodlines.

Leaning on her staff, Chyralane drew herself straight, taller than any man of her House. It was a presence she exploited. "We must concede that we face the threat of a Kheldish dynasty." She went to her cabinet and poured two goblets of wine, one of which she handed to Iphithus. "Handurin is certainly of that blood, given his mother. And yet all may not be as it seems. There may be more Staubaun there than Emyli has let us know." Chyralane allowed an icy smile as she looked out across the snow-dusted rooftops outside her high window. "Her ill-fated attempt to install Erwan as Lord of Gignastha not only resulted in his death but left her prisoner for three months to Ral of Leseos. We would do well to remember this."

As Iphithus sipped at his wine, a lift of his head showed that the speculation intrigued him. What had happened at Gignastha had been buried under layers of concealment on both sides for twenty years. "Are you suggesting that Handurin is the bastard of Ral Erruneos?"

"Perhaps." Chyralane's memory of Ral consisted of a single meeting with a sleek, handsome man with cruel eyes and a fit, hard body. He'd been an exceptional falconer. "Ral was a ruthless brute who would have killed Emyli but for fear of her father's vengeance. It would not be the first time a woman's violation was kept secret and her bastard attributed to a dead husband. The question, however, is not Handurin's lineage. His claim to Essera's Throne comes to him by way of Marc Frederick, through Emyli. Ral's bastard or Erwan's miscegenation matters naught. The danger is not that Handurin might rule. He's young and will follow his alliances. Only a fool would put him aside, and Dorilian is not a fool." She shrugged eloquently. "I can think of far worse outcomes for the Seven Houses than that we must endure a half-Kheldish Prince with a legitimate claim back to Endurin and the backing of the godborn Sordaneons." *The Rill, at least, will be secure and not used as a weapon against us.*

"What danger do you see, if not that he is as Kheld at heart as Stefan?"

"That he takes a Kheld bitch as his queen."

It interested Chyralane to watch those male eyes harden. Though Staubaun men often took the sexually alluring Kheld women for purposes of pleasure, they had no other place for them. Iphithus clearly took her point. "A wise king would take a queen from one of the great Houses," he assessed. "I am certain the Sordaneon will direct him to choose a consort suitable to his station—and peace among his nobles." He laughed, but nervously. "Indeed, given the way things have gone thus far, I would be surprised if Dorilian did not personally choose the woman for him and witness the consummation."

Chyralane lifted an arched eyebrow, her expression

contemptuous. "That man has yet to choose a Hierarchessa for himself. He is hardly attending his own dynastic imperatives, much less those of Essera." She frowned and moved across her room to the table at the center. There, she settled herself in her high-backed chair with its cushions of mink. "There is a Kheld woman I wish you to remove from Handurin's following."

"A woman? Is he interested in her?"

Chyralane turned her head, lifting her glass with a shrug that dismissed the notion as her reason. "Perhaps. What man is not interested in a beautiful woman? What alarms me is that this one's association with Handurin gives the impression she has consequence."

Iphithus looked intrigued. "I remember her. Her name is Aubrey Amundda. As you say, a beautiful woman. She is related to Nalf Rhys and Robdan Aelfricson and has extensive—and influential—clan connections. Handurin considers her a confidante. No one, however, has reported any interaction to suggest anything more between them."

"It is not from him I wish to remove her."

"Indeed? Has some lord nearer to home taken a fancy to her? As Handurin's cousin, her marriage would bring valuable connections to the Prince"—his gaze narrowed—"and maybe even shares in Trestethion's Rill slots."

"Just do as I require, Iphithus."

Iphithus nodded, then sighed. The golden rings on his fine hand glinted as he stroked it through his silvered hair. "I will need to be careful. She spends this night in Dazunor-Rannuli, she and some Kheld kin of hers."

Chyralane turned, her lips parting in surprise. "She is here?"

"Yes. She and her kinsman, Arne Anseldson of whom I spoke, returned from Lacenedon with the Rill order. They accompanied the Rill from Trestethion this afternoon on restored service and arrived to great fanfare in the city. And with a full contingent of Sordani troops to secure the station, I might add. Dorilian is as trusting as ever." Iphithus's nostrils flared. "The Khelds are staying at the house of one Egidius Mogens, a merchant with trade ties to Amallar who clearly hopes to profit by the association. At the moment, they are dining with the Dannuthi ambassador."

Chyralane gazed from her window. The Rill gleamed in ivory arches against the night sky. "He wields it like he wields his sword, sparingly, but each cut a masterstroke. See how he has Khelds bring the Rill to Dazunor-Rannuli, the insult of their doing so, the undermining of our place." That her opponent was brilliant merely made the game riskier, as well as necessary. "And tell me, where is Dorilian in all this news from the north?"

Faced with familiar ground again, Iphithus paced to the shimmering tapestry that only a closer look revealed to be a richly illustrated map, each Esseran domain and major city depicting a detailed scene associated with it. He indicated a coastal city, its harbor teeming with ships, its streets peopled by noble men and women and white-mounted Princes bearing light in their hands. Above them all arched fantastic shapes. "Common knowledge is he will ride to Stauberg to confront his enemy there. The Wall will most likely thwart him, but no one knows for certain. Whatever that plan, Erenor will find himself battling the Highborn this time."

"So our Sordaneon means to do battle," Chyralane murmured.

"Dorilian was never one to let sores fester while he decides on a course of action. I'm sure he fears further enemy encroachments over the winter that might impede him later. With Gweroyen yet free and parts of the Eleutheron in the hands of lords opposed to Erenor, Stauberg is vulnerable to attack from Lacenedon. Furthermore, Sordan has directed resources there, most notably his Neuberland army under Bersyas."

"The wolf and his pack. Very interesting. But will mortal forces prevail against Stauberg with Nammuor certain to intercede there? How foolish of Dorilian to put himself in such danger with no legacy to survive him." Chyralane cursed the divergence that had put Sordan so far out of Seven Houses's spheres of influence. Dorilian rejected every sway they might have had with him. *We rejected Sordan first. Our best blood sought purity in Essera and left the forsaken south to breed with lesser men. We thought doing so would weaken the Sordaneons and render them more easily influenced. But Mormantalorus showed more foresight. Nammuor wed his own sister to Dorilian.*

Chyralane's stomach soured as she thought of Daimonaeris's child, Dorilian's Heir but not his seed. *The Mormantaloran may yet gain the race—and Sordan too. Damn him! Dorilian should have denied the child or killed it along with its mother.*

Unaware of those musings, Iphithus continued to babble. "There's talk, and has long been talk, that he's a sorcerer himself. None truly know what happened at Permephedon, and then there is the way Stefan died."

"There was no Highborn magic in that." Chyralane dismissed the tale with a motion of her heavily ringed hand. The jewels she wore could have purchased a fleet of ships. "The World may well be as Dorilian Sordaneon perceives it and therefore doomed Stefan to the death that claimed him. So are we all fated. But the Highborn talent does not cast illusions; it creates truths. If Dorilian had truly thought Stefan a stag, Stefan would have stayed a stag even in death."

Iphithus regarded her with a smirk. "Then consider this truth: that Dorilian Sordaneon has fully manifested the Rill talent. Psilant Quirin himself acknowledges the event. Only Marenthro knows what it really means for a man to be a Rill Lord and his response to Dorilian's assumption of the Rill mythos has been notable for its restraint. Marenthro is watching and being careful." Iphithus leaned back in his chair and frowned at some recollection. "Quirin told me something most interesting. According to him, Marenthro claims that the Rill itself decided to stop running to Essera. There were no codes for the Epoptes to override because cessation was not initiated through the Overlay. The Rill *chose* not to run. The Entity is not known for making spontaneous decisions. So where did that come from?"

The answer, of course, had proclaimed itself. "Dorilian claims that to have been *his* decision."

"Exactly," said Iphithus.

The timeglass weights turned, the soft thunk barely heard. The great glass rotated gracefully on its axis and settled once more into place, another hour in its chamber.

"Marenthro could not tell which of them did it," Chyralane concluded. She looked away, toward the window and the Rill structures beyond.

Iphithus offered another possibility. "Perhaps it is a quality of the Rill that obscures the source of its impulses."

"Or," Chyralane said, something taking shape within her thoughts, "perhaps the wizard cannot detect any difference between them."

"Surely that's impossible."

"It is utterly possible."

"But the Entity is not human anymore. It hasn't been human for more than a thousand years. Those few who have touched the Rill's essence describe it as chillingly alien. And though I have yet to meet the man, those who know him claim that whatever else one may say about Dorilian Sordaneon, he is decidedly human."

Chyralane's laughter cut the room's cozy ambiance. "Is he? And what would we know of it if he were not? Think about it. Think about what the Highborn are to us. They breed male and only male, blood so holy we keep them apart, physically removed from the rest of our World. Is it for their sakes—or ours? We punish those who look upon or touch them without holy writ. We forbid all but the privileged few from getting too close. Why? Because they are intense, different, strange. Because we fear what experiencing them might bring, and what experiencing us might bring to them. Their blood kills our kind—our children when we seek to pass one as belonging to their race, our women in childbirth if all goes not perfectly. Godsblood, we call it, the deadliest poison of all."

Chyralane drank again from her golden cup, bathing her lips in rubies. Her mind wandered in halls of memories most of the Seven Houses had never shared.

"You forget whose daughter I am, where my girlhood was spent and with whom. I have seen for myself how Highborn Princes know each other's minds. I have seen them change lead to gold and produce swords from thin air. They feel each other's deaths. They heal from wounds that would kill us and regrow limbs and even organs. I once witnessed a Highborn Prince regrow his own entrails. They may be gods or just beautiful monsters, but they are *not* as we are." She looked out and toward the crowding dark over Dazunor-Rannuli. Winter nights came early and windows glowed orange with inner lights. "Yet this Sordaneon is human enough. Human enough to walk and talk among the barbarian Khelds and leave them none the wiser. He will serve us well—even splendidly—if we know how to use him."

Chyralane sighed heavily. The years had treated her kindly, but twelve decades had left their imprint on her flesh. She had not her Highborn father's gift of rejuvenation and was drawing near the end of her natural life. It was time for sleep. An hour would do. She waved her hand at Iphithus. "I do not want the Kheld woman to leave the city. Find her wherever she is and bring her to me."

# 31

The Rill cartel oppresses Dazunor-Rannuli with
monstrous power, at once omnipresent and secret. Like a
serpent of great beauty, the palaces of the Seven Houses
and Lords made rich by Rill trade encircle the city,
dazzling the eye with glittering scales while slowly
strangling the life from all who fall within their coils.
ROBDAN AELFRICSON, *JOURNAL OF THE ESSERAN WAR*

"There's all this talk of sorcery, but I have yet to see anything of it." Ambassador Misenos scanned his crowded hall as he surveyed the success of his Rill celebration party. The number of guests attending on short notice was exceptional. He had even scored a coup of sorts in getting Prince Handurin's Kheld emissaries to make an appearance. The pair—cousins, Misenos had been told, and cousins of the Prince as well—stood nearly at the center of the room, fielding conversation. "The Rill started up again," he commented to his companion, "but *that's* not sorcery!"

Dannuth's ties to Dazunor were ancient, but it was not itself a Rill center and the domain's importance in Dazunor-Rannuli was minor. Though not himself a lord of high rank, Misenos was half uncle to the current Bas. It so happened that his half nephew, the impetuous and idealistic young Bas Kerr, had elected to throw his lot in with Handurin, running off to join the Prince's army while Kerr's father, the beleaguered Grenant, held Kyrbasillon against the Regent. Kerr's gesture had contributed to a perception that Dannuth was somehow renegade and interesting. Besides, young Prince Handurin seemed more and more to be poised for something other than a quick defeat. If Kerr threw in with him, Misenos saw no harm in following.

"The sorcery is that he did it—and that we're accepting it." Lord Illarion was on his way out, having some business elsewhere.

"It?"

"The way Dorilian Sordaneon gave the Rill to Amallar."

"Oh, *that*." Misenos wished Lord Illarion hadn't brought that up. In truth, *that* did make Misenos uncomfortable. Just because it was precisely the sort of infuriating act that Dorilian always threw in their faces was no reason for Essera to dismiss it. After years of suffering the indignities of Stefan's miserable reign, empowering Khelds with the Rill didn't seem like the prudent thing for a man like Dorilian to do. It was, however, prudent to do precisely what Misenos was doing now—currying Kheldish attendance and favor in acknowledgment of the situation as it stood currently.

Misenos watched appreciatively as the Kheld woman tossed her head with laughter at something the ridiculous little Estol merchant with her had said.

"Well," he opined to Lord Illarion, "the day you devise how the rest of us can tell Dorilian Sordaneon what to do, you let us know. Better yet, you figure out how to do it, and we'll pay you handsomely to do it for us."

"You have just proven my point, coz. Good morrow." They exchanged arm clasps and Lord Illarion disappeared in the direction of the dock. In the distance, the silver components of the Rill sliced through the night, the sound of an arriving *charys* reaching Misenos a moment later. It was a reassuring sound, a dull reverberation as though from the distant anvil of a god. A very reassuring sound.

The party was just shifting from business to merriment when Aubrey decided she'd had enough wine, food, and conversation and would find a way to politely leave. Certainly she had stayed long enough to make her point. It had been a delightful surprise to find the invitation waiting for herself and Arne at Egidius Mogen's house. Neither of them was fooled as to what it meant. As Egidius had confirmed later in conversation, friendly gestures were not a Staubaun practice. In Dazunor-Rannuli, as in Askyllon, politics ruled what Staubauns did, both in motive and execution.

"It will be a fine party." Egidius had indicated that he would be attending himself. "Dannuth offends no one and is well respected, Misenos sets a splendid table, and as I recall their young Bas Kerr is off fighting alongside Handurin in his grand campaign to unite

Essera. And Sordan's ambassador will be there, Sinon Kouranos, a respected man. Your presence would send a suitably subtle message. Let everyone see that Khelds are civilized folk. I think you should go."

Egidius had helped to outfit Aubrey and Arne. Arne had only to say, "I have to get myself a set of fancy clothes, looks like. First Askyllon and now this, and I wager that's just the start!" for Egidius to gift him with the beginnings of an elegant wardrobe. Agreeing with Aubrey that it wouldn't do to look too lordly just yet, Arne nonetheless sported a new velvet and leather doublet threaded with gold in a pattern of oak leaves and acorns.

Khelds weren't backwoods anymore.

Aubrey turned away an offer of a glass of cordial and resumed speaking to the man with whom she'd been discussing Hans's plans for the Rill. "Ultimately, these matters will be decided at a joint conclave with all Rill domains and stakeholders," she said. "For now, Prince Handurin holds all contested and unassigned slots in trust until such time as this Kingdom is secure and at peace."

"The timing to be decided by Dorilian Sordaneon, you mean." The man, a lord who disliked having slots held in abeyance, curled his lip. "I'm surprised Khelds don't object more to *his* role in this." His dark eyes searched for a reaction to that charge, perhaps hoping to detect a flash of a hatred Khelds and Esseran nobles shared.

Bare months ago, Aubrey would have felt that hatred too. She still recognized those structures embedded in her response, underlying her ability to posture. She shaped her lips to convey a chilly smile. "About him, I have no opinion."

The man's answering smile was just as icy. With a nod, Aubrey removed herself from that conversation and turned away from the glittering company. The dress she wore belonged to one of Egidius Mogen's daughters. It was stunning but weighty. All those yards of deep emerald velvet quilted across the bodice with gold threads—trimmed on the arms and hem with purple satin and gold lace—were feeling heavier by the minute. Though less elegant than her Sordani gown, it better suited the occasion. This Rill celebration, hosted by a minor ambassador, had not attracted Dazunor-Rannuli's high aristocracy. No Denizens paraded here, no Basarchs and their ladies. Aubrey smiled to think that Sinon Kouranos, by virtue of representing a sovereign Highborn ruler, was probably the highest-ranking man in the room. Sordan's ambassador to the Archhalia even now held court at one end of the hall, his distinguished face remote and stern as he no doubt fielded the same concerns and questions Aubrey had endured all evening—except that to Sinon few would communicate how well his Hierarch was hated.

It was three weeks to the day since Aubrey had seen Dorilian. Three weeks since the pleasure of their bodies joining that night, legs and arms entangled in an act so ancient it transcended even the promise of love. But there had been love, or at least the start of it: hopeful, intimate, and new. Aubrey had felt it when Dorilian sought her promise to take the Rill to Bellan Toregh and not return north, to wait out the war in Amallar.

*I can't make that promise. Hans—*

*I will write to Handurin and he will understand. I am not exaggerating the danger to you.*

Askyllon and its treacheries were far away, but even so Aubrey felt a prickling of guilt. *If Dorilian finds out I did not stay in Amallar…*

She had delivered the key to Tharos but then… it had fallen to Aubrey to argue with the Seven Houses and their agent about securing priority for that evening's incoming loads from Bellan Toregh. And this invitation was important, wasn't it? All evening she had been winning over support from Esseran ladies and lords. Did Dorilian really expect Aubrey to stay in Amallar and be useless? The blade of that promise hung over even this glittering affair.

"These events can be endless." Egidius spoke up beside Aubrey. He held a silver chalice to his lip, sipping more of his host's seemingly endless supply of good Teremar wine. "But at least my contributions were good. My daughter told me you would look presentable in that dress."

"If you start complimenting me, I'll have to find other men to talk with."

"A pity. Clearly, I need to practice my flirting. It's just that your cousin appears to be enjoying the company more than you are." Egidius lifted a bushy eyebrow that directed Aubrey's attention to one of the room's two wall fountains.

Three young, golden-haired women had Arne backed against the fountain, laughing and flirting with him, swinging their skirts and flipping their hair. More likely than not they were merely curious and testing their female power on a new sort of man, but Aubrey could hardly fault Arne for enjoying the attention. Aubrey laughed as she imagined Arne's reaction should one of the girls actually indicate a desire to find some hidden corner.

"You aside, Egidius, Arne's company is less annoying than mine has been." Aubrey sought for how best to frame her complaint. "You always give me a smile. But all evening I've been beset by hoary old men with unsubtle offers, while the young ones have stayed away."

"Young men are more easily intimidated by beautiful women, but I think in your case it's more that they can sense when she already has a man." Egidius chuckled at the look Aubrey gave him. "An older man is more likely to believe he has enough worldly advantage to find success against a rival. Given the likely identity of your swain, the younger the man, the less interest he will have in crossing him. Future rulers make for damaging enemies."

*Hans.* Cam too had marked that rumor. Aubrey could have laughed but for the seriousness of the assumption being made. Already Hans battled a perception that he was too closely Kheld-bound, with suspicion that his Staubaun subjects might fail to gain equal standing in his court. Since returning to Dazunor-Rannuli, Aubrey could tell that belief had become more pervasive. She knew Hans was attempting to identify and garner much-needed Staubaun allies. That he had Sordaneon support and the backing of the Staubaun domains of the Sordaneon Hierarchate both helped and hindered him in that quest. His other primary allies remained Amallar and Trongor, though Merrydn and Rannul had recently entered the fold. To have Hans linked with Aubrey romantically was not in either of their interests, however useful it might be to her in warding off predatory lords.

"They stand a better chance of incurring his wrath for slighting me." Aubrey might as well speak lightly. "Prince Handurin is my cousin and brother in arms. He would be delighted if I caught some man's eye."

"I shouldn't think that would be difficult. We men are simple creatures; our interest is easily aroused. A woman need only encourage us. But you do not."

Aubrey was saved from having to reply by the arrival of their host, who wandered over after having given a few farewells at the door. Misenos looked pleased with the evening and himself.

"I haven't hosted a more joyful gathering in years," he announced, beaming. "Who could not be thrilled that the Rill has been restored to Dazunor-Rannuli? There will be talk of nothing else for days, even if the city is now filled with Sordan folk. We'll just have to get used to them, I suppose." He signaled a servant who trotted over with two flagons of wine. Peering at them, he chose one and had the boy fill his cup and Egidius's. "Please, do not refuse me, lady," Misenos said when Aubrey declined the offer of a cup. "Surely you will share a toast in your royal cousin's honor!"

Refusal would be impolite. The boy took a chalice from the several hanging at his belt and poured for her, the brilliant clear vintage dancing from earthenware lip to silver bowl.

"To Handurin," Misenos proposed, touching his cup to Aubrey's first. "May he live long, reign justly, and always be as popular as he is tonight."

"To Handurin." They downed their toasts as cheers, presumably of a similar sort, rose at the other end of the hall. Aubrey saw an appropriate opening to take her leave. In another few minutes, the dress would be unbearable. But more to the point, if she left now there was still time to detour to Cam and Ralen's party while Myron would still be there. She might even be on hand to hear Myron recite something. A famous poem or a new one, Aubrey hardly cared.

"Lord Misenos, thank you for this evening. It has crowned my stay in your city. Prince Handurin will be happy to learn that his name has been so warmly celebrated."

"It sounds as though you are taking leave, Lady." Misenos looked disappointed, though he accepted the chalice when passed.

Aubrey bowed her head with respect and gestured helplessly with her hands, as she had seen Staubaun women do. "I must. I have done far too much travel these last weeks and am tired. I will travel again to Amallar in the morning. Good Egidius," she said, "might I have use of your coach to take me back to your house?"

"Of course. Misenos, how might we alert my driver?"

Misenos signaled the footman at the door, indicating Egidius. The man nodded and ducked outside. "But lady," Mogens admonished, "Amallar in the morning? I thought you would be with us a day more at least!"

Aubrey smiled and let Misenos take both her hands in his, a Staubaun gesture of parting. "My cousin's business will not wait."

Aubrey made a last tour through the room, making her courtesy farewell to Sinon Kouranos and alerting Arne to her departure. Arne told Aubrey to wait for him, that they were to always travel together, but then he returned straightway to regaling his merry maidens. Aubrey bridled. If she waited for Arne, Myron might leave before she got there. If she went now, she would not stay at Cam and Ralen's very long, and would be back at Mogen's house before Arne's night here would end. The girls' giggles followed Aubrey all the way to the outer hall. There, a servant fetched her fur-lined wrap and the footman escorted her from the door to the coach. She gave him the address to which she wished to travel and entered when he held open the door, its panel emblazoned with Mogens' faux heraldic cup. It took some concentration to perform the intricate maneuvers needed to accommodate the voluminous skirt and wrap. How Staubaun women ever managed so much material, Aubrey did not understand.

Aubrey had settled on the tall rear bench and was still adjusting her skirt, the coach well underway, when she noticed she was not alone.

A shadow sat opposite her, gray in the night. Light reflecting off the canal showed her the suggestion of a man's face.

"Driver!" she cried. What was his name? "Lippion!" Though Aubrey moved for the door, the shadow moved faster, its hand closing over hers.

"Don't. And be silent," the muffled voice commanded. Aubrey's eyes had adjusted enough to the dark for her to see that the man was masked, his face covered by intricately carved leather molded to human features. "Lippion has been relieved of his post. The driver is mine."

She sank back against the padded bench, mind racing. "And who are you?"

"A courier. And you, my fine package, are being delivered to another. Put this on." A gloved hand extended something long and supple. A leather blindfold.

Aubrey took it but hesitated. She ran the smooth leather through her fingers and tried to play for time. Time to think, time to act. "Tell me where you are taking me."

"You are in no position to set conditions. Put it on. If you do not, I will render you unconscious and your ordeal will be that much longer."

Aubrey's stomach sank. She had heard of abductions such as this. As often as not, the women were taken to be raped or sold to lecherous men and were never seen alive again. Hadn't Nalf warned that her own grandmother had been abducted this way in Stauberg many years ago? She stalled, gathering details, her gaze finding and noting the dagger glinting at the stranger's belt. He was armed, while she had nothing but a small thin blade in her garter, not now within reach. But it would be, later....

"Yes, I'm armed, wench." He'd noted the direction of Aubrey's gaze. "And I will not hesitate to use it. Now, for the last time, put the blindfold on." Those shadowy hands moved with something, perhaps a needle tipped with a drug that would induce unconsciousness.

Yielding, Aubrey reluctantly tied the blindfold about her eyes and over the velvet headband she wore to hold back her long hair. With sure fingers, she knotted the ends behind her head, then felt the gloved fingers tug the leather facing down firmly over her eyes and check the firmness of the knot.

"Excellent. You are as smart as I was told." The man rapped on the coach wall, alerting the driver to proceed on a different course.

"If anything happens to me," Aubrey threatened through cold lips.

"In Dazunor-Rannuli, no one will care."

They proceeded in silence, the coach rumbling over stones, revealing that they remained in the city. When at last the coach stopped, she heard men approaching, but they, too, remained silent as they assisted Aubrey out of the coach. Their hands weren't cruel as they guided her across flagstones and up steps into a building. She didn't know if the shadowy man accompanied them or had turned her over to others. Footsteps echoed as she was led along a smooth, hard corridor, up one flight of stairs and then a second before walking along another hall. They paused. Aubrey heard a door open. She found herself propelled forward, then yanked to a stop. The men released their hold and retreated. Their footsteps exited behind her and the door closed.

Not waiting for whomever awaited her to announce themselves, she raised her hands to the blindfold and removed it.

The room to which her mysterious abductor had brought her was lush and extravagant. A ceramic brazier aglow with the twisting shapes of uncoiling serpents dominated the room's vaulted center. Walls of warm gold vied with dark blue. Velvet draping, rich and brown, obscured windows. What caught her attention, and held it, was a tall, aristocratic woman standing in shadows at the far end of the room beside an elaborately carved chair.

Aubrey had not been brought to see a man. Relief that she did not confront a familiar peril gave way to apprehension over what might be wanted instead.

"So, you are Aubrey Amundda." The woman's voice conveyed a cold and authoritative presence. "They say you speak excellent Stauba."

Aubrey nodded. Was this to be another, albeit bizarre, demand that she serve some high personage as an interpreter? "Yes, noble Lady, I do."

"How very uncommon." The woman stepped forward into the mellow light, revealing a patrician face with an aquiline nose and the gold-topaz eyes of the highest Staubaun breeding, closely akin to the Highborn. Aubrey did not doubt she spoke to one of the highest noblewomen in the city, if not the entire Triempery. "You are useful to your cousin, I am sure."

"Useful enough, yes, Lady."

"He even sent you to Sordan as part of his first delegation to the Hierarchate."

Surprised that this woman should know about it, or that word of her had spread to the enclaves of power in Essera, Aubrey demurred. "It was Amallar's delegation, and I was honored to represent my people."

A bare smile turned the aged lips. "Tell me, Kheld, what did you think of Sordan?"

Sensing a purpose behind the question, Aubrey answered carefully. "The City is lofty and beautiful. Far beyond anything I could have imagined. I was but there overnight and did not see much of it."

"Only the Sordaneon Serat, one of the wonders of the World. I was privileged to stay there once, many years ago. The views are breathtaking, water and sky. You can see why Amynas chose to make his City there." After wandering to the glowing ceramic brazier in the center of the room, the lady took up a delicately fashioned pot. She reached into it with aged fingers and tossed a handful of something onto the coals. The scent of oranges filled the air. "And did you meet the Sordaneons, by chance?"

The question was casual, and yet not so. Aubrey felt a wing tip of warning brush across her mind. "The Heir, Prince Levyathan, yes, Lady. He was most gracious. The Hierarch himself was not in Sordan at that time."

A soft smile did not touch those faded, golden eyes. "No, of course not. By that time, Dorilian had been for some weeks in Amallar."

Not many knew that. Only in the highest circles of Lacenedon, where the news had been confirmed by Dorilian himself, had Aubrey heard Staubauns remark on the Hierarch's exploit. It was that unbelievable. Most Staubauns and even the Khelds themselves still believed that Dorilian had worked his Rill magic in a night and probably from afar, from his Rill seat in Sordan or possibly Permephedon on his way north. Though Hans no longer feared revolt among his Kheld troops if they found out, he had not yet revealed how near to them Dorilian had been. Aubrey's every instinct urged her to deny it, but something in the old woman's manner proclaimed independent knowledge. Aubrey bowed her head and answered. "Indeed, he was, Lady, though not under that name. And he left before we knew who he was."

"Before *you* knew?"

Aubrey felt her heartbeat quicken. Though she had not meant to, she had revealed too much. "Yes."

The woman came to stand before Aubrey, formidable and towering, her costly robe with its threads of gold picking up a glow that itself spoke of great power. "But you met him there before he left, I can see that. I detect traces of that meeting in your eyes and the way you breathe. So tell me this—what did you think of him?"

The ceiling itself seemed to crowd close. This woman's questions wrapped about Aubrey like strands of a web. After allowing herself a moment to ponder, Aubrey answered. "I thought him a most unusual Trongorian."

The woman waited for more and, when no more was forthcoming, acknowledged that with a smile. She turned away. "You are a cunning little Kheld." Her aged hand pulled a cord on the wall. "But you have walked into rooms where you do not belong. You will be escorted from here much as you came."

"Excuse me, Lady, but I don't believe—"

The men entered the room with the quiet efficiency of those who often performed such tasks as they now did. The blindfold came over Aubrey's eyes, blocking out her last sight of the old female—cheekbones carved by shadows, lips thin and knowing— whose cold regard seared across the orange light of the brazier.

As she was turned around to be led away, Aubrey heard the old woman say in a murmured aside, "You know what to do."

# 32

The Staubaun heritage of the Highborn is a political asset.
Following the slaughter of Telarion's line and the dearly
bought defeat of the Aryati, the sons of Laakon chose
alliance with powerful Staubaun houses as a means of
securing the Esseran throne. This decision was fostered
by the new Kings' belief that the pure blood of the
ancestral World presented the most viable vessel for
perpetuating the legacy of Leur.
EPIRADES MALYRDEON, *On Men and Gods*

Chyralane watched the door close and felt a hard knot form about the core of the World she knew. So, that was the woman. An unexpected beauty, careful and intelligent, sophisticated enough to conduct her Stauberg-Randolph cousin's business in Staubaun circles. But Chyralane had seen something more in the creature's crude sensuality, the round fullness of the Kheld's breasts against the emerald velvet of her dress, the swell of her hips promising pleasures any man might find alluring. Seeing that, she knew she had feared with reason.

Was it possible? Had Dorilian Sordaneon, so cold all these years, at long last thawed ... and in a *Kheldish* maid's bed? Had the wench tasted those proud lips, felt the hard thrust of his body, and taken within her the holy promise of Dorilian's seed? Chyralane tightened her lips over the impulse to retch.

For years she had watched Dorilian and wondered. And not Chyralane alone. All Essera had watched and wondered... and feared. They had wondered if Dorilian liked women and what manner of beauty or intellect would appeal to his tastes, which kindred he would elevate when he finally chose to sire sons of his own, what alliances he would dignify and seal with his godborn blood. For all the ancient enmity the Seven Houses bore him, the precious Highborn birthright of which Dorilian was now the sole adult source tantalized imagination. Others of the Seven Houses had plotted Dorilian's death, but not Chyralane. His life held more possibility. The Sordaneons often married late and seldom sired offspring before their fifth decade. Labran had been in his sixties, Deben well into his fifties. And so Chyralane had been patient while Dorilian secluded himself in Sordan, lofty and remote in his City of Light, entangled by enemies without the recourse of physical battle, isolated within a protective shell of appropriately aligned nobles, advisors, and relations.

Chyralane knew better than all her peers the reasons Staubauns perpetuated the mystery and seclusion of the blood that ruled them. More than musty tradition lurked within the imperative: the Highborn should know no truth but Staubaun truth. Perceive no reality but Staubaun reality. Become no flesh but Staubaun flesh. That imperative had been enforced for so long, the World itself thought the Highborn could not know or be other than Staubaun. Until Handurin had come along, broken open Dorilian's isolation, and turned the World inside out. Nor did Chyralane delude herself to think it had begun there.

If she could not end what a wizard had begun, at least she could end one small part of it.

The corridors and stairwells were cool with winter once more. Aubrey felt herself ushered for some distance, then she was stopped, dragged into a room, pushed into a chair.

"What are you doing?" Desperation gave her strength and she struggled out of the chair, kicking it over. It crashed against the hard floor, scraping stone. Then hands seized her again and subdued her. "You Staubaun pig-bladders! Let me go!"

*Damn that blindfold!*

A strong arm wrapped around her neck, a hand grasping a fistful of her hair, pulling her head back.

"Here it is," a voice rasped, so close to Aubrey's face she could smell his stale breath. "Make her drink it."

Something cold pushed between Aubrey's lips. The rim of a cup, metal and heavy. The sour smell of wine mingled with that of anise as she clamped her jaw and lips against the invasion. Calling every bit of her strength, she turned her head sharply. Liquid splashed on her hair and the fur trim of her cloak. In that same moment, she felt the sting of a hand striking her face. Tears sprang to her eyes, but she kept her jaw tight and cursed the blindfold again for keeping her in darkness, not knowing who assailed her or with what. Or why.

"Damn little Kheld bitch!" The hand in Aubrey's hair tightened cruelly, her captor pulling her head back so far that she could barely breathe, much less move. If they chose to now, they could easily slit her throat.

"Don't mark her. Give it straight," the other man said. As she sought to twist in his hard grasp, the cup slipped and trickled more liquid down her chin.

A sudden grunt erupted from one of her captors. Boots and movement. Something struck the floor… metallic… the sharper ping of glass. Another chair crashed across the room. The ring of drawn steel. Abruptly, Aubrey found herself released, unbalanced, her weight carrying her to the floor. Her left elbow hit first, followed by blinding pain. She didn't care. Her hands were free.

Ripping the blindfold from her eyes, Aubrey tossed it aside, blinking in filtered light and shadow. With one well-practiced move, she pulled up her skirt and grabbed the thin dagger she wore strapped above her knee. Turning with knife in hand, she saw her surroundings for the first time: a bare guardroom with only a table and lantern, tall walls with high, narrow windows, and a floor of plain mudstone. She also saw a gold-haired man with a sword, flanked by three others, none of whom did more than glance at her. It was then that Aubrey noticed the two men on the floor, each sprawled in rapidly spreading pools of blood.

"Apparently, lady, you are worth fighting for." The man with the sword lowered his weapon. Its scabbard, hanging at his belt, glittered with gems. "Who are you, and why were these ruffians accosting you in this place?"

"I'm Aubrey Thegn Amundda." She kept her slim blade at the ready. "And I don't have the faintest idea where I am or why these joltheads attacked me. Unless," she thought quickly, "it's because I'm cousin to Prince Handurin of Dazunor."

Her rescuer exchanged a confirming glance with his men. As his gaze returned to Aubrey's, it showed eyes of rich clear brown, with more intensity than arrogance. Staubaun tall, with bright gold hair and that race's handsome features, he wore clothing of the kind that seemed to be the uniform of young Esseran Staubaun nobility: a brocade jacket trimmed with fur and leather, as well as leather leggings of rich color and detailed cut. His men were dressed less finely but were clearly not brigands.

"Now that you mention it, I have seen you in good company. It is why I followed you in the first place. I thought it odd someone would summon your coach—and replace the coachman." He sheathed his sword. "If you care to put away the knife, I will help you from the floor."

Aubrey eyed her three rescuers dubiously but slid her blade back into its sheath, then pulled her dress down to hide her thigh.

"I am Raphelon Illarion, and these my men at arms." Extending his hand, Raphelon helped Aubrey to her feet. "I care not who your cousin might be—it's still beyond strange that you should be beset in this way." His boot kicked something on the floor and he bent to pick it up. It was a tube of amber glass, encased in brass with a secure lock at the stopper. A pewter wine cup lay nearby, the drink spilled on the floor.

"What is it?" Aubrey tried to calm the shaking of her limbs.

"I don't know, but this may answer much." Raphelon wrapped the vial in a bit of cloth and added it to the contents of his hip pouch. "Whatever it is, I fear it was meant to do you harm. Come, you will be safer with me than you are here."

That Raphelon had killed to free her from her assailants told Aubrey enough to make the decision. With a nod, Aubrey accepted a steadying arm. She heard words, either orders or plans, spoken but hushed. As they left the room running Aubrey hurried to keep up with Raphelon's long-legged pace down the seemingly endless halls. Raphelon pulled Aubrey around one last corner and they plunged down a stairway clearly not meant for public use. A door at the bottom of the stairs opened onto a dark, narrow quay. They were at water level, with only water before them and lights across the way. The Lower Canal. A boat awaited, low-slung and narrow, meant for ferrying people, not goods.

Looking back and up over her shoulder to see from where she had come, Aubrey recognized the fearsome tall walls and distinctive gold-crowned dome and corner towers of the Customhouse. Fearing those dark walls more than this bright-haired young lord about whom she knew next to nothing, Aubrey climbed with Raphelon into the boat. The heavy skirt of her borrowed dress dragged in the water for a moment before she pulled in the sodden hem.

Two of the men poled them from the mooring. Seated in the middle, Aubrey faced her rescuer across the shadows and pulled her dark cloak closer about her shoulders. It smelled of wine and licorice, but at least it smelled better than the canal. "Why are you helping me?"

"Frankly, I could see no good reason for a well-born young Kheld woman, particularly one so clearly well connected, to be in the clutches of the Seven Houses. Their business seldom embraces your kind." Raphelon's gaze took in her elegant garb. "All I can conclude is that you caught some high lord's fancy."

Aubrey looked away, at the black water over which she rode, the remote dark walls of the merchant palaces. Above them, the Rill's surreal architecture shimmered with stark majesty.

Tiny waves slapped the side of the boat as Raphelon pondered both Aubrey and her silence. "Forgive me for saying this, but it's not the sort of thing I would expect of them. They're very much Purists."

"Sometimes, those are the worst. The stronger the prohibition, the stronger the appeal." Wasn't that part of Aubrey's own dilemma? That she should not even be *able* to think of Dorilian Sordaneon as someone she might bed?

"Yes, you're likely right."

The silent city slid by, palace walls crowding the canal, greenery-draped balconies overhanging dank water. Glowing rooms of light, carved of alabaster and fashioned from glass, crowned many of those towers. Centuries of Rill wealth closed in behind fortress walls.

"Are you a Purist?" Aubrey asked.

"Me?" Even as they glided into the shadows beneath a bridge, Aubrey marked Raphelon's self-deprecating smile. "I honestly don't know, which I suppose means I am not."

"Good," she said. "I haven't liked the ones I've met."

Raphelon laughed. "Come to think of it, neither have I. They despise what's noble along with what's crass. Marc Frederick was noble, and Stefan had his virtues. And Handurin is probably someone I should get to know."

"I think you should."

"I might. His association with the Sordaneon gives me pause. I don't know what to make of it." He looked up at something to which the tall soldier manning the boat's prow had grunted. "Here we are, lady." Raphelon stood and extended his hand as the boat bumped up against the side of a building and a small dock there. "We will rest an hour here, then be away."

"Away?" Using the offered hand for support, Aubrey also grasped the iron bracket in the wall and pulled herself and her voluminous garments up onto the landing. A small door there opened into the building. She followed Raphelon inside.

"No one escapes the Customhouse without pursuit. They may well think of me, knowing that I was there claiming business—but not, I think, that I will be here. Jereniell." He acknowledged a pale young woman, her skirt of rose cloth swirling about her legs and ankles, who entered from another doorway to meet them. Coils of golden hair held back by jeweled combs framed the round, sweet face of a girl but there was also something also more worldly, for she tilted her head and smiled knowingly at the tall young man.

"What have you rescued this time, Rafe?"

Raphelon grinned sheepishly. "A lady of the Kheld lands. Oh, and the Seven Houses may be looking for us." Aubrey looked to see if the men had closed the door behind them and was gratified that they had.

Removing his cap of leather and velvet, stitched with gold thread and trimmed with fur, the foremost of Raphelon's men bowed his blond head to Jereniell, then flicked his gaze to his lord. "If we are to leave, My Lord, I will go for our horses."

Raphelon quickly accepted that proposition. "This is as good a time to leave the city as any, Desmos. Tell the men we are going and join me in an hour. I'll send word to you at Misenos's."

Like shadows, Desmos and the two other men departed. Opening the door again, they climbed down into the boat and poled away on the canal's dark currents. Jereniell took Aubrey by the elbow, steering her and Raphelon from the cold stone room. Bare footsteps and a short hallway later, they stood in a sumptuously furnished chamber fashioned from glass. Opaque panels created intricately patterned walls, the glowing vault of the ceiling, even the staircase opposite, its magnificent balustrade twined with a profusion of glass flowers in perpetual bloom.

"My family is one of glassmakers," Jereniell told Aubrey with a smile. She must have noted Aubrey's surprise. "Though glass is but one form of our art."

Aubrey looked around in wonder at the multicolored splendor of the room, its walls hung with curtains of tiny strung glass beads mimicking flowing draperies of silk, shimmering with deep, glowing patterns. Light poured softly from waterglobes captured fantastic fixtures each more marvelous than the next. The window above the stairs, fashioned of many hundreds of pieces of tinted glass, brooded with dark beauty but would blaze to life in the light of day.

"Color is her art. Pigments. Jereniell is a chemist." Raphelon slipped onto a couch upholstered in fabric of apricot hue so rich and deep it burned like sunset. He reached into his belt pouch and pulled forth the vial he had picked up at the Customhouse. "What do you make of this, cousin?" He extended the slender tube. "The brigands besetting the lady tried to force her to drink wine with this in it."

Jereniell took the vial in her delicate fingers, turning it in the light. "Enerrach glass, ambered to protect the contents from light. Waxed stopper, which means it is probably an organic compound." She flipped open the brass fitting and removed the stopper, swirling the contents, which she then daintily sniffed. Her expression became guarded and she left the room for a moment, returning with a long, thin stick that she inserted into the liquid. Pulling it forth, she watched as the stick changed colors. "*Merethe.*"

"What's that?" Aubrey could see already that Raphelon looked as abruptly grim as Jereniell did.

"A rare drug, difficult to make and seldom used, but always against women." Jereniell replaced the vial's stopper, then capped it tightly by fastening the brass fittings. She set it in a rack of reddish wood she brought from one of the cabinets and placed it on the table, where it glinted like a cat's eye in the dark. "It's a devastatingly effective abortifacient."

"What?"

"Are you pregnant, lady?" Raphelon asked.

"Of course not!" Aubrey tried to control the feelings, including panic, which seized her. If she was....

"Apparently someone thinks so." Jereniell's expression offered support—and sympathy.

"Or simply wanted to make sure work of it, whether she is or not." Raphelon tapped the large ring on his left hand against the pebbled glass of the table beside him. His expression sharpened on Aubrey thoughtfully. "Whoever this lord is, he certainly doesn't want you to have his love child."

Aubrey glared at him. "You're assuming an awful damn lot! There is no lord, at least not one of that craven breed! And there is no child!" But an icy, terrifying realization set in. One of the powerful nobles of the Seven Houses had abducted and then interviewed her—and then ordered thugs to force her to drink a drug that would cause her womb to empty if she was with child.

There could be only one reason for it: the old woman had asked Aubrey about only one man.

Rumor must have flown from Askyllon. They wanted to make certain she would not bear a Highborn Heir. Aubrey tried to remember when she had last shown Mother's blood. She'd been menstruating when Hans had besieged Dazunor-Rannuli. More than six weeks ago. And then in Askyllon, Bas Hebron's men had made off with Aubrey's healer's case—and with it the supply of umbrelheart preventative she usually took after bedding a man.

Jereniell, seeing that Raphelon was about to speak, warned him off. Instead, she pressed Aubrey's hand in her pale one that seldom saw the light of day. "You drank none of it? Tell me truly. If you did, we must take steps to save your life."

"My life?" Aubrey forced herself to respond.

"*Merethe* opens blood vessels in the womb. The blood separates the child from the womb, which kills it, but often—almost always—the bleeding kills the mother as well. If you are not with child, the danger is less, but you would still bleed excessively."

"No. I swallowed none of it, not a drop."

Raphelon continued to look grim. "But why use so drastic a means? Surely there are easier ways to kill a woman, particularly one who is not expecting it. They used no ropes and little force. They were going to great length to make her death look to be of natural causes."

*Because they suspect who the father is.*

Aubrey shivered and looked away. *"Don't mark her. Give it straight."* The words suddenly took on new force. There were reasons upon reasons that these merchant princes would wish to make her death seem natural.

And all this because she had captured an attractive stranger one rainy day in Amallar, had drawn him to her in the forge, had followed the call of the Mother instead of her head. *How strange,* she thought.

"You were at the Dannuthi ambassador's party earlier."

Raphelon nodded when Aubrey gave him a surprised look. "I left before you did and was talking with Desmos when I saw what happened by the coaches. When I saw you get in, I was concerned enough to follow. And luckier still to find the coach in front of the Customhouse."

Drawing a breath to steady herself, Aubrey explained about the coach and her abduction. "At that point, I thought I was to be raped or sold to some vile man."

"That's usually the way of it."

Jereniell gaped from Raphelon to Aubrey, whose hand she still held. "How awful to know that such things happen! What an ordeal you've had! And by the hand of the Seven Houses."

"I was confused when I saw my surroundings. But still frightened. I didn't know where I was."

"Who did you see there? Anyone you can name?" Jereniell appeared to be still offended on Aubrey's behalf. Every question now sought avenues along which to pursue justice.

Aubrey shook her head. "I saw no one I knew. I've only been to the Customhouse of the Seven Houses twice before, with my cousin Hans, when he set the terms for renewing Rill service and negotiated for some boats."

Jereniell looked to Raphelon, who gave an acknowledging nod. "She is cousin to Prince Handurin and returned just yesterday afternoon after having played some part—all the city is speculating what—in restoring Rill service. Supplies for Handurin's army have been pouring in from Amallar and Sordan all night. Whatever deal he's struck with the Sordaneon, it appears it is being honored."

"I've been serving my cousin as translator and liaison," Aubrey said. "Not many Khelds speak Stauba well or want to learn it. That's changing, but not fast enough to give Hans the translators and interpreters he needs. I'm frequently called upon to convey messages or answer questions. In fact, I thought at first that was why I was brought there, because the old woman wanted to know something."

Raphelon's gaze sharpened. "Old woman?"

"Very tall and narrow. Strong features. She might have had gray hair, it looked like that at her temples, but she wore a tall headdress that covered it. When I was brought before her, the first words out of her mouth, after making sure of my name, were 'They say you speak excellent Stauba.'"

Raphelon's glance at Jereniell seemed meaningful, but neither added to the communication.

"She asked me all kinds of questions." A sudden drag of weariness assailed Aubrey, but she felt no desire at all for sleep. Her mind was galloping with too many thoughts, none of them restful.

Jereniell regarded Aubrey solemnly. "The old woman could be Chyralane Rannuleonis. She is Denizen of Phaer, head of that House. They are very high and powerful. Her father was a Highborn Prince, one of the Rannuli Malyrdeons, and her mother a high noblewoman of House Koillos. She sits on the Archhalia and would not involve herself in anything minor. This is certainly more than fear of some petty lord's inconvenient attachment or ill-gotten bastard. And it is more than a simple dislike of your influence over your cousin. The Seven Houses must think you a significant threat."

"And they chose *merethe*, let us not forget that." In the colored glows of the glass surrounding them, Raphelon's fair hair and face took on reflected hues, purple and apricot and one streak of red. "To even possess that drug is forbidden. Yet they risk it."

"It has been used in the past to kill royal heirs in the womb."

"They may feel the child is Handurin's, then." Raphelon regarded Aubrey with even greater interest.

"Hans? Oh, please. Nothing has ever happened between us that would produce a child!" Aubrey wondered how many more times she would need to say it. Or for how long.

"Very well, then, they fear that there is likely to be one if they do nothing." Raphelon's look matched Jereniell's for seriousness. "Clearly you and Handurin are linked in ways that make the Seven Houses uncomfortable. I heard comments enough after your visits to the Customhouse, when you accompanied him there. The Denizen of Hedys attended in person to hear Handurin's proposal for use of his House's barge fleet specifically because he wanted to see you for himself. To hear him now, you single-handedly secured his fleet for your Prince. Now Chyralane has seen for herself that you are accomplished and well educated, hardly the barbarian she might at first have thought. It is not impossible that Handurin might think you suitable for a royal wife. And who knows what talk has reached the cartel's ears to that end? They have spies in every quarter. It would be ridiculous to think Khelds do not have plans—openly or behind doors—to get Handurin with a Kheldish Queen as they did Stefan. One of your people's greatest fears has to be that their Prince will die without an Heir." Raphelon waited for an answer and, getting none, said, "Even you don't deny it."

How could she, remembering just about every conversation with her uncle Nalf since she'd arrived at Rhodhur from Saemoregh? It seemed all of Dazunor-Rannuli believed Hans was considering Aubrey for a wife. It might be to her advantage to let these Staubauns think that it was Hans the Seven Houses plotted to prevent from falling into a Kheldish marriage, not that she might have lain in Dorilian Sordaneon's bed. For now, thinking as they did, Jereniell and Raphelon were disposed to help. Aubrey didn't want to find out what they might think of the other possibility.

"I cannot take her back to Misenos or Mogens." Raphelon faced Jereniell and frowned as he contemplated his options. "They will be looking for her to return there. If Chyralane is involved, whatever follows will be persistent and deadly. I will need to stay either ahead of them or out of sight."

"Then you have no time to lose. Where will you go?" Jereniell looked nervous as sounds of activity rose from the courtyard outside the windows. Desmos must have arrived with the horses.

"It's best you don't know that. They may already have fingered me as the lady's benefactor. The Seven Houses and I are well acquainted." Raphelon rose and reached for his leather cloak again. "Have you traveling clothes for the lady?"

"Wait, Jereniell." Aubrey forestalled the young woman before she could run to another room for the things. "Do you have a father or brothers? Can you dress me as a man?"

Jereniell stopped and gave Aubrey an odd look. "A man?"

"I won't pass careful inspection, but Kheld women dress as our men when we travel. I'm perfectly comfortable in male clothing."

Raphelon shrugged to the look Jereniell threw him. "What do I care how she dresses? It might work for the better." He scrutinized Aubrey more closely. "Dare I hope you ride like a man as well?"

"I do. And handle a sword, if you can find me a blade."

Raphelon grinned. "That, I can do." He gestured, and Aubrey followed him into the next room, a towering chamber with wooden floors and panels, carpeted and lined with ancient weavings. One wall held nothing but books. Aubrey looked around in wonder. Robdan would be beside himself with happiness in such a place as this. Raphelon pressed something on one of the walls and the panel there swung open to reveal an array of weaponry. After a quick study of Aubrey, Raphelon chose one, hefting it then handing it over. "Try this."

Aubrey accepted the weapon with a flourish, earning a raised eyebrow at her facility. The blade was a good one, even better finished than her own, with a hilt of braided leather chased with embossed buttercups in gold. Raphelon handed over a matching belt and scabbard. Aubrey grinned back as she caressed the fine leather.

"You certainly seem to know your way around this place."

"My grandmother's kin. I usually stay with my father's cousins when in town, but I've spent many an hour of my wayward youth hiding in the Hebdomon draperies."

Jereniell appeared with an armful of clothing. There were silk shirts and leather breeches up to her chin. "These are my brother's. I pray they fit you reasonably."

"They'll be fine," Aubrey assured. But as she dressed just behind a closed panel door, cuffing the legs and belting the breeches with the sword belt she'd been given, she began thinking again. Glad as she was that this Raphelon had thwarted the designs of the Seven Houses, Aubrey wasn't sure her best path to safety lay with a man well known to them. Worse, by staying with him, Aubrey was putting Raphelon in danger as well. She was also endangering Jereniell and the entire house of Hebdomon.

"Get me a horse and direct me out of town, and I will make the rest of the way on my own. I will return the sword and horse." Aubrey came around the door to find Raphelon in close, hushed argument with Jereniell. Jereniell blushed as she pulled away. She was wearing a traveling cloak and boots. "Oh, I don't want this!" Aubrey declared. "Not her too."

Jereniell tossed her golden hair and drew on her gloves. "Only for part of the way. I heard talk of a train of supplies leaving for Rainill on the hour and, if Raphelon is wise, he will see to it that you join up with it. The convoy is accompanied by Sordani soldiers ultimately bound for the relief of Kyrbasillon." Jereniell lifted an eyebrow. "Even the Seven Houses would not pursue you then. As for myself, I figure someone has to let Aubrey's kin at Egidius Mogens's know what has become of her. My family is respected and I can travel about the city without raising suspicion. I will take the family guardsmen with me, of course."

Aubrey nodded, feeling a little chagrined. "Thank you, Lady Jereniell," she said. "I had wondered how I would let them know. And if you could return the dress I was wearing"—she sighed—"it isn't my own, but borrowed from one of Mogens's daughters. It's stained now, but I'm sure she would like it back."

"I thought I recognized it." Jereniell smiled in understanding. "Mogens bedecks his daughters like royalty."

Jereniell walked with Aubrey to the streetside courtyard of the stately house, where horses waited for them along with Raphelon and the already mounted men. Just before Aubrey passed through the deep doorway, Jereniell touched her arm, staying her. The knowing look returned to the young chemist's gaze. "If the Seven Houses truly have targeted you, this night will not dissuade them. They may attempt this drug again. There are signs to watch for: *merethe* is detected by hints of licorice, and it is generally administered in food or wine, something that will conceal the taste and smell. It is a strange choice for you, but if that is what they have chosen, be very careful. Drink clear water and eat simple food, and those only if you know from whose hand it came."

Moved by a goodwill she had never expected, Aubrey returned the smile Jereniell gave her. "I will. Thank you, Lady."

Jereniell looked around the doorway to where Raphelon was directing her escort and her own smile deepened. To Aubrey, she said, "He means well, but he must always have his way." She reached into her cloak and pulled out a small book. "Rafe would frown if he knew I did this, but it appears you have need. Khelds are not well versed in our ways, ill or good. Do you read Stauba also?"

"Yes."

"Then study this, and may it serve you well."

Jereniell pressed the palm-sized book into Aubrey's hands. It was leatherbound and well thumbed, its pages soft with use. The title embossed on the spine told the tale: *Surviving Poisons*.

With a grim smile, Aubrey accepted the book and tucked it under her jacket. She was learning much about Staubauns these days.

# 33

The west plain of Dazunor and the east plain of Tahlwent
are separated by the hills of the former Aryati megalopolis
of Gyges Minossa. After the Return, survivors reclaimed
strategic structures and founded several important cities
of the Staubaun repatriation: Trulo, Kyrbasillon,
Memlos, and Elithegh. At the urging of Ergeiron, the
Sons of Amynas secured intact grid points and core arrays
by building their cities and fortresses upon them.
EPIRADES, *HISTORY OF THE MALYRDEONS*

It was pouring rain when Hans caught up with his army at Tross. Prior to leaving Rainill, he had made sure of the new granaries and had established ties with local lords that would ensure regional stability. In return for the lords' fealty and tithes toward rebuilding the villages Erenor's men had destroyed, Hans promised they would keep their lands and be paid fair prices for their crops or livestock from his quartermasters.

"I can address them later for not standing up to Erenor or Mormantalorus," he told Nalf Rhys, who'd questioned the policy of letting men who'd stood by while tyrants slew entire villages profit by that cowardice. "They'll find that their families are not invited to my court, awarded favors, or seats on the principality's Lords' Council. For now, I need to make sure they don't make trouble for me by mounting insurrections while I'm chasing Zel through Dazunor."

The Kheld army had not engaged in battle in a week, though they had skirmished, meeting small pockets of soldiers they had soon noticed were designed to draw them toward the river. Seeing that, Fran had stopped pursuit and sent forth scouts, discovering a great body of men to the west, hidden behind the hills that crowded the Dazun like a dragon's neck barring their way. The Trongorian

Rangers, by far the best mounted fighting unit, made a push up the Road itself, toward Trulo, but turned back before reaching the hills. They returned white-faced, having ridden hard their steaming horses.

"Zel holds the Dazun Road." Farrl delivered the news even before dismounting his horse. He accompanied Hans and the other captains inside the farmhouse where Hans had made his lodging before telling them the rest. "The monster has again lined the road with Kheld villagers, as cruelly as before. Some victims still lived. But when my men tried to approach, we detected signs of wire."

"Wire!" Hans bit back his growing frustration. Soter had warned about the Mormantaloran tactic of stringing nearly invisible fine wire across roads, where it would slice into the legs and tendons of horses, laming them and slicing to ribbons the thrown riders. The need to watch for and remove wire would slow their progress.

"I feared the Mormantalorans lay in wait and would take aim at our men who approached on foot. So I retreated to a safe distance and had my archers put out of their misery any impaled souls who still moved."

"May Leur blind those that torture innocents!" cursed Euden Mezeon.

"How many? From the villages?" asked Nalf Rhys.

Farrl met Nalf's gaze evenly, grim eyes in a pale face. "I counted a hundred, then stopped because I could see no farther down the road." Fran paused to gather his thoughts, or perhaps to banish other thoughts from his mind, before turning to Hans. "I'm glad your lady mother is safe at Permephedon. I would fear for her at Zel's hand."

Hans nodded, reminded again that he had been in this World for nine months, in Essera for two months, and had yet to know more of his mother than could be conveyed in a handful of letters. Even the Khelds remembered Emyli primarily as a girl and young mother. She hadn't been a fixture at Stefan's court. From talking with Asphalladra, Hans understood Stefan had sent Emyli away on at least three occasions, once for having allowed Marenthro to hide Hans himself away.

"So we can't take the Dazun Road." Hans hadn't really expected it would be that easy. It made sense that Nammuor would escalate his campaign of terror. The Mormantalorans were invaders and the people they killed they considered subhuman. "What are the ways around Zel's position?"

"None that are good." Soter frowned. He stood at the rear, his shoulders braced against the wall, arms crossed on his chest as he pondered their dilemma. "There's the Dazun, but I fear it if the Sorcerer commands the waters."

"Which he's shown that he can," Euden Mezeon noted. "Also, the Malyrdeons installed river defenses near Trulo. A system of underwater machines and barricades that may have survived the flood and are controlled by Erenor. We're not equipped to move our entire fighting force by boat or barge, anyway."

"What vessels we do command are engaged already in conveying supplies," Hans agreed. In addition to barges owned by Cam and Ralen, Hans had procured the fleet of the Denizen of Hedys. For weeks now, the river had played a strong role in supplying Hans's troops. Fresh provisions, weapons, and horses could be brought in at liberated river ports. "Even if we could be sure of not encountering obstacles, it would take too long to gather the number of crafts needed and we would be obvious."

Young Bas Kerr looked up brightly. "We could ride into Dannuth. My father holds Kyrbasillon with the help of reinforcements from Sordan and Merrydn, with more coming."

While Hans welcomed the idea of more troops, he knew his army needed more speed, not less. It would take too long to go so far north, almost to the Hesperian Mountains—on the other side of which Stauberg's plain ran to the sea. Furthermore, doing so would expose his flank. Zel would move quickly to drive a wedge between the Stauberg-Randolph armies and the Dazun. Hans could not afford to have the enemy between his army and Dazunor-Rannuli.

He had to preserve his Rill access at all costs.

Hans leaned over the table, concentrating on the map skin with its beautifully inked details. "Why would we have to go so far north?" He traced the intervening lands with his fingertip. The soft hide of the map felt buttery and rich. "What are these hills, here? Just north of Omadawn. There's sure to be a way we could get through there and circle behind."

Kerr looked up unhappily. "Except that those hills are the reason Zel chose to block the Dazun Road where he did. These hills"—he tapped the markings where Hans's finger rested—"are called the Kragh. Difficult terrain to cross, sharp and crusted, densely forested. No trails and filled with dead ends and steep passes. Horrible for horses and worse for men. None go there."

Hans raised his head and looked Kerr in the eye. Though young, the lad was Bas of Dannuth and had knowledge of the region. "But an army could get through?"

Kerr hesitated. He brushed an unruly clump of white-gold hair out of his eyes. "I wouldn't know, Sire. As I said, none go there. There is no one to tell us if it can be done." He worried his lip for a moment, then explained. "It's not just the land that's horrible. Monsters dwell in those hills—creatures of blood and claw that kill all who trespass there. Legend has it that the Dog Men of the Kragh once hunted the Highborn and slew them, even the women and babes, for the Aryati. They seized Peleor, son of Derlon, and chained him for the Aryati to slay on the Rill mount at Simelon. For these deeds, the Highborn cursed the Dog Men and condemned them to be beasts, vowing they should remain so until they had washed the Highborn blood from their hands." Kerr's hard frown showed that he believed the tale. "They were given this land to live in by King Emrysen a thousand years ago. Every King since has forbidden people to have anything to do with them." Kerr looked at his companions bleakly. "None who enter these hills come back alive. The local people know better than to wander too near. The Dog Men are even more to be feared than Zel."

Hans moved his army as far as Omadawn, where he set crews to work taking down and burying the corpses of Zel's victims. Most of the villagers had been impaled after death, but they found some they could clearly see had been impaled while still alive, their faces set in contortions of unspeakable agony. The message Zel had intended worked its way through the initial rage of the advancing army, settling fear at the base of the brain, where it gnawed steadily at confidence and determination. Seeing how they might die, and how their bodies might be despoiled after death, disheartened many.

"I won't stay camped here another day," Hans told Fran and Nalf Rhys. "I don't care if there are monsters in the Kragh—they can't be any worse than this. Tomorrow, we move."

One bright note came in the form of the arrival of fresh troops and supplies from Dazunor-Rannuli, along with a brace of riders Hans had almost given up on seeing again. Hans recognized Arne's familiar roan, but Aubrey was riding an energetic gray instead of the well-bred bay she'd ridden from Amallar. With them were other riders whose horses' trappings proclaimed them to be Staubaun and noble. Aubrey and two of the Staubaun riders rode ahead to meet Hans, leaving Arne to direct the wagons to the quartermaster's flag.

"Aubrey!" Hans reached up to help Aubrey swing down from her horse and gave her a heartfelt hug. "I've been waiting for you and Arne to get back! You wouldn't believe what we've been through. The fighting has been ugly. You've brought supplies at just the right time! The men are exhausted and at least now they'll have good food and drink from home." Hans loosened his hold as Aubrey pulled away and only then noticed that they were being watched. "Hello," he said to the man who had joined them. Hans then nodded to the younger man standing to one side.

The former studied him with interest. "Prince Handurin."

Hans returned the study. Though of plain appearance, the newcomer's garments were superbly cut and sewn with telling details: embroidery of gold thread and heavy silk, fine buttons and richly finished metals in the buckles and light armor. Even without distinctions of wealth, this man possessed the arrogance of high birth. Furthermore, there was something measured about the way the man carried himself. Hans decided to learn more before being friendly. He looked to Aubrey for assistance.

She laughed. "My benefactor, Raphelon Illarion."

"Illarion." Hans paused to recall where he had heard the name before. He glanced again at the good-looking man. "And a benefactor?" This time Hans did smile.

"The lady needed assistance. I provided it." Raphelon indicated the young man at his side. "My man, Desmos Vallsiran. I also bring twenty men of my guard. More will follow if I send for them."

Hans saw that Raphelon would tell him nothing more. He nodded and hugged Aubrey again. "I'm glad you're back. I got word that the Rill is restored to Dazunor-Rannuli."

He wanted to see Arne right away and went with Aubrey and Raphelon to the quartermaster, who was assigning some just arrived wagons. With Arne was Gerd, who exclaimed his delight. "Hans! Or is that Prince, now? I can't remember such things. But I understand you need a cook and an innkeeper."

"I need a cook for sure," Hans told Gerd. "Snearly manages to burn even water."

"I've brought my pots and a full kitchen tent. We arrived in Rainill two days ago by barge! Aubrey helped me arrange it. And two whole wagons of hams!" Still as happy as if he'd been dropped into a busy fairground instead of a camp set up for war, Gerd bustled off to see to his hams.

"This is great, it really is," Hans told Arne, who looked no worse for his time in Lacenedon. Arne's grin was as refreshing as his arm clasp. "Good friends, good food. I'll fill you in later about Zel."

"You'd better, if he's the creature who did what we saw on the way in."

Other men rode up, a party of royal Dannuthi, no doubt alerted to the arrivals. Kerr's ivory steed cantered at their head.

"Prince Handurin!" Kerr dismounted in a blur of blue leathers to approach the group. A moment later he shouted, "Rafe!" Bypassing everyone else, Kerr raced up and grabbed Raphelon by the arms in a kinsman's greeting.

A broad grin brightened Raphelon's formerly solemn face. "Kerr, you Leur-crossed pup!"

"Rafe! I couldn't believe it when they told me you'd come! I had thought you were in Merath." Still grinning, Kerr turned back to Hans. "This is my cousin, Raphelon Illarion. He's Heir to Serrain."

Which accounted for Raphelon's caution. A man who might one day rule a domain would guard his loyalties as carefully as his life. Aubrey, however, swung around to confront the man she'd ridden into camp with.

"Heir to Serrain! You never told me that!" she protested.

"I told you my name."

"But it doesn't say where you're from," Aubrey asserted. Just ahead was the stone circle where Hans had set his tent. "At least with some men you know right away. Sordaneon. That tells you. No guessing with him. Even Stauberg-Randolph. But your name doesn't say a thing."

Kerr, looking embarrassed, interceded. "But it does! Illaria is a region of Serrain."

"It is?" Aubrey was already turning red.

"Yes," said Raphelon archly. "It is."

Hans and Arne broke out laughing. "This is great," Hans repeated, happy.

They parted with promises to reconvene for the evening meal. Raphelon, who knew the area well, told of hot springs nearby, and so Hans, Arne, and Kerr eagerly saddled up to go with him. Farrl's

Trongorian guard rode along, but at a distance, and it felt almost like a lark. The land had long been Staubaun ruled, and civilized, and the springs were ringed by stonework steps and smooth bathing ledges, the green surfaces of the pools sending forth clouds of mist into the crisp winter air.

"You don't look like Stefan." Raphelon sank down beside Hans in one of the pools that had a ledge just the right depth for sitting in water chest-deep. Arne and Kerr, though newly acquainted, splashed at each other in another pool nearby. "I expected you to be more Kheldish in appearance, even though I had heard otherwise." Raphelon paused. "My apologies if I have offended you. That's the downside of meeting people after having outside knowledge of them."

Hans nodded. Had he not done the same? "I know what you mean. I thought Dorilian would look more Staubaun than he does."

"Truly?" Raphelon cocked his head to the side, intrigued. "That is another thing I find astonishing, that you should know him at all. And that he has not yet had you killed. Apparently, you have yet to outlive your usefulness."

Surprised—not by the sentiment, which he'd encountered in a thousand variations, but that Raphelon should start their acquaintance in that way—Hans shook his head. "Dorilian and I understand each other."

"I never thought I would see the day when Khelds agreed to work with him. Six months ago, I would have said there was no possible way it could be done." Raphelon settled back and propped his head against the ledge. "I knew Stefan well. I liked him at first. I found that more difficult after he executed Rheger Dannutheon and his Heir. They were relatives and… well, you see, I still believe in Highborn rule. Most of my caste do, not least because our rule is historically predicated on theirs. We will always damn Stefan for having done away with the Malyrdeons."

"He also tried to kill the Sordaneons. He sent assassins."

"More than once. Stefan and Dorilian were always at each other's throats. Therein lies the irony, I suppose."

"Do you believe Dorilian murdered Marc Frederick? And Stefan?"

Raphelon grimaced. A long moment passed before he spoke. "I must answer carefully here, I think. Clearly you do not believe it, or you would not associate with him. So let me be blunt: I never thought he committed the murders at Permephedon. My maternal grandsire was Highborn and died at that Council. I know something of Highborn ways, and I know that they experience each other's deaths. If Dorilian were truly there—and I believe he was—the deaths would have affected him profoundly. I was also close enough to my Highborn kin to know Dorilian did not hate Marc Frederick as much as people say he did."

"He didn't. He tried to save him."

"Did he? I should be more surprised." Raphelon sucked his lips briefly, frowning at the water. "I do not personally know Dorilian, but I cannot believe anyone of that blood would eradicate his own race simply to gain a Hierarchate to which he was already Heir and legitimately ruled in all but name. He had by that point largely rid Sordan of Essera's yoke. Marc Frederick had aided him in that accomplishment, and Dorilian had little else to gain. Rheger never spoke against Dorilian after that day. He advocated. So if Marenthro says someone else did those murders, I believe that. Nammuor's plans for Sordan were well known, and we all see with whom Erenor now stands."

"It took Khelds a while to see what Erenor was up to." Hans swept his hands through the warm water but still felt chilled, so he sank until it was up to his shoulders. That was better.

"It took all of us longer than it should have," Raphelon acknowledged. "The Khelds, and many others, believed falsehoods because those pointed to a man they wished to hate. We here in Essera were no better. But I know too that Dorilian plagued Stefan and wanted him gone. I believe Dorilian wished to settle matters in Neuberland and seat himself on Essera's throne. His ambition is well established. And I thought it possible he played a hand in Stefan's death. I arrived at the lodge from Aral with Erenor that day. My brother Lucien was one of the men who was executed within the hour for the murder. I talked with him. He told me what he saw." Raphelon shook his head, his gaze haunted by horror. "Nammuor is reputed to be a sorcerer, true. But Stefan by then was his creature—why kill him? Dorilian is not incapable of murder, I think. And the Sordaneons are the most powerful of a breed we believe can alter reality if they are so determined."

Shouts from Arne and Kerr informed Hans that his friends were having fun. For him this interlude was for other things. He laid his head back against the smooth stone ledge, polished by eighteen centuries of other bodies doing just as he did now. "Then we will have to agree to hold different opinions." The blue sky overhead had the robin's-egg tinge of winter, when the sun swung low across the belly of the world. "I have no doubts about Dorilian. None at all. He didn't kill my grandfather or my brother."

"No doubt at all?"

"Not a one. He was Stefan's enemy, but he didn't kill him."

"Then I pray you are right—and that your faith in him will not come back to bite you."

In the next pool, Arne had taken to throwing yellow-tinged mud at Kerr, while Farrl stood by laughing. Desmos lounged on the rocks near the Trongorian, the two men staying armed while the others bathed. Three more guards stood along the path leading to the pools.

"It's hard to believe we're in the grip of war," Raphelon observed. "When I was a boy, we never thought about such things. War was something that happened in Neuberland. Or it was something the Sordaneons tried their hand at on occasion. Now I look at Kerr and I see someone too young for war."

"He'd disagree with you."

"He'd be wrong. We're all too young for war. Don't think me a pacifist. I have used my sword in combat. I just dislike the thought of dying, dislike it intensely. Especially if it involves the kind of dying I saw along the road to Omadawn."

Zel's terror tactics were taking their toll. Hans recalled the field of corpses impaled at the side of the road. "I won't let that happen to my men. I won't lead them into Nammuor's hell. I'll do this another way."

"And what way is that? Zel holds the Dazun Road. You yield that, and he slices you off from your Rill supply line and your allies across the river. Dazunor-Rannuli falls to Nammuor and for all we know the Sordaneon has a means to stop the Rill yet a second time should that happen. You cannot risk your supply line. So you are committed to the Dazun Road. With Zel dug in at Trulo, you cannot advance. The enemy besieging Kyrbasillon are dangerously near. Meanwhile, Nammuor could conceivably bring troops east from Tahlwent or south from Stauberg."

"There has to be a way." Hans turned over, letting the warm, mineral-laden water swirl under his belly. He rested his chin on his arms as they clasped the rock edge. "Dorilian will keep the enemy north of us busy for a while. Both Nammuor and Erenor see him as the greater threat and there's more to be gained defeating him than me. Defeat him and they not only secure all the lands to the north, but they also damage the mythos of Highborn invincibility. Kill or capture him and Sordan would be crippled, maybe mortally so. He's so very much the hope and embodiment of his City and nation."

"I saw him but once, at the Archhalia the day it bestowed the regency on Erenor. He is a true Highborn Prince in every way, including excessive pride. He may even have their powers. I saw that when he lit the Thrones of the Three." Lazily, Raphelon turned over also, water beading on his shoulders, and faced Hans across his wet hands and arms. "What do you think? Can he surmount the Wall at Stauberg?"

Hans had heard more about this Wall the deeper into Staubaun lands he had gone, but he was far from understanding it. "I don't know. I do know that Dorilian thinks he can, and I've learned not to underestimate him." He paused, then asked, looking at the thoughtful Heir to one of the domains bordering the Stauberg Principality. "Have you seen this Wall?"

Raphelon smiled. "Of course. Do you mean to say you have never been to Stauberg?"

"Until I was nine, I spent my childhood in Gustan and Amallar, with a few summers at Trulo. I never was at Stauberg. I only saw the Rill from a distance one time, from the river, and not again until I went to Sordan. And at Dazunor-Rannuli, of course, when I took the city. I still haven't ridden it. And I have never seen the Wall."

"You *are* a barbarian!" Raphelon snickered.

"That's exactly what Dorilian said!"

Raphelon stopped laughing then and looked merely amused. "Did he, really? Then you are truly doomed if a Highborn Prince has pronounced you such." He chuckled and lounged back in the water. "The Wall is barely to be described. At times, it looks to be not of this World. It changes shape according to forces we do not know or understand. School texts say it is part of the mechanism of the Creation that keeps the World's Rifts from opening. Ergeiron anchored his transformation to Stauberg's shield wall, and thereby created a living and immortal Wall. It is tall and white and utterly beautiful. I do not think its spell can be broken without destroying it, and that, my Prince, would be a crime against the very World."

# 34



"I cannot believe the Sordaneon plans to take Stauberg." Euden slid yet another map across the table. Hans had convened his captains over breakfast to make the day's plans. "Erenor sits as prettily in Stauberg as any man ever has. He has the sea to his back and the Wall to guard him. An Entity cannot be overcome by ordinary means. The Wall is more the Sordaneon's foe in taking Stauberg than any army could ever be."

"Or as the Kragh will be for us," observed Kerr. He jabbed without interest at the remaining chunk of ham on his plate and gave Aubrey a sideways glance. Obviously, he was curious about this new woman in their midst. Hans knew Kerr had seen Kheld women bearing arms in camp, but Aubrey was someone he'd only heard about before that day.

Hans leaned forward, elbows on his knees. "One thing Dorilian Sordaneon does better than anyone is to keep his enemies guessing. Stopping the Rill was brilliant. No one wondered where I was for weeks. And now that the Rill's back up and running, they're wondering what else he can do."

"I think we're all wondering that," said Arne.

Hans glared, wondering what Arne had seen in Lacenedon that made him so willing to knock an important meeting off topic. "Look, I think it's good that Nammuor must watch the Hierarch's every move—because that means Nammuor isn't focused much on *us*. To him, I'm just a nuisance playing toy soldiers... and you, my captains and generals, are the toy soldiers. That's why we stand to gain an advantage if we can flank Zel. We'll catch Nammuor's troops by surprise."

Soter Kometes stood near the brazier with his arms folded. He had expressed his own opinion earlier but raised it again. "If you but wait a few days—or a week, Your Royal Highness—you will have more troops. Highly skilled horsemen, infantry, and commanders well versed in warfare. All armed to the teeth. Pandaros Vidyamemnon is the Hierarch's best general." A courier had reached them that afternoon, bearing news from Dazunor-Rannuli that Sordan's second force out of Neuberland had crossed the Rannul and bypassed the city on its way into Dazunor.

Fran Gorseddson slammed down his water mug. "We don't need your stinking army!" he snarled. "Hans can do this on his own!"

Soter coldly returned the Neuberlander's glare. That Hans had so far been respectful of his counsel allowed Soter to dismiss such outbursts.

"There may be advantage in waiting, Prince Handurin." Euden's calm voice and grave presence smoothed ruffled Staubaun feathers. "The Mormantaloran forces besieging Kyrbasillon have been displaced by an army from Rannul and are poised to come down at us from Dannuth. If we go into the Kragh and fail, we risk much."

Hans shook his head. "If we succeed, we gain more."

"Well, I don't trust the lot!" Nalf Rhys snorted. "Sordan troops aren't our own, and the ones we have of that lot are enough. They stay out of our way. But we don't need ten thousand more of them. I don't like it that we'll have Sordan at our backs and Southlanders two sides to the river. But I know this: Sordan will fight the Southlanders. There's no love lost between 'em and they won't let 'em go back through to take their Rill! I say get us through the Kragh and leave them to fight each other!" Nalf looked around the table to see who might agree with him. Aubrey's answer was to give Nalf a gentle headshake.

Raphelon sighed. He rose to his feet and signaled to Kerr as he reached for his cloak. "It may be that I can help you in this, Prince Handurin. I have some knowledge of this region you speak of. King Stefan told me how your grandsire, Marc Frederick, had made a visit to the Kragh the year before his untimely passing. Stefan wanted to determine if he might do the same. I took a small force into the area to find out if there was a path into the hills. There is one, little known but to the local folk. It is marked with the bones and skulls of men, and I did not follow it further. I have heard only rumors that Stefan may have acted upon that intelligence. If I may have leave to retire for the night, I will sketch what I recall, and in the morning, I will lead you there."

"Thank you, Lord Illarion," Hans said. Raphelon's offer of aid was welcome but surprising. Other Staubauns had been more resistant to the idea. Hans hadn't yet gotten used to believing that men like Raphelon Illarion might look to him as their leader. "I can't help but feel we can make it work."

"I certainly hope so." Raphelon offered an unconvincing smile. He exchanged a rueful look with Aubrey. "After what we saw on the way in, I have no wish to ride into battle along the Dazun Road."

A pounding of hoofs and clatter of harness loudly announced the arrival of yet another courier. Every day, it seemed, came a steady stream of missives, though seldom at this late an hour. Hans turned as the tent guard captain announced, "Courier!" and held aside the flap for the rider to enter.

The man was Kheld, road-worn and breathing hard.

"Prince Handurin! News from Dazunor-Rannuli, about Bynum! The city's yours! Taken! Sordan's Hierarch, Dorilian Sordaneon, did it single-handed by killing a monstrous beast with his bare hands!"

"It wasn't with bare hands." Hans was glad the meeting had dispersed, because he was ready to use his hands to strangle the next person who said that, and especially Arne, who remained behind. Aubrey had gone outside to talk with Raphelon and Kerr. "Didn't you listen to what Soter and Euden said? Dorilian wore special armor created by one of his god ancestors, and he used an artifact sword made of *tullun*. A blade made of that stuff cuts through anything. And don't start up about if he'd pulled this kind of thing in Amallar—because I didn't let you say it the first time."

"And I get why you didn't, keeping that secret. But don't you think it's kind of scary that he can do things like that?"

"No, because he's not doing them to us. I'm already sick to death of Nalf and Fran saying things to rile up our people against him."

"It'd help—a lot!—if he'd stop doing the kinds of things that get people riled. It's unnerving the way he keeps changing."

That was clear. But Hans felt exactly the opposite of Arne. Hans felt vindicated—and surer than ever about why Marenthro had sent him to Sordan.

*I knew Dorilian had powers. I just knew!*

He looked up when Aubrey re-entered the tent. It was great to be with friends again. However strong the relationships Hans was forging with the commanders and important folk among the people he was leading, nothing ever felt as whole and true as being with Arne and Aubrey. He didn't even mind not having the tent to himself or that there were now three cots where there had been one, not even that part of the tent was partitioned off to give Aubrey privacy. For the first time in weeks, Hans didn't feel that he would be spending the night with strangers. It capped the day perfectly to have Gerd appear on Aubrey's heels, bearing a tray laden with steaming cobblers and rice puddings.

"A Kheld never ends the day without a sweet." Gerd put down the tray before he dashed off to tend to the hungry throng besieging his cook tent. Hans thought he had never seen a happier man.

"Good old Gerd!" Arne sighed contentedly as he spooned into an apple plum cobbler. Aubrey and Hans each took bowls of rice pudding.

"I hope he thought to offer these to the Staubaun captains and the Trongorians." Hans wanted to be sure his allies were being as well treated as him. He could be fairly certain the Kheld contingent wasn't suffering; he'd seen them heading toward the kitchen as a group after the conversation had broken up.

"They say an army marches on its stomach." Aubrey slid a spoonful of pudding between her lips.

"I'll be lucky if mine goes anywhere, then. If Gerd has his way, I'll have the fattest army in Essera!" But Hans wasn't unhappy with the prospect of a change in the way he'd been eating. Snearly was enthusiastic but he was no cook. As everyone enjoyed the warmth of the brazier and the desserts, Hans reached into his jacket and retrieved the letters Arne had brought earlier.

There was a hefty stack of official missives, including several pledges or petitions bearing royal and noble seals of Esseran Lords. Hans singled out the one from Hebron to read. There were also three letters from Robdan. And then there were two letters, written on the smooth, heavy vellum Hans now knew to be Sordan's alone. Aware of his friends watching him, he broke Dorilian's letters first, smiling as he began reading the flowing, beautiful writing. He hadn't figured out yet if the writing was Dorilian's own or that of his secretary.

"He says Askyllon is cold and he's hoping Stauberg will be warmer." Hans laughed. "And I can read between the lines that he thinks Hebron is a pompous ass. Get this, 'Hebron proposes subjecting Stauberg to siege by damming the Stariel River, thus depriving the city of fresh water. It fell to me to point out that such a strategy would proceed well into the next decade even if the project went uninterrupted. I pray Stauberg falls quickly. I can imagine no grimmer scenario than spending the winter with him. Of late I have even thought fondly of Endelarin.'"

Arne broke out in a grin. "Now that would liven up old Essera!"

"People in these parts are paranoid enough about Ardaen after two wars. And Dorilian and Endelarin together would probably generate more weirdness than anyone could handle." Hans broke the seal on the second letter.

*That your lady cousin sought me out in Lacenedon by her own choice, I have no doubt. As you were not wise enough to see that she stayed out of my path, be wise enough to see that she not place herself there again. I have sent her from Essera to spare you the trouble.*

Now Hans knew for certain whose handwriting he'd been reading.

He folded the letter again but kept it in his hand.

"What does it say?" The timber of Aubrey's voice suggested she knew it was about her. But Arne, when Hans looked at him, wore the expression of someone who would rather be elsewhere.

Hans didn't see the point of keeping Arne at hand. Not for this conversation. "One of us should return the dishes to Gerd, I think," he said.

Arne took the hint graciously. He picked up all their dessert dishes and cast a knowing look at Aubrey as he headed from the tent. They heard the Trongorians on duty parting to let Arne pass, then closing spears after.

"Dorilian claims he sent you from Essera," Hans said, low. "He wants you as far away as possible. I don't need to know the details; just tell me you didn't insult him in front of half the Royal North."

Aubrey looked at him aghast. "You think that I would?"

"Not on purpose. But you might have said something out of turn because of how you knew him in Amallar. Aubrey," Hans folded his hands on the table, "I'm not trying to accuse you. I'm just making sure this is about what I think it is, not something more... public."

Aubrey sighed. "It was nothing like that, though it was public enough. I danced with him."

Hans tried to understand. Anything Dorilian did, however casual it might seem, acquired importance in Staubaun eyes. In Sordan, on First Day, the Hierarch had led the dances. "He's a good dancer." Hans smiled, hoping to help Aubrey relax. "I think it's expected."

Aubrey laughed, extending her legs and wiggling her tent slippers. "I still have all my toes, at least." Then her expression turned serious again. "Hans," she said, not letting him look away from her, "I was the *only* one he danced with."

Hans tried to imagine it, and found he didn't have to. He'd *dreamed* it: Dorilian in all his royal Highborn attire, Aubrey in a glittering dress. Yearning and hunger, hair filling his hands, lips meeting. Hans shook his head, clearing the thought, refusing to go further.

"Is he angry?" Aubrey wanted to know.

"I don't know," Hans said truthfully. He hadn't picked up on any emotional undertones. "If he was, he wouldn't put it on paper. What I think he wants is for you to be someplace he doesn't have to worry about you."

With a sigh, Aubrey folded her arms across her body, hugging herself. Hans wished he could interpret her expression.

"You can start back in the morning," Hans wished Dorilian didn't want it this way. Had anyone else asked this of Hans, he would have refused. He enjoyed Aubrey's company and, after their weeks apart, realized how much he had come to rely on her advice. Aubrey had been second only to Sinon in helping handle the Seven Houses and negotiate restoration of Rill service to Dazunor-Rannuli. Even Arne credited Aubrey with having influenced Egidius Mogens into becoming the first Dazunor-Rannuli magnate to openly provision Hans's army. The idea of being known as 'the

King's Merchant' had greatly appealed to Egidius. "I'll ask Raphelon to escort you back. He's royal and has his own men. I like him and trust him. Once in Dazunor-Rannuli, you can catch the Rill back to Bellan Toregh."

Aubrey shook her head. "No, Hans, I can't." She lifted her face defiantly. "It's too dangerous for me to go to Dazunor-Rannuli, even to just catch the Rill. Ask Rafe if you don't believe me."

Hans frowned, wondering what had happened there but deciding that this wasn't the time for interrogation. "I believe you." He crossed over and sat beside Aubrey on the cushions. "I should never have sent you with Arne to Lacenedon. When I said I wanted Dorilian to be real to you, I didn't mean this real."

"I know." Aubrey sank against Hans, body warm but tense. "Let's look on the bright side. Khelds are now just as real to him."

"Do you really think so?"

"Yes, I do."

It was part of what Hans had hoped to accomplish in Amallar, in what now seemed like an age ago. In the long view, his plan had succeeded. He doubted it would be enough. "Most Khelds still hate Dorilian, unfortunately. They still think he killed Marc Frederick and Stefan. They blame him for Neuberland. They think because he can use magic weapons he's inhuman, some sort of monster. And they barely tolerate the fact that I consider him an ally. Aubrey, if word of this gets out, you'll be considered a traitor to your family's honor—a Staubaun whore. Worse, you'll be *his* whore. I don't even want to be around if ever Fran or Nalf Rhys find out!"

Aubrey's shudder made Hans want to put his arm around her.

"Listen," Hans said, "I'm not your King yet and I know that I can't order you against your will. I wouldn't do it even if I could. But Dorilian's right thinking you'd be safer in Amallar. Even if some kind of rumor did get down that way, you'd be far enough away from things that you could deny it there."

"And I would go if I thought I could reach Amallar safely. But I think the way will be watched. Hans," she pleaded, "I can become just as invisible here until we get to Gustan. Then I can use the Bogs to slip across the river."

Aubrey's continued apprehension alerted Hans to something else. Now he had to know. "What happened in Dazunor-Rannuli that you're so afraid you're being pursued?"

It took two false starts before Aubrey was able to speak. "Dorilian didn't want me to go there. He... he said not to go, but I did. The first Rill shipment was delayed and the priorities were challenged and I wanted to fix that. I made the mistake of staying too long and appearing in public. And then I was foolish and tried to go off on my own. The Seven Houses abducted me and brought me to someone. I have reason to think it was Chyralane Rannuleonis. She's Denizen of Phaer, a very powerful woman."

"I know who she is." Hans quickly sorted through information Sinon had given him about an aborted plot to coerce Hans's marriage to one of the cartel's daughters.

"She questioned me about Dorilian, very subtly, but I think she had heard some rumor from Askyllon. Then she ordered her men to take me away. She also ordered them to kill me. They tried to poison me." Aubrey huddled over, head bowed and hands in her hair. "If Raphelon hadn't come by with his men... if they hadn't slain the men trying to kill me.... I owe him my life."

"Does Raphelon know why the Seven Houses did what they did?"

Aubrey shook her head. "No. He thinks...." She gave Hans a weak smile. "He thinks it's because I'm linked romantically with you."

Hans felt a sick drop at the center of his stomach, not at the speculation, which he understood, but at the very real possibility that Raphelon was right about the response to it. The Seven Houses had already shown that they would move quickly to cut short an association they considered unsuitable. He managed a faint grin. "I guess I've come up in the world if the Denizens would consider a love interest of mine worth killing."

The coals in the brazier crackled. What an odd conversation they were having, and yet it felt right. Hans had always been able to talk with Aubrey, always been able to share feelings.

"But I think it's true. I think people fear that more—or, at least, more of them fear it. They see us together." Aubrey pushed her hair back from her face. "I read my runes the morning after I left Dazunor-Rannuli with Rafe, after Arne caught up with us and we joined up with Gerd and the others. My stones foretold danger should I try to go to Amallar. Only your rune sign coincided with the rune for safety."

Hans wasn't prepared to argue with Aubrey's runes. And

Dorilian was far away. While the Seven Houses had been quick to act on opportunity and would do so again, they might feel it imprudent to pursue Aubrey now that she had reached Hans's sphere of protection. She was indeed safest with him for the moment. "In that event, I hope your reading was a good omen." Hans helped Aubrey up from the floor and they both prepared to seek their cots for the night. At the tent flap, Hans told the soldier that if he saw Arne Anseldson, he should tell him to return. In the tent again, he stopped for a moment to warn Aubrey. "Where we're going tomorrow is supposed to be anything but safe."

Raphelon shivered against the driving ice that drenched the party. Sidling his horse as close as he could to Hans's, he leaned over and pointed out the barely seen shape of the Kragh. "There it is. Just under that crag, there's a narrow defile leading into the Howling Hills. That is the way in."

Hans nodded. "And you're telling me there's a way through?"

"Local folk say there is. The valley of the Hyllorhose lies on the other side."

Hans glanced behind him. Just down the hill, past his Trongorians, the combined force of Khelds, Dannuthians, the small Merrydni contingent, and Soter's handful of Sordani troops massed in a former rye field.

Riding at Han's left stirrup, Kerr huddled miserably in his hooded cloak and added another thought. "Most of us will have to wait here, I think. At least until we know for sure."

"I don't think we'll have to wait long for an answer," Hans decided. The skies had darkened again. No matter what way they went now, the weather would be nasty. Ice covered Hans's shoulders.

"If we meet any Dog Men we'll just have to take them on," Arne ventured from his place at Hans's right flank. If it was that or get stuck between Zel and the Seven Houses holed up in Dazunor-Rannuli, Arne was game for it. "After what Aubrey and I left behind in Dazunor-Rannuli, I don't trust that lot with anything Kheld—and that includes all our asses."

Seated on her gray mare beside Arne's gelding, Aubrey pondered the distant, weather-darkened land. Hans had watched that very morning in his tent when Aubrey had laid the Wheel and pronounced omens of meeting but not battle. Now Hans watched her face as she turned thoughtful.

"Go in peace," she suggested, repeating what she'd said before. "Announce ourselves with banners. Bring an armed guard of men but not a war party."

"We might wish for a war party," said Kerr. "They're savages at best and live like animals among the rocks, breeding brats and kidnapping mates from the folk around here—or those they catch passing through."

"They abduct women?" Hans turned a worried look at the women among his troops.

"Men too, for their women." Desmos, Raphelon's aide, added a rare aside. He, like Raphelon and Kerr, had grown up in the region. "They have to breed outblood or they spawn monsters."

"But if we have to go straight at the enemy, we'll be forced to meet them on the Road. Right where the damn Southlanders want us," Fran noted.

"And where they're dug in every other ditch and pothole," Arne pointed out.

The only other way was to go north to the edge of the high mountains, where more enemy troops waited. Fran and Arne were right. They had no choice.

"We go through the Kragh," Hans decided. "Fran, Euden—you wait here." Hans ignored the scowls from both men. "If we don't send word of a way through the Kragh, you must decide whether to battle Zel on the road or retreat to Dazunor-Rannuli."

When the groups parted, a bare two dozen rode into the bowl while the others stayed behind to watch and wait. Hans urged his horse down the hill, taking the lead. "Let's go."

# 35

Our first generations were not bred; we were altered. The Aryati warped something inside men, turned something that was human into something that was not. In this, the Masters said, they did no differently than Leur did. The godborn too are monsters.

HROLAF, *BLOOD CODEX OF THE HEN KYON*

The land fell steeply into the valleys of the Kragh. From the rise where farm fields ended, for as far north as eyes could see, puckered and densely forested hills led into mist-shrouded, taller crags. The tallest of these, the Maw, mounded and flattened, pushed like a shoulder above the sunken land.

The land had been shattered. The rocks looked like those Hans had seen around Rhodhur, splintered and crumbling, overgrown by greenery. Vines spilled down cliffs in ropes of yellowed leaves, twining with rivulets of ground water. The path they followed suggested others came this way, even to ruts that pointed to wagon traffic. As the day pushed into afternoon and they passed deep into the hills, however, they saw no one. Hans had taken Aubrey's suggestion and deployed men bearing the standards of his coalition. Raphelon, for all that he preferred plain clothes for travel, had draped his horse with the colors and saddle banner of Serrain. Soter Kometes contributed Sordan's green and silver ensigns. With Hans riding in a show of Stauberg-Randolph colors and Kerr those of Dannuth, they made an impressive and colorful company.

Raphelon pointed to skulls—human and animal, darkened by years and green with moss—nailed to trees along the path where it entered into a narrow gorge. "There," he said. The track leading into the cleft looked well traveled.

Hans nodded. But when he and others sought to guide their mounts into the shadowed passage, the horses would go no farther, sidling and snorting.

"What is—?" Hans started.

He didn't finish. The very trees erupted around to every side, shapes dropping or running onto the road behind and before the mounted party. The horses shied in alarm. Before Hans or any of the others could react to what was happening, they were twice outnumbered and fully encircled by figures draped with hoods and clothed in skins. No faces could be seen.

Emerging in the fore, one of the attackers rose to grasp Hans's horse by its bridle. The startled mount tried to whirl away but its captor held fast. Hans looked down in alarm, peering directly into the open hood.

What looked back at him was not a man.

Manlike, perhaps, though the face was tawny and bestial, bearded to the point of being furred, and its teeth yellowed and fanged. The ochre eyes were rimmed blood red; however, burning within, Hans saw the spark of intelligence, something canny and knowing. The creature then looked at Aubrey, but only a look that marked her as different and, for that reason, of interest.

"Who comes to our land?" Deep and rough, the voice was passably human and spoke heavily accented Stauba.

"I am Handurin Stauberg-Randolph, Prince of Dazunor." Hans did his best to speak boldly. "I come in peace. I seek only to pass through your land, to fight my enemy on the other side."

"The False Prince," the Dog Man said.

Surprised, Hans hesitated. He didn't know to whom the term referred, himself or Erenor. "Will you grant us passage and show us the way?"

"Grant passage, they ask." The Dog Man looked to his fellows with what appeared to be a sneer. "Show them the way. Why should we? Danger attends your entry here and your brother burns in perfidy." Below narrowed yellow eyes, his smile looked sickly and wicked. "Come to Gloanneach and see Baran if you would gain the way. Baran will answer you under the High Place."

Gloanneach was drenched in rain, a cluster of squat stone buildings with roofs of thatch, perched on a craggy hillside looking out across a river-bottomed gorge at the massive hump of the Maw. Hans could see how the guardian fissures and chasms of the Kragh's fortress hills might have swallowed thousands of men, never to disgorge them, but they had also hidden this place.

Most of Gloanneach's villagers looked human, although Hans detected enough differences to understand the genesis of local legends. He saw many inhabitants with odd features or unusual postures, stopped along the road or in doorways and windows to watch the arrival of men on horseback bearing banners and weapons. The villagers spoke to each other in their strange guttural tongue, but there was no shouting, either of hostility or welcome. In an open area before a great lodge built of stone and logs, the Dog Man who had spoken to Hans stopped the delegation and bid them dismount to enter.

Within the hall, lit by torches at the far end of the long room, a large figure sat on a high seat made of horns. Splendid skins hung from the shining points of the chair back, where heavy antlers framed the seated shape. Unlike the Dog Man who had escorted Hans—the distorted, furred figure who hunkered now at the foot of that seat—Baran was more obviously a human. Tall and solid, the great head of red hair and full red beard marked Baran at once as the man Raphelon said locals also called Redhargh. Only Baran's eyes, a gold too yellow to be Staubaun and flecked with black, hinted at the taint that lurked within his line.

"Stauberg-Randolph, you say." Baran assessed Hans, who stood at the foot of the platform on which the great horned chair rested. Baran raised an eyebrow and passed around a look to his gathered chieftains. The faintly bestial creatures—some more so, some less—stood in a half circle to each side of the clan chair. "That's a name to take note of for good and ill. And some of these followers of yours be Khelds, for I know the breed. It is not a stock we see much of—nor welcome."

Not a few among the chieftains sharpened their interest.

"The people with me come from many lands." Hans was glad to have Aubrey, Arne and Nalf all wearing fine attire and standing to his left side. The Staubauns stood to his right.

"Who are the lords?" Baran demanded.

"Kerr Staubaun Aigelleros, Bas of Dannuth." Hans introduced the youth, who bowed his golden head to their host. All around them, eyes glowed from that ring of shadowy faces, marking each person. "Raphelon Staubaun Illarion, Heir of Serrain. Soter Staubaun Kometes, of Sordan, in the service of the Hierarch." Each man bowed when named.

Again, that imposing head rose. "Noble names all. The Highborn fathered their mothers, these lords of Essera. We honor the blood that is in them and know the worth of Grenant in his battle against the Regent." Baran's yellow eyes fixed on Soter. "In the service of your Hierarch, Godborn Dorilian, the Sordaneon?"

At the speaking of that name, something rippled through the room, shadows leaning, crouching, passing the name from lip to ear in speculations the guests could not decipher.

"Yes." Soter again bowed his head.

"Is it true, then, what rumor says—that the breach is mended and Derlon's godborn heir has himself returned to Essera?"

That intelligence must have traveled strange winds to have reached this forgotten corner. "It's true," Hans answered. Again, he noted whispers pass on strange lips, darting as tiny bees bearing hidden meaning. "Dorilian and I came north together."

"And what does that mean, we're left to wonder. The last of his blood, or nearly so, and you the last of yours. The World must have a death wish." Baran grasped the polished staff of wood and bone a chieftain handed to him and tapped it against the stone floor, silencing the growing hum arising from his followers. His heavy face folded in furrows of thought. "You are of murdered Stefan's blood, this we can see, and you lead his folk. But I can see you do not share his heart."

"He was my brother. I honor his memory, but my heart is my own."

"Be sure of it." Baran's yellow eyes gleamed. "We remember him well. He came to us near his end, fleeing his demons, seeking answers. But the Kragh provides no refuge for Godborn-killers. We are not so isolated that we do not know the shape of the World outside or see the markers of its passage. The Mormantaloran's evil we have watched from afar and with fear. He has been long in coming, but we knew the day would dawn when the shadow of the Aryati would return to lay claim to the land where once they ruled. We smelled the Sorcerer's rot long before it claimed the mind of he who slew the Princes of Stauberg and Dannuth. Approach me, Handurin, if you are who you claim to be." Though aware of the concerned looks his companions gave him, Hans stepped up the first step of the platform, closer to the hulking figure on its chair of horns. Baran held out his hand. Broad, with short fingers. "Give me your hand," that rough voice demanded.

The Dog Men watched. Hans hesitated. He had not come this far only to let courage fail him. If Baran meant ill, Hans could not see it. The only path to trust was trust itself. Hans laid his hand in Baran's broad grip.

Out of habit, Hans expected a handclasp. But Baran simply pulled the hand near, close enough to bend his great head over it. Nostrils flaring, Baran inhaled, filling an impressive barrel chest. What that air told Baran, Hans dared not guess. The Dog Man appeared to have accepted already that Hans was Stefan's brother. A long moment passed. Then, slowly, Baran nodded.

"He is true," Baran declared to the room. "He does not have his brother's stench." Baran's feral gaze turned full on Hans again. Something new burned within it, hot and welcoming. "Bring your army into the Kragh, Handurin of the Stauberg-Randolphs. You shall have Cortogh here to guide you past the Maw. No one knows the ways better."

The Dog Man who had guided them to Gloanneach bent his thick neck and gave Hans a cold, utterly inhuman smile.

Hans bowed to Baran, and nodded to Cortogh. "Thank you, sir," he said. "Aside from harsh tales, I knew nothing of your people until this day. Now I owe you a debt of service. Perhaps, when this war is done, we can sit together and speak of the things that have estranged your people from mine."

"I'll do you one better, grandson of my friend," Baran said. "Have your men go ahead of you, for our ways are narrow and it will take a day and then some for so many to pass. As you are their Prince, you and your kinsfolk and friends shall stay here at this place tonight and be my guests. You and I will talk."

Hans dismissed the greater part of the party, including the Trongorians, with directions to summon the army to follow Cortogh. The Khelds, he knew, would be willing enough to do it; they were in a strange land and greatly dreaded the prospect of facing Zel. Most of the Kheld troops trusted Hans completely and believed him fated by Lud to succeed; with just a little encouragement, they would do exactly as Hans wished of them. The small Sordani force, too, would do whatever Soter directed. Only Esseran Staubaun forces, steeped since childhood in those tales of horror that so terrified the outlying villages, might balk and prove unwilling. In the end, Farrl and Soter rode out to reassure Euden and put to rest any fears that the Dog Men had taken them captive. Desmos would vouch to the Serrain and Dannuthi troops that their respective lords were also safe. Hans kept only Raphelon and Kerr and three Kheld companions with him: Arne, who refused to leave him, Aubrey, because Hans wanted her with him for so important a meeting, and Nalf, whose status as elder kinsman appealed to the Dog Men's deep respect for both family and years.

Hans wondered what Baran wished to speak about, though he could guess. The Kragh was a land apart by its own choice and that of its neighbors, not subject in any meaningful way to Staubaun rule. Yet Hans sensed in these hill folks a yearning to escape their disenfranchisement.

"We run off with fewer women than the towns say," big, red-bearded Baran told them later when Hans and the others joined as dinner guests in his private quarters. "The truth is, midwives throughout this region know we take in women, and their babes, without question. We treat them well, raise the young ones. But the families would rather think we carry off the girls to bear our twisted brats and many is the girl who will tell them so." Baran scowled with angry remembrance of the many things of which his people stood accused.

The six humans sat around a pit in the center of a room in Baran's great stone house that sat at the highest point in Gloanneach. Tapestries with forest scenes clothed the stone and timber walls. An immense chimney of pottery flared above the fire at the center of the pit, collecting smoke and sending it through the roof. Outside, the wind moaned through deep fissures and valleys.

Baran's daughter—yellow-eyed with a large, broad nose and dark hair—ushered out a brace of children, yapping in a strange speech. She returned with a round pot of some kind of cider and portions of bread.

"You mentioned a curse." Hans ventured. "Do you know what it is that has cursed your people?" The possible reasons, in this land, were too many to guess.

"That we exist," said Baran's daughter. Bitterness hardened her voice.

"Measure your words, Fellesma." Baran swung his great head around with a scowl. "Do not afflict our guests with your misery. These are matters neither you nor they yet understand." Fellesma, proud but obedient, dropped her gaze again and resumed pouring grog into their cups. Baran returned his attention to those who dined with him. "You have heard nothing of our history. Your folk speak of us as if we have none, as if our history consists of your experience of us. We are more ancient than that." His yellow gaze caught fire with remembrances, things persistent and deep, that dwelled beyond the reach of men. "The Dog Men of Gweroyen, that's what our forefathers were called. Hen Kyon is our proper name, the one the Masters gave us. The Aryati made us during Exile. How, we do not know. Nor do we know by what means they continued to produce us after the Return in their great city on the sea. We were created to help them in their wars against the Godborn. We have senses that know Godborn kind and can seek them out even in hiding. When the Hegemons rose against the Highborn Princes and slew the King Telarion, it was we who found his hiding place. We dragged him and his sons from their dwelling under the lake and brought them to our Masters. We identified the hidden, that the Aryati might cut them into pieces. It was we who bound Peleor to the Rill tree with his own entrails, spread wide his flayed skin, so Derlon, his father, might taste his poisoned blood. Terrible were we in our service to the Masters.

"But the Hegemons of Gweroyen were thrown down, Iddolea their city destroyed, and all that they had done was scattered to the wind. Including us, their servants. The Bane Beasts, the Hounds of the Aryati… now it was we who were cursed by the Godborn to be the hunted, until the debt of blood be repaid. Lords loyal to the Godborn slew all of our kind that they could. Some few of us survived, escaped across the ice and fled into the Mountains of the Evening Star. From there, we vanished into the wild, deep hills. That was eighteen hundred years ago. Then the land was empty, and we roamed all Tre-Dannuth, but hatred of us has driven us to this place no others want." Baran picked up a thin, sharpened stick threaded with meat and bread and dipped it in a bright red broth that had been set before them.

Hans lifted a skewer and dipped it. The broth, thick and spicy, flavored tender meat and soaked into firm cubes of bread. He pronounced it good, prompting the rest of his hungry companions to follow his example, and soon all were dipping and eating.

Baran appeared pleased. "We are not dogs. No canine blood mixed with ours, despite the name they gave us. I do not know what we are, but there remains in us the curse the Aryati set in our bones. We cannot eradicate it unless we eradicate ourselves. Life is too strong for that. We love, we laugh, we mate. When we mate with each other, the results are unpredictable and sometimes too deformed to live. Some few are marvelous. But when we mate outside our blood, the children are strong, though they bear our mark and often cannot pass outside these hills."

It was easy enough for Hans to identify what had happened. Using their godlike science, the remnants of which he now knew to have survived centuries after the Return, the Aryati had engineered a variant of human that had persisted through generations.

"Did the Highborn—the Godborn—ever forgive you?" Hans asked.

Baran looked at Hans sharply. "You would know as much as I. We never caused them trouble or harm after our Aryati Masters died. When they prevailed against their enemy, we witnessed their power and because of it worship that blood still. We know what they are. The King Emrysen summoned our leaders to him and took our promise never to allow others to use us against the Godborn again, and in exchange he and his kindred gave us this place and promised to take no vengeance on us. But he did not lift the curse. We have kept our promise. They have kept theirs." He stabbed again at the broth.

Something somber—maybe memories, maybe concern— showed in Baran's gaze when he looked back at Hans. "I don't know where the Mind of Leur now resides, but I do know this: when the Godborn Princes ceased to live in these lands, Essera became a worse place for it. There was order where the Godborn ruled. Men knew where they stood and what they believed in. Now, we have Staubaun lords—some are good and some are thieves. They don't keep promises. Same for the Khelds." Raphelon and Kerr, though they exchanged glances, looked thoughtful. When Nalf Rhys moved as if to speak, Baran silenced him with a great raised hand, each finger bearing heavy rings of gold. "Sorry, Handurin, if your kin and friends here disagree."

Fellesma brought over a warm, moist cloth on which Hans wiped clean his hands. One by one Fellesma did the same with the other guests. Although she did not speak, there was nothing subservient in her manner or the way her gaze assessed them, each in turn.

"There were noble Khelds when Marc Frederick ruled," Baran continued. "But many who came after were intent on plunder, and your brother I count with them. Men can't keep promises if they refuse to remember who made them or if they think history is written by tongues, not events. No man's boasts outlive his deeds."

Nalf's frown had deepened the whole time Baran had been speaking. "Well, there aren't any more Highborn, Godborn, or whatever you want to call them to be had, you know, and we can't do anything about that." No doubt that for Nalf everything said was beyond fantastic, referring to curses and ancient evils long passed into legend. "They're all gone but for the Sordaneons now, more's the pity. Their Hierarch says he's got no mind for Essera except getting the Mormantaloran out, and just as well, because we don't want either of them! None of us do. And Hans Thegn here will do things a sight better than Stefan. Seems to me we don't need Highborn Princes in Essera—especially that Sordaneon!"

The few other Dog Men in the room, seated on the periphery and merely attentive until then and intent on their food while their leader spoke for them, grew even more still. The wind had picked up outside and pushed at the house, but the dwelling was so sturdily built that only the rain pelting the windows gave notice.

"Think you not, Kheld man? Think you not?" Baran chewed pensively on his stick, then tossed it into the flames, where it caught fire and glowed for a moment before sinking in the ashes. He fixed Nalf with his gaze, at once feral and deeply human, then turned his massive head to Hans. "Let me tell you this tale, Stauberg-Randolph, and you decide if you need this Sordaneon. I met him when he was at Gustan that one season years ago. Not much older than a boy then and sullen too. Disliked Khelds with a passion, as I recall, and they liked him even less. But though he was Godborn he gave us our due and never treated me or mine less than we are. He sees clear to the bone. The Old King had a plan for him and nourished him with a steel hand and tolerance. Marc Frederick knew what he had. See that, young Prince?" Baran jabbed his finger at the hulk of the Maw outside the window. There was still light, but barely, coming from the west. Through the grainy, rough glass they could barely make out the mounding hilltop beyond a curtain of heavy rain. "That's a Rill mount."

They all looked hard at the hill but saw none of the now-familiar signs of Rill presence. No ghostly limbs stretched high above the naked hilltop. No pale building crowned the Maw. Raphelon's gaze, thought filled and wondering, shifted from the Maw to Kerr before returning to that rain-shrouded hill.

Hans looked back to Baran, who nodded, his mouth sliding into a bitter smile that bared yellowed teeth. "I was with the Old King and the Sordaneon Prince the day the diggers struck the thing. It's all cinder, that hilltop. *Skellai*. They dug out a part of it, white as bones. I heard for myself when the Sordaneon said it was Rill stuff they'd found. He would know. But there's no Rill can run to it. They found the approaches broken or toppled, all but a handful of them, going east, going west. So it's just there. Unusable."

The room had gone silent. From the edges of the room, the Dog Men watched the guests with whom they'd shared their secret. Hans thought they were seeking reaction. He peered at his companions, then back out the window at a hill that now was more than a hill.

Somewhere in the brooding night, looked down upon by that hulking landmark, Hans's army was on the move, shadows through a shadow land.

"They buried it again, didn't they?" Hans murmured.

Baran nodded. "They returned it to underground and never called it forth from its slumber. Derlon is deadly to our kind." Baran pondered the thing visible beyond the window and so did Hans. The very room had changed. There was something haunted about the Maw now that Hans knew what it was. He listened as Baran continued. "Now hear me out. There is a fungus in our forest that grows over a great area. It covers entire valley floors. Sometimes, at far intervals, it will send up its fluorescence, black caps and red gills. But they do not hint at the extent of the thing— the rest of it grows underground, out of sight. You walk among the trees, and grass and fern, and never know it is there. But if you dig into the earth, you will turn over black filaments of the thing, oozing red like blood. We call it bloodthreads." He pointed at the window. "I don't know what the Old King was trying to do here, but I can guess. The memories of my people are thick; we remember the Godborn race of old. We remember the gods. Derlon Sordaneon's body is in that thing that runs between Permephedon and Sordan. If you could cut it, such parts of it as can still bleed would bleed Godborn blood. Whatever properties Godborn flesh has, it shares. It grows. It heals on its own. And it knows its own. It took Derlon's cells many years to do, many centuries, but he has grown throughout the entire system. The crowns you see, the stations being used because they served the early needs of Staubaun-kind, are nothing. They are just hairs on the surface of the Rill beast. The rest is underground."

Hans recalled the schematic he had seen at Sordan, the red lines, the blue ones, green and gold. Spokes and hubs of ancient purpose. "You mean the Rill—"

"Is everywhere. It underlies all the lands—and maybe more. The Aryati knew this. They feared what Derlon could become. What he *would* become. They had a plan to poison him, early, when it could still be done, but their effort failed. Now the Rill is truly Immortal and a god. But it is still Godborn—Highborn, yes, and still Sordaneon." Baran leaned forward and drew a line in the air, then indicated the space below it. "Beneath the land, under the hills, the Rill stuff slumbers. What do you think would make it erupt to the surface, send forth new growth, new empires?"

A chill seized Hans. What Baran was talking about—Hans had never heard was possible. That the Rill lived, yes. That it was a being, even that it was a god. Yet it had always run along a course determined by preexisting arches and mounts. Or had it? What if the Rill could regrow parts of itself? Dorilian had. He'd regrown two fingers. Appendages of human flesh. What if he could persuade the Rill....

Abruptly, Hans understood. By the way Raphelon and Kerr stared at the window, Hans knew that they did too.

"Dorilian is not the Rill." Only when he'd said it did Hans realize he'd used the same words the Seven Houses had said. Had sought to deny. *Who is to say he is not?* Sinon Kouranos had answered. The fears and ambitions of the Seven Houses, the Cibulitans, the Epoptes, took shape in Hans's mind. To command the power of that god... Godborn.

*What if he can?*

All around Baran, faces human and only barely that, regarded him with glowing eyes. Aubrey made a point of putting her cup to her lips and Hans wondered if her thoughts burned even as his did. Though Nalf snorted, Arne shot Hans a look that asked how much of this he'd known

"I wonder," Baran said. "The day we covered the Rill rock again, I got him to talk to me. Rill Lord. Even then, they thought he might be that. There's Rill stuff in his blood, but he did not want to wake it. Said he might be able to wake the thing at the heart of the Maw, but that he could not create structures out of earth or air. I thought he was more afraid of succeeding than failing. Said that if he stood too long in the Rill's song, or it got into him, he would become part of it, or some such thing. Some Godborn thing." Baran paused and poured more drink for his guests, signaling Fellesma to bring more bread. "So what do I hear now but that the Rill stopped running—and when it starts again, it runs to Amallar. Men say that the Sordaneon awakened a dead Rill crown there. On the wind I hear Staubauns whisper that the Sordan Lord has found the power that ever lurked in his kind, the power they worship and fear, the same power we—who know the Godborn better— worship and honor. The power he told me of that day twelve years ago."

"Are you trying to tell us the cursed Sordaneon could bring the Rill to this place?" Nalf Rhys demanded. Beside him, Aubrey sat silent and watchful, her face carefully clear of anything she might be thinking. And Kerr and Raphelon looked at each other, glances thick with hidden, Staubaun thoughts.

Baran nodded, slowly, his wonder at the Kheld's simplicity obvious. "To bring the Rill *any* place. Any place it once ran. Possibly places it never did. Maybe he's not the one who can do it. But what—just imagine—what if he is? You may not want him, Kheldman, but ponder this: the next face of the World will not look like this one. It may well look like what's in the Sordaneon's dreams." Baran pointed to Hans, and all of them, and said, "Already, I think, it does. So know this, also: I would be damned, and my people with me, if we'd side with those who would move against him."

"I want to preserve the Highborn too, Baran Hen Kyon," Hans said quietly. The Dog Man's tale gripped strangely, in ways Hans could already tell would be profound. Whatever assurances the Dog Men's chieftain wanted, Hans was willing to give. *Wanted* to give. "I'm not trying to kill them. I want to save them. Dorilian Sordaneon is my friend." Hans's companions looked at him hard, then, in surprise. He had not used that word in reference to Dorilian before.

"Friend, you say?" Baran assessed sharply, a second question underlying the words. "Friendship counts for little. Erenor was Stefan's friend."

"Ours is binding. Sealed by blood."

Baran raised his head. "*His* blood?"

"And mine. We swore our oath in it." Hans was aware of the others looking at him with differing expressions, from Kerr's simple astonishment that Dorilian would do such a thing to Aubrey's look of something that at last made sense, to Nalf Rhys's barely concealed snort of disgust. The Dog Men's eyes burned fiercely, a ring of feral gold, so intently did they watch.

"Oaths sworn on that blood become Law," said Baran.

"I could no more betray him than betray myself."

"This I know. And for that, I have let you through the Kragh, and my children to guide you, that you might find the destiny you seek. Their god is with *you*, Handurin of the Stauberg-Randolphs. We owe the Godborn recompense for the evil we did them in the past. Maybe this will satisfy that debt."

# 36

The palaces of the Staubaun Lords are vast and open; the purpose of their dwellings is to make visitors feel small. The deeper I ride into Staubaun lands, the more I know that I do not belong in them.
ROBDAN AELFRICSON, *JOURNAL OF THE ESSERAN WAR*

Robdan had taken great care to sketch the city of Bynum faithfully, though he soon recognized that his attempt would never capture its beauty. To make up for his lack of talent as an artist, he filled in the margins by jotting notes: the Little Sister, Lake Kalasdossa, so deep it was widely believed to be bottomless; *righil*, the white and sapphire-blue winter flowers that grew between stones; the Blythagoran Serat, pillared dwelling of the Malyrdeon Princes, of white marble and blue granite with ornaments of purest gold. Not least did he note the city itself, beautiful Bynum, its spires dwarfed by the jagged white peaks of the Ulnossi, from the crags of which it was said a Highborn Prince had once destroyed the city, many centuries ago, during the Fall of Aryati-ruled Gweroyen. The only remaining evidence of Bynum's destruction was a blackened tower, long ago blasted and ruined, preserved within a park. Robdan had visited the glassy ruin, its twisted shape rising like smoke from the snow, and something about it had struck ice through his heart.

It looked to him as though the tower had been riven top to bottom. Despite the terror it held for him, he had drawn the tower in his journal.

Since leaving Amallar with Dorilian, Robdan had grown accustomed to being the only Kheld among Staubauns. After their initial suspicions about him had been satisfied, the Hierarch's

Sordani officers and soldiers had proven to be generous, assisting Robdan at times even when not asked. Admittedly, Dorilian's acceptance of him as an advisor, which remained surprisingly high, had much to do with Robdan's standing. Lacenedon's lords, by contrast, had yet to warm to having a Kheld in their midst and they remained distant, though seldom discourteous. For his part, Robdan practiced his best manners and remained mindful of his hosts' customs. He bathed daily, knowing that Staubauns were fastidious about hygiene and Khelds were widely criticized for not bathing enough. Beards, according to Staubaun society, were uncouth, an indication of lesser blood, and so Robdan shaved daily. In matters of dress, he adopted the most basic modes of Staubaun attire while avoiding all pretense of putting on airs.

Robdan never tried to pretend he was one of them or give Staubauns reason to think he hoped to raise himself to rank above them in any way. Stefan's policy of elevating his Kheld relations to the nobility had left a great distaste. Robdan harbored no such ambition and avoided giving even the appearance of having such thought. If ever there had been a question of his suitability, he set minds to rest whenever he sat astride a horse. It was a rare noble of any birth who did not sit on a horse as easily as his own favorite chair. Robdan had gone through a dozen horses ill matched to his lack of riding skill, until at last Bas Hebron's kindly Master of Horse had found for him a mount that had formerly been ridden by some local lord's young daughters, an older beast of short stature and narrower back. From that point on, Robdan rode with more ease, however much other men laughed at him.

Not that it had mattered what manner of beast he rode. As an ambassador attached to the Hierarch's household, Robdan saw no combat and was glad for that. Dorilian's progress across the Royal North had been swift. Bersyas had been sent south, skirting Serrain and into the low foothills of the Hesperians, there to harry Erenor's flanks while securing vital grain stores and mountain passes. That accomplished, Bersyas had rejoined them at Bynum. Hebron's generals, Illan Misenos—who was native to that region—and Orzemon Pessaeras had pressed in advance, engaging Erenor's forces at every step along the Golden Road. In this way, Dorilian and his allies succeeded in their goal of not allowing the enemy to consolidate forces in one place.

In every skirmish and battle thus far, Robdan had stayed to the rear—his smaller horse stationed alongside Dorilian's great one—watching the field. From that vantage, he had seen for the first time the reality of war, of men hewing other men, slashing and killing. The spectacle had sickened him and more than once he had dismounted to flee behind a shrubbery to empty his stomach. Though some men had looked upon Robdan's weakness with disdain, Dorilian had forbidden ridicule. "Leave him be. Master Aelfricson rightly gives these deeds their due. What we commit this day is butchery." Dorilian would turn his own horse from the field once the victory was certain. "Those men are to be pitied. Their leaders throw them away on the battlefield."

All leading to the other day and Dorilian's surprising slaughter of a monster. To the rise of legends and the freeing of this city, of storied Bynum. Outside the city's manses and villas, fields teemed with tents and horses. Above them flew the colors of the combined armies of Dorilian's alliances.

Robdan was grateful that the taking of Bynum brought with it a respite of several days. The city itself had not been securely held by Erenor, and much of the fighting within the city had been between Erenor's troops and an uprising of the populace led by citizens who still honored the Malyrdeon alliance with Marc Frederick. Though the rebels remained wary of the Sordaneon presence among them, remembering years not long past when that name had roused bitter contention, they were heartened that the holy blood of Amynas and Leur supported their cause. Bynum was cleansed of the Regent's forces in just two days.

"Erenor's name is hated by those who are good and true," one of the rebels told Robdan. They stood to watch the first formal meeting between their leaders and the Sordaneon Hierarch. Following his battle with the beast, Dorilian had healed quickly and so well that none would ever guess he had been hurt. Robdan noted with surprise that the rebels were men of high Staubaun blood, many with noble names. He had expected rebels like those from Neuberland, rough men drawn from the edges, not the center, of their society.

"Was he not once one of your own?" Robdan asked.

"He was. Until the young Princes died. That turned it. Erenor thought he could force our Princess Palaistea to wed him. Stefan wanted it for him too—the villain. Our Princess had too great a spirit to wed beneath her. Some say Stefan set afire the Danae Palace and her sons with it just to force her. Others say Erenor did that deed himself." The man's mouth turned downward as he frowned. "But none really know what happened that night—or ever will."

Palaistea Lacenedonea had been a Highborn Prince's daughter, her sons destined to rule Lacenedon. She had taken as her husband the much older Highborn Prince of Stauberg, Enreddon Malyrdeon, whose first two wives had died in childbirth presenting him with stillborn Heirs. By all accounts deeply in love with her husband, Palaistea had within five years given birth to two sons, the second just days after Enreddon's death at Permephedon. One boy had been declared Heir to Stauberg, the other to Lacenedon. Only six years later, both boys were dead, perished in a fire for which blame had flown in a thousand directions. Some had pointed to Stefan, whose battle to diminish Highborn power had grown increasingly contentious and who had subsequently taken the Stauberg title for himself; others suspected Erenor for his thwarted ambition. Still others pinned blame on Hebron, who had assumed the younger Prince's title and taken the throne of Lacenedon. And a few of course accused Dorilian, who they said wished to slay Essera's true Princes to smooth the way for his own claim.

"I didn't know the Princess," Robdan admitted. "I felt great pity, though, when I heard of her end, and that her sons were dead with her." He, like many Khelds, was fond of children. His people had held the Malyrdeons held in high regard, so that news of those deaths had been received with widespread sadness.

The man with Robdan sighed. "Spend your pity for our troubled land, Kheld. Once we were mighty, even as Sordan is now, ruled by Princes akin to gods. Now the Wall shall never speak again, for all those who might hear it are dead, and we shall never have another ruler of holy blood—unless *he* sires a son for us." He indicated Dorilian, even now receiving the rebel leaders. "But alas, his gift is the Rill, and that god runs to lands other than ours."

To that Robdan had no words, perhaps wisely. Increasingly in these northern lands, he sensed profound sadness that the days when the Highborn had ruled and the Wall had reigned were ended.

In the days that followed, soldiers mended their battle gear and their wounds and bathed in the healing springs for which the city was famous. When Bersyas invited Robdan to accompany him one day to try the fabled waters for himself, Robdan leaped upon the opportunity. For a man who had killed so many Khelds in

Neuberland, Bersyas demonstrated by far the most acceptance. It was a thing Robdan found strange, though not beyond explanation. *He knows us better for having fought us,* Robdan decided, but was less sure about what his own response should be. Rumors abounded that Bersyas had taken Kheld women willingly and unwillingly to his bed and that he was the unacknowledged father of several children by these women. Such claims disturbed Robdan as much as the killings.

As Robdan laid aside his folded dark clothes in the changing room, he tried to assume the casual air of the men he was with, for whom undressing in front of other men was neither new nor strange. He only partially succeeded. His physical differences, apparent even when fully clothed, were now uncomfortably intimate. Unlike Staubauns, who were tall and possessed little to no body hair, Robdan was short and his body had more hair on it than all of them put together, including their heads. Bersyas, with his warrior's build and pure Staubaun birth, had no hair on his limbs or upper torso. As Bersyas jumped into the pool, Robdan kept his towel about his hips and eased into the warm, lapping water. Robdan sat upon the ledge to let warmth seep into his bones and smiled in perfect happiness.

As a child and then a young man, Robdan had always wanted to see other lands and ways of life. And behold! He was doing so now, albeit in the midst of war, finding ease in the warm waters of Bynum in the middle of winter, beneath the snow-capped mountains of Staubaun legend, the Ulnossi. Not only that, Robdan traveled in the company of a Highborn Prince, a Sordaneon Hierarch no less, with many lords and generals. Robdan would have to thank Hans in his next letter for giving him a gift beyond price. He closed his eyes and savored contentment as his weariness melted away, his breathing become easier as warm, moist air filled his nostrils and then his lungs. Even the air had the sharp, fresh bite of distant spring. Dimly, he attended the arrival of others, a hollow echo of new voices filling the stone chamber. Only gradually did he become aware that some of the men had come to stand over him.

"This pool is fouled."

Robdan looked up at a tall man with the imposing body of a warrior, whose cold dark gaze fixed on his as though Robdan were something low and vile. The man spoke in the classical cadence of the wellborn.

"You, Kheld, get out that this pool may be fit for proper men."

Sitting up, water plastering his chest hair to his skin, Robdan moved to speak, only to find another speaking for him. Tall and glistening, Bersyas stood in water lapping at his hips. "He stays. This man is Prince Handurin's representative. He's the Hierarch's guest—and mine."

"The Sordaneon's guest, you say?" A second man spoke with a barely concealed sneer. "I don't see that one in the water with him."

"The Thrice Royal heard that the baths are frequented by louts." Bersyas remained unflustered.

"Louts, are we? Because we do not bathe with *that*?" said the first man. "Get it out before we take our fists to it."

Though Robdan feared what these men might do if he got within an arm's length of them, he knew what mattered most would be that he comport himself with dignity. His service to the Archhalia had taught him not to presume that Staubauns would treat him fairly, whatever he did. That Bersyas looked grim and prepared to stand his ground provided no reason to issue a challenge. There were reasons more compelling than this insult for Sordan to be at odds with Essera, and Robdan wished to do nothing that would make those matters worse.

"This is a fine place, but I prefer not to put its healing properties to the test. I will go, General Bersyas, if these men will stand away."

Without so much as a show of hesitation, the men stood aside, giving Robdan a clear path to the door. Perhaps they understood now, belatedly, who the man with Robdan was and feared possible consequences. Their comments about Dorilian had been ill thought and Sordan's general Bersyas carried a reputation nearly as fierce as that of his Hierarch.

Leaving puddles of water on the stone floor, Robdan retreated to the outer room, where he found his clothing undisturbed. Already he could feel the cold outside stealing through the walls and under doors. He was nearly dressed when Bersyas came in after him.

"There is one lie laid to rest: the baths at Bynum are not always warm. You should not have left," Bersyas said. "They would have relented."

Robdan bit back a frown and shook his head. "And what good in that? If they relent to you—or to your Hierarch—it means little. They'll think no better of men like me."

"Do they think better of you if you allow them to drive you away?"

Robdan sat on the stone bench so he might dry his feet. Only then would he pull on his socks and boots. "It may look as though I'm a coward and they will think that," he acknowledged, not without a twinge at the thought. "I don't seek battle, and I dislike argument. And it may be that I'm quick to concede matters I deem unimportant. What a few Staubauns in Bynum think of me or of Khelds matters less to me than that there be accord in the Hierarch's armies. His true enemy, and mine, is out there"—Robdan waved vaguely at the windows and the white lands to be seen if one looked out of them—"not in here. And I would like to keep it that way." He pulled on his boots as Bersyas, looking unconvinced, moved to dress.

As they left the baths for the cold street outside, Robdan had more to say. "Though these men want no Khelds in their bath, their attitudes come more from ignorance than malice. The Sorcerer we battle wants no Khelds in the World at all, and he would slay us to the last of our kind or see us in wretched slavery, never to be treated as human again. I can tolerate a few slurs from the tongues of fools if it means getting rid of the monster."

The mounted force that rode up to the ninety-nine steps of the Blythagoran Serat glittered with the heavy mail and arms of a dedicated fighting force. Four hundred strong and bearing the standards of the Sordaneon Hierarch himself, they pulled to a halt before the steps, their commander dismounting.

"That is Tutto Rhunnard, Bas of Kolgya," Legon informed Robdan. They waited together at the top of the steps, upon the broad fountain-lined court leading to the heavily guarded keep. "Bas Tutto stands high in the Thrice Royal's confidence. He is the Hierarch's swordmaster and an old retainer from his grandsire Sebbord's household."

Tutto paused only long enough to pull free a bundle he had carried before him on the horse, shouldering it before turning to mount the steps. Every Sordani soldier guarding the Serat, even the highest officers among them, lowered their weapons and bowed deeply. The Lacenedoni soldiers, knowing that the man being so honored must be at the very least a nobleman, did the same. When Tutto approached him, however, Robdan saw with surprise that he looked not upon a Staubaun lord, but one with the bronzed skin and stocky, compact build of a southern Estol. From beneath a helm of silver, dark eyes stabbed flint-hard from a scarred brown face as gnarled and knotted as old tree roots.

Legon stepped forward and nodded to Tutto as an equal. Robdan opted for a bow. Tutto barely gave Robdan a glance but fixed his gaze on Legon.

"So, he's decided finally to seek my advice. None too soon if Stauberg hosts the evil we think it might. It was a fell day when that city forgot its holy foundations and built for itself towers of shame." Robdan fought the urge to recoil as Tutto's stony gaze fell again on him. "So it's true, what a year ago we would have dismissed as madness: Khelds have proven to be the key to Essera."

Robdan followed as Legon led Tutto between the towering columns standing at the Serat's entrance, through doors patterned with intricate designs of men and deeds, into the massive building's interior. The atrium opened before them in tall rises of pillars clad in gold beneath a domed ceiling formed of bars and fans of clear blue glass. The effect, even on gray days, was that of standing beneath a summer sky.

"Handurin clears the fields in Dazunor, we hear." Legon pursued the conversation with Tutto. Robdan hoped to hear something good on that front. "Please tell me you have some news, having recently come that way."

Tutto nodded. His gaze swept past the impressive details of the Serat's vast, open space to the western landscape visible through the columns of the palisade. Many thousands camped in orderly ranks along the river. Smoke curled thick from campfires and the air was filled with the distant noise of an army preparing, once more, to move. "Talk at Permephedon was that Handurin had driven Zel back to Trulo," Tutto reported. "But that army can go no further. Zel holds the way between the Dazun and the Kragh."

Robdan had heard of the Kragh and had even, on his journeys to and from the Archhalia, ridden within sight of that feared region of crusted hills. More than local topography made it fearsome, though he recalled that Marc Frederick had made little of the talk of monsters dwelling there. These men looked less convinced.

"Sweep north then to Kyrbasillon?" Legon ventured a guess as to Hans's options.

"Only if he is a fool. They would then ride into the enemy's jaws." Turning his head to Robdan, Tutto said, "The time is coming when we will see what Khelds are made of—if they be fierce fighters or find victory only when victory is easy."

"I believe my people will prove hardy in battle," Robdan defended his people's honor, "even if they are less skilled than yours."

Tutto adjusted the bag on his shoulder. "Less skill can mean less heart. A warrior's heart is tempered in battle. He learns simplicity in thought and action; his will hardens through adversity. Such things come from having fought hard and won harder, not from good food and soft nights and victories handed over with the intent of luring quarry near." They passed beneath the carved figures of ancient Princes holding aloft great orbs, waterglobes spilling light into these inner chambers. "Handurin is not my concern. Dorilian is." Tutto turned to Legon. "You say he is well?" Tutto's rasping voice held a note of warning that he would brook no more softness in that answer than he would in combat.

Robdan noted Legon's tense mouth and clipped words. "I take it you know about the battle monster."

"The one he killed with his bare hands."

"Go, ask him about it. What did he tell me? That it died—and he did not." A dubious glance passed between the two men.

"So I must ask him directly to get a straight answer. And his reception here, among these Esserans?"

"Bas Hebron has extended the Thrice Royal every comfort and courtesy and I have overseen every detail of his protection. His only complaint is with the food. Erenor's men have emptied Bynum's storehouses and picked clean the countryside. Our liege eats the best of what they have, though it is not very good."

Tutto's scarred face creased with purpose. "No matter. I have brought along with me a supply of what he will need."

Legon stopped so sharply that Robdan nearly ran into him. "Do not beset him," Legon warned, a fell light in his narrowing gaze. "You know as well as I do how little he likes Sebbord's brew."

"The godborn are not as other men. He would do well to nourish a liking for what best nourishes him." Robdan noted that Tutto faced Legon without blinking, though it meant looking up. "Don't tell *me* he hasn't been dabbling with the gifts of his line, not when the Rill popped up among mud huts and barbarians and the countryside runs with tales of him being a legend in battle."

"Who is to say? All saw him kill the damn beast with that sword." Legon scowled. "He wore the Armor, and you know as much about that as I do." Robdan trotted to keep up as they began walking again. "If you want to know more about him tapping into the Rill, ask the Kheld. He was with him in Amallar and since."

"Is that so? What would a Kheld know of such things?"

Robdan nearly withered beneath the abrupt scrutiny of the heavily armored—and armed—man stalking at his side.

Squaring his shoulders with the dignity of his meager knowledge, Robdan answered. "I cannot claim to know much, but I was with His Thrice Royal Grace at Bellan Toregh—mud huts and barbarians, as you call it—when he awakened the Rill."

"Were you? There, you say. So tell me—how did he do that?"

Caught off guard, Robdan struggled to answer. "I cannot tell you. He made me promise."

"Promise?"

"Not to say anything about what I saw, to anyone. I'm sorry. Besides, I didn't see much at all. I fainted full away. The air inside was bad and it was hard to breathe—"

"The air was bad, you say?" Tutto regarded Robdan with an inquisitor's keen attention, a weighing that also included more knowledge than he had thus far revealed. "It would be so when voided for a Leur age. Then I will own you were there or you would not know as much… or have given such a promise. What I do not understand is why he would have you with him. It's not like him to carelessly show his ways."

"Nor did he wish it then. I begged him to let me stay with him," Robdan admitted. He saw the other men exchange disbelieving glances. "It was dark and cold, you see—nasty wet weather. I'm not a young man, and perhaps he was afraid I would catch my death of a chill."

"And he should have let you. A Kheld in the Rill sanctum!" Snorting, Tutto shook his head and shared a glare of disapproval with Legon. "And engaging a beast in battle to save a resort town. It shall be his downfall yet, his soft heart!"

# 37

Place two enemies in proximity and they will meet—and
those we carry within ourselves meet soonest.
EPIRADES, *DISCOURSE ON DUALITY*

Prince Regent Erenor's emissary approached along a lane lined
with soldiers. Foremost among these, the Sordaneon Eagle Guard
presented a solid front of emerald green livery and silver mail, their
fearsome blades a shining wall, drawn and held at the ready.
Opposite them stood the soldiers of Lacenedon and Gweroyen in
their garb of blue, gold, black, and white, swords also ready,
forming an avenue of death for any who came with ill intent. At the
end of that road waited the tents of the domains whose armies now
bore down upon Stauberg. Above the sky-blue awning that
overarched the seated commanders could be seen the toothed crown
of Kossa Kallitelh. Upon a dais were five chairs, one higher than the
four others. Dorilian, dressed in the royal emblems of his Sordan
Hierarchate, a circlet of clear blue and gold fire upon his head,
presided in the higher chair. Bas Hebron Ursenos of Lacenedon and
the Bas of Gweroyen, Estevan Niarchos, sat to either side. Beside
them sat the rebel Archon of the Eleutheron, Megall Uranaeos, and
Hebron's stout ally, the Bas of Pessach. Also seated near the dais to
the side of these five, in a place of dignity unprecedented for his
kind, was Robdan Aelfricson, serving as his Prince's eyes and ears.

Erenor's representative, who had ridden to the camp holding
only a short white staff and notched banner of an emissary,
dismounted and submitted to a search and escort. Beside him, a
second man dressed in blue and also bearing a staff submitted to the
same. When the search revealed no weapons or devices, they were

given leave to proceed down the corridor of steel. Four thousand eyes watched their every footfall, assessed their every movement, and stood ready to kill. At the foot of the dais, the representatives stopped, each lowering to one knee. From there the Regent's emissary lifted his gaze to the men seated there.

He spoke, however, to but one man. As well he should.

"Greetings, Son of Amynas, Derlon's Heir, Hierarch of Sordan and Sansordan, from my liege, Erenor Tholeros, Prince of Stauberg and Tahlwent, and Regent full sworn of this land." He removed his helm barred with diplomatic blue, his fair hair and features shining in the gloom of afternoon. "I am Kolax Staubaun Menullos, Enlad of Glavir. I convey to you my Prince's request—"

"Don't name your master a prince—not to me." Dorilian spoke with tones of ice, aware the chill that resulted would cause all who heard it to shudder. "I know he is not one."

Kolax flushed. "He is titled—"

"Titles he stole from a murdered child and a murdered queen. He presumes much if he thinks I wish to end this war other than with his head on a pike."

The man bowed lower still. "As I was saying, my Prince—"

"Call him that again and it will be *your* head on that pike."

A deep breath later, Kolax resumed. "My Lord proposes to meet on the morrow at the crossroads of Skalis, under terms of truce, for the purpose of discussing the means by which this conflict might be ended without further bloodshed."

"I should think the means obvious: he must surrender."

"To what end? He would hear this answer from your own lips, Thrice Royal, and seal it with your words. He regrets that you and he have not spoken together as Pri—as noble adversaries should— and that you would base your sacred judgments upon hearsay."

"His association with my enemy is not hearsay. His usurpation of the Stauberg titles is not hearsay. Neither is his opposition to the rightful Heir of this Kingdom."

"My Lord anticipated your reluctance, Thrice Royal, and so he bade me offer this: that if you meet with him at the crossroads, he will free one royal hostage."

All witnessed the birth of intrigue. Dorilian narrowed his gaze, assessing if this be a bluff or an offer with meat within. "Who would your paltry master have that I might be interested in seeing freed?"

Kolax raised his head, nearly bold. "Princess Palaistea Malyrdeonis."

"Impossible!" Hebron, whose cousin the Princess was, rose from his seat. "Palaistea died years ago along with her sons in the flames that consumed the Danae Palace. Erenor himself declared her death."

The emissary looked respectfully to the Bas, to whom he bowed his head in acknowledgment, then returned his attention to the Hierarch. "She did not die, Thrice Royal, but lives, a royal prisoner to my Lord. You can yourself ascertain the truth of my words."

Dorilian focused on the man. Believers would claim he looked through the skull and touched the very stuff of thought. That was not precisely true. Still, decades had passed since any of the men in attendance had seen the Highborn thus ascertain the truth behind men's words and now the sight unnerved them. Memories of the vanished powers of the departed Malyrdeons stirred them; they had already seen Dorilian demonstrate other abilities attributed to him. The emissary turned pale, but none could say what it was he felt.

But Dorilian tasted the brightness of unshadowed truth.

"He has her." Dorilian sank back in his chair.

"She lives?" asked Hebron, astonished.

"His words shine true. The fiend has apparently kept her alive. Perhaps even for this."

Dorilian wondered if he alone noted the flicker of a new and previously unsuspected game. He wondered too at the manifold responses to his ability to detect such nuances. Hebron was agape with worship—nor was he alone. Estevan too wore a watchful and anxious wonder. More interesting was Robdan, who gazed up at Dorilian as if he waited on the fullness of some answer.

Hebron's proud face hardened with resolve. "If you fear treachery, as I do, Thrice Royal, you will refuse this parley. Palaistea is close kin to me. By right, if she lives, Lacenedon is hers, and Stauberg also. I will ride in your stead."

"You and I will ride together." Dorilian warded off Hebron's impending protest. "It is not Erenor who plays this card. Nor is it you with whom he seeks this parley. Even with the small party we shall mount, I will be well protected against such treacheries as might be brought against me." Dorilian eyed the emissary, who surely knew the game being played. Reassurances of safety were but the lure. To meet at Skalis was Erenor's plan to remind his foes

that they would now have to confront the formidable defenses of
Stauberg's Wall. Giving a hand signal to Tutto to make the
arrangements, Dorilian rose. He remained long enough to watch
Tutto advance upon the now white-faced Kolax Menullos.

"The Thrice Royal has spoken," Tutto stated. "Your Lord of a
Thousand Lies will have his parley. Now here are the terms—and
if you do not hold to them, may Leur blacken your tongues to
match your hearts, that men may know you by them forever."

# 38



It took two days to traverse the Kragh, days during which some of them had not slept. But they were through it. Aubrey was glad to see the land open before them in a vista of river and mist, broad forests interspersed with cultivated fields. The main road from Trulo to Kyrbasillon wound through the valley below, where it passed within sight of the western hills of the Kragh. They were still on the near side of the River Hyllorhose and the Kragh's sinister hills ascended at their backs, forming misty, forbidding crags subject to stories even more terrible than those told by villagers to the east. The Dog Men, about twenty of whom, led by Cortogh, now traveled with them, had scouted ahead and declared they were but a day north of Trulo.

For all its apparent wildness, the land Hans and his army had entered was civilized. Though densely forested, the tall hills of western Dazunor boasted sheltered valleys and lofty, broad hilltops, home to prosperous farms and villages. As befitted a region long under Staubaun settlement, lordly villas overlooked many of the gemlike lakes for which the region was famous.

"The Glainoi, the Shining Hills." Kerr announced the land proudly, for Dannuth lay directly to the north and was formed of the same rich terrain.

"Why are they called shining?" Arne asked. He had told Aubrey that from what he could see of them, they looked like any other hills, fog-shrouded and damp.

Raphelon answered from where he rode beside Aubrey, rescuing Kerr from an unroyal display of ignorance. "Some would say it is because of the many lakes that shine in the sun, and the leafy forest with its jewellike spring and fall colors." He spoke with the authority of familiarity, then smiled. "But mostly they are called the Shining Hills because of the number of princely estates in the region. Many of the houses are as splendid as anything you would see in Dazunor-Rannuli or the Eleutheron. In some areas, the hills are crowned with golden rooftops. Even the towns, they say, are gilded. This was a land much favored by the Highborn and high Staubaun royalty before our ranks were decimated."

"All of the great Highborn Houses have dwellings here." Kerr's face turned abruptly thoughtful. "I remember my grandfather had one. After the Malyrdeon Princes died, however, most of the Highborn estates were given away to false nobility as appeasement to looters." He stopped speaking at that point, realizing that what he'd said might offend some with whom he rode.

Though Nalf Rhys frowned in Aubrey's direction, he said nothing and gestured Fran to silence too. It was likely Nalf remembered that Kerr's grandfather, Ostemun, Dannuth's Highborn ruler, had died at Permephedon with Marc Frederick. Ostemun's brother, Rheger, and Rheger's son, Elhanan, had then met their god on Stefan's order of execution. Several royal Dannutheon estates had gone to Kheldmen. Even if Stefan had been right to seize the lands of Dannuth's Highborn traitors, this was not the time to rub it in.

"There are fine places in this land." Nalf spoke to Aubrey later as they made camp for the night in a sheltered bend of the river, its water clear and cold, fed by deep lakes in the hills. "It's been a few years, but I've walked on floors of gold here and slept on beds so lofty I nearly broke my neck getting out of them. Even the stables have water that runs from the spout! At least in these parts there's a chance we can get decent accommodations."

But Aubrey pondered what she had seen of the puckered land

before them, and what caught her mind were visions of great walled houses armed and waiting, landed Staubaun lords and men loyal to Erenor holding strong on the hilltops. The rich lands between the Dazun River and the mountains formed Dazunor's Staubaun heart, and even before Stefan's death they had stood against the Kheldish folk who dwelled so near to them across the Dazun. Even if Hans won the looming battle against the Mormantaloran's army, securing the King's Road to Gustan, Hans might find himself reclaiming the Glainoi region estate by bloody estate.

Aubrey knew Hans must win decisively, so decisively that his enemies lost heart. So decisively that people would turn their eyes to their new King, see his victory and his alone, and forget that Dorilian Sordaneon was laying siege to Stauberg.

Although Hans seemed to think nothing of it and trusted Dorilian so fully that faith itself caused wonder, Aubrey knew the Staubauns in Hans's company still looked north nervously. They regarded Stauberg as the ancient seat of Highborn blood—and Labran Sordaneon's prison. In their minds, that specter of vengeance and the Highborn myth it carried burned hotter than any vow of trust.

With the Cortogh leading the way, Hans kept to the ravines leading out of the region. As they rode, Cortogh regarded Aubrey intently, watching her for many minutes at a time, though never constantly. He would sometimes do other things, like talk with Hans while loping at the shoulder of Hans's horse or trot ahead to scout out the trail before them. When Cortogh would return, however, after stationing his own kind and directing the advance troops, he would resume watching Aubrey with eyes yellow as ripened goldenrod. Aubrey took to staring back and noted that when she did so, Cortogh would always drop his gaze. To her mind, it was no mystery why he watched. As one of few women among so many men, Aubrey understood there would be some of that. Cortogh's gaze, however, was not that of other men. Mindful that the Hen Kyon helped them, wand Baran had pledged his folk with vows of honor, Aubrey didn't go to Hans about how much his new ally disturbed her. She would deal with the matter herself.

As they made camp for the night in the last hidden place before they would emerge onto the river plain to flank Zel's position, Aubrey saw Cortogh squatting by the riverbank, washing his hands in the water, for once not staring. She walked over in plain view but placed so none would overhear them.

"Why do you watch me all the time?" she demanded.

Cortogh jerked his head around, looking up as Aubrey stood over him, woman proud. His feral eyes lidded with secrets. "You are different. Other women will not look. They pretend they do not see me or they run away."

"I'm taking you at your word that you're honorable."

"Honor." Cortogh lifted his head to sniff the breezes that sifted down from the hills, carried on the wind. "That is an empty promise from a Kheldman's lips."

"I am not a Kheld*man*."

Thin lips stretched in a pained-looking smile. "Neither is he who seeded you. Is it the Prince's child that's in you?"

She stared. As Aubrey studied Cortogh's not-human face, with its elongated, wide nose and jaws, high and broad between wide-set eyes, seeing the knowing set of his gaze, she felt the first stirrings of panic. What no human but she could yet detect, this creature had. Cortogh's brutish senses read the signs of pregnancy in Aubrey's scent as easily as others would eventually read the changes in her body's shape. Behind her, she sensed the activity of the camp going about its business of travel and war. Her kinsmen were there, and her friends—but there were enemies too. As soon as her pregnancy became known, her life would again be in danger. Hans's Staubaun allies hoped for him to make a marriage with one of Essera's high houses. They might move upon rumor alone to prevent what they thought was a Stauberg-Randolph bastard—and the truth would endanger everything. Aubrey moved closer to Cortogh, observing how his nostrils widened as his gaze followed each step and movement.

"Maybe I don't know who the father is." Aubrey rested her hand on her sword hilt, knowing Cortogh would miss nothing of the nuances or actions. "Don't you know that a Kheldwoman's child could be any man's?"

"But your child is not any man's." Cortogh plunged his hands into the water again and washed them briefly before pulling them out, water dripping from nails that curved like claws. His semblance of a smile curled into a grimace more resentful than fierce. "Keep your woman's pride. I will not tell your secret. Secrets are safest where none will look. The young Prince is our hope as well as yours."

"Your hope?"

Cortogh rose. He was taller, Aubrey noticed with surprise. She had always been on horseback before, while he walked. In the dying light of day, his fur took on an even redder hue than usual. "To lift the curse. To bring us back into the World and make it so we are no longer hunted like beasts." He snorted and moved up the bank. "You follow him for love and because he has the blood of Khelds in his veins. We do not care about that. We but want to remove our debt."

"There are no Highborn Princes here. And Sordan's rides to battle in the north."

"Against that which should have been destroyed long ago." The failing sun slashed Cortogh's nonhuman face with light as he looked around at the shrouded hills. "Maybe it isn't enough to have not hunted them, to have accepted our lives and lived apart, in isolation, watching while others took up the hunt. Maybe we should have protected them, the Prince of Dannuth and his son. They say the Khelds walked in their blood and spat on their corpses."

Picking up his skin bag and shouldering it, Cortogh walked away without a glance back.

"You're sure we're still secret?" Hans queried Cortogh that night when he huddled with his generals and Cortogh around a clean-burning fire. Hans had kept the bulk of his men back in the folded valley of the Hyllorhose, though they were still on the Kragh side and had moved their equipment into hiding. Back in the hills, no one would see their fires and he planned to move forward before dawn.

"They don't know you are here. My people have shielded their presence. No scouts got through to see us." Cortogh traced a crude map in the dirt before them, marking a symbol for each position with his claw. "Over here, on the other side, they are set to be fooled. They have sent spies to the Kettle, riders who will find villagers who say some men tried to go to the Kragh but were sent back in pieces, and that you went north. You were wise to send part of your army that way."

"The best lies have some truth," Hans had accepted Fran Gorseddson's suggestion that they employ a diversion and had sent a company of his least experienced troops north toward Dannuth and the relief of Kyrbasillon. Under the command of young officers eager to prove themselves in their Prince's service and just as eager not to venture into the Kragh, that force was accompanied by some of the least mobile aspects of war: camp followers, bootjacks, cattle, and the larger wagons.

"The army you seek is encamped here." Cortogh scratched crossed swords in the dust. "This is the river, this the road."

"They will still probably get wind of us before we reach them." Raphelon frowned over the makeshift map, the features of which could be matched against what was known of the road and surroundings. There had also been reconnaissance from two of Cortogh's more human-looking brethren who had gone ahead to scout the enemy's positions. "But they will have to abandon their fortifications and split their forces."

Hans nodded, resisting the impulse to grin. "Zel built his breastworks facing east on the road."

"He's going to be real surprised," Arne agreed. He'd said something earlier about being glad they were out of the hills—and how the prospect of battle was less terrifying to him now than it had been only weeks before.

"They can turn the archers around fairly quickly," Soter noted, "but not the firepits. In fact, those will now be at their rear."

"We'll push them back into their own ranks, with *skifr* and spear, and our own archers too," Nalf Rhys contributed. He was eager to try out the spear catapults he'd acquired in Dazunor-Rannuli.

"And the Mormantaloran's cavalry will have to change their staging on a sword edge, come around this way. We can use this wetland, here, to guard against them flanking us east," Euden Mezeon added. He nodded his satisfaction that the plan would succeed.

"I want to move lightning fast," Hans told them. "The element of surprise is only as good as our ability to make sure they don't have a chance to adapt a strategy against us."

The morning dawned with mists along the river, the Hen Kyon leading the way to the lowlands where Zel's army held Trulo so securely.

<h1 style="text-align:center">39</h1>

If you yearn for war, prepare yourself for death. Or glory,
death's companion—because all deaths are glorious when
soldiers fall in battle. At least, that is what you will be told
by those who do not die.
Jonthan Stauberg-Randolph, letter to his nephew Stefan

When a soldier wearing travel-stained Mormantaloran leathers galloped up to the gate of the war works surrounding Trulo, riding a lathered horse and asking for General Zel, the General's men took the messenger to a fortified residence west of the city. There, as was his recent habit, Zel had spent the night savoring the charms and comforts of his mistress—the lovely Lady Iolanthe, Enladris of Narkissal—and the luxuries of that estate, easily the most splendid in the region. In the first gray before dawn, the messenger saw nothing of that grand house other than how well the stonework flooring was laid. All else was globe light and shadows.

"Great General, I bring you these words of warning from Lord Gan of Zarad." The gasping man fell to one knee and bowed low, helmet still on his head. The General's guard officers, roused from their own beds, had followed the messenger into the bedchamber and now stood behind him, a ring of half-clothed men and hastily grabbed weapons. "There is no army advancing on the Beldan. Prince Handurin is not there."

"What do you mean Handurin is not there?" The Stauberg-Randolph Prince had to be somewhere, and Zel knew where he was not. Not at Trulo. Not on the Dazun. Not in the Kragh, surely. That left only the plain of Beldan or its approaches. He reached for his robe. If he made quick work of this interruption, he could call the toothsome Io out from behind the chamber hangings and start his morning in a manner more to his liking.

The dirt-stained messenger would not raise his gaze but stared at the richly carpeted floor. "Lord Gan sent a force to sortie against them. What he found was not an army. Their numbers are swollen by camp followers, farmers—it only looks like a great army from afar. They dragged boards and palettes across the ground to raise dust as they went."

"A decoy?" Zel glanced sharply to his guards. They looked even more alarmed than he was and had nothing to suggest. He reached for his boots and gestured for the messenger to continue.

"The Prince's standard is there, but there is no sign of him—or the Trongor troops that travel with him. There are Khelds, but no Kheld horse soldiers or the main units of their archers and infantry. Although we could see banners of Merrydn and Dannuth, and some men wearing those colors, we soon noticed that the men wearing them were not soldiers but rabble. Handurin must have recruited folk from the farms and towns of the region. That horde has only enough soldiers to skirmish and run and persuade us they have purpose; the rest are armed with the blades they cook with. The real army is nowhere to be found. Gan does not know if they circle him—or you. Great General, I rode two days and nights and killed three horses to tell you this."

"Then kill three more! Ride back to Gan and tell him to slaughter whatever he's found. Then he's to find that cursed half-breed Prince and put an end to this pretense that he's worth fighting!" Zel stormed to his feet and glared at his guard. "Ready my horse. And send word ahead to Trulo. I want to meet with my officers to devise a plan. We need to know if Handurin braved the Kragh—and if he did, we need to know if he survived it. I'm going to contact Nammuor."

Zel watched the soldiers scurry away like mice glad to be free of the cat but terrified by knowing a serpent approached. *Run, little mice. Find Handurin and let the serpent gorge on* him *instead—until he gorges on the Sordaneon.*

Only that man's blood, Zel knew, would satisfy the Eye of Fire.

The riders from Narkissal had not yet reached the Mormantaloran perimeter forces when the first wave of Kheld infantry poured down the hills. The sentries in the hills had been silenced by the

Hen Kyon hours before and no warning had been sent. The Mormantalorans scrambled in surprise as the Khelds ran against the lightly protected watchtowers north of the city.

From Trulo, a hastily mounted cavalry rode forth to support an infantry just as hastily roused from their tents. In the misty chill of an icy dawn, the horse soldiers of Merrydn and Dannuth joined those of the Khelds in racing east along the river, using Raphelon's directions to follow the barely remembered Old Road through the marshes. Catching the enemy yet again by surprise, the horsemen attacked the rear of the Mormantaloran troops manning the mighty war works Zel had erected to bar the Dazun Road. The towering catapults and massive spoked barriers showed only their backs to attackers that had come from behind. Though the great firepits glowed, the Mormantalorans had received neither sign nor word to set any to blazing.

"Overturn the oil!" a Southlander captain shouted and his men leaped to the task, upending the great, machine-mounted vats so that gouts of black liquid spilled into the marsh. Other men, divining their captain's plan, tossed torches onto the spreading shadow on the water. Flames raced across the marsh in a curtain.

Raphelon reined in his horse as tongues of fire appeared between his Dannuthians and the rushing force of Kheldish infantry. He signaled to his men in alarm. "We're cut off!" The fire would spread toward the river, following the sluggish current. "To the Road!" he shouted, for there was safety to be found if they could gain the bridge there and defeat the enemy holding the highway.

Harnesses clacked and saddles creaked as Aubrey brought her mounted rangers to a halt on the wooded hillside. She doubted the trees, denuded as they were of leaves, would do much to conceal them. The Dog Men were better hidden, their rough garb blending with the landscape nearly as well as their furred skins. It had not been Aubrey's choice to secure this small cluster of buildings on the road leading to Trulo, a mere outpost on an unimportant road. She had argued to ride into battle. Her Saemoregh men were battle-hardened veterans of dozens of skirmishes in Neuberland as well as the now many-weeks-old campaign in the north. There was hardly a man among Hans's command who handled weapons better than Aubrey's lot and certainly none who were braver. Not only had her arguments fallen on deaf ears but she had also found herself outnumbered. First Nalf expressed his concerns for Aubrey's safety and then, not surprisingly, Raphelon had voiced firm opposition. Only Wodd had spoken to support her. Cortogh, however, had sealed Aubrey's fate. He had insisted Aubrey not enter battle and had by means of a silent, yet unmistakable, snarl conveyed that he would reveal the pregnancy if she pressed Hans on the matter. If that news got out, Hans would reduce Aubrey's activities to the point of uselessness.

*He would never risk Dorilian's child. His efforts to keep me close are bad enough already.*

"Not a day passed while you and Arne Thegn were away that Prince Handurin didn't complain about your absence," Wodd advised. His face was more heavily bearded now and streaked with silver, but his gaze was just as unswerving as ever. "He wishes you at his side for good counsel and your quick way with words. He doesn't see you as a soldier. Nor should he," Wodd added with a lift of his eyebrow.

"I don't want to be locked away, the way Staubauns do their women."

Wodd nodded and thought for a long moment. "Consider then that Hans Thegn has sent you on a mission with fierce, clawed creatures only he seems to trust, into country we cannot be sure is free of enemies, so that you may put your expertise in service to the Mother to the good of our lads. If that's being locked away, I would re-examine what Staubauns do."

All right. She wasn't being locked away, but Aubrey still glared at the back of Cortogh's head, wishing she had never heard of Dog Men and that she had never captured Cortogh's interest. It was only because of Cortogh's threat that Aubrey had allowed Hans to send her to the rear of the fighting, protecting the healers. Wodd wasn't wrong about the role being worthwhile. As a healer herself, trained at Aurdollen, Aubrey understood the importance of having a secure place to treat the wounded. That Hans gave as much thought to this aspect of war as he did to battle plans heightened her respect for him. It was just that she disliked being forced into a secondary role, yet another woman who could not fight.

Fighting was what she did best.

The hooded line of Cortogh's head lifted, then swung Aubrey's way. "Soldiers come along the road." Cortogh's voice never failed

to astonish her, growling and deep. Hans had chosen to keep the
Dog Men contingent, sent by Baran to aid his army, out of the
battle. Among other things, the Dog Men frightened most of the
soldiers and all of the horses. Aubrey, feeling plenty of anger but
no fear toward Cortogh, had agreed to work with the Dog Men in
securing the outpost.

"Southlanders?" she asked. Cortogh would know what she
meant, having learned the word over the last two days.

"Yes." Cortogh signaled and his soldiers came forward from
among the trees. Aubrey nodded to Wodd, indicating that it was
necessary to lead her force down the other side of the hill. The
horses would handle better if not too close to the beastlike
creatures.

Whatever was coming on the road, they would encounter
Kheldish steel.

"We got first advantage, but they are a fierce fighting force." Nalf
Rhys gave his report to Hans and a handful of the other mounted
captains atop a ridge overlooking the marshes and the road. As
daylight grew stronger, they could see more and more of the battle.
It was not unfolding precisely as they had hoped. "See how they
have dug in at the east end of the marsh, with their spears to the
river. Unless we can defeat those troops, our men will take the
town only to have the Southlanders come back at them!"

For that reason and more, the fire in the marshes alarmed Hans
the most. Not only had it divided Raphelon and the Dannuthi
horsemen from reinforcement by the Kheld riders and taken away
their option of flight, but the smoke produced by the fire was
drifting west to where the foot soldiers fought the Mormantalorans
in their own camp. He watched Arne below on his roan horse,
marshaling his archers and directing the assault on Trulo in tandem
with Farrl's Trongorians. Unseen to the north, Aubrey and her
rangers teamed with the Hen Kyon to capture an outpost that
could be used by the healers and nonfighting forces. Fran and his
Neuberland riders were also in that area, cutting off the Trulo
garrison from retreating west along the Dazun Road. Hans thought
it best to keep to his practice of having the affiliated northern
troops attack only the Mormantalorans. They would have no
hidden loyalties there and fewer repercussions later should there

be charges that one domain had inflicted harm on another. Even as Prince of Dazunor, it favored Hans to keep his politics clear. *I will not let Rafe or Kerr be criticized in their own lands that they did my dirty work. My Khelds and the Trongorians are my right arm in battle. Let the local lords rage against them and me.*

Hans tried to see the signs of Nammuor's presence, thinking there might be some trace of his malevolent adversary clinging to Trulo or his troops on the battlefield. All Hans discerned was misery. The gray stone of a city at war, the violence of men fighting and killing each other, the strained loyalties of neighbor against neighbor. For a moment, he glimpsed the fabric of it: societies and loyalties torn asunder, to emerge scarred if they emerged at all. He could now put a face to the lesson of Sordan. *Essera oppressed them and nearly destroyed the Sordaneons, but Sordan emerged stronger. Changed, but stronger. And the scars of that battle then are what allow me to succeed now. Those scars gave me the Rill and an ally… and they gave me Amallar.*

Marc Frederick becoming Essera's King had given Hans Nammuor as well.

Nammuor was not at Trulo, however—of that Hans was surpassingly sure. He no longer doubted that he would know when Nammuor was near. He had felt the prickling of that proximity at Rainill when confronted by Nammuor's device-wearing spy and, since then, had endured his share of disturbing dreams. The latter had begun to occur more frequently, perhaps because Hans was now nearer to Nammuor's strongholds in Tahlwent. In those dreams Hans saw Stefan, Marc Frederick—and Nammuor too. By that same measure, he felt confident he would not face Nammuor here. Nammuor spent his attention farther north, where royal Stauberg waited with sorcery of its own and Dorilian Sordaneon flaunted a destiny the Diadem could not ignore.

*It's been a good plan so far*, Hans wanted to say to the man who had conceived it. *Fighting on two fronts buys us time and costs our enemy opportunity. I would not have made it this far had you not been so bold. But what does it gain you?*

Hans became aware of Kerr, seated on an ivory horse at Hans's side, guards not far behind, pointing in alarm. On the field below, Hans saw signs of the battle shifting. As Nalf had predicted, a portion of the Mormantaloran army that had been posted along the river had found its way around the embattled Dannuthi and Merrydni cavalry. Even now, they fought their way toward the rear of the Kheldish force engaged in the camp. Smoke from the marsh fire prevented the Kheld soldiers from seeing the approaching foe.

"They'll be taken from behind!" Kerr panicked, jerking up his horse's head and looking about for relief troops. There were none to be seen. All of the army was fully engaged in the battle.

A sound of horns burst over the clashing forces to the east, barely heard by either combatant force above the din of their own fierce fighting. Hans heard it, however, and turned his horse toward the sound. On the field, the men of Merrydn and Trongor continued to fight. But the Khelds stopped and milled just as the enemy did, reacting with alarm as a horde of heavily armed, mounted men poured down from the ridges overlooking the Dazun Road to join in the battle. Above the tide of horsemen whipped banners of emerald and silver.

Sordan's army rode into the fray.

A wave of horses bearing riders with brandished spears and broadswords slammed into the underbelly of the hastily reversed Mormantaloran defenses, the first few hundred driving a wedge through the confused ranks, then turning back upon them. Cresting the ridge behind that leading phalanx was the arrival of thousands more. With elated hurrahs and cries of victory, the revived Khelds and Hans's Esseran forces plunged anew into the fighting. Everywhere one looked on the field, the Mormantalorans were now fighting for their lives.

A party of riders separated from the no longer beleaguered Khelds and rode up the hill to where Hans and a handful of his officers watched. Nalf Rhys waved his sword from astride his blood-splattered horse.

"By Lud's own fire, they did come!" Nalf swore as he joined Hans. "Half across the world to fight on our side!" The wild incredulity on Nalf's face changed to a roar of victory as the enemy force broke into disarray only to be hewn down on every side. Still in wonder, Nalf turned his gaze once more to the Dazunor hills from which help had come so unexpectedly. He grasped Hans by the arm. "Look!" He pointed.

Along the far ridge, well to the rear of the army on the field, rode a small group of men. In their midst could be seen four men on white horses. They carried the command banners of Sordan and its subject domains of Tollech and Ildurria. Floating beside them was the red and black royal banner of Ardaen, its golden ship blazing in the sun. Man by man, Hans's captains joined him to watch the colorful approach. More of Nalf's chieftains reined in, followed by Euden Mezeon, whose cavalry now pressed toward the city under leadership of his captains. Hans urged his steed ahead of his companions as the newcomers—several commanders and what appeared to be a noble in attendance—drew nigh and pulled to a prancing halt before him.

"Hello, Handurin!" Endelarin hailed from the most elaborately caparisoned horse Hans had ever seen. The Ardaenan king's brilliant purple garments, in keeping with the crimson and purple ribbons on his mount, stood out against the more somber armor and mail of the soldiers who accompanied him. Indeed, Endelarin clashed with the blue sky itself. "See what I brought? An army! Never say I did you no favors."

Hans laughed, as much from relief as anything else. Those with him, Kheld and Staubaun, merely looked amazed, both by the man and his proclamation. "This is Dorilian's army, Endelarin Nemenor." Hans grinned with an ease he would never have predicted several months ago, when he had been Endelarin's nervous companion at dinner in Sordan. "And I would wager my treasury that he sent it without any approval of yours."

"So it is, and so he did." Endelarin chuckled and turned a toothy and conspiratorial smile to the Sordani commander riding beside him. "A pity Prince Handurin is not colorblind—had he mistaken you and your men for Ardaenan, you would have owed me a daughter. Now instead I shall need an intercession with your Hierarch when he hears of our wager." With a regal sweep of his hand, Endelarin addressed Hans and indicated the other man. "Handurin Stauberg-Randolph, Prince of Dazunor and whatever else, I give you Pandaros Staubaun Vidyamemnon, Bas of Ildurria, General of Sordan's Second Eagle, and as noble a man as ever commanded an army. He's a third cousin to the Sordaneons."

Pandaros swept off his helmet, revealing the fully mature handsomeness of a man of his race. Above his long, straight nose, piercing and tawny eyes conveyed a solid intelligence and strength. "By the grace of my Thrice Royal Hierarch, Dorilian Sordaneon, I present to Your Royal Highness of Dazunor this army, which he has commanded be lent to your cause immediately."

Hans inclined his head slightly in acceptance. "Next time I see your Hierarch, I'll have to thank him. I pray it will be soon. Until then, I accept your assistance and that of your men in returning this land to its rightful rule." Hans indicated the field. "As you can see, you have already made an impact."

"What did I say?" Endelarin addressed Pandaros, who as he studied the field nodded agreement with Hans's assessment. "Young Handurin is well spoken and not one bit bad-tempered. Not like Stefan at all! And for some strange reason no one can fathom, he has taken a liking to your Hierarch."

Pandaros gave Hans a warmer look. "His Majesty of Ardaen seeks to put to rest any past reservations as to the wisdom of this alliance. I might have expressed how little I knew of the man upon whom it would fall to uphold my Hierarch's trust. Now that I have met you, I see I hesitated needlessly." With a bow of his head, Pandaros greeted the other commanders as Hans introduced them.

On the field below, Hans's army had met with the Sordani force and both armies now concentrated on slaying the remaining enemy. Some few of the latter had been captured, primarily by the Merrydn and Dannuthi troops. Neither the Khelds nor the Trongorians were showing quarter.

*They lost their families and friends.* Hans decided to let those troops finish what they had started. He had asked the Khelds to show restraint in other battles and they had honored his wishes. Now he honored theirs. *These Mormantalorans slaughtered entire villages, thousands of innocents, and they knew what they did. They would gladly carry their war into Amallar, kill me and my family. Even if I could find a way to provide for prisoners, I would not wish to spend precious resources on these.*

The battle had been clearly and swiftly won. Already troops had moved into position to secure the town. General Pandaros asked leave and rode with his officers to rejoin the main body of his troops. Hans nodded to each request as his captains also dispersed. Kerr rode off with his guard to join and congratulate Raphelon. The Trongorians were on the field and for their part the Khelds saw no lapse in protocol to leave the present King of Ardaen and the future King of Essera in conversation. Hans smiled when he saw he had no guards at all.

"I hope the war with Ardaen is officially over," he noted to Endelarin, "because if it isn't, you have a grand chance to get rid of *this* Esseran Prince!"

"Don't say that too loudly!" Endelarin looked about in alarm.

"There are some who would credit it!" Then he lifted an eyebrow. "If it is any consolation, I will point out that you are better armed."

Looking more closely, Hans saw that Endelarin wore no weapons. "Don't you at least wear a sword?"

Endelarin shook his head. "I know it's not kingly to say so, but I'm not good with swords. All but died of one, once, and swore off the things except for bestowing royal fripperies. I leave the swordplay to those who are skilled." He eyed Hans's weapon and how he wore it. "I see you've gotten better."

"Well, Dorilian trained me, and it paid off." Hans indicated the base camp being set up below. "Let's go down there. I want to stay on top of how my troops take control of the city." Together they rode down the hill. "If you don't wear weapons, how do you protect yourself, then? I mean, do you even have any guards?"

"Of course! I would be a poor excuse for a king without them. A full phalanx in fancy armor. But I left them in a village some ways back to keep them from even the hint of fighting. The last thing either of us wants is a charge that you have allied with Ardaen and Ardaenan troops helped you defeat Nammuor the Nihilistic—who, by the way, would be the first to mount just such an accusation. He dislikes that Ardaenan ships assist Sordan with controlling the Kolpos. No, my boy, no! I'm here on official business, would you believe it. I'm delivering important letters"—Endelarin patted the breast of his jacket, beneath which the missives surely lay—"and the ship I left behind in the village has a cargo I was told to deliver to you personally."

"Me?"

"A gift from Levyathan Sordaneon that he wants to be sure ends up with you and no one else. As I wanted to see how things were going here in the north, I volunteered my services."

"And let me guess: he accepted because you're family."

Endelarin chuckled. "Hardly. No, he did so because I'm bound by promises—Highborn ones! Not to mention I'm in a unique position to discuss wider issues. Ardaen is a participant in this war, though not formally. Our Queen has received and taken good advice about that. Even so, our aid to Trongor is steadfast and we are clear about our sovereign investment in the Kolpos. Because Nammuor yet hopes to keep our ships from disrupting his supply lines in the Northsea, he's being careful with us. Ardaen has yet to engage directly in Essera."

They reached the bottom of the hill. Hans's Kheld standard-bearer finally remembered his position and rejoined him, followed not long after by the first of the victorious captains. Euden Mezeon pulled his ivory horse to a halt before Hans and reported that Trulo was being cleared of any remaining enemies. Esseran troops would be the first to occupy the city. Hans saw a party of Khelds approaching, a cluster of dark horses led by one of shining gray. That sight, at least, made him smile—until he remembered that he had ordered Aubrey away from the battle. Endelarin turned to see what had brought about the change of expression and immediately perked.

"A lovely creature. If you don't want her—"

"Hands off, Endelarin," Hans said quickly. It was clear by now that Aubrey didn't have many rangers with her, but neither did she look like she was fleeing disaster.

Aubrey's hood flew back as she reined in before them. "Guess who wasn't in Trulo?" she asked before anyone else could speak. "Zel!"

"Zel!" Euden exclaimed in surprise.

"What do you mean, Zel?" Hans asked. "What about him?" They'd been operating under the assumption that the Mormantaloran general was with his army.

Aubrey patted her horse and smiled smugly as two more Kheld captains rode up. "My men and I caught him on the road. They and the Dog Men are bringing him in. And don't worry that I've forsaken my duty. Our wounded are so few, and our men so intent that none of the enemy survive the field, the healers have little to do. Fran is providing protection enough."

"I'm surprised he didn't capture Zel himself. His men are securing the Dazun Road."

"Zel wasn't trying to escape. He was trying to ride back this way along the road where I was. He and five men. They fought like mad dogs, but we took two alive. Zel and one of his captains." Aubrey frowned and looked puzzled. "The captain told Cortogh they were trying to get back into Trulo."

Two messengers rode up to join them, bringing reports of success from every part of the field. Only a small number of Mormantalorans, most thought to be officers and elite guards, had escaped into the hills west of Trulo.

"Zel could have fled into the hills with them—but he didn't," Hans wondered. "There's someone or something in the city that Zel wanted to get to." But what? Whatever it was had to be important, and more, important enough to risk everything. "Did the General have anything on him?"

Aubrey looked to Wodd, who had reined up beside her. "Caught him by surprise, we did, Hans Thegn, and took these off him quick. Put them in a dark bag, the Dog Man told us." Wodd held out a pouch of heavy, soiled leather. "He's down to skin and hair, that one, and still hissing like a cat because of it."

Hans took the pouch carefully. It was important Zel have nothing of sorcery on him. It was just as important to find out what those things were, even if doing so was a dangerous task. Swinging down from his horse, Hans went to the wreck of what had been a Mormantaloran war machine and pulled loose a block of wood. Taking a cloak one of the Khelds fetched for him from a fallen soldier, Hans covered the block, then signaled everyone to stand back. Slowly and with great care, he emptied the contents of the sack onto the cloak. Several jeweled objects tumbled forth to glitter in the sun: a dagger with a gem-studded grip, Zel's golden helmpiece with its yellow crystal ablaze, bracelets encrusted with semiprecious stones in the shape of snakes with vivid scales, and a ring with a ruby the size of an eagle's eye.

While Endelarin hung back and looked on with concern, others approached. Euden Mezeon dismounted and stepped forward.

"Take care, Sire. These objects may be traps or *lr* weapons. If you would allow me to examine them—"

Hans saw the wisdom in that. Euden had been among the first to identify the deadly crystal back in Rainill. "What experience do you have with such things?"

"*Lr* crystals? I possess only knowledge that is common to those born into noble rank. Our educations do not include the use of them; only Epoptes do so. But I can tell you that this"—Euden flicked the large yellow jewel in the helmpiece—"is not one."

"You can tell just by looking?"

"It takes a practiced eye, but Merrydn's treasury holds many *lr* devices, to which our Prince gave our teachers access," Euden confided as Hans along with Aubrey and Wodd gave him their full attention. "Among these is Merrydn's Crown, a powerful enhancer with many *lr* crystals. See this setting? It's entirely wrong for a *real* mage crystal. It has no way to tap the energy. This setting is strictly ornamental, with barely the pretense of a psi-interface." He held it up to his forehead so they could see the effect.

"It just looks like an enhancer," Hans concluded, beginning to understand.

Euden nodded. "It would seem Zel let people *think* it was a *lr* crystal, especially his officers and his troops. In that way he convinced them that their every move was being watched."

An effective way to keep an army in line. Hans could imagine Zel standing as his troops paraded past, each man seeing the flashing yellow jewel on his brow. They would think Nammuor himself reviewed them and would blast with lightning any that opposed his will. Probably it had happened, while Zel was wearing a real crystal, setting the example. But this crystal was false, had always been false. Now that Hans also looked closely, he could see that what Euden said was true: the setting looked nothing like the one Aedes Kopelates had worn when he had spied on and attempted to assassinate the Esseran leadership at Rainill.

"So *this* is just a gaudy headpiece, as are these." Euden dismissed the helm by placing it aside, along with the dagger and bracelets. "Snakes are the heraldic symbol of Orm, which is where Zel is from, and as you can see again there are no settings. But this"—Euden plucked a long pin from the fur trim of his heraldry-embroidered cape and picked the ring from the other items, lifting it and holding it before Hans—"could be something."

"What?"

Euden allowed a grim smile. "Trulo has a communications array."

Grinning that he understood, Hans held out the pouch, snapping it closed only after Euden had deposited the ring. "Bring along these other things," Hans said to Wodd, who took the bag in hand. To Aubrey, Hans added, "This battle isn't lost yet, as far as Nammuor knows. And I think we have to be very careful about how we tell him the news."

"You need to do something about Zel." Raphelon confronted Hans as they walked along the colonnade overlooking the river. The battle was over, the city won. Hans could now get down to figuring out what to do with it.

Trulo's Golden Palace sprawled behind the colonnade, its classic angles and open porticos crowning the city with a lofty majesty famed throughout Essera. Relieved by the arrival of Sordan's Second army, Raphelon's Serrain troops, along with Kerr's five hundred Dannuthians, had been the first to enter the town once it surrendered. With the Mormantalorans guarding the Serat having long since fled, the troops concentrated on securing the grounds and buildings of the former headquarters. Despite widespread fear instilled by the departing occupiers that Khelds would soon be running through the town to loot and kill, many of the palace servants had remained behind to get the royal dwelling running again. Word of Handurin's clemency toward those towns and peoples who surrendered to him had been whispered even behind the backs of the Mormantaloran high command.

Raphelon continued to argue Zel's fate. "The Khelds are crying for his blood. If it were not for their fear of the Dog Men guarding the man, they would have already torn him limb from limb."

"He deserves it." Hans had no trouble conjuring mental images of the thousand corpses, most of them Kheld, lining the road from Rainill to Omadawn.

"That may be." Raphelon was clearly trying to be sensitive to Hans's deep loyalty to his Kheld kin and forces. "Even so, it would be impolitic for him to die like an animal. It matters not that he killed other people like beasts. Listen to me"—Raphelon hastened to explain—"the manner of his death will reflect on you, not him."

*In Staubaun eyes.* Hans recognized the underlying truth of Raphelon's plea. *How Zel dies will tell Staubauns how I will deal with them. The Khelds will care less about the mechanics of his death, so long as he dies. Zel's death will speak loudest to the Staubauns. And to Nammuor, loudest of all.*

Hans had met Zel just minutes earlier, prior to having him hauled away to a cell for safekeeping. In that moment, Hans had known that he would kill him.

He had seen this man's face before.

"Prince Handurin!" One of the Trongorians raced along the walkway on which they stood. The walkway looked out over the frosty Dazun, at misty Amallar and the small boats that dared the river by celebrating the victory. "We found the array. It's in a locked room in a tower attached to nowhere else. Captain Farrl sent us to tell you!"

Nodding briskly to the man, Hans sent him on yet another errand. "Find Euden Mezeon," Hans directed as he and Raphelon set off to learn what the searchers had found. "And clear the people from that part of the palace until we know what this device will do."

"*Lr* relays used to be more common, located in every Highborn domain," Pandaros Vidyamemnon told Hans just before Euden Mezeon arrived, completing the group that would examine the tower. Sordan and Merath, and Raphelon for Serrain, along with Arne and Aubrey for the Khelds. Hans wanted every faction included in important discoveries or decisions. Prominently positioned at the center of the small, circular room it occupied, the relay device rested upon an intricately wrought stand of gleaming greenish metal. Everything about it looked strange but for the familiar golden tint of the crystals embedded in its mysteriously configured base. "Sordan destroyed its array—and three others— the day our Hierarch was taken hostage and your grandfather became King. And the one in Gignastha was destroyed by its Prince when Khelds took the city."

Hans met Arne's cautionary gaze, warning that being reminded about Gignastha never sat well. Sure enough, Euden looked uncomfortable, so Hans pushed past that. "But this one remains."

"As do others in Essera," Euden confirmed. "Stauberg. Merath. Kenelm. Dazunor-Rannuli."

"Aral?"

Euden nodded.

Hans wished he knew more about this hidden means of communications. Aryati devices made him more nervous than they did his comrades, perhaps because he had more idea of what they might be capable of doing. "Tell me how these things work. What do they do?"

"They are located in Highborn palaces and were until recently used only by the Highborn. They sent important messages... news... secret orders." Euden frowned when Aubrey knelt to study the underside of the device. Not one to be excluded from anything Hans might want included in notes, Aubrey now insisted on seeing the array for herself. "I have never used one, personally. My Prince did so, and now my Princess, most often as a task given to secretaries trained by the Brotherhood of Epoptes. One doesn't need to be Highborn to operate an array. The devices send messages by way of cylinders—like this one." Looking about, Euden found a cabinet and located an example, which he picked up without hesitation and handed to Hans.

Hans took the metallic object. It appeared to be made of brass and had a familiar shape. "It looks like the message cylinders we use for coded communications."

"Patterned after these. But you will notice these cylinders are more sophisticated. Plain housings but with keyed bases for designating destinations."

Tipping the object to look at the ends more closely, Hans saw the pattern to which Euden referred. Flat gemstones, bracketed by metallic geometric shapes that could be turned to any number of configurations. Hans's hand wrapped easily around the thing, which had surprisingly little weight. "I wonder where this one goes to."

"Stauberg, I would say. Possibly Dazunor-Rannuli or Aral," ventured Raphelon. His face looked grave. "Stauberg has a full array of such devices. They conveyed the King's word through the Triempery. Stefan used them through a keyed ring. Erenor would have that now, and last year he gave Nammuor run of that city."

And its wealth of devices once controlled by the Highborn Malyrdeons. Hans sighed. He knew what that meant. "Now we know how he's been receiving news about me. I bet the array in Dazunor-Rannuli is controlled by the Seven Houses, at least since the Malyrdeons died. Sinon suggested the Epoptes might control it, but maybe it was never in their hands." Hans regarded the device anew. "Can Nammuor take the Stauberg array with him if he leaves or gets driven out?"

"I don't see how. The *lr* crystals in an array are absolutely site specific; it is part of how they work," Euden explained. "Once the crystals are set, arrays cannot be moved, but they can be rigged with reflectors, bounce things elsewhere."

"Like Bynum?" Hans asked. "Could we use it to communicate with our allies in the Royal North?"

Euden grimaced. "Possibly, though I do not know for certain."

"And are there any dangers? To using it?"

"Few, if used correctly. Perhaps we can find a secretary who has not yet fled." Euden sighed deeply. "There is some risk that the *lr* energy of the crystals could be reversed by a malfunction—or an adept, as we saw at Rainill. If that were to happen, the destruction would be considerable. It would be a shame to dismantle it. This array would be useful once Nammuor is no longer about!"

Raphelon looked aghast that Euden would even suggest destroying the priceless artifact.

Hans put that fear to rest. "I think we can just cordon off this part of the palace and resign ourselves to the possibility of losing it. Chances are good right now that Nammuor doesn't even know we might have it. But we don't know what Nammuor will do once he does know. He might send a *lr* weapon through or reverse the energy or some other destructive thing—unless he knows we know how to use the array and could send it right back. Any message he might send would be just lies and treachery."

Hans turned to Arne. "Fran's just outside, right? With the guard?" When Arne nodded, Hans said, "Bring him in."

Witnesses matter when princes flex their muscles. For flexing his muscles Hans chose witnesses who would attest to his fairness. Pandaros, who would talk with Dorilian. Arne and Aubrey for the Khelds. Euden and Raphelon would let the Esseran allies know what happened here.

But Fran Gorseddson wasn't there either for the Khelds or to be a witness. Hans wanted him for something else. He looked Fran in the eye.

"If I have Zel brought in here, will you do whatever I ask?"

"As long as it involves killing him."

Taking Fran aside, to a table still strewn with battle plans and the remains of a meal that had never been finished, Hans made evident what he wanted. He then sent Euden to bring in the prisoner. Hans also sent those of his guard who had stayed outside the room to see that the north wing of the palace be evacuated.

"With all respect, my Prince—what's that about?" Raphelon demanded. "If you mean to do what I think—"

But Hans shook his head and signaled for him and the other Staubaun leaders to continue their trust in him. "This is yet Nammuor's game," he said to Raphelon for all to hear, "and I'm playing it."

Minutes later, Zel stood before them, wearing plain but clean clothing and accompanied by Euden Mezeon. Euden had seen to Zel's safety after removing him from custody of the Dog Men, and Zel showed no fear for his life. With the pride of a man who did not yet fully acknowledge his defeat, he refused to kneel and fought to remain standing.

"Let him stand," Hans said, his memory hard edged and certain. *Dorilian was standing when this man leered into his eyes.*

"Prince Handurin," Zel acknowledged. He used inflections that conveyed his derision. "Now that I have seen you, I will own that at least one rumor is true: you are a pretty boy."

Fran would have slain the man on the spot, except that Hans stayed that impulse with a halting wave of his hand. He wanted Zel alive—for now. Hans wanted to look into those eyes and see what would look back at him. "Do you remember," he asked, "how you killed Marc Frederick? The Highborn Princes? The Kheld leaders? You and Nammuor and two other men?"

Zel stiffened and went silent. Hans knew why. Even those who spoke loudest that Nammuor had done those murders had never said anything about there being companions to the deed. Dorilian himself might not know the names of the men who had nearly slain him that day.

"You're mad!" Zel looked around at the faces of those with him in the room, all hating him but listening, stunned, to what they were hearing.

Hans stared into those dark, cold eyes. He had wanted to be sure, and now he was. The same eyes. The same indifferent hatred. The same thin white scar above Zel's lip. Hans had seen these proofs through other eyes, but he had seen them. "Am I? Then prove yourself. Tell them how you got the scar across your belly."

Zel stiffened and struggled as first Arne and then Euden, on Hans's signal, laid hold of Zel's arms and held him so that Fran could pull open his garments. The scar was there as Hans had known it would be, carved straight as a sword blade across the pale skin.

"I got that in battle." Zel's dark eyes took on a staring, hunted look. The others gathered in the room seemed to have become statues, so still were they standing.

"Oh, it was a battle. A battle to the death. A battle of sorcery and steel. Do you remember what you did that day to the man who gave you that wound?"

Zel's breathing was uneven now, but he lifted his head defiantly. "I wasn't there!" he snarled. "Neither were you!"

Relinquishing the defiant Zel, Hans said to his startled onlookers, "I'm going to send Nammuor a message. You won't understand the meaning of it, but he will. Beside the table!" he directed Arne and Euden.

"Handurin, no!" Raphelon protested, but he found Pandaros blocking him and Aubrey's hand upon his arm. To Raphelon's agonized stare, Aubrey shook her head, telling him not to leap to conclusions. Hans was not about to take this man's life.

"Sordan put him up to this!" Zel screamed to anyone who would listen. "Don't you see? The damned Sordaneon filled his ears with lies!" It took both Arne and Euden to hold Zel as Fran Gorseddson jammed the Mormantaloran general's hand up against the table, two fingers above, the thumb and others below. "I didn't kill your fucking King! Stop! Handurin, I didn't do it. If you know anything, you know that—"

"I do know. I know that Nammuor killed them all. He and his sister who poisoned the wine. But you did torture someone: the only man to survive it."

White-lipped, Zel's round wild gaze locked on Hans's.

"You cut off his fingers." Closing his ears to Zel's shouts and struggles, Hans turned to Fran, who stood by with his sword already drawn. "Do it."

Zel's scream punctuated the sound of Fran's sword biting into the wood of the table, neatly severing both fingers.

Hand still on Raphelon's arm, Aubrey blinked, then swallowed. Though Arne released Zel, now keening in pain and fallen to his knees, he looked up with new understanding. Hans had told Arne that Dorilian had lost two fingers to a sword blow. And Hans had just gotten Zel to admit to being at the Demise, to being part of those murders. Zel hadn't denied what Hans said about who had killed Marc Frederick and the Highborn Princes, or the Kheld leaders.

Zel hunched on his knees beside the table, clutching his bleeding hand, his face white with pain and memories of deeds he had thought forever behind him. When Hans came to stand over him, Zel looked up again at the Prince who had gotten both confession and retribution from him. He no longer hoped for his life. Dorilian Sordaneon had healed from his mutilation. Zel would have no need.

"Send these to your Master," Hans directed Zel. Between his thumb and forefinger, gold against a square of blue velvet cloth, he held the ruby ring taken from Zel earlier. Hans extended it. "Do it and I promise you a quicker death. If you don't, I will still find a way to send them, but first I will turn you over to the Khelds. They've been sharpening a stake for you and I won't stop them from using it."

Zel placed his severed fingers in a cylinder, rotated the base rings, and set it on the tray. He then used the setting in the ruby ring to activate the crystal array. Light blazed about the rim of the tray, encircling the contents, then ascended. Whatever had been on the tray was gone. Hans didn't doubt that the cylinder with Zel's fingers had gone to Stauberg—and Nammuor. Zel would want his master to know his fate.

"Cordon off this wing of the palace, quickly." Hans directed Pandaros to that task. He indicated that Euden and the others, and especially white-faced Raphelon, should accompany him as witnesses to what happened next. Of all the tales that would fly from this day, none would say that the Khelds had slaughtered Salkren Zel. With Fran and Arne dragging Zel, they made for the Summer Wing in its isolated location overlooking the river. There, on the snow in front of the royal residence, Hans handed a sword to the man who stood ready to pay the price of his defeat.

"I give you a soldier's death, Zel—not because you deserve it, but because I would not burden my people with the death they would give you."

"How did you know?" After taking the sword, Zel acknowledged Hans, gaze and words both asking a question to which he still wanted an answer. "Dorilian Sordaneon went mad. He never speaks about it. He may not even remember."

Hans mouthed the answer: "I was there."

But the question lingered in Zel's eyes even after he had driven the sword into his own heart.

# 40



Robdan noticed that the sky had brightened by the time they arrived at the crossroads, though clouds still canopied above with an insincere threat of snow. A light dusting already powdered the valley floor, far below blue-shadowed mountains standing like teeth to the north. The road from Bynum wound in a dark ribbon toward the Wall city and its outlying towns. Even at this distance, the Wall loomed white and tall with its own announcement of invincibility. What amazed Robdan most was seeing the legendary battlements in motion. Ethereal components silently tumbled and slid as the Wall's massive planes and angles rearranged.

"The city itself is warmer"—Bas Hebron pulled his collar more closely about his neck against the cold lash of the wind—"and less windy." His laconic lift of an eyebrow suggested that, to him, the Wall was an ordinary sight. "The Wall moderates even the wind off the sea."

The sea! Robdan stood in his stirrups as much as he dared and gazed at the indistinct horizon. To look upon the fabled waters of the salt sea! Old Tobold and Cedrec had boasted of that.

Dorilian noticed the way Robdan craned for a glimpse of water and laughed. "You won't see it yet, Master Aelfricson. Stauberg is built on cliffs above the coast."

"Cliffs? But... how can it have a harbor, then?" Robdan had seen drawings in his books.

Hebron snorted in derision and gave a knowing look to Legon, who also rode with them. The rest of their escort, a full company of the Eagle Guard, remained within view but well behind their Hierarch. "The city sits above a natural harbor more than well suited to that function. There is not a better ship haven in Essera. Stauberg's harbor is large enough for a thousand ships, in keeping with the local tides."

Robdan surrendered to perplexity. "Tides?"

"Next he shall need me to explain to him the moon." Hebron smirked.

"Nothing a book cannot explain better," Dorilian reasoned. "He can procure one in Stauberg. The Royal Library must surely have a hundred volumes on the subject."

"No doubt it does, Thrice Royal."

They faced the city in silence, seemingly in wait. Soon Robdan saw why: the approach of five horses with riders. The Wall, dwarfing them, shifted into new shape at their backs. Robdan swallowed and sat straighter in the saddle. Other than having seen the emissary who had brought the offer of parley to the Hierarch, Robdan had not encountered the enemy directly. Even his horse had fled from the possibility. Now, as he waited, shivering and cold on his small horse, he began to understand that the form the enemy would take would be a known one.

Horses approached: three black as night, draped with crimson saddlecloths; two of snowiest ivory arrayed with the bright blue of Esseran royalty; all large-boned and swift. Three of the riders wore rich garments of gold and crimson under winter garb of luxurious furs, and two wore gold helms. The other went bareheaded. The remainder, upon the ivory horses, wore Stauberg colors. One rode sideways in the saddle and was proclaimed by her skirt to be a woman. By the time these approaching riders drew within hailing distance, Robdan recognized the man and knew who the woman must be.

But for the harried, ambitious look on his face, Erenor Staubaun Tholeros might have been considered handsome. He wore his aristocratic breeding in full measure—fair-haired, brown-eyed, with the tall, straight body so often seen in Staubaun men. Vivid blue and gold clothing visually affirmed his assumption of the ruling Stauberg name and titles. Though Erenor's claim of having Highborn ancestors was spurious, his coat and standards incorporated the star and crown of the Malyrdeons, and upon his head he wore a gleaming crown of gold set with crystals bright as stars and bearing a single blue gem. Robdan had last seen the crown on Stefan's head and knew it to be the Stauberg Coronal. Ergeiron's Crown. Yet even that sight did not arouse as much anger and offense as seeing the woman who rode at Erenor's side, her horse's reins gripped in his hand.

Palaistea Lacenedonea é Malyrdeonis had been beautiful. What looked back at them from within the hood of the heavy winter cloak was not. The face that had enchanted a generation was now a mass of ridges and scars and the hands clasping the saddle horn were but mitts, tiny and fingerless. Though she clearly lived, the fire that had destroyed the Danae Palace had all but destroyed Palaistea as well.

Erenor broke the silence first, raising his right arm and solemnly speaking with the distinctive tenor that had always made listening to him in the Archhalia a pleasure.

"Hail, Dorilian Sordaneon, Thrice Royal Hierarch of Sordan!"

Dorilian guided his horse forward a few paces to acknowledge the salute. "Congratulations, Erenor Tholeros, Usurper." Disdain hardened his tone. "I particularly admire the headpiece—I have one much like it at home."

The bareheaded Mormantaloran smiled.

Erenor's eyelids narrowed with displeasure at the insult. "You are in simple form today, Thrice Royal. You might be mistaken for a commoner. I expected more pomp — perhaps Derlon's Armor of which we have heard so much, or even the Sordan Coronal to remind us of *your* godborn blood."

"I have no need of signifiers, as evidenced by your greeting." Dorilian shifted his attention to the woman at Erenor's side. "I believe the terms for this meeting were that Princess Palaistea be released to us."

The Princess raised her hooded head, her open eye bright with apprehension. Though the orb surrounding it was dark and scarred, that eye shone clear gold, a coin without tarnish.

"Are you certain this is she, Thrice Royal?" Hebron asked in a lowered voice, his suspicions attuned to deception. "Her appearance is much... changed."

"Yes, I am sure." Dorilian intensified his study of Erenor's captive. "Princess, taking custody of your person is the condition upon which I agreed to meet with these men. Will you come with us in completion of that condition?"

Palaistea nudged her horse forward, only for Erenor to tighten his hand on the reins, holding it back. The captive's swaddled form bobbled, then caught her balance. Someone in the Sordan and Lacenedon ranks swore. Palaistea's intent had been clear and Dorilian's expression was not the only one to darken.

"The promised meeting has not yet taken place," Erenor pointed out. Pale daylight gleamed on the polished buttons of his jacket and across the elaborate harnesses of the horses. Erenor's cold smile proclaimed his advantage.

"You craven lackey," Dorilian said. "My promise once given will not be broken. Your game insults us—the stakes are not so high that we need play." Dorilian raised his hand, signaling the troops behind him that the meeting was no longer considered friendly. He began to turn his horse.

"Hold!" The bareheaded Mormantaloran spoke. "Let her go!"

Erenor blanched. Robdan marked anger and, more surprising, fear. But Erenor threw down the reins. At once, Palaistea urged her horse forward again. To be certain of the beast, for Palaistea did not have hold of the reins or any way to control it, Hebron rode forward to meet her and took the horse in hand, leading it back with him as he rejoined his comrades. Taking no chance that Erenor or his party might change their minds, Hebron immediately signaled the Eleutheron lord Megall forward, so that he might take Palaistea back to the waiting troops. Robdan noted that Legon didn't even glance at what Hebron or the others did. The hawk-eyed commander of Dorilian's bodyguard kept his attention only on his Hierarch and the men facing him. Dorilian, too, though he had signaled his men on the ridge behind them to wait, never took his gaze from Erenor's party, having fixed on the person of the Mormantaloran who had spoken.

"Nammuor."

The man who had smiled earlier lifted his pale head in answer and Robdan felt a chill that penetrated to his soul. Nammuor was a man in body, tall and slender but loosely built beneath his heavy winter garb, with a laziness of form suggesting that he had lost the need and even the reflex for decisive movement. His skin, almost as white as his hair, gleamed pale across strong bones, and his eyes, black and penetrating, possessed depths that spoke of centuries rather than the middle years attested to by his appearance. Two things kept his face from classic perfection—a golden jewel the size of a man's thumb-tip, ringed by raised and puckered tissue above his left eye, and a thin white scar running from right eyebrow to left jaw, disfiguring his long and slightly aquiline nose.

As Nammuor rested his gaze upon Dorilian, his full mouth flitted with acknowledgments.

"Hail, Sordaneon. I'm surprised to see you without your current lapdog. Where is young Handurin these days?"

"You're the sorcerer. You tell me."

"Safely out of the way, I assume. Mine and yours."

"Yes."

"You don't trust me to play fair." Nammuor absently patted his mount's smooth black neck. He used the left hand. Any who looked could see that it was missing the third finger. "I wouldn't take advantage of the boy. He has nothing I want. Not yet, that is."

"You qualify your statement well."

"Let me revise the statement: he has *one* thing I want." A flash of displeasure burned in Nammuor's pitch-black eyes. "My sister's murderer."

"You're the only true murderer here. I but thwarted a thief."

"You cut off her head."

"That must have been disappointing when she fled to you, to get only her head and not the parts that carried my Heir."

Robdan turned to see if Legon or Hebron was as stunned as he by the accusation—and the cold delivery of its answer. Neither man looked surprised. Rumor that Dorilian had slain his wife was both widespread and oddly intangible. A deed nearly forgotten.

Nammour's eyes narrowed. "Your Heir and mine also. Does the boy even know that?"

Dorilian scowled and pulled his ivory horse a few steps aside. "You clearly have nothing useful to say to me."

"You agreed to parley."

"Then parley and cease these useless inquiries that I shall not answer."

Nammuor cocked his head, eyes narrowing. "How confident you are. You and your web of petty alliances armed with naught but Highborn pride. But even you cannot hope to take Stauberg! No mere man can surmount Ergeiron's Wall."

"The Wall is Immortal. Its defenders are not."

"You never were a fool so don't play one now. The city is impregnable. You throw yourself against it needlessly. Your losses will be heavy, Dorilian."

"Against the Wall... I estimate as much as a third of my forces," Dorilian admitted. Neither Hebron nor Legon blinked at that assessment, but Robdan, who had not thought of Stauberg in terms of the numbers of men that might die in taking it, struggled to keep his dismay from showing.

Nammuor laughed. "Only a third? Better to say half. Or maybe all. And your own life not the least of them, my dear Sordaneon. Although," a devouring smile curved Nammuor's mouth, "I have already ordered to have your life very carefully preserved."

Robdan noticed how Dorilian's skin paled, though he answered easily. "I will never fall into your hands. And I don't intend to preserve your life should you fall into mine. Nor Erenor's either. Nor any who fight with you, however noble their names. I don't believe in leaving alive those who would take up sword against me."

"Then do as you see fit. But know that you stand to lose this battle along with all your misplaced hopes. Or have you, of all people, forgotten the powers at my disposal?"

Though others froze at those words, Dorilian scoffed. "You're bluffing," he said. "I know you won't use your wretched device. You don't even have it with you. This crossroad is safely within the Wall's presence or I would not have agreed to meet you here."

Nammuor's dark eyes narrowed shrewdly in appraisal. "Very well, I have an offer for you."

"Speak it."

"Handurin wants Stauberg. I will give him the city."

"No!" Erenor's harsh cry broke the frozen stillness of the empty plain. "You cannot do that! Stauberg is mine!"

Nammuor bestowed upon Erenor a glance thick with disdain. "Stauberg is *mine*. I but let you pretend it is yours. Don't make me regret my indulgence. Surely even you can see that our Sordaneon presents an opportunity. I am a reasonable man, Dorilian," Nammuor continued, returning his attention to the man before him. "And I respect you in ways you have yet to appreciate. I am sure we can come to an agreement that will satisfy every Lord and Kheld in Essera. I am willing to give Stauberg to Handurin, acknowledge him as King of this land. I will even agree this day to withdraw my forces from Essera as a sign of my honorable intentions. Don't you think that is a reasonable offer?"

"Surface sparkle. I think I've heard but half of it."

Nammuor spread his red-sleeved arms magnanimously. "But I would do so! Forswear everything north of the Randpor. And I would ask but a small proof of Handurin's good faith, a very small gesture for so great a Kheldish King. One hostage."

Dorilian played along. "Only one? How unexpectedly generous. Who did you have in mind?" He and every man in his company already knew the answer.

"You."

"And predictable too."

Nammuor's laugh barely frosted the air. "You wouldn't be coming cheap. What a splendid price! Imagine, one man ransoming Stauberg—indeed, all of Essera! Frankly, I don't think Handurin is worth it."

"Neither do I."

"Yet you intend to spend thousands of lives to capture this same city for him, for Stefan's even more callow brother?"

"I do. He is worth *their* lives."

Hebron exchanged glances then with Legon and Robdan, pondering that answer and its possible implications.

"What a cold man you have become. You are harder than when we last met. It is almost becoming on you." Something in Nammuor's voice dripped like honey, warm and superficially sincere. Robdan found himself lulled by it, but also aware of what it tried to do.

When Legon and Hebron, sensing something amiss, moved to ride nearer, Dorilian signaled them to stay where they were.

Nammuor frowned petulantly. "Why do you distrust me so?" His expression grew wistful in the smooth pale light. "I honor your blood as others do not. I promise you will not be mistreated. You will be provided every comfort, every luxury—"

"Every torment your twisted mind can conceive. Come, Nammuor, we are not strangers."

"So, you fear me after all."

That truth forced a thin smile of admission. "I would be a fool not to recognize your viciousness. None know better than I what you are capable of. Yet I am such that you cannot beguile me as you can the weak-minded fools who follow you or poor misbegotten Stefan and his hunting party. Haven't you noticed that things assume their true shapes around me? You cannot rearrange molecules and persuade me that you can heal. Neither can you mislead any who stand near to me. Is this the first time Erenor has seen your disfigurements? Or Palaistea's? So leave aside these persuasions and attend the matter, or else consider this parley done and depart."

"What I have to say, I will say only to you."

Looking disgusted, Dorilian shook his head. Robdan heard a muffled under-breath curse.

Nammuor persisted. "Let me come forward to speak to you alone."

Legon tossed aside obedience and kneed his horse forward. "Don't do it," he warned. He looked as afraid as Robdan had ever seen him.

With a sigh, Dorilian lifted his head and looked past Nammuor's company, to where the Wall lifted its white shape over the heads of Erenor and the other three men.

"Move your men back, and I will move mine," Dorilian told Nammuor. "We will talk right here."

Robdan withdrew with Hebron and Legon a full ten horse lengths to where the Hierarch's guard waited. Even the soldiers' mounts were restive, their harnesses clinking in the crisp winter air.

"Why is he humoring that monster?" Hebron demanded between tightly clenched teeth. He tugged at his gloves, and Robdan thought he wished more to draw his blade.

"It helps to be close to something if you want to take its temperature. If he is correct about the Wall's protection, then Nammuor cannot use his device or work sorcery here," Legon answered.

"But what if he's *wrong*?"

Something grim hardened Legon's lips. None of them wished to find out the consequences if that were the case. "Why do you think he did not wear the Armor today? There are twenty archers behind us trained to take down a target at twice this distance. Their arrows are tipped with spring-loaded heads that expand upon impact, releasing a chemical that will cause his blood to clot almost instantly. If it even so much as looks like Nammuor can take him, our orders are to kill Dorilian first."

Ten years had not erased their last meeting. It seemed to Dorilian that the smoking ruin of Permephedon's Arcana still crackled and smoldered to every side of this windswept, winter-bound land. Sordan and the Rill were unreachable, and he heard not the wind but the silent screams of his dying kindred. All that was missing was Nammuor's foul, blood-drinking crown.

Though the Diadem of the Devaryati was not present, the thing still looked back at Dorilian through Nammuor's not wholly human gaze. By looking into the eyes of the host Dorilian glimpsed the parasite, and by listening to Nammuor's taunts and gloats he discerned the working of its mind. Though it was fascinating to watch, it was also horrifying.

Tilting his head, Nammuor eyed Dorilian with barely concealed hatred. "Why are you doing it? Why have you left the safety of Sordan and the Rill behind to put yourself in my path? Are you really that arrogant?"

"Not at all. Not about this."

"But why? For Essera? You hate this land and its people. You hate them rightly! When I say I want your blood, they offer to help! This degenerate populace sold itself long ago for far less than it will cost you to free them." Nammuor snorted, puffs of air rising white from his nostrils. "And what is this Handurin to you? Marc Frederick's grandson? A ghost, a shadow, maybe even a hope—but he is *not* Marc Frederick. Even Marenthro cannot remake that dead King."

*Damn him.* Nammuor aimed for the heart. Dorilian battled laden memories. Now was not the time to remember Marc.

Nammuor did not miss the wince. "How pathetic you are. He used you the way they all want to use you, gifting you with robes of fantasies you yearn to believe. And now you have tied yourself to yet another of his grandsons who will only betray you in the end." Now it was Nammuor's turn to taunt. "Everyone sees it but you. Once Handurin has Essera and his Kingship is secure, he will heed what his Khelds say of you, that you killed his grandfather at Permephedon, his brother at Aral. That you conspire against him and will kill him next. Who around him will not speak against you? If I were to approach him, he might be tempted to take the price I offer and sell you to me."

It was a good thing Dorilian had mastered that fear. He had confronted it by turns in Sordan, at Rhondda, and finally in Amallar. He trusted damn few people with his life, but Handurin, Dorilian realized with fleeting surprise, was one of them.

A blood-red ruby flashed on Nammuor's finger as he

unconsciously lifted it to his cheek and traced the thin line of his disfigurement. "You will plague me to the end. I curse the day I gave my sister to your wretched family."

"So do I, because I've damned you every hour since that day."

"That's where it started, isn't it? You have always resisted my attempts to rule you—any attempt, by anyone. Well, I value you all the more for it. Handurin has no reward to equal your worth. Leave him. I would have you away from his defeat, if only because it will be swifter and more final with you gone. In return for that cooperation, I will bequeath Sordan to you for your domain—an independent Kingdom, a free nation, an empire of its own that you may govern as you see fit, without interference. I will ask no tribute, take no hostages, make no war, nor will I place restrictions on your alliances, be they trade or sovereign. You will be autonomous, allied with Mormantalorus and the new Kingdom to be created in Essera and ruled by *our* Heir—a Triempery such as this World has never seen. A true Triempery of Staubaun peoples. I am prepared to negotiate a treaty to that effect which would bind me more absolutely than death binds the living, sworn upon the very power I employ to be turned against me if I prove false. You know it can be done." Nammuor moved his horse nearer. "Do I interest you now?"

Dorilian sensed the threads of Nammuor's intent. Behind that scarred visage, scarred by Dorilian and forever warped where he was concerned, he glimpsed what went unspoken. Lies upon lies, the heart of the game they played—and the soul of perversion. Nammuor knew Dorilian would be interested in none of these things. Yet Nammuor moved about him like a master about a game board, pondering the next move. Touching this piece, touching that, only to seize at the last moment the piece he meant to capture.

"Are you enjoying your game?" Dorilian did not need to read Nammuor's mind to know that it was time to go. "I would sooner see Sordan fall, the Rill silenced forever, and myself dead on Stauberg's icy field than any fate you would prescribe!"

"My dear Dorilian, you have no choice!" Nammuor leaned over and grasped the reins of Dorilian's horse to prevent his leaving. "You have no fate, no future! I don't want you dead—far from it! Your life is more precious to me than you can imagine. What I don't understand is why you are throwing yourself away on a half-Kheld Prince to a lost Triempery. But I will destroy your plans at Stauberg and let the fields run red with blood if that is what it will take to finally break you. And whatever the outcome of this battle, I shall see your Kheldish Prince destroyed as well, just as I saw to it that Marc Frederick and the rest of the bastard Stauberg-Randolphs met their fates at my hand."

"I will oppose you in that as well."

Laughter, disdainful and cruel, greeted that answer. "And why should you do that when you stand to gain a throne with him dead? It seems you require me to kill him for you." Nammuor waited for a reply that was not forthcoming, and his expression grew cold again. "No matter, our hour is at hand. By whatever gods, your life will be mine!"

Nammuor's gaze burned red now, his face pale with a light not of the World alone. Other light surrounded them, other energies not manifested ordinarily in the World. Dorilian realized what Nammuor was trying to do, sensed the vortex striving to take shape but being distorted by the Wall's shield of countering forces. The vortex dissipated and was not attempted again.

The horses, alarmed by the shifting energies around them, pranced in place, but Nammuor held fast. "You have become a magnificent creature. Highborn blood in all its glory, Rill Lord and Hierarch and protected by your Entities, every inch the Leur Prince you were born to be," Nammuor admitted. "Who would have guessed? It was my mistake to have let you escape me at Permephedon. I have paid dearly for that error, and I will not let it happen again. Next time, I will not be gentle."

Nammuor's black eyes fixed on Dorilian like a predator's, beckoning the unwary things of the world. Dorilian had seen that look before. He jerked the reins away but not quickly enough to prevent Nammuor from grabbing his wrist. Suddenly there was fear, blinding terror crawled out of the gutters of a haunted past as Nammuor pulled the arm to full extension and pressed his mouth to the exposed flesh at Dorilian's wrist. Every muscle knotted in revulsion at that moist contact as Nammuor made a soft noise in his throat and sank his teeth to the bone, biting hard and deep before Dorilian could wrench his arm back. Nammuor laughed, wearing a triumphant smile red with Dorilian's blood. Dorilian stared at his bloodied wrist in horror.

"That's what I want from you," Nammuor delighted. "Yours and the boy's. And then, truly, Leur's Creation will know its doom!"

Nammuor wheeled his black horse into a gallop back toward the distant city, the rest of his parleying party following. Only

Erenor looked back, to deliver a mocking salute before spurring to catch up to his swift-riding companions.

Alone and cold, sickened by a confrontation he should have declined, Dorilian slumped in his saddle, trembling against the warm neck of his horse, clutching its harness to keep himself from falling. Knowing that others watched him and would be alarmed, he forced his torso upright. Drawing deep breaths of icy air helped. Disturbed stones clicked alongside him and he pulled back from the roiling dissonance of his body to see Legon and the Kheld, Robdan, had joined him.

"I told you, and everyone, to stay where you were," Dorilian said.

Robdan swallowed once, then nodded. "I know, Thrice Royal, but I thought, maybe, you could use some help. And, well," he looked over his shoulder, "Commander Legon is here to stop me."

"I would kill him now," Legon agreed, "were I convinced you did not need him for your alliance."

Dorilian signaled agreement that Legon had chosen correctly.

Robdan uncapped his flask and extended it. "Hrisian spirits," he explained.

Before Legon could intercept the offer, Dorilian took the flask and put it to his lips. The liquor burned a path down his throat but helped clear his head. It wasn't quite as effective as Tutto's damnable nectar, but it helped—and it tasted better. Ignoring Legon's scowl, Dorilian took a second, longer draught before he returned the flask. As he did so, Robdan stared openly at his wrist. A thin line of red had appeared on the outer leather of his glove, drops falling to the snowy ground below. Dorilian quickly took up the reins.

"Disarm the archers," he said to Legon. "We had best get back to camp. It grows dark early and we don't want to be blundering about when night falls."

Legon rode back to fulfill the order.

"So that was him? The enemy?" Robdan remained at hand.

"Yes."

"What did he offer you?"

The Kheld was damn bold to ask. Dorilian glared down. "Something that was not his to give. Something I refuse to give him."

But not something Nammuor could not take.

# 41



*She has another eye.*

Tutto noted how Palaistea gripped the writing stick with the stumps of both hands. Still seated on her horse, which was being held by a groom, she stared straight ahead at the line of soldiers on the ridge and wrote awkwardly in large letters. Earlier, she had refused Tutto's attempt to leave her with attendants and gestured to her throat. By that, he'd known Palaistea wanted paper and graphite. A Highborn daughter, she spoke their signs. Tutto had brought a wood plank, paper, and a cartographer's graphite stick.

*He alone can set me free.* The crude letters were uneven, but their message was clear. So was the way Palaistea never once looked at the paper.

Tutto marked the way Palaistea fixed her eye elsewhere. It was not that she was unaware. She did not turn her gaze upon Tutto because she feared what his expressions or actions might betray. She did this because she wore a *lr* crystal. Anything Palaistea saw, or heard, would be known to the one who keyed it.

*Lr* crystals were high Aryati sorcery and required mage skills to create. Only a handful of mages existed who might possess the skill to create one powerful enough to work remotely, much less fashion a device subtle enough to be hidden. Tutto had no doubt who had done so with Palaistea. With an eye trained to detect mage work, he scanned Palaistea's garments, the elaborate embroidery decorating her heavy cloak, the high, jeweled neckline of her gown. It could be any of those jewels, if the setting needed for a remote crystal were concealed by the embroidery. Perhaps her captors gambled that because of her birth and her disfigurement Dorilian's security would not make Palaistea remove her garments. Tutto would have her do so anyway, but later. The jewel of this matter, however, transmitted images and sounds and—if it was what Tutto thought it might be—it would be exposed.

"The parley has ended. My Hierarch returns, Royal Highness." As Tutto spoke, he moved into Palaistea's field of vision and afforded himself a hard look at her face.

Palaistea's good eye, its lashes darkened by cosmetics, remained large and brilliant gold, alive with intelligence and feeling. Though her face bore the terrible scars of burns, the one half was not as ruined, and skin as smooth and clear as pearl covered one cheek, part of the brow, and half of her nose. In what might have seemed but a vanity, for it was a fashion among Staubaun women, three exquisite yellow jewels punctuated the elegant line of her one perfect eyebrow.

Giving no sign that he had noted the embellishment, Tutto gestured toward the parting ranks of men to show Palaistea that, indeed, those who had ridden to the parley had returned. Tutto remounted his own horse and watched the Lacenedoni groom lead Palaistea's mount along with them as the arrayed forces fell into line, following Dorilian and his escort back to the encampment.

Once at their camp, Tutto walked over to Dorilian's horse and held it as he dismounted. "You must speak with the Princess." He pitched his voice so it would not reach beyond the two of them. He'd positioned himself so his lips could not be read. "Exercise caution, Sire: she wears a *lr* device. She wrote a message unseen by the thing. It said only you could set her free."

Dorilian turned back toward his horse, taking something from the gear it bore and using that movement to conceal his face while they spoke. Tutto had been his tutor in *lr* crystals for too many years not to be trusted with Aryati manipulations and their limitations. "Set her free of what, I must now wonder."

"None of us will ever know as much from her lips as you can dredge from behind her eyes. I will search her thoroughly before I bring her to you."

# 42



Erenor heard the clink of glasses, the ripple of liquid flowing from one hollow vessel into another, the softer sound of a body settling onto cushions. He looked around to see Nammuor lounging comfortably on the long divan, holding out a half-filled goblet of wine to him and cradling one for himself in his other hand. Erenor sighed and flung the drapery back across the window, unable to decide which view he despised more, the one outside or the one inside. He might be Prince of Stauberg, but he hated this city nearly as much as Stefan ever had. Walking over to the divan, Erenor took the proffered drink, but he remained standing and paced nervously before the nearest of three fireplaces. This room and seventeen others formed the State apartments of the Asae Eranos, and they were imbued with a history as sumptuous as the luxury they afforded. That sense of history emanated from tapestries and patterned carpets depicting the most fabled of legends, numerous portraits of long-dead rulers still watching over the rooms where they had been born and in which most of them had also died. Erenor glared at the benevolent King gazing out from above the mantelpiece, reading condemnation in the eyes of past ages.

"Come, Erenor," Nammuor scolded. "Old Eremanthus is not so grim as all that. Enjoy your glass. It is one of the best vintages out of Nalapar. Or have you developed a thirst for Teremari wine?"

Erenor detected the double meaning and turned away, causing Nammuor to smirk. Feeling a sudden chill, Erenor rubbed his free hand on his silken sleeve: he had begun to lose his attraction for Nammuor of late. Increasingly, too, he realized how fully his own position depended on the Mormantaloran ruler. It had not started out that way. Erenor had thought himself to be clever—clever at manipulating Stefan, clever at usurping leadership in Essera—but now he saw that he was no more than the tool that had brought Nammuor to these shores.

*He rules here now, and I serve only in that it amuses him to own me.*

"What brings on this sudden melancholy?" Nammuor asked without any serious interest. "Do you begin to pine for fair Palaistea?"

Erenor blanched. He recalled the moment Nammuor had brought her to Stauberg, full knowing the Wall would remove the illusion. *You would see her truly in his presence, anyway,* the Sorcerer had noted. Though he had known about Nammuor's disfigurements, Erenor had never suspected hers. Frozen, he had watched Palaistea's beauty replaced by monstrousness: her face a reddened, hideous half mask, her graceful body distorted with long contracted scars, her hands shrunk down to fingerless stumps, her legs footless.

And he had been in bed with that creature.

No wonder it had shrieked every time he had been with it. It had been in pain.

"You should have told me she was badly maimed. A mass of scars! Instead you deceived me—all of us! You said you had healed her!"

Nammuor's impassive face betrayed nothing of feeling, neither compassion nor amusement. "And so I did. Is it my fault human flesh scars when it heals? That her flesh did not restore its lost parts? You found her pleasing enough." He sipped his wine and appeared to study the cup. A pair of twining female shapes formed the bowl's stem. "Dorilian will find her less so. He may be ambitious, but he craves beauty for his bed and takes no pleasure in hurting women. There will be no royal coupling there to threaten your precious claim to this city."

"Do not mock me."

"Then do not press me on matters where your opinion matters not. Palaistea was ever a piece for me to play. Stop complaining about how I played her."

Nammuor's attention turned to the device mounted on the low table before him. Just the sight of it made Erenor's stomach turn. Another mirror, much like this one, had been instrumental in Palaistea's conflagration. This one presented a marvelous plate of silver twice the size of a human face and set about the perimeter with filigrees of *audum*, that rare metal used by the Aryati to fashion their sorcerous machines. At equidistant points about the mirror glimmered seven topaz orbs large enough to fill a man's palm. Each was keyed to a *lr* crystal. Images from the one active crystal moved within the polished surface of the mirror. Two of the topaz orbs, blackened, recalled those crystals that had malfunctioned or been destroyed. Nammuor frowned at that sight, as much as that of the man before him. "Do you now distrust me, Erenor?"

Sighing, Erenor shook his head, as much to deny that suspicion to himself as to Nammuor. "No, Master." He framed his answer carefully. "But I begin to understand what I am to you."

"Is that all?" The blatant scorn in Nammuor's soft voice caused Erenor to stiffen. "Then you are slow, my dear usurper, very slow indeed. Dorilian Sordaneon has long carried that understanding with him."

*And avoided its claws,* Erenor added in his thoughts, *for all the good it will do him in the end.* Nammuor's venomous fangs would fasten onto Dorilian whatever steps might be taken to avoid them. It was but a matter of time now. Their meeting this afternoon had been a battle of wills, and Erenor could still see the results of that confrontation burning in Nammuor's black eyes. What he saw disturbed him.

"Does my puppet prince now regret the price of furthering his ambitions?" Nammuor's white hair gleamed against the divan's dark embroidery.

"You know I am your man, if only because no other will have me. You heard him. I am a dead man should I ever fall into his hands." Erenor leaned his elbows on the mantel and took a long sip from his propped glass. The sweet wine warmed a hollow course through his bowels. "You play a treacherous game with Sordan. You should have killed him on the parley field this afternoon and assured the success of tomorrow's battle."

Nammuor looked at Erenor incredulously, freezing in the midst of tasting his own drink. "What? And have his blood on my hands?"

"Why not? You had it in your mouth."

Nammuor laughed. "A far sweeter scenario. Have you ever tasted Highborn blood, Erenor?" A snicker followed when Erenor put aside his cup, no longer able to look at or sip the wine. "No? I can see you have not. Not many have. It's delicious, truly sweet and rich and rare. Most remarkable. One could develop a taste for it."

*As you have.* Erenor waved his hand as if that might ward off the image in his brain. "Suck him dry if you wish. But I fear Dorilian's presence near Stauberg. He's not without support from the populace. He flaunts his descent from Derlon the Rill-Giver as though it were a banner. And the people have missed the old glory of the Highborn Houses. The pomp. The stability. They look upon Dorilian Sordaneon, his victories and his Rill—that he can wear and use his god's thrice-cursed Armor—with growing favor. They've forgotten what it was to fear him. They believe the old rumor that the Sordaneons might someday bring the Rill to Stauberg." If they looked out the windows, they would see the massive structures standing silently over the city, overarched by the shimmering curtain of the Wall.

"Your people are sentimental, I'm afraid." Nammuor scowled at mention of the Rill. "Labran killed that dream when Marc Frederick imprisoned him here. How it must gall them that Amallar now has the Rill while they go begging."

It was Erenor's turn to laugh. "On the contrary. The Sordaneon curse is on every lip. 'The filthy Khelds will get the Rill before ever Stauberg does!' That's what Labran said. And now, what do they see? The fucking Rill runs to Trestethion! Sordan's heart and mind are turned."

"To his own advantage only."

"What does that matter? The Mind of Leur has spoken! His reality is our reality. If the Rill now goes to Trestethion, why not here? Dorilian has proven himself a true Rill Lord, the first any can remember. He clearly has the ability to commune with the Rill. What we do not know is the extent of his ability to *command* it." Erenor seized a rare chance to goad his partner in this increasingly ill-fated endeavor. "Who knows but that Dorilian could open the Rill again to Mormantalorus? No wonder you want him kept alive."

Nammuor turned his goblet in his hand, again and again, watching the reflections. "Yes." His black eyes narrowed and he surveyed Erenor much less kindly than before. "And not for that reason only. But make no mistake. He will do none of it willingly.

Not to Mormantalorus and not to this miserable seat. I don't believe you or your people understand the depth of Dorilian Sordaneon's contempt for our race or how useless Stauberg is to him. There's very little Staubaun left in him. There never was much, diluted as his blood is, but it's been replaced with something else. I saw that this afternoon. He's Highborn—and only that! God or demon, he now has no allegiance to anything Staubaun, and that boy Handurin has turned him loose on Essera. On me! If Dorilian takes Stauberg, it will not be to liberate it but so that he might throw it—and us—away. Give the whole of Essera to that Kheldish Prince and, with it, Staubaundom's last chance to flower again. Dorilian Sordaneon is not just a man—he is barely that, if our own legends are true. He is a *bloodline*, the last exhalation of a lineage born to a power and a godhood even he does not yet realize. If I cannot bring his Highborn blood back into the Staubaun race so that it again breeds true, if I cannot control how that godhead unfolds within our race, then I will do what I should have done years ago—and what Stefan tried to do too late. I will destroy Dorilian and all that race utterly, as one would any other parasite."

A knock sounded at the door. Moments later, a red-robed mage appeared, bearing a gleaming cylinder in his hands. Bowing low, he extended it to Nammuor.

"From Trulo, Master," the man intoned. He kept his eyes lowered, lids tattooed red.

"News from Zel," Nammuor said.

Erenor picked up his wine cup again, his smile resuming. Handurin had long since outlived any purpose Erenor had once had for him.

"Dare I hope we can confront Dorilian in the morning with news that his puppet Prince has lost his crown?"

Nammuor caressed the warm skin of the metal casing before he opened the chamber. And froze.

Erenor came over to see what caused Nammuor to stare. Nestled within the message chamber were two bloodied fingers… the first and second fingers, the latter tattooed with a serpent, cut from some man's left hand and still joined by one knuckle and a strip of waxen skin.

# 43

The first time I saw Dorilian Sordaneon, he had just
turned sixteen. He simply appeared unannounced at
Marc Frederick Stauberg-Randolph's anniversary
celebration. He then proceeded to insult all the guests.
The King, I recall, was less insulted than amused—and
already plotting how best to seize the advantage.
PRINCESS PALAISTEA, *BEFORE THE STORM*

Dorilian met Palaistea Malyrdeonis in a tent that ordinarily housed two young officers of the Sordaneon horse ranks. Those men had been reassigned and their possessions removed. Tutto had let Palaistea know the tent was now hers and settled her there. He had also sent trained bondslaves to see to Palaistea's comfort. Nammuor could guess what he liked as to why she had not been housed with the Hierarch's household or that of her cousin, Hebron of Lacenedon.

A *lr* crystal—or rather three of them.

Dorilian brought only five men to his meeting with Palaistea. In addition to the ever-present Legon, he included Hebron and Robdan. Hebron was Palaistea's cousin and close kin, and Robdan... Dorilian wanted the Kheld to see what Nammuor truly was. What the monster had done... and what he was still doing. The final man, Tutto, had searched the Princess for weapons and would do so again just prior to the actual meeting. The search had confirmed there was no other larger crystal than the set gracing her eyebrow. Tutto presented his information during the walk from Dorilian's command tent to the one where they would find Palaistea.

"They're a matched string, each gem too small for anything but surveillance only. However...." Tutto had been trained by device mages and looked grim as he recalled what he knew. "If the energy in the string were reversed, it could harm the wearer and any within several feet of her. My thought is they have gambled that this aspect would go undetected. If you and Bas Hebron stand where I direct you to, you should be safe."

"Too small for translocation?" Dorilian inquired about the other known application.

"Portions of the crystals are beneath the lady's skin and possibly set in bone, so they might be larger than they appear. I couldn't examine them closely without revealing we had detected them. But if the crystals are high level, the three together might be enough to transport one person."

"Transport?" The quiet voice reminded them that Robdan was also with them. Dorilian's inclusion of Robdan at meetings no longer raised eyebrows, but Robdan's habit of standing quietly on the fringes of conversations irritated a few people to no end.

"Carry a body from one point to another," Tutto growled. "Usually to no good."

Hebron broke into a worried frown. "What are the dangers to her?"

"Preset triggers. Malfunction of the base device with energy reversal. Most of all, Nammuor's intentions, which can only be foul." Tutto left no doubt in any of their minds as to who had set the crystals or forced Palaistea to wear them.

"But why send her to us wearing one of these?" Fitful firelight carved deep shadows into Hebron's saturnine face as they approached the Princess's tent. "Surely Erenor and the Sorcerer know we would take precautions with any released hostage, that she would not be questioned in your quarters or allowed to listen in on important conversations or any talk that would reveal our plans. To what purpose has he employed fell magic?"

Dorilian thought the answer clear. "They are not interested in our plans. They are interested only in their own. Nammuor wants Palaistea's path to cross with mine. You can be sure she knows something he wants me to discover."

Dorilian nodded to Tutto to go ahead and conduct his weapons search.

Hebron paused for a long breath, then said, low and afraid, "The Malyrdeon Princes, her sons... Stefan refused to allow Rheger or Elhanan—or yourself—to examine the corpses."

Dorilian refrained from snapping immediately at the man. Speculation that Palaistea's sons had not died in the fire had never completely been laid to rest. He bit his tongue only because he, unlike Hebron, had never had to live with the possibility of having other heirs with more valid claims to his lands or titles step forward. "If she can decide that matter once and for all, be assured I will do so." Dorilian gave Hebron a warning scowl. "Yet you misunderstand Nammuor if you think his game is with you, or Lacenedon, or Essera at all. His politics are ice cold, and if he had held that piece you think he might, he would have played it long before now and hung the Royal North in Staubaun glory upon Enreddon Malyrdeon's Heir. Nothing would defeat Handurin, or you, more easily."

Dorilian paused outside Palaistea's tent before entering, directing Hebron inside before he muttered, so only Legon and Robdan could overhear. "I have not been away from fishing so long that I do not recognize bait."

Palaistea sat upon a chaise that had been set up for her, her body propped with pillows. With back straight and head high, she looked up at the entrance of visitors. Yards of purple wool, provided by Tutto, wrapped Palaistea with an elegance not unlike that of the court clothes she had once worn. She wore a golden circlet of rank atop a sheer veil that concealed the worst of the scarring on her nearly bald head.

"Your Thrice Royal Grace," she acknowledged.

The words, though roughly shaped and barely understandable as human, surpassed expectation. Given her earlier demeanor, they had feared Palaistea might be past speech. For those who remembered her voice, it would have seemed kinder if she had been.

"Gracious Princess." Dorilian granted the full rank Palaistea had held after the death of her husband. Enreddon Malyrdeon, Prince of Stauberg and the Eleutheron, had been Dorilian's equal in rank. Palaistea and Dorilian had not known each other well and had only met three times, most recently at Dazunor-Rannuli twelve years before. Now he could barely recall the beauty Palaistea had been. Tufts of wispy pale hair grew in patches on her scarred head and her one eye looked out of the only unburned expanse of skin on her ruined face. "We had thought you dead."

Her scarred slit of a mouth grimaced. Or smiled. "We thought you... a murderer."

Affront flared, then stilled. She did not think that now.

She raised the red lump that was her left hand and gestured for

Dorilian to come near. Tutto put a hand on his arm, but Dorilian shook his head. He sensed no malice in this woman, nothing of untruth, and the crystals were quiescent. What he did feel was Palaistea's anguish, her urgency, and that he was the focus of it. He knelt before Palaistea, aware of the mixed feelings in the men who watched. Tutto's fear of the crystals; Legon's concern that kneeling to anyone, even she, did not befit Dorilian's station; Hebron's approval for the recognition extended to his royal cousin; Robdan Aelfricson's curiosity and quiet appreciation for what he witnessed. Nothing that if it bled through would do harm.

*Follow her lead.* The wisdom of Dorilian's grandfathers guided him. *She knows our ways. If she is open, her mind will reveal its secrets.* Either Nammuor knew that Palaistea would tell Dorilian something or she knew something that Nammuor wished unlocked. But what? Tutto was right to think that what Dorilian wished to do could prove dangerous. *Nammuor does nothing without his own purposes. He's waiting for her to be careless—or for me to be.*

"My Lord Sordaneon," the tortured voice rasped. But it was the thought behind those words that spoke most acutely. *You, at least, remain of them.* With shattering clarity, he felt himself examined, hungrily devoured by Palaistea's gaze. Dorilian saw himself through her. The Sordaneon eagle breastplate he wore and that it was a part of Derlon's Armor. The emerald and green insignia of his Hierarchate. The Rill Stone glinting green fire on his hand. His features telling those who knew what to look for who he was, what he was. Somewhere far away, perhaps in Stauberg, Nammuor noted these things as well.

"It has been a long time, cousin." In her ardent gaze, Dorilian sensed that Palaistea wondered if he could do what she required. The empathic gifts of the Highborn race, though widely revered, did not appear in every man born to that blood. Because he had fostered rumor that he lacked talent, only his most trusted retainers knew for certain what abilities Dorilian possessed. He reached out to Palaistea, pressed his thoughts into hers.

He felt a flaring awareness, surprise even as Palaistea recognized the thing she had looked for. *Highborn, yes. The blood runs true!* As that thought and others raced through her anguished mind, he sensed them all: joy mingled with fear, then hard logic and relief. *The other cannot read minds!*

Neither could Dorilian. But he could read emotions, detect

strong thoughts or mental images. When Palaistea reached for him, he allowed her contact. Too soon.

*My father! My husband! My sons!*

Palaistea's mind was an assault, a maelstrom of all that she had suffered and lost. *Permephedon. Enreddon. Her babies. Danae burning to the ground.* Recoiling from so much overwhelming emotion and the chaotic images that broke through his belatedly mounted defenses, Dorilian severed contact to protect them both. He kept his face impassive but knew his gaze would say too much. He looked away. Palaistea recognized what had happened and covered for them both.

"I am... hideous... am I not?" The look in her eye when Dorilian met it again was all steel. Palaistea would not let Nammour know the extent to which he succeeded.

"Appearance is not a barrier."

"It was... sorcery's fire."

Palaistea's response sounded natural, something she might try to tell him, something Nammuor of course already knew—and it was the entry Dorilian needed. Once more Palaistea's mind opened with images. *Heat... noise... flame... a woman's voice, her own, screaming her sons' names.* This time, however, Dorilian asserted control as Sebbord had taught him, using methods honed by the Highborn through the ages. *The Mind is of my own making. All things happen in the same moment. I control this one.* As he had done with Levyathan so many times before—as he had done one time and one time only with Marc Frederick—Dorilian fashioned a synaptic divergence, an open-ended matrix into which he channeled the confused stream of Palaistea's feeling and thought, pressing his thoughts alongside hers, instilling calm and order. But he could make nothing of the chaos.

"I cannot help you," he whispered. He exposed his open frustration, as much for Nammuor's benefit as anything. Let Nammuor think Dorilian was getting nowhere.

Palaistea's mouth gaped with sobs. Her one bright eye spilled tears. "Touch me... cousin," her broken voice pleaded, "touch me so I can feel it."

So much of her body had been burned, so much of her skin reduced to eschar, then immobilizing scars. The sensory nerves had been destroyed. Even if someone touched such thickened, changed skin as covered her now, Palaistea would detect only pressure or pain, never anything delicate or tender. Certainly, her captors had never done so. Knowing what she needed, Dorilian lifted his left hand, the Rill Stone a steady gleam in the low light, and gently laid his fingertips to the one patch of skin he could see that was still as he remembered, just beneath Palaistea's golden eye. Her tears wet his skin as she moved her head, pressing more insistently against his touch.

She knew the difference of Highborn skin upon hers, had felt it before and known it intimately. Her father's touch; her husband's; her sons'. This time Dorilian was prepared for the moment their minds touched. Open, trusting, her mind opened to his as Marc's once had, as Levyathan's still could—a brilliantly hued, flowing tapestry of memory and need. And Dorilian saw. In that moment. He saw everything.

As Palaistea's single eye met Dorilian's stricken, aware gaze, the sickened reeling in his mind, he sensed one thing more. Her tears still bathed his fingers but there was now a film of energy between his skin and hers. *Not now!* Even as he reached for the suddenly blazing *Ir* crystals above Palaistea's eye, hoping to pluck just one, to disrupt the field, Legon and Tutto leaped forward.

"No! Let me!" Dorilian shouted, but the two men had already grabbed his arms and pulled him away. Even Hebron held him back while at the same time staring at his now screaming cousin. A net of golden light spun from the three glowing crystals to form a glittering matrix and Palaistea dissolved in a wail before their eyes. Where the woman had been, only a malignant shadow of something remembered remained.

Struggling in the grip of the men, Dorilian railed at them. "Do you know what you've done? Do you even know? I could have saved her!"

Legon's jaw clamped stubbornly as he released his grip. Hebron retreated backward several steps. Only Tutto dared to continue to hold Dorilian. "The three crystals had already linked. Any disruption would have turned her inside out. The only thing you could have done was kill her! And maybe yourself in the bargain!"

"And better so! I've seen what that monster's been doing to her!" Dorilian turned away. He could not meet their eyes as he added, "Better she was dead than where she is now. And I have seen that the World would be better dead than if I were to fall into his hands."

# 44

My father believed he had been handed an extraordinary
opportunity to reinvent the Mind.
EMYLI STAUBERG-RANDOLPH, *REFLECTIONS ON KINGSHIP*

The battle for Trulo had been decisive and bloody. The Khelds
had been unmerciful in slaughtering enemy troops and,
afterward, bodies in the Pearlsnake Marshes piled three deep. The
Mormantalorans, knowing their lives would not be spared, fought
even harder. Encircled and trapped in the sucking ground of the
marshes, they had died to the man. The bog so ran with blood that
for generations it would be said only blood peat could be gotten from
it. That spring and for years after, bog eels multiplied astoundingly
and grew fat, but townspeople would refuse to eat them, though they
did not balk at selling them by bargefuls to other towns or lands.

Hans, to secure Dazunor's official capitol, decided to leave Euden
Mezeon's troops and a regiment of Dannuthi soldiers headed by Serrain
officers. At the very least, the presence of fellow Esserans would
reassure Trulo's inhabitants that they would not be turned over to
foreigners. The remainder of Hans's army and that of Sordan now
under his command would forge ahead on the two-day march to
Gustan. The village and the Manor Marc Frederick had built there
would be a strong position. Using signal flags, Hans had already
arranged for Kheld reinforcements from across the river to join him.
Endelarin, however, declined to accompany him. After turning over
the letters entrusted to him, Endelarin stayed only long enough to
bring in the river yacht on which he had sailed from Dazunor-Rannuli
and present Hans with the promised gift from Levyathan.

"The lad insisted," Endelarin maintained. He and Hans waited in an elegantly appointed parlor of a warehouse fronting the docks, where Endelarin's yacht was being readied for its return voyage.

Hans held a long-necked string instrument in his hand. A lute of sorts, full bellied, beautifully made of golden polished woods and gleaming frets. "He remembered." Hans adjusted his hold and played a few chords, the beginning of a tune, something Geraldine had taught him. Though this World had never heard the melody he strummed, he thought it sounded at home. "I spent an afternoon with Levyathan in Sordan, playing songs on an instrument like this," Hans added with a smile. "I taught him a few old Dominioner tunes. I think he was surprised I could play."

"He might have been. Though it seems to me music runs in your family."

"I don't know about that. Levyathan was probably humoring me. I mean, have you heard him play? Seen his fingerwork? He's far better than I will ever be." Hans cradled the instrument again and gave a few more strums to the strings. The lute needed tuning. "I wonder why he wanted me to have this."

"Who knows? But you can be sure it will come in useful one day, perhaps to woo a female to wander near." Endelarin laughed at the blush and Hans's look of censure. "I will not bring it up again. Just be aware there are Malyrdeon Princesses working behind palace curtains to secure your future."

"My *future*?"

"More like the Kingdom's. A wife, a *Queen*. It's a time-honored tactic. The current candidate is Elhana Malyrdeonea, daughter of Dannuth's royal line. Stefan had her removed as Stauberg's Princess, but her lineage could not be higher. You could do worse for a wife if you're prepared to wait a few years. She's two years old, so you have some time."

Hans had no time for contemplating any future other than defeating Nammuor and driving Erenor out of Essera—and he couldn't even imagine a future that included being betrothed to a two-year-old. To his relief, a broad figure filled the warehouse's doorway and Ralen Ornichos stepped inside. Ralen inclined his head deeply enough to signal respect. "If your Royal Majesties—"

"Is my ship ready?" Endelarin perked.

"*My* ship is," Ralen corrected. Endelarin didn't own a ship on the Dazun. He had taken passage from Dazunor-Rannuli on Ralen's yacht and would be returning the same way.

"Good man." After Ralen departed, Endelarin turned to Hans. "If I may be so bold, let me congratulate you on having done remarkably well so far. Nammuor never established control of the river; he left that to Erenor. It appears everyone here in Essera underestimated you and Dorilian too. People haven't figured out yet whose fool of a gamble has paid off—yours or his."

"Both?" Hans suggested.

"It certainly looks that way. I suppose we will know when all is done."

They walked together onto the quay. Farrl and three Trongorians, and an equal number of Ardaenan guards, fell into protective positions as escorts. Now that the Mormantalorans had retreated to strongholds nearer Aral and their supply lines by sea, the city of Trulo had become as secure as any of Hans's armed camps. Gustan remained, but it was a shallow water port and even Zel had called the Manor too confounding a presence for any military purpose.

"Are you headed back to Ardaen?" Hans asked.

"I should. I probably will, though my main role these days is ambassadorial. The Queen prefers to handle the military herself—and for me to stay far away."

"What about your family?" Hans asked. "Don't they miss you?"

"Not in any meaningful way. To them I'm mostly a rumor."

And possibly a rumor to much of Ardaen as well. Though Hans had studied Ardaen's history in Sordan, mostly about how Ardaen had lost the Second War and the Sordaneons gained Caerdon along with their controversial lineage, he had spent time at Rhodhur studying up with Robdan's book collection. Ardaen was ruled by a king for some matters—but greater influence was held by the king's sister, who ruled as queen. The king was always succeeded by a nephew, not a son. Hans didn't know if Endelarin himself had any children at all.

The deck of the two-masted schooner at the dock was lined with Ardaenan guards who placed hands on sword hilts and shouted greeting to their king. Endelarin beamed and waved appreciatively. To Hans he noted quietly, "They look happy enough, but how not? Though they would die for me, I never put them in that position." Gray eyes agleam with mirth, he offered one last bit of advice. "If you keep chasing Nammuor, one day you will catch him. I hope you have a plan for that. Which reminds me"—Endelarin reached into his jacket and pulled out an envelope of tawny leather embellished with emerald and black ribbons—"I was also charged to give you this. I'm not certain, but I think it may be intended to help."

"More messages?" Arne slumped down onto the upholstered bench opposite Hans. They were in the Prince of Dazunor's private apartment with wine to drink and a bank of softly crackling flames warming the marble-fronted fireplace. Endelarin had set sail back upriver. And Arne had arrived wearing some kind of velvet cloak and embroidered jacket over stained Kheld leathers. Hans didn't have the heart to tell him he looked ridiculous.

Hans had spent the remainder of his day conferring with Euden Mezeon and Kerr, who would be staying behind in Trulo for at least the next week to shore up logistics with some of Pandaros's officers. Only now that he was back in his suite of rooms in the Golden Palace did Hans have time to look at the envelope.

"Endelarin gave it to me. It's from Levyathan." Hans turned the letter over in his hands before breaking the seal. The contents were... interesting. Odd though it seemed to receive a letter from the Sordaneon Heir, it made sense that Levyathan would have access to the same paper and ink.

"Something wrong?"

"No, just unexpected." Angling his legs onto the cushioned divan, Hans leaned against the pillows at his back and laid out the note again to read it.

The letter began with congratulations on his victories thus far... and ended with a warning. *Nammuor and Dorilian must soon meet and our circumstances become more fraught. With Dorilian away from the City, Sordan's Serat is no longer refuge enough should Nammuor attack in earnest. I must seek the protection afforded by the Rill. With the blessing of the Epoptes, who now fear my brother's demise more than they fear his power, I occupy a sanctuary on the Rill mount and maintain my presence in Sordan that way. Nammuor cannot use the Diadem within Rill fields, and so I will be safe from him.*

*I pray that you and Dorilian soon join forces again. Each of you is stronger with the other and I fear for him most of all. Nammuor's malice toward him is the stuff of nightmares.*

And questions. *For your friendship toward my brother, I offer you a brother's gift. You deserve to know your truths. Ask your Lady Mother these things: To what other name are you heir? Where were you born? Who killed your father?*

Hans folded the paper again. Just when he'd hoped his world would finally begin to make sense, the damn kid had given him more questions—but no answers.

Reflections from his wineglass, the way light from the gilded sides played in the ruddy liquid, reminded Hans of blood. Of war. He was always reflective after a battle, and Levyathan's letter had given him fresh fuel for thought. The questions raised were not entirely new ones. Arne and others had brought to Hans's attention speculations that Staubauns wouldn't dare ask to his face. Always before, he had dismissed them. "How much do you know about my family, Arne?"

"Your family? Not much. I mean, not as much as you do."

"Meaning the Sordaneons would know more?"

"Probably. They got their cursed spies everywhere." Arne reached over to pick up a long-necked amphora from the table. "You've got all this fancy wine, so you might as well drink it." He splashed some into Hans's cup.

"Enough! Enough!" Hans moved his goblet out of range. A stream of wine hit the cushions and ran over the brilliant blue upholstery, bringing an expression of dismay to Arne's face. "I don't want to drink too much. I have to move with my army in the morning," Hans explained. Using the soft sash of the robe he was wearing, he helped Arne mop up the red stain. "The letter just got me thinking about my family, is all. Do you remember anything at all about me?"

"You?" Arne settled back among his cushions, though he put aside the bottle. Wine had never been his drink. "Just bits and pieces. People talked mostly about Stefan, but I knew you existed."

"Do you know where I was born?"

"Not precisely. Somewhere in Essera, I figure. Does it matter?"

Hans sighed. Arne wasn't being particularly helpful. "I don't know. The question came up and it occurred to me that I don't even know where I was born."

"Not everyone does."

"But other people know where they were born. I bet you do. And Dorilian knows where he was born," Hans pointed out.

"Well, of course he does. Sordaneons are always born in Sordan," Arne said. His face screwed up with a new thought. "Aren't they?"

Hans decided he would have to take Levyathan's advice after all. "I'll just have to ask my mother."

"Why, there's your answer! Mothers always know that sort of thing. She can probably tell you the weather on the day you were conceived, what she ate the night before, and how many contractions it took to deliver you."

"And who my father is."

In this room of regal splendor overlooking Essera's dark, patient lands, Arne frowned. "Well, everyone knows that. It was Erwan Cedrecson, just as with Stefan, and before we came north I never heard anyone say anyone else."

Hans took another sip of wine. "Yeah. About that—"

Arne's frown deepened. "That bunch of lies the Gignasthans tell? Nobody puts much stock in that. Besides, you heard what Sinon said: as far as your Kingship goes, it doesn't matter."

Maybe not. And that people questioned Hans's paternity apparently worked in his favor... a little. All Essera knew Stefan was Erwan the Rebel's son. About Hans, they weren't as sure. Hans was in the middle of a war and it was probably just as well that both sides found their own way to claim him.

*One thing no one questions is that I'm Emyli's son and Marc Frederick's sole remaining Heir. So maybe they don't need to know... not for me to do what I must do.*

But *he* needed to know.

"It must be strange for Levyathan." Hans took another deep drink of wine. It went down heavily this time and he knew better than to want more. He had never liked alcohol particularly, and right now it was feeding his growing melancholy. "Knowing that he's related to Nammuor by blood."

"It never seemed to me like he makes much of it," said Arne.

"It's just that Levyathan seems old for a boy. Hopeful, but sad."

"Guess he would be. Look at all that happened the day he was born."

*My private hell*, Dorilian had called Permephedon. That day. So many Highborn deaths that the event had forced itself into the mind of half the population of the Triempery. Including that of the newborn Levyathan? Hans shuddered to even think of that.

*That day scarred me too. Stayed with me. It's with me even more now because I made Marenthro show me what happened.*

With a sigh, Hans rose and walked to the window. He felt the dark edge of a mood that had haunted him all evening creeping under the skin of his military victory and the celebrations that had followed in his wake. Dotting the dark curve of the river Dazun, orange lights glinted like strings of eyes, winking as lines of boats making the journey from Amallar, bringing supplies and men, passed in front of them. He was, at this moment, ruler of all he surveyed. Amallar and Dazunor were his. Merrydn and Rannul were allies. So were Serrain and Dannuth. Now only Tahlwent and Aral and Nammuor yet awaited beyond the hills and over the mountains, between Hans's armies and the sea. And Dorilian. Nammuor had not used his Diadem or his power against Hans and his army of Khelds and their allies, Hans felt certain, because Nammuor waited on another.

*I'm just another annoying Stauberg-Randolph.* But Levyathan had not dismissed him—and neither had Dorilian.

Turning his back on the night, Hans gave Arne a tired smile. "I used to think Dorilian held my fate in his hands. Now I'm beginning to think I was wrong. The day is still coming that will determine the fate of us all."

"I wouldn't disagree with that, given all that I've seen." Arne stood and stretched. He picked up the blue cloak and velvet jacket he'd removed while they talked.

"What did you do?" Hans asked about the new attire. Pearls and other gems glinted on the jacket breast and hems. "Plunder a tailor?"

Arne grinned. "Won it in a bout of gaming last night with Pandaros and Endelarin."

"Endelarin!"

"He may be a king and all, but he's got no luck at throwing wands. Pandaros carried off a crown."

Hans laughed. Someone, at least, was having luck. He, on the other hand, was flagging badly. "Don't lose it all in your next set. Half the army out there would welcome the chance to win your gold." He formally dismissed his friend and listened long enough at the door to hear the excitement of some of the Trongorian guards when Arne suggested pulling together some lads for a game.

*At least they'll have fun tonight. I'm too tired!*

Retreating to a bedchamber that had slept only Princes and Kings until Erenor's regency and the Mormantaloran occupation, Hans shut the door behind him and gazed upon the bed with an amazement no more or less for having glimpsed it earlier. The sumptuously hung bed, all silk and furs, could have slept an entire Kheldish family with room to spare. The servants had turned it down and warmed it, a kind of flawless attention Hans had seen before in Sordan and Dazunor-Rannuli. He ran his hand over the unblemished white northern seal fur covering the bed, marveling at its silky softness and that he could feel every hair. Exhausted, glad he had taken a bath earlier, he slipped out of his garments and between the sheets. In few hours he would need to awaken again, be on the road...

He would take Arne with him. Arne could ride even if hung over. And Aubrey too. Sordan's newly arrived troops had her on edge about potential rumors. After what had happened at Dazunor-Rannuli, it was understandable that she would want to get away from Staubauns for a bit. Aubrey's Saemoregh riders could be Hans's guard, along with the Trongorians. Everyone else could follow behind. He would put Nalf in charge of the Khelds. Hans had already planned to leave Euden at Trulo because the Staubaun populace wouldn't mind him... and Pandaros and Sordan's Second could bring up the rear, guard against any surprise from Mormantalorus or threat to Trulo. The Khelds would proceed to Gustan, find a place for the next base camp.

Yes. Hans would do that.

Sleep came slowly, laden with dreams. Nammuor lurked on the edges of perception, laughing with blood-stained teeth. Zel was dead, but it wasn't Zel's blood that colored this harrowing landscape... there was a woman... and not blood but fire.

*Palaistea.* The name unfolded before Hans, known yet never known. A woman draped in purple, hideously scarred. He reached to her and the world was fire, a great staircase in flames; a floor burned through and gave way, throwing him in the maelstrom as he shouted names he did not know. Pain. Terror. *Touch me, that I may feel it.* His skin found hers and the images that flooded Hans then bore no description.

Nammuor, ravening, his voice like a nightmare. Blood and horror and pain, pustules broken open and draining... a woman's weeping. Healing and madness and Nammuor in the night, every night, until Palaistea had done what was wanted, until she had conceived. The way the villain gloated and kept her at his side, finger stroking under her eye. Bearing her child surrounded by enemies, the scars on her belly rupturing... nearly dying, alone, wanting that. But Nammuor nursed Palaistea back. *The next one will be godborn*, Nammuor promised and raped her while wearing another man's face. Every night that Nammuor came, he wore the face of the man he would give her. The man upon whom every night he visited unspeakable atrocities before the illusion fell from his victim and he committed the maimed body to the ovens and gutters and dogs.

*No!* But Hans could not get rid of it, would never banish the images in his brain. Those memories were his memories now. Dorilian, violated and violating… with children, with animals… with Nammuor himself, even with Hans. Killed in a thousand gruesome ways… torn apart… eviscerated… burned… dissolving in acid…

"No!" Hans lurched to his hands and knees in the bed, drenched and shaking. He gasped fresh air into his lungs as if that could banish the foulness of the nightmare still clinging to him. He knew he had screamed when people rushed in. Arne. Two of the guards. Servants coming in on their heels.

"What's wrong? Hans, what happened?" Arne raced to the bed, his gaze raking the room. A drawn sword was in his hand.

Hans dropped back onto the bed, pulled the blanket over his body. "I'm all right," he insisted. "I'm awake. Send them away." The guards retreated and Arne signaled that the servants should leave, which they did. To them Hans was a stranger, brother to a King they had served faithfully.

"What happened?" Arne asked again, less alarmed now. He sheathed his sword but wouldn't leave until he had heard the reason for Hans's distress. Hans welcomed the clean, cool touch of Arne's hand on his shoulder. It made the world seem more solid and real.

"I saw something. Something horrible." Hans wondered how much he should tell Arne, then reasoned there was nothing he couldn't tell him. He gazed upon that trusted face. "I glimpsed a corner of Nammuor's mind. I don't know how it happened. But I saw what Nammuor has planned for Dorilian, the way he's going to kill him." Those memories broke free again and Hans's body quaked as he clutched the blankets. It was all he could do to keep his voice from cracking as he added, in a whisper too small for what he had seen, "He'll make sure it takes years."

# 45

Marenthro first appears in the histories as a companion of
Amynas. Only in later texts does the relationship become
clearer.
ZAMENES, *CIBULITUS AND THE FIRST TRIEMPERATE*

Stauberg slept uneasily, crowned by a thousand torches, secure
within her fabled fortifications that, in the night, soared cold and
white as some great beast's bones. A faint sheen clung to it and
overarched the city in giant spreading wings. Perhaps the Wall
sensed the two men on the ridge overlooking the frozen white river
and the city beyond, but none within the city's fastness detected
them or would have cared if they had. On the eve of battle,
sentinels on each side stood a vigilant guard.

"That's a hell of a Wall."

Dorilian nodded. "Yes, Tutto, it is. And it stands rooted in a
dead man's prayer."

"Now you've lost me."

"Only for the moment. If I succeed tonight, tomorrow Ergeiron
himself will be our herald." Dorilian settled the Sordan Coronal
upon his head. Derlon's Crown. He had not worn the device before
this because he hadn't wanted the enemy to know he had it with
him—or speculate on his ability to use it. The central green stone
glinted in the starlight, as did the seven stones set within its ring of
points.

"I know you too well to try to turn your mind, yet I fear this
thing you do." Like his Hierarch, Tutto wore a heavy gray cloak
that blended with the night and surrounding stone from which the
snow had melted. "Didn't I guard your back in Neuberland when

you followed your temper instead of good advice? I spent a year under guard in Merath for that. And I killed two men on the steps at Holy Permephedon itself when you went to see Stefan there. Spilled blood on sacred ground, I did. You do what you will, and I am with you. But what good will I be here on this godsforsaken hillside if you are found in the city? That would be the end of you, no matter your godborn ways."

"I won't be found. Stauberg has places it has itself forgotten. I will be keeping company with ghosts." Dorilian strapped the Gweroyen Sword—which he had not worn or used since Bynum— across his back and adjusted the drape of his cloak so that it covered the weapon but did not impede his access to it.

"I tell you still, I fear this Sorcerer. You are not yet his match."

"Maybe I am and will prove it tonight. He cannot read minds, Tutto, nor can he detect where I might be. He no doubt thinks I am hiding in my tent, guarded to the teeth, too afraid to sleep and on the edge of madness over his evil actions this day."

Even now, it took sheer force of will for Dorilian to block out those images Nammuor had known Palaistea would share with him. If he thought about such horrors, doing so might well reduce him to despair. His ordeal at Permephedon and its aftermath, the deaths he had survived and the ones he had caused, had taught him ways to deal with nightmares. He owned the mental barricades to keep Palaistea's revelations at bay. What preyed most on his mind now were the echoes. The memory of being helpless as Palaistea was wrenched back into the hands of her captors. The memory of being helpless as Marc Frederick was killed before his eyes.

"Let that be proof to you that I am right." Tutto was not giving up. "That creature is but treachery and more treachery! If there is a trap lying in wait for you, she is the bait. Promise me you will not seek to rescue her."

"Upon all my Highborn ancestors, Tutto, I swear to you my only goal this night is the one we discussed. No man even dreams what I will do here tonight." He gave Tutto a final nod. "Be but here when I wish to return."

Dorilian faced the city, focusing on it. The Wall did not, could not, block a Son of Amynas. One of its own, perhaps even its creation. Through the matrix of the Coronal, his mind seized Stauberg, pulled it near. He shifted place within the firmament and the sky vanished.

The time had come to remind the World of what Dorilian was. Odd that it should begin with grave robbing.

The Panagaos of Stauberg stood empty. Even by day, it was not a place frequented by soldiers and at night it was frequented by no one. Only scholars ever sought its tiled halls, its shelves of books and scrolls, the maps upon its storied walls. A vaulted ceiling arched in ghostly ribs overhead, upheld by triple ranks of pillars. Alabaster crowned with gold, newly restored to their former glory. Great windows, set high in the walls, allowed the fitful light of the Wall to spill into the vastness and play with the shadows of the place.

Dorilian crouched down in the darkness, letting his momentary weakness pass. Moving bodily through the firmament required more energy than other manipulations, even with the power of the Sordan Coronal to enhance his innate ability. Here the Rill was quiescent, though he could touch that also. He pulled from his pocket a small flask of Tutto's brew and drank from it. The liquid was gaggingly sweet, but he swallowed and was pleased when his body absorbed it almost instantly. He would need strength later. Rill might. For now, at least, he could make do with lesser means.

*Light.*

The *orbus* filled Dorilian's hand and illuminated golden hues to every side.

Dorilian cast barely a glance at floors inlaid with bloodstone and obsidian. He crossed the wide circle of the rotunda to the staircase that led down to the lower levels and the archives—and the first reading room. There, in a chamber formed by the still-standing foundations of the original building, he would find what he sought.

The restoration work had been done under the guidance of Cibulitan scholars and Esseran architects, by craftsmen Dorilian had contracted painstakingly and in secret through intermediaries so removed from his sphere that all in Stauberg thought the work was the doing of Erenor himself. Even Erenor thought it. But the Hierarch's agents remained undiscovered, in large part because it had not occurred to Stauberg that Sordan would have an interest in her monuments. For three years, Dorilian had read monthly reports from Palimia on the library's progress. He knew what the workers had uncovered, even if they did not. In the center of the room, ringed by a mosaic floor inscribed with sacred text, elevated upon a simple slab, sat a great stone basin planted with an ancient tree. Seedling of a tree that once grew in Mena'thessalia, in the World That Was, before Mena'tantaureus was even given birth in the Mind of Leur, the tree's branches reached to the glass ceiling above. Its leaves preserved memory, it was said, and its bark was inscribed with the past. But it was what slept beneath the slab that interested him.

"*Asthava navij'anyi, Epirades.*" Dorilian invoked the tongue that had been spoken long before Stauba had taken shape from its ruin. "Knowledge does indeed have deep roots." He closed his hand, dousing the *orbus*. In this room domed by glass, there was Wall light enough to see by.

He drew his sword, the room ringing with the sound, and swung it high overhead, then with both hands brought it down on the exposed corner of the slab. The bright long blade cut cleanly into the stone, cleaving it so deeply that the slab cracked, then split, one corner breaking away in pieces, some of which fell within. Kneeling, Dorilian peered into the gaping hollow beneath the slab and detected, within that darkness, the unmistakable gleam of a sarcophagus. There was just enough room to pry at the lid. He did so on his hands and knees, with his sword, needing to know. Ordinary remains would be dust by now. As he slid the lid back, his gaze fell upon flesh as intact as that of a living man. But the skin, when he held an *orbus* to it, was dry and fragile, that of the dead. Satisfied, he eased the lid back into place.

None had known about him, this Highborn scholar buried with his books at the foot of Stauberg's storied Tree, where school children sat to learn their lessons and stare up at the silver boughs. Now that tree reared a ghostly canopy and Dorilian contemplated the unthinkable.

*Forgive me, brother. I do what I must.*

Sheathing the sword, Dorilian reached into the jagged opening he had created and placed his hands on the ancient alabaster. Focusing through the Sordan Coronal he wore, he brought forth the power that was in him, reached for the Rill, and envisioned Permephedon.

"Enjoy the brief reunion, Epirades," Dorilian murmured.

Permephedon's foundations arched over his head and it was not imagination that he felt entombed. In this Vault of Incorruption, among a thousand lifelike corpses lying in perfectly preserved repose on beds of gold and finest silk, the sarcophagus of Ergeiron's scholarly grandson looked like a relic of even more ancient times.

Dorilian did not look at the bier to his right. He didn't wish to look again upon Marc's corpse. Or those of Rheger and Elhanan. Ghosts, at least, still spoke to him as if alive. What would he gain by eroding memory with truth?

Sensing the moment he ceased to be alone, Dorilian turned.

Marenthro stood at his side. They had not confronted each other or spoken since before Marc Frederick had died. "So, you found him," the wizard observed.

"It took me six years. And three hundred books. And a treasury of gold to pay for the 'renovation' of the Panagaos. But yes, I found him." Dorilian removed his hand from the sarcophagus of the man he had found.

"Exhuming bodies isn't your usual line of work."

"It's difficult to find grave diggers in Stauberg at this time of night. I don't intend to take it up as a practice."

Marenthro walked up to the sarcophagus, ran his hand over the smooth surface and the symbols carved there. "Poor Epirades. All he ever wanted was to be left in peace so he might mind his books. He never imagined that his resting place would decide so important a battle. And now, because you have removed his corpse from the city, you can surprise Nammuor with his fleet still in the harbor."

"Did you ever doubt I would move my fleet as well as my army?"

"No. Not ever."

Dorilian accepted that with a nod. On some level, he and Marenthro had always understood each other. He backed away, ready to leave.

Marenthro placed a hand on his arm. "Dorilian, don't go just yet."

"Unhand me."

Marenthro heeded the warning. "You did not come here by mundane means. You've been teaching yourself—"

"Don't berate me either."

"—taking chances. No one knows your native abilities better than I, who knows where they come from and where they can lead. Don't play with your life. With all our lives."

"All *their* lives," Dorilian corrected. "You're Immortal. The Creation itself could burn to ash and you would be an ever-living cinder."

Marenthro sighed. "You have a rare talent, and not just for dismissing me. For years I've suspected your device affinity, but you hid yourself too well for me to affirm it. Until now. Circumstances are forcing you to reveal yourself." His gaze never strayed from the man to whom he spoke. "You're just beginning down a path your ancestors tested but never mastered. Ability is not the same as prowess. What will you do when you must open the channels completely? Power like yours is raw and unpredictable, even when trained."

"I know that. Why do you think I've held back?"

"You can't always hold back. At some point, you won't be able to. If you attempt to use it, the godhead and the power it conveys will become manifest. Maybe it already has. How close are you?"

"Look at me and tell me what you see." Marenthro's copper gaze held his. Dorilian knew why the wizard could not answer.

"Are you so possessed that you don't see the danger?"

Dorilian laughed. "Are you trying to intervene? If so, you're too late. Who are you trying to save?"

"I think you know that answer."

Dorilian looked away. He didn't want to stay in this place, and he did not want to engage in verbal sparring. Not with Marenthro, and not over this.

"I've been watching you. You're *hierarchos*," Marenthro persisted. "Not just the Leur talent innate to the Highborn—you have the Aryati range as well. Device affinity. As Derlon did."

"I don't want to hear this."

"You *are* this."

"Maybe I simply *am*!" Even as he shouted, Dorilian was disgusted with himself for losing his temper. "I am. I exist. I live. I may be more than that, but what I am…. Isn't that enough, wizard? What more do you want out of a line you almost destroyed? Be content that I stand here to listen to you at all."

"You listen because you know I'm right. I have the answers you need, even those you are afraid to seek. Why do you hold me at arm's length?"

"Because I must. Just because you cannot accept my decision doesn't mean I have to explain it." Dorilian knew he must go. Stauberg awaited him, as well as Nammuor who, for now, did not yet grasp the nature of the enemy he faced. It was Dorilian's one advantage—if he played it well. But neither did he want to leave Marenthro with an argument.

"I like Handurin," he said, giving the wizard that to console him. "He has a noble heart, like his grandfather, and a penetrating mind. He will always see things clearly."

"Yes. Even you."

"Isn't that why you sent him to me?" Dorilian sighed and felt some of the harshness leave him. "Too many deaths stand between us for even Handurin to set right. You cannot remedy the past by throwing him my way, but maybe I can use him to put right what went wrong. Perhaps it is you who needs to examine your intercessions and ask yourself if all the misery was worth it. As you sit here in the center of your webs and pluck at the strands, examine why your futures no longer show *me*."

With that, Dorilian focused and was gone.

# 46



What is a city?
A dream fed by demons, a hope built on lies, and a history
written in stone.
ISSAHAN, *PASSAGE TO BATRAZ*

Tutto greeted Dorilian on the cold dark slope, a sharp wind whipping his cloak and the saddlecloths on the horses that stamped nearby. Without a word, Tutto handed Dorilian a large flask of ambrosia and waited until he had taken a good long drink.

"What did you do to the Wall?"

"I held it fast to its Promise." Capping the flask, Dorilian handed it back and walked to his horse. There was much yet to do and generals with whom he must now meet. The weariness in his bones would wait. "Ergeiron and I understand each other, Tutto. I am brother to that thing he became, and on the morrow I will prove it. Tonight, no man of Highborn blood, be he living or dead, dwells in Stauberg."

Together they looked across the river plain to Stauberg's glittering palisades. The Wall was visibly diminished, no longer shining, its soaring ramparts of power gone.

Wherever Ergeiron had fled, his remnants were fading.

Stauberg's Wall was just a wall.

Robdan entered Dorilian's campaign tent and looked around until his eyes adjusted to the low light. It was before dawn and Robdan had yet to clear all the sleep from his brain. Dorilian sat in a chair beside a table strewn with documents and weights to hold them down, pens and blotters nestled among leather and paper. He summoned Robdan to his side.

"Handurin said you were to be his eyes and ears. And so you shall be. You will ride with my party into battle today."

"Into battle?" Robdan wished his voice had not quavered. "You mean, we won't be just looking on this time?"

"No, Master Aelfricson. Today, I will myself go into battle."

It was not the news Robdan had expected. "Against beasts?"

"No. I do not expect there to be any."

"Oh, good. I mean... I wouldn't know how to fight one. Or fight anything—I don't know much about war." Dorilian already knew this, of course. "I deal with books, not swords. I don't even own a weapon."

Dorilian looked at Robdan thoughtfully, with just a trace of a smile. "Although I will insist that you be armed, Master Aelfricson, I don't expect either of us to engage the enemy in single combat. Even so, you should be as prepared to fight as any other man on the field. Have you ever used a weapon?"

"A slingshot. In my youth." It didn't bear mentioning that Robdan's youth had been long ago.

"You are a better man for never having had to use steel. I think I was born knowing how, such has been my need." Dorilian turned to reach behind him, then laid a blade, belt, and scabbard on the table. "Use this one. It is well made, and should you find yourself in battle it would meet the test."

Robdan picked up the short sword. Everything about its weight and purpose felt wrong. "It's not the quality of the blade that worries me, but the temperament of the bearer. I lack the hand for it." He pulled the blade from its sheathing and found that it was indeed finely made, of bright steel edged in the Sordan manner, and beautifully balanced. It almost seemed light. The hilt, wrapped in brown leather polished from use, fit his hand well.

Dorilian approached. He grasped the sword and, taking Robdan's hand, repositioned it. "Like this," he said. "You should be able to rotate the wrist and keep the same line."

"I hope I remember this in battle."

"You won't have to remember if you make a habit of holding it correctly. Let the hand remember." Dorilian stood and retrieved one of his own weapons from a nearby rack. Using his left hand, he tossed the blade in the air. Effortlessly, he snatched it in his right hand. "See," he said, showing Robdan his grip. "It becomes as natural as picking up a cup for a drink."

Robdan admired both the demonstration and the blade itself. Sleek in design and heavy, it was a weapon meant for intimidation.

Dorilian shifted stance with a swordsman's ease. "Attack me," he directed.

"Sire! No!" Robdan only realized after speaking that he'd called the Hierarch by the same familiar title his close retainers did. "I could not conceive of such a thing."

In truth, Robdan had never attacked a soul, for any reason. It was impossible for him to think of pitting himself against Dorilian, a Highborn Prince dressed for what might be the greatest battle of their age. Dorilian wore heraldic silks emblazoned with eagles, his body shielded by armor famed throughout the World.

But Dorilian only frowned. "Robdan, I am so much more skilled than you that, believe me, you could not lay a blade on me were that your sole goal in life. I but want to show you defensive moves. I did no less with Handurin, and he has survived thus far to become quite good with a sword."

Robdan felt his cheeks warm with blood. "But I don't want to become good, Thrice Royal. Only not get killed and not look too foolish. Fighting you puts me at risk of both. And, well, I am an educated man. I know that to raise a sword against you is itself a death sentence."

"Not if I order it. Besides, there's no one to see, and I have no reason to kill you. Attack me."

Awkwardly, the weapon unfamiliar to his hand, his balance new at every step, Robdan lifted the blade and struck. Dorilian brought his sword to bear and slid the oncoming weapon down, bringing the metal to the floor. Again Robdan thrust, and again he found his weapon swept downward and to the side. Gaining boldness from his lack of success, he tried once more, then a fourth time. Each time, Dorilian matched the stroke and performed the same maneuver. No matter what Robdan did, the result was the same. And then, suddenly, Dorilian reversed and attacked.

Leaping back, Robdan stumbled against a chest and staggered before he found his footing.

"The tip," Dorilian told him. "Not the hand. Never look at the hand. Nor the shaft of the blade. Focus on and bring down the tip, force it away from your body."

Many minutes later, after modest success, Robdan stepped back, winded, his arm tired of swinging. He gestured that he was done for.

Dorilian, too, laid down his sword. "I tell you truly, Master Aelfricson—you are no danger to any man so long as you fight like that."

"Lud smile upon them." Robdan could say nothing more, he was so occupied by gasping for air.

"I have more in store for you than this." Dorilian turned a chair. Thankful, Robdan accepted the seat. "Your safety is best assured, for now, by staying at my side. You are unused to battle, and the situation will be less confusing around me than elsewhere. There is one problem with that, however."

"A problem?" Robdan wondered what new trouble awaited.

"Yes. You will be seeing things no Kheld has ever seen. Things few outside of the Highborn kind have ever seen." Shadows of questions lingered in Dorilian's gaze, though he sounded resolute enough. "It's time to bring truth out of the realms of myth and into the light of day."

"Sometimes you speak in riddles."

"I've sought concealment for so long, I no longer know my own true shape."

Whatever Dorilian feared, he also looked determined to reveal.

Robdan thought it best to profess his own ignorance. "I think there's a reason you keep me with you. Maybe it's that I, at least, am profoundly convinced you're human."

"Tomorrow may change your mind."

"If it changes everyone's, perhaps."

"I will change the World as we know it. What history has forgotten, I will now cause it to remember." Dorilian sighed and picked up a weight of glass filled with a faint, shimmering light. Keeping his fingers on the beautiful thing, he placed it on the table between them. "Stauberg's Wall is no longer invulnerable. Last night, I removed its heart."

"Its *heart*?" Why, all at once, did the air within this tent feel so very still?

"A long-dead and ancient Highborn Prince named Epirades. Last night, I went into the city and found his resting place. When I left, I took his corpse with me. And when I took him with me, the Wall lost something essential to one very special aspect of its purpose. Something people have forgotten. Ergeiron's Wall doesn't exist to protect Stauberg. It exists to separate Time and the Rift. It protects Stauberg because Ergeiron made a Promise. Ergeiron promised his Wall would protect Stauberg as long as any of Highborn blood were in the city."

"But there have been no Highborn in Stauberg since the Princes of Dannuth died," Robdan said. That the Wall persisted had been one of Stefan's great triumphs, proof that the Highborn mythos was merely a story designed to deceive—and that the Rill would be similarly tractable.

"Indeed, they were murdered. But you are wrong about no Highborn being in the city. All who believed that were wrong. So were those who thought the Wall would stand only while the Malyrdeons lived. Epirades was still in Stauberg, buried for centuries, forgotten. Highborn *blood* is immortal. While Epirades slept eternal in his modest sepulcher, his blood immortal within his corpse, Ergeiron continued to keep his Promise." Dorilian shrugged. "Now Epirades sleeps elsewhere, and no more of Highborn blood rests within the city. There is nothing in Stauberg for Ergeiron to protect." As Dorilian spoke, he removed his fingers from the orb and the light within the glass died. Dark, it hunkered like a gray stone between them.

"The Wall… *died*?"

"It ceased. It ceased there—or, more properly, it ceased *now*. The men of Stauberg have completely forgotten the true nature of the magic that girded their city and raised them above all others. The edifice that remains, the original city wall built by Aryati engineers, is mighty, but it is no longer inhabited by a god. It can be broken, and I am so made that I can break it. Stauberg might as well be Eastmeary Brenna for all the difficulty my army will have in taking it."

Robdan regarded Dorilian apprehensively, not sure of what this meant. He had learned these last many weeks to look beyond Dorilian's words. What Robdan found there now caused his mouth to go dry. Was it joy—or fear? With its fabled Wall broken, Stauberg might well find its will to fight broken also and be taken easily. But Nammuor still dwelt within that place, and anything might yet happen. Robdan remembered Dorilian on the parley field the day before, facing an amused Nammuor and trading words that hinted at terrible power. What had he overheard? One sorcerer speaking to another? The rumors that fueled Robdan's thoughts were legion.

"You want me to be there to relate truthfully all that I witness."

"Yes. That's all I ask. This is a day Essera will never forget, and you have the singular privilege of being the sole Kheld to bear witness. I should call that remarkable."

Robdan rose to the sound of troops passing outside and took his new sword and belt in hand. Strange as it would be to do so, he knew he would wear it. As he turned to go, he noticed a sword, long and gleaming, laid out on the nearby bed. It was not the one Robdan had parried against, nor like it. Not like it at all. This blade was massive, intricate, shining metal the color of mist. Latticed with overlays, the hilt carved in polished curves was a thing from a time come and gone, or maybe yet to come. Robdan recognized it not only because he had seen Dorilian use it to slay a great beast but also because images of that blade appeared often in studies of ancient things.

*Dorilian plans to use it!* Astonished by what he'd just seen, Robdan stepped out into a camp mobilized for war. *The great sword that legend says was saved from being lost after the Aryati slew the Highborn King Telarion and his sons.* A slain Prince's young daughter had fled with the sword and it had become the possession of the Sordaneons, her sole dowry upon her marriage to Deben I. Beautiful and storied, it had served as the State Sword of Sordan for more than sixteen hundred years. Beside it had rested a crown of white gold and emerald fire.

Why had Dorilian brought these things here? The storied sword and the princely device of power that was the Sordan Coronal?

Because he meant to use them, surely. But for what—a battle or a coronation?

Robdan had already mounted and taken his place with Dorilian's entourage when Dorilian emerged from his tent and swung easily onto the great ivory war horse Legon Rebiran held for him. Dorilian's appearance evoked both awe and confusion. He wore Derlon's Armor: The fabled Eagle breastplate of the Sordaneon rulers spread its silver wings across his chest and gauntlets of smooth molded metal sheathed his forearms from wrists to elbows. Greaves of that same silver metal covered his legs from above the knees to the tops of fine boots crafted from panels of thick emerald leather carved and silvered in wonderous design. Though Dorilian's belt was that of a prince, not a soldier, and a regal cape of emerald velvet—lined with silver ermine and hemmed with sable, chased with his Hierarchate's silver eagle—fell from his shoulders, he looked ready for war. In place of a helm such as a warrior might wear, Sordan's emerald crown blazed upon his brow. Across his back, Dorilian had strapped a silver ghost of a sword only those who had witnessed him in battle at Bynum had seen before. Those that had knew that sword to be the stuff of legend.

Robdan tried to decipher the glance that passed between Legon and Tutto. That look said they had known this day would come.

Dorilian paid no attention to the multitude of his army but looked beyond them at dawn-tinged Stauberg framed against a dark sky. When he rode through his gathered troops to take position at their head, past his own soldiers and those of his allies, men more likely than he to die that day, their cheers faded on their lips.

It had been two hundred and eighty years since a Highborn Prince had openly ridden into battle. What the armies arrayed at Stauberg were seeing now, no person living, save Marenthro in Permephedon, had ever seen. They wore the aspect of a host that knew they marched into history.

The sight of Stauberg seemed just as chilling. The Wall no longer soared above the city or draped its famed towers with power. Instead the city looked diminished, stripped of its crowning glory. Stripped even of light. The wall that remained, high and black, had been built with forgotten Aryati technology during the first century following the Return. Maintained as the sacred seat of Ergeiron's stunning transformation, the old fortification lifted pristine ramparts around Stauberg's old city but—unlike the Wall—did not enclose all the centuries-old hamlets and neighborhoods that had grown around the city. Throughout the night residents had fled into the city and now those neighborhoods stood undefended.

Bersyas and Hebron's generals moved their troops forward in two prongs, clearing the road and then the great boulevard leading to the massive Gate of the Transformation, carved from blocks of blue agate with images of Ergeiron's deeds. Other forces proceeded to widen the military corridor, going house to house. The main army stopped moving when it reached a large park overlooking the city, just out of long-bolt range from troops lining the black battlements. Between the mighty forces and extending to the monumental Gate was a broad, open approach. With a gesture, Dorilian sent Legon forth bearing the cropped flag of an emissary. The emerald and silver banner flickered on the wind.

Robdan kept his horse near that of Tutto and was glad of the army arrayed between him and the enemy. Stauberg was a formidable city and there remained a chance soldiers might pour forth from the gate. Sunlight glinted from the thousands of spears and swords being displayed along the ramparts. Larger, more fearsome weapons hunkered on the heights.

"Is that the Wall, what's left of it?"

Tutto humphed. "What stands before us is not the Wall, but a relic of the Aryati from before Ergeiron underwent his transformation. You look upon why the Entity is called a Wall and not a Guardian or Shield."

"I saw it for the first time yesterday from a distance and not in its full glory."

"Well, I have seen the Wall's full glory, and right now I prefer it this way."

Legon reined in before the gate. His voice bellowed toward the city's defenders and back toward the army they faced. "By the mercy of Leur and his Thrice Royal Highborn Grace, Dorilian Derlon Amynas Sordaneon, Hierarch of Sordan and descended of the gods, you are given this opportunity to lay down arms and accept his amnesty—in return for embracing the terms of his peace!"

Movement at the top of the gate preceded the appearance of Erenor, bright-helmed and wearing Stauberg colors, flanked by his generals.

"Tell your master that we will not lay down arms and that we mean to oppose him! This city is autonomous—Ergeiron's own— and it will not bow and scrape to Labran's forsaken line nor that of a Kheldish pretender!"

Legon dipped his flag, announcing that he would return with that answer.

"Wait!"

A flash of red, glimpsed beneath a cloak of gray, heralded Nammuor's arrival. He did not look at Legon, who had halted and now waited below. Instead, the Sorcerer looked out across the open space at the troops.

"I would speak with you, Sordaneon!" Robdan knew not by what means Nammuor projected his voice, only that it—like Erenor's— carried across great distance. The Aryati had possessed such means.

From his place at the head of the Sordani and Lacenedoni forces, Dorilian lifted his gaze to Stauberg.

"What's he doing?" Robdan whispered to Tutto. Dorilian had removed his heavy cloak, which Tutto had taken, and now urged his horse forward and was cantering to join Legon.

"Just watch. He has their measure. They don't have his."

The ramparts bristled, soldiers and citizens alike seeking to catch a glimpse of the enemy. Of *him*. Dorilian knew the stories the northlands told of him, knew them all by heart. Derlon's Heir and Labran's image, thrust upon Essera against its will. Rill Lord and rebel. Neuberland's bane. Marc Frederick's failed experiment. Permephedon's traitor and Stefan's nemesis. Madman and mystery. And Highborn, bearing the blood of Leur in his veins—always, for them, that fact resounded. Years ago, he had traveled to Stauberg and met the man who would shape his life, but none of these people would reflect on that. They remembered only his adolescent ambition upon which a generation had heaped judgment and condemnation.

What they had forgotten was their own legends.

Dorilian stopped his horse in front of his massed troops, between them and the city and within hailing distance. A hand gesture from him signaled Legon to return. Flag lowered, Legon cantered back to the line.

Then Dorilian, facing the city, lifted his head and slowly spread wide his arms, hands open, empty, in the age-old acknowledgment of men who need no swords.

Nammuor laughed. His dark voice floated down like a caress.

"What did you do to negate Ergeiron's magic? Or is it true what the populace is saying—that Ergeiron refuses to stand against one of his own brother's blood?"

"I defer to Ergeiron—wherever he is." Dorilian's voice also carried to those on both sides.

Nammuor spread his own hands, indicating the rampart's defenders. "You play to the masses, Dorilian. It is ever what you do best. To men who cannot even see what you are. But you… you see what *we* are. Ergeiron may have retreated, but I sense that he resides here still, within this structure our ancestors raised from the depths of the world. He underwent his transformation here in this very spot! He's still *alive* within the Aidion at the heart of this fortress. His mighty and unbreachable corpus inhabits this city. If you attack, will he not defend himself? You and your men are flesh and blood—whereas this stuff"—Nammuor smote the battlement upon which he stood—"holds Ergeiron's immortal flesh! Mere men cannot scale it and even you cannot break it!"

*The blustering fool.* "Have I your answer?"

"Yes!" Erenor grabbed a spear from one of his guards and flung it, straight and sure, at Dorilian. The weapon spun wickedly but fell far short. The best spearman in the land could not have thrown it far enough to reach Dorilian as he sat unchallenged astride his ivory horse.

"So be it."

"Sordaneon!"

Nammuor's command went unheeded as Dorilian urged his horse into an easy lope back to his army. At the front line of cavalry, on a modest rise in full view of the city and the body of his troops, he wheeled the beast around and stopped. Then he dismounted. He looked back toward the city along a broad boulevard of stone and ice. Two men rushed forward to hold his horse.

The time had come to awaken the World again. For too long it had slumbered, its truths forgotten or exchanged for lies.

*Remember.*

Facing Stauberg, Dorilian gestured to his troops, the combined armies standing about him in a crescent of many colors, armor and weaponry glinting even in the faded winter sun.

"*They* cannot shatter your Wall!" Dorilian's voice carried as Nammuor's had, clear to them all. "But I *can*!"

Footstep. Heel. Muscles of the calf, then thigh. The Armor activated and Dorilian launched. To anyone watching, he would appear to be a blur. Midpoint between Stauberg and his troops, from a slight rise of ground from which he could see the Gate of Transformation and also the ghostly shapes of Rill rings above the distant harbor, Dorilian arrested his momentum, stopped, and took up his stance. Practices unfolded in his memory, so many—the King's House in Sordan, cliffsides at Rhondda. He could do this.

Feet apart, body angled toward the city, Dorilian extended his left arm, his palm turned skyward. The Rill Stone on his hand flashed bright as a star as he laid himself open to the Rill. Here on Stauberg's plain, as in its harbor, his Entity slept beneath the surface, but Dorilian could touch Derlon's dreams. The Rill's sleeping power. All at once, throughout the city and the fields surrounding it, the temperature dropped and the ground itself gave forth an emanation, shimmering currents that wavered before his eyes. Before everyone's eyes. Streams of light spun out of the air on high and up from the earth pooled in Dorilian's ungloved hand and clothed his arm. With every ounce of will, he pulled the collected energy into a ball of white fire.

*Now.* Ergeiron had created him. Created *this.* Now Ergeiron must suffer the consequences.

Using his other hand, Dorilian drew the device sword from behind his back. Green-white, bejeweled with emeraldine, the blade gleamed against the snow with an ice all its own. He held it aloft, then swung it in an arc over his head, pulling back his arm so the blade's tip touched the ball of fire in his hand.

The sword blazed purple and white, snaked with light. Energy leaped from the white ball in Dorilian's hand, crackling across the plain like a living, many-tentacled thing, growing as it went. Becoming a wave. That wave slammed against Stauberg's outer fortification as writhing fire, penetrating the seamless black stone with such fury that it became a mass of seething fissures.

As Nammuor had asserted, Ergeiron—though now invisible— still inhabited the transformed wall. Inhabited... and suffered. With a fearsome noise the Wall shattered.

Defenders screamed, many falling into the destruction. Those uninjured by the blast fled the ramparts. A gaping breach appeared, smoking and filled with clots of Wall debris, opening the way into the city.

Did Entities feel pain? Dorilian now knew the answer. As the stunned army at his back watched, nearly as awestruck as Stauberg's defenders, Dorilian ignored the distant throb of the Wall's torment and turned. He extended his hand again, this time toward the northern fortifications. Again, the air turned cold. Again, energy flowed from air and ground into a swirling ball of white fire in his hand—singing power into his skin—and again he brought down the sword in a deliberate arc.

Tendrils snaked across the plain like a demon's tongue, turning another section of the towering wall to rubble. A fine red mist billowed onto the field, drifting into an immense and eerie silence filled only with Stauberg's distant calamity.

Ergeiron's Immortal Wall, Stauberg's glory for two thousand years, having stood against the Aryati and formidable even without its otherworldly extensions, lay in ruins.

The deed done, Dorilian let his left arm drop until it hung, Rill Stone quiescent again, at his side. Only the Gweroyen Sword still gleamed like a living thing, held aloft, a deadly force in his right hand.

Bersyas, who had been watching him, seeing that Dorilian had finished and recognizing the moment, roused his men. "Now!" Bersyas shouted. He spurred his horse forward and led the advance rank of his fighters into the breach Dorilian had created. On the opposite flank, Lacenedon's general also urged his men on and both armies, with cries of victory and newly heartened, poured across the remaining distance. All gave Dorilian a wide berth.

Only when the advancing armies had outrun his location did Dorilian permit himself to show weakness. The amount of Rill power he had summoned, and used, rivaled that of the Debens. Had he not prepared himself so well in advance, weakened the Wall ahead of time... He dropped to his knees, his head resting against his grip on the sword.

*Are you happy now with what I've done?* he silently asked of the Entity he had just crippled. *Nammuor will have to flee now. He knows you're merely wounded and, because of that, he will not choose to face me here.*

Which was just as well. Dorilian at the moment didn't think he could rise from his knees.

Cursing, Tutto grabbed up the reins of Dorilian's horse and handed them to Legon. "Come on!" he barked. Leaving the stunned Hebron and the Esseran Lords on the rise, they galloped forward to their Hierarch. Robdan, not knowing where he should go, and not wanting to be left alone among Staubauns, urged his horse after them. Sounds of fighting rolled from the city, screams and the distant clashing of weapons.

As the wind whipped cold around them, Tutto dismounted, spread the royal Eagle cloak he had carried with him, and threw it around his kneeling liege. Dorilian gave a grateful glance.

"My thanks, Tutto."

Tutto grunted. He unhooked the large bag he'd carried behind his saddle. "I thought I'd seen all your pretty tricks!" he snapped. "Fireballs and targets, eh? Get the Rill to heed your will—there's a good one. Use the Armor to slay a beast. But where did *that* come from? You just laid to ruin the Immortal Wall! Not even Sebbord ever did such as that! Your own uncle only laid low the damn Vermillion Aqueduct!"

"When Ergeiron withdrew his protection, that wall became mere stone again—just like the Aqueduct."

"Well, you certainly laid it as low." Tutto handed Dorilian a flask and gestured for him to drink. "Good malt, so sweet it would choke a honeybee. If you don't get your blood back up, you'll be good for nothing. Let's get some food into you now."

This time the glance he earned was far less grateful. But Dorilian drained the full contents of the flask. "I'm better already," he said before he handed it back. He looked toward Stauberg, from which smoke and shouting reached their position.

"Not nearly enough. Not after a display like that. Sebbord would have my ass on a pike if I let you do more than lift a cup."

"Sebbord is dead."

"Your grandfather, my liege"—Tutto reminded stiffly—"died a very old man. And he ate like a godborn Prince to the end of his days."

Despite Tutto's objections, Dorilian rose to his feet and prepared to mount his horse. Robdan saw no further sign of weakness. The mounted Eagle Guard, held back from the fighting, stood at the ready nearby. Hebron and the Lacenedoni nobles, seeing Dorilian standing and purposeful once more, rode up.

"It will be a rout in the city, Thrice Royal." Hebron's manner already reflected a change in how he viewed Dorilian. "The enemy is disorganized. They have fled from the fortifications. We may enter without undue danger."

Dorilian swung astride his horse. He looked at the city, its white palaces and beautiful towers rising above its mottled, broken Wall. He too heard and saw signs of the fighting being waged within. "You may take the city with my blessing, so long as it is in Handurin's name. However, the time is not yet right for me to enter there."

"But surely, Thrice Royal—"

Dorilian shook his head. "Don't think me afraid. I hold the advantage and Nammuor still has his ships. But he will find them no refuge. My fleet arrived from Maskos this morning."

"Your fleet!"

In landbound Lacenedon, with its vast seas of grass, how easily they had forgotten that Sordan ruled the Kolpos by its ships.

"When will you enter the city, Thrice Royal?" one of the others asked.

"When it is won and time to secure it."

Though the Lords of the Royal North looked unsure, they clearly did not want to delay when there was a victory to be had. Making hasty bows, they rode off to pursue their interests in Stauberg's fall. Foremost in Hebron's mind would be to search for his cousin, the royal hostage Palaistea.

Robdan could barely believe he was witnessing such events or that he might soon walk Stauberg's fabled streets and look upon its many wonders. Though his uncle Tobold had served at Marc Frederick's court here—and there had been, for at least a hundred years, a sizable Kheld presence in the city—Robdan doubted any Khelds remained. The city's inhabitants had slain any they could get their hands on following the murders of the Malyrdeon Princes. That in itself gave Robdan pause. He would be safest to stay near Dorilian and, with any luck, he would still set eyes on the salt sea.

But he would not see Ergeiron's Wall, one of the wonders of the World. Not now. He sighed, then looked over to see Dorilian gazing back at him.

"Why the long face, Master Robdan?" Dorilian appeared amused. "Stare not too mournfully at that ruin. Am I the only one who has not forgotten that the Wall *is* Ergeiron—and that Ergeiron, an Entity, is Immortal?"

A chill seized Robdan. He wondered if he could ever get used to this man he now knew could hurl sorcery through the air—and know men's minds. "Then the Wall is not dead?"

"No. I did not kill the Wall. I but drove Ergeiron to vacate this mortal foundation. And then I *breached* it. All that's needed for Ergeiron to return the Wall to its former state is a restoration of its reason for being here. Its Promise. Which is why I will not ride into Stauberg just yet."

Robdan blinked as he remembered the conversation that morning. Dorilian had explained it already. He could not yet enter Stauberg because *he* was Highborn. A man of godborn blood.

Just by Dorilian's presence in the city, the Wall would be reborn.

# 47

It is easy for people to overlook that the Wall is not truly a
wall at all, but merely the most visible aspect of a reactive
Entity devoted to maintaining the integrity of Leur's
Creation. Because the Wall exists along structures of
Time, its dimensions are not immediately apparent and
many of its functions are more hidden than those of the
Rill, which is similarly oversimplified.
EPIRADES, *PROGENITORS OF THE ESSERAN KINGDOM*

Dorilian entered Stauberg within the hour. In advance of his
arrival, he secured the city's perimeter to bar looters and
thieves from tarnishing his victory. Not least of those he would
forbid entrance would be any who had fled the city in advance of
the battle. They had trusted neither their Wall nor their liberators,
and to his mind they deserved banishment until their loyalty could
be established.

"Fighting has ceased in all but the harbor district." Tutto had
been in communication with the victorious troops.

"Did any enemy ships escape?"

"None. Our warships bottled them in."

They were a small party, Dorilian and his Eagle bodyguard along
with his entourage, though by the time they reached the Wall, they
were of sufficient number to draw notice. Word spread quickly and
soon the streets leading to the Gate of Transformation were lined
with people, inhabitants and soldiers alike, come to see the Hierarch
set foot in the city. Dorilian bypassed the famed Gate, though it lay
open, choosing instead the first of the great breaches he had created.
His horse picked its way through and around the smoking rubble.
He dismounted just before the Wall itself and bade a guard to lead
his horse the rest of the way. Dorilian directed the same of Robdan
and Legon and all but a few of his bodyguard.

"Enter ahead of me, or I will not guarantee where you will be after."

Robdan walked slowly and stumbled but a little as he passed through the breach. Only now did he realize fully what a formidable fortification Stauberg's wall was, even now when uninhabited by a god: half a league thick and taller than any structure in Amallar save Rill-crowned Bellan Toregh. Freshly broken and gaping, the edges of the rupture shimmered as might starlit water. Glistened. Robdan reached out his fingers to touch a piece of shorn stone. The surface yielded slightly and he pulled his hand away. The Wall was not cold but warm, of a texture more like damp clay than rock. In those places where the dying light of day fell upon it, it had a color like blood. Even the smell of it was not that of stone but had the disturbing complexity of soil and flesh and living things.

Dorilian entered the breach only when everyone else had fully passed into the city. He would not endanger those who trusted him when he did not himself know what to expect. Leaving behind a handful of soldiers who would ensure that none entered after him, he stepped within the matrix of the Entity. Ergeiron's reality smote him like a wave crashing down upon a ship at anchor, surging against Dorilian's tiny being in a mighty current. He was glad to have his own weight anchored to mighty bedrock.

*Time.* The Wall's physical stuff existed simultaneously throughout Time. The stratum it occupied in the Creation had appeared, legend had it, upon the birth of the Three. Born with them, it existed no further into the Past than They and extended only into Futures in which the Highborn existed. When the Sons of Amynas had Returned, Ergeiron had founded Stauberg in a place to access that stratum, facing the Rift and the sea. The Entity had become manifest as such upon Ergeiron's transformation, and from that day its corpus had allowed generations of Malyrdeons to examine their past and peer into their futures.

Brother to the Rill, the Wall still stood, though all those who might have spoken to it were now gone. *Gone for us,* Dorilian realized. Not necessarily gone for all or forever. Other lives, past and maybe even to come, bespoke Ergeiron still. Ergeiron might even now be telling Endurin that Dorilian stood within this breach.

Dorilian placed the hand upon which the Rill Stone burned with green fire onto the Wall's warm, damp matrix. He did not fear the pairing. The Rill inhabited too much of Dorilian now for the Wall to do more than press against his boundaries. *Know me*, he willed thought into silent stone. *Tell them. Make sure that he will be here—and that I will meet him.*

For Ergeiron had told the Wall Lords about Dorilian. Of that, Dorilian was sure. It was from that knowledge—against him, because of him, perhaps even to assure that Dorilian would be born or destroyed—that Endurin had brought Marc Frederick to the World.

Robdan still lingered at the edges of those who had entered ahead of the Hierarch. He had finished looking in wonder at so many great buildings arrayed between palace-crowned hills and faced the broken wall again when Dorilian emerged from the breach.

A crack like thunder accompanied a burst of blue as Dorilian continued to walk forward, toward Robdan and Legon. Robdan staggered backward as the glow enveloped the fissured wall—then spread. Azure light raced through the shattered structure, a lattice of spider-silk veins, until the substrate itself seemed aglow. In the breach through which they had just passed, climbing over rubble, the body of the Wall extruded new corpus into the gap. Pieces that had fallen, whether near or far, leaped suddenly and of unnatural will back into place. Like a wound in a living thing, the rupture began to seal itself from within. Dorilian, confident and reverent, stepped in front of his men and faced the Entity. He lifted the shining Gweroyen Sword aloft—not in challenge, Robdan realized, but in salute. The sword blazed with the same blue light that shone from the Wall.

"Ergeiron!" Dorilian cried, and the name was taken up by those around him. The name of the son of Amynas and Leur resounded as residents of Stauberg came forth from their houses and places of hiding. Exclamations of wonder flooded the streets of a city shocked by the suddenness of its defeat.

"Look!" they cried. "The Wall! The Wall!"

The Wall proved itself a living thing and surged as though Creation itself flowed through it. With a sound heard throughout the city, the solid matrix groaned, then swelled, flowing thickly to seal the great wounds Dorilian had made. Slowly at first and then with such speed that things happened one on top of another, the Wall rebuilt itself. The dazed populace poured into the streets to witness their Entity's resurrection. The Wall's regeneration slithered and climbed, its groans became a hum and then, in a burst of pure magic, a clear tone of completion. No longer broken, its breaches healed as if they'd never existed, the Wall sheathed itself in brilliant adamantine and threw up white arches like bones. It raced away from its foundations, spreading outward to its former perimeter. Finally, with a clear high sound none in any mortal lifetime had ever heard, the structure spun a veil of shimmering translucence overhead, pale against the chill rose sky.

Dorilian lowered his sword.

From this day, thousands could proclaim witness of what they had seen.

A Highborn Prince had returned to Stauberg. Had conquered and thrown down their Wall and then restored it.

Every person within Dorilian's sight, every man and woman in the street, every soldier and noble, his own or formerly an enemy, had fallen to their knees and pressed their faces to the ground in abject worship. Moved by that same wonder, Robdan knelt and lowered his head.

"My ships will be harder to replace than your men!"

Erenor's blood, already cold, ran colder as Nammuor's rage erupted. Soldiers and scholars scattered to every side as he and Nammuor stormed into the map room on the top floor of Stauberg's Harbor House. The room evoked the sea. A floor paved with tiles of lapis and pale-yellow stone, a compass at its center, was overarched by a smooth plaster ceiling, lines as flowing as water itself, washed with blues and pastels. From the center of that ceiling rose the golden arches of the building's landmark dome. But Nammuor beheld neither the room's beauty nor its tranquility. Men fled the room rather than look upon his pale, furious face.

Erenor took little satisfaction from the extent to which Nammuor had underestimated their adversary. Dorilian's war ships bottled Nammuor's ships within the harbor, launching fire against the amassed vessels. They had known Sordan's navy was in northern waters, worrisome as sharks prowling the dark seas of Maskos, but Nammuor had dismissed the threat. He had counted on the invincibility of Stauberg's Wall to keep his fleet safe until, if needed, they could sail out in sorcerous force. Now he raged that he should have known the Highborn thing would betray him.

Maybe it had.

*It let Nammuor in.* Erenor could fathom no other explanation. *The Wall exists through the entirety of the Second Creation, including Time—the Past and the Future. It let the slayer of its sons enter because it knew what would happen. The Wall anticipated Dorilian.*

Erenor had followed Nammuor in the mad hope of still working a victory, but now could hardly believe what he was hearing and seeing. He had half hoped Nammuor had kept his cursed Diadem in the city and would put it on after leaving the darkened Wall. Anything to turn the tide in their favor. Instead, Nammuor not only had not used his device but seemed intent on escape.

"The battle has just begun!" Erenor still wore full battle regalia, in command of an army in complete disarray. With the Wall breached, Stauberg's soldiers had fallen back to defend the harbor and royal Mount. Those soldiers, that was, who had not already thrown down their weapons rather than face godborn might. "Surely you do not intend to concede the city!"

"I do! Because of *that*!" Nammuor pointed out the nearest window. A curtain of blue light had just bisected the harbor. As the veil of light danced across the outer islands to touch the silent sentinels of the Rill mount, its angles shot skyward, creating wonder.

A tone like morning and trumpets penetrated the Harbor House walls as the familiar shape of the Wall reasserted.

"Put on your Diadem!"

Nammuor laughed. A mad sound. "Do you think I have it *here*? That I would bring it inside the bowels of an Entity to be trapped or destroyed? The Wall was supposed to keep Dorilian *out*!"

Klaxons of alarm, warnings of fire, sounded from the harbor. Not every missile lobbed would hit a ship. Soon the entire harbor would be in flames.

"But you're a sorcerer, aren't you?" Erenor stalked after Nammuor. "You burned Zepheron's ship! Caused the Dazun to rage! You can still save this city! You have other devices. I know you do. Defeat *him*! They think he's a god! Slay Dorilian and they will despair. Or is your paltry sorcery useless against him?"

"Useless?" Robe flaring around his furious form, Nammuor turned on Erenor. "The Wall protects him! It protects him *here*.

He knew this and he planned every step of this defeat—especially trapping my fleet. And you! You are finished. But he has not trapped me! I will have my revenge and take him at a time and a place of my choosing. Next time he will not have the Wall on which to stake his godborn ass."

"So you cannot take him with sorcery the way you hoped. Kill him! He's flesh and blood!"

With a snarl, Nammuor waved his hand.

The gesture threw Erenor bodily across the vast room, hard against the sea-colored wall, sword clanging to the floor. The golden gem buried at Nammuor's left temple blazed. With a flick of his fingers, Nammuor caused Erenor's sword to leap from the floor. Erenor barely saw the flash of metal before the sword penetrated his mail, then his ribcage, pinning him upright to the wall. Mouth open, gaping as blood bubbled around the entry wound made by his sword, he stared at the man who advanced upon him.

"Just how should I kill Dorilian?" Nammuor snarled, his black eyes burning with a mad violence Erenor had never dreamed would turn upon him. "Like that, you yapping common dog? Or like this?" He pointed and the great globe across the open room exploded, its pieces flying at Erenor as he struggled, pinned like an insect to the wall. White marble chunks struck him full force, crushing flesh and bone.

Crying out as his body sagged and bled, legs broken, Erenor grappled with the sword that held him to the wall, slicing his hands as he pulled at the blade. His guards, running to see what was happening, just as quickly backed away and fled for their own lives. No reason remained for them to stay and fight. If they had not thought Stauberg lost before, they knew it now.

"Or this!" Nammuor gestured to a mirror behind him. The huge, framed glass shattered, silvered shards leaping as a host of daggers through the air. Erenor screamed as the razor-sharp fragments stabbed his flesh in a hundred places, fixing his limbs to the wall, piercing his gut, his neck, his cheek. "Or maybe this?"

As Nammuor laughed maniacally, flame from the room's three fireplaces erupted into the air, then raced across the intervening distance to wrap Erenor in tongues of fire. Silk melted and burned and exposed blistered skin before the flames died against chain mail and leather. Nailed by steel and glass to the wall, his windpipe pierced and his body ruined, Erenor no longer resisted his torture.

Nammuor sneered and licked his lips. "You don't die nearly as appealingly as he will. You will die like the lowborn flesh you are. He would live much longer, his godborn flesh regenerating to repair each new wound. Imagine. He'd grow new skin, new flesh, new bones. New organs. He might take days—weeks—to die. You fool, I don't want to kill him—I very much want him to *suffer*. And his trickery here today makes me want that all the more. Maybe I did not catch him here the way we had planned, but next time we meet he will have no Wall, no Rill, and no escape."

Nammuor walked up to where Erenor hung, voiceless, fire still alive and burning slowly into skin beneath charred mail. Nammuor paused to admire his handiwork, tracing a thumb across Erenor's bloodied mouth. "How like Stefan you proved to be, thinking you could be a king. Dorilian's new sorcery amuses me, puppet. Much, much more than your whore-mongering ways. Even Stefan had more pride than you." With a sneer, he turned away. "Dorilian is welcome to Stauberg. I appreciate the irony of his taking it. But I will not be trapped within these walls now that he has entered the city."

Erenor blinked but could no longer lift his head. Blood frothed on his lips.

Nammuor reached under Erenor's chin, lifting his victim's head. "Who knows? Maybe the Sordaneon will make creative use of his newfound powers to end your miserable life."

Just before Erenor's head dropped again, he saw Nammuor draw a circlet ringed with *Ir* gems from his robe. Place it upon his brow. Touch it to fold light and space. When Nammuor was gone, only the shrill sounds of fighting closing in from the streets below filled Erenor's hearing.

# 48



Dorilian winced as he tested his right arm, bending it to better assess how well the strain he'd placed on his bicep was healing. Using Derlon's Armor had been a risk, and doing so led to… mishaps. But he had needed to defeat the Wall and liberate Stauberg. Take it—and look invincible doing so. In a war of gods, symbolic statement mattered.

The Malyrdeon Mount and its royal palaces had sustained little damage. Most of Erenor's troops had broken and run, and those that did not surrender had fled the city, leaving the palatial hill to be occupied by Dorilian's troops. The Mormantalorans, better organized and having less hope for their lives, had dug into positions overlooking the harbor, there to be uprooted in bitter clashes through the night. Darkness fell upon a city mostly silent, ruled by its Wall and its ghosts—stained red by the light of Nammuor's burning ships.

High above the city, the pale edifice of the Asae Eranos with its great throne hall, loomed. Within the palace's storied towers ranged hallways wonderful and adorned, passages bathed only by Wall light and the tormented reflections of flames from distant battles. With its corridor of golden pillars and its vaulted ceiling hung with the finery of centuries, the throne hall known as the Hall of the Victorious Three nevertheless loomed lifeless and empty, its stone-paved floor smoothed by darkness to a sheen of gray silk. It had the air of a crypt, a place long closed and gone to dust.

Dorilian walked the length of the celebrated hall and sensed its dust break about his feet, could feel it in his lungs and nostrils even though this chamber had been used and kept in order by a succession of false rulers. The Hall of the Victorious Three owned no dust save for that in his mind. No phantoms but those he knew to haunt his memories. He had left Legon and his Eagle Guard at the door to assure he would be alone with ghosts. On the paved area before the throne stood a low raised plinth bearing a fabled device carved of ghostly crystal, unused since the death of Endurin Malyrdeon.

*They broke the prime arrays in Sordan and Mormantalorus when they broke the Triempery*, Dorilian recalled. Broke the means of seeing and speaking with each other from afar. Only this prime remained along with a score of lesser arrays meant only for the sending of cylinders.

The array being useless, he bypassed it. Instead he ascended the steps of the midnight blue dais to the Star Throne of the Malyrdeons, vacant beneath its canopy of cerulean onyx and the faceted gleam of the Eternity Orb that rode above the throne's headpiece. Absently, he let his fingers drift across the shining gold arm of the Star Throne itself. Before this night, only his gaze had ever touched it. Twelve years ago, he had knelt at the foot of this platform, in acknowledgement of the one seated here, Marc Frederick. Before meeting him, Dorilian had knelt to but one man, his father. There had been no dishonor in that. But the Fur-Faced King? The usurper? Dorilian had balked, performing according to the dictates of prudence rather than respect—until respect had demanded its due and he had bent that formerly reluctant knee willingly.

*Last I saw this room, you were its master.* Dorilian turned his gaze along the great hall's length, seeing it again in his mind, ablaze with full light and glory, filled with people and pageantry. *I was but Deben's troublesome Heir that no one but you were willing to confront. In the end I stood beside you. Little did we know your death would be the price of that.*

Dorilian had never beheld an emptier chair. Even a royal throne served a simple function, after all, and that function was not to make a man a king. It struck Dorilian that he had known only one King. Fools had sat on this throne since and they had been as nothing to him. He touched the sweeping carvings, seeking traces of the one man he had never ceased to hope he might recover.

*This was your proper seat. Would you mind so very much?*

More likely, it would amuse him. Marc Frederick had always known who held the more valid claim. Removing the sword from his back and balancing the weapon beside his hand, Dorilian sat in the empty chair. Not one of his Sordaneon ancestors had ever planted his ass upon this throne or done what he now did, unwitnessed. In other times, it would have been an act of treason. Some would still call it so. He was glad there were no Khelds here to see him, that he had installed Robdan in a comfortable room in another tower. From the throne, the room's magnificent architecture opened to Dorilian like a story untold, the yawning spaces between the great pillars reminding him of Permephedon's Vault of Incorruption. Following the Wall's breaching and before entering the city, he had returned from there yet again, with Epirades's body, which he had instructed Tutto to restore in secret to its beloved resting place.

Now even that whim felt empty. With the passing of the Malyrdeons, Stauberg was and always would be a city of the dead.

Awareness prickled along the edge of Dorilian's extended senses, an alien energy. Another presence intruded here—a *lr* device not in this room but in contact with a device that *was*. Dorilian grimaced at the prime array and gazed into the murk until Nammuor's image, sculpted not of flesh but of energy writ upon air, appeared on the paved court before him.

"You suit the Throne," Nammuor observed. Though he was bare headed, not wearing the deadly Diadem he so loved, a bruised indentation from the device marred his high brow. It wasn't Highborn truth that exposed the long scar across Nammuor's face and the missing finger on his left hand; prime arrays did not display illusions.

"How are you doing this?" Dorilian asked. "Did you find some way to upgrade the array at Aral?"

A slight smile. "Scorn these arts I command if you wish, but they have their uses."

Aryati arts, forbidden and almost forgotten. Nammuor and his acolytes aside, only the Epoptes and Sages at Permephedon and Sordan still pursued such lost knowledge. Dorilian frowned. Mormantaloran magecraft was not known to include arrays.

"Do you hear them?" Nammuor turned his head as if listening. "They proclaim you in the streets. Dorilian Highborn. Rill Lord. The Sorcerer King. *Their* King. Do you really mean to deny what Stauberg offers with open hands?"

"It would suit you too well if I did not."

Nammuor's soulless eyes glittered. "There are some things well worth a loss. Seeing you as you are now, grown into your power, arrayed with your devices, is one of them. You have proven a better adversary than I expected. Stauberg is yours. I concede it to you."

Dorilian bit back a snort. "You are quick to concede what you have already lost."

"I will not concede you."

"Or claim what you will never have."

Nammuor's teeth flashed through the gloom. "Don't be so sure of that. Some things are just a matter of time."

"Is that why you've appeared before me? A pathetic shade? To argue the point?"

"Don't tell me you haven't considered Essera for yourself."

Dorilian leaned back in the throne. That his posture felt completely natural was not simply a matter of good furniture design. "You haven't unearthed any secrets. I put forth the Sordaneon claim at the Archhalia more than a year ago, following Stefan's demise."

"And withheld it, a bare month after, in favor of Handurin," Nammuor reminded. "Why? Why throw all this away?"

"Because Stauberg is nothing to me. It's a bauble, naught but a false promise of power. Besides, Handurin is more of a threat to you than I am."

"Handurin is not a threat to anyone but himself... or maybe those ridiculous Khelds that lap at his every footfall." Nammuor's expression soured as if he'd bitten a moldy grape. "Any fool can see that he is little more than your tool in this venture, a grass soldier. That callow youth is defenseless without you. He has nothing you have not given him or otherwise made possible for him to attain— not his return, not his alliance, not even his precious Amallar. You made it all possible. You've taken up the patrimony of Leur and you're spending it on a pointless gamble!" Nammuor's raised voice, anger threading through his words, barely registered in that high chamber. "Once you held your sacred blood above that of lesser men. In those days, you let fools go begging. Stefan, for one."

Dorilian felt the bite of truth. "You liked that too well. He was your cruelest weapon against me. You should have let him live for that alone. You got greedy. You listened to your minion and threw in your hand."

"No, I forced yours. I brought you out of hiding. Now, they will all know what you are—you and your cursed breed."

That, too, was truth. "It could not be otherwise. I won't let you destroy us simply because I don't want to be their god."

"Destroy you?" Nammuor laughed at the accusation. His image paced before the throne, a petitioner and ambassador. "I've stayed my hand against you time and time again. You are Leurspawn and precious to me in all your facets. Others are more careless of you than I would be. I would put your gifts to far better use than you have."

"Your only wish is to murder me."

"True, but I might seek to preserve your grotesque bloodline first."

Dorilian marked Nammuor's petulant frown. "Has lovely Melenthas been complaining to you? Did you really think I would not see it? She was a very poor actress. I would say offhand that you lust for me more than she ever did."

"You would not be wrong."

Dorilian closed his hand about the hilt of the Gweroyen Sword where it glinted in the fitful light. "Leave. Take your falsehoods and insinuations with you."

Nammuor lifted his shining head and laughed, the sound filling the ancient hall. "I will, but not before I remind you that this thing I wear has marked you for mine; whether you accept that path or not, you cannot escape. Stefan saw to it that you and I would be forced to each other in the end. He slew all other options and made you *necessary*. If he hadn't, I would have killed you by now—or haven't you noticed that I have not been trying?"

Nammuor crossed the shadowed floor, his footfalls unheard in a silence so deep that thoughts pounded like surf. In his current form, no living man could stop him. Dorilian marveled at the art that had achieved this visitation. Nammuor's *lr* image mounted the steps of the dais and knelt as might a petitioner. He looked up with glowing eyes.

"I'm sure that by now the masses in that city are shouting your name! They want a Son of Amynas to rule them, a Highborn King upon a Highborn Throne. Stauberg is your place. Your throne. Your destiny, which not even Wall Lords could circumvent. The blood of Leur and Amynas is that of Immortals and God-Kings—even your iron will cannot make it less." The cruel mouth curved with remembrances. "You will not be easy for me. At Permephedon I had you in my power, I touched you and did not detect what you were. I would that I had taken more than your fingers then. Now you think you have put yourself out of my reach. But have you? This sorcery you wield intrigues me, but it will not make you safe. Nor will it protect that foolish Prince you foster. The next battle will be on my terms. I will destroy your Stauberg-Randolph Prince on the fields of Elithegh, and then, when you are without allies or recourse, I will come for you."

Nammuor rose, soundless as smoke, dark for all his silvered looks, and disappeared into the surrounding night. Nammuor had been but a shade, an image projected onto the very motes of dust before Dorilian's eyes—that could not hold its shape beyond Dorilian's willingness to entertain it. Nor had Nammuor worn his Diadem. He had not risked it even as a projection within the bounds of Stauberg's Wall Entity. Even in that form the Wall would have tried to destroy the god-infested thing.

Yet another phantom. Among a host.

Dorilian released his pent breath and felt the chill slide from his skin. He had won this battle, yes—but worse awaited. Gods were come to the field.

Willing his thoughts away, Dorilian again gazed about the room. Here in Stauberg's fastness, ghosts crowded near, the shades of men Dorilian had seen die. Some had been adversaries. Some few might have been friends but for his youthful resentments and determination to create enemies. Remnants of those Malyrdeon lives clung to these stones and provided witness.

"Did you know then that I would survive you?" In the encompassing silence Dorilian sensed a Wall truth. He acknowledged it. "Endurin's endgame doomed you all. It sent you to Permephedon to die—and it left me to survive."

How much had those ancient Wall Lords foreseen? The Wall's revelations were mere glimpses, never a whole picture. Had the Wall shown the Malyrdeons their lives would be rendered to enhance the weapon Nammuor wielded? If so, they should have fought harder.

Instead, they had embraced their Wall, entrusted themselves to it. They had left this battle to Dorilian, even though they had seen him alone but for the Rill. And for what? Hoping for an Entity to reemerge?

Feeling hollowed, Dorilian sank back in the throne and clung to his dream of a life without chains. The only certainty was that he would not find it here. He rose, retrieved his sword and descended the dais, his footfalls echoing. Dorilian walked to the center of the chamber and lifted his hand, generating an *orbus* bright enough to illuminate the high vaults of the ceiling.

A display of royal flags hung the length of the great corridor, a thousand years of majesty and empire, but the standard of the Stauberg-Randolphs did not float at their head above the throne. Erenor's obscenity of a banner hung in its place.

Now at last Dorilian mourned Stefan.

It should be Marc's banner there, the soaring symbol of the Stauberg-Randolphs a promise to be seen by all. Dorilian would not leave Stauberg until it was restored. He would not leave *Essera*.

Iron clanged to announce the great double doors to the chamber had opened, enabling men to intrude on his solitude. He closed his fingers to dowse the *orbus* as Legon trotted to his side.

"They would not be stopped."

No, these intruders honored no restraints on their privilege. Two of the men held aloft cressets that provided light enough to see by. Dorilian gazed upon a foursome of somber faces. Hebron. Megall of Bynum. A man named Gavril, Lord of the Eleutheron region of Laregh. Standing with them and looking uncomfortable was Estevan, the Bas of Gweroyen. In their hands they clutched their belts and weapons. Dorilian tensed his arm, prepared to draw the Gweroyen Sword. He put nothing past them.

Nearly as one, all four men dropped to their knees and laid their sheathed swords upon the shimmering, torchlit floor.

"Thrice Royal. Know where we stand—in this city, on this day. We have seen our great Entity itself proclaim your birthright. We, the Lords and peoples of the Royal North, descendants of the Returned and subjects of the God Born, uphold your rightful claim. We wish you to be our King."

---

## *END*

---

Kindly turn the page for a preview of the exciting finale to the Triempery Revelations:

# THE RILL LORD

"Show me." Hans lifted his eyes to Dorilian's suddenly startled ones. "Show me what you can do."

Dorilian looked at him for so long that Hans found himself holding his breath, waiting on that calm assessment. He watched as scrutiny collapsed inward, Dorilian consulting yet other considerations.

Hans persisted. "I know I'm not Highborn, I don't have the right—"

"It's not that. There are other things."

"Like what?"

Dorilian appeared to be caught upon the horns of answers he did not know how to give. "Like Marenthro, for instance," he said finally, looking annoyed. "Where has he been? It is he you should be asking. Has it even occurred to you that you might have talent of your own?"

A draft blew through the room and the fire blazed briefly higher on the grate.

"Talent? Me?" Hans scoffed. "I saw Marenthro a few days ago and he said nothing about that. Any talent I might have is probably too small for him to work with. I've heard about my family having some ability. People keep telling me my grandfather did. But he wore the Leur's ring… and I don't. The Epoptes said I probably can't."

"Epoptes?" Dorilian snorted. "As soon talk about beetles in a box trying to understand the universe. You have talent enough." Dorilian pondered the Rill Stone ring on his hand, then flicked a glance at Hans. "Let's play catch," he said, as if that decided it. He rose and visually searched the items of the house, seeking something to his liking.

Despite himself, Hans smiled. It sounded childish.

"You said you wanted to see. I think we should start simply. We can work our way up to eradicating barns and farmhouses." Dorilian picked up a small child's toy, forgotten behind a cushion. Shabby, brown and soft, it vaguely resembled a bear. He bounced it in his hand, then tossed it easily toward Hans. "Catch!" he commanded.

With the old habit of childhood, Hans put up his hands and

caught it neatly. He then sat there, on the edge of his seat, looking at Dorilian expectantly. "What do I do now?"

"You toss it back."

Hans did.

"You forgot to say 'Catch!'" Dorilian pointed out. He tossed it to him again. "Catch!"

"This is pretty silly." Hans caught the stuffed bear a second time.

"Do you want to continue or not?"

"Yes. I just don't understand."

"Understanding comes second, not first, with most things we do. When an infant starts to walk, it's not necessary that he understand the process. We do it because we can, not because we understand it."

"Catch!" Hans said, firing the bear back to him.

As they tossed the bear back and forth, Hans sought new paths of conversation. It would distract him from thinking that what he was doing looked ridiculous. "Robdan told me you faced Nammuor himself. He called him terrifying."

"With reason. The man is a monster. And I do not just say that. The Undying Crown is robbing him of what little humanity he ever had. His eyes have ceased to be human."

"But you defeated him. Catch!"

"Is that what you think?" Dorilian perched the bear on the arm of his chair, where it sat, its seed eyes bright from reflected firelight. "I didn't defeat Nammuor, Handurin. We never exchanged more than words. It was Erenor who lost his army at Stauberg. Erenor's men defended that city, and Erenor's fate rested on the success of that defense. It was Erenor who perished there. Nammuor lost his northern fleet and one division of his elite soldiers. I dealt him a blow—a significant blow, by destroying his fleet. More than that, I removed Stauberg from his influence and the north of Essera is out of contention. But defeated? No. That ravening thing is still full-fledged and powerful, and his garrison was not at Stauberg. His army is well-armed and trained, and it lies at hand still at Aral and Elithegh."

"We've got good armies. Yours and mine," Hans pointed out. Maybe he had started out with a ragtag army, but the forces Hans commanded now were battle-hardened and sharp. "My Staubaun divisions are growing daily with the influx of local lords and their men. And the Khelds have become fierce fighters. Their victories at Dazunor-Rannuli and Trulo have given them confidence like they've never had before."

"They've never had military success on this scale. Nor have they ever had so much at stake."

"They want a Kheld king. And they see that goal in reach."

"They may prove as monstrous as Nammuor."

Hans laughed. "Regretting our alliance?"

"No. Only the paucity of choices."

*Catch!*

Hans lifted his hands and caught the soft body of the bear. Then he realized what had happened. "You didn't say that out loud!"

Was Dorilian laughing? "But you did hear me say it."

**THE RILL LORD** IS
COMING IN 2026 FROM FOREST PATH BOOKS
https://forestpathbooks.com

# Author's Acknowledgements

I've said it before, and I'll say it again. A lot of people go into the creation of a world, a story, and a book. *The Walled City* is the result of a lot of hard work and, in some cases, a bit of serendipity.

My brother David Steele inspired the character of Davon Artos, the Sordani engineer who devises a way for Hans and his army to cross the flooded Dazun. As far as I know, David has no experience with either floods or bridge building—but he's an engineer and seemed like a good choice on which to model the character.

I owe so many heartfelt thanks to the people who find ways to let me know this series gives them joy. For example, avid readers like Dwyer Freeman and Nichole Whiteman at Thomas Wharton Elementary School in Lancaster, Pennsylvania are always eagerly waiting to read the next book. Your enthusiasm for this series inspires me. Shout outs also to the reviewers whose favorable opinions on the books of this series have led readers to venture into the story. Kay's Hidden Shelf gave *Sordaneon* a lovely and generous video review. Jordan Buxton's reviews of *Sordaneon* and *The Kheld King* are great intros to the story. And readers really should treat themselves to Joseph Poopinski's reviews of the series.

Many thanks also to my wonderful publisher Forest Path Books for believing in this series—especially now as it leaps toward its conclusion. Forest Path keeps my books in stock and offers signed editions. Next year there will be a completed series to offer!

Thanks also to the many artists who help bring the world of the Triempery to life. I must start of course with Larry Rostant, whose book covers for this series have been brilliant. Each beautiful cover concisely presents the core elements of the story. I also commission illustrations for each book; readers can look on my website or social media to see the amazing images created for *The Walled City* by Jamie Noble. His illustration of Cortogh, the Dog Man, is perfect and has become a fan favorite. For *The Walled City*, I commissioned maps of Essera and also of the city of Dazunor-Rannuli from Dominique44. Her maps really bring the world to life!

It's impossible to give enough praise to Christina Wooden, who has read and made significant contributions to every book in the Triempery series. Every reader of my work can thank her for editing my wayward commas into submission. And last but never least is my husband, Steve. If anyone ever has a right to complain about the amount of time I spend writing, editing, revising, creating social media content, commissioning artists, corresponding with other writers and fans... it's Steve. Instead, he fully supports me. He has read, edited, and made suggestions for every book in the series, often more than once. He has my thanks, and I hope he has yours too.

# ABOUT THE AUTHOR

**L.L. Stephens** has been writing science fiction and fantasy full time for several years. Published works include a debut novel in the deep dark past, short stories under various pen names, articles in medical journals, and pamphlets for everything from local politicians to a major international airport.

The Triempery series, which includes *Sordaneon*, *The Kheld King*, *The Second Stone*, *The God Spear* and *The Walled City* is a six-book series and life work. Look for the final book, *The Rill Lord*, in 2026. For excerpts from existing or upcoming books, lore, maps, and other related content, visit the L.L. Stephens website, *triempery.com*, or L.L.'s giveaway-happy social media.

# TRIEMPERY APPENDIX
## CHARACTERS

## MALYRDEONS—Past/Historical

*Ariande* Granddaughter of Endurin. Mother of Marc Frederick.

*Cienorr* Son of Ergeiron & founder of the Mormantalorus Nuarchate.

*Emrysen* Wall Lord & great-grandson of Ergeiron, who bestowed a conditional pardon on the Hen Kyon.

*Endurin* Last true Wall Lord & last Malyrdeon King of Essera. Endurin's Heir, Estevan, died unexpectedly, leaving only a natural daughter, who fled to sea & was caught in the Rift. Endurin later brought her son Marc Frederick back to the World.

*Epirades* Grandson of Ergeiron, a famous scholar who founded the Panagaos Library.

*Ergeiron* One of The Three, sons of Leur & Amynas. After his brother Derlon gave life to the Rill, Ergeiron founded the Wall, sealing dangerous Time Rifts opened during the Gweroyen War, protecting the Malyrdeon stronghold at Stauberg, & serving as a means by which his descendants could discern past & future events.

*Erremon* King of Essera, great grandson of Emrysen. Slain by Ardaenan King Thorondar in the First War with Ardaen

*Erydon* Great-great grandson of Emrysen, who granted the Khelds the wilderness of Amallar for their homeland.

*Telarion* Son of Ergeiron & founder of the Stauberg Principate, first Esseran king & ancestor of current Malyrdeons.


## MALYRDEONS—Present (and Associated Characters)

*Apollonia Halasseon* Queen of Essera; daughter of Elegiros, Prince of Tahlwent. Wife of Marc Frederick & mother of Jonthan. Deceased.

*Austell* Wall Lord, third cousin of Endurin & distaff cousin to Marc Frederick. Brother of Enreddon II. Died in the Demise.

*Elegiros Halasseon* Prince of Tahlwent; third cousin to Endurin. Father of Apollonia. Died in the Demise.

*Elhana* Daughter of Elhanan & Margarid. Exiled by Stefan.

*Elhanan* Son of Rheger Dannutheon; Wall-gifted; one-time tutor of Stefan & Dorilian at Permephedon. Husband of Margarid & father of Elhana. Killed by Stefan.

*Enreddon II* Prince of Stauberg; cousin to Endurin & distaff cousin to Marc Frederick. Scholarly, but not Wall-gifted, Enreddon supported Endurin when the aged king named Marc Frederick to be his Heir. Both of Enreddon's wives died in childbirth, failing to produce living sons. Later wed Palaistea. Died in the Demise.

*Ionais* Princess of Merrydn; daughter of Regelon & betrothed of Jonthan Stauberg-Randolph. Aunt by marriage to Hans.

*Margarid* A princess of Gweroyen who weds Elhanan. Daughter of Kathanos. Sister to Estevan IV Niarchos. Mother of Elhana, infant Princess of Dannuth & Stauberg. Exiled by Stefan.

*Ostemun Dannutheon* Prince of Dannuth; distant cousin to the Stauberg Malyrdeons. Sired three daughters. Grandfather to Kerr & Raphelon. Died in the Demise.

*PALAISTEA* Princess of Lacenedon; daughter of Lakron. Married Enreddon II. Mother to Eldon II & Enreddon III, Heirs to Stauberg & Lacenedon. Believed deceased.

*REGELON MERRYDEON* Prince of Merrydn; matrilineal cousin to Sebbord Teremareon. Father of Ionais, betrothed of Marc Frederick's son Jonthan. Died in the Demise.

*RHEGER DANNUTHEON* Prince of Hespera & later Prince of Stauberg; brother to Ostemun. Father of Elhanan. One of few Malyrdeons known to use an enhancer for translocation. Killed by Stefan.

*SAPPHIA* A Princess of Lacendeon who wed Rheger Dannutheon. Mother of Elhanan. Grandmother o Elhana. Exiled by Stefan following Rheger's death.

## SORDANEONS — Past

*DEBEN I/II/III* Son, grandson & great-grandson of Derlon (collectively known as the Three Debens), ushered in a Golden Age of Rill expansion & Triemperal growth that secured the Sordaneon dynasty. Builder/creators of Leseos, Bynum, Gignastha, & the Vermillion Aqueduct.

*DERLON* One of The Three; known as the Rill-Giver because he integrated his immortal body & life with remnants of the Rill, facilitating its rebirth. Epoptes believe Derlon's integration still directs the Rill's actions, though he has lost the ability to interact with other beings.

*PELEOR* Son of Derlon; slain by the Aryati, who poisoned his blood & spilled it on the mount at Simelon to be absorbed by the Rill. His blood still stains the platform & Rill structures.

*TARLON* Hierarch of Sordan during the Second War with Ardaen. The youngest of his three sons wed an Ardaenan princess to secure the truce. Tarlon was the last manifested Rill Lord, able to communicate with & influence the Entity. Opened the Rill node at Randpory Crossing.

## SORDANEONS — Present (and Associated Characters)

*BERSYAS GARHELEON* One of Dorilian's generals. Commands the 7th Viper.

*DAIMONAERIS* Princess of Mormantalorus. Daughter of Camas, the Mormantaloran Nuarch; half-sister of Nammuor. Married Dorilian. Mother of Levyathan II. Deceased.

*DEBEN IV* Son of Labran, & Ermenthalia, daughter of Mezentius, Prince of Suddekar. Later Hierearch of Sordan. Deeply paranoid, Deben had not set foot outside of Sordan's Serat in thirty-five years. Married Valyane, daughter of Sebbord Teremareon. Father of Dorilian & Levyathan I. Died in the Demise.

*DELEUS* Son of the Heir to Suddekar; great-grandson of Mezentius & grandson of Sebbord. Although a first (& second) cousin to Dorilian, Deleus is not Highborn.

*DELOS* Deben IV's twin brother. Son of Labran. Used the Lacenedon Crown to break the Vermillion Aqueduct & end the siege at Gignastha. Died after that deed from plasm shock.

*DORILIAN* Son of Deben IV & Valyane. Brother of Levyathan I. At the age of seven, witnessed his mother's murder. His precocious physical & empathic gifts allowed him to save his neonate brother. Determined to right wrongs done to his family. Reigning Hierarch of Sordan.

*ERMENTHALIA* Daughter of Mezentius & a Mormantaloran princess. Wife of Labran, mother of Deben IV & Delos. Bears title of Gracious Hierarchessa. Inclined to favor alliance with Mormantalorus, from which her mother hailed. Incarcerated in Sordan for treason.

*FAHME* Princess of Sordan. Noemi's daughter by Heran. Adopted by Dorilian.

*HAESKOS PERISKLERON* Dorilian's Admiral.

*LABRAN* Grandson of Tarlon; his mother was a princess of Ardaen. He wed Ermenthalia, daughter of Mezentius, Bas of Suddekar, & is father of Deben IV & grandfather of Dorilian. He objected to Endurin Malyrdeon naming Marc Frederick as Heir to Essera & at Marc Frederick's coronation refused to acknowledge him as King. Labran fought his way into the Rill node at Permephedon & was able to command the Rill to stop running, creating wide-spread panic. Taken captive by Marc Frederick & considered too dangerous to release, Labran was imprisoned at Stauberg, far from any active Rill nodes.

*LEGON REBIRAN* Son of Terveryen, Bas of Anit-Rebir. Youngest of six sons. Sent to Sebbord as a boy to enter Sordaneon service. Dorilian's friend. Commander of the Eagle Guard.

*LEVYATHAN I* Son of Deben IV & Valyane. Grandson to Labran & Sebbord. Brother to Dorilian. When enemies poisoned his mother, Levyathan was born months too soon to survive. Although saved by Dorilian, Levyathan's development was affected, & he suffered neurological deficits. Deceased.

*LEVYATHAN II* Son of Daimonaeris & Deben IV, raised by Dorilian as his own son. Heir to Sordan.

*MEZENTIUS* Bas of Suddekar. Wed a Mormantalorean princess. His eldest daughter Ermenthalia wed Labran & gave birth to Deben IV. Died in the Demise.

*NOEMI* Wet nurse & governess to the infant Levyathan I. Mother of Fahme. Deceased.

*PALLAS TROPHONEOS* Speaker of the Sordan Halia.

*PANDAROS VIDYAMEMNON* One of Dorilian's generals. Commands the 1ˢᵗ Viper

*PITAR KISTHODA* Arch Epopte/Arch Mage; chief at Dazunor-Rannuli.

*QUIRIN CHRYSOLEMNOS* Psilant, or leader, of the Brotherhood of Epoptes

*SEBBORD* Prince of Teremar. Possibly Rill-gifted, Sebbord trained as an Epopte & rose to the level of Archmage in service to the Rill. He wed twice & sired three daughters. Grandfather of Dorilian, Levyathan, Deleus & Tiflan. Murdered by the Seven Houses.

*SINON KOURANOS* Marc Frederick's administrator in Sordan during that city's occupation; later governor of Neuberland. Stefan's Archhalial Ambassador. Shifted allegiance to become Dorilian's Archhalial Ambassador.

*SOTER KOMETES* Military advisor assigned to assist Hans

*TERVERYEN REBIRAN* Bas of Anit-Rebir. Father of Legon & Cressida.

*THAROS ODAKKON* Epopte at Sordan.

*THURAYA LARES* Sage Physician; Dorilian's house physician.

*TIFLAN MOREVYEN* Bas of Teremar. Grandson of Sebbord but not Highborn. Seven feet tall, he is Dorilian's first cousin & a loyal ally.

*TUTTO RHUNNARD* An Estol who served as Sebbord's sword master & now serves Dorilian. Later Bas of Kolgya.

*VANEUS PINDAR* Dorilian's ambassador to Merrydn.

*VALYANE* Princess of Teremar. Sebbord's daughter, wife to Deben IV. Mother of Dorilian & Levyathan I. Murdered by the Seven Houses.

## STAUBERG-RANDOLPH (and associated characters)

*EMYLI* Daughter of Marc Frederick & Thora; was betrothed to Deben IV Sordaneon but ran away at age 14 with charismatic Kheld rebel Erwan Cedrecson. The pair wed & Emyli gave birth to Erwan's son, Stefan. To free Erwan from prison,

Emyli helped Kheld rebels gain access to the stronghold of Gignastha, resulting in three Highborn deaths & the bloody siege of that city. She later gave birth to her second son, Handurin.

*GARETH MORGEN*  Marc Frederick's steward, in charge of his household. Currently runs Emyli's household.

*HANS/HANDURIN*  Son of Emyli, reputed son of Erwan. Grandson of Marc Frederick. Brother to Stefan. During Stefan's reign, Hans was hidden in one of the World's archived pasts.

*JONTHAN*  Son of Marc Frederick & Apollonia. Prince of Dazunor. Married Ionais, princess of Merrydn. Their union was childless. Deceased.

*MARC FREDERICK*  King of Essera; great-grandson of Endurin Malyrdeon through Estevan II & Brenna Almarresda. Son of Ariande Malyrdeon & William Randolph. Considered a Malyrdeon in recognition of his relation to them, but he is not Highborn. Marc Frederick first married Thora, a Kheld woman. After Thora died of a miscarriage, he wed the Highborn princess Apollonia as a condition to becoming Endurin's Heir. He has two children: Emyli, his daughter by Thora, & Jonthan, his son by Apollonia. Died in the Demise & interred in the Vault of Incorruption.

*MARENTHRO*  Wizard of Permephedon; ageless & possibly immortal. No one knows much about him save that he is apparently benign & possesses both Wall & Rill affinity. Responsible for finding Marc Frederick for Endurin & bringing him back to this World. Hides Handurin in a past & brings him back after Stefan's death.

*STEFAN*  Son of Emyli & Erwan; grandson of Marc Frederick & adopted by him after Jonthan's death. Succeeded Marc Frederick as King of Essera. Married Nilla Lowenda but left no living heirs. Killed by Nammuor & Erenor.

*TREVOR ALLEN*  Captain of King's Guard, later of Emyli's guard.

## MORMANTALORUS (and associated characters)

*BAMATU*  Archmage at Aral.

*CORAM BARZANES*  Was with Nammuor at the Demise. Nammuor's emissary to Stefan. An adept in mage arts.

*NAMMUOR*  Ruler of Mormantalorus, half-brother to Daimonaeris. Reputed to have Aryati blood. Recovered the lost Diadem of the Devaryati. Responsible for the Demise. Intent on collecting the blood & life forces of the remaining Highborn.

*SALKREN ZEL*  Mormantaloran general. With Nammuor at the Demise.

## SEVEN HOUSES (and associated characters)

*CHYRALANE RANNULEON*  Denizen of Phaer, most prominent of the Seven Houses. Daughter of a Highborn prince of Rannul. Married a Lord of Phaer. Opposed to any action that would lessen the cartel's control over the Rill. Very tall.

*GERON THOPTIS*  Denizen of House Hedys.

*IPHITHUS KHEPRION*  House of Phaer. Nephew & heir to Chyralane.

*PHILEMON LEANDER*  Wealthy Staubaun merchant, aspiring to nobility. His daughter married the Denizen of House Haralambdos. Sordaneon aligned.

*RHYNOS TYBENOS*  Denizen of House Koillos.

*THIRZAN ESDRAS*  Denizen of House Haralambdos.

# ESSERAN STAUBAUNS (and associated characters)

*ALBAN ESKEROS* Gignasthan lord whose lodge Dorilian used during his rebellion.

*ALGO MISENOS* Nobleman related to the Aigelleros family in Dannuth; currently Dannuth's ambassador to Dazunor.

*ARTON METAGORAS* Third son of the Archon of Eddethel (Merrydn). Assistant to Cullen Brodheson. Wed Euella Phaeros. Executed for Stefan's murder.

*ASPHALLADRA VELOS* Youngest daughter of the Archon of Chennor; wed Cullen Brodheson. Mother to Ranwulf & Allysa.

*BURELAN PHAEROS* Late Bas of Rannul. Grandson of the last Prince of Rannul. Slain by Stefan's forces during the Rannul War.

*DESMOS VALLSIRAN* Raphelon's attendant & man at arms.

*EGIDIUS MOGENS* Merchant/broker in Dazunor-Rannuli; aligns with Hans & the Khelds.

*ERENOR THOLEROS* Cousin to the Halasseon rulers of Tahlwent; grandson of a natural daughter of Elegiros. Friend of Stefan. Currently Bas of Aral & Prince Regent for Handurin.

*ESTEVAN IV* Bas of Gweroyen. Son of Kathanos Niarchos. Maternal grandson of Estevan III, last Highborn Prince of Gweroyen.

*EUELLA PHAEROS* Burelan's sister. Forced by Stefan to wed Arton Metagoras. Current Basarchessa of Rannul.

*GRENANT AIGELLEROS* Minor lord loyal to Ostemun. Wed Raeva, eldest of Ostemun's daughters. Father of Kerr.

*GWENNA* Hebron's mistress.

*HEBRON URSENOS* Cousin to Lakron, late Prince of Lacenedon, & Palaistea. Current Bas of Lacenedon.

*JARON VELOS* Archon of Chennor. Father of Asphalladra & Zoranna. Ambitious nobleman intent on arranging high-ranking mates for his three daughters.

*JERENIELL HEBDOMON* Noblewoman dwelling in Dazunor-Rannuli; cousin to Raphelon. An accomplished chemist who creatres colors for glassmaking.

*KATHANOS NIARCHOS* Archon of Peleddor. Father of Estevan. Friend of Emyli.

*KERR AIGELLEROS* Son of Grenant & Raeva. Grandson of Ostemun. Nephew of Rheger & cousin of Elhanan & Raphelon. Bas of Dannuth.

*KONDROS BRAGORD* Ally of Erenor.

*LAAVI* Maid-in-training in the fortress of Askyllon who assists Aubrey.

*LUCIEN ILLARION* Heir to Serrain. Supporter of Stefan. Executed for Stefan's murder.

*MACHON EPIROSI* Archon of Penrhu. Breeder of blood horses.

*MEGALL URANAEOS* A Lord of Bynum; one of the rebels against Erenor

*RALEN ORNICHOS* Staubaun trader & barge owner working the Dazun River. Lives in Dazunor-Rannuli with his Kheld partner Cam Gereggson.

*MYRON* Famous Esseran poet.

*PALIMIA ATTORA* Daughter of a high-ranking Sordani noble killed to facilitate confiscation of his estates. Later married Eldonus Kastryon. Mistress to Marc Frederick, & later Dorilian. Deceased.

*PHELLAN ILLARION* Bas of Serrain, married to Linne, one of Ostemun Dannutheon's daughters. Father of Lucien & Raphelon.

*RAPHELON ILLARION* Younger brother to Lucien. Cousin to Kerr. Current Heir to Serrain.

*Zepheron Elmarachos* Admiral of Essera's Royal Navy. Zepheron & his ship were famously destroyed at sea by Nammuor.

# KHELDS (and Associated Characters)

*Arne Anseldson* Friend & companion to Hans; a slave whose freedom Hans purchased on the way to Sordan. Son of Wyneghan. Nephew of Robdan Aelfricson.
*Aubrey Amundda* Daughter of Amund Rhys & Vallsa Elslethboern. Niece of Nalf Rhys. Cousin of Cullen Brodheson. Friend of Nilla & Lark. Inherited a king's grant in Neuberland.
*The Bog Crone* Mythical old woman who lives in the Bogs/Fens. Aubrey, Lark, & Nilla encountered the Bog Crone, who then read their runes upon her Wheel.
*Brec Anseldson* Arne's older brother. Son of Wyneghan. Nephew of Robdan Aelfricson. Nephew of Robdan Aelfricson.
*Cam Gereggson* Esseran Kheld. Barge owner & merchant on the Dazun River. Lives in Dazunor-Rannuli with his Staubaun partner Ralen
*Cedrec Aelfricson* Late Kheld representative to the Triemperal Archhalia. Father to Erwan. Grandfather to Stefan & Hans. Died at the Demise.
*Cullen Brodheson* Cousin & best friend to Stefan, for whom he was Keeper of the King's Trade. Enlad (later Archon) of Heddros & Wyre. Wed Asphalladra. Father of Ranwulf & Allysa. Cousin of Aubrey Amundda. Executed for Stefan's murder.
*Erwan Cedrecson* Son of Cedrec Aelfricson; ran off with young Emyli Stauberg-Randolph. She later bore his sons, Stefan & Hans. Died at Gignastha.
*Fran Gorseddson* Foremost general of Neuberland's Kheld forces. Friend & former lover of Aubrey Amundda.
*Gerd Ralfson* Innkeeper at Rhodhur Hall. Formerly cooked for Cullen Brodheson.
*Lark Rappeleye* Friend of Aubrey & Nilla. High clan; Rune Daughter.
*Lowen Toboldson* Son of Tobold & father of Nilla. Executed for Stefan's murder.
*Mother Ewlys* One of the Old Mothers of Rhodhur's Barrowwood.
*Mother Aegdnis* Chief of Rhodhur's Old Mothers.
*Mother Ednowa* Old Mother at Bellan Toregh.
*Nalf Rhys* Current Thegnard (leader) of the Thegnkeld, the foremost clan of Amallar. Follower of Stefan. Uncle of Aubrey.
*Nilla Lowenda* Daughter of Lowen Toboldson & niece of Goff Horvadson. Marries Stefan. Murdered by Erenor.
*Orem Darm* Headman of the Darm clan, who dwell & prosper along the Dazun & Floh rivers.
*Robdan Aelfricson* Cedrec's youngest brother; a scribe & diplomat. Great-uncle to Stefan & Hans. Amallar's Ambassador to the Archhalia.
*Ressany Robdansda* Robdan's oldest daughter; widow of Bren Forbasson, a Kheld noble executed for Stefan's murder. Holder of good land. Mother of seven.
*Snearly Darm* A young Darm lad who becomes Hans's attendant.
*Tobold Forbasson* Thegnard of the Thegnkeld. Died at the Demise.
*Trella Robdansda* Robdan's middle daughter, mother of Remi
*Wytha Robdansda* Robdan's youngest daughter.
*Wodd* Chief of Aubrey Amundda's holdermen; his wife Hild serves as steward of Aubrey's holding in Neuberland.

## OTHER CHARACTERS

*BARAN REDHARG* Hen Kyon leader, Lord of Gloanneach. Looks nearly fully human.
*CORTOGH* Hen Kyon warrior. Son of Baran. Has a fierce bestial appearance.
*ENDELARIN NEMENOR* King of Ardaen, brother to the throne queen. Romantic
& rumored to have one hundred wives. Cousin to the Sordaneons & fond of
reminding them of it.
*FARRL HENNEK* Captain of Trongor.
*FELLESMA* Hen Kyon woman. Daughter of Baran. Sister of Cortogh & like him
is less human in appearance.
*GALANTHIAS HELAOSUN* King of Merced, father of Melenthas. The island nation
of Merced, while economically allied with Sordan, embraces ties with Nammuor.
*GERALDINE STOLL-BECKER* One of Hans's two moms, along with Irmgard, who
lived in the Dominion, a country in one of the Archived Pasts where Hans was
hidden. Deceased.
*HERBERTH TAMMET* Elector of Trongor.
*IRMGARD STOLL-BECKER* One of Hans's two moms, along with Geraldine, who.
lived in the Dominion, a country in one of the Archived Pasts where Hans was
hidden. Deceased.
*JOOAR ZETHARNNA* A prince of Lahgael, not in the line of succession. Governor
of Ben Aranath.
*MELENTHAS HELAOSUN* Princess of Merced, daughter of King Galanthius.
Prospective bride for Dorilian Sordaneon.
*THAA* Non-human. Rift Guardian; the Dark Watcher. Aligned with Marenthro.
*TYE* One of Farrl's men who guards Hans.

## ENTITY-BOUND DEVICES

*THE LEUR'S RING* Fashioned from the body of The Leur as last living act. Rejects
non-Leur flesh & can only be worn by the Highborn. Used at coronations to
identify the true king of Essera (Heir of Ergeiron). Manipulates real world/Leur's
Creation. Removes barriers. Opens doors. Reveals truth & restores Leur's reality.
*THE RILL STONE* Device created by Derlon, who encapsulated his immortal
blood in Rill matrix. The Rill Stone will identify a Sordaneon who wears it by
glowing green. The Rill recognizes Sordaneon wearers & will not arm itself or
lock locations against them. Can be used to burn a permanent Eagle mark onto
any other substance, including human skin.
*THE WALL STONE* Shard of the Wall containing Ergeiron's immortal essence.
The Wall Stone connects directly to the Wall, regardless of proximity, & must be
used carefully by individuals open to its gifts. Allows wielder to peer into discreet
temporal flows. The Wall Stone unlocks the Aidion & provides access to the
Archive, which it assists in revealing.

## OTHER ENTITIES

*THE DIADEM* The Undying Crown. Also known as the Diadem of the Devaryati.
Pre-Devastation device created in secret by the Aryati from the immortal core that
remained of Vllyr after that god was destroyed by Amynas & the Leur. Generates &
commands arcane forces. Vastly powerful when fully tapped into an immortal being.
Retains vestige of Vllyr's godhood. Malevolently self-aware & fixated on destroying

that which destroyed Vllyr. Succeeded in corrupting the Aryati, destroying Mulsor & the First Creation.

## GREATER ENHANCERS

*LACENEDON CROWN* Also called Ulnossi's Bane. Used by Delos Sordaneon to break the Vermillion Aqueduct.

*MORMANTALORUS CORONAL* Also called the Crown of Fire; Ciennor's Crown. Now in possession of Mormantalorus & its ruler.

*RANNUL'S CROWN* Also called the Circle Kissed by the Sun. Euella gives this to Dorilian for his safety because she knows he can use it. *SORDAN CORONAL* Also called Derlon's Crown. Most powerful of the Greater Diadems. Now in possession of the Sordaneons.

*STAUBERG CORONAL* Also called the Star Crown; Ergeiron's Crown. Now in possession of the Malyrdeons.

## OTHER DEVICES

*DERLON'S ARMOR* The fabled Eagle Breastplate, helm, gauntlets & greaves. When activated sheaths the wearer's torso & limbs. Kinetic negation. Any blow to the armor is absorbed. Invincible to nearly all weapons.

*RINGS OF ORDER* Three rings created by Derlon Sordaneon before the Inception. Used in accessing Rill stations & communicating with the Overlay. The Head Epopte (Psilant) keeps one of the rings, the First Ring of Order. Two Arch Epoptes/Mages hold the others.

*SWORD OF AMYNAS* Also known as Derlon's Sword or the Gweroyen Sword. Greatest of the tullun blades crafted from Vllyr's skeleton. Devastatingly effective when paired with more powerful enhancers.

## BACKGROUND — Highborn Origins

*ARYATI* Human strain engineered to replicate the powers & immortality of Leur. Creators of greater & lesser devices that generate quasi-magical powers. The Aryati rose to extraordinary heights through genetic manipulation & technology but were arrogant & acquisitive; they ultimately destroyed their world. A remnant of the Aryati survived into the new Creation but most were slain following their defeat by the Highborn during the Gweroyen Wars. The survivors scattered. No pureblood Aryati survive but the strain persists in noble Staubaun lineages.

*LEUR* Immortal beings that created the World. Elusive & mostly hidden from humans until technological advances revealed them. Leur magic built the Five Cities, each in a day, &, combined with Aryati technology, engineered the living matrix of the Rill. During the Devastation brought by the Aryati, the Leur race sacrificed itself to create the temporal disjunction that preserved the Creation. The lone Leur survivor mated their immortal bloodline with that of the Aryati clone-prince Amynas, conceiving three immortal sons known as The Three.

*MALYRDEON* Descendants of Ergeiron, one of the three sons of the gods Amynas & Leur; Ergeiron settled in what is now Stauberg, where he created the Wall as a barricade against the Rift. The Wall exists throughout all Time. Some descendants of Ergeiron are able to "walk the Wall" & by that means divine future events or reveal the truth or import of past events.

*Sordaneon* Descendants of Derlon, second of the three sons of the gods Amynas & Leur. Derlon settled Sordan, home to one of the surviving Five Cities of Leur, from which he gave life to the Rill by melding his immortal body with that of the vast machine. The descendants of Derlon carry the potential to connect with & communicate with the Rill, which would allow them to alter the god-machine's operation & physical structure.

# HUMAN RACES

*Estol* An amalgamation of races; the general population. Disdained as mongrels by Staubauns, Estols nonetheless rise to positions of influence & become minor nobility. Most are servants, laborers, soldiers & craftsmen. Because they are of mixed blood, Estols can have any human color of eyes, hair, or skin.

*Highborn* Males descended from the immortal sons of Leur & the human Amynas. Leur traits pass only to male offspring, who must mate with human females to reproduce. For this reason, the adage is that the Highborn take the race of their mothers. Almost exclusively, the Highborn have chosen to reproduce using Staubaun lineages.

*Kheld* A barbaric people that entered Essera through the Rift during a period of instability following the First War with Ardaen. Khelds generally have blue or green eyes. They also have dark hair, sturdy builds & are shorter. Adult males are usually bearded. Their language is completely separate, as are their ways of life. Kheld naming differs from the Staubaun, as does their system of inheritance.

*Nemenor* A seafaring people that forms the ruling families of Ardaen, Callorn, Lahgael, & the Isles of Maskos. Traditional enemies of the Triempery in the past, a marriage by treaty to a younger son of the Hierarch of Sordan instilled Ardaenan Nemenor blood into the lineage of the Highborn Sordaneons.

*Staubaun* A people originally created by (and related to) the Aryati & still manifesting some traits of the parent race. Some can wield lesser devices. Tall, fair-skinned, brown or gold-eyed blondes, beardless (with little body hair), Staubauns are intelligent & long-lived. They also, after generations of success & prosperity, tend to be rich & privileged.

# NONHUMAN RACES

*Hen Kyon* The Dog Men, created by the Aryati as hunters & servants, specifically to track down & kill the magic-gifted offspring of Amynas & Leur. Intelligent & reclusive, the Hen Kyon are bipedal, often with fur covering parts or all of their bodies. The most true-to-breed have long, wolfish faces with well-developed olfactory organs. They have incredible stamina & strength, & can interbreed with humans, from which race they were originally fashioned. The Hen Kyon nearly eradicated the young Highborn race. Though they later repented their deeds, the Dog Men were abhorred & hunted nearly into extinction until the Malyrdeon King Emrysen cloaked them in obscurity & gave them the haunted wilds of the Kragh in which to live unmolested. They have since become feared & avoided.

*Leur* A magical race, as explained above, creators of the original World & the tripartite Creation they fashioned to salvage it from destruction. Originally the Leur people inhabited the area now known as the Bogs, a marshy delta where the Dazun River flows into the sea. The last Leur was slain by the Devaryati & the race is now only legend.

## PLACES (background)

**D**ALN **B**ARRIER  Created by Leur to separate the World in Time. Past World/ Gsch/Current World.

**F**IVE **C**ITIES  Eternal cities built in the First Creation by Leur & continuing in the Second Creation. Îs (vanished), Permephedon, Sordan, Mormantalorus, & Mulsor (destroyed).

**G**SCH  The World of Fire. The moment of Devastation, forever happening, never completed. A single moment in Time that has both already occurred & will never occur.

**(M**ENA**)**TROHJANA  The Second Creation. The present World that moves forward in Time.

**(M**ENA**)**TANTAUREUS  Archived world/Past world, living remnant of the First Creation. Birthplace of Marc Frederick.

**M**ULSOR  Destroyed in the Devastation. As a Leur creation part of it remains eternal. A ghost city whose appearance portends doom.

**T**HE **R**IFT  Transient instabilities in the Daln Barrier that permit passage between the Past World & the Current World. The appearance of Mulsor is one such occurrence.

**T**RIEMPERY  A confederation comprised of three aligned Highborn empires: Essera, Sordan, & Mormantalorus.


## ESSERA

**A**IDION  Heart of the Wall. Located under the shrine at the Gate of Transformation. It is the place where gifted Malyrdeons walk the Wall.**S**TAUBERG  Capital city of Essera. Home of the Malyrdeons. Major seaport. Location of the Wall. Site of a dormant Rill mount.

**A**MALLAR  Semi-autonomous domain of the Khelds. Considered part of Essera.

**A**MUNDHAL  Kings grant holding of Aubrey Amundda. Near Saemoregh.

**A**NNECH  Frontier holding allied with Gobba, increasingly at odds with Essera.

**A**RAL  Capital of Tahlwent. Major sea port.

**A**SAE **E**RANOS  The Malyrdeon Serat or Malyrdeon Tower. Royal palace in Stauberg.

**A**SKYLLON  Fortress in Lacenedon, on north shore of Ulan-Sana lake.

**A**URDOLLEN Sanctuary near Rhodhur & site of a school for girls.

**B**ELLAN **T**OREGH Town on eastern edge of Amallar. Site of a dormant Rill mount.

**B**EARD **F**EN  Kheld neighborhood in Dazunor-Rannuli

**T**HE **B**OGS  Kheld term for The Fan; endless marshes of terminal Dazun River.

**B**YNUM  Foremost city of the Eleutheron, on south shore of Ulan-Sana lake.

**C**USTOMHOUSE  Seven Houses seat in Dazunor-Rannuli.

**D**ANAE **P**ALACE  Princess Palaistea's seat. Near Bynum. Now destroyed.

**D**ANNUTH  Principality in Essera, holding of the Dannutheon Princes.

**D**AZUNOR  Principality in Essera, holding of Essera's Heir.

**D**AZUNOR-**R**ANNULI  Pre-eminent city in Essera due to its position on the Dazun River & presence of a major Rill node. Home of the Seven Houses.

**D**AZUN **R**IVER  Largest river north of the Telarkan Mountains. Major economic resource & highway. Has no navigable egress to the sea.

*EASTMEARY BRENNA* City in Amallar.

*ELITHEGH* Fortified castle near Gustan.

*ELEUTHERON* Domain also ruled by the Prince of Stauberg. Rich & deep in history.

*EMRYSEN PALACE* Esseran monarch's residence in Dazunor-Rannuli, on the Upper Canal

*ENNSA* Capital city of Gweroyen.

*FLOH* River that flows through Bellan Toregh. Tributary of Dazun River.

*GATE OF TRANSFORMATION* Original city gate of Stauberg. Transformed by Erge-iron & now site of a shrine.

*GIGNASTHA* Former Principality in Essera. Made a Crown Protectorate after its Highborn Princes were murdered by Kheld rebels.

*GOBBA* Frontier holding east of Neuberland, loosely affiliated with Essera.

*GOLDEN PALACE* Highborn palace in Trulo.

*GWEROYEN* Domain in Essera, north of Stauberg. Former stronghold of the Ary-ati.

*GUSTAN* Town on the Dazun River near the Fan.

*GUSTAN MANOR* Marc Frederick's personal residence, which he designed & built using materials from his home world.

*HALASSEON SERAT* Palace of the Halasseon Princes.

*HIGH CITADEL* Central redoubt of Permephedon's city core. Also called Maren-thro's Tower. The Leur Arcana & Harmonic Hall are here, as are the Archhalia Chambers.

*THE HILL* Temple complex at Aurdollen devoted to the Mother. Children conceived under the Hill, through anonymous couplings sanctified by the Mother's Priestesses, are considered destined for fortunate lives.

*HORCROD* Fortress in Lower Neuberland.

*HYLLORHOSE RIVER* West of the Kragh; flows into the Dazun near Trulo.

*.IDDOLEA* Destroyed city in Gweroyen. Former capital of the Aryati.

*ILLYSTRI PALACE* Malyrdeon palace in Dazunor-Rannuli, located on island in the Lago

*JEWEL TOWER* Malyrdeon tower. Floats above the Mirror in Permephedon's city core.

*KENELM* Capital city of Lacenedon. Site of a dormant Rill mount.

*KRAGH* Badlands of high hills & dangerous gorges. Home of the Hen Kyon.

*KYRBASILLON* Capital city of Dannuth. Famous for its beauty & public places. Four gateways of Virtue: Arch of Mercy, Arch of Truth, Arch of Courage, Arch of Justice.

*LACENEDON* Domain in Essera, north & east of Permephedon.

*LAGO* Lake in heart of Dazunor-Rannuli near the Rill mount.

*LESEOS* City-State. Former Principality of Essera, now a semi-autonomous Basar-chate. Rill city. Located south of Amallar & west of Gignastha.

*LOWER CANAL* Main canal of Dazunor-Rannuli. Largely commercial properties along it.

*LOWER NEUBERLAND* Part of the Principality of Gignastha, south of Gignastha & bordering Randpory, the northernmost territory of Sordan.

*THE MAW* Huge hill in the Kragh

*MERRYDN* Principality in eastern Essera. Located where the Rannul River flows into the Dazun River. Home to the Merrydeon Princes.

*Merath* Capital city of Merrydn. Famous for its palace & walls of blue stone. Home of a dormant Rill mount

*Neuberland* Esseran domain/protectorate. Kheld & Staubaun populations often in dispute over land.

*Old Fort* Stronghold on high ground overlooking the Dazun Road.

*Orqho* Mines in southern Amallar near Leseos.

*Permephedon* City-State presided over by Marenthro. One of the three remaining Five Cities. Neutral seat of the Triempery & home of the Triemperal Archhalia. Northernmost Rill city & a major Rill hub.

*Pessach* Domain north of Lacenedon bordering the Cjta, or Ice Lands.

*Rannul* Domain in Essera.

*Rhodhur* Capital of Amallar. Site of Rhodhur Hall.

*Rillhome* Sordaneon palace in Dazunor-Rannuli

*The Sacred Grove* Oak grove & temple complex near Aurdollen devoted to the god Lud. Home of the Faeduadan Priesthood.

*Serrain* Domain in Essera, just west of Permephedon

*Saemoregh* Kheld town in Neuberland.

*Sar'Pryannis* Poisoned lake in Gignastha. Gignastha is built on cliffs overlooking this lake

*Simelon* Capital city of Serrain. Site of a dormant Rill mount.

*Sordaneon Tower* Sordaneon hold in Permephedon's city core. Congruent with the Rill, which it is near.

*Tahlwent* Principality in Essera. South of Stauberg & on the sea. Home to the Halasseon Princes.

*Terna* Capital city of Rannul.

*The Fan* Egress of Dazun; fens, marshes & channels that go nowhere. Also called the Bogs. No one knows how or where the Dazun empties into the sea (or even if it does).

*Trulo* Major city on Dazun River. Seat of the Princes of Dazunor. Site of the destroyed Aryati city of Gyges.

*Upper Canal* Large canal north of the Rill mount & Lago, where the wealthy live.

*Vermillion Aqueduct* Raised by Deben II Sordaneon to provide water to Gignastha & also power the locks securing the impregnable gate of the Watergilt Palace. Broken by Delos Sordaneon during the Gignastha War.

# SORDAN

*Amroset* Capital city of Ardaen.

*Anit-Rebir* Domain located north of Teremar. Mountainous.

*Ardaen* Monarchy located on large peninsula west of Trongor. Seafarers known as the Sea Kings.

*Askorras* Capital of Teremar.

*Batraz* Capital city of Suddekar; location of the Palace of Dawn.

*Ben Aranath* River port of Lahgael on the Sorandruil.

*Caerdon* Principality. Former region of Ardaen, ceded to the Sordaneon Hierarchate as part of a treaty & now included among the Hierarch's title domains.

*Callorn* Region of Ardaen.

*Hestya* River port in Teremar. Site of an active Rill mount.

*THE INCEPTION* Sordan's Rill mount. Largest Rill complex, where Derlon's presence has fully completed its transformation. Multiple levels, platforms, & crown of portals.

*ILDURRIA* Domain located on northern shore of Sarkuan.

*ILMAR* Domain of Sordan. Located at mouth of Sorand'ruil.

*IRIDONOS* Fabled treasure city of the Aryati, rumored to lie in poisoned Sansordan.

*IVERNESSE* Capital city of Ilmar.

*KING'S HOUSE* Palace near the Serat, connected to the Va Haira. Former residence of the Malyrdeons.

*KOLPOS* Gulf between Sansordan & Ardaen. Also known as the Gulf of Mulsor.

*LAHGAEL* Kingdom of the Gae, a Nemenor-Estol people allied with Sordan.

*MERCED* An independent island kingdom near Ardaen, loosely allied with Ardaen.

*NEREID PALACE* Sordaneon palace in Ivernesse.

*OGARTH* Capital city of Trongor. Site of a dormant Rill mount.

*THE PRISM* Rainbow-laced waterfall & gorge on grounds of the Serat.

*RANDPORY CROSSING* By agreement a free trade city-state because of its Rill mount.

*RANDPORY RIVER* Navigable river that forms the border between the Sordan Hierarchate & Trongor.

*RHONDDA* Sordaneon estate on Sordan island. Personal estate of Dorilian.

*SANSORDAN* Domain attached to Hierarchate. Largely desert/wasteland. Western coast poisoned by destruction of Mulsor.

*SARKUAN* Lake surrounding Sordan.

*SKALMRIMVOR* (see Caerdon)

*SORDAN* One of the three remaining Five Cities. Called the City of Light, City of Amynas. Site of the Inception, originating point of the Rill, & a major Rill node. Island city surrounded by a large & very deep lake.

*SORDANEON SERAT* Palace of the Sordaneon Hierarchs, in Sordan, & congruous with the Rill. Portions of the palace are part of the immortal Citadel forming the core of the city.

*SORAND'RUIL* River that flows from Sarkuan to the sea.

*SUDDEKAR* Principality located on the southern shore of Sarkuan. Borders Mormantaloran domain of Othgol. Home of the Suddekeon Princes.

*TEREMAR* Principality located on eastern shore of Sarkuan. Rich & powerful, home of the Teremareon Princes.

*TIRIS* Estate on Sordan island given by Dorilian to Daimonaeris.

*TOLLECH* Principality located north of Ildurria.

*TRONGOR* Independent nation of sea folk located on Kolpos north of Sansordan, west of Randpory, & south of Amallar. Separated from latter by the Telarkan Mountains.

*TULAMANTA* Palace at Askorras.

*VA HAIRA* First Creation underground passage connecting the Rill, Citadel, Serat & other pre-Return structures in Sordan's city core.

*VIRIDIAN RIVER* Man-made river contained within the Serat. Site of numerous features, including a waterfall over the Serat walls.

*WELL OF BIRDS* Located in a courtyard of the Sordaneon Serat.

# MORMANTALORUS

*DZALARAD* The volcano.

*ILGAON* Main tower of the Citadel of Mormantalorus, where Nammuor creates his arcane crystals & devices using the energy of the volcano.

*MAGISTRY* Part of Ilgaon tower where mage work is done.

*MORMANTALORUS* One of the three remaining Five Cities. Sits on an active volcano & is livable only because the City itself creates an environment conducive to human habitation. The environment immediately outside the city's bubble is toxic.

*NALAPAR* Eastern domain of Mormantalous.

*NUARCH'S TOWER* Residential tower of the Citadel of Mormantalorus.

*ORM* Domain. Borders Suddekar.

*OTHGOL* Domain. Borders Teremar.

*TELEG* Southernmost domain of Mormantalorus.

*ULAN-JANA* Mountainous domain south of Teremar & northeast of Mormantalorus. Gifted by Nammuor to Dorilian & Daimonaeris on their wedding.

*XEBBETH* Large island domain west of Mormantalorus.

## WORDS & TERMS found in the Books

*CHARYS* Rill conveyance. Created by the Rill at need & uncreated when no longer needed.

*CRUIHCIL* Kheld unit of government; leaders in a community charged to speak for that community as a whole or at a Witan.

*DEIKNYA* An oval medallion created by Marenthro that displays the royal or noble house to which that person is bound. Given exclusively to Highborn, royal, or high nobility.

*FAETHA* Kheld word meaning 'learned female'; one who has formally studied under the Mother; term of respect.

*FAEDU* Kheld word meaning 'learned male'; one who has dedicated themselves to the god Lud & are bound to the Faeduadan priesthood.

*FRA'DON* Means 'royal brother.' Used by the Highborn for another of their kindred.

*GYNEKOS* used for a Highborn lineage that has reverted to purely human. This happens when a Highborn sires daughters instead of sons.

*OLD MOTHER* Kheld term of respect for an elder female who has taken up formal devotion to the Mother at one of the Motherhomes. Many Old Mothers hold politically important positions.

*ORBUS/ORBI* Balls of light Highborn princes generate in their hands. A minor power.

*THRICE ROYAL* Proper form of address for a Highborn prince regardless of age or rank. Highborn are considered royal three times over: Father. Mother. Entity. Generally, a Highborn prince is born to a royal father & mother, though the latter is not always the case… but it usually is.

*TULLUN* Material created from the god Vllyr's skeleton. Can be sharpened to an edge that can cut anything but itself. Shaped by the Aryati into blades from daggers to swords. The Sword of Amynas is a *tullun* blade mated with device matrices.

# INDEPENDENT PUBLISHERS ROCK!

We appreciate your purchase of a Forest Path Book. We do our best to cultivate distinctive and compelling stories for our readers.

If you enjoy our authors' efforts, kindly consider that a reader review at your favourite retailer can help spread the word.

To keep track of our latest releases, sales, & happenings, please join:

## INTO THE FOREST
*https://forestpathbooks.com/into-the-forest*
(the Forest Path Books reading group and newsletter)

When you sign up for the newsletter, as our "thank you!" you'll receive a code for 25% off your first purchase at our store.

*https://forestpathbooks.com*